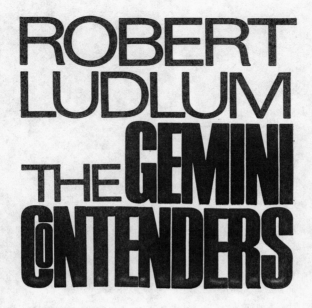

ROBERT LUDLUM
THE GEMINI CONTENDERS

THE DIAL PRESS
NEW YORK

For Richard Marek, Editor.

Brilliance cloaked in great humor. Perception beyond any writer's imagination. Simply, the best there is.

And for lovely Margot, who makes it all perfect.

BOOK ONE

PROLOGUE

DECEMBER 9, 1939
SALONIKA, GREECE

One by one the trucks struggled up the steep road in the predawn light of Salonika. Each went a bit faster at the top; the drivers were anxious to return to the darkness of the descending country road cut out of the surrounding forests.

Yet each of the five drivers in the five trucks had to control his anxiety. None could allow his foot to slip from a brake or press an accelerator beyond a certain point; eyes had to be squinted, sharpening the focus, alert for a sudden stop or an unexpected curve in the darkness.

For it was darkness. No headlights were turned on; the column traveled with only the gray light of the Grecian night, low-flying clouds filtering the spill of the Grecian moon.

The journey was an exercise in discipline. And discipline was not foreign to these drivers, or to the riders beside the drivers.

Each was a priest. A monk. From the Order of Xenope, the harshest monastic brotherhood under the control of the Patriarchate of Constantine. Blind obedience coexisted with self-reliance; they were disciplined to the instant of death.

In the lead truck, the young bearded priest removed his cassock, under which were the clothes of a laborer, a heavy shirt and trousers of thick fabric. He rolled up the cassock and placed it in the well behind the high-backed seat, shoving it down between odd items of canvas and cloth. He spoke to the robed driver beside him.

"It's no more than a half mile now. The stretch of track parallels the road for about three hundred feet. In the open; it will be sufficient."

"The train will be there?" asked the middle-aged, powerfully built monk, narrowing his eyes in the darkness.

"Yes. Four freight cars, a single engineer. No stokers. No other men."

"You'll be using a shovel, then," said the older priest, smiling but with no humor in his eyes.

"I'll be using the shovel," replied the younger man simply. "Where's the weapon?"

"In the glove compartment."

The priest in the laborer's clothes reached forward and released the catch on the compartment panel. It fell open. He put his hand inside the recess and withdrew a heavy, large-calibered pistol. Deftly, the priest sprung the magazine out of the handle, checked the ammunition, and cracked the thick steel back into the chamber. The metallic sound had a finality to it.

"A powerful instrument. Italian, isn't it?"

"Yes," answered the older priest without comment, only the sadness in his voice.

"That's appropriate. And, I suppose, a blessing." The younger man shoved the weapon into his belt. "You'll call his family?"

"I've been so ordered——" It was obvious that the driver wanted to say something more, but he controlled himself. Silently he gripped the wheel more firmly than necessary.

For a moment the moonlight broke through the night clouds, illuminating the road cut out of the forest.

"I used to play here as a child," said the younger man. "I would run through the woods and get wet in the streams . . . then I would dry off in the mountain caves and pretend I had visions. I was happy in these hills. The Lord God wanted me to see them again. He is merciful. And kind."

The moon disappeared. There was darkness once more.

The trucks entered a sweeping curve to the west; the woods thinned out and in the distance, barely visible, were the outlines of telegraph poles, black shafts silhouetted against gray night. The road straightened and widened and became one with a clearing that stretched perhaps a hundred yards from forest to forest. A flat, barren area imposed on the myriad hills and woodlands. In the center of the clearing, its hulk obscured by the darkness beyond, was a train.

Immobile but not without movement. From the engine came curls of smoke spiraling up into the night.

"In the old days," said the young priest, "the farmers would herd their sheep and cart their produce here. There was always a great deal of confusion, my father told me. Fights broke out constantly over what belonged to whom. They were amusing stories. . . . There he is!"

The beam of a flashlight shot out from the black. It circled twice and then remained stationary, the white shaft directed now at the last freight car. The priest in laborer's clothes unclipped a pencil light from his shirt pocket, held it forward and pressed the button for precisely two seconds. The reflection off the truck's windshield briefly illuminated the small enclosure. The younger man's eyes were drawn swiftly to the face of his brother monk. He saw that his companion had bitten his lip; a rivulet of blood trickled down his chin, matting itself in the close-cropped gray beard.

There was no reason to comment on it.

"Pull up to the third car. The others will turn around and start unloading."

"I know," said the driver simply. He swung the wheel gently to the right and headed toward the third freight car.

The engineer, in overalls and a goatskin cap, approached the truck as the young priest opened the door and jumped to the ground. The two men looked at each other and then embraced.

"You look different without your cassock, Petride. I'd forgotten how you looked——"

"Oh, come now. Four years out of twenty-seven is hardly the better part."

"We don't see you often enough. Everyone in the family remarks about it." The engineer removed his large, calloused hands from the priest's shoulders. The moon broke through the clouds again; the spill lighted the trainman's face. It was a strong face, nearer fifty than forty, filled with the lines of a man constantly exposing his skin to the wind and the sun.

"How's mother, Annaxas?"

"Well. A little weaker with each month of age, but alert."

"And your wife?"

"Pregnant again and not laughing this time. She scolds me."

"She should. You're a lustful old dog, my brother. But better to serve the church, I rejoice to say." The priest laughed.

"I'll tell her you said that," said the engineer, smiling.

There was a moment of silence before the young man replied. "Yes. You tell her." He turned to the activity taking place at the freight cars. The loading doors had been opened and lanterns hung inside, shedding their muted light sufficiently for packing, but not bright enough to be obvious outside. The figures of robed priests began walking swiftly back and forth between the trucks and the doors, carrying crates, boxes of heavy cardboard framed with wood. Prominently displayed on each crate was the crucifix and thorns of the Order of Xenope.

"The food?" inquired the engineer.

"Yes," answered his brother. "Fruits, vegetables, dried meats, grain. The border patrols will be satisfied."

"Then where?" It was not necessary to be clearer.

"This vehicle. In the middle section of the carriage, beneath tobacco nets. You have the lookouts posted?"

"On the tracks and the road; both directions for over a mile. Don't worry. Before daybreak on a Sunday morning, only you priests and novices have work to do and places to go."

The young priest glanced over at the fourth freight car. The work was progressing rapidly; the crates were being stacked inside. All those hours of practice were showing their value. The monk who was his driver stopped briefly by the muted light of the loading door, a carton in his hands. He exchanged looks with the younger man, then forced his attention away, back to the carton which he swung up into the well of the freight car.

Father Petride turned to his brother. "When you picked up the train, did you speak with anyone?"

"Only the dispatcher. Naturally. We had black tea together."

"What did he say?"

"Words I wouldn't offend you with, for the most part. His papers said the cars were to be loaded by the fathers of Xenope in the outlying yards. He didn't ask any questions."

Father Petride looked over at the second freight car, on his right. In minutes all would be completed; they would be ready for the third car. "Who prepared the engine?"

"Fuel crews and mechanics. Yesterday afternoon. The orders said it was a standby; that's normal. Equipment breaks down all the time. We are laughed at in Italy. . . . Naturally, I checked everything myself several hours ago."

"Would the dispatcher have any reason to telephone the freight yards? Where supposedly we are loading the cars?"

"He was asleep, or practically so, before I left his tower. The morning schedule won't start——" the engineer looked up at the gray black sky "——for at least another hour. He'd have no reason to call anyone, unless the wireless reported an accident."

"The wires were shorted out; water in a terminal box," said the priest quickly, as if talking to himself.

"Why?"

"In case you did have problems. You spoke to *no one* else?"

"Not even a drifter. I checked the cars to make sure none were inside."

"You've studied our schedule by now. What do you think?"

The trainman whistled softly, shaking his head. "I think I'm astounded, my brother. Can so much be . . . so arranged?"

"The arrangements are taken care of. What about the time? That's the important factor."

"If there are no track failures the speed can be maintained. The Slav border police at Bitola are hungry for bribes; and a Greek freight at Banja Luka is fair game. We'll have no trouble at Sarajevo or Zagreb; they look for larger fish than food for the religious."

"The time, not the bribes."

"They *are* time. One haggles."

"Only if *not* haggling would seem suspicious. Can we reach Monfalcone in three nights?"

"If your arrangements are successful, yes. If we lose time we could make it up during the daylight hours."

"Only as a last resort. We travel at night."

"You're obstinate."

"We're cautious." Again the priest looked away. Freight cars one and two were secure, the fourth would be loaded and packed before the minute was up. He turned back to his brother. "Does the family think you're taking a freight to Corinth?"

"Yes. To Navpaktos. To the shipyards on the straits of Patrai. They don't expect me back for the better part of a week."

"There are strikes at Patrai. The unions are angry. If you were a few days longer, they'd understand."

Annaxas looked closely at his brother. He seemed startled at the young priest's worldly knowledge. There was a hesitancy in his reply. "They'd understand. Your sister-in-law would understand."

"Good." The monks had gathered by Petride's truck, watching him, waiting for instructions. "I'll join you at the engine shortly."

"All right," said the trainman as he walked away, glancing at the priests.

Father Petride removed the pencil light from his shirt pocket and in the darkness approached the other monks at the truck. He searched out the powerfully built man who was his driver. The monk understood and stepped away from the others, joining Petride at the side of the vehicle.

"This is the last time we speak," said the young priest.

"May the blessings of God——"

"Please," interrupted Petride. "There's no time. Just commit to mem-

ory each move we make here tonight. *Everything*. It must be duplicated
exactly."

"It will be. The same roads, the same orders or trucks, the same
drivers, identical papers across the borders to Monfalcone. Nothing will
change, except one of us will be missing."

"That's the will of God. For the glory of God. It's a privilege beyond
my worth."

There were two master padlocks on the truck's panel. Petride had
one key; his driver held the other. Together they approached the locks
and inserted the keys. The irons sprung; the locks were lifted out of the
steel hasps, the hasps slapped up, and the doors opened. A lantern was
hung high on the edge of the panel.

Inside were the crates with the symbols of the crucifix and thorns
stenciled on the sides between the strips of wood. The monks began to
remove them, maneuvering like dancers—robes flowing in the eerie light.
They carried the cartons to the loading door of the third freight car.
Two men leaped up into the heavy-beamed deck of the car and started
stacking the boxes at the south end.

Several minutes later half the truck was empty. In the center of the
van, separated from the surrounding cartons, was a single crate draped
in black cloth. It was somewhat larger than the cases of produce and
not rectangular in shape. Instead, it was a perfect cube: three feet in
height, three in width, and three in depth.

The priests gathered in a semicircle in front of the open panels of the
truck. Shafts of filtered white moonlight mingled with the yellow spill of
the lantern. The combined effect of the strange admixture of light, the
cavernous truck, and the robed figures made Father Petride think of a
catacomb, deep in the earth, housing the true relics of the cross.

The reality was not much different. Except that what lay sealed inside
the iron vault—for that was what it was—was infinitely more meaningful
than the petrified wood of the crucifixion.

Several of the monks had closed their eyes in prayer; others were
staring, transfixed by the presence of the holy thing, their thoughts suspended, their faith drawing sustenance from what they believed was
within the tomblike chest—itself a catafalque.

Petride watched them, feeling apart from them, and that was how it
should be. His mind wandered back to what seemed only hours ago, but
was in reality six weeks. He had been ordered out of the fields and
taken to the white concrete rooms of the Elder of Xenope. He was
ushered into the presence of that most holy father; there was one other
priest with the old prelate, no one else.

"Petride Dakakos," the holy man had begun, sitting behind his thick wooden table, "you have been chosen above all others here at Xenope for the most demanding task of your existence. For the glory of God and the preservation of Christian sanity."

The second priest had been introduced. He was an ascetic-looking man with wide, penetrating eyes. He spoke slowly, precisely. "We are the custodians of a vault, a sarcophagus, if you will, that has remained sealed in a tomb deep in the earth for over fifteen hundred years. Within that vault are documents that would rend the Christian world apart, so devastating are their writings. They are the ultimate proof of our most sacred beliefs, yet their exposure would set religion against religion, sect against sect, entire peoples against one another. In a holy war. . . . The German conflict is spreading. The vault must be taken out of Greece, for its existence has been rumored for decades. The search for it would be as thorough as a hunt for microbes. Arrangements have been made to remove it where none will find it. I should say, most of the arrangements. You are the final component."

The journey had been explained. The *arrangements*. In all their glory. And fear.

"You will be in contact with only one man. Savarone Fontini-Cristi, a great *padrone* of northern Italy, who lives in the vast estates of Campo di Fiori. I, myself, have traveled there and spoken with him. He's an extraordinary man, of unparalleled integrity and utter commitment to free men."

"He is of the Roman church?" Petride had asked incredulously.

"He is of no church, yet *all* churches. He is a powerful force for men who care to think for themselves. He is the friend of the Order of Xenope. It is he who will conceal the vault. . . . You and he alone. And then you . . . but we will get to that; you are the most privileged of men."

"I thank my God."

"As well you should, my son," said the holy father of Xenope, staring at him.

"We understand you have a brother. An engineer for the railroads."

"I do."

"Do you trust him?"

"With my life. He's the finest man I know."

"You shall look into the eyes of the Lord," said the holy father, "and you will not waver. In His eyes you will find perfect grace."

"I thank my God," said Petride once again.

He shook his head and blinked his eyes, forcing the reflections out of his mind. The priests by the truck were still standing immobile; the hum of whispered chants came from rapidly moving lips in the darkness.

There was no time for meditation or prayer. There was no time for anything but swift movement—to carry out the commands of the Order of Xenope. Petride gently parted the priests in front of him and jumped up into the truck. He knew why he had been chosen. He was capable of such harshness; the holy father of Xenope had made that clear to him.

There was a time for such men as himself.

God forgive him.

"Come," he said quietly to those on the ground. "I'll need help."

The monks nearest the truck looked uncertainly at one another. Then, one by one, five men climbed into the van.

Petride removed the black drape that covered the vault. Underneath, the holy receptacle was encased in the heavy cardboard, wood framing, and the stenciled symbols of Xenope; identical except for size and shape to all the other crates. But the casing was the only similarity. It required six strong backs, pushing and pulling, to nudge it to the edge of the van and onto the freight car.

The moment it was in place, the dancelike activity resumed. Petride remained in the freight car, arranging the crates so that they concealed the holy thing, obscuring it as one among so many. Nothing unusual, nothing to catch the eye.

The freight car was filled. Petride pulled the doors shut and inserted the iron padlock. He looked at the radium dial of his wristwatch; it had all taken eight minutes and thirty seconds.

It had to be, he supposed, yet still it annoyed him: His fellow priests knelt on the ground. A young man—younger than he, a powerful Serbo-Croat barely out of his novitiate—could not help himself. As the tears rolled down his cheek, the young priest began the chant of Nicaea. The others picked it up and Petride knelt also, in his laborer's clothes, and listened to the holy words.

But not speaking them. There was no *time! Couldn't they understand?*

What was happening to him? In order to take his mind off the holy whispers, he put his hand inside his shirt and checked the leather pouch that was strapped to his chest. Inside that flat, uncomfortable dispatch case were the orders that would lead him across hundreds of miles of uncertainty. Twenty-seven separate pages of paper. The pouch was secure; the straps cut into his skin.

The prayer over, the priests of Xenope rose silently. Petride stood in front of them and each in turn approached him and embraced him and held him in love. The last was his driver, his dearest friend in the order. The tears that filled the rims of his eyes and rolled down his strong face said everything there was to say.

The monks raced back to the trucks; Petride ran to the front of the train and climbed up into the pilot's cabin. He nodded to his brother who began to pull levers and turn wheels. Grinding shrieks of metal against metal filled the night.

In minutes the freight was traveling at high speed. The journey had begun. The journey for the glory of one Almighty God.

Petride held on to an iron bar that protruded from the iron wall. He closed his eyes and let the hammering vibrations and rushing wind numb his thoughts. His fears.

And then he opened his eyes—briefly—and saw his brother leaning out the window, his massive right hand on the throttle, his stare directed to the tracks ahead.

Annaxas the Strong, everyone called him. But Annaxas was more than strong; he was good. When their father had died, it was Annaxas who had gone out to the yards—a huge boy of thirteen—and worked the long, hard hours that exhausted grown men. The money Annaxas brought home kept them all together, made it possible for his brothers and sisters to get what schooling they could. And one brother got more. Not for the family, but for the glory of God.

The Lord God tested men. As He was testing now.

Petride bowed his head and the words seared through his brain and out of his mouth in a whisper that could not be heard.

I believe in one God, the Father Almighty, maker of all things both visible and invisible, and in one Lord, Jesus Christ, Teacher, Son of God, Only begotten of the Father. God of God, Light of Light, Very God of Very God, begotten not made. . . .

They reached the sidings at Edhessa; a switch was thrown by unseen, unauthorized hands, and the freight from Salonika plunged into the northern darkness. The Yugoslav border police at Bitola were as anxious for Greek news as they were for Greek bribes. The northern conflict was spreading rapidly, the armies of Hitler were maniacs; the Balkans were next to fall, everyone said so. And the unstable Italians were filling the piazzas, listening to the screams of war mouthed by the insane Mussolini and his strutting *fascisti*. The talk everywhere was of invasion.

The Slavs accepted several crates of fruit—Xenope fruit was the best in Greece—and wished Annaxas better fortune than they believed he would have, especially since he traveled north.

They sped through the second night north into Mitrovica. The Order of Xenope had done its work; a track was cleared on which no train was scheduled and the freight from Salonika proceeded east to Sarajevo, where a man came out of the shadows and spoke to Petride.

"In twelve minutes the track will be shifted. You will head north to Banja Luka. During the day you'll stay in the yards. They're very crowded. You'll be contacted at nightfall."

In the crowded freight yards at Banja Luka, at precisely quarter past six in the evening, a man came to them dressed in overalls. "You've done well," he said to Petride. "According to the dispatcher's flagging schedules, you don't exist."

At six thirty-five a signal was given; another switch was thrown, and the train from Salonika entered the tracks for Zagreb.

At midnight, in the quiet yards of Zagreb, another man, emerging from other shadows, gave Petride a long manila envelope. "These are papers signed by *Il Duce*'s *Ministro di Viaggio*. They say your freight is part of the Venice *Ferrovia*. It is Mussolini's pride; no one stops it for anything. You will hold at the Sezana depot and pick up the *Ferrovia* out of Trieste. You'll have no trouble with the Monfalcone border patrols."

Three hours later they waited on the Sezana track, the huge locomotive idling. Sitting on the steps, Petride watched Annaxas manipulate the valves and levers.

"You're remarkable," he said, meaning the compliment sincerely.

"It's a small talent," replied Annaxas. "It takes no schooling, just doing it over and over."

"I think it's a remarkable talent. I could never do it."

His brother looked down at him; the glow of the coals washed over his large face, with the wide-set eyes, so firm and strong and gentle. He was a bull of a man, this brother. A decent man. "You could do anything," said Annaxas awkwardly. "You have the head for thoughts and words far beyond mine."

"That's nonsense," laughed Petride. "There was a time when you'd slap my backside and tell me to tend to my chores with more brains."

"You were young; that was many years ago. You tended to your books, you did that. You were better than the freight yards; you got out of them."

"Only because of you, my brother."

"Rest, Petride. We must both rest."

They had nothing in common any longer, and the reason they had nothing was because of Annaxas's goodness and generosity. The older brother had provided the means for the younger to escape, to grow beyond he who provided . . . until there was nothing in common. What made the reality unbearable was that Annaxas the Strong understood the chasm between them now. In Bitola and Banja Luka he had also insisted they rest, not talk. They would get little sleep once they crossed the borders at Monfalcone. In Italy there would be no sleep at all.

The Lord God tested.

In the silence between them, in the open cabin, the black sky above, the dark ground below, the incessant straining of the engine's fires filling the night outside, Petride felt an odd suspension of thought and feeling. Thinking and feeling once-removed, as though he were examining another's experiences from some isolated perch, looking down through a glass. And he began to consider the man he would meet in the Italian Alps. The man who had provided the Order of Xenope with the complicated schedules of transportation through northern Italy. The expanding circles within circles that led inexorably across the Swiss borders in a way that was untraceable.

Savarone Fontini-Cristi was his name. His estate was called Campo di Fiori. The Elders of Xenope said the Fontini-Cristis were the most powerful family in Italy north of Venice. Quite possibly the richest north of Rome. The power and the wealth certainly were borne out by the twenty-seven separate papers in the leather pouch strapped so securely around his chest. Who but an extraordinarily influential man could provide them? And how did the Elders reach him? Through what means? And why would a man named Fontini-Cristi, whose origins had to be of the Roman church, deliver such assistance to the Order of Xenope?

The answers to these questions were not within his province, but nevertheless the questions burned. He knew what lay sealed in the vault of iron in the third freight car. It was more than what his brother priests believed.

Far more.

The Elders had told him so he would understand. *It* was the holiest of compelling motives that would allow him to look into the eyes of God without doubt or hesitation. And he needed that assurance.

Unconsciously, he put his hand under the coarse shirt and felt the pouch. A rash had formed around the straps; he could feel the swelling and the rough, abrasive surface of his skin. It would be infected soon.

But not before the twenty-seven papers did their work. Then it did not matter.

Suddenly, a half mile away on the northern track, the Venice *Ferrovia* could be seen speeding out of Trieste. The Sezana contact raced out of the control tower and ordered them to proceed without delay.

Annaxas fired up and throttled the idling locomotive as rapidly as possible and they plunged north behind the *Ferrovia* toward Monfalcone.

The guards at the border accepted the manila envelope and gave it to their superior officer. The officer shouted at the top of his lungs for the silent Annaxas to fire up quickly. *Proceed!* The freight was part of the *Ferrovia!* The engineer was not to delay!

The madness began at Legnago, when Petride gave the dispatcher the first of Fontini-Cristi's papers. The man blanched and became the most obsequious of public servants. The young priest could see the dispatcher searching his eyes, trying to unearth the level of authority Petride represented.

For the strategy devised by Fontini-Cristi was brilliant. Its strength was in its simplicity, its power over men based in fear—the threat of instant retaliation from the state.

The Greek freight was not a Greek freight at all. It was one of the highly secretive investigating trains sent out by Rome's Ministry of Transportation, the inspectors general of the Italian rail system. Such trains roamed the tracks throughout the country, manned by officials ordered to examine and evaluate all rail operations and submit reports that some said were read by Mussolini himself.

The world made jokes about *Il Duce*'s railroads, but behind the humor was respect. The Italian rail system was the finest in Europe. It maintained its excellence by the time-honored method of the fascist state: secret efficiency ratings compiled by unknown investigators. A man's livelihood—or absence of it—depended on the judgments of the *esaminatori*. Retentions, advancements, and dismissals were often the results of a few brief moments of observation. It stood to reason that when an *esaminatore* revealed himself, absolute cooperation and confidentiality were given.

The freight from Salonika was now an Italian train with the covert imprimatur of Rome as its shield. Its movements were subject only to the authorizations contained in the papers supplied the dispatchers. And the orders within those authorizations were bizarre enough to have come from the convoluted machinations of *Il Duce* himself.

The circuitous route began. The towns and villages fled by—San

Giorgio, Latisana, Motta di Levenza—as the freight from Salonika entered tracks behind Italian boxcars and passenger trains. Treviso, Montebelluna, and Valdagno, west to Malcesine on the Lago di Garda; across the large expanse of water on the sluggish freight boat and immediately north to Breno and Passo della Presolana.

There was only frightened cooperation. Everywhere.

When they reached Como the circling stopped and the dash began. They sped north on the land route and swung south to Lugano, following the tracks on the Swiss borders south and west again to Santa Maria Maggiore, crossing into Switzerland at Saas Fee, where the freight from Salonika resumed its identity, with one minor alteration.

This was determined by the twenty-second authorization in Petride's pouch. Fontini-Cristi had once again provided the simple explanation: The Swiss International Aid Commission at Geneva had granted permission for the Eastern church to cross borders and supply its retreat on the outskirts of Val de Gressoney. What was implied was that the borders would soon be closed to such supply trains. The war was gaining a terrible momentum; soon there would be no trains whatever from the Balkans or Greece.

From Saas Fee the freight rolled south into the yards at Zermatt. It was night; they would wait for the yards to close operations and a man who would come to them and confirm that another switch had been thrown. They would make the incursion south into the Italian Alps of Champoluc.

At ten minutes to nine a trainman appeared in the distance, coming out of the shadows across the Zermatt freight yard. He ran the last several hundred feet and raised his voice.

"Hurry! The rails are clear for Champoluc. There's no time to waste! The switch is tied to a master line; it could be spotted. Get *out* of here!"

Once more Annaxas went about the business of releasing the enormous pressures built up in the fires of the iron fuselage, and once again the train plunged into the darkness.

The signal would come in the mountains, high near an Alpine pass. No one knew just where.

Only Savarone Fontini-Cristi.

A light snow was falling, adding its thin layer to the alabaster cover on the moonlit ground. They passed through tunnels carved out of rock, swinging westward around the ledges of the mountains, the steep gorges menacingly beneath them on their right. It was so much colder. Petride had not expected that; he had not thought about temperatures. The snow and the ice; there was ice on the tracks.

Every mile they traveled seemed like ten, every minute that passed could have been an hour. The young priest peered through the windshield, seeing the beam of the train's searchlight reflecting off the falling snow. He leaned out; he could see only the giant trees that rose up in the darkness.

Where *was* he? Where was the Italian *padrone*, Fontini-Cristi? Perhaps he had changed his mind. O merciful God, that could not be! He could not allow himself to think such thoughts. What they carried in that holy vault would plunge the world into chaos. The Italian knew that; the Patriarchate had total confidence in the *padrone*. . . .

Petride's head was aching, his temples pounded. He sat on the steps of the tender; he had to control himself. He looked at the radium dial of his watch. *Merciful God!* They'd traveled too far! In a half hour they'd be out of the mountains!

"There is your signal!" shouted Annaxas.

Petride leaped to his feet and leaned over the side, his pulse wild, his hands trembling as he gripped the roof ladder. Down the track no more than a quarter of a mile, a lantern was being raised and lowered, its light flickering through the thin sheets of snow.

Annaxas braked the locomotive. The belching engine drew out its roars like the subsiding giant furnace it was. In the snow-lit, moonlit distance, aided by the beam of the locomotive's single headlight, Petride saw a man standing next to an odd-shaped vehicle in a small clearing at the side of the rails. The man was dressed in heavy clothing, collar and cap of fur. The vehicle was both a truck and not a truck. Its rear wheels were much larger than those in front, as though belonging to a tractor. Yet the hood beyond the windshield was not a truck's hood, or a tractor's, thought the priest. It resembled something else.

What was it?

Then he knew and he could not help but smile. He had seen hundreds of such pieces of equipment during the past four days. In front of the strange vehicle's hood was a vertically controlled cargo platform.

Fontini-Cristi was as resourceful as the monks in the Order of Xenope. But then the pouch strapped to his chest had told him that.

"You are the priest of Xenope?" Savarone Fontini-Cristi's voice was deep, aristocratic, and very used to authority. He was a tall man and slender beneath the Alpine clothing, with large, penetrating eyes recessed in the aquiline features of his face. And he was a much older man than Petride thought he would be.

"I am, *signore*," said Petride, climbing down into the snow.

"You're very young. The holy men have given you an awesome responsibility."

"I speak the language. I know that what I do is right."

The *padrone* stared at him. "I'm sure you do. What else is left for you?"

"Don't you believe it?"

The *padrone* replied simply. "I believe in only one thing, my young father. There is but a single war that must be fought. There can be no divisions among those who battle the fascist. *That* is the extent of what I believe." Fontini-Cristi looked up abruptly at the train. "Come. There's no time to waste. We must return before daybreak. There are clothes for you in the tractor. Get them. I'll instruct the engineer."

"He doesn't speak Italian."

"I speak Greek. Hurry!"

The freight car was lined up with the tractor. Laterally operated chains were placed around the holy vault, and the heavy iron receptacle encased in strips of wood was pulled, groaning under the tension, out onto the platform. It was secured by the chains in front; taut straps buckled over the top.

Savarone Fontini-Cristi tested the harnessing on all sides. He was satisfied; he stood back, the beam of his flashlight illuminating the monastic symbols stenciled on the encasement.

"So after fifteen hundred years it comes out of the earth. Only to be returned to the earth," said Fontini-Cristi quietly. "Earth and fire and sea. I should have chosen the last two, my young priest. Fire or the sea."

"That is not the will of God."

"I'm glad your communication is so direct. You holy men never cease to amaze me with your sense of the absolute." Fontini-Cristi turned to Annaxas and spoke fluently now in Greek. "Pull up so that I may clear the tracks. There's a narrow trail on the other side of the woods. We'll be back before dawn."

Annaxas nodded. He was uncomfortable in the presence of such a man as Fontini-Cristi. "Yes, Your Excellency."

"I'm no such thing. And you're a fine engineer."

"Thank you." Annaxas, embarrassed, walked toward the engine.

"That man is your brother?" asked Fontini-Cristi softly of Petride. "Yes."

"He doesn't know?"

The young priest shook his head.

"You'll need your God then." The Italian turned swiftly and started for the driver's side of the enclosed tractor. "Come, Father. We have work to do. This machine was built for the avalanche. It will take our cargo where no human being could carry it."

Petride climbed into the seat. Fontini-Cristi started the powerful engine and expertly shifted gears. The platform in front of the hood was lowered, permitting visibility, and the vehicle lunged forward, vibrating across the tracks into the Alpine forest.

The priest of Xenope sat back and closed his eyes in prayer. Fontini-Cristi maneuvered the powerful machine through the rising woods toward the upper trails of the Champoluc mountains.

"I have two sons older than you," said Fontini-Cristi after a while. And then he added, "I'm taking you to the grave of a Jew. I think it's appropriate."

They returned to the Alpine clearing as the black sky was turning gray. Fontini-Cristi stared at Petride as the young priest climbed out of the strange machine. "You know where I live. My house is your house."

"We all reside in the house of the Lord, *signore*."

"So be it. Good-bye, my young friend."

"Good-bye. May God go with you."

"If He chooses."

The Italian pushed the gearshift into place and drove quickly down the barely visible road below the tracks. Petride understood. Fontini-Cristi could not lose a minute now. Every hour he was away from his estate would add to the questions that might be asked. There were many in Italy who considered the Fontini-Cristis to be enemies of the state.

They were watched. All of them.

The young priest ran through the snow toward the engine. And his brother.

Dawn came over the waters of Lago Maggiore. They were on the Stresa freight barge; the twenty-sixth authorization in the pouch was their passport. Petride wondered what would greet them in Milan, although he realized that it did not really matter.

Nothing mattered now. The journey was coming to an end.

The holy thing was in its resting place. Not to be unearthed for years; perhaps to be buried for a millennium. There was no way to tell.

They sped southeast on the main track through Varese into Castiglione. They did not wait for nightfall . . . nothing mattered now. On the outskirts of Varese, Petride saw a roadsign in the bright Italian sunlight.

CAMPO DI FIORI. 20 KIL.

God had chosen a man from Campo di Fiori. The holy secret now belonged to Fontini-Cristi.

The countryside rushed by; the air was clear and cold and exhilarating. The skyline of Milan came into view. The haze of factory smoke intruded on God's sky and lay suspended like a flat, gray tarpaulin above the horizon. The freight slowed and entered the tracks of the depot sidings. They held at a stop until a disinterested *spedizioniere* in the uniform of the state railroads pointed to a curve in the rails where a green disc snapped up in front of a red one. It was the signal to enter the Milan yards.

"We're here!" shouted Annaxas. "A day's rest, then home! I must say you people are remarkable!"

"Yes," said Petride simply. "We're remarkable."

The priest looked at his brother. The sounds of the freight yard were music to Annaxas; he sang a Greek song, his whole upper body swaying rhythmically to the sharp, fast beats of the melody.

It was strange, the song Annaxas sang. It was not a song of the railroads; it belonged to the sea. A chanty that was a favorite of the fishermen of Thermaïkós. There was something appropriate, thought Petride, about such a song at such a moment.

The sea was God's source of life. It was from the sea that He created earth.

I believe in one God . . . maker of all things. . . .

The priest of Xenope removed the large Italian pistol from under his shirt. He took two steps forward, toward his beloved brother, and raised the barrel of the weapon. It was inches from the base of Annaxas's skull.

. . . both visible and invisible . . . and in one Lord, Jesus Christ . . . only begotten of the Father. . . .

He pulled the trigger.

The explosion filled the cabin. Blood and flesh and things most terrible flew through the air and matted onto glass and metal.

. . . substance of the Father . . . God of God . . . light of light . . . very God of very God. . . .

The priest of Xenope closed his eyes and shouted in exaltation as he held the weapon against his own temple.

". . . *begotten, not made! I will look into the eyes of the Lord and I shall not waver!*"

He fired.

PART
ONE

1

DECEMBER 29, 1939
MILAN, ITALY

Savarone walked past his son's secretary into his son's office and across the heavily carpeted floor to the window overlooking the vast factory complex that was the Fontini-Cristi Industries. His son, of course, was nowhere to be seen. His son, his *eldest* son, was rarely in his office; he was rarely in Milan, for that matter. The first son, the heir-apparent to all of Fontini-Cristi, was incorrigible. And arrogant, and far too concerned with his own creature comforts.

Vittorio was also brilliant. A far more brilliant man than the father who had trained him. And that fact only served to further infuriate Savarone; a man possessing such gifts had greater responsibilities than other men. *He* did not settle for the daily accomplishments that came naturally. He did not carouse and whore and gamble at roulette and baccarat. Or waste sleepless nights with the naked children of the Mediterranean. Neither did he turn his back on the events that were crippling his country, veering it into chaos.

Savarone heard a slight cough behind him and turned. Vittorio's secretary had come into the office.

"I've left word for your son at the Borsa Valori. I believe he was to see his broker this afternoon."

"You may believe it, but I doubt you'll find it on his calendar." Savarone saw the girl flush. "I apologize. You're not accountable for my son. Although you've probably done so, I suggest you try whatever private numbers he's given you. This is a familiar office to me. I'll wait." He removed his overcoat of light camel's hair and his hat, a Tyrolean of green felt. He threw them on the armchair at the side of the desk.

"Yes, sir." The girl left quickly, closing the door behind her.

It *was* a familiar office, thought Fontini-Cristi, although it had been necessary to call it to the girl's attention. Until two years ago, it had been his. Very little remained of his presence, now; only the dark wood paneling. All the furniture had been changed. Vittorio had accepted the four walls. Nothing else.

Savarone sat in the large swivel chair behind the desk. He did not like such chairs; he was too old to let his body be suddenly turned and sprung back by unseen springs and hidden ball bearings. He reached into his pocket and took out the telegram that had brought him to Milan from Campo di Fiori, the telegram from Rome that said the Fontini-Cristis were marked.

But marked for what? By whom? On whose orders?

Questions that could not be asked on the telephone, for the telephone was an instrument of the state. The state. Always the state. Seen and unseen. Observing, following, listening, prying. No telephone could be used and no answer given by the informer in Rome who employed the simple codes.

We have received no reply from Milan, therefore we take the liberty of wiring you personally. Five shipments of aircraft piston hammers defective. Rome insists on immediate replacement. Repeat: immediate. Please confirm by telephone before the end of the day.

The number "five" referred to the Fontini-Cristis, because there were five men in the family—a father and four sons. Anything to do with the word "hammer" meant sudden, extreme danger. The repetition of the word "immediate" was self-explanatory: not a moment could be lost, confirmation of receipt was to be made by telephone to Rome within minutes of the telegram's arrival in Milan. Other men would then be contacted, strategies analyzed, plans made. It was too late now.

The wire had been sent to Savarone that afternoon. Vittorio must have received his cable by eleven. And yet his son had neither replied to Rome nor alerted him in Campo di Fiori. The end of the day was at hand. Too late.

It was unforgivable. Men daily risked their lives and the lives of their families in the fight against Mussolini.

It had not always been so, thought Savarone, as he stared at the office door, hoping that any second the secretary would reappear with news of Vittorio's whereabouts. It had all been very different once. In the beginning, the Fontini-Cristis had endorsed *Il Duce*. The weak, indecisive Emmanuel was letting Italy die. Benito Mussolini had offered an alternative; he had come himself to Campo di Fiori to meet with the patriarch of the Fontini-Cristis, seeking alliance—as Machiavelli once so sought the backing of the princes—and he had been alive, and committed, and filled with promise for all Italy.

That was sixteen years ago; since that time Mussolini had fed upon his own rhetoric. He had robbed the nation of its right to think, the people of their freedom to choose; he had deceived the aristocrats—used

them and denied their common objectives. He had plunged the country
into an utterly useless African war. All for the personal glory of this
Caesar Maximus. He had plundered the soul of Italy, and Savarone had
vowed to stop him. Fontini-Cristi had gathered the northern "princes"
together, and quietly the revolt was taking place.

Mussolini could not risk an open break with the Fontini-Cristis. Unless the charge of treason could be sustained with such clarity that even
the family's most avid supporters would have to conclude they had been
—if nothing else—stupid. Italy was gearing for its own entry into the
German war. Mussolini had to be careful. That war was not popular,
the Germans less so.

Campo di Fiori had become the meeting place of the disaffected.
The sprawling acres of lawns and forests and hills and streams were
suited to the clandestine nature of the conferences which generally took
place at night. But not always; there were other gatherings that required
the daylight hours, where younger men were trained by other experienced younger men in the arts of a new, strange warfare. The knife, the
rope, the chain, and the hook. They had even coined a name for themselves: *partigiani.*

The partisans. A name that was spreading from nation to nation.

These were the games of Italy, thought Savarone. "The games of
Italy" was what his son called them, a term used in derision by an arrogant, self-centered *aristocratico* who took seriously only his own plea-
sures. . . . No, that was not entirely true. Vittorio also took seriously
the running of Fontini-Cristi, as long as pressures of the marketplace
conformed to his own schedules. And he made them conform. He used
his financial power ruthlessly, his expertise—the expertise he had
learned at his father's side—arrogantly.

The telephone rang; Savarone was tempted to pick it up, but he did
not. It was his son's office, his son's telephone. Instead, he got out of
the terrible chair and walked across the room to the door. He opened it.
The secretary was repeating a name.

". . . Signor Tesca?"

Savarone interrupted harshly. "Is that Alfredo Tesca?"

The girl nodded.

"Tell him to stay on the telephone. I'll speak with him."

Savarone walked rapidly back to his son's desk and the telephone.
Alfredo Tesca was a foreman in one of the factories; he was also a *partigiano.*

"Fontini-Cristi," Savarone said.

"Padrone? I'm glad it's you. This line is clear; we check it every day."

"Nothing changes. It only accelerates."

"Yes, *padrone.* There's an emergency. A man has flown up from Rome. He must meet with a member of your family."

"Where?"

"The Olona house."

"When?"

"As soon as possible."

Savarone looked at the overcoat and the green felt hat he had thrown over the chair. "Tesca? Do you remember two years ago? The meeting at the apartment on the Duomo?"

"Yes, *padrone.* It will be six o'clock soon. I'll be waiting for you."

Fontini-Cristi hung up the telephone and reached for his overcoat and his hat. He put them on and checked his watch. It was five forty-five; he had to wait a few minutes. The walk across the concrete lot to the factory was short. He had to time it so that he entered the building at the height of the crowds; when the day shift was leaving and the night shift came to work.

His son had taken full advantage of *Il Duce*'s war machine. The Fontini-Cristi Industries operated around the clock. When the father had reproached the son, the son had replied, "We don't make munitions. We're not geared for that. The conversion would be too expensive. We make only profits, father."

His son. The most capable of them all had a hollowness in him.

Savarone's eyes fell on the photograph in the silver frame on Vittorio's desk. Its very existence was a cruel, self-inflicted joke. The face in the picture was that of a young woman, pretty in the accepted sense, with the pert, set features of a spoiled child growing into spoiled maturity. She had been Vittorio's wife. Ten years ago.

It had not been a good marriage. It had been more an industrial alliance between two immensely wealthy families. And the bride brought little to the union; she was a pouting, self-indulgent woman whose outlook was guided by possessions.

She died in an automobile crash in Monte Carlo, early in the morning after the casinos had closed. Vittorio never talked about that early morning; he had not been with his wife. Another had.

His son had spent four years in turbulent discomfort with a wife he could not stand, and yet the photograph was on his desk. Ten years later. Savarone once asked him why.

"Being a widower lends a certain respectability to my life-style."

It was seven minutes to six. Time to begin. Savarone walked out of his son's office and spoke to the secretary. "Please call downstairs and have my car brought around to the west gate. Tell my chauffeur I have a meeting at the Duomo."

"Yes, sir. . . . Do you wish to leave a number where your son can reach you?"

"Campo di Fiori. But by the time he calls, I'll no doubt be asleep."

Savarone took the private elevator to the ground floor and went out the executive entrance onto the concrete. Thirty yards away his chauffeur was walking toward the limousine with the crest of Fontini-Cristi on the door panels. The two men exchanged looks. The chauffeur nodded slightly; he knew what to do. He was a *partigiano*.

Savarone crossed the yard, aware that people were watching him. That was good; that was the way it had been two years ago when *Il Duce*'s secret police were tracking his every move, trying to unearth the whereabouts of an antifascist cell. The factory whistles blew; the day shift was released and within minutes the yard and the corridors would be crowded. The incoming workers—due at their stations at six fifteen—were flooding through the west gate.

He climbed the steps to the employees' entrance and entered the crowded, noisy corridor, removing his coat and hat in the confusion. Tesca stood by the wall, halfway toward the doors that led to the workers' lockers. He was tall and slender, very much like Savarone, and he took Savarone's coat and hat and helped Fontini-Cristi into his own worn, three-quarter-length raincoat with a newspaper in the pocket. Then he handed Savarone a large cloth visor cap. The exchange was completed without words in the jostling crowds. Tesca accepted Savarone's assistance in putting on the camel's hair coat; the employer saw that the employee had taken the trouble—as he had done two years ago—to change into pressed trousers, shined shoes, and a white shirt and tie.

The *partigiano* entered the flow of human traffic to the exit doors. Savarone followed ten yards behind, then stood immobile on the crowded platform outside the constantly opening doors, pretending to read the newspaper.

He saw what he wanted to see. The camel's hair coat and the green Tyrolean hat stood out among the worn leather jackets and frayed workers' clothing. Two men beyond the throngs signaled each other and began the chase, making their way through the crowd as best they could in an effort to catch up. Savarone squeezed himself into the stream of workers and arrived at the gate in time to see the door of the Fontini-Cristi limousine close and the huge automobile roll into the traffic of the Via di Sempione. The two pursuers were at the curb; a gray Fiat pulled up and they climbed in.

The Fiat took up the chase. Savarone turned north and walked swiftly to the corner bus stop.

The house on the riverfront was a relic that once, perhaps a decade ago, had been painted white. From the outside it looked dilapidated, but inside the rooms were small, neat, and organized; they were places of work, an antifascist headquarters.

Savarone entered the room with the windows overlooking the murky waters of the Olona River, made black by the darkness of night. Three men rose from straight-backed chairs around a table and greeted him with feeling and respect. Two were known to him; the third, he presumed, was from Rome.

"The hammer code was sent this morning," said Savarone. "What does it mean?"

"You *received* the wire?" asked the man from Rome incredulously. "All telegrams to Fontini-Cristi in Milan were intercepted. It's why I'm here. All communications to your factories were stopped."

"I received mine at Campo di Fiori. Through the telegraph office in Varese, I imagine, not Milan." Savarone felt a minor relief in knowing his son had not disobeyed. "Have you the information?"

"Not all, *padrone*," replied the man. "But enough to know it's extremely serious. And imminent. The military is suddenly very concerned with the northern movement. The generals want it crippled; they intend to see your family exposed."

"As what?"

"As enemies of the new Italy."

"On what grounds?"

"For holding meetings of a treasonable nature at Campo di Fiori. Spreading antistate lies; of attempting to undermine Rome's objectives and corrupt the industrial arm of the country."

"Words."

"Nevertheless, an example is to be made. They demand it, they say."

"Nonsense. Rome wouldn't dare move against us on such tenuous grounds."

"That is the problem, *signore,*" said the man hesitantly. "It's not Rome. It's Berlin."

"*What?*"

"The Germans are everywhere, giving orders to everyone. The word is that Berlin wants the Fontini-Cristis stripped of influence."

"They look to the future, don't they," stated one of the other two men, an older *partigiano* who had walked to the window.

"How do they propose to accomplish this?" asked Savarone.

"By smashing a meeting at Campo di Fiori. Forcing those there to bear witness to the treasons of the Fontini-Cristis. That would be less difficult than you think, I believe."

"Agreed. It's the reason we've been careful. . . . When will this happen? Do you have any idea?"

"I left Rome at noon. I can only assume the code word 'hammer' was used correctly."

"There's a meeting tonight."

"Then 'hammer' was called for. Cancel it, *padrone.* Obviously, word got out."

"I'll need your help. I'll give you names . . . our telephones are unsafe." Fontini-Cristi began writing in a notebook on the table with a pencil supplied by the third *partigiano.*

"When's the meeting scheduled?"

"Ten thirty. There's enough time," replied Savarone.

"I hope so. Berlin is thorough."

Fontini-Cristi stopped writing and looked over at the man. "That's a strange thing to say. The Germans may bark orders in the Campidoglio; they're not in Milan."

The three partisans exchanged glances. Savarone knew there was further news he had not received. The man from Rome finally spoke.

"As I said, our information is not complete. But we know certain things. The degree of Berlin's interest, for example. The German High Command wants Italy to openly declare itself. Mussolini wavers; for many reasons, not the least of which is the opposition of such powerful men as yourself——" The man stopped; he was unsure. Not, apparently, of his information, but how to say it.

"What are you driving at?"

"They say that Berlin's interest in the Fontini-Cristis is Gestapo inspired. It's the Nazis who demand the example; who intend to crush Mussolini's opposition."

"I gathered that. So?"

"They have little confidence in Rome, none in the provinces. The raiding party will be led by Germans."

"A German raiding party out of *Milan?*"

The man nodded.

Savarone put down the pencil and stared at the man from Rome. But his thoughts were not on the man; they were on a Greek freight from Salonika he had met high in the mountains of Champoluc. On the cargo that train carried. A vault from the Patriarchate of Constantine, now buried in the frozen earth of the upper regions.

It seemed incredible, but the incredible was commonplace in these times of madness. Had Berlin found out about the train from Salonika? Did the Germans know about the vault? *Mother of Christ,* it had to be kept from them! And all—*all*—*like* them!

"You're sure of your information?"

"We are."

Rome could be managed, thought Savarone. Italy needed the Fontini-Cristi Industries. But if the German intrusion was linked to the vault from Constantine, Berlin would not consider Rome's needs in the slightest. The possession of the vault was *everything*.

And, therefore, the protection of it essential beyond all life. Above all things its secret could not fall into the wrong hands. Not now. Perhaps not ever, but certainly not now.

The key was Vittorio. It was always Vittorio, the most capable of them all. For whatever else he was, Vittorio was a Fontini-Cristi. He would honor the family's commitment; he was a match for Berlin. The time had come to tell him about the train from Salonika. Detail the family's arrangements with the monastic Order of Xenope. The timing was right, the strategy complete.

A date marked in stone, etched for a millennium, was only a hint, a clue in case of a sudden failing of the heart, death from abrupt natural or unnatural causes. It was not enough.

Vittorio had to be told, charged with a responsibility beyond anything in his imagination. The documents from Constantine made everything else pale into insignificance.

Savarone looked up at the three men. "The meeting will be canceled tonight. The raiding party will find only a large family gathering. A holiday dinner party. All my children and their children. However, for it to be complete, my oldest son must be at Campo di Fiori. I've tried calling him all afternoon. Now you must find him. Use your telephones. Call everyone in Milan if you have to, but *find him!* If it gets late, tell him to use the stable road. It wouldn't do for him to enter with the raiding party."

2

DECEMBER 29, 1939
LAKE COMO, ITALY

The white, twelve-cylinder Hispano-Suiza, its off-white leather top rolled halfway back, uncovering the front, red leather seat, took the long curve at high speed. Below on the left were the winter-blue waters of Lake Como, to the right the mountains of Lombardy.

"*Vittorio!*" shrieked the girl beside the driver, holding her wind-shocked blonde hair with one hand, her collar of Russian pony with the other. "I'll be undone, my lamb!"

The driver smiled, his squinting gray eyes steady on the onrushing road in the sunlight, his hands expertly, almost delicately, feeling the play in the ivory steering wheel. "The Suiza is a far better car than the Alfa-Romeo. The British Rolls is no comparison."

"You don't have to prove it to *me,* darling. My God, I refuse to look at the speedometer! And I'll be an absolute mess!"

"Good. If your husband's in Bellagio, he won't recognize you. I'll introduce you as a terribly sweet cousin from Verona."

The girl laughed. "If my husband's in Bellagio, he'll have a terribly sweet cousin to introduce to *us.*"

They both laughed. The curve came to an end, the road straightened, and the girl slid over next to the driver. She slipped her hand under the arm of his tan suede jacket, enlarged by the heavy wool of the white turtleneck sweater beneath; briefly she placed her face against his shoulder.

"It was sweet of you to call. I really had to get away."

"I knew that. It was in your eyes last night. You were bored to death."

"Well, God, weren't *you?* Such a dreary dinner party! Talk, talk, talk! War this, war that. Rome yes, Rome no, Benito always. I'm positively sick of it! Gstaad closed! St. Moritz filled with Jews throwing money at everyone! Monte Carlo an absolute fiasco! The casinos are closing, you know. Everybody says so. It's all such a *bore!*"

The driver let his right hand drop from the steering wheel and reached for the fold of the girl's overcoat. He separated the fur and caressed her inner thigh as expertly as he fingered the ivory steering wheel. She moaned pleasantly and craned her neck, putting her lips to his ear, her tongue darting.

"You continue that, we'll end up in the water. I suspect it's damned cold."

"You started it, my lovely Vittorio."

"I'll stop it," he said smiling, returning his hand to the wheel. "I won't be able to buy another car like this for a long time. Today everything is the tank. Far less profit in the tank."

"Please! No war talk."

"You'll get none from me," said Fontini-Cristi, laughing again. "Unless you want to negotiate a purchase for Rome. I'll sell you anything from conveyor belts to motorcycles to uniforms, if you like."

"You don't make uniforms."

"We own a company that does."

"I forgot. Fontini-Cristi owns everything north of Parma and west of Padua. At least, that's what my husband says. Quite enviously, of course."

"Your husband, the sleepy count, is a dreadful businessman."

"He doesn't mean to be."

Vittorio Fontini-Cristi smiled as he braked the long white automobile for a descending curve in the road toward the lakeshore. Halfway down, on the promontory that was Bellagio, stood the elegant Villa Lario, named for the ancient poet of Como. It was a resort lodge known for its extraordinary beauty, as well as its marked exclusivity.

When the elite moved north, they played at Villa Lario. Money and family were their methods of entry. The *commessi* were diffident, soft-spoken, aware of their clientele's every proclivity, and most alert as to the scheduling of reservations. It was uncommon for a husband or a wife, a lover or a mistress, to receive a quiet, cautioning phone call suggesting another date for arrival. Or rapid departure.

The Hispano-Suiza swerved into the parking lot of blue brick; two uniformed attendants raced from the heated booth to both sides of the automobile, opening the doors and bowing.

The attendant at Vittorio's side spoke. "Welcome to Villa Lario, *signore.*"

It was never nice-to-see-you-again-*signore*.

Never.

"Thank you. We have no luggage. We're here only for the day. See to the oil and petrol. Is the mechanic around?"

"Yes, sir."

"Have him check the alignment. There's too much play."

"Of course, *signore*."

Fontini-Cristi got out of the car. He was a tall man, over six feet in height. His straight, dark-brown hair fell over his forehead; his features were sharp—as aquiline as his father's—and his eyes, still squinting in the bright sunlight, were at once passive and alert. He walked in front of the white hood, absently feeling the radiator cap, and smiled at his companion, the Contessa d'Avenzo. Together they crossed to the stone steps leading up to the entrance of Villa Lario.

"Where did you tell the servants you were off to?" asked Fontini-Cristi.

"Treviglio. You are a horse trainer who wants to sell me an Arabian."

"Remind me to buy you one."

"And you? What did you say at your office?"

"Nothing, really. Only my brothers might ask for me; everyone else waits patiently."

"But not your brothers." The Contessa d'Avenzo smiled. "I like that. The important Vittorio is hounded in business by his brothers."

"Hardly! My sweet younger brothers have between them three wives and eleven children. Their problems are continuously and forever domestic. I think sometimes I'm a referee. Which is fine; they keep occupied and *away* from business."

They stood on the terrace outside the glass doors that led to the lobby of Villa Lario and looked down at the enormous lake and across to the mountains beyond.

"It's beautiful," said the contessa. "You've arranged for a room?"

"A suite. The penthouse. The view's magnificent."

"I've heard of it. I've never been up there."

"Few people have."

"I imagine you lease it by the month."

"That's not really necessary," said Fontini-Cristi, turning toward the huge glass doors. "You see, as it happens I own Villa Lario."

The Contessa d'Avenzo laughed. She preceded Vittorio into the lobby. "You are an *impossible, a*moral man. You get richer from your own kind. My God, you could blackmail half of Italy!"

"Only *our* Italy, my dear."

"That's enough!"

"Hardly. But I've never had to, if it relieves your mind. I'm merely a guest. Wait here, please."

Vittorio walked over to the front desk. The tuxedoed clerk behind the marble counter greeted him. "How good of you to come to see us, Signor Fontini-Cristi."

"Are things going well?"

"Extremely so. Would you care to——?"

"No, I should not," interrupted Vittorio. "I assume my rooms are ready."

"Of course, *signore*. As you requested, an early supper is being prepared. Caviar Iranian, cold pressed duck, Veuve Cliquot twenty-eight."

"And?"

"There are flowers, naturally. The masseur is prepared to cancel his other appointments."

"And . . . ?"

"There are no complications for the Contessa d'Avenzo," answered the clerk quickly, rapidly. "None of her circle is here."

"Thank you." Fontini-Cristi turned, only to be stopped by the sound of the clerk's voice.

"Signore?"

"Yes?"

"I realize you do not care to be disturbed except in emergencies, but your office called."

"Did my office say it was an emergency?"

"They said your father was trying to locate you."

"That's not an emergency. It's a whim."

"I think you may be that Arabian, after all, lamb," mused the contessa out loud, lying beside Vittorio in the feather bed. The eiderdown quilt was pulled down to her naked waist. "You're marvelous. And so patient."

"But not patient enough, I think," replied Fontini-Cristi. He sat up against the pillow, looking down at the girl; he was smoking a cigarette.

"Not patient enough," agreed the Contessa d'Avenzo, turning her face and smiling up at him. "Why don't you put out the cigarette?"

"In a little while. Be assured of it. Some wine?" He gestured at the silver ice bucket within arm's reach. It stood on a tripod; an open bottle draped with a linen towel was pushed into the melting crushed ice.

The contessa stared at him, her breath coming shorter. "You pour the wine. I'll drink my own."

In swift, gentle movements, the girl turned and reached under the soft quilt with both hands to Vittorio's groin. She raised the cover and placed her face underneath, over Vittorio. The quilt fell back, covering her head as her throaty moans grew louder and her body writhed.

The waiters cleared away the dishes and rolled out the table, a *commesso* lighted a fire in the fireplace and poured brandy.

"It's been a lovely day," said the Contessa d'Avenzo. "May we do it often?"

"I think we should set up a schedule. By your calendar, of course."

"Of course." The girl laughed throatily. "You're a very practical man."

"Why not? It's easier."

The telephone rang. Vittorio looked over at it, annoyed. He rose from the chair in front of the fireplace and crossed angrily to the bedside table. He picked up the instrument and spoke harshly. "Yes?"

The voice at the other end was vaguely familiar. "This is Tesca. Alfredo Tesca."

"Who?"

"One of the foremen in the Milan factories."

"You're *what?* How *dare* you call here! How did you get this number?"

Tesca was silent for a moment. "I threatened the life of your secretary, young *padrone*. And I would have killed her had she not given it to me. You may fire me tomorrow. I am your foreman, but I am a *partigiano* first."

"You *are* fired. *Now*. As of this moment!"

"So be it, *signore*."

"I want no part——."

"Basta!" shouted Tesca. "There's no time! Everyone's looking for you. The *padrone*'s in danger. Your whole *family*'s in danger! Go to Campo di Fiori! At once! Your father says to use the stable road!"

The telephone went dead.

Savarone walked through the great hall into the enormous dining room of Campo di Fiori. Everything was as it should be. The room was filled with sons and daughters, husbands and wives, and a thoroughly boisterous crowd of grandchildren. The servants had placed silver trays of antipasto on the tops of marble tables. A tall pine that reached the high beamed ceiling was a magnificent Christmas tree, its myriad lights and glittering ornament filling the room with reflections of color that bounced off the tapestries and the ornate furniture.

Outside in the circular drive in front of the marble steps of the entrance were four automobiles illuminated by the floodlights that beamed down from the eaves. They could easily be mistaken for anyone's automobiles, which was what Savarone intended. For when the raiding party arrived, all it would find was an innocent, festive family gathering. A holiday dinner. Nothing else.

Except an imperiously aggravated patriarch of one of Italy's most powerful clans. The *padrone* of the Fontini-Cristis, who would demand to know who was responsible for such a barbarous intrusion.

Only Vittorio was missing; and his presence was vital. Questions might be raised that could lead to other questions. The unwilling Vittorio, who scoffed at their work, could become an unjustified target of suspicion. What was a holiday family dinner without the eldest son, the primary heir? Further, if Vittorio appeared *during* the intrusion, arrogantly reluctant—as his custom—to give an account of himself to anyone, there could be trouble. His son refused to acknowledge the extent, but Rome *was* under Berlin's thumb.

Savarone beckoned his next eldest, the serious Antonio, who stood with his wife as she admonished one of their children.

"Yes, father?"

"Go to the stables. See Barzini. Tell him that if Vittorio arrives during the fascists' visit, he's to say he was detained at one of the plants."

"I can call him on the stable phone."

"No. Barzini's getting on. He pretends it's not so, but he's growing deaf. Make sure he understands."

The second son nodded dutifully. "Yes, of course, father. Anything you say."

What in God's name had his father *done?* What *could* he do that would give Rome the confidence, the *excuse,* to move openly against the house of Fontini-Cristi?

Your whole family is in danger.

Preposterous!

Mussolini courted the northern industrialists; he needed them. He knew that most were old men, set in their ways, and knew he could achieve more with honey than vinegar. What did it matter if a few Savarones played their silly games? Their time was past.

But then there was only one Savarone. Separate and apart from all other men. He had become, perhaps, that terrible thing, a symbol. With his silly, goddamned *partigiani.* Ragtail lunatics who raced around the fields and the woods of Campo di Fiori pretending they were some kind of primitive tribesmen hunting tigers and killer lions.

Jesus! *Children!*

Well, it would all come to a stop. *Padrone* or no *padrone,* if his father had gone too far and embarrassed them, there would be a confrontation. He had made it clear to Savarone two years ago that when he assumed the reins of Fontini-Cristi, it meant that all the leather was in his hands.

Suddenly Vittorio remembered. Two weeks ago, Savarone had gone to Zürich for a few days. At least, he *said* he was going to Zürich. It wasn't really clear; he, Vittorio, had not been listening closely. But during those few days, it was unexpectedly necessary to get his father's signature on several contracts. So necessary that he had telephoned every hotel in Zürich, trying to locate Savarone. He was nowhere to be found. No one had seen him, and his father was not easily overlooked.

And when he returned to Campo di Fiori, he would not say where he had been. He was maddeningly enigmatic, telling his son that he would explain everything in a few days. An incident would take place in Monfalcone and when it occurred, Vittorio would be told. Vittorio *had* to be told.

What in hell was his father talking about? *What* incident at Monfalcone? Why would *anything* taking place at Monfalcone concern them? Preposterous!

But Zürich wasn't preposterous at all. Banks were in Zürich. Had Savarone manipulated money in Zürich? Had he transferred extraordinary sums out of Italy into Switzerland? There was specific laws against that these days. Mussolini needed every *lira* he could keep. And God knew the family had sufficient reserves in Berne and Geneva; there was no lack of Fontini-Cristi capital in Switzerland.

Whatever Savarone had done, it would be his last gesture. If his father was so politically involved, let him go somewhere else and proselytize. America, perhaps.

Vittorio shook his head slowly in defeat, as he steered the Hispano-Suiza onto the road out of Varese. What was he thinking of? Savarone was—Savarone. The head of the house of Fontini-Cristi. No matter the son's talents or expertise, the son was not the *padrone.*

Use the stable road.

What was the point of that? The stable road started at the north end of the property, three miles from the east gates. Nevertheless, he would use it; his father must have had a reason for giving the order. No doubt as implausible as the foolish games he indulged in, but a surface filial obedience was called for; the son was going to be very firm with the father.

What had happened in Zürich?

He passed the main gates on the road out of Varese and proceeded to the intersecting west road three miles beyond. He turned left and drove nearly two miles to the north gate, turning left again into Campo di Fiori. The stables were three-quarters of a mile from the entrance; the road was dirt. It was easier on the horses, for this was the road used by riders heading for the fields and trails north and west of the forest at the center of Campo di Fiori. The forest behind the great house that was bisected by the wide stream that flowed from the northern mountains.

In the headlights he saw the figure of old Guido Barzini waving his arms, signaling him to stop. The gnarled Barzini was something: a fixture at Campo di Fiori who had spent his life in the service of the house.

"Quickly, Signor Vittorio!" said Barzini through the open window. "Leave your car here. There's no more time."

"Time for what?"

"The *padrone* spoke to me not five minutes ago. He said if you drove in now, you were to call him on the stable telephone before you went to the house. It's nearly half past the hour."

Vittorio looked at the dashboard clock. It was twenty-eight minutes past ten. "What's going on?"

"Hurry, *signore! Please! The fascisti!*"

"What *fascisti?*"

"The *padrone*. He'll tell you."

Fontini-Cristi got out of the car and followed Barzini down the stone path into the entrance of the stables. It was a tack room; bits and braces and halters and leather were hung neatly on the walls, surrounding countless plaques and ribbons, proof of the superiority of the Fontini-Cristi colors. Also on the wall was the telephone that connected the stables to the great house.

"What's going on, father? Have you any idea who called me in Bellagio?"

"*Basta!*" roared Savarone over the telephone. "They'll be here any moment. A German raiding party."

"*Germans?*"

"Yes. Rome expects to find a *partigiano* meeting taking place. They won't, of course. They'll intrude on a family dinner. *Remember!* A family dinner party was on your calendar. You were detained in Milan."

"What have Germans got to do with Rome?"

"I'll explain later. Just remember——"

Suddenly, over the telephone, Vittorio heard the sounds of screeching tires and powerful motors. A column of automobiles was speeding toward the great house from the east gates.

"*Father!*" yelled Vittorio. "Has this anything to do with your trip to Zürich?"

There was silence over the phone. Finally Savarone spoke. "It may have. You must stay where you are——"

"What happened? What happened in Zürich?"

"Not Zürich. Champoluc."

"What?"

"Later! I have to get back to the others. Stay where you are! Out of sight! We'll talk when they leave."

Vittorio heard the click. He turned to Barzini. The old stable master was riffling through a low chest of drawers filled with odd bits and braces; he found what he was looking for: a pistol and a pair of binoculars. He pulled them out and handed both to Vittorio.

"Come!" he said, his old eyes angry. "We'll watch. The *padrone* will teach them a lesson."

They ran down the dirt road toward the house and the gardens above and behind it. When the dirt became pavement they cut to their left and climbed the embankment overlooking the circular drive. They were in darkness; the whole area below bathed in floodlights.

Three automobiles sped up the east-gate road; long, black, powerful vehicles, their headlights emerging out of the darkness, swallowed by the floodlamps that washed the area in white light. The cars entered the circular drive, careening to the left of the other automobiles, stopping suddenly, equidistant from each other in front of the stone steps that led to the thick oak doors of the entrance.

Men leaped out of the cars. Men dressed alike in black suits and black overcoats; men carrying weapons.

Carrying *weapons!*

Vittorio stared as the men—seven, eight, nine—raced up the steps to the door. A tall man in front assumed command; he held his hand up to those behind, ordering them to flank the doors, four on each side. He pulled the bell chain with his left hand, his right holding a pistol at his side.

Vittorio put the binoculars to his eyes. The man's face was turned away toward the door, but the weapon in his hand came into focus. It was a German Luger. Vittorio swung the binoculars to those on both sides of the doors.

The weapons were all German. Four Lugers, four Bergmann MP38 submachine guns.

Vittorio's stomach suddenly convulsed; his mind caught fire as he watched in disbelief. What had Rome *permitted?* It was incredible!

He focused the binoculars on the three automobiles. In each was a man; all were in shadows, only the backs of their heads seen through the rear windows. Vittorio concentrated on the nearest car, on the man inside that car.

The man shifted his position in the seat and looked back to his right; the light from the floodlamps caught his hair. It was close-cropped, grayish hair, but with a white streak shooting up from his forehead. There was something familiar about the man—the shape of the head, the streak of white in the hair—but Vittorio could not place him.

The door of the house opened; a maid stood in the frame, startled by the sight of the tall man with a gun. Vittorio stared in fury at the scene below. Rome would pay for the insult. The tall man pushed the maid aside and burst through the door, followed by the squad of eight men, their weapons held in front of them. The maid disappeared in the phalanx of bodies.

Rome would pay dearly!

There were shouts from inside. Vittorio could hear his father's roar and the subsequent shouted objections of his brothers.

There was a loud crash, a combination of glass and wood. Vittorio reached for the pistol in his pocket. He felt a powerful hand grip his wrist.

It was Barzini. The old stable master held Vittorio's hand, but he was looking over his shoulder, staring below.

"There are too many guns. You'll solve nothing," he said simply.

A third crash came from below, the sound nearer now. The left panel of the huge oak double door had been thrown open and figures emerged. The children, first, bewildered, some crying in fear. Then the women, his sisters and his brothers' wives. Then his mother, her head defiant, the youngest child in her arms. His father and his brothers followed, prodded violently by the weapons in the hands of the black-suited men.

They were herded onto the pavement of the circular drive. His father's voice roared above the others, demanding to know who was responsible for the outrage.

But the outrage had not begun.

When it did, the mind of Vittorio Fontini-Cristi snapped. Cracks of thunder deafened him, streaks of lightning blinded him. He lunged forward, every ounce of his strength trying to wrench his hand free of Barzini's grip, twisting, turning, trying desperately to free his neck and his jaw from Barzini's stranglehold.

For the black-suited men below had opened fire. Women threw themselves over the children, his brothers lurched at the weapons that shattered the night with fire and death. The screams of terror and pain and outrage swelled in the blinding light of the execution grounds. Smoke billowed; bodies froze in midair—suspended in blood-soaked garments. Children were cut in half, the bullets ripping out mouths and eyes. Pieces of flesh and skull and intestine shot through the swirling mists. A child's body exploded in its mother's arms. And still Vittorio Fontini-Cristi could not free himself, could not go to his own.

He felt dead weight pressing him downward, then a clawing, choking, pulling at his lower jaw that blocked all sound from his lips.

And then the words pierced through the cacophony of gunshot and human screams below. The voice was tremendous, its thunder chopped by the firepower of submachine guns, but not stopped.

It was his father. Calling to him over the chasms of death.

"*Champoluc* . . . Zürich is *Champoluc*. . . . Zürich is the *river* . . . *Champoluuuc*. . . ."

Vittorio gnashed his teeth down on the fingers inside his mouth, pulling his jaw out of its socket. He wrenched his hand free for an instant—the hand with the weapon—and tried to raise the pistol and fire below.

But suddenly he could not. The sea of heaviness was over him again, his wrist twisted beyond endurance; the pistol was shaken loose. The enormous hand that had gripped his jaw was pushing his face into the cold earth. He could feel the blood in his mouth, over his lips, mingled with dirt.

And the horrible scream from the abyss of death came once more.

"*Champoluc!*"

And then was stilled.

3

DECEMBER 30, 1939

"Champoluc . . . Zürich is Champoluc . . . Zürich is the river. . . ."

The words were screams and they were blurred in agony. His mind's eye was filled with white light and explosions of smoke and deep red streaks of blood; his ears heard the screams of jolting shock, and terror, and the outrage of infinite pain and terrible murder.

It had happened. He had borne witness to the tableau of execution: strong men, trembling children, wives and mothers. His own.

Oh, my God!

Vittorio twisted his head and buried his face into the coarse cloth of the primitive bed, the tears flowing down his cheeks. It was cloth, not cold rough dirt; he had been moved. The last thing he remembered was his face being pressed with enormous strength into the hard ground of the embankment. Pressed down and held furiously immobile, his eyes blinded, his lips filled with warm blood and cold earth.

Only his ears bearing witness to the agony.

"Champoluc!"

Mother of God, it had happened!

The Fontini-Cristis were massacred in the white lights of Campo di Fiori. All the Fontini-Cristis but one. And that one would make Rome pay. The last Fontini-Cristi would cut the flesh, layer by layer, from *Il Duce*'s face; the eyes would be last, the blade would enter slowly.

"Vittorio. Vittorio."

He heard his name and yet he did not hear it. It was a whisper, an urgent whisper, and whispers were dreams of agony.

"Vittorio." The weight was on his arms again; the whisper came from above, in the darkness. The face of Guido Barzini was inches from his, the sad strong eyes of the stablemaster were reflected in a shaft of dim light.

"Barzini?" It was all he could manage to say.

"Forgive me. There was no choice, no other way. You would have been killed with the rest."

"Yes, I know. Executed. But *why?* In the name of God, *why?*"

"The Germans. That's all we know at the moment. The Germans wanted the Fontini-Cristis dead. They want you dead. The ports, the airfields, the roads, all of northern Italy is sealed off."

"Rome allowed it." Vittorio could still taste the blood in his mouth, still feel the pain in his jaw.

"Rome hides," said Barzini softly. "Only a few speak."

"What do they say?"

"What the Germans want them to say. That the Fontini-Cristis were traitors, killed by their own people. That the family was aiding the French, sending arms and monies across the borders."

"Preposterous."

"Rome is preposterous. And filled with cowards. The informer was found. He hangs naked from his feet in the Piazza del Duomo, his body riddled, his tongue nailed to his head. A *partigiano* placed a sign below; it says, 'This pig betrayed Italy, his blood flows from the stigmata of the Fontini-Cristis.' "

Vittorio turned away. The images burned; the white smoke in the white light, the bodies suspended, abruptly immobile in death, a thousand sudden blots of thick red; the execution of children.

"Champoluc," whispered Vittorio Fontini-Cristi.

"I beg your pardon?"

"My father. As he was dying, as the gunfire ravaged him, he shouted the name, Champoluc. Something happened in Champoluc."

"What does it mean?"

"I don't know. Champoluc is in the Alps, deep in the mountains. 'Zürich is Champoluc. Zürich is the river.' He said that. He shouted it as he died. Yet there's no river in the Champoluc."

"I cannot help you," said Barzini, sitting up, the anxiety in his questioning eyes and in the awkward rubbing together of his large hands. "There's not a great deal of time to dwell on it, or to think. Not now."

Vittorio looked up at the huge, embarrassed farmhand sitting on the side of the primitive bed. They were in a room built of heavy wood. There was a door, only partially open, ten or fifteen feet away, on his left, but no windows. There were several other beds; he could not tell how many. It was a barracks for laborers.

"Where are we?"

"Across the Maggiore, south of Baveno. On a goat farm."

"How did we get here?"

"A wild trip. The men at the riverfront drove us out. They met us with a fast car on the road west of Campo di Fiori. The *partigiano* from Rome knows the drugs; he gave you a hypodermic needle."

"You carried me from the embankment to the west road?"

"Yes."

"It's more than a mile."

"Perhaps. You're large, but not so heavy." Barzini stood up.

"You saved my life." Vittorio pressed his hands on the coarse blanket and raised himself to a sitting position, his back against the wall.

"Revenge is not found in one's own death."

"I understand."

"We must both travel. You out of Italy, me to Campo di Fiori."

"You're going back?"

"It's where I can do the most good. The most damage."

Fontini-Cristi stared for a moment at Barzini. How quickly the unimaginable became the practical reality. How rapidly did men react savagely to the savage; and how necessary was that reaction. But there was no time. Barzini was right; the thinking would come later.

"Is there a way for me to get out of the country? You said all of northern Italy was sealed off."

"All the usual routes. It is manhunt mounted by Rome, directed by the Germans. There are other ways. The British will help, I am told."

"The British?"

"That is the word. They have been on *partigiano* radios all through the night."

"The British? I don't understand."

The vehicle was an old farm truck with poor brakes and a sliding clutch, but it was sturdy enough for the badly paved back roads. It was no match for motorcycles or official automobiles, but excellent for traveling from one point to another in the farm country—one more truck carrying a few livestock that lurched unsteadily in the open, slatted van.

Vittorio was dressed, as was his driver, in the filthy, dung-encrusted, sweat-stained clothes of a farm laborer. He was provided with a dirty, mutilated identification card that gave his name as Aldo Ravena, former *soldato semplice* in the Italian army. It could be assumed his schooling was minimal; any conversation he might have with the police would be simple, blunt, and perhaps a touch hostile.

They had been driving since dawn, southwest into Torino, where they swung southeast toward Alba. With no serious interruptions they would reach Alba by nightfall.

At an *espresso* bar in Alba's main piazza, San Giorno, they would make contact with the British; two operatives sent in by MI6. It would be their job to get Fontini-Cristi down to the coast and through the patrols that guarded every mile of waterfront from Genoa to San Remo. Italian personnel, German efficiency, Vittorio was told.

This area of the coast in the Gulf of Genoa was considered the most conducive to infiltration. For years it had been a primary source route for Corsican smugglers. Indeed the *Unio Corso* claimed the beaches and rocky ocean cliffs as their own. They called this coast the soft belly of Europe; they knew every inch.

Which was fine as far as the British were concerned. They employed the Corsicans, whose services went to the highest bidders. The *Unio Corso* would aid London in getting Fontini-Cristi through the patrols and out on the water where, in a prearranged rendezvous north of Rogliano on the Corsican coast, a submarine from the Royal Navy would surface and pick him up.

This was the information Vittorio was given—by the ragtail lunatics he had scorned as children playing primitive games. The unkempt, wild-eyed fools who had formed an untenable alliance with such men as his father had saved his life. *Were* saving his life. Skinny peasant thugs who had direct communication with the far-off British . . . far off and not so distant. No farther than Alba.

How? Why? What in the name of God were the English doing? Why were they doing it? What were men he had barely acknowledged, hardly spoken to in his life before—except to order and ignore—what were *they* doing? And *why?* He was no friend; no enemy, perhaps, but certainly no friend.

These were the questions that frightened Vittorio Fontini-Cristi. A nightmare had exploded in white light and death, and he was not capable of fathoming—even wanting—his own survival.

They were eight miles from Alba on a curving dirt road that paralleled the main highway from Torino. The *partigiano* driver was weary, his eyes bloodshot from the long day of bright sunlight. The shadows of early evening were now playing tricks on his eyes; his back obviously ached from the constant strain. Except for infrequent fuel stops he had not left his seat. Time was vital.

"Let me drive for a while."

"We're nearly there, *signore*. You don't know this road; I do. We'll enter Alba from the east, on the Canelli highway. There may be soldiers at the municipal limits. Remember what you're to say."

"As little as possible, I think."

The truck entered the light traffic on the Via Canelli and maintained a steady speed with the other vehicles. As the driver had predicted, there were two soldiers at the municipal line.

For any of a dozen reasons, the truck was signaled to stop. They pulled off the road onto the shoulder of sand and waited. A sergeant approached the driver's window, a private stood laconically outside Fontini-Cristi's.

"Where are you from?" asked the sergeant.

"A farm south of Baveno," the *partigiano* said.

"You've come a long way for such a small delivery. I count five goats."

"Breeding stock. They're better animals than they look. Ten thousand *lire* for the males; eight for the females."

The sergeant raised his eyebrows. He did not smile as he spoke. "You don't look like *you're* worth that, *paisan*. Your identification."

The partisan reached into his rear pocket and pulled out a worn billfold. He withdrew the state card and handed it to the soldier.

"This says you're from Varallo."

"I come from Varallo. I work in Baveno."

"*South* of Baveno," corrected the soldier coldly. "*You,*" said the sergeant, addressing Vittorio. "Your identification."

Fontini-Cristi put his hand into his jacket, bypassing the handle of his pistol, and removed the card. He handed it to the driver, who gave it to the soldier.

"You were in Africa?"

"Yes, sergeant," replied Vittorio bluntly.

"What corps?"

Fontini-Cristi was silent. He had no answer. His mind raced, trying to recall from the news a number, or a name. "The Seventh," he said.

"I see." The sergeant returned the card; Vittorio exhaled. But the relief was short-lived. The soldier reached for the handle of the door, yanked it downward and pulled the door open swiftly. "Get out! Both of you!"

"What? Why?" objected the partisan in a loud whine. "We have to make our delivery by nightfall! There's barely time!"

"Get *out.*" The sergeant had removed his army revolver from the black leather holster and was pointing it at both men. He barked his orders across the hood to the private. "Pull him out! Cover him!"

Vittorio looked at the driver. The partisan's eyes told him to do as he was told. But to stay alert, be ready to move; the man's eyes told him that also.

Out of the truck on the shoulder of sand, the sergeant commanded both men to walk toward the guardhouse that stood next to a telephone pole. A telephone wire sagged down from a junction box and was attached to the roof of the small enclosure; the door was narrow, and open.

On the Via Canelli the twilight traffic was heavier now; or it seemed heavier to Fontini-Cristi. There were mostly cars, with a scattering of trucks, not unlike the farm trucks they were driving. A number of drivers slowed perceptibly at the sight of the two soldiers, their weapons drawn, marching the two civilians to the guardhouse. Then the drivers speeded up, anxious to be away.

"You have no right to stop us!" cried the partisan. "We've done nothing illegal. It's no crime to earn a living!"

"It's a crime to give false information, *paisan.*"

"We gave no false information! We are workers from Baveno, and, by the Mother of God, that's the truth!"

"Be careful," said the soldier sarcastically. "We'll add sacrilege to the charges. Get inside!"

The roadside guardhouse seemed even smaller than it appeared from the Via Canelli. The depth was no more than five feet, the length perhaps six. There was barely enough room for the four of them. And the look in the partisan's eyes told Vittorio that the close quarters was an advantage.

"Search them," ordered the sergeant.

The private placed his rifle on the floor, barrel up. The partisan driver then did a strange thing. He pulled his arms across his chest, protectively over his coat, as though it were a conscious act of defiance. Yet the man was not armed; he had made that clear to Fontini-Cristi.

"You'll steal!" he said, louder than was necessary, his words vibrating in the wooden shack. "Soldiers steal!"

"We're not concerned with your *lire, paisan*. There are more impressive vehicles on the highway. Take your hands from your coat."

"Even in Rome reasons are given! *Il Duce,* himself, says the workers are not to be treated so! I march with the fascist guards; my rider served in Africa!"

What was the man doing? thought Vittorio. *Why was he behaving so? It would only anger the soldiers.* "You try my patience, pig! We look for a man from Maggiore. Every road post looks for this man. You were stopped because the license on your truck is from the Maggiore district . . . Hold out your arms!"

"*Baveno!* Not Maggiore! We are from *Baveno!* Where are the lies?"

The sergeant looked at Vittorio. "No soldier in Africa says he was with the Seventh Corps. It was disgraced."

The army guard had barely finished when the partisan screamed his command.

"*Now, signore!* Take the other!" The driver's hand swept down, lashing at the revolver in the sergeant's grip, only inches from his stomach. The suddenness of the action and the shattering roar of the partisan's voice in the small enclosure had the effect of an unexpected collision. Vittorio had no time to watch; he could only hope his companion knew what he was doing. The private had lurched for his rifle, his left hand on the barrel, his right surging down to the stock. Fontini-Cristi threw his weight against the man, slamming him into the wall, both hands on the side of the soldier's head, crashing the head into the hard, wooden surface. The private's barracks cap fell off; blood matted instantly throughout the hairline and streaked down over the man's head. He slumped to the floor.

Vittorio turned. The sergeant was wedged into the corner of the tiny guardhouse, the partisan over him, pistol-whipping him with his own weapon. The soldier's face was a mass of torn flesh, the blood and ripped skin sickening.

"*Quickly!*" cried the partisan as the sergeant fell. "Bring the truck to the front! Directly to the front; squeeze it between the road and the guardhouse. Keep the motor running."

"Very well," said Fontini-Cristi, confused by the brutality as well as the swift decisiveness of the last thirty seconds.

"And, *signore!*" shouted the partisan, as Vittorio had one foot out the door.

"Yes?"

"Your gun, please. Let me use it. These army issues are like thunder."

Fontini-Cristi hesitated, then withdrew the weapon and handed it to the man. The partisan reached over to the crank-telephone on the wall and ripped it out.

Vittorio steered the truck to the front of the guardhouse, the left wheels by necessity on the hard surface of the highway; there was not sufficient room on the shoulder to pull completely off the road. He hoped the rear lights were sufficiently bright for the onrushing traffic—far heavier now—to see the obstruction and skirt it.

The partisan came out of the guardhouse and spoke through the window. "Race the motor, *signore*. As loud and as fast as you can."

Fontini-Cristi did so. The partisan ran back to the guardhouse. Gripped in his right hand was Vittorio's pistol.

The two shots were deep and sharp; muffled combustions that were

sudden, terrible outbursts within the sounds of the rushing traffic and
racing motor. Vittorio stared, his emotions a mixture of awe and fear
and, inexplicably, sorrow. He had entered a world of violence he did
not understand.

The partisan emerged from the guardhouse, pulling the narrow door
shut behind him. He jumped into the truck, slammed the door panel,
and nodded to Vittorio. Fontini-Cristi waited several moments for a
break in the traffic, then let out the clutch. The old truck lurched forward.

"There is a garage on the Via Monte that will hide the truck, paint it,
and alter the license plates. It's less than a mile from the Piazza San
Giorno. We'll walk there from the garage. I'll tell you where to turn."

The partisan held out the pistol for Vittorio. "Thank you," said Fontini-Cristi awkwardly, as he shoved the weapon into his jacket pocket.
"You killed them?"

"Of course," was the simple reply.

"I suppose you had to."

"Naturally. You'll be in England, *signore*. I, in Italy. I could be
identified."

"I see," answered Vittorio, the hesitancy in his voice.

"I don't mean disrespect, Signor Fontini-Cristi, but I don't think you
do see. You people at Campo di Fiori, it's all new to you. It's not new
to us. We've been at war for twenty years; I, myself, for ten."

"War?"

"Yes. Who do you think trains your *partigiani?*"

"What do you mean?"

"I am a Communist, *signore*. The powerful, capitalist Fontini-Cristis
are shown how to fight by Communists."

The truck was rushing forward; Vittorio held the wheel firmly, astonished but strangely unmoved by his companion's words.

"I didn't know that," he replied.

"It's peculiar, isn't it?" said the partisan. "No one ever asked."

4

The *espresso* bar was crowded, the tables full, the voices loud. Vittorio followed the partisan through the mass of gesturing hands and reluctantly parted bodies to the counter; they ordered coffee with Strega.

"Over there," said the partisan, indicating a table in the corner with three laborers seated around it, their soiled clothes and stubbled faces testifying to their status. There was one empty chair.

"How do you know? I thought we were to meet two men, not three. And British. Besides, there's not enough room; there's only one chair."

"Look at the heavyset man on the right. The identification is on the shoes. There are splotches of orange paint, not much but visible. *He's* the Corsican. The other two are English. Go over and say 'Our trip was uneventful'; that's all. The man with the shoes will get up; take his seat."

"What about you?"

"I'll join you in a minute. I must talk with the *Corso*."

Vittorio did as he was told. The heavyset man with the drippings of paint on his shoes got up, heaving a sigh of discomfort; Fontini-Cristi sat down. The British across from him spoke. His Italian was grammatically proper but hesitant; he had learned the language but not the idiom.

"Our sincerest regrets. Absolutely dreadful. We'll get you out."

"Thank you. Would you prefer speaking English? I'm fluent."

"Good," said the second man. "We weren't sure. We've had precious little time to read up on you. We were flown out of Lakenheath this morning. The *Corsos* picked us up in Pietra Ligure."

"Everything's happened so fast," said Vittorio. "The shock hasn't worn off."

"Don't see how it could," said the first man. "But we're not clear yet. You'll have to keep your wits about you. Our orders are to make bloody sure we get you to London: not to come back without you, and that's a fact."

Vittorio looked alternately at both men. "May I ask you why? Please understand, I'm grateful, but your concern seems to me extraordinary. I'm not humble, but neither am I a fool. Why am I so important to the British?"

"Damned if we know," replied the second agent. "But I can tell you, all hell broke loose last night. *All* night. We spent from midnight till four in the morning at the Air Ministry. All the radio dials in every operations room were beaming like mad. We're working with the Corsicans, you know."

"Yes, I was told."

The partisan walked through the crowds to the table. He pulled out the empty chair and sat down, a glass of Strega in his hand. The conversation was continued in Italian.

"We had trouble on the Canelli road. A checkpoint. Two guards had to be taken out."

"What's the A-span?" asked the agent on Fontini-Cristi's right. He was a slender man, somewhat more intense than his partner. He saw the puzzled expression on Vittorio's face and clarified. "How long does he think we have before the alarm goes out?"

"Midnight. When the twelve o'clock shift arrives. No one bothers with unanswered telephones. The equipment breaks down all the time."

"Well done," said the agent across the table. He was rounder in the face than his fellow Englishman; he spoke more slowly, as if constantly choosing his words. "You're a Bolshevik, I imagine."

"I am," replied the partisan, his hostility near the surface.

"No, no, please," added the agent. "I like working with you chaps. You're very thorough."

"M.I.-*Sei* is polite."

"By the way," said the Britisher on Vittorio's right, "I'm Apple; he's Pear."

"We know who you are," said Pear to Fontini-Cristi.

"And my name's not important," said the partisan with a slight laugh. "I'll not be going with you."

"Let's run through that, shall we?" Apple was anxious, but controlled to the point of being reserved. "The going. Also, London wants to set up firmer communications."

"We knew London would."

The three men fell into a professional conversation that Vittorio found extraordinary. They spoke of routes and codes and radio frequencies as though they were discussing prices on the stock exchange. They touched on the necessity of *taking-out, eliminating* various people in specific positions—not men, not human beings, but *factors* that had to be killed.

What kind of men were these three? "Apple," "Pear," a Bolshevik with no name, only a false identification card. Men who killed without anger, without remorse.

He thought of Campo di Fiori. Of blinding white floodlights, and gunfire and death. *He* could kill now. Viciously, savagely—but he could not speak of death as these men spoke of it.

". . . get us to a trawler known to the coastal patrols. Do you understand?" Apple was speaking to him, but he had not been listening.

"I'm sorry," said Vittorio. "My mind was elsewhere."

"We've a long way to go," said Pear. "Over fifty miles to the coast, then a minimum of three hours on the water. A lot can happen."

"I'll try to be more attentive."

"Do better than try," replied Apple, his tone one of controlled irritation. "I don't know what you've done to the Foreign Office, but you happen to be a high-priority subject. It's our asses if we don't bring you out. So *listen!* The Corsicans will take us to the coast. There will be four changes of vehicles——"

"Wait!" The partisan reached over the table and gripped Apple's arm. "The man who was seated with you, the paint-spattered shoes. Where did you pick him up? *Quickly.*"

"Here in Alba. About twenty minutes ago."

"Who made contact first?"

Both Englishmen looked at each other. Briefly, with instant concern. "He did," said Apple.

"Get out of here! Now! Use the kitchen!"

"*What?*" Pear was looking over at the *espresso* counter.

"He's leaving," said the partisan. "He was to wait for me."

The heavyset man was making his way through the crowds toward the door. He was doing so as unobtrusively as possible; a drinker going to the men's room, perhaps.

"What do you think?" asked Apple.

"I think that there are a great many men throughout Alba with paint on their shoes. They wait for strangers whose eyes stray to the floor." The Communist rose from the table. "The contact code was broken. It happens. The Corsicans will have to change it. Now, *go!*"

The two Englishmen got out of their chairs, but not with any overt sense of urgency. Vittorio took his cue and stood up. He reached out and touched the partisan's sleeve. The Communist was startled; his eyes were on the heavyset man; he was about to plunge into the crowds.

"I want to thank you."

The partisan stared for an instant. "You're wasting time," he said.

The two Britishers knew exactly where the kitchen was, and therefore the exit *from* that kitchen. The alley outside was filthy; garbage cans were lined against the dirty stucco walls, refuse overflowing. The alley was a link between the Piazza San Giorno and the street behind, but so dimly lit and strewn with trash it was not a popular shortcut.

"This way," said Apple, turning left, away from the piazza. "Quickly now."

The three men ran out of the alley. The street was sufficiently filled with pedestrians and shopkeepers to provide them with cover. Apple and Pear fell into a casual walk; Vittorio followed suit. He realized that the two agents had maneuvered him between them.

"I'm not sure the Bolshie was right," said Pear. "Our *Corso* might simply have spotted a friend. He was damned convincing."

"The Corsicans have their own language," interjected Vittorio, excusing himself as he nearly collided with an oncoming stroller.

"Couldn't he tell by talking to him?"

"Don't do that," said Apple incisively.

"What?"

"Don't be so damned polite. It hardly goes with the clothes. To answer your question, the Corsicans employ regional contacts everywhere. We all do. They're minor level, just messengers."

"I see." Fontini-Cristi looked at the man who called himself Apple. He was walking casually, but his eyes kept shifting about in the night-cloaked street. Vittorio turned his head and looked at Pear. He was doing precisely what his countryman was doing: observing the faces in the crowds, the vehicles, the recesses in the buildings on both sides of the street.

"Where are we going?" asked Fontini-Cristi.

"To within a block of where our Corsican told us to be," replied Apple.

"But I thought you suspected him."

Pear spoke. "They won't see us because they don't know what to look for. The Bolshevik will catch the *Corso* in the piazza. If everything's on the up-and-up, they'll arrive together. If not, and if your friend is competent, he'll be the only one."

The shopping area curved to the left, into the south entrance of the Piazza San Giorno. The entrance was marked by a fountain, the circular pool at its base littered with discarded papers and bottles. Men and women sat on the ledge dipping their hands in the dirty water; children shouted and ran on the cobblestones under their parents' watchful eyes.

"The road beyond," said Apple, lighting a cigarette, gesturing toward the wide pavement seen through the spray of the fountain, "is the Via Ligata. It leads to the coastal highway. Two hundred yards down is a side street where the *Corso* said a taxi would be waiting."

"Would the side street, by any chance, be a dead end?" Pear asked the question with a degree of disdain. He did not really expect an answer.

"Isn't that a coincidence? I was wondering the same thing. Do let's find out. You," said Apple to Vittorio, "stay with my partner and do *exactly* as he says." The agent threw the match to the ground, inhaled deeply on his cigarette, and walked rapidly over the cobblestones toward the fountain. When he was within several feet of the pool, he slowed down, and then, to Vittorio's astonishment, he disappeared, lost entirely in the crowds.

"He does that rather in top form, doesn't he?" said Pear.

"I can't make him out. I don't see him."

"Not supposed to. A good race-and-melt, done in the proper light, can be very effective." He shrugged. "Come along. Keep abreast and chatter a bit. And gesture. You people wave your hands like mad."

Vittorio smiled at the Englishman's bromide. But as they walked into the crowds, he was conscious of moving hands and flailing arms and sudden exclamations. The Britisher knew his Italians. He kept pace with the agent, fascinated by the man's decisiveness. Suddenly, Pear grabbed Vittorio's sleeve and yanked him to the left, propelling them both toward a newly vacated space on the fountain's ledge. Fontini-Cristi was startled; he thought their objective was to reach the Via Ligata as rapidly and as unobtrusively as possible.

Then he understood. The Britisher's experienced, professional eyes had seen what the amateur's had not seen: the signal.

Vittorio sat on the agent's right, his head down. The first objects that came into focus were a pair of worn shoes with the splotches of orange paint on the scuffed leather. A single pair of immobile shoes in the moving shadows of moving bodies. Then Vittorio raised his head and froze. The partisan driver was cradling the heavyset body of the Corsican contact, as though succoring a friend who had drunk too much. But the contact was not drunk. His head was slumped, his eyes open, staring downward into the moving darkness. He was dead.

Vittorio leaned back on the ledge, mesmerized by the sight below. A steady, narrow stream of blood was soaking the back of the Corsican's shirt, rolling down the stone of the fountain's inner wall, mingling with the filthy water, forming circles and swirling half circles in the intermittent light of the piazza's street lamps.

The partisan's hand gripped the cloth, bunching the shirt around the blood-soaked area, knuckles and wrist drenched. And in his grip was the handle of a knife.

Fontini-Cristi tried to control his shock.

"I was hoping you'd stop," said the Communist to the Englishman.

"Nearly didn't," replied Pear in his overly grammatical Italian. "Until I noticed the couple leap up here." The agent indicated the ledge on which he and Vittorio sat. "They're yours, I presume."

"No. When you were closest, I told them my friend was about to vomit. It's a trap, of course. Fishnet variety; they don't know what they'll catch. They broke the code—last night. There are a dozen or so *provocatori* in the area, flushing out what targets they can. A roundup."

"We'll tell the Corsicans."

"It won't do much good. The code changes tomorrow."

"The taxi's the snare, then?"

"No. The second bait. They're not taking chances. The taxi drives the targets into the net. Only the driver knows where; he's upper level."

"There must be others nearby." Pear brought his hand to his mouth; it was a gesture of thought.

"Certainly."

"But which ones?"

"There's a way to find out. Where's Apple?"

"In the Via Ligata by now. We wanted to separate in case you had trouble."

"Join him; the trouble wasn't mine."

"Yes. I can see that——"

"*Mother of God!*" exclaimed Vittorio under his breath, incapable of silence. "You're holding a dead man in the middle of the piazza and you chatter like women!"

"We have things to say, *signore*. Be quiet and listen." The partisan returned his eyes to the Englishman, who had barely taken notice of Fontini-Cristi's outburst. "I'll give you two minutes to reach Apple. Then I'll let our *Corso* friend here slide into the pool, back up, knife visible. There'll be chaos. I'll start the shouting myself. It will carry. It'll be enough."

"And we keep our eyes on the taxi," interrupted Pear.

"Yes. As the shouting grows, see who speaks together. See who leaves to investigate."

"Then take the bloody taxi and be off," added the agent with finality.

"Good show! I look forward to working with you again." The Britisher rose; Vittorio did the same, feeling Pear's hand on his arm.

"You," said the partisan, looking up at Vittorio while cradling the limp, heavyset body in the noisy, jostling, shadow-filled darkness. "Something to remember. A conversation in the midst of many people is often the safest. And a blade in a crowd is the hardest to trace. Remember these things."

Vittorio looked down at the man, not sure whether the Communist meant his words to be insulting or not.

"I'll remember," said Vittorio.

They walked swiftly into the Via Ligata. Apple was on the other side, slowly making his way toward the side street where the Corsican contact said the taxi would be waiting. The street lamps were dimmer than in the piazza.

"Hurry, now. There he is," said Pear in English. "Take longer steps, but don't run."

"Shouldn't we go over and meet him?" asked Vittorio.

"No. One person crossing the street is less obvious than two. . . . All right. Stop now."

Pear removed a box of matches from his pocket; he struck one. The instant it flared, he waved it out, throwing it to the pavement—as if the flame had seared his finger—and immediately struck a second, holding it to the cigarette he had placed in his lips.

Less than a minute passed before Apple joined them by the wall of a building. Pear told him the partisan's strategy. The three walked in silence, between the strollers, down the pavement to the end of the block opposite the side street. Across, in the dim white wash of the streetlights, was the taxi, thirty feet from the corner.

"Isn't that a coincidence," said Apple, lifting his foot to a low ledge on the building, pulling up his sock. "It's a dead end."

"The troops can't be far away. Is your pillow attached? Mine isn't."

"Yes. Fix yours."

Pear turned into the building and removed an automatic from inside his jacket. With his other hand he reached into his pocket and withdrew a cylinder about four inches long, with perforations on the iron surface, and twisted it into the barrel of his weapon. He replaced the gun inside his jacket just as the cries from the piazza began.

There were only a few at first, almost indistinguishable. And then a crescendo of sound erupted.

"*Polizia!*" "*A quale punto polizia!*" "*Assassinio!*" "*Omicidio!*" Women and children ran out of the square; men followed, shouting orders and information at no one and everyone. Among the screams came the words: *"Uomo con arancia scarpe,"* a man with orange shoes. The partisan had done his job well.

And then the partisan himself was among the crowds running down the pavement. He stopped ten feet from Fontini-Cristi and the two Englishmen and roared in a loud voice to any who would listen.

"I *saw* him! I saw *them!* I was right *next* to him! This man—his shoes were *painted*—they put a knife into his back!"

From the dark recess of a building a figure came dashing across the street, heading for the partisan. "You! Come here!"

"What?"

"I'm with the police. What did you see?"

"The police. Thank God! Come with me! There were two men! In sweaters——"

Before the official could adjust, the partisan started to race back toward the entrance of the piazza through the crowds. The policeman hesitated, then looked across the dimly lit street. Three men were talking together several yards in front of the taxi. The policeman gestured; two of the men broke away and started after the officer, who was now racing toward San Giorno and the disappearing partisan.

"The man left at the car. He's the driver," said Apple. "Here we go."

The next moments were a blur. Vittorio followed the two agents across the Via Ligata into the side street. The man at the taxi had climbed into the driver's seat. Apple approached the car, opened the door, and without saying a word raised his gun. A muted explosion burst from the mouth of his revolver. The man slumped forward; Apple rolled him over the seat toward the opposite door. Pear spoke to Fontini-Cristi.

"Into the back. Quickly, now!"

Apple turned the ignition; the taxi was old, the engine new and powerful. The automobile's make was the usual Fiat, Vittorio thought, but the motor was a Lamborgini.

The car lurched forward, turned right at the corner and gathered speed on the Via Ligata. Apple spoke over his shoulder, addressing Pear. "Check the glove compartment, will you? This bloody wreck belongs to some very *important people.* I daresay it would do well at Le Mans."

Pear lunged from the seat in the speeding car, over the felt back, and across the corpse of the Italian. He pulled open the glove compartment panel, grabbed the papers, bunching them together in his hand. As he pushed himself off the dashboard, the car swerved; Apple had swung the wheel to pass two automobiles. The body of the dead Italian fell across Pear's arm. He gripped the lifeless neck and threw the corpse violently back into the corner.

Vittorio stared at the scene, sick and uncomprehending. Behind them a heavyset man floated in death in a piazza fountain, the handle of a knife protruding from his blood-soaked shirt. Here, in an unmarked, speeding police car disguised as a taxi, a man slumped in the front seat, a bullet in his lifeless body. Miles away in a small guardhouse on the Via Canelli, two other men lay dead, killed by the Communist who had saved his life. The continuing nightmare was destroying his mind. He held his breath, desperately trying to find an instant of sanity.

"Here we are!" shouted Pear, holding up a rectangular sheet of heavy paper he had been studying in the inadequate light. "By God, it's a clean wicket!"

"An inland passport, I expect," said Apple, slowing down for a curve in the road.

"Indeed it is! The bloody *veicolo* is assigned to the *ufficiale segreto!* That bunch has access to Mussolini himself."

"It had to be something like that," agreed Apple, nodding his head. "The motor in this tacky box is a bloody marvel."

"It is a Lamborgini," said Vittorio quietly.

"What?" Apple raised his voice to be heard over the roar of the engine on the now straightaway road. They were approaching the outskirts of Alba.

"I said it's a Lamborgini."

"Yes," replied Apple, obviously unfamiliar with the engine. "Well, you keep coming up with things like that. Things Italian, that is. We're going to need your words before we reach the coast."

Pear turned to Fontini-Cristi. The Englishman's pleasant face was barely discernible in the darkness. He spoke gently, but there was no mistaking the quiet urgency in his voice.

"I'm sure this is all very strange to you, and damned uncomfortable, I should think. But that Bolshevik had a point. Remember what you can. The most difficult part of this work isn't the *doing;* it's getting *used* to the doing, if you see what I mean. Just accepting the fact that it's real, that's the leg up a fellow needs. We've all been through it, go through it constantly, as a matter of fact. It's all so bloody outrageous, in a way. But someone's got to do it; that's what they tell us. And I'll say this: You're getting some very practical on-the-job training. Wouldn't you agree?"

"Yes," said Vittorio softly, turning front, his eyes mesmerized by the onrushing road outlined by the beams of the headlights, and his mind frozen by the sudden question he could not avoid.

Training for what?

5

DECEMBER 31, 1939
CELLE LIGURE, ITALY

It was two hours of madness. They turned off the coastal highway and
carried the body of the dead driver into a field, stripping it naked,
removing all identification.

They returned to the highway and sped south toward Savona. The
road checks were similar to those on the Via Canelli: single guard-
houses next to telephone booths, two soldiers in attendance at each.
There were four checkpoints; three were passed easily. The thick,
official document that proclaimed the vehicle assigned to the *ufficiale
segreto* was read with respect and not a little fear. Fontini-Cristi did the
talking at all three posts.

"You're damned quick," said Apple from the front, shaking his head
in agreeable surprise. "And you were right about staying back there.
You roll down that window like a Punjab prince."

The road sign was caught in the headlights.

ENTRARE MONTENOTTE SUD

Vittorio recognized the name; it was one of those medium-sized towns
surrounding the Gulf of Genoa. He recognized it from a decade ago,
when he and his wife had driven down the coast road on their last trip
to Monte Carlo. A journey that had ended a week later in death. In a
speeding car at night.

"The coast's about fifteen miles from here, I think," said Apple hesitantly, interrupting Fontini-Cristi's thoughts.

"Nearer eight," corrected Vittorio.

"You know this area?" asked Pear.

"I've driven to Cap Ferrat and Villefranche a number of times." *Why
didn't he say Monte Carlo; was the name too much of a symbol?* "Usually on the Torino road, but several times on the shore route from
Genoa. Montenotte Sud is known for its inns."

"Then would you know a dirt road that cuts north of Savona—through some hills, I gather—into Celle Ligure?"

"No. There are hills everywhere. . . . But I know Celle Ligure. It's on the waterfront just beyond Albisolla. Is that where we're going?"

"Yes," said Apple. "It's our backup rendezvous with the Corsicans. In case anything happened, we were to make our way to Celle Ligure, to a fishing pier south of the marina. It'll be marked with a green wind sock."

"Well, *something* happened, as they say," interjected Pear. "I'm sure there's a *Corso* wandering around Alba wondering where we are."

Several hundred yards ahead in the glare of the headlights, two soldiers stood in the center of the road. One held a rifle at port arms; the other had his hand raised, signaling them to stop. Apple slowed the Fiat, the transposed motor emitting the low sounds of its decelerating power. "Do your bitchy act," he said to Vittorio. "Be arrogant as hell." The Britisher kept the car in the center of the road, a sign that the inhabitants expected no interruption; pulling off to the side was unnecessary.

One of the soldiers was a lieutenant, his companion a corporal. The officer approached Apple's open window and saluted the unkempt civilian smartly.

Too smartly, thought Vittorio.

"Your identification, *signore*," said the soldier courteously.

Too courteously.

Apple held up the thick official paper and gestured toward the back seat. It was Vittorio's cue.

"We are the *ufficiale segreto*, Genoa garrison, and in a great hurry. We have business in Savona. You've done your job; pass us through immediately."

"My apologies, *signore*." The officer took the heavy paper in Apple's hand and scrutinized it. He creased the folds as his eyes scanned downward in the very dim light. He continued politely. "I must see your identifications. There is so little traffic on the road at this hour. All vehicles must be checked."

Fontini-Cristi slammed his hand down on the top of the front seat in sudden irritation. "You're out of order! Don't let our appearances fool you. We're on official business and we're late for Savona!"

"Yes. Well, I must read this——"

But he was *not* reading it, thought Vittorio. A man in inadequate light did not fold a page of paper *toward* him; if he folded it at all, it would be *away*—to catch more light. The soldier was stalling. And the corporal had moved to the right front of the Fiat, his rifle still held across his chest; but the left hand was now lower on the barrel grip. Any hunter knew the stance; it was ready-at-fire.

Fontini-Cristi sat back in the seat, swearing furiously as he did so. "I demand your name and the name of your commanding officer!"

In the front, Apple had edged his shoulders to the right, trying to see into the rearview mirror, unable to do so without being obvious. But in his pretended anger, Fontini-Cristi had no such difficulty. He whipped his hand up behind Pear's shoulders, as if his irritation had reached the breaking point.

"Perhaps you did not hear me, soldier! Your name and that of your commanding officer!"

Through the rearview mirror he saw it. Quite far in the distance, beyond the clear range of the mirror, not easily seen through the window itself. A car had pulled off the road . . . so far off, it was half into the field bordering the highway. Two men were getting out of the front seat, the figures barely visible, moving slowly.

". . . Marchetti, *signore*. My commanding officer is Colonel Balbo. Genoa garrison, *signore*."

Vittorio caught Apple's eye in the rearview mirror, nodded slightly, and moved his head in a slow arc toward the back window. At the same time, he tapped his fingers rapidly on Pear's neck in the darkness. The agent understood.

Without warning, Vittorio opened his door. The rifle-bearing corporal jerked his weapon forward. "Put that *down, caporale*. Since your superior sees fit to take up my time, I will put it to use. I am Major Aldo Ravena, *ufficiale segreto,* from Rome. I will inspect your quarters. I will also relieve myself."

"*Signore!*" shouted the officer from across the Fiat's hood.

"Are you addressing me?" asked Fontini-Cristi arrogantly.

"My apologies, major." The officer could not help himself; he stole a quick glance to his right, to the road behind. "There are no facilities inside the guardhouse."

"Surely you are not immaculate in your bowels, man. The fields must be inconvenient. Perhaps Rome will install such facilities. I'll see."

Vittorio walked swiftly toward the door of the small structure; it was open. As he expected, the corporal went with him. He walked rapidly through the door. The instant the corporal entered behind him, Fontini-Cristi turned and jammed the pistol up under the man's chin. He pushed the weapon into the flesh of the corporal's throat and with his left hand grabbed the barrel of the rifle.

"If you so much as cough, I'll have to kill you!" whispered Vittorio. "I don't wish to do that."

The corporal's eyes widened in shock; he had no stomach for heroics. Fontini-Cristi held the rifle and gave his order quietly, precisely.

"Call the officer. Say I'm using your telephone and you don't know what to do. Tell him I'm calling the Genoa garrison. For that Colonel Balbo. *Now!*"

The corporal shouted the words, conveying both his confusion and his fear. Vittorio pressed his back against the wall by the door. The reply from the lieutenant betrayed the officer's own fear; perhaps he had made a dreadful mistake.

"I am only following orders! I received orders from Alba!"

"Tell him Colonel Balbo is coming to the telephone," whispered Fontini-Cristi. *"Now!"*

The corporal did so. Vittorio heard the footsteps of the officer running from the Fiat to the guardhouse.

"If you wish to live, Lieutenant, remove your pistol belt—just unbuckle both straps—and join the corporal at the wall."

The lieutenant was stunned. His jaw dropped, his lips parted in fright. Fontini-Cristi prodded him with the rifle, lancing the barrel into his stomach. The bewildered officer winced and gasped and did as he was told. Vittorio called outside, in English.

"I've disarmed them. Now I'm not sure what to do."

Pear's half-whispered shout came back. "What to *do?* My God, you're a bloody marvel! Send the officer back outside. Make sure he knows we have our weapons on him. Tell him to return to Apple's window right off. We'll take it from there."

Fontini-Cristi translated the instructions. The officer, prodded by the barrel of Vittorio's pistol, lurched out the doors and crossed swiftly in front of the car's headlights to the driver's window.

Ten seconds later the officer's shouts were heard on the road outside.

"You men from Alba! This is not the vehicle! A mistake has been made!"

A moment passed before other voices replied. Two voices, loud and angry.

"What happened? Who are they?"

Vittorio could see the figures of two men come out of the darkness of the field. They were soldiers and held guns at their sides. The officer answered.

"These are *segreti* from Genoa. They, too, look for the vehicle from Alba."

"Mother of Christ! How many *are* there?"

Suddenly, the officer pushed himself away from the window, screaming as he dove for the front of the automobile.

"*Shoot! Open fire!* They are——"

The muffled explosions of the British pistols erupted. Pear leaped out of the right rear door, covered by the automobile, and fired at the approaching soldiers. A rifle answered; it was a wild shot that thumped into the tarred surface of the road, triggered by a dying man. The checkpoint lieutenant sprang to his feet and started to race toward the opposite field into the darkness. Apple fired; three muted reports accompanied the sharp, abrupt flashes of his weapon. The officer screamed and arched his back. He fell into the dirt off the road.

"*Fontini!*" yelled Apple. "Kill your man and get out here!"

The corporal's lips trembled, his eyes watered. He had heard the muted explosions, the screams, and he understood the command.

"No," said Fontini-Cristi.

"Goddamn you!" roared Apple. "You do as I *say!* You're under *my* orders! We've no time to waste *or* chances to take!"

"You're wrong. We would waste more time and take greater risks if we could not find the road into Celle Ligure. This soldier will surely know it."

He did. Vittorio drove, the soldier beside him in the front seat. Fontini-Cristi knew the area; if they ran into trouble, he could handle it. He had proved that.

"Relax," said Vittorio in Italian to the frightened corporal. "Continue to be helpful; you'll be all right."

"What will happen to me? They'll say I deserted my post."

"Nonsense. You were ambushed, forced at the point of a gun to accompany us, to act as a shield. You had no choice."

They drove into Celle Ligure at ten forty; the streets of the fishing village were nearly deserted. The majority of its inhabitants began their days at four in the morning; ten at night was late. Fontini-Cristi drove into the sandy parking area behind an open fish market that fronted the wide ocean street. Across was the main section of the marina.

"Where are the sentries?" asked Apple. "Where do they meet?"

At first the corporal seemed confused. Vittorio explained. "When you are on duty here, where do you turn around?"

"I see." The corporal was relieved; he was obviously trying to help. "Not here, not at this section. Up farther; I mean, down farther."

"*Damn* you!" Apple was forward in the back seat. He grabbed the Italian by the hair.

"You'll get nowhere like that," said Vittorio in English. "The man's frightened."

"So am I!" countered the agent. "There's a dock across there with a green wind sock on it, and a boat in that dock we have to find! We don't know what's happened behind us; there are soldiers on the piers with weapons—one shot would alert the whole area. And we have no idea what orders have been radioed the water patrols. *I'm damned* frightened!"

"I remember!" cried the corporal. "On the left. Up the street on the left! The trucks stopped and we would walk through to the piers and wait for the man on duty. He would give us the patrol sheet and be relieved."

"Where? *Exactly* where, Corporal?" Pear spoke urgently.

"The next street. I'm sure of it."

"That's roughly one hundred yards, wouldn't you say?" asked Pear, looking at Fontini-Cristi. "And the street below this another one hundred, give or take some."

"What's your idea?" Apple had released the corporal, but kept his hands menacingly on the top of the seat.

"Same as yours," replied Pear. "Take the sentry at midpoint; less chance of his being seen there. Once he's out we walk south to the wind sock, where, I trust, a Corsican or two will show themselves."

They crossed the ocean road into an alley that led to the dock complex. The smell of fish and the sounds of half a hundred boats creaking in rhythmic rest in their slips filled the darkness. Nets were hung everywhere; the wash of the sea could be heard beyond the planked walkway that fronted the piers. A few lanterns were swaying on ropes over decks; a concertina played a simple tune in the distance.

Vittorio and Pear walked casually out of the alley, their footsteps muted by moist planks. Apple and the corporal remained in the shadows. The walkway was bordered by a railing of metal tubing above the lapping water.

"Do you see the sentry?" asked Fontini-Cristi softly.

"No. But I hear him," answered the agent. "He's rapping the pipe as he walks. Listen."

It took Vittorio several seconds before he could distinguish the faint metal sounds among the rhythmic creakings of wood on water. But they were there. The unconscious, irregular tattoo of a bored man performing a dull task.

Several hundred feet south on the walkway, the figure of the soldier came under the spill of a pier light, his rifle angled down to the deck through his left arm. He was beside the railing, his right hand aimlessly tapping out his steps.

"When he gets here, ask him for a cigarette," said Pear calmly. "Pretend you're drunk. I will, too."

The sentry approached. The instant he saw them he snapped up his rifle and cracked the bolt, holding his position fifteen feet away.

"*Halt!* Who's *there?*"

"Two fishermen without cigarettes," replied Fontini-Cristi, slurring his words. "Be a nice fellow and give us a couple. Even one; we'll share it."

"You're drunk," said the soldier. "There's a curfew tonight on the piers. How come you're here? It was on the loudspeakers all day."

"We've been with two whores in Albisolla," answered Vittorio, lurching, steadying himself on the railing. "Only things we heard were music on a phonograph and creaking beds."

"Very nice," mumbled Pear.

The sentry shook his head in disapproval. He lowered his rifle and approached, reaching into the pocket of his tunic for cigarettes. "You *Ligurini* are worse than the *Napoletani*. I've done duty there."

Behind the soldier, Vittorio could see Apple coming out of the shadows. He had forced the corporal to lie down on his back in the corner of the alley; the corporal would not move. In Apple's hands were two spools.

Before Vittorio could realize what was happening, Apple sprang out of the passageway, his arms stretched, angled upward. In two swift moves, the agent's hands whipped over the sentry's head, and with his knee jammed into the small of the soldier's back, he yanked violently, causing the guard to arch spastically and then collapse.

The only noise was an abrupt, horrible expunging of air, and the quiet fall of the man's body into the soft, moist wood.

Pear rushed to the corporal; he held his pistol against the soldier's temple. "Not a sound. Understood?" It was a command that left no room for debate. The corporal rose silently.

Fontini-Cristi looked down in the dim light at the guard on the walkway. What he could see he wished he had not seen. The man's neck was severed half off his body, the blood was pouring out in a dark-red stream from what had been the man's throat. Apple rolled the body through a wide space in the railing. It hit the water with a muffled splash. Pear picked up his rifle and spoke in English.

"Off we go. Down this way."

"Come on," said Fontini-Cristi, his hand on the trembling corporal's arm. "You have no choice."

The green wind sock was limp, no breeze billowing its cloth. The pier was only half filled with boats; it seemed to extend farther out into the water than the others. The four of them walked down the steps, Apple and Pear in front, their hands in their pockets. The two Englishmen were obviously hesitant. It was apparent to Vittorio that they were concerned.

Without warning or sound, men suddenly appeared on both sides of them, their weapons drawn. They were on the decks of the boats; five, no, six men dressed as fishermen.

"Be you George the Fifth?" said the gruff voice of the man nearest the agents, standing on the deck of a small trawler.

"Thank *God!*" said Pear in relief. "We've had a nasty time of it."

At the spoken English, weapons were replaced in belts and pockets. The men converged, a number talking at once.

The language was Corsican.

One man, obviously the leader, turned to Apple. "Go to the end of the pier. We've got one of the fastest trawlers in Bastia. We'll take care of the Italian. They won't find him for a month!"

"No!" Fontini-Cristi stepped between the two men. He looked at Pear. "We gave our word. If he cooperated, he lived."

Apple replied, instead, his whispered voice drawn out in irritation. "Now, you see here. You've been a help, I'll not deny it, but you're not running this show. Get out to the bloody boat."

"Not until this man is back on the walkway. We gave our word!" He spoke to the corporal. "Go back. You won't be harmed. Strike a match when you reach a passageway to the ocean road."

"And if I say *no?*" Apple continued to grip the soldier's tunic.

"Then I'll remain here."

"*Damn!*" Apple released the soldier.

"Walk with him part way," said Fontini-Cristi to the Corsican. "Make sure your men let him pass."

The Corsican spat on the pier.

The corporal ran as fast as he could toward the base of the dock. Fontini-Cristi looked at the two Englishmen.

"I am sorry," he said simply. "There's been enough killing."

"You're a damn fool," replied Apple.

"Hurry," said the Corsican leader. "I want to get started. The water's rough beyond the rocks. And you people are crazy!"

They walked out to the end of the long pier, one by one jumping over the gunwale onto the deck of the huge trawler. Two Corsicans remained on the dock by the pilings; they unwound the thick greasy ropes while the gruff captain started the engines.

It happened without warning.

A fusillade of gunfire from the walkway. Then the blinding shaft of a searchlight shot out of the darkness, accompanied by the shouts of soldiers at the base of the pier. The voice of the corporal could be heard.

"Out *there!* At the end of the dock! The *fishing trawler!* Send out the alarms!"

One of the Corsicans was hit; he plunged to the ground, at the last second freeing the rope from the piling.

"The *light!* Shoot out the light!" screamed the Corsican from the open wheelhouse, revving the engines, heading for open water.

Apple and Pear unscrewed their silencers for greater accuracy. Apple was the first to raise himself over the protection of the gunwale; he squeezed his trigger repeatedly, steadying his hand on the wooden rail. In the distance the searchlight exploded. Simultaneously, fragments of wood burst around Apple; the agent reeled back, screaming in pain.

His hand was shattered.

But the Corsican had steered the fast-moving trawler out into the protective darkness of the sea. They were free of Celle Ligure.

"Our price goes up, English!" shouted the man at the wheel. "You whoreson bastards! You'll pay for this craziness!" He looked at Fontini-Cristi crouched beneath the starboard gunwale. Their eyes met; the Corsican spat furiously.

Apple sat back sweating against a pile of ropes. In the night light reflecting the ocean's spray, Vittorio saw that the Englishman was staring at the bloody mass of flesh that was his hand, holding it by the wrist.

Fontini-Cristi got up and crossed to the agent, tearing off part of his shirt as he did so. "Let me wrap that for you. Stop the bleeding——"

Apple jerked his head up and spoke in quiet anger. "Stay the hell away from me. Your goddamned principles cost too much."

The seas were heavy, the winds strong, the rolls violent and abrupt. They had plowed through the drenching waves of the open water for thirty-eight minutes. Arrangements had been made, the blockade run; the trawler's engines were now idling.

Beyond the swells, Vittorio could see a small flashing blue disc: on

for a beat, off for a beat. The signal from a submarine. The Corsican on
the bow with the lantern began his own signal. He lowered and raised
the lamp, using the gunwale as a shutter, imitating the timing of the blue
disc half a mile away over the waters.

"Can't you radio him?" Pear shouted his question.

"Frequencies are monitored," replied the Corsican. "The patrol
boats would circle in; we can't bribe them all."

The two vessels began their cautious pavane over the rough seas, the
trawler making most of the moves until the huge undersea marauder
was directly off the starboard rail. Fontini-Cristi was hypnotized by its
size and black majesty.

The two ships drifted within fifty feet of each other, the submarine
considerably higher on the mountainous waves. Four men could be seen
on the deck; they were hanging on to a metal railing, the two in the center trying to manipulate some kind of machine.

A heavy rope shot through the air and crashed against the midships
of the trawler. Two Corsicans leaped at it, holding on desperately, as if
the line had a hostile will of its own. They lashed the rope to an iron
winch in the center of the deck and signaled the men on the submarine.

The action was repeated. But the second rope was not the only item
that had been shot from the submarine. There was a canvas pouch with
metal rings on the edges, and from one of these rings was a thick coil of
wire that extended back to the crew on the sub's deck.

The Corsicans ripped open the canvas pack and pulled out a shoulder harness. Fontini-Cristi recognized it immediately; it was a rig used
to cross crevasses in the mountains.

Pear, bracing himself as he lurched forward on the rolling deck,
approached Vittorio.

"It's a bit skin-crawling, but it's safe!" he yelled.

Vittorio shouted back "Send your man Apple first. His hand should
be looked after."

"You're the priority. And frankly, if the damn thing doesn't hold, I'd
rather we find out with you!"

Fontini-Cristi sat on the iron bunk inside the small metal room and
drank from the thick china mug of coffee. He pulled the Royal Navy
blanket around his shoulders, feeling the wet clothes beneath. The discomfort did not bother him; he was grateful to be alone.

The door of the small metal room opened. It was Pear. He carried an
armful of clothing which he dropped on the bunk.

"Here's a dry change for you. It wouldn't do for you to croak off with pneumonia now. That'd be a clanker in the balls, wouldn't it?"

"Thank you," said Vittorio, getting up. "How's your friend?"

"The ship's doctor is afraid he'll lose the use of his hand. The doctor hasn't told him, but he knows."

"I'm sorry. I was naïve."

"Yes," agreed the Britisher simply. "You were naïve." He left, leaving the door open.

From the narrow metal corridors outside the tiny metal room, there was a sudden eruption of noise. Men raced by the door, all running in the same direction, fore or aft, Fontini-Cristi could not tell. Over the ship's intercom a piercing, deafening whistle shrieked without letup; metal doors slammed, the shouting increased.

Vittorio lunged at the open door; his breathing stopped. The panic of helplessness under the sea gripped him.

He collided with a British sailor. But the sailor's face was not contorted in panic. Or fear. Or anything but carefree laughter.

"*Happy New Year,* mate!" cried the sailor. "Midnight, chum! We're in 1940. A bloody new decade!"

The sailor raced on to the next hatchway, which he opened with a crash. Beyond, Fontini-Cristi could see the mess quarters. Men were gathered around holding out mugs into which two officers were pouring whiskey. The shouts merged into laughter. "Auld Lang Syne" began to fill the metal chambers.

The new decade.

The old one had ended in death. Death everywhere, most horribly in the blinding white light of Campo di Fiori. Father, mother, brothers, sisters . . . the children. *Gone.* Gone in a minute of shattering violence that was burned into his mind. A memory he would live with for the rest of his life.

Why? *Why?* Nothing made sense!

And then he remembered. Savarone had said he had gone to Zürich. But he had not gone to Zürich; he had gone somewhere else.

In that somewhere else lay the answer. But what?

Vittorio walked into the small metal room of the submarine and sat down on the iron ridge of the bed.

The new decade had begun.

PART
TWO

6

JANUARY 2, 1940
LONDON, ENGLAND

Sandbags.

London was a city of sandbags. Everywhere. In doorways, windows, storefronts; piled in mounds on street corners. The sandbag was the symbol. Across the Channel, Adolf Hitler vowed the destruction of all England; quietly the English believed his threat, and quietly, firmly, they steeled themselves in anticipation.

Vittorio had reached the Lakenheath military airfield late on the previous night, the first day of the new decade. He had been taken off an unmarked plane flown out of Majorca and whisked into operations, the purpose of which was to confirm his identity for the Naval Ministry. And now that he was safely in the country, the voices suddenly became calm and solicitous: Would he care to rest up after his grueling journey? Perhaps the Savoy? It was understood that the Fontini-Cristis stayed at the Savoy when in London. Would a conference tomorrow afternoon at fourteen hundred hours be convenient? At the Admiralty, Intelligence Sector Five. Alien operations.

Of course. For God's sake, *yes!* Why have you English done what you've done? I must know, but I will be silent until you tell me.

The Savoy desk provided him with toilet articles and nightclothes, including a Savoy robe. He had drawn a very hot bath in the enormous hotel tub and immersed himself for such a length of time the skin on his fingertips wrinkled. He then proceeded to drink too many glasses of brandy and fell into bed.

He had left a wake-up call for ten but, of course, it was unnecessary. He was fully alert by eight thirty; showered and shaved by nine. He ordered an English breakfast from the floor steward and while waiting, telephoned Norcross, Limited, on Savile Row. He needed clothes immediately. He could not walk around London in a borrowed raincoat, a sweater, and the ill-fitting trousers provided by an agent named Pear on a submarine in the Mediterranean.

As he hung up the phone, it struck Vittorio that he had no money other than ten pounds courtesy of Lakenheath dispersals. He assumed his credit was good; he would have funds transferred from Switzerland. He had not had time to concentrate on the logistics of living; he had been too preoccupied with staying alive.

It occurred to Fontini-Cristi that he had many things to do. And if only to control the terrible memory—the infinite pain—of Campo di Fiori, he had to keep active. Force his mind to concentrate first on the simple things, everyday things. For when the great things came into focus he could go mad pondering them.

Please, dear God, the *little* things! Spare me the time to find my sanity.

He saw her first across the Savoy lobby while waiting for the day manager to arrange for immediate monies. She was sitting in an armchair, reading the *Times,* dressed in the stern uniform of a branch of the women's service, what branch he had no idea. Beneath the officer's visor cap her dark brunette hair fell in waves to her shoulders, outlining her face. It was a face he had seen before; it was a face one remembered. But it was a younger version of that face that stuck in his mind. The woman was, perhaps, in her middle thirties; the face he recalled had been no more than twenty-two or twenty-three. The cheekbones were high, the nose more Celtic than English—sharp, slightly upturned, and delicate above the full lips. He could not see the eyes clearly, but he knew what they looked like: a very intense blue, as blue as he had ever seen a woman's eyes.

That's what he remembered. Angry blue eyes staring up at him. Angry and filled with disdain. He had not encountered that reaction often in his life; it had irritated him.

Why did he remember? When was it?

"Signor Fontini-Cristi." The Savoy manager walked briskly out of the cashier's arch, an envelope in his hand. "As you requested, a thousand pounds."

Vittorio took the envelope and shoved it in the raincoat pocket. "Thank you."

"We've arranged for your limousine, sir. It should be here shortly. If you'd care to return to your suite, we'll ring you the moment it arrives."

"I'll wait here. If you can put up with these clothes, I can."

"Please, *signore.* It is always a great pleasure to welcome a member of the Fontini-Cristis. Will your father be joining you this trip? We trust he's well."

England marched to the sudden drums of war and the Savoy inquired about families.

"He'll not be joining me." Vittorio saw no point in further explanations. The news had not reached England, or if it had, the war dispatches made it insignificant. "By the way, do you know that lady over there? The one seated. In the uniform."

The manager unobtrusively glanced across the sparsely crowded lobby. "Yes, sir. She's Mrs. Spane. I should say *was* Mrs. Spane; they're divorced. I believe she's remarried now. Mr. Spane is. We don't see her often."

"Spane?"

"Yes, sir. I see she's with Air Defense. They're a no-nonsense group, they are."

"Thank you," said Vittorio, dismissing the manager courteously. "I shall wait for my car."

"Yes, of course. If there's anything we can do to make your stay more pleasant, don't hesitate to call upon us."

The manager nodded and walked away. Fontini-Cristi looked again at the woman. She glanced at her watch, and then returned to her reading.

He remembered the name Spane because of its spelling, and because of the spelling, he remembered the man. It had been eleven, no, twelve years ago; he had accompanied Savarone to London to observe his father in negotiations with British Haviland—the observation a part of his training. Spane had been introduced to him one night at Les Ambassadeurs, a youngish man two or three years older than he was. He found the Englishman mildly amusing but basically tiring. Spane was a Mayfair product quite content to enjoy the fruits of ancestral labors without contributing much of anything himself, other than his expertise at the races. His father had disapproved of Spane and said as much to his eldest son, which, quite naturally, goaded the son into a brief acquaintanceship.

But it had been brief, and Vittorio suddenly remembered why. That it had not first come to mind was merely further proof that he had blocked her existence from much of his memory: not the woman across the lobby, but his wife.

His wife had come to England with them twelve years ago, the *padrone* feeling that her presence would have a restraining influence on a headstrong, wandering son. But Savarone did not know his daughter-in-law that well; he did later, but not at the time. The heady atmosphere of Mayfair at the height of the season was a tonic to her.

His wife was attracted to Spane; one or the other seduced one or the other. He had not paid much attention; he had been occupied himself.

And somewhere along the way there'd been a disagreeable confrontation. Recriminations had been hurled, and the angry blue eyes had stared up at him.

Vittorio walked across the lobby toward the armchair. The Spane woman glanced up as he approached. There was a moment of hesitancy in her eyes, as if she were unsure. And then she *was* sure and there was no hesitance at all; the disdain he recalled so vividly replaced the hesitation. Their eyes locked for a second—no more—and she returned to the newspaper.

"Mrs. Spane?"

She looked up. "The name is Holcroft."

"We've met."

"We have. It's Fontini——" She paused.

"Fontini-Cristi. Vittorio Fontini-Cristi."

"Yes. A long time ago. You'll forgive me, but I've a full day. I'm waiting for someone and I shan't have the chance to get through the paper again." She went back to her reading.

Vittorio smiled. "You dismiss me efficiently."

"I find it quite easy to do so," she replied without looking at him.

"Mrs. Holcroft, it *was* a long time ago. The English poet says that nothing so becomes change as the years."

"The English poet also maintains that leopards do not change their spots. I'm really quite occupied. Good day."

Vittorio started to nod his departure when he saw that her hands trembled ever so slightly. Mrs. Holcroft was somewhat less confident than her demeanor implied. He was not sure why he stayed; it was a time to be alone. The terrible memories of white light and death burned; he did not care to share them. On the other hand, he wanted to talk. To someone. About anything.

"Is an apology offered for childish behavior twelve years ago a decade too late?"

The lieutenant glanced up. "How *is* your wife?"

"She died in an automobile crash ten years ago."

The look in her eyes was steady; the hostility lessened. She blinked in discomfort, mildly embarrassed. "I'm sorry."

"It is my place to apologize. Twelve years ago you were seeking an explanation. Or comfort. And I had neither to give."

The woman allowed herself the trace of a smile. Her blue eyes had an element—if only an element—of warmth in them. "You were a very arrogant young man. And I'm afraid I had very little grace under pressure. I came to have more, of course."

"You were better than the games we played. I should have understood."

"That's a very disarming thing to say. . . . And I think we've said enough about the subject."

"Will you and your husband have dinner with me tonight, Mrs. Holcroft?" He heard the words he had spoken, not sure he had said them. It was the impulse of the moment.

She stared at him briefly before answering. "You mean that, don't you?"

"Certainly. I left Italy in somewhat of a rush, courtesy of your government, as these clothes are the courtesy of your countrymen. I haven't been to London in several years. I have very few acquaintances here."

"Now that's a provocative thing to say."

"I beg your pardon?"

"That you left Italy in a rush and you're wearing someone else's clothes. It raises questions."

Vittorio hesitated, then spoke quietly. "I would appreciate your having the understanding I lacked ten years ago. I would prefer those questions not be raised. But I'd like to have dinner with you. And your husband, of course."

She held his gaze, looking up at him curiously. Her lips curved into a gentle smile; she had made her decision. "My husband's name was Spane. Holcroft's my own. Jane Holcroft. And I'll have dinner with you."

The Savoy doorman interrupted. "Signor Fontini-Cristi, your car has arrived, sir."

"Thank you," he replied, his eyes on Jane Holcroft. "I'll be right there."

"Yes, sir." The doorman nodded and walked away.

"May I pick you up this evening? Or send my car for you?"

"Petrol's getting scarce. I'll meet you here. Eight o'clock?"

"Eight o'clock. *Arrivederci.*"

"Until then."

He walked down the long corridor at the Admiralty, escorted by a Commander Neyland who had met him at the entrance desk. Neyland was middle-aged, properly military, and quite impressed with himself. Or perhaps he was not at all impressed with Italians. In spite of Vittorio's fluency in English, Neyland insisted on using the simplest terms, and raising his voice as though addressing a retarded child. Fontini-Cristi was convinced that Neyland had not listened to his replies; a man did not hear of pursuit, death, and escape, and respond with such banalities as "You don't say." . . . "Odd, isn't it?" . . . "The Genoa gulf can be choppy in December, can't it?"

As they walked, Vittorio balanced his negative reaction to the commander with his gratitude for old Norcross on Savile Row.

Where the commander floundered, Norcross performed. The old tailor had clothed him in a matter of hours.

The little things; concentrate on the every*day* things.

Above all, maintain a control that bordered on ice during the conference with whatever, or whoever, comprised Intelligence Sector Five. There was so much to learn, to understand. So much that was beyond his comprehension. In the cold recital of the events that were the horror of Campo di Fiori, he could not let the agony cloud his perceptions; the recital, therefore, *would* be cold and understated.

"Through here, old man," said Neyland, indicating a cathedral-arched doorway that was more reminiscent of some venerable men's club than a military building. The commander opened the heavy door, gleaming with brass hardware, and Vittorio walked in.

There was nothing about the large room that belied the concept of a subdued but richly appointed club. Two huge windows overlooked a courtyard; everything was heavy and ornate: the drapes, the furniture, the lamps, and to some degree the three men who sat at the thick mahogany table in the center. Two were in uniform—the insignia and breast decorations duly proclaiming advanced ranks unknown to Fontini-Cristi. The man in civilian clothes had an archly diplomatic look about him, complete with a waxed moustache. Such men had come and gone in Campo di Fiori. They spoke in soft voices, their words ambiguous; they were seekers of elastic. The civilian was at the head of the table, the officers seated at the sides. There was one empty chair, obviously for him.

"Gentlemen," said Commander Neyland, as if he were announcing a petitioner at the Court of St. James, "Signor Savarone Fontini-Cristi of Milan."

Vittorio stared at the fatuous Englishman; the man had not heard a word he said.

The three men at the table rose as one. The civilian spoke. "May I introduce myself, sir. I am Anthony Brevourt. For a number of years I was the crown's ambassador of the Greek court of George the Second in

Athens. On my left, Vice Admiral Hackett, Royal Navy; on my right, Brigadier Teague, Military Intelligence."

At first there were formal nods of acknowledgment, then Teague broke the formality by coming around his chair, his hand held out for Vittorio.

"I'm glad you're here, Fontini-Cristi. I received the preliminary reports. You've had a hell of a time of it."

"Thank you," said Vittorio, shaking the general's hand.

"Do sit down," said Brevourt, indicating the expected chair to Vittorio and returning to his own. The two officers took their seats— Hackett rather formally, even pompously; Teague quite casually. The general withdrew a cigarette case from his pocket and offered it to Fontini-Cristi.

"No, thank you," said Vittorio. To smoke with these men would imply a casualness he neither felt nor wanted them to think he felt. A lesson from Savarone.

Brevourt quickly continued. "I think we'd better get on with it. I'm sure you know the subject of our anxieties. The Greek consignment."

Vittorio looked at the ambassador. And then at the two officers. They were staring at him, apparently in anticipation. "The Greek? I know nothing of a 'Greek consignment.' However, I know the gratitude I feel. There are no words to express it in either language. You saved my life; men were killed doing so. What more can I say?"

"I think," said Brevourt slowly, "that we should like to hear you say something about an extraordinary delivery made to the family Fontini-Cristi by the Eastern Brotherhood of Xenope."

"I beg your pardon?" Vittorio was stunned. The words had no meaning for him. Some extraordinary error had been made.

"I told you. I was the crown's ambassador to Athens. During the tenure of my office, diplomatic liaisons were formed throughout the country, including, of course, the religious. For, in spite of the turmoil Greece is experiencing, the church hierarchy remains a powerful force."

"I'm sure it does," agreed Vittorio. "But I have no idea why it concerns me."

Teague leaned forward, the smoke curling in front of his face, his eyes riveted on Fontini-Cristi. "Please. We've done our share, you know. As you've said—I think quite properly—we saved your life. We sent in our best men, paid thousands to the *Corsos,* took considerable gambles in dangerous waters with a submarine—of which we have precious few—and activated a barely developed aircraft escape route. All these just to get you out." Teague paused, put down his cigarette and smiled ever so slightly. "All human life is sacred, perhaps, but there are limits to the expenditures one makes to prolong it."

"Speaking for the navy," said Hackett with controlled irritation, "we followed blindly, given only the barest facts, urged by the most commanding figures in the government. We jeopardized a vital area of operations; a decision that could cost a great many lives in the near future. Our expense was considerable. And the full tally's not in yet."

"These gentlemen—the government itself—acted on my most urgent entreaties," said Ambassador Anthony Brevourt with measured precision. "I was convinced beyond any doubt that *whatever* the cost, it was imperative to get you out of Italy. Quite simply put, Signor Fontini-Cristi, it was not your life. It was the information you possess relative to the Patriarchate of Constantine. That is my conduit. Now, if you please, the location of the delivery. Where is the vault?"

Vittorio returned Brevourt's stare until he could feel the sting in his eyes. No one spoke; the silence was strained. Things were being alluded to that moved the highest echelons of government and Fontini-Cristi knew he was the focus. But that was all he knew.

"I cannot tell you what I know nothing about."

"*The freight from Salonika.*" Brevourt's voice was cutting. The flat of his hand descended delicately on the table, the soft slap of flesh against the wood as startling as it was abrupt. "Two dead men in the railroad yards of Milan. One a priest. Somewhere beyond Banja Luka, north of Trieste, past Monfalcone, somewhere in Italy, or Switzerland you met that train. Now *where?*"

"I met no train, *signore.* I know nothing of Banja Luka, or Trieste. Monfalcone, yes, but it was only a phrase, and meaningless to me. An 'incident' would 'take place at Monfalcone.' That was all. My father did not elaborate. His position was that I would be given the information *after* the incident at Monfalcone. Not before."

"What of the two dead men in Milan? In the railroad yards." Brevourt would not let up; his intensity was electric.

"I read of the two men you speak of—shot in the Milan freight yards. It was a newspaper story. It did not seem terribly important to me."

"They were *Greeks.*"

"I understand that."

"You *saw* them. They made the *delivery* to you."

"I saw no Greeks. No delivery was made to me."

"Oh, my God!" Brevourt drew out the words in a pained whisper. It was obvious to all at the table that the diplomat was suddenly gripped in his own particular fear; he was not feigning for negotiable effect.

"Easy," said Vice Admiral Hackett vacuously. The diplomat started to speak again, slowly, carefully, as though marshaling his thoughts.

"An agreement was made between the Elders of Xenope and the Italian Fontini-Cristis. It was a matter of incalculable priority. Sometime between December ninth and sixteenth—the dates the train left Salonika and arrived in Milan—it was met and a crate removed from the third freight car. Of such value was this cargo that the train's itinerary was prepared in isolated stages. There was only a single master plan, itself a sequence of documents, held by one man, a priest of Xenope. These, too, were destroyed before the priest took his own life and that of the engineer. Only he knew where the transfer was to be made, where the crate was to be removed. He and those responsible for removing it. The Fontini-Cristis." Brevourt paused, his deepset eyes riveted on Vittorio. "These are facts, sir; given to me by a courier from the Patriarchate. Coupled with the measures my government has taken, I presume they are sufficient to convince you to give us the information."

Fontini-Cristi shifted his position in the chair and looked away from the quietly intense face of the ambassador. He was sure the three men thought he was dissembling; he would have to dissuade them of that. But first he had to think. So this was the reason. An unknown train from Salonika had caused the British government to take extraordinary measures to—what had Teague said?—prolong his life. Yet it was not his life that was important, as Brevourt had made clear. It was the information they assumed he possessed.

Which, of course, he did not.

December 9 through 16. His father had left for Zürich on the twelfth. But Savarone had not been in Zürich. And he would not tell his son where he had been. . . . Brevourt might well have cause for his anxieties. Still, there were other questions; the pattern was unclear. Vittorio turned back to the diplomat.

"Bear with me. You say Fontini-Cristis. You use the plural. A father and four sons. The father's name was Savarone. Your Commander Neyland inaccurately introduced me by that name."

"Yes." Brevourt was barely audible, as if he were being forced to confront a conclusion he refused to accept. "I was aware of that."

"So Savarone is the name you received from the Greeks. Is that correct?"

"He could not have done it alone." Again Brevourt spoke hardly above a whisper. "You're the eldest son; you run the companies. He would have advised you. He needed your help. There were over twenty separate documents to be prepared, we know that. He *needed* you!"

"It is what you apparently—perhaps desperately—wish to believe. And because you believed it, you took extraordinary measures to save my life, to get me out of Italy. You obviously know what happened at Campo di Fiori."

Brigadier Teague spoke. "We picked it up first through the partisans. The Greeks weren't far behind. The Greek embassy in Rome was keeping close tabs on the Fontini-Cristis; it wasn't told why, apparently. The Athens conduit reached the ambassador and he, in turn, got in touch with us."

"And now you are implying," said Brevourt icily, "that it was all for nothing."

"I'm not implying it. I'm stating it. During the period you spoke of, my father said he was traveling to Zürich. I'm afraid I wasn't paying much attention at the time, but several days later I had an urgent reason to ask him to return to Milan. I tried contacting him; I called every hotel in Zürich; he was nowhere to be found. He never told me where he was, where he had been. That's the truth, gentlemen."

The two officers looked at the diplomat. Brevourt leaned slowly back in his chair—it was a gesture of futility and exhaustion; he stared at the table top. Finally, he spoke.

"You have your life, Signor Fontini-Cristi. For all our sakes, I hope the cost was not too great."

"I can't answer that, of course. Why was this agreement made with my father?"

"*I* can't answer *that*," replied Brevourt, his eyes still on the table. "Apparently someone, somewhere, believed he was resourceful enough, or powerful enough, to carry it off. Either or both of which have been borne out. Perhaps we'll never know. . . ."

"What was on the train from Salonika? What was in the vault that caused you to do what you did?"

Anthony Brevourt raised his eyes and looked at Vittorio and lied. "I don't know."

"That's preposterous."

"I'm sure it must appear that way. I know only the . . . implications of its significance. There is no price on such things. It's an abstract value."

"And on that judgment you made these decisions, convinced your highest authorities to make them? Moved your government?"

"I did, sir. I would do it again. And that's all I'll say on the subject."

Brevourt rose from the table. "It's pointless to go on. Others may be in touch with you. Good day, Signor Fontini-Cristi."

The ambassador's action startled the two officers, but they said nothing. Vittorio got out of his chair, nodded, and walked silently to the door. He turned and looked at Brevourt; the man's eyes were noncommittal.

Outside, Fontini-Cristi was surprised to see Commander Neyland standing at attention between two enlisted men. Intelligence Sector Five, Alien Operations, was taking no chances. The door of the conference room was being guarded.

Neyland turned, astonishment in his face. He obviously expected the meeting to last far longer.

"You've been released, I see."

"I didn't think I was being held," answered Vittorio.

"Figure of speech."

"I never realized how unattractive it was. Are you to escort me past the desk?"

"Yes, I'll sign you out."

They approached the Admiralty's huge entrance desk. Neyland checked his watch, gave Vittorio's last name to the guard. Fontini-Cristi was asked to initial the departure time; he did so, and as he stood up from the desk he was greeted by the commander's very formal salute. He nodded—formally—turned and walked across the marble floor to the huge double doors to the street.

He was on the fourth step when the words came to him. They shot through the swirling mists of white light and the shattering staccato of gunfire.

"Champoluc . . . Zürich is Champoluc . . . Zürich is the river!"

And then no more. Only the screams, and the white light, and the bodies suspended in death.

He stopped on the marble step, seeing nothing but the terrible visions of his mind.

"Zürich is the river! Champoluc. . . ."

Vittorio controlled himself. He stood motionless and breathed deeply, vaguely aware that people on the pavement and the steps were staring at him. He wondered if he should walk back through the doors of the Admiralty and down a long corridor to the cathedral arch that was the conference room of Intelligence Sector Five.

Calmly he made his decision. *Others may contact you.* Let the others come. He would not share with Brevourt, the seeker of elastic who lied to him.

* * *

"If I may, Sir Anthony," said Vice Admiral Hackett, "I believe there was a great deal more ground we might have covered——"

"I agree," interrupted Brigadier Teague, his irritation showing. "The admiral and I have our differences, but not in *this,* sir. We barely scratched the surface. We made an extraordinary investment and got nothing for it; there was more to be had."

"It was useless," said Brevourt wearily, walking slowly to the draped window overlooking the courtyard. "It was in his eyes. Fontini-Cristi told the truth. He was stunned by the information. He knows nothing."

Hackett cleared his throat, a prelude to judgment. "He didn't strike me as foaming at the mouth. He seemed to take it rather in stride, I'd say."

The diplomat stared absently out the window as he replied quietly. "If he had foamed at the mouth, I would have kept him in that chair for a week. He behaved precisely the way such a man reacts to deeply disturbing news. The shock was too profound for theatrics."

"Granting your premise," said Teague coldly, "it does not eliminate mine. He may not *realize* what he knows. Secondary information often leads to a primary source. In our business it nearly always does. I must object, Sir Anthony."

"Your objection is noted. You're perfectly free to make further contact; I made that clear. But you'll learn no more than we did this afternoon."

"How can you be so *sure?*" asked the Intelligence man quickly, his irritation rapidly turning into anger.

Brevourt turned from the window, his expression pained, his eyes in reflection. "Because I knew Savarone Fontini-Cristi. Eight years ago in Athens. He was a neutral emissary, I think is the term, from Rome. The only man Athens would trust. The circumstances are not relevant here; the methods of Fontini-Cristi are. He was a man possessed with a sense of discretion. He could move economic mountains, negotiate the most difficult international agreements, because all parties knew his word was better than any written contract. In a strange way, it was why he was feared; beware the man of total integrity. Our only hope was if he had called in his son. If he had needed him."

Teague absorbed the diplomat's words, then leaned forward, his arms on the table. "What was on the train from Salonika? In that damned vault?"

Brevourt paused before answering. The two officers understood that whatever the ambassador was about to say, it was *all* he would say.

"Documents hidden from the world for fourteen centuries. They could tear the Christian world apart, setting church against church . . . nation against nation, perhaps; forcing millions to choose sides in a war as profound as Hitler's."

"And by so doing," interrupted Teague in the form of a question, "dividing those who fight Germany."

"Yes. Inevitably."

"Then we'd better pray they're not found," concluded Teague.

"Pray strenuously, general. It's strange. Over the centuries men have willingly given their lives to protect the sanctity of those documents. Now they've disappeared. And all who knew where are dead."

PART THREE

7

The telephone rang on the antique desk in the Savoy suite. Vittorio was at the casement window overlooking the Thames, watching the barges make their way slowly up and down the river in the afternoon rain. He checked his watch; it was exactly four thirty. The caller had to be MI6's Alec Teague.

Fontini-Cristi had learned many things about Teague over the past three weeks; one was that the man was punctual to a fault. If he said he would telephone *around* four thirty, then he would do so *at* four thirty. Alec Teague ran his life by a clock; it made for abrupt conversations.

Vittorio picked up the telephone. "Yes?"

"Fontini?" The Intelligence man was also given to brevity when it came to names. Apparently he saw no reason to add the Cristi when the Fontini was sufficient.

"Hello, Alec, I've been expecting you."

"I've got the papers," said Teague rapidly. "And your orders. The Foreign Office was reluctant. It's an equal wager whether they were concerned for your well-being, or whether they thought you'd present the crown with a bill."

"The latter, I can assure you. My father drove 'hard bargains,' I think is the term. Frankly, I've never understood the phrase; can bargains be soft?"

"Damned if I know." Teague was not really listening. "I think we should meet right off. How's your evening?"

"I'm having dinner with Miss Holcroft. Under the circumstances I can cancel, of course."

"Holcroft? Oh, the Spane woman."

"I think she prefers Holcroft."

"Yes, can't blame her. He's a bloody fool. Still, you can't deny the ceremony."

"She's doing her best to, I believe."

Teague laughed. "Damned gutsy girl. I think I'd like her."

"Which means you don't know her, and you want *me* to know you've had me followed. I never mentioned her married name to you."

Teague laughed again. "For your own benefit, not ours."

"Shall I cancel?"

"Don't bother. When will you be finished?"

"Finished?"

"Dinner. Damn, I forgot; you're Italian."

Vittorio smiled. Alec's recollection was made in complete sincerity. "I can see the lady home by ten thirty . . . ten o'clock. I gather you wish to meet tonight."

"I'm afraid we have to. Your orders call for you to leave tomorrow. For Scotland. In the morning."

The restaurant in Holborn was named Fawn's. Black curtains were drawn tautly across the windows, stretched and tacked, inhibiting any light from spilling a single shaft into the street. He was in the bar, seated at a corner stool with a clear view of the lounge and the shrouded entrance. She would arrive any minute now and he smiled at himself, realizing that he wanted to see her very much.

He knew when it had begun with Jane—their swiftly developing relationship that would shortly lead to the splendid comfort of the bed. It was not their meeting in the Savoy lobby; nor was it their first evening together. Those were pleasant distractions; he had sought no more, wanted no more.

The beginning was five days later when he had been sitting alone in his rooms. There'd been a knock on the foyer door. He had opened it; Jane was standing in the hallway. In her hand was a slightly worn copy of the *Times*. He had not seen it.

"For God's sake, what happened?" she asked.

He had shown her in without answering, unsure of her meaning. She'd handed him the newspaper. In the lower left corner of the front page was a brief article circled in red pencil.

MILAN, Jan. 2 (Reuters)—A news blackout has been lowered on the Fontini-Cristi Industries here as government officials moved in assuming managerial control. No member of the Fontini-Cristi family has been seen, and the police have sealed off the family estate at Campo di Fiori. Rumors abound as to the fate of this powerful dynasty headed by the financier Savarone Fontini-Cristi and his eldest son, Vittorio. Reliable sources indicate they may have been killed by patriots, infuriated by recent company decisions many felt were inimicable to Italy's interests. It was reported that the mutilated body of an "informer" (unseen by this journalist) was found hanging in the Piazza del Duomo, with a sign that would seem to confirm the rumors of execution. Rome has issued only the statement that the Fontini-Cristis were enemies of the state.

Vittorio had put down the paper and walked across the room, away from the girl. He knew she meant well; he did not fault her concern. Yet he was profoundly annoyed. The anguish was his alone and he did not care to share it. She had intruded.

"I'm sorry," she'd said quietly. "I presumed. I had no right to do that."

"When did you first read this?"

"Less than a half hour ago. It was left on my desk. I've mentioned you to friends. I saw no reason not to."

"And you came right over?"

"Yes."

"Why?"

"I cared," had been her simple answer. The honesty of it had touched him. "I'll go now."

"Please——"

"Do you want me to stay?"

"Yes. I think I do."

And so he had told her. In measured tones at first, his sentences gathering momentum as he approached the hideous night of white light and death that was Campo di Fiori. His throat was dry. He did not wish to go on.

And Jane did a strange thing. Separated by the short distance between their opposing chairs, making no move to diminish that separation, she forced him to continue.

"For God's sake, *say* it. *All* of it."

She whispered, but the whisper was a command and in his confusion and anguish he accepted it.

When he was done, relief swept over him. For the first time in days an unbearable weight had been lifted. Not permanently, it would return; but for the moment he had found his sanity; really found it, not an imposed pretense that left his breath always a little short.

Jane had known what he had not understood. She had said it.

"Did you think you could go on keeping it inside? Not saying the words; not hearing them. What kind of man do you think you *are?*"

What kind of man? He did not really know. He had not actually thought about the kind of man he was; it was not a question that had concerned him beyond certain limits. He was Vittorio Fontini-Cristi, first son of Savarone. Now he would find out what else he was. He wondered whether Jane could be a part of his new world. Or whether the hate and the war would be all-consuming. He knew only the war—and the hate—were his springboards back to life.

Which was why he had encouraged Alec Teague when the MI6 man contacted him after the disastrous conference with Brevourt at Intelligence Sector Five. Teague wanted background material—seemingly unimportant conversations, offhand remarks, oddly repeated words—anything that might have a bearing on the train from Salonika. But Vittorio wanted something, too. From Teague. So he spaced out the isolated scraps of information: a river that might or might not have anything to do with Zürich, a district in the Italian Alps that bore the name Champoluc, but possessed no river. Whatever the puzzle was, its pieces remained separate. Still Teague probed.

And while he probed, Vittorio drew out the conceivable options MI6 might have for him. He was fluent in English and Italian, more than proficient in French and German; he had an intimate working knowledge of a score of major European industries, had negotiated with the leading financial figures throughout Europe. Certainly there was *something*.

Teague said he would look. Yesterday Teague said he would call him today at four thirty; there might be something. This afternoon at precisely four thirty Teague had called; he had Vittorio's "orders." There *had* been something. Fontini-Cristi wondered what it was, and even more, why the abruptness of his departure for Scotland.

"Have you been waiting long?" asked Jane Holcroft, suddenly standing beside him in the dimly lit bar.

"I'm *sorry*." Vittorio was; he had not seen her in the lounge. Yet he had been staring at the door. "No, not at all."

"You were miles away. You looked right at me and when I smiled, you scowled. I trust it's not indicative."

"Good heavens, no. You were right; I was miles away. In Scotland."

"I beg your pardon?"

"I'll tell you about it at the table. What I know, which is very little."

They were led to their table and ordered drinks. "I've told you about Teague," he said, lighting her cigarette, holding the flame of the match for his own.

"Yes. The man from Intelligence. You didn't say a great deal about him. Only that he seemed to be a good chap who asked a lot of questions."

"He had to. My family required it." Fontini-Cristi had not told Jane about the freight from Salonika; there was no point. "I've been pestering him for several weeks to find me a job."

"In the service?"

"In any service. He was a logical man to approach; he knows people everywhere. We both agreed I have qualifications that might be useful to someone."

"What will you be doing?"

"I don't know, but whatever it is, it begins in Scotland."

The waiter arrived with their drinks. Vittorio nodded his thanks, aware that Jane kept her eyes on his face.

"There are training camps in Scotland," she said quietly. "Several are listed as highly classified. They're quite secret and heavily guarded."

Vittorio smiled. "They can't be *too* secret."

The girl returned his smile, the full explanation in her eyes, only half of it in her words. "There's an elaborate system of air defense warning-relays throughout the areas. Overlapping sectors; extremely difficult for aircraft to penetrate. Especially single-engine light aircraft."

"I forgot. The Savoy manager said you were no-nonsense people."

"We're also given extensive training in all existing systems. As well as those in development stages. Systems vary considerably from sector to sector. When are you leaving?"

"Tomorrow."

"I see. For how long?"

"I don't know."

"Of course. You said that."

"I'm to meet with Teague tonight. After dinner, but there's no need to rush. I'm not seeing him until ten thirty. I presume I'll know more then."

Jane was silent for several moments. She locked her eyes with his and then spoke simply. "When your meeting with Teague is over, will you come to me? To my flat? Tell me what you can."

"Yes. I will."

"I don't care what time it is." She placed her hand over his. "I want us to be together."

"So do I."

Brigadier Alec Teague removed his creased officer's cap and army overcoat and threw them on the Savoy chair. He unbuttoned his tunic and his collar and loosened his tie. He lowered his large, powerful frame into the soft couch and exhaled a sigh of relaxation. He grinned at Fontini-Cristi, who stood in front of an opposing armchair and held his palms up in supplication.

"Since I've been at it since seven this morning, I do think you should offer me a drink. Whiskey neat would be splendid."

"Of course." Vittorio crossed to the small bar against the wall, poured two short glasses, and returned with the drinks.

"Mrs. Spane's a most attractive woman," Teague said. "And you're quite right, you know, she does prefer her maiden name. At the Air Ministry the 'Spane' is in brackets. She's called Flying Officer Holcroft."

"Flying Officer?" Vittorio did not know why but the title seemed faintly amusing to him. "I hadn't thought of her in such military terms."

"Yes, I see what you mean." Teague finished his drink quickly and placed his glass on the coffee table. Vittorio gestured for a refill. "No more, thank you. It's time for serious talk." The Intelligence man looked at his wristwatch; Fontini-Cristi wondered if Teague really scheduled himself to the precise half-minute for social conversation.

"What's in Scotland?"

"Your place of residence for the next month or so. Should you accept the terms of employment. The pay's not exactly what you're accustomed to, I'm afraid." Teague grinned again. "As a matter of fact, we rather arbitrarily placed it at a captain's rate. I don't have the figures in my head."

"The figures aren't my concern. You say I have a choice, but before you said that my orders had arrived. I don't understand."

"We have no hold over you. You can reject the employment and I'll cancel the orders. It's as simple as that. However, in the interests of time, I made the purchase first. Frankly, to be sure it *could* be made."

"All right. What is it?"

"That's rather difficult to answer quickly. If at all, really. You see, it's pretty much up to you."

"To *me?*"

"Yes. The circumstances surrounding your getting out of Italy were unique, we all understand that. But you're not the only continental who's fled Europe. We've got dozens and dozens. And I'm not talking about the Jews and the Bolsheviks; they're in the thousands. I'm referring to scores of men like yourself. Businessmen, professionals, scientists, engineers, university people who, for one reason or another—we'd like to think it was moral repugnance—couldn't function where they lived. That's about where we are."

"I don't understand. Where are you?"

"In Scotland. With forty or fifty ragtail continentals—all quite successful in their previous livelihoods—in search of a leader."

"And you think I am *he?*"

"The more I think about it, the more convinced I become. Rather natural qualifications, I'd say. You've moved in the monied circles, you speak the languages. Above all, you're a businessman, you've developed markets all over Europe. Good heavens, man, the Fontini-Cristi Industries are *enormous;* you were its chief executive. Adapt to the conditions. Do what you've done splendidly for the past half-dozen years or so. Only do it from the *opposite point of view. Mis*management."

"What *are* you talking about?"

The brigadier continued, speaking rapidly. "We have men in Scotland who've worked in scores of occupations and professions in all the major cities in Europe. One step always leads to another, doesn't it?"

"That's what you're counting on, isn't it? We both ask questions."

Teague leaned forward, suddenly reflective. "These are hectic and complicated times. There are more questions than there are answers. But one answer was right in front of our eyes only we didn't see it. We were training these men for the wrong things! That is, we weren't sure *what* we were training them for; vaguely for underground contacts, routine information runs, it was amorphous. There's something better; damned ingenious, if I say so myself. The strategy, the concept is to send them back to *disrupt* the marketplace, create havoc—not so much physical sabotage, we've enough people doing that, but bureaucratic chaos. Let them operate in their former bailiwicks. Accounting offices consistently out of balance, bills of lading constantly inaccurate, delivery schedules at sixes and sevens, mass confusion in the factories: exemplary *mis*management at all *costs!*"

Teague was excited, his enthusiasm infectious. It was difficult for Vittorio to keep his concentration on the essence of his original question. "But why do I have to leave in the morning?"

"To put it bluntly, I said I might lose you if there were any further delays."

"Further? How can you say that? I've been here less than——"

"Because," broke in Teague, "no more than five people in England know why we *really* got you out of Italy. Your complete lack of information about the train from Salonika has them stunned. They took an extraordinary gamble and lost. What you've told me leads nowhere; our agents in Zürich, Berne, Trieste, Monfalcone . . . they can trace nothing. So I stepped in with a different version of why we got you out and saved a few heads in the bargain. I said this new operation was *your* idea. They leaped at it! After all, you are a Fontini-Cristi. Will you accept?"

Vittorio smiled. " 'Mismanagement at all costs.' That is a credo I doubt has a precedent. Yes, I do see the possibilities. Whether they are enormous—or theoretical—remains to be seen. I accept."

Teague smiled slyly. "There's one thing more. About your name——"

"Victor Fontine?" Jane laughed beside him on the couch in the Kensington flat, warmed by the glow of the burning logs in the fireplace. "That's British cheek if I ever heard it. They've *colonized* you."

"And made me an officer in the process," chuckled Captain Victor Fontine, holding up the envelope and dropping it on the coffee table. "Teague was amusing. He approached the subject rather the way one expects from the cinema. 'We must find you a *name*. Something immediately recognizable, easy to use in cables.' I was intrigued. I was to be given a code name, something quite dramatic, I imagined. A precious stone, perhaps, with a number. Or an animal's name. Instead, he merely Anglicized my own and lopped it off." Victor laughed. "I'll get used to it. It's not for a lifetime."

"I don't know if I can, but I'll try. It's rather a letdown, frankly."

"We must all sacrifice. Am I correct in assuming a *capitano* is a higher rank than a flying officer?"

"The 'flying officer' has no intention of giving orders. I don't think either of us is very military. Nor is Kensington. What about Scotland?"

He told her sketchily, keeping what facts he knew unspecific. As he spoke, he saw and could feel her unusually light-blue eyes probing his, looking beyond the offhand phrases, knowing surely there was more, or would be. She was dressed in a comfortable lounging robe of pale yellow that accentuated her very dark brown hair and emphasized the blue of her eyes. Underneath the robe, between the wide lapels, he could see the soft white of her nightgown and he knew she meant him to see it, and to want to touch her.

It was so comfortable, thought Fontine. There was no sense of urgency or maneuver. At one point during his monologue he touched her shoulder; she slowly, gently reached up and held his hand, her fingers caressing his. She led his hand down to her lap and cupped it with her other hand as he finished.

"So there we have it. 'Mismanagement at all costs' wherever it can be inflicted."

She was quiet for a moment, her eyes still probing, and then she smiled. "It's a marvelous idea. Teague's right, the possibilities are enormous. How long will you be in Scotland? Did he say?"

"Not specifically. A 'number of weeks.'" He withdrew his hand from hers and casually, naturally reached around her shoulders and drew her to him. Her head rested on his upper chest; he kissed her soft hair. She pulled back and looked up at him—her eyes still searching. She parted her lips as she moved toward him, taking his hand and casually, perfectly naturally, leading it between the lapels of her robe, inside over her breast. When their lips met, Jane moaned and widened her mouth, accepting the full moisture of his own.

"It's been a long time," she whispered finally.

"You're lovely," he replied, stroking her soft hair with his hand, kissing her eyes.

"I wish you didn't have to go away. I don't want you to go."

They stood up in front of the small couch. She helped him take off his jacket, pausing to press her face against his chest. They kissed again, holding each other at first gently, and then with gathering strength. For the briefest time, Victor placed his hands on her shoulders and moved her back; her lovely face was below him and he spoke into her blue eyes. "I'll miss you terribly. You've given me so much."

"And you've given me what I was afraid to find," she answered, her lips forming a gentle, quiet smile. "Afraid to look for, actually. Good heavens, I was petrified!"

She took his hand and they walked across the room to a doorway. Inside was the bedroom; a single ivory lamp shone on a night table, its yellowish white glow throwing light up on the walls of soft blue and across the ivory-colored, simple furniture. The silk spread over the bed was, again, blue and white and filled with the intricate circles of a floral design. It was all so peaceful, so away, so lovely, as Jane was lovely.

"This is a room of great privacy. And warmth," said Fontine, struck by simple beauty. "It's an extraordinary room, because it's your room and you care for it. Do I sound foolish?"

"You sound Italian," she answered softly, smiling, her blue eyes filled with love and urgency. "The privacy and the warmth are for you to share. I want you to share them."

She walked to one side of the bed, he to the other. Together they folded back the silk spread; their hands touched and they looked at each other. Jane walked around the bed to him. As she did so, she reached up and unbuttoned the top of her negligee, and then untied the ribbon of her gown. The fabric fell away, her round, full breasts emerged from the folds of silk, the nipples pink, taut.

He took her into his arms, his lips seeking hers in moist, soft excitement. She pressed her body against his. He could never remember being so completely, so totally aroused. Her long legs trembled and once again she pressed against him. She opened her mouth, her lips covered his, low moans of sweet pleasure coming from her throat.

"Oh, God, *take* me, Vittorio. Quickly, *quickly,* my love!"

The telephone rang on Alec Teague's desk. He looked at the office clock on the wall, then at his wristwatch. It was ten minutes to one in the morning. He picked up the receiver.

"Teague here."

"Reynolds in surveillance. We have the report. He's still in Kensington at the Holcroft flat. We think he'll stay the night."

"Good! We're on schedule. Everything according to plan."

"I wish we knew what was said. We could have set it up, sir."

"Quite unnecessary, Reynolds. Deposit a file-insertion for the morning: Parkhurst at the Air Ministry is to be contacted. Flying Officer Holcroft is to be given flexible consideration, including a tour of the Loch Torridon warning relays in Scotland, if it can be arranged quietly. Now, I'm off for some sleep. Good night."

8

Loch Torridon was west of the northwest highlands on the edge of the water, the source of the loch in the sea leading to the Hebrides. Inland there were scores of deep ravines, with streams rolling down from the upper regions, water that was icy and clear and formed pockets of marsh. The compound was between the coast and the hills. It was rough country. Isolated, invulnerable, patrolled by guards armed with weapons and dogs. Six miles northeast was a small village with a single main street that wound between a few shops and became a dirt road on the outskirts.

The hills themselves were steep, the abrupt inclines profuse with tall trees and thick foliage. It was in the hills that the continentals were put through the rigors of physical training. But the training was slow and laborious. The recruits were not soldiers but businessmen, teachers, and professionals, incapable of sustaining harsh physical exertion.

The common denominator was a hatred of the Germans. Twenty-two had their roots in Germany and Austria; in addition, there were eight Poles, nine Dutch, seven Belgians, four Italians, and three Greeks. Fifty-three once-respectable citizens who had made their own calculations months earlier.

They understood that one day they would be sent back to their homelands. But as Teague had noted, it was a formless sort of objective. And this undefined, seemingly low-level, participation was unacceptable to the continentals; undercurrents of discontent were heard in the four barracks in the middle of the camp. As the news of German victories came with alarming rapidity over the radio, the frustrations grew.

For God's sake! When? Where? How? *We are wasted!*

The camp commander greeted Victor Fontine with not a little wariness. He was a blunt officer of the Regulars and a graduate of MI6's various schools of covert operations.

"I won't pretend to understand much," he said at first meeting. "My instructions are muddy, which is what they're supposed to be, I imagine. You'll spend three weeks, more or less—until Brigadier Teague gives us the order—training with our group as one of the men. You'll do every-thing they do, nothing out of the ordinary."

"Yes, of course."

With these words Victor entered the world of Loch Torridon. A strange, convoluted world that had little in common with anything he had experienced in his life before. And he understood, although he was not sure why, that the lessons of Loch Torridon would merge with the teachings of Savarone and shape the remaining years of his life.

He was issued regulation combat fatigues and equipment, including a rifle and a pistol (without ammunition), a carbine bayonet that doubled as a knife, a field pack with mess utensils, and a blanket roll. He moved into the barracks, where he was greeted casually, with as few words as possible and no curiosity. He learned quickly that there was not much camaraderie in Loch Torridon. These men lived in and with their imme-diate pasts; they did not seek friendship.

The daylight hours were long and exhausting; the nights spent memo-rizing codes and maps and the deep sleep necessary to ease aching bod-ies. In some ways Victor began to think of Loch Torridon as an exten-sion of other, remembered games. He might have been back at the university, in competition with his classmates on the field, on the courts, on the mats, or up on the slopes racing downhill against a stopwatch. Except that the classmates at Loch Torridon were different; most were older than he was and none had known even vaguely what it was like to have been a Fontini-Cristi. He gathered that much from brief conver-sations; it was easy to keep to himself, and therefore to compete against himself. It was the cruelest competition.

"Hello? My name is Mikhailovic." The man grinning and speaking to Victor sank to the ground, breathing heavily. He released the straps of his field pack and let the bulky canvas slip from his shoulders. It was midpoint in a ten-minute break between a forced march and a tactical maneuver exercise.

"Mine's Fontine," replied Victor. The man was one of the two new recruits who had arrived in Loch Torridon less than a week ago. He was in his mid-twenties, the youngest trainee in the compound.

"You're Italian, aren't you? In Barracks Three?"

"Yes."

"I'm Serbo-Croat, Barracks One."

"Your English is very good."

"My father is an exporter—was, I should say. The money's in the English-speaking countries." Mikhailovic pulled out a pack of cigarettes from his fatigues pocket and offered it to Fontine.

"No, thanks. I just finished one."

"I ache all over," said the Slav, grinning, lighting a cigarette. "I don't know how the old men do it."

"We've been here longer."

"I don't mean you. I mean the others."

"Thank you." Victor wondered why Mikhailovic complained. He was a stocky, powerfully built man, with a bull neck and large shoulders. Too, something about him was odd: there was no perspiration whatsoever on Mikhailovic's forehead, while Fontine's own was matted with sweat.

"You got out of Italy before Mussolini made you a lackey to the German, eh?"

"Something like that."

"Machek's taking the same road. He'll run all of Yugoslavia soon, mark my word."

"I didn't know that."

"Not many people do. My father did." Mikhailovic drew on his cigarette, his eyes across the field. He added quietly, "They executed him."

Fontine looked compassionately at the younger man. "I'm sorry. It's painful, I know."

"Do you?" The Slav turned; there was bewilderment in his eyes.

"Yes. We'll talk later. We must concentrate on the maneuver. The object is to reach the top of the next hill through the woods without being tagged." Victor stood and held out his hand. "My first name's Vittor—Victor. What's yours?"

The Serbo-Croat accepted the handshake firmly. "Petride. It's Greek. My grandmother was Greek."

"Welcome to Loch Torridon, Petride Mikhailovic."

As the days went by, Victor and Petride worked well together. So well, in fact, the compound sergeants paired them off against superior numbers in the infiltration exercises. Petride was allowed to move into Victor's barracks.

For Victor, it was like having one of his younger brothers suddenly return to life; curious, often bewildered, but strong and obedient. In some ways Petride filled a void, lessened the pain of his memories. If there was a liability in the relationship it was merely one of excess on the Serbo-Croat's part. Petride was an excessive talker, forever questioning, always volunteering information about his personal life, expecting Victor to reciprocate.

Beyond a point, Fontine could not. He simply was not so inclined. He had shared the anguish of Campo di Fiori with Jane; there would be no one else. Occasionally he found it necessary to reprimand Petride Mikhailovic.

"You're my friend. Not my priest."

"Did you have a priest?"

"Actually, no. It was a figure of speech."

"Your family was religious. It must have been."

"Why?"

"Your real name. 'Fontini-Cristi.' It means fountains of Christ, doesn't it?"

"In a language several centuries old. We're not religious in the accepted sense; not for a long time."

"I'm very, *very* religious."

"It's your right."

The fifth week came and went and still there was no word from Teague. Fontine wondered if he'd been forgotten; whether MI6 had developed second thoughts over the concept of "mismanagement at all costs." Regardless, life at Loch Torridon had taken his mind off his self-destructive memories; he actually felt quite strong and capable again.

The compound's lieutenants had devised what they called a "long-pursuit" exercise for the day. The four barracks operated separately, each taking forty-five degrees of the compass within a ten-mile radius of Loch Torridon. Two men from each barracks were given a fifteen-minute head start before the remaining recruits took chase; the object being for the hunted to elude the hunters for as long as possible.

It was natural for the sergeants to choose the best two from each barracks to begin the exercise. Victor and Petride were the first eluders in Barracks Three.

They raced down the rocky slope toward the Loch Torridon woods.

"Quickly now!" ordered Fontine as they entered the thick foliage of the forest. "We'll go left. The *mud;* step into the mud! Break as many branches as you can."

They ran no more than fifty yards, snapping limbs, stamping their feet into the moist corridor of soft earth that angled through the woods. Victor issued his second command.

"Stop! This is far enough. Now, carefully. We'll make footprints up onto the dry ground. . . . That's enough. All right, step backward, directly on the prints. *Across* the mud. . . . Good. Now, we'll head back."

"Head back?" asked the bewildered Petride. "Head back where?"

"To the edge of the woods. Where we entered. We've still got eight minutes. That's enough time."

"For what?" The Serbo-Croat looked at his older friend as if Fontine was amusingly mad.

"To climb a tree. Out of sight."

Victor selected a tall Scotch pine in the center of a cluster of lower trees and started up, shinnying to the first level of branches. Petride followed, his boyish face elated. Both men reached the three-quarter height of the pine, bracing themselves on opposite sides of the trunk. They were obscured by the surrounding branches; the ground beneath, however, was visible to them.

"We've nearly two minutes to spare," whispered Victor, looking at his watch. "Kick any loose limbs away. Rest your weight solidly."

Two minutes and thirty second later, their pursuers passed far below them. Fontine leaned forward toward the young Serbo-Croat.

"We'll give them thirty seconds and then climb down. We'll head for the other side of the hill. A section of it fronts a ravine. It's a good hiding place."

"A stone's throw from the starting line!" Petride grinned. "How did you think of it?"

"You never had brothers to play games with. Race-and-hide was a favorite."

Mikhailovic's smile disappeared. "I have many brothers," he said enigmatically, and looked away.

There was no time to pursue Petride's statement. Nor did Victor care to. During the past eight days or so, the young Serbo-Croat had behaved quite strangely. Morose one minute, antic the next; and incessantly asking questions that were beyond the bounds of a six-week friendship. Fontine looked at his watch. "I'll start down first. If there's no one in sight, I'll yank the branches. That's your signal to follow."

On the ground, Victor and Petride crouched and ran east at the edge of the woods, the base of the starting hill. Three hundred yards, around the circle of the hill was a slope of jagged rock that overlooked a deep ravine. It was carved out of the hill by a crack of a glacier eons ago, a natural sanctuary. They made their way literally across the gorge. Breathing hard, Fontine lowered himself into a sitting position, his back against the stone cliff. He opened the pocket of his field jacket and took out a pack of cigarettes. Petride sat in front of him, his legs over the side of the ledge. Their isolated perch was no more than seven feet across, perhaps five in depth. Again, Victor looked at his watch. There was no need to whisper now.

"In half an hour, we'll climb over the crest and surprise the lieutenants. Cigarette?"

"No, thank you," replied Mikhailovic harshly, his back to Fontine. The note of anger could not be overlooked. "What's the matter? Did you hurt yourself?"

Petride turned. His eyes bore into Victor. "In a manner of speaking, yes."

"I won't try to follow that. You either hurt yourself or you didn't. I'm not interested in manners of speech." Fontine decided that if this was to be one of Mikhailovic's periods of depression, they could do without conversation. He was beginning to think that beneath his wide-eyed innocence, Petride Mikhailovic was a disturbed young man.

"You *choose* what interests you, don't you, Victor? You turn the world off at will. With a switch in your head, all is void. Nothing." The Serbo-Croat stared at Fontine as he spoke.

"Be quiet. Look at the scenery, smoke a cigarette, leave me alone. You're becoming a bore."

Mikhailovic slowly pulled his legs over the ledge, his eyes still riveted on Victor. "You must not dismiss me. You cannot. I've shared my secrets with you. Openly, willingly. Now you must do the same."

Fontine watched the Serbo-Croat, suddenly apprehensive. "I think you mistake our relationship. Or, perhaps, I've mistaken your preferences."

"Don't insult me."

"Merely clarification——"

"My time has *run out!*" Petride raised his voice; his words formed a cry as his eyes remained wide, unblinking. "You're not blind! You're not deaf! Yet you pretend these things!"

"Get out of here," ordered Victor quietly. "Go back to the starting line. To the sergeants. The exercise is over."

"My name," Mikhailovic whispered, one leg pulled up beneath his powerful, crouching body. "From the beginning you refused to acknowledge it! *Petride!*"

"It is your name. I acknowledge it."

"You've never heard it before? Is that what you're saying?"

"If I have, it made no impression."

"That's a lie! It's the name of a priest. And you *knew that priest!*" Again the words floated upward, a cry shouted in desperation.

"I've known a number of priests. None with that name——"

"A priest on a *train!* A man devoted to the glory of God! Who walked in the grace of His holy work! You cannot, *must* not deny him!"

"*Mother of Christ!*" Fontine spoke inaudibly; the shock was over-powering. "Salonika. The freight from Salonika."

"Yes! That most holy train; documents that are the blood, the *soul* of the *one incorruptible, immaculate* church! You've taken them from us!"

"You're a priest of Xenope," said Victor, incredulous at the realiza-tion. "My God, you're a monk from Xenope!"

"With all my heart! With all my *mind* and *soul* and *body!*"

"How did you get here? How did you penetrate Loch Torridon?"

Mikhailovic pulled his other leg up; he was fully crouched now, a mad animal prepared to spring. "It's irrelevant. I must know where that vault was taken, where it was hidden. You'll tell me, *Vittorio Fontini-Cristi!* You've no choice!"

"I'll tell you what I told the British. I know *nothing!* The English saved my life; why would I lie?"

"Because you gave your word. To another."

"Who?"

"Your father."

"No! He was killed before he could say the words! If you know any-thing, you know that!"

The priest of Xenope's eyes became suddenly fixed. His stare was clouded, his lids wide, almost thyroid. He reached under his field jacket and withdrew a small, snub-nosed automatic. With his thumb he snapped up the safety. "You're insignificant. We're both insignificant," he whispered. "We're nothing."

Victor held his breath. He pulled his knees up; the split second approached when he would have the one opportunity to save his life, when he would lash his feet out at the maniacal priest. One boot at the weapon, the other at Mikhailovic's weighted leg, sending him over the precipice. It was all there was left—if he could do it.

Abruptly, the vocal intrusion startling, the priest spoke, his tone chantlike, transfixed. "You're telling me the truth," he said, closing his eyes. "You have told me the truth," he repeated hypnotically.

"Yes." Fontine took a deep, deep breath. As he exhaled, he knew he would plunge both legs out; the moment had come.

Petride stood up, his powerful chest expanding beneath the soldier's clothes. But the weapon was no longer aimed at Victor. Instead, both Mikhailovic's arms were extended in an attitude of crucifixion. The priest raised his head to the skies and shouted.

"*I believe in one God, the Father Almighty! I will look into the eyes of the Lord and I shall not waver!*"

The priest of Xenope bent his right arm and put the barrel of the automatic to his temple.

He fired.

"You got your first kill," said Teague casually, sitting in a chair in front of Fontine's desk in the small, enclosed cubicle.

"I did not kill him!"

"It doesn't matter how it happens, or who pulls the bloody trigger. The result's the same."

"For the wrong reason! That *train*, that damned, *unholy train!* When will it stop? When will it *go away?*"

"He was your enemy. That's all I'm saying."

"If he was, you should have known it, spotted it! You're a fool, Alec."

Teague shifted his legs in irritation. "That's rather harsh language for a captain to employ with a brigadier."

"Then I'd be delighted to purchase your command and set it right," said Victor, returning to the papers in manila folders on his desk.

"One doesn't do that in the military."

"It's the only reason for your continuity. You wouldn't last a week as one of my executives."

"I don't believe this." Teague spoke in astonishment. "I'm sitting here being cashiered by a ragtail guinea."

Fontine laughed. "Don't exaggerate. I'm only doing what you asked me to do." He gestured at the manila folders on the desk. "Refine Loch Torridon. In that process, I've tried to learn how this priest of Xenope, this Mikhailovic, got in."

"Have you?"

"I think so. It's a basic weakness with every one of these dossiers. There are no clear financial appraisals; there are endless words, histories, judgments—but very few figures. It should be corrected wherever possible before we make our final personnel decisions."

"What on earth are you talking about?"

"Money. Men are proud of it; it's the symbol of their productivity. It can be traced, confirmed in a dozen different ways. Records abound. Where possible, I want financial statements on every recruit in Loch Torridon. There was none on Petride Mikhailovic."

"Financial——"

"A financial statement," completed Fontine, "is a most penetrating look into a man's character. These are businessmen and professionals, by and large. They'll be anxious to oblige. Those that are not we'll question at length."

Teague uncrossed his legs, his voice respectful. "We'll get at it, there are forms for that sort of thing."

"If not," said Victor glancing up, "any bank or brokerage house can supply them. The more complex, the better."

"Yes, of course. And beyond this, how are things going?"

Fontine shrugged, waving his hand again over the pile of the folders on the desk. "Slowly. I've read all the dossiers several times, making notes, cataloging by professions and related professions. I've detailed geographical patterns, linguistic compatibilities. But where it's all led me, I'm not sure. It'll take time."

"And a lot of work," interrupted Teague. "Remember, I told you that."

"Yes. You also said it would be worthwhile. I hope you're right."

Teague leaned forward. "I have one of the finest men in the service to work with you. He'll be your communications man for the whole show. He's a crackerjack; knows more codes and ciphers than any ten of our best cryptographers. He's damned decisive, a shark at quick decisions. Which is what you'll want, of course."

"Not for a long time."

"Before you know it."

"When do I meet him? What's his name?"

"Geoffrey Stone. I brought him up with me."

"He's in Loch Torridon?"

"Yes. No doubt checking the cryp's quarters. I want him in at the beginning."

Victor was not sure why but Teague's information disturbed him. He wanted to work alone, without distraction. "All right. I imagine we'll see him at the dinner mess."

Teague smiled again and looked at his watch.

"Well, I'm not sure you'll want to dine at the Torridon mess."

"One never *dines* at the mess, Alec. He eats."

"Yes, well, the cuisine notwithstanding. I've a bit of news for you. A friend of yours is in the sector."

"Sector? Is Loch Torridon a sector?"

"For air warning-relays."

"Good Lord! *Jane* is here?"

"I found out the night before last. She's on tour for the Air Ministry. Of course, she had no idea you were in this area, until I reached her yesterday. She was in Moray Firth, on the coast."

"You're a terrible manipulator!" Fontine laughed. "And so obvious. Where the devil *is* she?"

"I swear to you," said Teague with convincing innocence, "I knew nothing. Ask her yourself. There's an inn on the outskirts of town. She'll be there at five thirty."

My God, I've missed her! I've really missed her. It was rather extraordinary; he had not realized how deeply he felt. Her face with its sharp yet delicate features, her dark, soft hair that fell so beautifully around her shoulders; her eyes, so intensely blue; all were etched in his mind. "I assume you'll give me a pass to leave the compound."

Teague nodded. "And arrange a vehicle for you. But you've a while before you should drive off. Let's spend it on specifics. I realize you've only begun, but you must have reached a conclusion or two."

"I have. There are fifty-three men here. I doubt twenty-five will survive Loch Torridon, as I believe it should be run——"

They talked for nearly an hour. The more Fontine expanded his views, the more completely, he realized, did Teague accept them. Good, thought Victor. He was going to make many requests, including a continuing hunt for Loch Torridon talent. But now his thoughts turned to Jane.

"I'll walk you to your barracks," Teague said, sensing his impatience. "We might drop in at the officers' club for a minute—I promise no longer. Captain Stone will be there by now; you should meet him."

But it was not necessary to stop off at the officers' bar to find Captain Geoffrey Stone. As they walked down the steps of the field complex, Victor saw the figure of a tall man in an army overcoat. He stood about thirty feet away in the compound, his back to them, talking to a sergeant major. There was something familiar about the officer's build, a kind of unmilitary slouch in the shoulders. Most striking was the man's right hand. It was encased in a black glove obviously several sizes too large to be normal. It was a medical glove; the hand was bandaged beneath the black leather.

The man turned; Fontine halted in his tracks, his breath suspended.

Captain Geoffrey Stone was the agent named Apple, who was shot on the pier in Celle Ligure.

They held each other. Neither spoke, for words were extraneous. It had been ten weeks since they'd been together. Ten weeks since the splendid, exciting moments of lovemaking.

At the inn, the old woman who sat in a rocking chair behind the front desk had greeted him.

"Flying Officer Holcroft arrived a half hour ago. 'A trust you're the captain, though the clothes dinna' say it. She said you're t' go up, if you're a mind to. She's a direct lass. Dinna' care for sly words, that one. Top of the stairs, turn left, room four."

He had knocked softly at the door, the pounding in his chest ridiculously adolescent. He wondered if she was possessed by the same tension.

She stood inside, her hand on the door knob, her inquisitive blue eyes bluer and more searching than he could remember ever having seen them. The tension was there, yet there was confidence, too.

He stepped in and took her hand. He shut the door; they closed the distance between them and slowly reached for each other. When their lips touched, all the questions were put to rest, the answers obvious in silence.

"I was frightened, do you know that?" whispered Jane, holding his face in her hands, kissing his lips tenderly, repeatedly.

"Yes. Because I was frightened, too."

"I wasn't sure what I was going to say."

"Neither was I. So here we are talking about our uncertainties. It's healthy, I suppose."

"It's probably childish," she said, tracing his forehead and his cheek with her fingers.

"I think not. To want . . . to *need* . . . with such feeling is a thing apart. One is afraid it may not be returned." He took her hand from his face and kissed it, then kissed her lips and then her soft dark hair that fell, framing the soft smooth skin of her lovely face. He reached around her and pulled her to him, holding her close, and whispered "I *do* need you. I've missed you."

"You're a love to say it, my darling, but you don't have to. I don't require it, I won't ask for it."

Victor pulled away gently and cupped her face, staring into her eyes, so close to his. "Isn't it the same with you?"

"Very much the same." She leaned into him, her lips against his cheeks. "I think of you far too often. And I'm a very busy girl."

He knew she wanted him as fully and completely as he wanted her. The tension each had felt was transferred to their bodies, release to be found only in the act of love. Yet the swelling, aching urgency in them did not demand swiftness. Instead, they held each other in the warm excitement of the bed, explored each other in tenderness and growing insistence. And they talked softly in whispers as their excitement grew.

Oh, God, he loved her so.

* * *

They lay naked under the covers, spent. She rose on her elbow and reached across him, touching his shoulder, tracing the skin with her fingers down to his thighs. Her dark hair fell over his chest; behind it, below her delicate face and penetrating blue eyes, her breasts were suspended over his flesh. He moved his right hand and reached for her, a signal that the act of love would begin again. And it suddenly occurred to Vittorio Fontini-Cristi, as they lay naked together, that he never wanted to lose this woman.

"How long can you stay in Loch Torridon?" he asked, pulling her face down to his.

"You're a horrid manipulating spoiler of not-so-young girls," she whispered, laughing softly in his ear. "I am currently in a state of erotic anxiety, with the memory of thunderbolts and erogenous pleasure still rippling up my most private—and you ask me how long I can stay! Forever and ever, of course. Until I return to London in three days."

"Three days! It's better than two days. Or twenty-four hours."

"For what? To reduce us both to babbling idiots?"

"We'll be married."

Jane raised her head and looked at him. She looked at him for a long time before she spoke, her eyes locked with his. "You've been through a great deal of sorrow. And terrible confusion."

"You don't want to marry me?"

"More than my *life,* my darling. God, more than all the world. . . ."

"But you don't say yes."

"I'm yours. You don't have to marry me."

"I *want* to marry you. Is it wrong?"

"It's the rightest thing I can imagine. But you have to be sure."

"Are *you* sure?"

She lowered her cheek on his. "Yes. It's you. *You* must be sure."

With his hand he swept her soft dark hair away from her face and answered her with his eyes.

Ambassador Anthony Brevourt sat behind the enormous desk in his Victorian study. It was nearly midnight, the household retired, the city of London dark. Everywhere men and women were on rooftops and on the river and in the parks talking quietly into wireless sets, watching the skies. Waiting for the siege they knew would come, but had not yet begun.

It was a matter of weeks; Brevourt knew it, the records projected it. But he could not keep his attention on the horrors that would reshape history as inevitably as the events moved forward. He was consumed by another catastrophe. Less immediately dramatic, but in many ways no less profound. It was contained in the file folder in front of him. He stared at the handwritten code name he had created for himself. And a few—very few—others.

SALONIKA

So simple in the reading, yet so complex in meaning.

How in God's name could it have happened? What were they thinking of? How could the movements of a single freight crossing half a dozen national borders be untraceable? The key had to be with the subject.

From below, in a locked drawer of his desk, a telephone rang. Brevourt unlocked the drawer and pulled it open. He lifted the receiver.

"Yes?"

"Loch Torridon," was the flat reply.

"Yes, Loch Torridon? I'm alone."

"The subject was married yesterday. To the candidate."

Brevourt momentarily stopped breathing. Then inhaled deeply. The voice on the other end of the line spoke again. "Are you there, London? Do you hear me?"

"Yes, Torridon. I heard you. It's more than we might have hoped for, isn't it? Is Teague pleased?"

"Not actually. I think he would have preferred a convenient relationship. Not the marriage. I don't think he was prepared for that."

"Probably not. The candidate might be considered an obstruction. Teague will have to adjust. Salonika has far greater priority."

"Don't you ever tell M.I.-Six that, London."

"At this juncture," said Brevourt coldly, "I trust all files relative to Salonika have been *removed* from M.I.-Six. That was our understanding, Loch Torridon."

"It is correct. Nothing remains."

"Good. I'll be traveling with Churchill to Paris. You may reach me through the official Foreign Office channel, Code Maginot. Stay in contact; Churchill wants to be kept informed."

9

LONDON

Fontine entered the stream of pedestrians moving toward Paddington Station. There was a numbness in the streets, a sense of disbelief that resulted in pockets of silence. Eyes searched other eyes, strangers took notice of the other strangers.

France had fallen.

Victor turned into Marylebone; he saw people buying newspapers in silence. It had happened; it had *really happened*. Across the Channel was the enemy—victorious, invincible.

The Dover boats from Calais held no crowds of laughing tourists on holiday any longer. Now there were different journeys; everyone had heard of them. The Calais boats sailed under cover of night, as men and women, some bloodied, some whole, all desperate, crouched below decks, hidden by nets and canvas, bringing out the stories of agony and defeat that were Normandy, Rouen, Strasbourg, and Paris.

Fontine remembered Alec Teague's words: *The concept, the strategy is to send them back to disrupt the marketplace . . . create havoc! Mismanagement at all costs!*

The marketplace was now all of Western Europe. And Captain Victor Fontine was ready to send out his Loch Torridon mismanagers of that marketplace.

Of the original fifty-three continentals, twenty-four remained; others would be added—slowly, selectively—as losses demanded. These twenty-four were as diverse as they were accomplished, as inventive as they were devious. They were German, Austrian, Belgian, Polish, Dutch, and Greek, but their nationalities were secondary. Labor forces were shipped across borders daily. For in Berlin, the *Reichsministerium* of Industry was pressing into service people from all occupied territories— it was a sweeping policy that would accelerate as new lands were brought under control. It was not unusual for a Hollander to be working in a Stuttgart factory. Already—only days after Paris fell—Belgians were being shipped to captured plants in Lyon.

Acting on this knowledge, the underground leaders were scouring the labor-transfer lists. Objectives: Find specialized temporary "employment" for twenty-four skilled professionals.

In the confusion that resulted from the German obsession for maximum productivity, positions were unearthed everywhere. Krupp and I.G. Farben were exporting so many experts to get factories and laboratories rolling in conquered countries that German industrialists complained bitterly to Berlin. It led to haphazard organization, slipshod management; it reduced the effectiveness of German plants and offices.

It was into this morass that the French, Dutch, Belgian, Polish, and German undergrounds infiltrated. Job recruitment directives were sent by espionage couriers to London, for the scrutiny of Captain Victor Fontine.

Item: Frankfurt, Germany. Messerschmidt subsupplier. Three plant foremen sought.

Item: Kraków, Poland. Axle division, automobile plant. Draftsmen needed.

Item: Antwerp, Belgium. Railroad yards. Freight and scheduling divisions. Management scarce.

Item: Mannheim, Germany. Government printing offices. Bilingual technical translators needed imperatively.

Item: Turin, Italy. Turin Aircraft. Source partigiano. *Mechanical engineers in short supply.*

Item: Linz, Austria. Berlin claims consistent overpayment fabrics company. Cost accountants needed.

Item: Dijon, France. Wehrmacht legal department. Lawyers demanded by occupation forces. . . . (So like the French, Victor had thought. In the midst of defeat, the Gallic mind sought debate in practical legalities.)

And so they went. Scores of "requirements," dozens of possibilities that would grow in numbers as the German demands for productivity grew.

There was work to be had, to be done, by the small brigade of Loch Torridon continentals. It was now merely a question of proper allocations and Fontine would personally oversee the specifics. He carried in his briefcase a very small strip of reusable tape that could be attached to any part of the body. The adhesive had the tensile strength of steel, but could be removed by a simple solution of water, sugar, and citrus juice.

Within that tape were twenty-four dots, each containing a microfilm. On each microfilm was a microscopically reduced photograph and a brief résumé of talents. They would be used in concert with the under-

ground leaders. Twenty-four positions of employment would be found
. . . temporary, to be sure, for such skilled personnel would be desirable in many locations during the coming months.

But first things first, and the first item on Fontine's agenda was a business trip of undetermined length. He would be parachuted into France, in the province of Lorraine near the Franco-Swiss border. His first conference would take place in the small town of Montbéliard, where he would stay for several days. It was a strategic geographical point, affording maximum accessibility for the underground from northern and central France and southern Germany.

From Montbéliard he would head north on the Rhine as far as Wiesbaden, where contingents of anti-Reichists from Bremen, Hamburg, Berlin, and points north and west would gather for meetings. From Wiesbaden he would take the underground's routes east to Prague, then northwest into Poland and Warsaw. Schedules would be created, codes refined, official work papers provided for eventual duplication in London.

From Warsaw he would return to Lorraine. The decision would then be made whether to head south into his beloved Italy. Captain Geoffrey Stone was against it in principle. The agent Fontine had known as Apple made that clear. All things Italian filled Stone with loathing, his revulsion traced to a pier in Celle Ligure and a hand shattered because of Italian naïveté and betrayal. Stone saw no reason to waste their resources on Italy; there were too many other pressure points. The nation of incompetents was its own worst enemy.

Fontine reached Paddington and waited for the Kensington bus. He had discovered buses in London; he had never taken public conveyances in his life before. The discovery was partly defensive. Whenever official cars were used, they were shared, calling for conversation between the passengers. None was called for on a bus.

There were times, of course, when he carried highly sensitive material home to read, when Alec Teague simply refused to allow him his newfound indulgence. It was too dangerous. Tonight had been a case in point, but Victor had fought his superior; the official car had two other riders and he wanted to think. It was his last night in England. Jane had to be told.

"For heaven's sake, Alec! I'll be traveling several thousand miles in hostile territory. If I lose a briefcase that's chained to my wrist with a combination lock on a London bus, I think we're all in for immense trouble!"

Teague had capitulated, checking the chain and the lock himself.

The bus pulled up and he climbed in, threading his way down the crowded corridor to a seat in the front. It was by a window; he looked out and let his thoughts dwell first on Loch Torridon.

They *were* ready. The concept *was* valid. They *could* place their personnel in succeeding managerial positions. All that remained was the implementation of the strategy. He would accomplish a great deal of that on his trip. He would find the right positions for the right personnel . . . the chaos and the havoc would shortly follow.

He was primed for the moment of departure. Yet he was not really prepared for the one thing that faced him now: telling Jane the moment had finally come.

He had moved into her Kensington flat when he returned from Scotland. She'd rejected his offer of considerably grander quarters. And these past weeks were the happiest in his life.

And now the moment had come and fear would replace the comfort of daily existence together. It made no difference that thousands upon thousands were going through the same experience; there was no comfort in mathematics.

His stop was next. The June twilight washed the trees and scrubbed the houses. Kensington was peaceful, the war remote. He got off the bus and started down the quiet street when suddenly his attention was drawn away from the entrance gate. He had learned over the past months not to betray his concern, so he pretended to wave to an unseen neighbor in a window across the way. By doing so, while squinting his eyes against the setting sun, he was able to see more clearly the small Austin sedan parked on the opposite side of the street fifty yards diagonally in front of him. It was gray. He had seen that gray Austin before. Exactly five days ago. He remembered vividly. He and Stone had been driving up to Chelmsford to interview a Jewess who had worked for the Kraków civil service until just before the invasion. They had stopped at a service station outside of Brentwood.

The gray Austin sedan had driven in behind them to the pump beside theirs. Victor had noticed it only because an attendant who sold the driver petrol was caustic when the pump registered less than two gallons . . . and the Austin's tank was full.

"That's bein' a mite greedy," the attendant had said.

The driver had looked embarrassed, turned the ignition, and sped out on the highway.

Fontine had noticed because the driver was a priest. The driver of the gray Austin across from him now was a priest. The white collar could be seen clearly.

And the man, he knew, was staring at him.

Fontine walked casually to the gate of the house. He lifted the latch, entered, turned, and closed the gate; the priest in the gray Austin sat motionless, his eyes—behind what appeared to be thick glasses—still directed at him. Victor approached the door and let himself inside. The moment he was in the hallway he shut the door and moved quickly to the narrow column of windows that flanked the doorframe. A blackout curtain was draped over the glass; he parted the edge and looked out.

The priest had inched his way over to the right window of his car and was looking out and up at the front of the building. The man was grotesque, thought Fontine. He was extremely pale and thin, and the lenses of his glasses were thick.

Victor let the curtain fall back and walked rapidly to the staircase, climbing the steps two at a time to the third floor, their floor. He could hear music within; the radio was on; Jane was home. As he closed the door behind him, he heard her humming in the bedroom. There was no time to shout greetings; he wanted to get to the window. And he did not wish to alarm her if he could avoid it.

His binoculars were in the bookshelf on the fireplace wall. He pulled the case from its recess between a section of books and took out the binoculars, went to the window and focused the glass below.

The priest was talking to someone in the back seat of the small automobile. Fontine had not seen anyone else in the car. The rear seat was in shadow and he had been concentrating on the driver. He edged the binoculars behind the priest and refined the focus.

Victor froze. The blood rushed to his head.

It was a nightmare! A nightmare that repeated itself! *Fed* upon itself!

The streak of white in the close-cropped hair! He had seen that shock of white from an embankment . . . inside an automobile . . . under the glaring lights . . . soon to erupt in smoke and death!

Campo di Fiori!

The man in the back seat of the gray Austin below had been in another back seat! Fontine had looked down at him from the darkness as he was now looking down at him thousands of miles away in a Kensington street! One of the German commanders! One of the German executioners!

"Good heavens! You startled me," said Jane, walking into the room. "What are you——?"

"*Get Teague on the telephone! Now!*" shouted Victor, dropping the binoculars, struggling with the combination lock on his briefcase.

"What *is* it, darling?"

"Do as I say!" He fought to keep control. The numbers came; the lock sprang open.

Jane stared at her husband; she dialed rapidly, asking no further questions.

Fontine raced into the bedroom. He pulled his service revolver from between a pile of shirts and tore it from its holster, running back into the living room toward the door.

"Victor! Stop! For God's sake!"

"Tell Teague to get over here! Tell him a German from Campo di Fiori is below!"

He ran out into the corridor and raced down the narrow staircase, manipulating his thumb beneath the barrel of the weapon, unlatching the safety. As he reached the top of the first flight, he heard the gunning of an engine. He yelled and plunged down to the hallway, to the front door, yanking furiously at the knob, pulling the door open with such force that it crashed against the wall. He ran outside to the gate.

The gray Austin was speeding down the street; pedestrians were on the sidewalks. Fontine chased it, dodging two oncoming cars, their tires screeching as they braked. Men and women shouted at him; Victor understood. A man racing in the middle of the street at seven in the evening with a gun in his hand was a cause for violent alarms. But he could not dwell on such thoughts; there was only the gray Austin and a man in the back seat with a shock of white in his hair.

The *executioner.*

The Austin turned right at the corner! Oh, God! The traffic on the thoroughfare was light, only a few taxis and private cars! The Austin accelerated, speeding, weaving between the vehicles. It jumped a traffic light, narrowly missing a delivery truck which jolted to a stop, blocking all vision beyond.

He had lost it. He stopped, his heart pounding, sweat pouring down his face, his weapon at his side, But he had not lost everything. There were six numbers on the gray Austin's license plate. He'd managed to distinguish four of them.

"The automobile in question is registered to the Greek embassy. The attaché assigned to it claims it must have been removed from the embassy grounds late this afternoon." Teague spoke rapidly, annoyed not only with his conceivably false information but with the entire incident itself. It was an obstruction, a serious obstruction. The Loch Torridon operation could not tolerate barriers at this moment.

"Why the German? Who is he? I know *what* he is." Victor spoke quietly, with enormous feeling.

"We're putting on every trace we can come up with. A dozen experienced field men are pulling the files. They're going back years, getting everything we have. The description you gave the artist was good; his sketch quite accurate, you said. If he's there, we'll find him."

Fontine got out of the chair, started for the window and saw that heavy black drapes had been drawn, shutting in all light. He turned and looked absently at a large map of Europe on Teague's wall. There were dozens of red mark-pins protruding from the thick paper.

"It's the train from Salonika, isn't it?" He asked the question softly, not needing an answer.

"That wouldn't explain the German. If he is a German."

"I *told* you," interrupted Victor, turning to face the brigadier. "He was there. In Campo di Fiori. I remembered then that I'd thought I'd seen him before."

"And you've never been able to recall where?"

"No. There are times when it drives me mad. I don't *know!*"

"Can you associate? Go back. Think in terms of cities, or hotels; start with business dealings, contracts. Fontini-Cristi had investments in Germany."

"I've tried all that. There's nothing. Only the face, and that not terribly clear. But the white streak in the hair, that's what stays in my mind." Wearily, Victor returned to the chair and sat down again. He leaned back, both hands over his closed eyes. "Oh, God, Alec, I'm frightened to death."

"You've no reason to be."

"You weren't in Campo di Fiori that night."

"There'll be no repetition in London. Or anywhere else, for that matter. Tomorrow morning your wife will be escorted to the Air Ministry, where she will turn over her workload—files, letters, maps, everything—to another officer. The ministry has assured me the transition can be concluded by early afternoon. Thereupon, she'll be driven to very comfortable quarters in the countryside. Isolated and totally secure. She'll stay there until you return, or until we find your man. And break him."

Fontine lowered his hands from his eyes. He looked questioningly at Teague. "When did you do this? There's been no time."

Teague smiled, but it was not the unsettling smile Victor was used to. It was, if anything, gentle. "It's been a contingency plan since the day you were married. Within hours, as a matter of fact."

"She'll be safe?"

"No one in England more so. Frankly, I've a twofold motive. Your wife's safety is directly related to your state of mind. You've a job to do, so I'll do mine."

Teague looked at the wall clock, then at his wristwatch. The clock had lost nearly a minute since he'd last adjusted it. When *was* that? It must have been eight, ten days ago; he would have to bring it back to the watchsmith's in Leicester Square.

It was a foolish preoccupation, he supposed, this obsession with time. He'd heard the names: "Stopwatch Alec," "Timer Teague." His colleagues often chided him; he wouldn't be so damned concerned with time if he had a wife and small ones clattering about. But he had made that decision years ago; in his profession he was better off without such attachments. He was no monk. There had, of course, been women. But no marriage. It was out of the question; it was a hindrance, an obstacle.

These passive thoughts gave rise to an active consideration: Fontine and *his* marriage. The Italian was the perfect coordinator for the Loch Torridon operation, yet now there was an obstacle—his wife.

Goddamn it! He had cooperated with Brevourt because he really *did* want to use Fontini-Cristi. If a convenient relationship with an English girl served both objectives, he was willing to go along. But not *this* far!

And now, where the hell was Brevourt? He had given up. He had faded away after having made extraordinary demands of Whitehall in the name of an unknown freight from Salonika.

Or had he merely pretended to fade away?

It seemed that Brevourt knew when to cut his losses, when to back away from an embarrassing failure. There'd been no further instructions regarding Fontine; he was now the property of MI6. Just like that. It was as though Brevourt wanted to put as much distance as possible between himself and the Italian *and* the goddamned train. When the report of the infiltrating priest of Xenope was given to Brevourt, he feigned only a mild interest, ascribing the episode to a lone fanatic.

For a man who had moved his government to do what it did, that wasn't natural. Because the priest of Xenope had not acted alone. Teague knew it; Brevourt knew it, too. The ambassador was reacting too simply, his sudden disinterest too obvious.

And that girl, Fontine's wife. When she appeared, Brevourt had snapped up her existence like a true MI-Sixer himself. She was a short-range anchor. She could be appealed to, used. If Fontine's behavior became suddenly strange, if he entered into or sought abnormal contacts that could be traced to the train from Salonika, she was to be called in and given her instructions: *report everything*. She was an English patriot; she would comply.

But no one had even considered a marriage. That *was* mismanagement-at-all-costs! Instructions could be given to a convenient mistress; they were not given to a wife.

Brevourt had taken this news with an equanimity that was again unnatural.

Something was happening that Teague did not understand. He had the uncomfortable feeling that Whitehall was using MI6 and that meant using him, tolerating Loch Torridon because it might lead Brevourt to a greater objective than the scattered disruption of enemy industry.

Back to the train from Salonika.

So two parallel strategies were being played out: Loch Torridon, and the search for the documents of Constantine. They allowed him the former; he was dismissed from the latter.

Dismissed and left with a married Intelligence officer—the most vulnerable kind.

It was ten minutes to three in the morning. In six hours he would be driving down to Lakenheath with Fontine to see him off.

A man with a streak of white in his hair. A sketch that eluded thousands of photographs and file descriptions, a hunt that led nowhere. A dozen MI6 staffers were down in the archives continuing the search. The field agent who broke the identity would not be overlooked when choice assignments were passed around.

His telephone rang, startling him.

"Yes?"

"It's Stone, sir. I think I have something."

"I'll be right down."

"If it's all the same to you, I'd prefer coming up. It's a bit mad. I'd rather see you alone."

"Very well."

What had Stone found? What could be so odd that it required in-house security?

"Here is the sketch Fontine approved, general," said Captain Geoffrey Stone, standing in front of Teague's desk, placing the charcoal portrait on the blotter. An envelope was clamped awkwardly between his arm and his chest, above the immobile, gloved right hand. "It matched nothing in the Himmler files, or any other German—or German-related—sources, including collaborationist circles in Poland, Czechoslovakia, France, the Balkans, and Greece."

"And Italy? What of the Italians?"

"That was our first consideration. Regardless of what Fontine claims to have seen that night in Campo di Fiori, he *is* Italian. The Fontini-Cristis made enemies among the fascists. But we found nothing, no one faintly resembling the subject in question. Then quite frankly, sir, I began thinking about the man. His marriage. We didn't expect that, did we, sir?"

"No, captain. We did not expect that."

"A small vicarage in Scotland. A church of England ceremony. Not exactly what one would have thought."

"Why not?"

"I've worked the Italian sectors, general. The Catholic influence is most pervasive."

"Fontine's not a religious man. What in hell are you driving at?"

"Just that. Everything's a question of degree, isn't it? One never is just this or just that. Especially a man who has wielded such power. I went back to *his* file; we've photostats of every damned thing we could lay our hands on. Including his marriage application and certificate. Under the heading of 'denomination' he inserted one word: 'Christian.' "

"Get to the point."

"I'm doing so. One thing always leads to another. An immensely wealthy, powerful family in a Catholic country, and the surviving son purposely denies any association with its church."

Teague narrowed his eyes. "Go on, captain."

"He *was denying*. Perhaps unconsciously, we don't know. 'Christian' is not a denomination. We were looking for the wrong Italians, pulling out the wrong files." Stone raised the envelope with his left hand, unwound the small string and opened the flap. He took out a newspaper clipping, a cropped photograph of a bareheaded man with a shock of white in his dark hair. The bareheaded man wore the black robes of the church; the picture was taken at the altar of St. Peter's. The man was kneeling, facing the cross. Above him was a pair of outstretched hands. They were holding the three-cornered hat of a cardinal.

"My God!" Teague looked up at Stone.

"The Vatican files. We keep records of all ecclesiastical elevations."

"But *this*——"

"Yes, sir. The subject's name is Guillamo Donatti. He's one of the most powerful cardinals in the Curia."

10

MONTBÉLIARD

The aircraft began its ninety-degree turn. They were at 3,000 feet, the night clear, the wind stream rushing past the open hatch with such force Fontine thought he would be sucked out before the red light above him was extinguished, replaced by the sudden glare of the white bulb that was his signal to leap. He gripped the handles at the sides of the hatch, bracing himself; his thick boots were pressed against the steel deck of the Haviland bomber; he waited to jump.

He thought of Jane. At first, she'd objected strenuously to her confinement. She had earned her position at the Air Ministry, weeks and months of "just plain damned hard work," were now taken away in a matter of hours. And then she abruptly stopped, seeing, he was sure, the pain in his eyes. She wanted him back. If isolation in the countryside would help his return, she would go.

He thought, too, of Teague; partially of what he said, mostly of what he did not say. MI6 had a line on the German executioner, the man-monster with the streak of white in his hair who had coldly observed the horror of Campo di Fiori. The service assumed him to be a ranking member of the *Geheimdienst Korps,* Himmler's secret police, a man who stayed far in the background, never expecting to be identified. Someone who had been stationed at the German consulate in Athens, perhaps.

"Assumed." "Perhaps." Words of equivocation. Teague was concealing information. For all his experience, the Intelligence man could not hide his omissions. Nor was he entirely convincing when he subtly introduced a subject that had little to do with anything:

"——it's standard procedure, Fontine. When a man goes on assignment we list his religious affiliation. Just like a birth certificate or a passport——"

No, he had no formal affiliation. No, he was not Catholic, nor was that extraordinary; there *were* non-Catholics in Italy. Yes, Fontini-Cristi was a derivative combination that was translated as the "fountains of Christ"; yes, the family for centuries had been allied with the church, but a number of decades ago had broken with the Vatican. But, no, he did not place undue emphasis on the break; he rarely thought about it.

What was Teague after?

The red light went off. Victor bent his knees as he had learned to do, and held his breath.

The white bulb flashed. The tap came—sharp, assured, solid. Fontine whipped his hands into reverse grips on the latch handles, leaned back, and propelled himself through the open hatch into the furious slipstream of the aircraft. He was buffeted away from the huge fuselage, the force of the wind crashing into his body with the sudden velocity and weight of a giant wave.

He was in free fall. He forced his legs into a V, feeling the harness of his chute cutting into his thighs. He thrust his arms forward and diagonally out at his side. The spread-eagle configuration did what it was supposed to do: It stabilized his fall through the sky, just enough for Victor to concentrate on the dark earth below.

He saw them! Two tiny flares to his left.

He pulled his right hand in against the rushing air and tugged at a small ring beside the parachute release. There was a momentary flash above him, like an instantly fading spit of a Roman candle. It would be enough for those on the ground to get a sighting. The moment fell back into darkness; he yanked the rubber handle of the parachute release. The billowing folds of cloth shot out of the pack; the massive jolt came, causing him to expunge his breath, his every muscle taut in counterthrust.

He floated, swinging in quarter circles in the night sky, toward the earth.

The conferences in Montbéliard went well. It was strange, thought Victor, but in spite of the crude, even primitive surroundings—an abandoned warehouse, a barn, a rock-strewn pasture—the conferences were not unlike smoothly run management meetings, with himself acting as a visiting consultant from the home office. The objective of each conference with the teams of underground leaders who made their covert treks into Lorraine was the same: projected recruitment for the pool of skilled personnel now in exile in England.

Management personnel were in demand everywhere, for everywhere within the Third Reich's expanding sphere production facilities were instantly appropriated and geared for maximum output. But there was a major flaw in the German obsession for immediate efficiency: Control remained in Berlin. Requests were processed by the *Reichsministerium* of Industry and Armaments; orders were cleared and issued hundreds of miles away from the place of origin.

Orders could be intercepted enroute; requests could be altered at the source, within the ministries; infiltrated at the clerical level.

Positions could be created; personnel could be replaced. In the chaos that was the Berlin fever for instant, total efficiency, fear was inherent. Orders were rarely questioned.

Everywhere the bureaucratic environment was ripe for Loch Torridon.

"You will be taken to the Rhine and put aboard a river barge at Neuf-Brisach," said the Frenchman, going to the small window in the rooming house overlooking Montbéliard's rue de Bac. "Your escort will bring the papers. I understand they describe you as river garbage, strong back and small head. A loading stevedore who spends most of his waking hours drunk with very cheap wine."

"That should be interesting."

THE RHINE

It wasn't. It was grueling, physically exhausting, and made almost intolerable by the stench below decks. German patrols prowled the river, stopping vessels continuously, subjecting crews to brutal interrogations. The Rhine was an underground courier route; it took no great perception to know that. And because the river "garbage" deserved no better, the patrols took delight in wielding clubs and rifle stocks when bones and flesh were the objects of impact. Fontine's cover was successful, if revolting. He drank enough rancid wine and induced sufficient vomit to give his breath the putrid foulness of a confirmed, unkempt alcoholic.

What kept him from losing his sensibilities altogether was his escort. The man's name was Lübok, and Victor knew that whatever risks he was taking, Lübok's were far greater.

Lübok was a Jew and a homosexual. He was a blond-haired, blue-eyed, middle-aged ballet master whose Czechoslovakian parents had emigrated to Berlin thirty years ago. Fluent in the Slovak languages, as well as German, he held papers identifying him as a translator for the Wehrmacht. Along with the papers were several letters on High Command stationery that proclaimed Lübok's loyalty to the Reich.

The papers and the letterheads were genuine, the loyalty false. Lübok operated as an underground courier across the Czechoslovakian and

Polish borders. At such times he wore his homosexual inclinations outrageously on his sleeve; it was common knowledge that such circles
existed in the Officer *Korps*. Checkpoints never knew who was favored
by powerful men who preferred to bed with other men. And the middle-
aged ballet master was an encyclopedia of truths, half-truths and gossip
as they pertained to the sexual practices and aberrations practiced by
the German High Command in any given sector or zone he entered. It
was his inventory; it was his weapon.

Lübok had volunteered for the Loch Torridon assignment, to be the
MI6 escort out of Montbéliard, through Wiesbaden, east to Prague and
north to Warsaw. And as the journey progressed and the days and the
miles went by, Fontine was grateful. Lübok was the best. Beneath the
well-tailored suits was a powerful man whose acid tongue and withering
stare guaranteed a hot but intelligent temper.

WARSAW, POLAND

Lübok drove the motorcycle with Victor in the sidecar, dressed in the
uniform of a Wehrmacht *Oberst* attached to Occupation Transport.
They sped out of Lódz on the road to Warsaw, reaching the final checkpoint a little before midnight.

Lübok performed outrageously before the patrols, dropping the
names of *Kommandanten* and *Oberführerin* in acid rapidity, implying all
manner of recriminations if their vehicle was detained. The embarrassed
guards were not anxious to test him. The bike was waved through; they
entered the city.

It was chaos. Although it was dark, rubble could be discerned everywhere. Street after street was deserted. Candles shone in windows—most
electricity was out. Wires sagged, automobiles and trucks were immobilized—scores overturned, lying like giant steel insects waiting to be
impaled on a laboratory table.

Warsaw was dead. Its armed killers walked in groups, themselves
afraid of the corpse.

"We head for the Casimir," said Lübok softly. "The underground's
waiting for you. It's no more than ten streets from here."

"What's the Casimir?"

"An old palace on the Kraków Boulevard. In the middle of the city.
For years it was the university; now the Germans use it for barracks
and offices."

"We go in *there?*"

Lübok smiled in the darkness. "You can put Nazis in universities, but it guarantees no instruction. The maintenance crews for all the buildings and the grounds are *podziemna.* Underground, to you. At least the beginnings of one."

Lübok squeezed the motorcycle between two staff cars on the Kraków Boulevard, halfway down the block, across from the main gate to the Casimir. Except for the guards at the gatehouse, the street was deserted. Only two streetlamps were working, but within the Casimir's grounds floodlights shot up from the grass, lighting the ornate facades of the buildings.

Out of the shadows walked a German soldier, an enlisted man. He approached Lübok and spoke quietly in Polish. Lübok nodded; the German continued diagonally across the wide boulevard up toward the Casimir gate.

"He's with the *podziemna,*" said Lübok. "He used the correct codes. He said you should go in first. Ask for Captain Hans Neumann, Block Seven."

"Captain Hans Neumann," repeated Victor. "Block Seven. What then?"

"He's tonight's contact in the Casimir. He'll take you to the others."

"What about you?"

"I'm to wait ten minutes and follow. I'm to ask for an Oberst Schneider, Block Five."

Lübok seemed concerned. Victor understood. Never before had they been separated at their point of contact with the underground leaders. "This is an unusual procedure, isn't it? You look troubled."

"They must have their reasons."

"But you don't know what they are. And that fellow didn't tell you."

"He wouldn't know. He's a messenger."

"Do you sense a trap?"

Lübok leveled his gaze at Fontine. He was thinking as he spoke. "No, that's not really possible. The commandant of this sector has been compromised. On film. I won't bore you with details, but his proclivity for children has been duly recorded. He's been shown the results and told negatives exist. He lives in fear, and we live with *him.* . . . He's a Berlin favorite, a close friend of Göring's. No, it's not a trap."

"But you're worried."

"Needlessly. He *had* the codes; they're complicated and very precise. I'll see you later."

Victor got out of the cramped sidecar and started across the boulevard toward the gates of the Casimir. He stood erect, the picture of arrogance, prepared to arrogantly display false papers that would gain him admittance.

As he walked across the Casimir's floodlit grounds, he could see German soldiers strolling in pairs and threes down the paths. A year ago these men might have been students and professors, recapping the events of the academic day. Now they were conquerors, peacefully removed from the devastation that was everywhere outside the walls of the Casimir. Death, hunger, and mutilation were within the sound of their commands, yet they talked quietly on clean paths, oblivious to the consequences of their acts.

Campo di Fiori. There were floodlights at Campo di Fiori. And death with mutilation.

He forced the images out of his mind; he could not allow his concentration to be weakened. The entranceway with the filigreed arch framing the thick double doors below the number seven was directly ahead. A Wehrmacht guard stood at attention on the single marble step.

Fontine recognized him: the soldier who had whispered in Polish to Lübok on the Kraków Boulevard.

"You're efficient," said Victor softly in German.

The guard nodded, reached for the door and opened it. "Be quickly now. Do use the staircase to the left. You will be met on the first landing."

Fontine walked rapidly through the door into the huge marble hall, crossed to the stairs, and started up. Halfway to the landing he slowed his pace. A silent alarm went off in his brain.

The guard's voice, his use of German. The words were odd, strangely awkward. *Be quickly. . . . Do use the staircase. . . .*

Watch for the lack of idiom, the excessively grammatical, or conversely, unmatching end syllables. Loch Torridon.

The guard was not German. Yet why should he be? He was from the *podziemna.* Yet, again, the *podziemna* would not take chances. . . .

Two German officers appeared on the landing, their pistols drawn and leveled down at him. The man on the right spoke.

"Welcome to the Casimir, Signor Fontini-Cristi."

"Please don't stop, *padrone.* We must hurry," said the second man.

The language they spoke was Italian, but their speech was not native. Victor recognized the source. The officers above him were no more German than the guard was German. They were *Greek.* The train from Salonika had reappeared!

There was the crack of a pistol bolt behind him, followed by rapid footsteps. Within seconds, the barrel was jammed into the small of his back, propelling him farther up the staircase.

There was no way he could move, no diversion he could employ, to distract his confronters. Weapons covered him, eyes watched his hands, bullets were locked in chambers.

Above, somewhere in an unfamiliar corridor, he heard laughter. Perhaps if he shouted, raising alarms of an enemy within the enemy camp; the concentric circle of thought was numbing.

"Who are you?" *Words*. Begin with words. If he could raise his voice in sequence, natural sequence that would minimize the chance of triggers pulled. "You're not German!"

Louder. *Now* louder.

"What are you *doing* here?"

The barrel of the pistol slid up his back and was jabbed into the base of his skull. The jolt caused him to stop. A closed fist punched him in the left kidney; he lurched forward, caught by the silent, staring Greeks in front of him.

He started to shout; there was no other way. The laughter above was growing louder, nearer. Other men were descending the staircase.

"I warn you——"

Suddenly, both his hands were yanked back, his arms bent and locked, the wrists turned inward. A large, coarse cloth was shoved into his face, saturated with acrid, foul-smelling liquid.

He was blinded; a breathless vacuum was being imposed on him, without light, without air. His tunic was ripped away, the cross strap pulled up from his chest. He tried to lash out his arms.

As he did so, he could feel the long needle entering his flesh; he was not sure where. Instinctively, he raised his hands in protest. They were *free;* and they were useless as his resistance was useless.

He heard the laughter again; it was deafening. He was aware of being propelled forward, and downward.

But that was all.

"You betray those who saved your life."

He opened his eyes; images came into focus slowly. There was a burning sensation in his left arm, or shoulder. He reached for it; the touch was painful.

"You feel the antidote," said the voice of the blurred figure somewhere in front of him. "It raises a welt, but it isn't harmful."

Fontine's eyes began to clear. He was sitting on a cement floor, his back against a wall of stone. Across from him, perhaps twenty feet away, a man stood in front of an opposite wall. They were on some kind of raised platform in a large tunnel. The tunnel appeared to be deep underground, carved out of rock, both ends disappearing into darkness. On the floor of the tunnel were old, narrow tracks; they were cracked, rusted. Light came from several thick candles inserted in ancient brackets on the walls.

His focus refined, Fontine concentrated on the man across from him. He wore a black suit; around his neck was a white collar. The man was a priest.

He was bald, but not from age. The head was shaved; the man was no more than forty-five or fifty, the face ascetic, the body slender.

Beside the priest was the guard in the Wehrmacht uniform. The two Greeks impersonating German officers stood by an iron door in the left wall facing the tunnel. The priest spoke.

"We've followed you since Montbéliard. You're a thousand miles from London. The English can't protect you. We have routes south they know nothing about."

"The English?" Fontine stared at the priest trying to understand. "You're from the Order of Xenope."

"We are."

"Why do you fight the English?"

"Because Brevourt's a liar. He breaks his word."

"Brevourt?" Victor was stunned; nothing made sense. "You're out of your mind! Everything, *everything* he's done in *your name!* For *you.*"

"Not for us! For England. He wants the vault of Constantine for *England!* Churchill demands it! It's a more powerful weapon than a hundred armies, and they all know it! We would never see it again!" The priest's eyes were wide, furious.

"You believe that?"

"Don't be an ass!" spat the monk from Xenope. "As Brevourt breaks his word, we broke Code *Maginot*. Messages were intercepted; communications between . . . shall we say, interested parties."

"You're *crazy!*" Fontine tried to think. Anthony Brevourt had faded away; there'd been no word from him—or about him—in months. "You say you've followed me since Montbéliard. *Why?* I don't have what you want! I never did have it! I know nothing about that goddamned train!"

"Mikhailovic believed you," said the priest softly. "I don't."

"Petride——" The sight of the child monk taking his own life on the rocky ledge in Loch Torridon came back to Victor.

"Petride was not his name——"

"You killed him!" said Fontine. "You killed him as surely as if you'd pulled the trigger yourself. You're insane! All of you."

"He failed. He knew what was expected. It was understood."

"You're *sick!* You infect everyone you touch! You can believe me or not, but I'm telling you for the last time! I don't have the information you want!"

"Liar!"

"You're mad!"

"Then why do you travel with Lübok? Tell me that, Signor Fontini-Cristi! Why Lübok?"

Victor recoiled; the shock of Lübok's name caused him to arch his back against the stone. "Lübok?" he whispered incredulously. "If you know his work, you know the answer to that."

"Loch Torridon?" asked the priest sarcastically.

"I never heard of Lübok before in my life. I only know he does his job. He's a Jew, a . . . he takes great risks."

"He works *for Rome!*" roared the priest of Xenope. "He conveys offers to Rome! *Your* offers!"

Victor was silent; his astonishment was so complete he had no words. The monk of Xenope continued, his voice low, penetrating. "Strange, isn't it? Of all the escorts in the occupied territories, Lübok is chosen. He just shows up in Montbéliard. Do you expect us to believe that?"

"Believe what you will. This is madness."

"It is *betrayal!*" the priest shouted again, taking several steps away from the wall. "A degenerate who can pick up a telephone and blackmail half of Berlin! And most outrageous—for you—a dog who works for the monster of——"

"*Fontine! Dive!*" The piercing command came from the black hole of the tunnel. It was screamed in Lübok's high-pitched voice, the sound bouncing off the receding walls of rock, overriding the shouts of the priest.

Victor reeled and sprang forward, rolling down the stone wall, crashing from the platform to the hard ground by the old rusted track. Above him he heard the spits of bullets shattering the air, followed by two thunderous explosions of unsilenced Lugers.

In the flickering light he could see the figures of Lübok and several others lurch out of the darkness, angling their weapons, taking rapid, accurate aim; firing and spinning back into the protection of the rock.

It was over in seconds. The priest of Xenope had fallen; he was hit in the neck, his left ear blown off his head. He had crawled to the ledge of the platform, dying, staring down at Fontine. In imminent death his whispered voice was a rasp.

"We . . . are not your enemies. For the mercy of God, bring the documents to us——"

A final, muted spit was heard; the priest's forehead exploded above his staring eyes.

Victor felt a grip on his left arm; it caused shooting pains throughout his shoulder and chest. He was being yanked to his feet.

"*Get up!*" was Lübok's command. "The shots may have been heard. Run!"

They raced into the tunnel. The beam of a flashlight pierced the black, held by one of Lübok's men up ahead. The man whispered his instructions in Polish. Lübok translated for Fontine, who ran beside him.

"About two hundred yards down there's a monks' cave. We'll be safe."

"A *what?*"

"Monks' cave," answered Lübok, breathing heavily. "The history of the Casimir goes back centuries. Escapes were needed."

They crawled on their hands and knees through a narrow, dark passageway cut out of rock. It led to the depths of a cave. The air was instantly different; there was an opening somewhere beyond in the darkness.

"I have to talk to you," said Victor quickly.

"To answer your questions, Captain Hans Neumann is a devoted officer of the Reich with a cousin in the Gestapo. Oberst Schneider wasn't on the roster; that was sticky. We knew it was a trap. . . . In all honesty we didn't expect to find you in the tunnel. That was a stroke of luck. We were on our way to Block Seven." Lübok turned to his comrades. He spoke first in Polish, then translated for Fontine. "We'll stay here for a quarter of an hour. That should be time enough. Then we'll proceed to the rendezvous in Seven. You'll conduct your business on schedule."

Fontine grabbed Lübok's arm and led him away from the *podziemna* men. Two of the men had turned on their flashlights. There was enough light to see the middle-aged courier's face, and Victor was grateful for that.

"It wasn't a German trap! Those men back there were Greek! One was a priest!" Fontine whispered, but there was no mistaking his intensity.

"You're mad," said Lübok casually, his eyes a perfect blank.

"They were from *Xenope*."

"From what?"

"You heard me."

"I heard you, but I haven't the faintest idea what you're talking about."

"Goddamn you, Lübok! Who are you?"

"Many things to many people, thank heavens."

Victor grabbed the blond-haired Czech by the lapels of his jacket. Lübok's eyes became suddenly distant, filled with cold anger. "They said you worked for Rome. That you would convey offers to Rome! *What* offers? What does it mean?"

"I don't know," replied the Czech slowly.

"Who do you work for?"

"I work for many people. *Against* the Nazis. That's all you have to know. I keep you alive and see that you complete your negotiations. How I do it is none of your business."

"You know *nothing* about Salonika?"

"It is a city in Greece, on the Aegean Sea. . . . Now, take your hands off me."

Fontine relaxed his grip but still held on. "Just in case—in *case*—the many people you speak of include men interested in that train from Salonika. I know *nothing*. I never did."

"If the subject ever comes up, and I can't imagine why, I'll convey the information. Now may we concentrate on your negotiations in Warsaw? We must complete them tonight. In the morning arrangements have been made for two couriers to fly out on the Berlin military shuttle. I'll check the airfield myself before daybreak. We'll get off at Müllheim. It's near the Franco-Swiss border, a night's trip to Montbéliard. Your business in Europe is finished."

"*Fly* out?" Victor removed his hands. "On a German plane?"

"Courtesy of a very distraught Warsaw commandant. He's seen too many motion pictures in which he was a prominent player. Sheer pornography."

11

AIR CORRIDOR, MUNICH WEST

The trimotored Fokker was stationary as maintenance crews checked the engines and a fuel truck filled the tanks. They were in Munich; they had left Warsaw early in the morning with a stop at Prague. Most of the passengers had gotten off at Munich.

Müllheim was next, the last leg of their journey. Victor sat uncomfortably beside a seemingly relaxed Lübok in the quiet cabin of the aircraft. There was one other passenger: an aging corporal on leave to Stuttgart.

"I'd like it better if there were a few more hitchhikers," whispered Lübok. "With so small a number, the pilot may insist everyone stay on board at Müllheim. He could gas up quickly and be on his way. He takes on most of his passengers in Stuttgart."

He was interrupted by the sound of clattering footsteps on the metal stairs outside the aircraft. Raucous, uninhibited laughter accompanied the unsteady clattering and grew louder as the new passengers approached the cabin door. Lübok looked at Fontine and smiled in relief. He returned to the newspaper provided by the attendant and sank back in the seat. Victor turned; the Munich contingent came into view.

There were three Wehrmacht officers and a woman. They were drunk. The girl was in a light-colored cloth coat; she was pushed through the narrow door by two of the Wehrmacht and shoved into a seat by the third. She did not object; instead she laughed and made funny faces. A willing, participating toy.

She was in her late twenties, pleasant-looking but not attractive. There was a frantic quality in her face, an intensity that made her appear somehow frayed. Her light-brown, windswept hair was a little too thick; it had not fallen free in the wind. The mascara about her eyes was too pronounced, the lipstick too red, the rouge too obvious.

"What are *you* looking at?" The question was shouted above the roar of the revving motors. The speaker was the third Wehrmacht officer, a broad-chested, muscular man in his thirties. He had walked past his two comrades and addressed Victor.

"I'm sorry," said Fontine, smiling weakly. "I didn't mean to be rude."

The officer squinted his eyes; he was a brawler, it was unmistakable. "We've got a *fancy* one. Listen to the lace-pants!"

"I meant no offense."

The officer turned to his comrades; one had pulled the not-unwilling girl over on his lap, the other was in the aisle. "The lace-pants meant no offense! Isn't that nice?"

The two fellow officers groaned derisively. The girl laughed; a little too hysterically, thought Victor. He turned front, hoping the Wehrmacht boor would go away.

Instead, a huge hand reached over the seat and grabbed him by the shoulder blade. "That's not good enough." The officer looked at Lübok. "You two move up front."

Lübok's eyes sought Victor's. The message was clear: Do as the man ordered.

"Certainly." Fontine and Lübok rose and walked swiftly up the aisle. Neither spoke. Fontine could hear the uncorking of bottles. The Wehrmacht party had begun.

The Fokker sped down the runway and left the ground. Lübok had taken the aisle seat, leaving him the window. He riveted his eyes on the sky, withdrawing into the cocoon of himself, hoping to produce a blankness that would make the journey to Müllheim pass more swiftly. It could not pass swiftly enough.

The blankness would not come. Instead, involuntarily, he thought of the Xenope priest in the underground tunnel of the Casimir.

You travel with Lübok. Lübok works for Rome.

Lübok.

We are not your enemies. For the mercy of God, bring the documents to us.

Salonika. It was never far away. The vault from Constantine was capable of violently dividing men who fought a common enemy.

He heard laughter from the rear of the cabin, then a whispered voice behind him.

"*No!* Don't turn around. *Please!*" It was the flight attendant, barely audible through the narrow space between the seats. "Don't get up. They're *Kommandos*. They just let off steam, so don't concern yourselves. Pretend there is nothing!"

"*Kommandos?*" whispered Lübok. "In Munich? They're stationed north, in the Baltic zones."

"Not these. These operate across the mountains in the Italian sectors. Execution teams. There are many——"

The words struck with the impact of silent thunderbolts. Victor inhaled; the muscles of his stomach hardened into a wall of stone.

. . . *execution teams.* . . .

He gripped the armrests of his seat and arched his back. Then, pressing his back into the seat, he stretched his neck and turned his eyes toward the rear of the cabin, over the metal rim of the headrest. He could not believe what he saw.

The wild-eyed girl was on the floor, her coat open; she was naked except for torn undergarments, her legs spread, her buttocks moving. A Wehrmacht officer, his trousers and shorts pulled down to his knees, lowered himself on her, his penis stabbing. Kneeling above the girl's head was a second Wehrmacht, his trousers removed, an erection protruding from the opening in his shorts. He held the girl by the hair and lanced his erection around the flesh of her face; she opened her mouth and accepted it, moaning and coughing. The third Wehrmacht was sitting, bent over on the armrest above the rape. He was breathing in gasps through parted lips, his left hand extended, rubbing the girl's naked breasts in a rhythm that matched the masturbating motions of his right hand.

"*Animali!*" Fontine lunged from the seat, ripping Lübok's fingers from his wrist, hurling himself forward. The Wehrmacht were stunned beyond movement, their shock total. The officer on the armrest gaped. Victor's open hand gripped his hair and crashed the man's head into the steel rim of the seat. The skull cracked; an eruption of blood sprayed the face of the Wehrmacht lying between the spread legs of the girl. The officer caught his knees in his trousers; he fell forward on top of the girl, his hands lashing out to grab support. He rolled on his back, crushing the girl in the narrow aisle. Fontine raised the heel of his right boot and propelled it into the soft throat of the Wehrmacht. The blow was pulverizing; the veins in the German's neck swelled into huge tubes of bluish-black under the skin. His eyes rolled up into his sockets, the eyeballs white gelatine, blank and horrible.

The screams of the girl beneath were now mingled with the cries of agony from the third officer, who had sprung forward, propelling himself off the Fokker's deck toward the rear bulkhead. The man's underwear was matted with blood.

Fontine lunged; the German rolled hysterically away. His bloody, trembling hand reached under his tunic; Victor knew what he was after: the four-inch *Kommando* knife, strapped next to his flesh beneath his armpit. The Wehrmacht whipped out the blade—short, razor sharp—and slashed it diagonally in front of him. Fontine rose from his crouch, prepared to leap.

Suddenly an arm was lashed around Victor's neck. He struck back with his elbows, but the grip was unbreakable.

His neck was yanked back and a long knife sped through the air and imbedded itself deep in the German's chest. The man was dead before his body slumped to the floor of the cabin.

Abruptly Fontine's neck was released. Lübok slapped him across the face, the blow powerful, stinging his flesh.

"Enough! Stop it! I won't die for *you!"*

Dazed, Victor looked around. The throats of the other two Wehrmacht had been cut. The girl had crawled away, vomiting and weeping between two seats. The flight attendant lay sprawled in the aisle—dead or unconscious, there was no way to tell.

And the old corporal who had stared at nothing—in fear—only minutes ago, stood by the pilot's cabin door, a pistol in his hand.

Suddenly the girl started screaming as she got to her feet. "They'll *kill* us! Oh, God! Why did you do it?"

Stunned, Fontine stared at the girl and spoke quietly with what breath he had left. *"You?* You can ask that?"

"Yes! Oh, my God!" She pulled her filthy coat around her as best she could. "They'll kill me. I don't want to die!"

"You don't want to live like *that."*

She returned his stare maniacally, her head trembling. "They took me from the camps," she whispered. "I understood. They gave me drugs when I needed them, wanted them." She pulled at her loose right sleeve; there were scores of needle marks from her wrist to her upper arm. "But I understood. And I lived!"

"Basta!" roared Victor stepping toward the girl, raising his hand. "Whether you live or die is immaterial to me. I didn't act for you!"

"Whatever you did is done, Captain," said Lübok quickly, touching his arm. "Snap out of it! You've had your confrontation, there can be no more. Understand?"

Fontine saw the strength in Lübok's eyes. Breathing heavily, Victor pointed in astonishment at the fortyish corporal who stood silently by the cabin door, his weapon drawn. "He's one of you, isn't he?"

"No," said Lübok. "He's a German with a conscience. He doesn't know who or what we are. At Müllheim he'll be unconscious, an innocent bystander who can tell them whatever he likes. I suspect it will be nothing. Stay with the girl."

Lübok took charge. He went back to the bodies of the Wehrmacht and removed identification papers and weapons. In the tunic of one, he found a hypodermic kit and six vials of narcotics. He gave them to the girl, who sat by the window next to Fontine. She accepted them gratefully and without so much as looking at Victor, she proceeded to break a capsule, fill the hypodermic, and insert the needle into her left arm.

She carefully repacked the kit and shoved it into the pocket of her bloodstained coat. She leaned back and breathed deeply.

"Feel better?" asked Fontine.

She turned and looked at him. Her eyes were calmer now, only contempt showing in them. "You understand, Captain. I don't *feel*. There are no feelings. One just goes on living."

"What will you do?"

She took her eyes away from him and returned to the window. She answered him quietly, dreamily—out of contact. "Live, if I can. It's not up to me. It's up to you."

In the aisle the flight attendant stirred. He shook his head and got to his knees. Before he could focus, Lübok was in front of him, his gun at the attendant's head.

"If you want to stay alive, you'll do exactly as I say at Müllheim."

Obedience was in the soldier's eyes.

Fontine got up. "What about the girl?" he whispered.

"What about her?" countered Lübok.

"I'd like to bring her out with us."

The Czech ran an exasperated hand through his hair. "Oh, Christ! Well, it's that or killing her. She'd identify me for a drop of morphine." He looked down at the girl. "Get her to clean up. There's a raincoat in the back. She can put it on."

"Thanks," said Victor.

"Don't," replied Lübok. "I'd kill her in a second if I thought it was a better solution. But she could be valuable; she's been with a *Kommando* unit where we didn't know one existed."

The Resistance fighters met the automobile on a back road of Lörrach, near the Franco-Swiss border. Victor was given clean but ragged clothes to replace the German uniform. They crossed the Rhine at nightfall. The girl was taken west to a Resistance camp in the hills; she was too drugged, too erratic to make the trip south to Montbéliard.

The flight attendant was simply taken away. Fontine kept his own counsel. There'd been another corporal from another army on a pier in Celle Ligure.

"I leave you now," said Lübok, crossing to him on the riverbank. The Czech's hand was extended.

Fontine was surprised. The plan had been for Lübok to go with him to Montbéliard; London might have new instructions for him. He took Lübok's hand, protesting.

"Why? I thought——"

"I know. But things change. There are problems in Wiesbaden."

Victor held the Czech's right hand with his own, covering it with his left. "It's difficult to know what to say. I owe you my life."

"Whatever I did, you would have done the same. I never doubted that."

"You're generous as well as brave."

"That Greek priest said I was a degenerate who could blackmail half of Berlin."

"Could you?"

"Probably," answered Lübok quickly, looking over at a Frenchman who was beckoning him to the boat. He acknowledged with a nod of his head. He turned back to Victor. "Listen to me," he said softly, removing his hand. "That priest told you something else. That I worked for Rome. You said you didn't know what that meant."

"I don't, specifically. But I'm not blind; it has to do with the train from Salonika."

"It has *everything* to do with it."

"You do work for Rome, then? For the church?"

"The church is not your enemy. Believe that."

"The Order of Xenope claims *it* is not my enemy. Yet certainly I have one. But you don't answer my question. Do you work for Rome?"

"Yes. But not in the way you think."

"Lübok!" Fontine grabbed the middle-aged Czech by the shoulders. "I *have* no thoughts! I don't *know!* Can't you understand that?"

Lübok stared at Victor; in the dim night light his eyes were searching. "I believe you. I gave you a dozen opportunities; you seized none of them."

"Opportunities? *What* opportunities?"

The Frenchman by the boat called again, this time harshly. "You! Peacock! Let's get out of here."

"Right away," replied Lübok, his eyes still on Fontine. "For the last time. There are men—on both sides—who think this war is insignificant compared to the information they believe you have. In some ways I agree with them. But you don't have it, you never did. And this war must be fought. And won. In fact, your father was wiser than all of them."

"Savarone? What do you——?"

"I go now." Lübok raised his hands, with strength but no hostility, and removed Victor's arms. "For these reasons, I did what I did. You'll know soon enough. That priest in the Casimir was right: there are monsters. He was one of them. There are others. But don't blame churches; they are innocent. They harbor the fanatics, but they're innocent."

"Peacock! No more delay!"

"Coming!" said Lübok in a shouted whisper. "Good-bye, Fontine. If for one minute I thought you were not what you say you are, I would have wracked you myself for the information. Or killed you. But you are what you are, caught in the middle. They'll leave you alone now. For a while."

The Czech touched Victor's face briefly, gently, and ran down to the boat.

The blue lights flashed above the Montbéliard field at precisely five minutes past midnight. Instantly two rows of small flares were ignited; the runway was marked, the plane circled and made its approach.

Fontine ran across the field carrying his briefcase. By the time he reached the side of the rolling plane, the hatch was open; two men were standing in the frame, gripping the sides, their arms extended. Victor heaved the briefcase inside and reached up, making contact with the arm on his right. He ran faster, jumped, and was pulled in through the opening; he lay face down on the deck. The hatch was slammed shut, a command shouted out to the pilot, and the engines roared. The plane sprang forward, the tail of the fuselage rising in seconds, and seconds later they were airborne.

Fontine raised his head and crawled to the ribbed wall outside the hatch. He pulled the briefcase to his side and breathed deeply, letting his head fall back against the metal.

"Oh, my God!" came the words spoken in shock out of the darkness. "It's *you!*"

Victor snapped his head to the left, in the direction of the indistinguishable figure who spoke with such alarm in his voice. The first shafts of moonlight came from the windows of the open pilot area. Fontine's eyes were drawn to the right hand of the speaker. It was encased in a black glove.

"Stone? What are you doing here?"

But Geoffrey Stone was incapable of answering. The moonlight grew brighter, illuminating the hollow shell that was the aircraft's fuselage. Stone's eyes were wide, his lips parted, immobile.

"Stone? It *is* you?"

"Oh, Jesus! We've been tricked. They've done it!"

"What are you talking about?"

The English continued in a monotone. "You were reported killed. Captured and executed in the Casimir. We were told that only one man escaped. With your papers——"

"Who?"

"The courier, Lübok."

Victor got to his feet unsteadily, holding on to a metal brace that protruded from the wall of the vibrating aircraft. The geometric pieces were coming together. "Where did you get this information?"

"It was relayed to us this morning."

"By whom? Who picked it up? Who relayed it?"

"The Greek embassy," replied Stone barely above a whisper.

Fontine sank back down to the deck of the plane. Lübok had said the words.

I gave you a dozen opportunities; you seized none. There are men who think this war is insignificant. . . . For these reasons I did what I did. You'll know soon enough. . . . They'll leave you alone now. For a while.

Lübok had made his move. He had checked an airfield in Warsaw before daybreak and sent a false message to London.

It did not take a great deal of imagination to know what that message accomplished.

"We're immobilized. We've exposed ourselves and been taken out. We all watch each other now, but no one can make a move, or admit what we're looking for. No one can afford that." Brevourt spoke as he stood by the leaded window overlooking the courtyard in Alien Operations. "Checkmate."

Across the room, standing by the long conference table, was a furious Alec Teague. They were alone.

"I don't give a *damn*. What concerns me is your blatant manipulation of Military Intelligence! You've placed an entire network in jeopardy. Loch Torridon may well have been crippled!"

"Create another strategy," said Brevourt absently, looking out the window. "It's your job, isn't it?"

"Damn you!"

"For God's sake, Teague, *stop* it!" Brevourt reeled from the window. "Do you for one minute think I was the final authority?"

"I think you compromised that authority! I should have been consulted!"

Brevourt started to reply, then stopped. He nodded his head as he walked slowly across the room to the table opposite Teague. "You may be right, general. Tell me, you're the expert. What was our mistake?"

"Lübok," said the brigadier coldly. "He faded you. He took your money and turned to Rome, then made up his own mind. He was the wrong man."

"He was your man. From your files."

"Not for that job. You interfered."

"He can go anywhere in Europe," continued Brevourt almost plaintively, as if Teague had not interrupted. "He's untouchable. If Fontini-Cristi broke away, Lübok could have followed him anywhere. Even into Switzerland."

"You expected that, didn't you?"

"Frankly, yes. You're too good a salesman, general. I believed you. I thought Loch Torridon *was* Fontini-Cristi's brainchild. How logical it all seemed. The Italian goes back under perfect cover to make his own arrangements." Brevourt sat down wearily, clasping his hands in front of him on the table.

"Didn't it occur to you that if such was the case, he would have come to us? To you?"

"No. We couldn't return his lands or his factories."

"You don't know him," concluded Teague with finality. "You never took the trouble. That was your first mistake."

"Yes, I expect it was. I've lived most of my life with liars. The corridors of mendacity. The simple truth is elusive." Brevourt suddenly looked up at the Intelligence man. His face was pathetic, his pallid skin taut, the hollows of his eyes proof of exhaustion. "You didn't believe it, did you? You didn't believe he was dead."

"No."

"I couldn't take the chance, you see. I accepted what you said, that the Germans wouldn't execute him, that they'd put a trace on him, find out who he was, use him. But the report said otherwise. So, if he *was* dead, it meant the fanatics in Rome or Xenope had killed him. They wouldn't do that unless—*unless*—they'd learned his secret."

"And if they had, the vault would be theirs. Not yours. Not England's. It was never yours to begin with."

The ambassador looked away from Teague and sank back in the

chair, closing his eyes. "Nor could it be allowed to fall into the hands of maniacs. Not now. We know who the maniac is in Rome. The Vatican will watch Donatti now. The Patriarchate will suspend activities; we've been given assurance."

"Which was Lübok's objective, of course."

Brevourt opened his eyes. "Was it really?"

"In my judgment, yes. Lübok's a Jew."

Brevourt turned his head and stared at Teague. "There'll be no more interference, general. Get on with your war. Mine is at a standoff."

Anton Lübok crossed Prague's Wenceslaus Square and walked up the steps of the bombed-out cathedral. Inside, the late afternoon sun streaked through the huge gaps of stone where *Luftwaffe* bombs had exploded. Whole sections of the left wall were destroyed; primitive scaffolds had been erected everywhere for support.

He stood in the far right aisle and checked his watch. It was time.

An old priest came out of the curtained apse and crossed in front of the confessional booths. He paused briefly at the fourth. It was Lübok's signal.

He walked down the aisle cautiously, his attention on the dozen or so worshipers in the church. None was watching him. He parted the curtains and walked inside the confessional. He knelt before the tiny Bohemian crucifix, the flickering light of the prayer candle throwing shadows on the draped walls.

"Forgive me, Father, for I have sinned," Lübok began softly. "I have sinned in excess. I have debased the body and blood of Christ."

"One cannot debase the Son of God," came the proper reply from behind the drapes. "One can only debase oneself."

"But we are in the image of God. As was Himself."

"A poor and imperfect image," was the correct response.

Lübok exhaled slowly, the exercise was completed. "You are Rome?"

"I am the conduit," said the voice in quiet arrogance.

"I didn't think you were the city, you damn fool."

"This is the house of God. Watch your tongue."

"And you revile this house," whispered Lübok. "All who work for Donatti revile it!"

"*Silence.* We are the way of Christ!"

"You're *dirt!* Your Christ would spit on you."

The breathing beyond the drapes was filled with controlled loathing.

"I shall pray for your soul," came the forced words. "What of Fontini-Cristi?"

"He had no other purpose but Loch Torridon. Your projections were wrong."

"That won't do!" The priest's whisper was strident. "He had to have other objectives! We're positive!"

"He never left my side from the moment we met in Montbéliard. There were no additional contacts other than those we knew about."

"*No!* We don't believe that!"

"In a matter of days it won't make any difference what you believe. You're finished. All of you. Good men will see to it."

"What have you done, *Jew?*" The voice behind the drapes was low now, the loathing absolute.

"What had to be done, priest." Lübok rose to his feet and put his left hand into his pocket. With his right he suddenly ripped the drapes in front of him.

The priest was revealed. He was huge, the black robes giving him the appearance of immensity. His face was the face of a man who hated deeply; the eyes were the eyes of a predator.

Lübok withdrew an envelope from his pocket and dropped it on the prayer stall in front of the stunned priest. "Here's your money. Give it back to Donatti. I wanted to see what you looked like."

The priest answered quietly. "You'd better know the rest. My name is Gaetamo. Enrici Gaetamo. And I'll come back for you."

"I doubt it," replied Lübok.

"Don't," said Enrici Gaetamo.

Lübok stood for a moment looking down at the priest. When their eyes were locked, the blond-haired Czech wet the fingers of his right hand and reached for the prayer candle, extinguishing its flame. All was darkness. He parted the drapes and walked out of the confessional.

PART FOUR

12

The cottage was on the grounds of a large estate west of Aylesbury in Oxfordshire. Tall metal poles strung with electrified barbed wire surrounded the area. Killer dogs guarded the enormous compound.

There was only one entrance, a gate at the base of a long, straight driveway flanked by open lawns. At the main house, a quarter of a mile from the gate, the drive split off right and left, then split again with several smaller roads leading to the various cottages.

There were fourteen cottages in all, houses built in and around the woods of the estate. The residents were men and women who needed the security: defectors and their families, double agents, couriers who'd been exposed—targets who'd been marked for an assassin's bullet.

Jane's cottage became their home and Victor was grateful for its remoteness. For nightly the *Luftwaffe* streaked through the skies, the fires of London grew, the battle for Britain had begun.

And so had Loch Torridon.

For weeks at a time, Victor was away from their miniature house in Oxfordshire, away from Jane, his mind at rest because she was safe. Teague moved the Loch Torridon headquarters into the cellars of MI6. Day and night had no essential meaning. Men worked around the clock with files and shortwave radios, and with complicated equipment that reproduced perfectly the documents required in the occupied lands: work papers, travel permits, clearances from the *Reichsministerium* of Armaments and Industry. Other men were called into the cellars and given their instructions by Captains Fontine and Stone. And they were sent to Lakenheath and beyond.

As was Victor on a growing number of occasions. At such times, he knew Alec Teague was right: *Your wife's safety is directly related to your state of mind. You have a job to do; I'll do mine.*

Jane could not be touched by the maniacs of Rome or Xenope. It was all that mattered. The freight from Salonika became a strange, painful memory. And the war went on.

AUGUST 24, 1940
ANTWERP, BELGIUM

(Intercepted dispatch—duplicate—Commandant: Occupation Forces, Antwerp, to Reichsminister Speer, Armaments.)

The railroad yards at Antwerp are chaos! Supply trains crossing Schelde River are overloaded through carelessness in shipping orders, causing cracks throughout bridge structure. Schedules and signaling codes altered without proper notice. From offices managed by *German personnel!* Reprisals ludicrous. No alien responsibility. Trains meet one another from opposing directions on the same tracks! Freights pull up for loading at sidings and depots where there are no trucks! No shipments! The situation is intolerable and I must insist that the *Reichsministerium* coordinate more thoroughly. . . .

SEPTEMBER 19, 1940
VERDUN-SUR-MEUSE, FRANCE

(Excerpts from letter received by the second command legal office of *Gesetzbuch Besitzergreifung*—from a Colonel Grepschedit, Verdun-Meuse.)

. . . It was agreed that we prepare specific rules of occupation to adjudicate disputes between ourselves and the conquered who laid down their arms. The regulations were circulated. We now find additional regulations—circulated by *your* offices—that contradict whole sections of the previous codes. We are in constant debate with even those who *welcome* us! Entire days are taken up with occupation hearings. Our own officers are faced with conflicting orders from your couriers—all under proper signatures and validated by your seals. We are at a boiling point over inconsequentials. We are going out of our minds. . . .

MARCH 20, 1941
BERLIN, GERMANY

(Extracted minutes of the meeting between accounts stabilizers of the *Finanzministerium* and the officials of *Reichsordnung*. File removed—duplicate.)

. . . The substance of Ordnance's unending difficulties are to be found with the *Finanzministerium*'s consistent errors in funds allocations. Accounts go unsettled for months, payrolls are miscalculated, monies are transferred to wrong dispersal depots—often to wrong geographical sectors! Whole battalions have gone without pay because the funds were somewhere in Yugoslavia when they should have been in Amsterdam! . . .

JUNE 23, 1941
BREST-LITOVSK, RUSSIAN FRONT

(Courier dispatch from General Guderian to his commander, General Bock, Hdqtrs: Pripet, Poland. Intercept: Bialystok. Not delivered.)

. . . In two days of the offensive we are within forty-eight hours of Minsk. The Dnieper will be crossed in a matter of weeks, the Don and Moscow not far beyond! The speed of our assault requires instant communications—in the main—radio communications, but there are increasing difficulties with our radio equipment. Specifically in what the engineers tell me is frequency calibration. More than half our divisional equipment is set in differing graduations. Unless extreme caution is taken, communications are sent out on unintended frequencies, often *enemy* frequencies. It is a factory problem. Our concern is that it is impossible to determine which equipment has malfunctioning calibrations. I, myself, initialed a communication to Kleist on Rundstedt's south flank and reached our forces in eastern Lithuania. . . .

FEBRUARY 2, 1942
BERLIN, GERMANY

(Removed from correspondence file of Manfried Probst, Official, *Reichsindustrie* from Hiru Kayanaka, attaché, Japanese Embassy, Berlin.)

Dear Reichsoffiziell Probst:

Since we are now comrades in battle as well as spirit we must attempt to strive further for the perfection expected of us by our leaders.

To the subject at hand, my dear *Reichsoffiziell*. As you know, our respective governments have entered into joint radar development experiments.

We flew—at great risk—our foremost electronic scientists to Berlin to enter conferences with your people. That was six weeks ago and

to date there have been no conferences whatsoever. I am now informed that our foremost scientists were flown to Greifswald on the
Baltic Sea by error. They are not concerned with the rocket experiments, but with radar, my dear *Reichsoffiziell.* Unfortunately, none
speak your language and the interpreters you assigned are less than
fluent in ours.

Word reached my desk an hour ago that our foremost scientists
are now on their way to Würzburg, where there are radio trans-
mitters. My dear *Reichsoffiziell,* we do not know where Würzburg is.
And our foremost scientists are not concerned with radio trans-
mitters, but with *radar!*

Can you please locate our foremost scientists? When are the
radar conferences? Our foremost scientists are traveling all over
Germany for what purpose? . . .

MAY 25, 1942

ST. VALÉRY-EN-CAUX, FRANCE

(Report filed by Captain Victor Fontine, who was dropped behind lines in the Héricourt district. Returned by trawler, Isle of
Wight.)

. . . The armaments shipments along the coastal regions are primarily offensive in nature, with little thought at this point given to
defensive weapons. The shipments are routed from Essen, through
Düsseldorf, across the border to Roubaix and then to the French
coast. The key is fuel. We have placed our people in the petrol depots. They are receiving continuous "instructions" from the *Reichsministerium* of Industry to divert shipments of fuel immediately out
of Brussels to Rotterdam, where rails will begin the journey to the
Russian front. At last report, there were fourteen miles of standard
armaments vehicles choking the roads between Louvain and Brussels, their tanks empty. And, of course, no reprisals. We estimate
that the ploy will be operable for another four days, at which point
Berlin will be forced to move in and our people will move out. Coordinate air strikes at this time. . . .

(Note: Loch Torridon Command. For record. Cleared, Brigadier
General Teague. Captain Victor Fontine granted leave upon return from Wight. Recommendation for majority approved——)

Fontine sped out of London on the Hempstead road toward Oxfordshire. He thought the debriefing session with Teague and Stone

would never end! *God!* The repetitions! His coadministrator, Stone, was always furious when he returned from one of his trips behind the German lines. It was work Stone had been trained to do, but now was impossible for him. His shattered hand ruled out such incursions and he spent his rage on Victor. He would subject Fontine to rapid, harsh, repetitive interrogation, looking for errors in every phase of a mission. What charity Victor once felt for the cryptographer had disappeared over the months. Months? Mother of Christ, it was nearly two and a half years!

But tonight Stone's delaying tactics were unforgivable. The *Luftwaffe* strikes over England had lessened, but they had not disappeared. Should the air raid sirens begin, it might be impossible for him to drive out of London.

And Jane was nearly due. The doctors had said it was a matter of a fortnight. That was a week ago, when he had flown out of Lakenheath to France and dropped into the grazing fields of Héricourt.

He reached the outskirts of Aylesbury and looked at his watch, holding it under the dim light of the dashboard. It was twenty minutes past two in the morning. They would both laugh at that; he was always coming back to her at ridiculous hours.

But he was coming back. He'd be at the compound in ten minutes.

Behind him, in the distance, he could hear the wail of the sirens rising and falling in plaintive fugues. There was not the jolting, breath-catching anxiety that used to accompany the terrible sound. The sound itself had taken on a weariness; repetition had dulled its terror.

He swung the wheel of the automobile to the right; he was now on the back road that led to the Oxfordshire estate. Another two or three miles and he'd be with his wife. His foot pressed down on the accelerator. There were no cars on the road; he could speed.

Instinctively, his ears listened for the distant rumbling of the bombing. But there was no faraway thunder, only the incessant whines of the sirens. Suddenly, there were sounds intruding where no sounds should be; he caught his breath, realizing instantly the return of forgotten anxiety. He wondered for a moment whether his exhaustion was causing tricks to be played. . . .

It was no trick! No trick at all! The sounds were overhead and unmistakable. He'd heard them too often, both over London and across the Channel in scores of different, covert locations.

Heinkel aircraft. Twin-engine, German, long-range bombers. They'd passed London. And if London was bypassed, it was a good bet that

Heinkels would take a northwest heading toward the Birmingham district and the munitions factories.

My God! The aircraft were *losing altitude*. They were pitching down in rapid descent.

Directly *above* him!

In *front* of him!

A bombing run! An airstrike in the countryside of *Oxfordshire!* What in God's name? . . .

Jesus! Oh, Jesus Christ!

The compound!

The one place in England without parallel in security. From the ground, but *not* from the skies!

A low-altitude air strike had been called against the compound!

Fontine held the accelerator to the floor, his body trembling, his breath coming in short, spurting expulsions, his eyes riveted to the onrushing road.

The skies exploded. The screams of diving aircraft mingled with the manmade thunder: detonation after detonation. Immense flashes of white and yellow—jagged, shapeless, horrible—filled the open spaces above and between the woods of Oxfordshire.

He reached the compound's gate, tires screeching as he braked the car into a turn. The iron gates were open.

Evacuation.

He stabbed the pedal to the floor and sped into the long straight drive. Beyond, fires were everywhere, explosions everywhere, people running in panic—everywhere.

The main house had taken a direct hit. The entire left front wall was blown out; the roof was collapsing in weirdly shapeless splendor, bricks and stone cascading to the ground. Smoke spread in vertical swirls of black and gray—fires beyond, spurting upward, jagged, yellow, terrifying.

A deafening crash; the car lurched, the ground swelled, the windows shattered, hurling fragments of glass—everywhere. Fontine felt blood streaking down his face, but he could see and that was all that mattered.

The bomb had struck less than fifty yards to his right. In the light of the fires he could see the ripped-out earth of the lawn. He swung the car to the right, skirting the crater, cutting across the grass toward the dirt road that led to their cottage. Bombs did not strike twice in the same zero target, he thought.

The road was blocked; trees had fallen, fires consuming them—everywhere.

He lurched out of the car and raced between the flaming barriers. He saw their cottage. A huge oak had been blown out of the ground, its massive trunk crashed into the pipe-tiled roof.

"Jane! Jane!"

God of hatred, do not do this to me! Do not do this to me again!

He smashed through the door, sending it hurtling off its hinges. Inside was total wreckage; tables, lamps, chairs were scattered, overturned, broken into a thousand fragments. Fires were burning—on the couch, in the open roof where the oak had crashed.

"Jane!"

"Here. . . ."

Her voice came from the kitchen. He raced through the narrow doorway and felt for an instant that he should fall to his knees in supplication. Jane stood gripping the edge of the counter, her back to him, her body shaking, her head nodding up and down. He rushed to her and held her shoulders, his face against her cheek, the spastic rhythm of her movements uninterrupted.

"My darling."

"Vittorio. . . ." Suddenly Jane contracted violently, gasping as she did so. "Sheets. . . . Sheets, my love. And blankets, I think I'm not sure, really——"

"Don't talk." He picked her up and saw the pain in her face in the darkness. "I'll take you to the clinic. There's a clinic, a doctor, nurses——"

"We can't get there!" she screamed. "Do as I say." She coughed in a spasm of pain. "I'll show you. Carry me."

In her hand she gripped a knife. Hot water had been running over the blade; she had been prepared to give birth alone.

Through the incessant detonations, Victor could hear the aircraft ascending, scrambling to higher altitudes. The strike was coming to an end; the distant, furious whines of Spitfires converging into the sector was a signal no *Luftwaffe* pilot overlooked.

He did as his wife told him to do, holding her in his arms, awkwardly gathering up whatever she ordered.

He kicked his way through the wreckage and the spreading flames and carried his wife out the door. Like an animal seeking sanctuary, he hurried into the woods and found a lair that was their own.

They were together. The frenzy of death that was several hundred yards away could not deter life. He delivered his wife of two male infants.

The sons of Fontini-Cristi were born.

* * *

Smoke spiraled up lazily, vertical coils of dignified, dead vapor interrupting the shafts of early morning sunlight. Stretchers were everywhere. Blankets covered the faces of the dead; the living and partly living were staring upward, mouths open, the shock imbedded. Ambulances were everywhere. And fire engines and police vehicles.

Jane was in an ambulance, a mobile medical unit, they called it. His sons were with their mother.

The doctor came out of the lean-to canvas extension of the strange vehicle and walked across the short stretch of lawn toward Victor. The doctor's face was haggard; he had escaped death but he lived with the dying.

"She's had a hard time of it, Fontine. I told her she would under normal circumstances——"

"Will she be all right?" interrupted Victor.

"Yes, she'll be all right. However, she'll need a long, *long* rest. I told her several months ago I suspected a multiple birth. She was not—shall I say—designed for such a delivery. In some ways it's rather amazing that she made it."

Fontine stared at the man. "She never mentioned that to me."

"Didn't think she would. You're in a precarious business. Can't have too much on your mind."

"May I see her?"

"Not for a while. She's solidly corked off; the infants are quiet. Let her be."

The doctor's hand was gently on his arm, leading him away from the ambulance toward what remained of the main house. An officer approached them and took Victor aside.

"We found what we were looking for. We knew it was here, or something like it. The strike was far too accurate. Even German instruments couldn't do it, and night pilotage was out; we checked. There were no markings, no flares."

"Where are we going? What are you talking about?" Victor had heard the officer speak, but the words were elliptical.

". . . high-arc transmitter."

The words still did not penetrate. "I'm sorry. What did you say?"

"I said the room's still standing. It's at the rear of the right wing. The bastard was operating a simple high-arc transmitter."

"A transmitter?"

"Yes. That's how the Huns came in on pinpoint. They were guided by a radio beam. The chaps at M.I.-Five and -Six had no objection to my showing you. As a matter of fact, I think they were pleased. They're afraid with all the confusion here someone'll disturb things. You can confirm that we haven't."

They threaded their way through the rubble and the intermittent piles of smoking debris to the right side of the large house. The major opened the door and they turned right down a corridor that seemed to be newly partitioned, as if for offices.

"A radio beam could bring a squadron into the area," said Fontine, walking beside the officer. "But only the area, not the target. These were bombers. I was on the road; they dove to the lowest levels. They would need more sophisticated equipment than a simple high-arc——."

"When I said there were no markings, no flares," interrupted the major, "I meant in a pattern; points A to B to C. Once they were over the target area, the bastard simply opened his window and shot up fireworks. He *did* use flares then. A fucking box full, from what we've found on the ground."

At the end of the corridor a door was flanked by two uniformed guards. The officer opened it and stepped inside; Victor followed.

The room was immaculate, miraculously no part of the surrounding carnage. On a table against the wall was an open briefcase, a circular aerial protruding out of it, attached to radio equipment beneath, secured in the case.

The officer gestured to his left, to the bed, not at first visible from the doorway.

Fontine froze. His eyes locked on the sight now in front of him.

On the bed was the body of a man, the back of his head blown off, a pistol beside his right hand. In his left hand was gripped a large crucifix.

The man was in the black robes of a priest.

"Damned strange," said the major. "His papers said he was a member of some Greek monastic brotherhood. The Order of Xenope."

13

He vowed it! There would be no more.

Jane and their two infant sons were taken secretly to Scotland. North of Glasgow, to an isolated house in the countryside of Dunblane. Victor would not rely on compounds *without-parallel-in-security,* nor on any guarantees from MI6 or the British government. Instead, he used his own funds, employed former soldiers, exhaustively screened by himself, and turned the house and grounds into a small but impenetrable fortress. He would not tolerate Teague's suggestions *or* objections *or* excuses. He was being pursued by forces he could not understand, an enemy beyond control, removed from the war and yet part of it.

He wondered if it would be so for the rest of his life. Mother of Christ, why didn't they believe him? How could he reach the fanatics and the killers and roar his denials? He knew nothing! *Nothing!* A train had left Salonika three years ago, at dawn on the ninth of December 1939, and he knew *nothing!* Only of its existence. Nothing more!

"Do you intend to remain here for the rest of the war?" Teague had come up to Dunblane for the day; they walked in the gardens behind the house, in sight of the high brick wall and the guards. It had been five months since they'd seen each other, although Victor permitted calls over redirected scrambler-telephones. He was too much a part of Loch Torridon; his knowledge was vital.

"You have no hold over me, Alec. I'm not British. I've sworn no allegiance to you."

"I never thought that was necessary. I did make you a major, however." Teague smiled.

Victor laughed. "Without ever having been formally inducted into the service? You're a disgrace to military tradition."

"Absolutely. I get things done." The brigadier stopped. He bent over to pick up a long blade of grass and rose, looking at Fontine. "Stone can't do it alone."

"Why not? You and I talk several times a week. I tell you what I can. Stone expedites the decisions. It's a sound arrangement."

"It's not the same and you know it."

"It will have to do. I can't fight two wars." Fontine paused, remembering. "Savarone was right."

"Who?"

"My father. He must have known that whatever was on that train could make men enemies even when they fought for a common survival."

They reached the edge of the path. A guard was thirty yards away across the lawn by the wall; he smiled and stroked the fur of a leashed Great Dane that snarled at the sight and scent of the stranger.

"One day it will have to be resolved," said Teague. "You, Jane, the children: You can't live with it for the rest of your lives."

"I've said that to myself more times than I can count. But I'm not sure how it can be."

"Perhaps I do. At least, I'm willing to try. And I have at my disposal the finest Intelligence service in existence."

Victor glanced at him, interested. "Where would you start?"

"The question is not where, but when."

"Then, *when?*"

"When this war is over."

"Please, Alec. No more words, no strategies. Or tricks."

"No tricks. A simple, uncomplicated agreement. I need you. The war has turned; Loch Torridon enters its most important phase. I intend to see that it does its job."

"You're obsessed."

"So are you. Quite rightfully. But you'll learn nothing of 'Salonika'—that's Brevourt's code name, incidentally—until this war is won, take my word for it. And the war *will* be won."

Fontine held Teague's eyes with his own. "I want facts, not rhetoric."

"Very well. We have identities you don't have, nor, for your own safety and the safety of your family, will I reveal them to you."

"The man in the car? In Kensington, Campo di Fiori. The streak of white? The *executioner?*"

"Yes."

Victor held his breath, controlling a nearly overpowering urge to grab the Englishman and force the words from him. "You've taught me to kill; I could kill you for that."

"To what end? I'd protect you with my life, and you know it. The point is, he's immobilized. Under control. If, indeed, he *was* the executioner."

Victor let his breath out slowly. The muscles in his jaw pained from the tension. "What other identities?"

"Two elders of the Patriarchate. Through Brevourt. They command the Order of Xenope."

"Then they're responsible for *Oxfordshire.* My *God,* how can you——?"

"They're *not,*" interrupted Teague quickly. "They were, if possible, more shocked than we were. As was pointed out, the last thing they wanted was your death."

"The man who guided those planes was a priest! From Xenope!"

"Or someone made to appear so."

"He killed himself," said Fontine softly, "in the prescribed manner."

"No one has a quota on fanatics."

"Go on." Victor began walking back on the path, away from the guard and the dog.

"These people are the worst kind of extremists. They're mystics; they believe they're involved in a holy war. Their war permits only confrontation by violence, not negotiation. But we know the pressure points, those whose word cannot be disobeyed. We can bring about a confrontation through Whitehall pressure, if need be, and demand a resolution. At least one that removes you from their concerns—once and for all. You can't do this by yourself. We can. Will you come back?"

"If I do, all this will be set in motion? I, myself, a part of the planning?"

"We'll mount it with the precision we mounted Loch Torridon."

"Has my cover in London been kept absolute?"

"Not a dent. You're somewhere in Wales. All our telephone calls are placed to the Swansea area and tripped north. Mail is regularly sent to a post office box in the village of Gwynliffen, where it's quietly put in other envelopes and returned only to me. Right now, if I'm needed, Stone places a call to a Swansea number."

"No one knows where we are? *No one?*"

"Not even Churchill."

"I'll talk with Jane."

"One thing," said Teague, his hand on Fontine's arm. "I've given my word to Brevourt. There'll be no more trips across the Channel for you."

"She'll like that."

Loch Torridon flourished. The principle of mismanagement-at-all-costs became a thorn in the German craw.

In the Mannheim printing plants, 130,000 *Commandmant Manuals for Occupation* came off the presses with all negatives dropped in vital restrictions. Shipments to the Messerschmidt factories in Frankfurt were routed to the Stuka assembly lines in Leipzig. In Kalach on the Russian front, it was found that three quarters of the radio equipment now operated on varying frequency calibrations. In the Krupp plants at Essen, engineering miscalculations resulted in malfunctions in the firing mechanisms of all cannon with the bore number 712. In Kraków, Poland, in the uniform factories, fabric bypassed a chemical saturation process and 200,000 units were sent out, subject to instant flammability. In Turin, Italy, where the Germans ran the aircraft plants, designs were implemented that caused metal fatigue after twenty hours of flight; entire sections of squadrons structurally collapsed in midair.

In late April of 1944, Loch Torridon concentrated on the offshore patrols throughout the coastal zones of Normandy. A strategy was conceived that would alter the patrol schedules as they were issued to the German naval personnel from the base at Pointe de Barfleur. Brigadier Teague brought the explosive report to Supreme Headquarters, Allied Command, and handed it personally to Dwight Eisenhower.

> The German coastal predawn patrols will be removed from Normandy zones during the first eleven days in June. That is the calendar target. Repeat: 1 June through 11 June.

The supreme commander responded appropriately. "I'll be goddamned. . . ."

Overlord was executed and the invading armies progressed. Under Badoglio and Grandi, the outlines of the Italian collaboration were negotiated in Lisbon.

It was a trip Alec Teague permitted Major Fontine. He was entitled to it.

And in a small room in Lisbon, a weary Badoglio faced Victor. "So the son of Fontini-Cristi brings us our ultimatum. There must be a certain gratification in that for you."

"No," replied Victor simply. "Merely contempt."

JULY 26, 1944
WOLFSSCHANZE, EAST PRUSSIA

(Excerpts from the Gestapo investigation of the assassination attempt on Adolf Hitler at the Wolfsschanze High Command Headquarters. File removed and destroyed.)

. . . The aides of the traitor, Gen. Claus von Stauffenberg, have broken. They described a widespread conspiracy implicating such generals as Olbricht, von Falkenhausen, Hoepner, and possibly Kluge and Rommel. This conspiracy could not have been coordinated without enemy assistance. All normal channels of communication were avoided. A network of unknown couriers was employed, and a code name surfaced, unheard of previously. It is of Scottish origin, the name of a district or a village: Loch Torridon. . . . We have captured . . .

Alec Teague stood in front of the map on his office wall. Fontine sat dejectedly in the chair by Teague's desk, his eyes on the brigadier across the room.

"It was a gamble," said Teague. "We lost. Can't expect to win every time. You've had too few losses, that's your trouble, you're not used to them." He removed three pins from the map and walked back to his desk. He sat down slowly and rubbed his eyes. "Lock Torridon has been an extremely effective operation. We have every reason to be proud."

Fontine was startled. "Past tense?"

"Yes. The Allied ground offensive toward the Rhine will commence maximum effort by October first. The Supreme Command wants no complications; they anticipate widespread defections. We're a complication, possibly a detriment. Loch Torridon will be phased out over the next two months. Terminated by the end of September."

Victor watched Teague as the brigadier made the pronouncement. A part of the old soldier died with the words. It was painful to watch Alec. Loch Torridon was his moment in the military sun; he would get no nearer, and jealousies were not out of the question regarding its termination. But decisions had been made. They were irrevocable, and to fight them *was* out of the question. Teague was a soldier.

Fontine examined his own thoughts. At first he experienced neither elation nor depression; more a suspension, as if time were abruptly arrested. Then slowly, painfully, there was the momentary feeling of what now? Where is my purpose? What do I do?

And then suddenly these vague concerns were swiftly replaced. The obsession that was never far from his mind came sharply into focus. He got out of the chair and stood in front of Alec's desk. "Then I call in your debt," he said quietly to Teague. "There's another operation that must be mounted 'with all the precision of Loch Torridon.' That's the way you phrased it."

"It will be. I gave you my word. The Germans can't last a year; surrender feelers already come from the generals. Six, eight months, and the war will be over. 'Salonika' will be mounted then. With all the precision of Loch Torridon."

14

It took twelve weeks to close the books and bring the men back to England. Loch Torridon was finished; twenty-two cabinets of accomplishments were all that remained. They were put under lock and seal and stored in the vaults of Military Intelligence.

Fontine returned to the isolated compound in Scotland. To Jane and the twins, Andrew and Adrian, named for the British saint and any of several acceptable Romans. But they were neither saintly nor imperial; they were two and a half years old, with all the energy that age implied.

Victor had been surrounded by the children of his brothers all his adult life, but these were *his*. In themselves they were different. They alone would carry on the Fontini-Cristis. Jane could have no more children; the doctors had agreed. The injuries at Oxfordshire were too extensive.

It was strange. After four years of furious activity and strain he was suddenly, abruptly, totally passive. The five months in '42 when he remained in Dunblane could not be considered a period of tranquility. Jane's recovery had been slow and dangerous; the fortifying of the compound had obsessed him. There'd been no letup of pressure then.

There was now. And the transition was unbearable. As unbearable as the wait for "Salonika" to begin. It was the inactivity that gnawed at him; he was not a man for idleness. In spite of Jane and the children, Dunblane became his prison. There were men outside, across the Channel, deep within Europe and the Mediterranean, who sought him as intensely as he sought them. There was nothing until that movement could begin.

Teague would not go back on his word, Victor understood that. But neither would he deviate from it. The end of the war would mark the commencement of the strategy that would lead to the men of Salonika. Not before. With each new victory, each new penetration within Germany, Fontine's mind raced. The war *was* won; it was not over, but it was won. Lives all over the world had to be picked up, the pieces put back together and decisions made, for years of living had to be faced. For him, for Jane, everything depended on the forces that sought a vault that came out of Greece five years ago—at dawn on the ninth of December.

The inactivity was his own particular hell.

During the waiting he had reached one decision: he would not return to Campo di Fiori after the war. When he thought of his house and looked at his wife, he saw other wives slain in the white mists of light. When he saw his sons, he saw other sons, helpless, terrified, riddled by gunfire. The tortures of the mind were too vivid still. He could not go back to the killing ground, or to anything or anyone associated with it. They would build a new life somewhere else. The Fontini-Cristi Industries would be returned to him, the Court of Reparations in Rome had sent word to London.

And he had sent word back through MI6. The factories, the plants, all lands and properties—except Campo di Fiori—would go to the highest bidder. He would make separate arrangements for Campo di Fiori.

It was the night of March 10. The children were asleep across the hall; the last of the winter winds blew in gusts outside the windows of their bedroom. Victor and Jane lay under the covers, the coals in the fireplace throwing an orange glow on the ceiling. And they talked quietly, as they always talked in the final hours of the day.

"Barclay's will handle everything," said Victor. "It's a simple auction, really. I've put a cellar on the total; however they want to divide the entire purchase is up to them."

"Are there buyers?" asked Jane, lying on her elbow, looking at him.

Fontine laughed softly. "Packs of them. Mostly in Switzerland, mostly American. There are fortunes to be made in the reconstruction. Those who have manufacturing bases will have the advantage."

"You sound like an economist."

"I sincerely hope so. My father would be terribly disappointed if I didn't." He fell silent. Jane touched his forehead, brushing aside his hair.

"What's the matter?"

"Just thinking. It'll be over with soon. First the war, then 'Salonika'; that will be finished, too. I trust Alec. He'll bring it off if he has to blackmail all the diplomats in the Foreign Office. The fanatics will be forced to accept the fact that I don't know a damn thing about their ungodly train."

"I thought it was supposed to be awfully godly." She smiled.

"Inconceivable." He shook his head. "What kind of god would allow it?"

"Checkmate, my darling."

Victor raised himself on the pillow. He looked over at the windows; a March snow was silently careening off the dark panes of glass, carried by the winds. He turned to his wife. "I can't go back to Italy."

"I know. You've told me. I understand."

"But I don't want to stay here. In England. Here I will always be Fontini-Cristi. Son of the massacred family of *padrones*. Equal parts reality, legend, and myth."

"You *are* Fontini-Cristi."

Victor looked down at Jane in the dim light of the fire. "No. For five years now I've been Fontine. I've gotten rather used to it. What do you think?"

"It doesn't lose too much in the translation," said Jane, smiling again. "Except, perhaps, a flavor of landed gentry."

"That's part of what I mean," he replied quickly. "Andrew and Adrian shouldn't be burdened with such nonsense. Times are not what they were; those days will never return."

"Probably not. It's a little sad to see them go, but it's for the best, I suppose." His wife suddenly blinked her eyes and looked questioningly up to him. "If not Italy, *or* England, then where?"

"America. Would you live in America?"

Jane stared at him, her eyes still searching. "Of course. I think that's very exciting. . . . Yes, it's right. For all of us."

"And the name? You don't mind really, do you?"

She laughed, reaching up to touch his face. "It doesn't matter. I married a man, not a name."

"You matter," he said, pulling her to him.

Harold Latham walked out of the old, brass-grilled elevator and looked at the arrows and the numbers on the wall. He had been transferred to the Burma theater three years ago; it had been that long since he'd been in the corridors of MI6-London.

He tugged at the jacket of his new suit. He was a civilian now; he had to keep reminding himself of that. Soon there would be thousands upon thousands of civilians—*new* civilians. Germany had collapsed. He'd wagered five pounds that the formal announcement of surrender would come before the first of May. There were three days to go, and he didn't give a damn about the five quid. It was over; that was all that mattered.

He started walking down the hallway toward Stone's office. Good old, poor old, angry Geoff Stone. The *Apple* to his *Pear*. Rotten fucking luck it was, old Apple's hand shot to bits because of a high-handed guinea; and so early on, too.

Still, it bloody well might have saved his life. An awful lot of two-handed operatives never came back. In some ways Stone was damned fortunate. As he had been fortunate. He had a few pieces of metal in his back and stomach, but if he was careful they said he'd do fine. Practically normal, they said. Discharged him early, too.

Apple and Pear had survived. They'd made it! *Goddamn,* that called for a month of whiskies!

He had tried to call Stone but hadn't been able to reach him. He telephoned for two days straight, both the flat and the office, but there was never an answer. There was no point in leaving messages; his own plans were so ragtail he wasn't sure how long he could stay in London.

It was better this way. Just barge in and demand to know why old Apple had taken so long to win the war.

The door was locked. He knocked; there was no answer. *Damn!* The front desk had Stone checked in; that was to say he hadn't checked *out* last night, or the night before, which was not unusual these days. Office couches were beds these days. All the Intelligence services were working around the clock, going through files, destroying records that could be embarrassing, and probably saving a few thousand lives in the process. When the dust of victory and defeat settled, informers were the least popular survivors.

He knocked louder. Nothing.

Yet there was light shining through the thin, lateral crack at the base of the door. Perhaps Stone had stepped out for a minute. To the W.C. or the cafeteria.

And then Latham's eyes strayed to the round lock cylinder. There was something odd, something wrong. A speck of dull gray seemed to cling to the brass, a tiny scratch above it, to the right of the keyhole. Latham looked closer; he drew a match and struck it, almost afraid to do what he was about to do.

He held the flame directly below the speck of gray matter. It melted instantly and fell away; solder.

It was also an obscure but time-tested device that Apple favored. He had used it on numerous occasions when they worked together. Come to think of it, Latham couldn't remember anyone else ever using it.

Melt the end of a small solder wire and shove the soft liquid into the lock with its key. It jammed the tumblers but did not prevent the key from going in.

It merely prevented any key from opening the lock. In quiet situations that called for a little time while a man raced out of a trap, it provided that time without raising any sudden alarms. A perfectly normal-looking lock malfunctioned; most locks were old. One did not break down a door; one called a locksmith.

Had Apple needed time? Was there a trap?

Something *was* wrong.

"Good Christ! Don't touch anything! Get a *doctor!"* shouted Teague, lunging into the office beyond the unhinged door. "And keep this tight!"

"He's dead," said Latham quietly at the brigadier's side.

"I know that," answered Teague curtly. "I want to know how *long* he's been dead."

"Who is he?" asked Latham, looking down at the dead man. The body had been stripped; only the undershorts and shoes remained. There was a single, clean gunshot wound in the upper center of the naked chest; the rivulet of blood had dried.

"Colonel Aubrey Birch. Officer of the vaults." Teague turned and spoke to the two guards holding the door. A third soldier had gone for the MI6 house surgeon on the second floor. "Put that door back. Admit no one. Say nothing. Come with me, Latham."

They rode the elevator to the cellars. Latham saw that Teague was not only in a state of shock, he was frightened.

"What do you think happened, sir?"

"I gave him his separation papers two nights ago. He hated me for it."

Latham was silent for a moment. Then he spoke without looking at Teague, his eyes straight ahead. "I'm a civilian, so I'll say it. That was a rotten, goddamned thing to do. Stone was once the best man you had."

"Your objection is noted," said the brigadier coldly. "You were the one they called Pear, weren't you?"

"Yes."

Teague glanced at the discharged Intelligence agent; the panel light indicated that the cellars had been reached. "Well, the apple soured, Mr. Pear. It became rancid. What concerns me now is how far the rot penetrated."

The door opened. They walked out of the elevator and turned right toward a wall of steel that closed off the corridor. In the center of the wall was a thick steel door, its frame was barely discernible. There was a plate of bulletproof glass in the upper section, a black button to the left, a thin rubber slot below, a metal sign above.

SECURITY AREA

No Admittance Without Proper Authorisation
Ring Bell—Place Authorisation In Vacuum Slot

Teague approached the glass, pushed the button and spoke firmly. "Code Hyacinth. No delays, please; make visual confirmation. This is Brigadier Teague. I'm accompanied by one Mr. Harold Latham, cleared by me."

There was a whirring sound. The steel door receded, then was slid manually to the side. An officer on the other side saluted.

"Good afternoon, general. There's been no Hyacinth report down here."

Teague acknowledged the salute with a nod of his head. "I'm delivering it myself, major. Nothing is to be removed until further orders. What does the duty ledger read on Colonel Birch?"

The officer turned to a metal desk that was attached to the metal wall. "Here it is, sir," he said, holding open a black leather notebook. "Colonel Birch signed out the night before last at nineteen hundred hours. He's due back in the morning. Oh seven hundred, sir."

"I see. Was anyone with him?"

The major looked again at the large notebook. "Yes, sir. Captain Stone, sir. His checkout time is the same."

"Thank you. Mr. Latham and I will be in Vault Seven. May I have the keys, please? And the combination figures."

"Of course."

Inside the metal room were twenty-two file cabinets. Teague stopped at the fourth cabinet against the far wall opposite the door. He looked at the page of figures in his hand and began manipulating the combination lock in the upper right corner of the cabinet. As he did so, he held out the page of figures for Latham.

"Save time," he said brusquely, his voice hoarse. "Locate the cabinet with the Brevourt file. B-r-e-v-o-u-r-t. Extract it."

Latham took the paper, returned to the left wall and found the cabinet.

The lock sprung. Teague reached over and pulled out the second cabinet drawer. Rapidly his fingers separated the files.

Then he separated them again. Slowly, allowing for no oversight.

It wasn't there. The file on Victor Fontine was gone.

Teague closed the cabinet drawer and stood erect. He looked over at Latham, who knelt by the bottom drawer of his cabinet, an open folder in his hand. He was staring at it, his expression one of stunned bewilderment.

"I asked you to find it, not to read it," said the brigadier icily.

"There's nothing to read," replied Latham quietly, removing a single page of paper from the folder. "Except this. . . . What the hell have you bastards *done?*"

The paper was a photostat. It had a black border, with room at the bottom for two seals of approval. Both men knew exactly what it was.

An order for execution. An official license to kill.

"Who's the target?" asked Teague in a monotone, remaining by the cabinet.

"Vittorio Fontini-Cristi."

"Who approved of it?"

"Foreign Office seal, Brevourt's signature."

"Who *else?* There must be *two!*"

"The prime minister."

"And Captain Stone is the assignee——"

Latham nodded, although Teague had not asked a question. "Yes."

Teague breathed deeply, closing his eyes for a moment. He opened them and spoke. "How well did you know Stone? His methods?"

"We worked together for eighteen months. We were like brothers."

"Brothers? Then I remind you, Mr. Latham, that in spite of your separation from the service, the Official Secrets Act still binds you."

15

Teague spoke into the telephone, his phrases precise, his voice cutting. "From the beginning he was your man. From the day we placed him in Loch Torridon. His interrogations, the endless questions, Lübok's name in our files, the traps. Fontine's every move was reported to you."

"I make no apologies," said Anthony Brevourt on the other end of the line. "For reasons you well know. 'Salonika' was, and still remains, a highest priority of the Foreign Office."

"I want an explanation for that order of execution! It was never cleared, never reported——"

"Nor was it *meant* to be," interrupted Brevourt. "That order was our backup. You may subscribe to your own immortality, brigadier, but we don't. Air raids aside, you're a strategist for covert operations; a potential mark for assassination. If you were killed, that order permitted Stone immediate access to Fontini-Cristi's whereabouts."

"Stone convinced you of that?"

There was a pause before the ambassador replied. "Yes. Several years ago."

"Did Stone also tell you he hated Fontine?"

"He didn't approve of him; he wasn't alone."

"I said *hated!* Bordering on the pathological."

"If you knew that, why didn't you replace him?"

"Because, damn it, he controlled it! As long as he had a reason to. He has *none* now."

"I don't see——"

"You're a goddamn fool, Brevourt! Stone left us a photostat; he kept the original. You're helpless and he wants you to know it."

"What are you talking about?"

"He's walking around with an official document that gives him a warrant to kill Fontine. Countermanding it now is meaningless. It would have been meaningless two *years* ago! He has the paper; he's a professional. He intends to carry out the assignment and place that document where you can't get it. Can the British government—can *you,* or the foreign secretary, or Churchill, himself, justify that execution? Would any of you care to even *comment* on it?"

Brevourt replied swiftly, urgently. "It was a contingency. That was *all* it was."

"It was the best," agreed Teague harshly. "Startling enough to cut through red tape. Sufficiently dramatic to break down bureaucratic walls. I can hear Stone mounting his argument."

"Stone must be found. He must be stopped." Brevourt's breathing could be heard over the line.

"We've reached one area of agreement," said the brigadier wearily.

"What are you going to do?"

"To begin with, tell Fontine everything."

"Is that wise?"

"It's fair."

"We expect to be kept informed. If need be, hourly."

Teague looked absently across the office at his wall clock. It was nine forty-five; moonlight streamed through the windows, no curtains blocked it now. "I'm not sure that's possible."

"*What?*"

"You're concerned with a vault taken out of Greece five years ago. I'm concerned with the lives of Victor Fontine and his family."

"Has it occurred to you," said Brevourt, drawing out his words, "that the two are inseparable?"

"Your conjecture is noted." Teague hung up and leaned back in his chair. He would have to call Fontine now. Warn him.

There was a knock on his door.

"Come in."

Harold Latham walked in first, followed by one of the best investigating officers in MI6. A middle-aged, former Scotland Yard forensic specialist. He carried a manila file folder in his hand.

A few weeks ago, Pear would not have walked into Teague's office smoking a cigarette. He did so now; it was important to him. Yet, thought Teague, Latham's hostility had lessened. Pear was first and foremost a professional. Civilian status would not change that.

"Did you find anything?" asked Teague.

"Scratchings," said Latham. "They may mean something, they may not. Your man here is sharp. He can lift a book off a pinhead."

"He knew where to point me," added the analyst. "He was familiar with the subject's habits."

"What have we got?"

"Nothing on the premises; his office was clean. Nothing but case work, dossiers marked for the ovens, all quite legitimate. His flat was something else. He was a thorough chap. But the arrangements of the hangers in the closets, the clothes in his bureau, the toilet supplies . . . they all indicate that Stone had been planning his departure for some time."

"I see. And these scratchings?"

Pear answered. The professional in him needed recognition. "Stone had a disagreeable habit. He would lie in bed making notes. Words, brackets, figures, arrows, names—doodling, I call it. But before he turned in he'd tear off the pages and burn them. We found a writing pad on the shelf of the bedside table. There was nothing on it, of course, but the Yarder here knew what to do."

"There were depressions, sir. It wasn't difficult; we lifted them under spectrograph." The officer handed Teague the folder across the desk. "Here are the results."

Teague opened the folder and stared at the spectrogram. As Pear had described, there were numbers, brackets, arrows, words. It was a disjointed puzzle, a wild diagram of incoherent meanderings.

And then the name leaped up from the mass of incoherence.

Donatti.

The man with the streak of white in his hair. The executioner of Campo di Fiori. One of the most powerful cardinals in the Curia.

"Salonika" had begun.

". . . Guillamo Donatti."

Fontine heard the name and it triggered the memory locked in his mind. The name was the key, the lock was sprung, and the memory revealed.

He was a child, no more than nine or ten years old. It was evening and his brothers were upstairs preparing for bed. He had come down in his pajamas to find a book, when he'd heard the shouting from his father's study.

The door was open, no more than a foot, and the curious child had approached it. What he saw inside so shocked his sensibilities that he stood there hypnotized. A priest was in front of his father's desk, roaring at Savarone, pounding the top of the desk with his fist, his face pinched in anger, his eyes wide in fury.

That anyone could behave this way in his father's presence, even—perhaps especially—a priest, so startled the child that he involuntarily, audibly gasped.

When he did the priest whipped around, the burning eyes looking at the child, and it was then that Victor had seen the streak of white in the black hair. He had run away from the living room and up the staircase.

The next morning Savarone had taken his son aside and explained; his father never left explanations suspended. What the violent argument referred to was obscured with time, but Fontine recalled that his father had identified the priest as Guillamo Donatti, a man who was a disgrace to the Vatican . . . someone who issued edicts to the uninformed and enforced them by fear. They were words a child remembered.

Guillamo Donatti, firebrand of the Curia.

"Stone's after his own, now," said Teague over the line from London, bringing Victor's focus back to the present. "He wants you, and whatever price you'll bring. We were looking in the wrong areas; we've traced him now. He used Birch's papers and got a military flight out of Lakenheath. To Rome."

"To the cardinal," corrected Fontine. "He's not taking chances with long-distance negotiations."

"Precisely. He'll come back for you. We'll be waiting."

"No," said Victor into the telephone. "That's not the way. We won't wait, we'll go after them."

"Oh?" The doubt was in Teague's voice.

"We know Stone's in Rome. He'll stay out of sight, probably with informer cells; they're used to hiding men."

"Or with Donatti."

"That's doubtful. He'll insist on neutral territory. Donatti's dangerous, unpredictable. Stone realizes that."

"I don't care what you're thinking, but I can't——"

"Can you circulate a rumor from reliable sources?" interrupted Fontine.

"What kind of rumor?"

"That I'm about to do what everyone expects me to do: return to Campo di Fiori. For unknown reasons of my own."

"Absolutely not! It's out of the question!"

"For God's *sake*," shouted Victor. "I can't hide out for the rest of my life! I can't live in fear that each time my wife or my children leave the house there is a Stone or a Donatti or an execution team waiting for them! You promised me a confrontation. I want it *now*."

There was silence on the line from London. Finally Teague spoke. "There's still the Order of Xenope."

"One step leads to another. Hasn't that been your premise all along? Xenope will be forced to acknowledge what *is,* not what it thinks *should* be. Donatti and Stone will be proof. There can be no other conclusion."

"We have men in Rome, not many——"

"We don't *want* many. Very few. My being in Italy must not be linked with M.I.-Six. The cover will be the Court of Reparations. The government wants to control our factories, the properties. The court bids higher every week; they don't want the Americans."

"Court of Reparations," said Teague, obviously writing a note.

"There is an old man named Barzini," continued Fontine. "Guido Barzini. He used to be at Campo di Fiori, he tended the stables. He could give us background. Put a trace on him in the Milan district. If he's alive, he'll be found through the *partigiani*."

"Barzini, Guido," repeated Teague. "I'll want safety factors."

"So do I, but very low profile, Alec. We want to force them out in the open, not further underground."

"Assuming the bait's taken, what will you do?"

"Make them listen. It's as simple as that."

"I don't think it is," said Teague.

"Then I'll kill them," said Victor.

The word went out. The *padrone* was alive; he had returned. In a small hotel several blocks from the Duomo, he was *seen*. Fontini-Cristi was in Milan. The news was known even in Rome.

There was a knock on the hotel door. Barzini. It was a moment Victor both looked forward to and dreaded. The memories of white light and death inadvertently came into focus. He suppressed them as he walked across the room to the door.

The old farmhand stood in the hallway, his once muscular body now bent and thin, lost within the coarse fabric of his cheap black coat. His face was wrinkled; the eyes were rheumy. The hands that had held Victor's writhing, lashing body to the earth, the fingers that had clawed at his face and saved his life, were withered, gnarled. And they shook.

To Fontine's sorrow and embarrassment, Barzini fell to his knees, his thin arms outstretched, grasping Victor's legs.

"It's true. You're alive!"

Fontine pulled him to his feet and embraced him. In silence he led the old man into the room, to the couch. Beyond his age, it was obvious that Barzini was ill. Victor offered food; Barzini asked for tea and brandy. Both were brought quickly by the hotel waiters, and when both were finished, Fontine learned the salient facts of Campo di Fiori since the night of the massacre.

For months after the German killings, the fascist troops kept the estate under guard. The servants were allowed to take their possessions and leave; the maid who had witnessed the shooting was murdered that night. No one was permitted to live in Campo di Fiori except Barzini, who was obviously mentally deficient.

"It was not difficult. The *fascisti* always thought everyone else was crazy but themselves. It was the only way they could think, and face themselves in the morning."

In his position of stablehand and groundkeeper, Guido was able to watch the activity at Campo di Fiori. Most startling were the priests. Groups of priests were permitted in; never more than three or four at a time, but there were many such groups. At first Guido believed they had been sent by the holy father to pray for the souls of the house of Fontini-Cristi. But priests on sacred missions did not behave as these priests behaved. They went through the main house, then the cottages and, finally, the stables, searching with precision. They tagged everything; furniture was pried apart; walls tapped for hollow sections and panels removed; floors ripped up—not in anger but as experienced carpenters might do; lifted and replaced. And the grounds were combed as though they were fields of gold.

"I asked several of the young fathers what they were looking for. I don't think they really knew. They always replied, 'thick boxes, old man. Cartons of steel and iron.' And then I realized that there was one priest, an older priest, who came every day. He was forever checking the work of the others."

"A man in his sixties," said Victor softly, "with a streak of white in his hair."

"Yes! That was he! How did you know?"

"He was expected. How long did the searching go on?"

"For nearly two years. It was an unbelievable thing. And then it stopped."

All activity stopped, according to Barzini, except German activity. The Wehrmacht Officer Corps appropriated Campo di Fiori, turning it into an elaborate retreat for the higher echelon commanders.

"Did you do as the Englishman from Rome told you, old friend?" Fontine poured Barzini more brandy; the trembling had partially subsided.

"Yes, *padrone*. For the past two days I have gone to the markets in Laveno, in Varese, and Legnano. I say the same to a few chosen loud-mouths: 'Tonight I see the *padrone!* He returns! I go to Milan to meet him, but no one is to know!' They will know, son of Fontini-Cristi." Barzini smiled.

"Did anyone ask you *why* I insisted you come to Milan?"

"Most did. I say only that you wish to talk with me privately. I tell them I am honored. And I am."

"It should be enough." Victor picked up the phone and gave a number to the hotel switchboard. While he waited for the call to be placed, he turned to Barzini. "When this is over, I want you to come back with me. To England, then America. I'm married, old friend. You'll like the *signora*. I have sons, two sons. Twins."

Barzini's eyes shone. "You have sons? I give thanks to God——"

There was no answer on the line. Fontine was concerned. It was *imperative* that the MI6 man be at that telephone! He was stationed halfway between Varese and Campo di Fiori. He was the contact for the others, spread out on the roads leading from Stresa, Lugano, and Morcote; he was the focal point of communications. Where the hell *was* he?

Victor hung up the phone and took his wallet out of his pocket. In a concealed recess was another telephone number. In Rome.

He gave it to the operator.

"What do you mean there's no answer?" asked the precise English voice that answered.

"Is there a clearer way to say it?" responded Fontine. "There *is* no *answer*. When did you last hear from him?"

"About four hours ago. Everything was on schedule. He was in radio contact with all vehicles. You got the message, of course."

"What message?"

There was a momentary silence. "I don't like this, Fontine."

"What *message?*"

"He said he might have been zeroed, but we weren't to worry. He'd reach you at the hotel when you arrived. He spotted up the car himself. It was on the road that passes the main gates at Campo di Fiori. He didn't reach you?"

Victor suppressed a desire to shout. "He didn't reach me. There were no messages for me. What car?"

"A green Fiat. The license was from Savona, that's on the Genoa gulf. One of the descriptions matched a Corsican in the police files. A contrabandist London believes worked for us. The others are also Corsos, we think. And *him.*"

"I presume you mean——"

"Yes. Stone's the fourth man."

Stone had taken the bait. Apple had gone back to Celle Ligure, back to the Corsicans to find his recruits. And Apple, the professional, had removed the contact in Varese.

Eliminate the couriers. Immobilize communications. Loch Torridon.

"Thank you," said Victor to the man in Rome.

"See *here*, Fontine!" came the harried voice over the telephone. "You're to do *nothing!* Stay where you are!"

Without answering, Victor replaced the phone and walked back to Barzini. "I need some men. Men we can trust, who are willing to take risks."

Barzini looked away; the old man was embarrassed. "Things are not what they were, *padrone*."

"*Partigiani?*" said Fontine.

"Mostly Communists. They're concerned with themselves now. With their pamphlets, their meetings. They——" Barzini stopped. "Wait. There are two men who don't forget. They hid in the mountains; I brought them food, news of their families. We can trust them."

"They'll have to do," said Victor, starting for the bedroom door. "I'm going to change clothes. Can you reach them?"

"There's a telephone number," answered Barzini, getting up from the couch.

"Call them. Tell them to meet me at Campo di Fiori. I assume there are guards."

"Only a nightwatchman now. From Laveno. And myself."

Fontine stopped and turned to Barzini. "Would these men know the back road north of the stables?"

"They can find it."

"Good. Tell them to start out now and wait for me on the bridle path at the rear of the stables. It's still there, isn't it?"

"It is still there. What are you going to do, *padrone?*"

Victor realized as he spoke that he was repeating the words he had used over the phone to Teague five days ago. "What everyone expects me to do." He turned and continued toward the bedroom.

16

The lessons of Loch Torridon were always present, thought Victor, as he stood in front of the hotel desk, his arms on the marble counter, watching the night clerk carry out his request. He had demanded a car for hire in a voice loud enough to draw attention. It was a difficult order considering the hour; vehicles were hard enough to come by during the day, much less in the middle of the night. But they could be had if the money was sufficient. Then, too, the argument at the front desk was sufficiently disagreeable to alert any observer. Also, there were the clothes he wore: dark gray trousers, boots, and a dark hunting jacket. It was not the hunting season.

There were only a few stragglers in the lobby; several businessmen making unsteady treks to their rooms after long, liquid conferences; a couple arguing over one or the other's behavior; a nervous, rich youth signing in with a whore who waited discreetly in a chair. And a dark, swarthy man with the hard leather face of the sea, who was across the lobby in an armchair reading a magazine, seemingly oblivious to the hotel's night scene. A Corsican, thought Victor.

It was this man who could carry the message to other Corsicans. To the Englishman named Stone.

It was simply a matter of coordinating the upcoming sequence. To make sure there was a green Fiat on the street, probably in shadows, ready to take up a discreet position when the rented car drove away. If there was no such automobile, Victor could find reasons to delay until it arrived.

No delay was necessary. The Fiat could be seen in the middle of the next block. Captain Geoffrey Stone was sure of himself. The auto was positioned in front of Fontine's car, heading west, toward the road to Varese. To Campo di Fiori.

Barzini sat in the front with Victor. The brandy had done its work. The old man's head kept falling to his chest.

"Sleep," said Victor. "It's a long drive and I'll want you rested when we get there."

They drove through the open gates and into the long winding en-

trance of Campo di Fiori. Although he was braced for it, the sight of
the house filled his chest with pain; hammering seared through his temples. He approached the execution grounds. The sights and sounds of
that agony returned, but he knew he could not permit them to over-
whelm him. The lessons of Loch Torridon: *Divided concentrations
were dangerous.*

He contracted the muscles of his stomach taut and stopped the car.

Barzini was awake, staring at him. The nightwatchman emerged from
the thick oak doors beyond the marble steps, the beam of his flashlight
examining the car and those inside. Barzini stepped out and spoke.

"I bring the son of Fontini-Cristi. He's the *padrone* of this house."

The watchman threw the beam over at Victor, who had gotten out of
the car and stood by the hood. His voice was respectful. And not a little
frightened.

"I am honored, *padrone.*"

"You may go home to Laveno," Fontine told him. "If you don't
mind, use the north road. You probably do anyway. It's the shortest
way."

"Much the shortest, *signore.* Thank you, *signore.*"

"There may be two friends waiting for me at the stables. Don't be
alarmed, I asked them to drive through the north gate. If you see them,
please tell them I'll be there shortly."

"Of course, *padrone.*" The nightwatchman nodded and walked rapidly down the marble steps into the drive. There was a bicycle in the
shadows by the shrubbery. He mounted and pedaled off into the darkness toward the stables.

"Quickly," said Victor, turning to Barzini. "Tell me. Are the telephones as they were? Is there still a line connecting the house with the
stables?"

"Yes. In your father's study and in the hall."

"Good. Go in and turn on all the lights in the hall and in the dining
room. Then go back to the study, keeping those lights out. Stay by a
window. When I reach your friends, I'll call you from the stables and
tell you what to do. Soon the Corsicans will appear. On foot, I'm sure.
Watch for small flashlights. Tell me what you see."

"Very well. *Padrone?*"

"Yes?"

"I have no gun. Weapons are outlawed."

"Take mine." Victor reached into his belt and removed his Smith &
Wesson. "I don't think you'll need it. Don't fire unless your life depends
on it."

Thirty seconds later the lights in the great hall shone through the stained-glass windows above the huge entrance doors. Victor hurried along the side of the house and waited by the edge of the building. The chandeliers in the dining room were switched on. The whole north section of the house was a blaze of light, the south section in darkness.

There were still no signs of life on the road; no beams of flashlights or flares or matches. It was as it should be. Stone was a professional. When he moved it would be with extreme caution.

So be it. *His* moves would be cautious also.

Victor ran into the north road toward the stables. He kept low to the ground and alert, listening for the unusual. Stone might have opted for the north gates as his means of entry, but it was unlikely. Stone was anxious; he would move in swiftly, close behind his quarry, and seal off the exits.

"*Partigiani.* It's Fontini-Cristi." Victor walked down the bridle path at the rear of the stables. The few horses left inside were old and weary, the whinnies intermittent.

"*Signore.*" The whisper came from the woods to the right of the path; Fontine approached. Suddenly a flashlight beam shot out from the opposite side. From the left. And another voice spoke.

"Stay where you are! Don't turn!"

He felt the hand of the man behind him on the small of his back, holding him steady. The flashlight moved forward over his shoulder, shining in his face, blinding him.

"It's him," said the voice in the darkness.

The flashlight was removed. Fontine blinked and rubbed his eyes, trying to erase the residual image of the blinking light. The *partigiano* came out of the darkness. He was a tall man, nearly as tall as Victor, dressed in a worn American field jacket. The second man came from behind; he was much shorter than his comrade and barrel-chested.

"Why are we here?" asked the tall man. "Barzini's old and doesn't think clearly. We agreed to watch you, warn you . . . nothing else. We do this because we owe Barzini much. And for old time's sake; the Fontini-Cristis fought against the fascists."

"Thank you."

"What do the Corsicans want? And this Englishman?" The second man moved to his friend's side.

"Something they believe I have, which I don't have." Victor stopped. From the stables there was a soft, tired snort followed by a series of hoof thumps. The partisans heard it, too; the flashlight was extinguished.

A crack of a limb. A pebble dislodged under a footstep. Someone approached, following the same path Fontine had taken. The partisans separated; the stocky man moved forward and disappeared into the foliage. His brother did the same in the opposite direction. Victor stepped to his right and crouched off the path.

Silence. The footsteps scratching over the dry earth became clearer. Suddenly the figure was there, only inches in front of Fontine, outlined in the forest night.

And then it happened. A powerful beam of light burst out of the darkness, piercing the opposite woods; at the same instant there was the sudden, muted spit of a pistol, its noise contained by a silencer.

Victor sprang up, lashing his left arm around the throat of the man, his right surging beyond for the weapon, forcing it downward. As the man's back arched, Victor crashed his knee into the base of the spine. The man's breath was expunged; Fontine yanked with all his strength at the taut neck in his hammerlock. There was a snap, sickening and final. The light rolled on the path.

The tall *partigiano* raced out of the woods, crushing the light underfoot, his pistol in his hand. He and Victor plunged into the foliage, both silently acknowledging the fear that their ally was dead.

He was not. The bullet had only creased his arm. He lay wild-eyed in shock, his mouth open, his breathing loud. Fontine knelt beside him, tearing off the partisan's shirt to check the wound. The man's friend remained standing, his gun on the stable path.

"Mother of Christ! You damn fool! Why didn't you *shoot* him?" The wounded *partigiano* winced in pain. "Another second and he would have killed me!"

"I had no weapon," replied Victor quietly, wiping the blood from the man's flesh.

"Not even a knife?"

"No." Fontine bound the wound and knotted the cloth. The *partigiano* stared at him.

"You've got balls," he said. "You could have waited out of sight. My comrade has a gun."

"Come on, stand up. There are two other *Corsi* somewhere. I want them. But without gunfire." Victor bent down and picked up the dead man's pistol. There were four bullets in the chamber; the silencer was one of the best. He beckoned the tall partisan off the path and spoke to both. "I'm going to ask a favor of you. You can refuse me and I'll understand."

"What is it?" asked the larger man.

"The other two Corsicans are back there. One's probably watching the main road, the other may be behind the house, in the gardens, there's no way to tell. The Englishman will stay out of sight, near the house. I'm sure the *Corsi* won't kill me. They'll watch every move I make, but they will not open fire."

"That one," said the wounded partisan, pointing to the dead man, "did not hesitate to pull his trigger."

"These *Corsi* know me by sight. He could see you weren't me."

The strategy was clean. Victor was the bait; he would walk openly down to the circular drive and turn into the gardens at the rear of the house. The partisans were to follow him, staying out of sight in the trees. If Fontine was right, a Corsican would be seen. And taken. Or killed silently. It did not matter; these *Corsi* murdered Italians.

The strategy would then be repeated on the main entrance road, the partisans crossing diagonally far behind the embankment, meeting him at a juncture a quarter of a mile away. Somewhere between the circular drive and the gates, the third and last Corsican would be stationed.

The positions were logical, and Stone was nothing if not a logical man. And thorough. He *would* seal off the exits.

"You don't have to do this for me," said Victor. "I'll pay generously, but I understand——."

"Keep your money," interrupted the wounded man, looking first at his comrade. "You didn't have to do what you did for me."

"There's a telephone in the stables. I must talk with Barzini. Then start down the road."

The surmise was confirmed. Stone had covered both roads and the gardens. And the remaining Corsicans were taken, their lives ended with partisan knives.

They met at the stables. Fontine was sure that Stone had been watching him from the embankment. The quarry was walking the killing ground; the return was painful. Loch Torridon had taught them both to anticipate reactions. It was a weapon.

"Where's your car?" Victor asked the *partigiani*.

"Outside the north gate," replied the tall one.

"You have my thanks. Get your friend to a doctor. Barzini will know where I can send a more concrete form of gratitude."

"You want the Englishman for yourself?"

"There'll be no trouble. He's a man with one hand, without his *Corsi*. Barzini and I know what to do. Get to a doctor."

"Good-bye, *signore*," said the tall man. "Our debts are canceled. To old Barzini. To you, perhaps. The Fontini-Cristis were good to this land once."

"Many thanks."

The partisans nodded a last time and made their way swiftly up the road into the darkness toward the north gate. Fontine went down the path and let himself into the stables through a side door. He walked by the stalls, past the horses and Barzini's small bedroom, into the tack room. He found a wooden box and began filling it with braces and bits and musty, framed citations from the walls. He crossed to the telephone by the door and pushed a button beneath it.

"All is well, old friend."

"Thank God."

"What about the Englishman?"

"He's waiting across the drive, in the high grass. On the embankment. The same——" Barzini stopped.

"I understand. I'm starting out now. You know what to do. Remember, at the door speak slowly, clearly. The Englishman hasn't spoken Italian in recent years."

"Old men talk louder than they must," said Barzini, humor in his voice. "Because we hear poorly, so must everyone else."

Fontine replaced the phone and checked the pistol the partisans had left him; it had been taken from a dead Corsican. He unscrewed the silencer and put the weapon in his pocket. He picked up the box and went out the tack room door.

He walked slowly down the road to the circular drive opposite the embankment. In front of the steps, in the spill of light from the windows, he paused, giving his arms a moment of rest, conveying the fact that the box was heavier than its size might indicate.

He continued up the steps to the large oak doors. He then did the most natural thing that came to him: he kicked at the right door.

In seconds the door was opened by Barzini. Their exchange was simple, without strain. The old man spoke clearly.

"You're sure I can't bring you something, *padrone?* A pot of tea, coffee?"

"No, thank you, old friend. Get some sleep. We have a lot to do in the morning."

"Very well. The horses will eat early today." Barzini walked past Victor to the steps and down into the circular drive. He turned left toward the stables.

Victor stood in the great hall; everything was as it had been. The Germans knew when not to mar a thing of beauty. He turned into the darkened south section, into the enormous drawing room toward the doors of his father's study. As he walked through the familiar space, he felt pains of anguish in his chest and the catching of breath in his throat.

He went into his father's study, Savarone's *sanctum sanctorum*. Instinctively, he turned right in the darkness; the huge desk was where it had always been. He put the box down and turned on the green-shaded lamp he remembered; it was the same lamp. Nothing had changed.

He sat down in his father's chair and removed the pistol from his pocket. He placed it on the desk, behind the wooden box, concealing it from the front.

The waiting had begun. And for the second time his life was in Barzini's hands. He could not imagine a firmer grip. For Barzini would not reach the stables. He would walk up the stable road and enter the woods, doubling back into the gardens, to the rear of the house. He would let himself in through one of the patio doors, and wait for the Englishman to come.

Stone was trapped.

The minutes dragged on. Absently, Fontine opened the drawers of his father's desk. He found sheets of Wehrmacht stationery, and methodically he placed them sheet by sheet in separate piles, a game of solitaire with huge blank playing cards.

He waited.

At first, he did not hear any sound. Instead, he felt the presence. It was unmistakable, filling the air between himself and the intruder. Then the creak of a floorboard pierced the silence, followed by two distant footsteps, bold, unconcealed; Fontine's hand moved toward the gun.

Suddenly, out of the dark space, a light-colored object came flying through the shadows toward him, *at* him! Victor recoiled as the object came into focus, trailing rivulets of blood in the air. There was a harsh slap—flesh against wood—and the horrible thing made contact with the top of the desk and rolled obscenely under the spill of the lamp.

Fontine expelled his breath in an instant of total revulsion.

The object was a hand. A severed right hand cut crudely above the wrist. The fingers were old and withered and clawlike in spastic contraction, the tendons iced at the instant of primitive surgery.

It was the hand of Guido Barzini. Thrown by a maniac who had lost his own on a pier in Celle Ligure.

Victor shot up from the chair, suppressing the revulsion that welled up beside him, stabbing for the gun.

"Don't touch that! You do, you're dead!" Stone's words were spat out in English. He crouched in the shadows across the room, behind a high-backed armchair.

Victor withdrew his hand. He had to force himself to think. To survive. "You killed him."

"They'll find him in the woods. It's odd *I* found him there, isn't it?"

Fontine stood motionless, accepting the awful news, suspending emotion. "Odder still," said Victor quietly, "that your Corsican didn't."

Stone's eyes reacted; only a flicker of recognition, but the reaction was there. "The walk you took. I wondered." The Englishman nodded his head. "Yes, you could have done that. You could have taken them out."

"I didn't. Others did."

"Sorry, Fontini. That doesn't wash."

"How can you be sure?"

"Because if there were others, you wouldn't use an old man for the last job; that's stupid. You're an arrogant son of a bitch, but you're not stupid. We're alone, all right. Just you and me and that box. *Christ!* It must have been in one hell of a hole. Enough people looked for it."

"Then you made your deal with Donatti?"

"He thinks so. Strange, isn't it? You took everything from me. I crawled out of Liverpool and made my way up, and you took it all away on a fucking guinea pier five years ago. Now I've got it all back and then some. I may hold the biggest auction anyone's ever heard of."

"For what? Old hunt prizes? Faded citations?"

Stone snapped the hammer of his weapon into firing position. His black glove slapped the back of the chair, his eyes bore through the shadows. "Don't make jokes!"

"No jokes. I'm not stupid, remember? And you're not in any position to pull that trigger. You've only got one chance to deliver the contents of that vault. If you don't, another order of execution can easily be issued. Those powerful men who hired you five years ago don't like embarrassing speculations."

"Shut up! *Stop it!*" Furiously, Stone raised the clawlike glove above the chair and smashed it down. "Those tactics won't work on me, you guinea bastard! I used them before you ever heard of Loch Torridon."

"Loch Torridon was based on *error*. Miscalculation! *Mismanagement!* That was its *premise*. Remember?" Fontine took a step backward, pushing the chair with his legs, extending his hands out in a gesture of helplessness. "Come on. Look for yourself. You wouldn't kill me before you saw what the bullet cost you."

"Move back! *Farther!*" Stone came around the chair, his immobile right hand stretched out directly in front of him like a protruding lance. His left hand held the weapon with the cocked hammer; the slightest squeeze of the trigger and the pin would spring forward, exploding the shell.

Victor did as he was commanded, his eyes riveted on the pistol. His moment would come; it had to come or there was nothing.

The Englishman approached the desk, each step the movement of a man filled with loathing and wariness, prepared to destroy at the split second of imbalance. He took his eyes from Fontine and stared at the top of the desk. At the severed, mutilated hand of Guido Barzini. At the box. At the pile of debris inside the box.

"No," he whispered. "*No!*"

The moment came: the shock of revelation was in Stone's eyes. It would not come again.

Victor sprang forward over the desk, his long arms plunging for the weapon; it had wavered with only a heartbeat, but that was all he could hope for.

The explosion was deafening, but Fontine's grip had deflected the shot. Only inches, but it was enough. The bullet shattered the top of the desk, hurling splinters of wood everywhere. Victor held Stone's wrist, wrenching with all the power he possessed, feeling and not feeling the blows delivered to his face and neck by the hard gloved hand. Stone brought his right knee up, pummeling Fontine's groin and stomach; the pistol would not be dislodged. The Englishman screamed and went into a paroxysm of frenzy. He would not, *could* not be bested by strength alone.

Victor did the only thing left for him. For an instant he stopped all movement, then yanked Stone's wrist forward as if jamming the pistol into his own stomach. As the gun was about to touch the cloth of his jacket, he suddenly twisted his body and Stone's wrist, inverting the weapon, and shoved it with his full weight upward.

The explosion came. For a second Fontine was blinded, his flesh ice cold with fireburn, and for that instant he believed he had been killed.

Until he felt the body of Geoffrey Stone collapse, pulling him downward to the floor.

He opened his eyes. The bullet had entered the flesh beneath Stone's jaw, its trajectory upward, through the skull, ripping open the top of Stone's head.

And next to the mass of blood and tissue was the severed hand of Guido Barzini.

He carried Barzini's body out of the woods and to the stables. He placed the mutilated corpse on the bed and covered it with a sheet. He stood over the body, for how long he would never remember, trying to understand pain and terror and love.

Campo di Fiori was still. For him its secret was buried, never to be known. The mystery of Salonika was a confidence Savarone had not shared. And the son of Savarone would no longer dwell on it. Let others do so, if they cared to. Let Teague take care of the rest. He was finished.

He walked down the north road from the stables to the drive in front of the house and climbed into the rented car. It was dawn. The orange summer sun broke over the Italian countryside. He took one last look at the home of his childhood and started the ignition.

The trees rushed by, the foliage became a blur of green and orange and yellow and white. He looked at the speedometer. Over eighty. Eighty-four kilometers an hour on the twisting entrance road cut out of the forest. He should brake the speed, he knew that. It was foolhardy, if not dangerous. Yet his foot would not obey his mind.

Oh, God! He had to get away!

There was a long hairpin curve that preceded the gate. In the old days—years ago—it was the custom to blow one's horn when one approached the curve. There was no cause to do so now; and he was relieved to find his foot relaxing its pressure on the pedal. Instinct was intact. Still, he took the curve at fifty, the tires screeching as he came out of the turn and headed for the gates. Automatically, on the straightaway, he accelerated. He would whip past the gateposts and swing out the road for Varese. Then Milan.

Then London!

He was not sure when he saw it. *Them.* His mind had wandered, his eyes on the immediate ground in front of the hood. He only knew that he slammed the brakes with such force he was thrown against the steering wheel, his head inches from the windshield. The car swerved, the tires screamed, dust billowed up from the wheels, and the automobile skidded diagonally through the gates, stopping only feet from the two black limousines that had converged out of nowhere, blocking the road beyond the stone posts.

His body was jolted back against the seat; the whole car shook in its sudden, violent arrest. Stunned, it took Fontine several seconds to shake off the effects of the near collision. He blinked his eyes, quickly regaining focus. His fury was suspended in astonishment at what he saw.

Standing in front of the two limousines were five men in black suits and white clerical collars. They stared impassively at him. Then the rear door of the limousine on the right opened and a sixth man got out. He was a man of about sixty, in the black robes of the church.

With a shock of white in his hair.

17

The cardinal had the eyes of a fanatic and the strained, clipped voice of a man possessed. He moved in slow, fluid motions, never permitting his audience's attention to waver. He was at once theatrical and ominous. It was a cultivated appearance, refined over the years in the corridors of the Vatican. Donatti was an eagle who fed on sparrows. He was beyond righteousness; he *was* righteousness.

At the sight of the man Victor lost control of himself. That this killer of the church could approach Campo di Fiori was an obscenity he could not stand. He lunged at the vile, cassocked figure, all sense of reason and survival and sanity itself destroyed in the instant of memory.

The priests were ready for him. They converged, as the limousines had converged, blocking his path of assault. They held him, twisting his arms high up behind his back; a hand with powerful fingers gripped his throat, forcing his head into an agonizing arch, choking off all speech, but not sight or hearing.

"The car," said Donatti quietly.

The two priests who were not restraining Fontine raced to the rented car and began the search. Victor could hear the doors and the trunk and the hood being opened. Then the ripping of upholstery and the crashing of metal as the car was torn apart. For nearly a quarter of an hour the ransacking continued. Throughout, Fontine's eyes were locked with the cardinal's. Only at the end of the search did the priest of the Curia look over at the automobile, when the two men approached and spoke simultaneously.

"There is nothing, Your Grace."

Donatti gestured to the priest whose powerful hand held Victor's throat. The grip was eased; Fontine swallowed repeatedly. His arms were still stretched taut behind his back. The cardinal spoke.

"The heretics of Constantine chose well: the apostates of Campo di Fiori. The enemies of Christ."

"Animal! Butcher!" Victor could barely whisper; the muscles of his neck and windpipe had been damaged severely. "You *murdered* us! I *saw* you!"

"Yes. I thought you might have." The cardinal spoke with quiet venom. "I would have fired the weapons myself, had it been required. And thinking thus, you are quite correct. Theologically, I was the executioner." Donatti's eyes grew wide. "Where is the crate from Salonika?"

"I don't know."

"You'll tell me, heretic. Believe the word of a true priest. You haven't got a choice."

"You hold me against my will! In the name of *God,* I presume!" said Fontine coldly.

"In the name of preserving the *mother church!* No laws take precedence over that. *Where is the shipment from Salonika?"*

The eyes, the high-pitched voice triggered the memory of years ago— a small child outside a study door. "If that knowledge was so important to you, why did you execute my father? He was the only one who knew. . . ."

"A *lie!* That is a *lie!"* Donatti caught himself, his lips trembling.

Fontine understood. A raw nerve had been exposed. An error of extraordinary magnitude had been made, and the cardinal could not bear to face it. "You know it's the truth," said Victor quietly. *"Now* you know it's the truth and you can't stand it. *Why?* Why was he *killed?"*

The priest lowered his voice. "The enemies of Christ deceived us. The heretics of Xenope fed lies to us." And once more Donatti roared abruptly. *"Savarone Fontini-Cristi* was the *communicator of those lies!"*

"What lies could *he* tell *you?* You never believed him when he told you the truth."

Again the cardinal trembled. He could barely be heard. "There were two freights out of Salonika. Three days apart. The first we knew nothing about; the second we picked up at Monfalcone, making sure that Fontini-Cristi would not meet it. We did not know then that he had already made contact with the first train. And now you will tell us what we wish to know. What we *must* know."

"I can't give you what I don't have."

Donatti looked at the priests and said one word. "Now."

Victor could never remember the length of time, for there was not time, only pain. Excruciating, harrowing, stinging, convulsive pain. He was dragged within the gates of Campo di Fiori and taken into the forest. There the holy apostolic priests began the torture. They started with his bare feet; every toe was broken, the ankles twisted until they cracked. The legs and knees were next: crushed, inverted, racked. And then the groin and stomach——*O God! He wished to die!*——And al-

ways, above him, blurred in the vision of tears of pain, was the priest of
the Curia with the shock of white in his hair.

"Tell us! Tell us! Enemy of Christ!"

His arms were sprung from their sockets. His wrists were turned inward until the capillaries burst, spreading purple fluid throughout the
skin. There were moments of blessed void, ended suddenly by hands
slapping him back to consciousness.

"Tell us! Tell us!" The words became a hundred thousand hammers,
echoes within echoes. *"Tell us! Enemy of Christ!"*

And all was void again. And through the dark tunnels of feeling, he
sensed the rhythm of waves and air and suspension. A floating that deep
within his brain told him he was near death.

There was a final, convulsive crash, yet he could not feel it. He was
beyond feeling.

Yet he heard the words from far, far away in the distance, spoken in
a chant.

*"In nomine Patris, et Filii et Spiritus sancti. Amen. Dominus vobis-
cum. . . ."*

Last rites.

He had been left to die.

There was the floating again. The waves and the air. And voices, indistinct, too far away to be really heard. And touch. He felt touching,
each contact sending shafts of pain throughout his body. Yet these were
not the touches of torture; the voices in the distance were not the voices
of tormentors.

The blurred images at last came into focus. He was in a white room.
In the distance were shining bottles with tubes cascading in the air.

And above him was a face. The face he knew he would never see
again. What was left of his mind was playing horrible tricks on him.

The face was crying; tears rolled down the cheeks.

His wife Jane whispered. "My love. My dearest love. Oh, *God,* what
have they done to you?"

Her beautiful face was next to his. Touching his.

And there was no pain.

He had been found by worried men of MI6. The priests had carried
him to a car, driven him to the circular drive, and left him to die in
Campo di Fiori. That he did not die was not to be explained by the doctors. He *should* have died. His recovery would take months, perhaps
years. And, in truth, he would never completely recover. But with care

he would regain the use of his arms and legs; he would be ambulatory, and that in itself was a miracle.

By the eighth week he was able to sit up. He concluded his business with Rome's Court of Reparations. The lands, the factories, the properties were sold for seventy-five million pounds sterling. As he had promised himself, the transaction did not include Campo di Fiori.

For Campo di Fiori he made separate arrangements, through a trusted lawyer in Milan. It, too, was to be sold but he never wanted to know the name of the buyer. There were two inviolate restrictions: The purchaser was to have nowhere in his history any connection with the fascists. Nor was he to have any association whatsoever, regardless of denomination, with any religious body.

On the ninth week an Englishman was flown over from London on instructions of his government.

Sir Anthony Brevourt stood at the foot of Fontine's bed, his jaw firm, his eyes compassionate and yet not without hardness. "Donatti's dead, you know. He threw himself off the balustrade of St. Peter's. Nobody mourns him, least of all the Curia."

"Yes, I knew that. At the end an act of insanity."

"The five priests who were with him have been punished. Three were excommunicated, prosecuted, and in prison for several decades. The other two are under life penance in the Transvaal. What was done in the church's name horrifies its leaders."

"It seems to me that too many churches permit the fanatics, then look back in astonishment, amazed at what was done in 'their names.' It's not restricted to Rome. Trappings often obscure purposes, don't they? That goes for governments, too. I want *questions answered!*"

Brevourt blinked several times at Fontine's outburst and replied rapidly, mechanically. "I'm prepared to offer them where I can. I've been instructed to withhold nothing."

"First, Stone. The order of execution has been explained; I have no comment. I want to know the rest. All of it."

"Precisely what you've been told. I didn't trust you. I was convinced when you first arrived in London that you'd made up your mind to reveal nothing about the train from Salonika. I expected you to make your own arrangements, on your own terms. We couldn't let that happen."

"Stone reported my movements then?"

"Every one. You made eleven trips across the Channel, and one to Lisbon. With Stone's help we had you covered each time. In the event of capture, we were prepared to negotiate an exchange with the enemy."

"Suppose I'd been killed?"

"In the beginning it was a risk we calculated, overshadowed by the fact that you might have bolted, made contact with regard to 'Salonika.' And in June of forty-two, after Oxfordshire, Teague agreed not to send you across any longer."

"What happened at Oxfordshire? The priest—if he *was* a priest—who led those planes in was Greek. From the Order of Xenope. Your first constituency, I believe."

Brevourt pursed his lips and breathed deeply. Admissions were being made that both pained and embarrassed him. "Stone, again. The Germans had tried for two years to locate the compound at Oxfordshire. He leaked the precise bearings to Berlin, and at the same time made his own arrangements with the Greeks. He convinced them there was a way to break you. It was worth trying; a broken man talks. He didn't give a damn himself about 'Salonika,' but the raid served his primary aim. He put a fanatic priest in the compound and coordinated the strike."

"For God's sake, *why?*"

"To kill your wife. If she'd been killed, even severely wounded, he assumed you'd turn on all things British, get out of M.I.-Six. He was right. You nearly did, you know. He hated you; blamed you for ruining a brilliant career. As I understand it, he tried to keep you in London that night."

Victor remembered the horrible night. Stone, the methodical psychopath, had counted the minutes, projected the speed of a car. Fontine reached for his cigarettes on the bedside table. "The last question. And don't lie to me. What was on the train from Salonika?"

Brevourt walked away from the bed. He crossed to the hospital window and was silent for a moment.

"Parchments, writings from the past which, if made public, could bring chaos to the religious world. Specifically, they would tear the Christian world apart. Accusations and denials would be hurled back and forth, governments might have to choose sides. Above everything, the documents in enemy hands would have been an ideological weapon beyond anything imaginable."

"Documents can do this?" asked Fontine.

"These documents can," replied Brevourt, turning away from the window. "Have you ever heard of the Filioque Clause?"

Victor inhaled. His mind went back over the years to the impartial lessons of his childhood. "It's part of the Creed of Nicaea."

"More properly, the Nicene Creed of the year 381; there were many councils, subtle alterations of the creed. The Filioque was a later addition that once and for all established the Christ figure as one substance with God. It's rejected by the Eastern church as misleading. For the Eastern church, especially the sects that followed the scholar-priest Arius, Christ as the son of God was the teacher; his divinity was not equal to God's. No such equality could exist for them in those times. When the Filioque was first proposed, the Patriarchate of Constantine recognized it for what it was: a doctrinal division that favored Rome. A theological symbol that was the excuse to divide and conquer new territories. And quite right they were. The Holy Roman Empire became a global force—as the globe was known. Its influence spread throughout the world on that single premise, this specialized divinity of Christ: *Conquer* in the name of *Christ*." Brevourt stopped, as if searching for words. He walked slowly back toward the foot of the bed.

"Then the documents in that vault," said Victor, "refute the Filioque? If so, they challenge the foundation of the Roman church and all the Christian divisions that followed."

"Yes, they do that," replied Brevourt quietly. "Collectively they're called the denials . . . the Filioque denials. They include agreements between crowns and caesars from as far away as Spain, in the sixth century, where the Filioque originated, for what many believe were purely political reasons. Others trace what they term the 'theological corruption.' . . . But if that was *all* they did, the world could live with them. Son of God, teacher, one substance. These are theological differences, subjects for biblical scholars to debate. They do more, I'm afraid. In the Patriarchate's fervor to deny the Filioque, it sent out priests to search the holy lands, meet with the Aramaic scholars, unearth everything that ever existed relative to Jesus. They unearthed more than they were looking for. There were rumors of scrolls written during the years just preceding and after the mark of the first century. They traced them, discovered several, and brought them back to Constantine. It is said that one Aramaic scroll raises profound and very specific doubts as to the man known as Jesus. He may never have existed at all."

The ocean liner headed toward the open waters of the Channel. Fontine stood at the railing and watched the skyline of Southampton. Jane was at his side, one hand gently around his waist, the other crossed in front of her, over his hand on the railing. The crutches with the large metal clasps that held his forearms were to his left, the shiny half circles of stainless steel glistening in the sunlight. He had designed them himself. If it was going to be necessary, as the doctors said, for him to use crutches for a year or more he could damn well improve on the existing product.

Their two sons, Andrew and Adrian, were with their nurse from Dunblane—one of those who had elected to sail to America with the Fontines.

Italy, Campo di Fiori, the train for Salonika were in the past. The cataclysmic parchments that had been taken from the archives of Xenope were somewhere in the vast range of the Italian Alps. Buried for a millennium; perhaps never to be found.

It was better that way. The world had passed through an era of devastation and doubt. Reason demanded that a calm be restored, at least for a while, if only on the surface. It was no time for the vault from Salonika.

The future began with the rays of the afternoon sun on the waters of the English Channel. Victor leaned toward his wife and put his face next to hers. Neither spoke; she held his hand in silence.

There was a commotion on the deck. Thirty yards aft the twins had gotten into a quarrel. Andrew was angry with his brother Adrian. Childish blows were exchanged. Fontine smiled.

Children.

PART
ONE
BOOK TWO

18

Men.

They were men, thought Victor Fontine as he watched his sons thread separately through the guests in the bright sunlight. And twins, second. It was an important distinction, he felt, although it wasn't necessary to dwell on it. It seemed years since anyone had referred to them as the twins. Except Jane and himself, of course. Brothers, yes; but not twins. It was strange how that word had fallen into disuse.

Perhaps the party would revive it for a while. Jane would like that. They were always the twins to Jane. Her Geminis.

The afternoon party at the North Shore house on Long Island was *for* Andrew and Adrian; it was their birthday. The lawns and gardens behind the house, above the boathouse and the water, had been turned into an enormous outdoor *fête champêtre,* as Jane called it. "A ruddy, grownup picnic! No one has them anymore. We will."

A small orchestra played at the south edge of the terrace, its music serving as an undercurrent to a hundred conversations. Long tables heaped with food were organized on the large expanse of manicured lawn; two bars did brisk business at either end of the rectangular buffet. *Fête champêtre.* Victor had never heard the term before. In thirty-four years of marriage, he had never heard it.

How the years had flown! It was as though three decades had been compressed into a time capsule and shot through the skies at incredible speed, only to land and be opened and scanned by participants who had merely grown older.

Andrew and Adrian were near each other now. Andy chatted with the Kempsons by the canapé table. Adrian was at the bar, talking to several young people whose clothes were the only vague evidence of their gender. It was right, somehow, that Andrew should be with the Kempsons. Paul Kempson was president of Centaur Electronics; he was well thought of by the Pentagon. As, of course, was Andrew. Adrian, no doubt, had been cornered by several university students who wanted to question the singularly outspoken attorney who was Victor's son.

Victor noted with a certain satisfaction that both twins were taller than those around them. It was to be expected; neither he nor Jane were short. And they looked somewhat alike, but not identical. Andrew's hair was very light, nearly blond; Adrian's was dark, auburn. Their features were sharp, a combination of his and Jane's, but each with his own identity. The only physical thing they shared in common was their eyes: they were Jane's. Light blue and penetrating.

At times, in very bright sunlight or in dim shadows, they could be mistaken for each other. But only at such times, under such conditions. And they did not seek them. Each was very much his own man.

The light-haired Andrew was in the army, a dedicated professional. Victor's influence had secured a congressional appointment to West Point, where Andrew had excelled. He'd made two tours of duty in Vietnam, although he despised the way the war was fought. "Win or get out" was his credo, but none listened, and he wasn't sure it made any difference. There was no way to win for losing. Saigon corruption was like no other corruption on the face of the earth.

Yet Andrew was not a spoiler within the ranks, either. Victor understood that. His son was a *believer*. Deep, concerned, unwavering: The military was America's strength. When all the words were said and done, there remained only the power at hand. To be used wisely, but to be *used*.

For the dark-haired Adrian, however, there was *no* limit to be placed on the use of words, and no excuse for armed confrontation. Adrian, the lawyer, was as dedicated in his fashion as his brother, although his demeanor might seem to deny it. Adrian slouched; he gave the appearance of nonchalance where none existed. Legal adversaries had learned never to be lulled by his humor or his seeming lack of concern. Adrian *was* concerned. He was a shark in the courtroom. At least he *had* been for the prosecutor's office in Boston. He was in Washington now.

Adrian had gone from prep school to Princeton to Harvard Law, with a year taken off to wander and grow a beard and play a guitar and sleep with available girls from San Francisco to Bleecker Street. It had been a year when Victor and Jane had held their collective breath, though not always their tempers.

But the life of the open road, the provincial confines of a half-dozen communes palled on Adrian. He could no more accept the aimlessness of unprovoked experience than Victor had nearly thirty years ago at the end of the European war.

Fontine's thoughts were interrupted. The Kempsons were heading over to his chair, excusing their way through the crowd. They would not expect him to get up—no one ever did—but it annoyed Victor that he could not. Without help.

"Damn fine boy," said Paul Kempson. "He's got his head on straight, that Andrew does. I told him if he ever wants to chuck the uniform, Centaur has a place for him."

"I told him he should *wear* his uniform," added Kempson's wife brightly. "He's such a handsome man."

"I'm sure he thinks it would be disconcerting," said Fontine, not at all sure. "No one wants to be reminded of the war at a birthday party."

"How long's he home for, Victor?" asked Kempson.

"Home? Here? Only for a few days. He's stationed in Virginia now. At the Pentagon."

"Your other boy's in Washington, too, isn't he? Seems I read something about him in the papers."

"Yes, I'm sure you did." Fontine smiled.

"Oh, then they're together. That's nice," said Alice Kempson.

The orchestra finished one number and began another. The younger couples flocked to the terrace; the party was accelerating. The Kempsons floated away with nods and smiles. Briefly, Victor thought about Alice Kempson's remark.

. . . *they're together. That's nice.* But Andrew and Adrian were not together. They worked within twenty minutes of each other but lived separate lives. At times, Fontine thought, *too* separate. They did not laugh together as they once did as children. As men, something had happened between them. Fontine wondered what it was.

Jane acknowledged for roughly the hundredth time that the party *was* a success, wasn't it. A statement. Thank heavens the weather held. The caterers had sworn they could erect the tents in less than an hour, if it was necessary, but by noon the sun was bright, the promise of a beautiful day confirmed.

Not, however, a beautiful evening. Far in the distance, over the water near Connecticut, the sky was gray. Weather reports predicted scattered-nocturnal-thundershowers-with-increasingly-steady-precipitation, whatever all *that* meant. Why didn't they simply say it would rain later on?

Two o'clock to six o'clock. Good hours for a Sunday *fête champêtre*. She had laughed at Victor's ignorance of the term. It was so pretentiously Victorian; the fun was in using it. It looked ridiculous on the invitations. Jane smiled, then stifled a laugh. She really *should* control her foolishness, she supposed. She was much too old for that sort of thing.

Across the lawn between the crowds, Adrian was smiling at her. Had he read her thoughts? Adrian, her dark-haired Gemini, had inherited her slightly mad English humor.

He was thirty-one years old. *They* were thirty-one years old. Where had those years gone? It seemed like only months ago they'd all arrived in New York on the ship. Followed by months of activity that had Victor flying all over the States and back to Europe, furiously building.

And Victor had done it. Fontine, Ltd. became one of the most sought-after consulting firms in America, Victor's expertise primarily aimed at European reconstruction. The name Fontine on a corporation's presentation was an industrial plus. Knowledge of a given marketplace was assured.

Victor had involved himself totally, not merely for the sake of pride, or instinctive productivity, but for something else. Jane knew it, and at the same time knew she could do nothing to help him. It took his mind off the pain. Her husband was rarely without pain; the operations prolonged his life, but did little to lessen the pain.

She looked at Victor across the lawn, sitting in his hard wooden chair with the straight back, the shiny metal cane at his side. He had been so proud when the two crutches were replaced by the single cane that made it possible for him to walk without being so obvious a cripple.

"Hi, Mrs. Fontine," said the young man with the very long hair. "It's one terrific party! Thanks for letting me bring my friends. They really wanted to meet Adrian."

The speaker was Michael Reilly. The Reillys were their nearest neighbors on the shore, about a half a mile down the beach. Michael was in law school at Columbia. "That's very flattering!"

"Hey, *he's great!* He wrapped up that Tesco antitrust in Boston when even the federal courts thought it was too loose. Everyone knew it was a Centaur company, but it took Adrian to nail it."

"Don't discuss it with Mr. Kempson."

"Don't worry. I saw him at the club and he told me to get a haircut. What the hell, so did my father."

"You won, I see."

Michael grinned. "He's mad as a bull but he can't say anything. I'm on the honors list. We made a deal."

"Good for you. Make him live up to it."

The Reilly boy laughed and leaned over, kissing her cheek. "You're outta sight!" He grinned again and left, beckoned by a girl at the edge of the patio.

Young people liked her, thought Jane. It was a comforting realization these days when the young found so little to like, or to approve. They liked her in spite of the fact that she refused to make concessions to youth. Or to age. Her hair was streaked—God, more than streaked—with gray; her face was lined—as it should be lined—and there were no discussions of a skin nip here, or a tuck there, as so many of her friends had done. She thanked her stars she'd kept her figure. All things considered, not bad for sixty . . . *plus,* damn it.

"Excuse me, Mrs. Fontine?" It was the maid; she'd come out of the turmoil that was the kitchen.

"Yes, Grace? Problems?"

"No, ma'am. There's a gentleman at the door. He asked for you or Mr. Fontine."

"Tell him to come out."

"He said he'd rather not. He's a foreign gentleman. A priest. I thought with so many people, Mr. Fontine——"

"Yes, you were right," interrupted Jane, understanding the maid's concerns. Victor did not relish walking among his guests as he was forced to walk. "I'll go see him."

The priest stood in the hallway, his black suit ill-fitting and old, his face thin and tired. He appeared awed, frightened.

Jane spoke coldly. She could not help herself. "I'm Mrs. Fontine."

"Yes, you are the *signora,*" replied the priest awkwardly, a large, stained envelope in his hand. "I have seen the pictures. I did not mean to intrude. So many automobiles."

"What is it?"

"I have come from Rome, *signora.* I bring a letter for the *padrone.* You will see that he gets it, please?" The priest held out the envelope.

Andrew watched his brother at the bar with the long-haired students, dressed in their uniforms of denim and suede, medallions around their necks. Adrian would never learn; his audience was useless. They were fakes. It was not simply the profusion of unkempt hair and the offbeat clothes that bothered the soldier; those were only symptoms. It was the pretense that went with these shallow expressions of nonconformity. By and large they were insufferable; antagonistic people with unkempt minds.

They spoke so intensely, so knowingly, of "movements" and "countermovements" as though they were participants, shifters of political thought. *This* world . . . the *third* world. And that was the biggest joke of all, because not one in ten thousand would know how to act as a revolutionary. They had neither the commitment nor the guts nor the savvy.

They were misfits who threw plastic bags of shit when no one paid attention to their ravings. They were . . . freaks, and, Christ, he couldn't stand the freaks. But Adrian did not understand; his brother looked for values where there weren't any. Adrian was a fool; but then he learned that seven years ago. Seven years ago he had discovered just how big a fool his brother was. Adrian was a misfit in the worst sense: He had every reason not to be.

Adrian glanced up at him from the bar; he turned away. His brother was a bore, and the sight of him proselytizing to that particular audience was distasteful.

The soldier hadn't always felt this way. Ten years ago when he'd gotten out of The Point he hadn't *hated* with the vehemence he felt now. He didn't think much of Adrian and his collection of misfits, but there was no hatred. The way the Johnson crowd began handling Southeast Asia, there was something to be said for the dissenters' attitude. *Get out.*

Translated: *Obliterate Hanoi. Or get out.*

He had explained his position time and again. To the freaks. To Adrian. But no one wanted to hear it from a soldier. "Soldierboy," that's what they called him. And "shell-head," and "missile-fingers," and "blast-ass."

But it wasn't the names. Anyone who'd gone through West Point and Saigon could handle that. Ultimately, it was their stupidity. They didn't simply turn off the people who mattered, they antagonized them, infuriated them, and finally *embarrassed* them. And *that* was the final stupidity. They drove even those who agreed with them into opposing positions.

Seven years ago in San Francisco, Andrew tried to make his brother see that, tried to make him understand that what he was doing was wrong and stupid—and very dangerous to the brother who was a soldier.

He'd gotten back from two and a half years in the Mekong Delta with one of the finest record sheets in the army. His company had the highest body count in the battalion; he'd been decorated twice, his first lieutenancy lasting a month before he was given his captain's bars. He was that rare commodity in armed forces: a young, brilliant military strategist from an immensely wealthy, influential family. He was on his way up to the top—where he belonged. He was being flown back for reassignment, which was another way of the Pentagon's saying: *That's our man. Keep your eye on him. Rich, solid, future Joint Chiefs mate-*

rial. A few more combat tours—in selected areas, a few short years—and it's the War College.

It never hurt the Pentagon to favor a man like him, especially when it was justified. The army needed men from powerful families, they had precious few.

But regardless of what the Pentagon favored or the army needed, G2 agents had shown up when he got off that plane in California seven years ago. They'd taken him to an office and given him a two-month-old newspaper. On the second page was a story about an insurrection at the Army's Presidio in San Francisco. Accompanying the article were photographs of the riot, one showing a group of civilians marching in support of the mutineering enlisted men. A face had been circled in a red pencil.

It was Adrian. It seemed impossible, but there he was! He wasn't supposed to be there; he was in his last year at law school. In Boston. But he was not in Boston, he was in San Francisco harboring three convicted deserters who had escaped; that's what the G2 men said. His twin brother was working for the *enemy!* Goddamn it, that's what they *were* and that's what he was *doing!* The Pentagon wouldn't look upon *that* with a whole lot of laughs. Jesus! His brother! His *twin!*

So G2 flew him up north and, out of uniform, he had wandered the streets of Haight-Ashbury until he'd found Adrian.

"These aren't men, they're confused kids," his brother said in a quiet bar. "They were never even told what their legal alternatives were; they've been railroaded."

"They took oaths like everybody else. You can't make exceptions," Andrew had replied.

"Oh, come on. Two of them didn't know what that oath meant, and the other one genuinely changed his mind. But nobody wants to listen. The judge advocates want examples, and the defense attorneys don't want to make waves."

"Sometimes examples *have* to be made," the soldier had insisted.

"And the law says they're entitled to competent counsel. Not barracks drinking buddies who want to look good——"

"Get with it, Adrian!" he interrupted. "There's a war out there! The firepower's real! Bastards like these cost *lives.*"

"Not if they're over here."

"Yes, they do! Because others will begin to wonder why they're over *there.*"

"Maybe they should."

"For Christ's sake, you're talking about *rights*, aren't you?" asked the soldier.

"You better believe it."

"Well, doesn't the poor son of a bitch on patrol in a rice paddy have any? Maybe *he* didn't know what he was getting into; he just went along because the law said he had to. Maybe *he* changed his mind. But he doesn't have time to think about it; he's trying to stay alive. He gets confused, he gets sloppy, he gets *killed!*"

"We can't reach everybody; it's one of the law's oversights, an abuse built into the system. But we do what we can."

Adrian would not give him any information seven years ago. He refused to tell him where the deserters were hidden. So the soldier said good-bye in the quiet bar and waited in a San Francisco alley until his brother came out. He followed Adrian for three hours through the acid streets. The soldier was an expert in tracking stray patrols in jungles; San Francisco was just another jungle.

His brother made contact with one of the deserters five blocks from the waterfront. The boy was a Black, with a growth of beard on his face. He was tall and thin and matched the photograph in Andrew's pocket. His twin gave the deserter money; it was a simple matter to follow the Black down to the waterfront, to a filthy tenement that was as good a hiding place as any in the area.

The phone call was made to the military police. Ten minutes later three convicted deserters were dragged out of the filthy tenement, to spend eight years in the stockades.

The misfit network went to work; the crowds gathered screeching their epithets, swaying to their adolescent, useless chants. And throwing their plastic bags of feces.

His brother came up to him in the crowds that night and for several moments just stared at him. Finally he said, "You've driven me back. Thanks."

Then Adrian had walked swiftly away to the barricades of would-be revolutionaries.

Andrew's reflections were interrupted by Al Winston, nee Weinstein, an engineer with an aerospace company. Winston had called out his name and was making his way over. Al Winston was heavy into air force contracts, and lived in the Hamptons. Andrew didn't like Winston-Weinstein. Whenever he ran into him he thought of another Jew— and compared them. The Jew he thought of was stationed at the Pentagon after four years under heavy fire in the worst sections of the Delta. Captain Martin Greene was a tough son of a bitch, a great soldier—not

a flabby Winston-Weinstein from the Hamptons. And Greene didn't
gouge profits from cost overruns; instead he watched them, catalogued
them. Marty Greene was one of *them*. One of Eye Corps.

"Many happy returns, major," said Winston, raising his glass.

"Thanks, Al. How are you?"

"Be a lot better if I could sell you boys something. I get no support
from the ground troops." Winston grinned.

"You do pretty well *off* the ground. I read where you're in on the
Grumman contract."

"Nickels and dimes. I've got a laser honing device that can be
adapted to heavy artillery. But I can't get to first base."

Andrew toyed with the idea of sending Winston-Weinstein to Martin
Greene. By the time Greene got finished with him, Al Winston would
wish he'd never heard of the Pentagon. "I'll see what I can do. I'm not
in procurement——"

"They *listen* to you, Andy."

"You never stop working, Al."

"Big house, big bills, rotten kids." Winston grinned again, then
stopped smiling long enough to get across his point. "Put in a word for
me. I'll make it worth your while."

"With what?" asked Andrew, his eyes straying toward the boathouse
and the Chris-Craft and the sailboats moored in the water. "Money?"

Winston's grin returned, now nervous, awkward. "No offense," said
the engineer softly.

Andrew looked at the Jew, thinking again of Captain Martin Greene
and the difference between the two men. "No offense," he said, walking
away.

Christ! Next to the freaks, he despised the *corrupters*. No, that wasn't
true. Next to the corrupters, he despised those who allowed themselves
to *be* corrupted. They were everywhere. Sitting in boardrooms, playing
the golf courses in Georgia and Palm Springs, lapping up the sauce in
the country clubs of Evanston and Grosse Pointe. They'd sold their
ranks!

Colonels, generals, commanders, admirals. The whole goddamned
military establishment was riddled with a new brand of thieves. Men
who winked and smiled and put their signatures on committee recom-
mendations, on procurements approvals, on contracts, on overruns. Because there were understandings made. Today's brigadier was tomorrow's "consultant" or "Washington representative."

Christ, it was easy to hate! The misfits, the corrupters, the corrupted. . . .

It was why Eye Corps was formed. A very small, select group of officers who were sick to death of the apathy and corruption and venality that pervaded every branch of the armed forces. Eye Corps was the answer, the medicine that would cure the sickness. For Eye Corps was compiling records from Saigon to Washington. The men of Eye Corps were putting it all together: names, dates, connections, illegal profits.

To hell with the so-called proper channels: up the chain of command. To the inspector general. To the secretary of the army. Who vouched for command? Who for the IG? Who in his right *mind* would vouch for the civilians?

No one they trusted. So they would do it themselves. Every general—every brigadier and admiral—*anyone* who tolerated any form of deviation would be smoked out and confronted with his crimes.

Eye Corps. That's what it was all about. A handful of the best young officers in the field. And one day they'd walk into the Pentagon and take over. None would dare stand in their way. The Eye Corps indictments would hang like grenades over the heads of the high brass. The grenades would explode if the brass didn't move out, leaving their chairs for men of the Eye Corps. The Pentagon belonged to them. They would give it meaning again. Strength. *Their* strength.

Adrian Fontine leaned on the bar and listened to the intense young students arguing, aware that his brother was staring at them. He looked up at Andrew; the soldier's cold eyes held their usual veiled contempt and then glanced away as Al Winston approached, raising his glass to the major.

Andrew was beginning to wear his contempt too openly, thought Adrian. His brother had lost some of his well-known cool; things aggravated the soldier too quickly these days.

God, how they'd veered from each other! They'd been so close once. The Geminis . . . brothers, twins, friends. The Geminis were the *best!* And somewhere along the line—in their teens, in prep school—it all started to change. Andrew began to think he was better than best, and Adrian became less than convinced he was adequate. Andrew never questioned his abilities; Adrian wasn't sure he had very many.

He was sure now. The terrible years of indecision were over; he'd passed through uncertainty and found his own way. Thanks in large measure to his very positive brother, the soldier.

And today, on their birthday, he had to confront his brother and ask some very disturbing questions. Questions that went to the core of Andrew's strength.

Core? It was appropriate; the sound was right, the spelling wrong.

Eye Corps was the name they'd uncovered. His brother was on the list. Eight self-deluded elitists who concealed evidence for their own purposes. A small band of officers who had convinced themselves they should run the Pentagon through what amounted to sheer blackmail. The situation might have been comic except that the evidence was there, and Eye Corps had it. The Pentagon was not above being manipulated by fear. Eye Corps was dangerous; it had to be ripped out.

They'd settle for that. They'd hand over a blanket subpoena to the army lawyers and let them handle it quietly. As long as the army lawyers did handle it and did not cover up. Perhaps it wasn't the time for demoralizing trials and long prison sentences. The guilt was so widespread and the motives so complex. But there was one irreducible condition. *Get the elitists out of uniform; clean your military house.*

Jesus, the irony of it! In San Francisco, Andrew had blown a crude whistle in the name of military law. Now, seven years later, he, Adrian, was blowing the whistle. Less crudely, he hoped, but the law was no less specific. The charge was obstruction of justice.

So much had changed. Nine months ago he was an assistant prosecutor in Boston, happy doing what he was doing, building a reputation that could lead to just about anywhere. Building it *himself*. Not having it *given* to him because he was Adrian Fontine, son of Victor Fontine, Limited; brother of West Point's celebrated Major Andrew Fontine, immaculate warrior.

Then a man had called him in early October, asking him to have drinks at the Copely bar late in the afternoon. The man's name was James Nevins and he was Black; he was also an attorney, and he worked for the Justice Department in Washington.

Nevins was the spokesman for a small contingent of harassed, disaffected government lawyers who burned under the tactics of the most politicized Justice Department in memory. The phrase "White House calling" simply meant another manipulation was taking place. The lawyers were worried, genuinely worried. Those manipulations were taking the country too close to the specter of a police state.

The lawyers needed help. From the outside. Someone to whom they could funnel their information. Someone who could organize and evaluate, who could set up and pay for a command center where they could meet privately and discuss their progress.

Someone, frankly, who could not be harassed. For reasons more obvious than not, one Adrian Fontine fit the bill. Would he accept?

Adrian hadn't wanted to leave Boston. He had his work; he had his girl. A slightly mad, brilliant girl he adored. Barbara Pierson, B.A., M.A., Ph.D. Associate Professor, Anthropology Laboratories, Harvard University. She of the quick deep laugh, the light-brown hair and the dark-brown eyes. They'd been living together for a year and a half; it wasn't easy to leave. But Barbara had packed for him and sent him on his way because she knew he had to go.

Just as he had to go seven, eight years ago. He had to leave Boston then, too. A depression had swept over him. He was the wealthy son of a powerful father; the twin brother of a man the army paraded in dispatches as one of the brightest young lights in the military.

What was left? For him? Who *was* he?

So he fled the trappings of a lifetime to see what he could find for himself. That was *his*. It was his own personal crisis; he couldn't explain it to anyone. And he ended up in San Francisco where there was a fight, a struggle he could understand. Where he could help. Until the immaculate warrior came along and ripped the scene apart.

Adrian smiled, remembering the morning after the terrible night in San Francisco. He'd gotten roaring drunk and woke up in the house of a legal aid lawyer in Cape Mendocino sick and vomiting.

"If you're who you say you are, you can do more than any of us," said the lawyer in Cape Mendocino that morning. "Hell, my old man was a janitor at the May Company."

In the seven intervening years Adrian had tried. But he knew he had only just begun.

"It's a constitutional ambiguity! Isn't that right, Adrian?"

"What? Sorry, I didn't hear what you said." The students at the bar had been arguing among themselves; now all eyes were on him.

"Free press versus pretrial bias," said an intense young girl, stumbling over the words.

"It's a gray area, I think," replied Adrian. "Each case is judged by itself."

The youngsters wanted more than he gave them, so they went back to yelling at each other.

Gray area. Saigon's Eye Corps had been a gray area only weeks ago. Rumors had filtered back to Washington that a small cadre of young senior officers were regularly harassing enlisted personnel on the docks and in the warehouses, insisting on copies of shipment manifests and destinations schedules. Shortly after, in one of the numerous, half-heartedly pursued antitrust cases at Justice, there was a plaintiff's allegation that records had been stolen from the corporation's Saigon offices, thus constituting illegally obtained evidence. The case would be dropped.

The lawyers at Justice wondered whether there was a connection between the strange group of officers who scoured the shipment manifests and corporations under contract to the Pentagon. Had the military gone that far? The conjecture was enough to send Jim Nevins to Saigon.

The Black attorney found what he was looking for. In a warehouse in the Tan Son Nhut cargo area. An officer was in the process of illegally transcribing security-related information on armaments supplies. Threatened with charges, the officer broke, and Eye Corps was revealed for everything it was. There were eight officers; the man caught knew the names of seven. The eighth was in Washington, that's all he knew.

Andrew Fontine headed the list of those identified.

Eye Corps. Nice fellows, thought Adrian. Just what the country needed; storm troopers out to save the nation.

Seven years ago in San Francisco his brother had not given him any warning before the action started, and the sirens came screaming into Haight-Ashbury. Adrian would be more considerate. He was going to give Andrew five days. There'd be no sirens, no riots . . . no eight-year sentences in the stockades. But the celebrated Major Andrew Fontine would be out of the army.

And although the work in Washington was nowhere near completed, Adrian would go back to Boston for a while. Back to Barbara.

He was tired. And sick with what faced him in an hour or so. The pain was real. Whatever else, Andrew was his brother.

The final guests had left. The orchestra was packing its instruments, and the caterers were cleaning up the lawn. The sky was growing darker, as much because of the threatening clouds over the water as by the approach of nightfall.

Adrian walked across the lawn to the flagstone steps and down to the boathouse. Andrew was waiting for him; he had told the soldier to be there.

"Happy birthday, counselor," said Andrew as Adrian came through the boathouse door. The soldier leaned against the wall beyond the boat slip, his arms folded, smoking a cigarette.

"Same to you," answered Adrian, stopping at the edge of the slip. "You staying tonight?"

"Are you?" asked Andrew.

"I thought I might. The old man looks pretty bad."

"Then I won't," said the soldier politely.

Adrian paused; he knew he was expected to speak. He wasn't quite sure how to begin, so instead he looked around the boathouse. "We had some good laughs down here."

"Did you want to reminisce? Is that why you asked me to come down here?"

"No. . . . I wish it were that simple."

The soldier flipped the cigarette into the water. "I hear you left Boston. You're in Washington."

"Yes. For a while. I keep thinking we'll run into each other."

"I doubt it," said the major, smiling. "We don't travel in the same circles. You working for a D.C. firm?"

"No. I guess you might say I'm a consultant."

"That's the best job in Washington." Andrew's voice was laced with quiet contempt. "Who are you counseling?"

"Some people who are very upset——"

"Oh, a consumer group; isn't that nice." It was an insulting statement. "Good for you!"

Adrian stared at his brother; the soldier returned the look. "Don't dismiss me, Andy. You're in no position to do that. You're in trouble. I'm not here to help you, I can't do that. I'm here to warn you."

"What the hell are you talking about?" asked the major softly.

"A deposition was taken from an officer in Saigon by one of our people. We have a complete statement about the activities of a group of eight men who call themselves Eye Corps."

Andrew bolted upright against the wall, his face pinched, his fingers stretched, curved, immobile. He seemed to freeze; he spoke barely above a whisper, spacing his words out. "Who is 'we'?"

"You'll know the origin soon enough. It's on the subpoena."

"*Subpoena?*"

"Yes. The Justice Department, a specialist division. . . . I won't tell you the individual attorneys, but I will tell you that your name heads the Eye Corps list. We know there are eight of you; seven have been identified, the eighth is at the Pentagon. In procurement. We'll find him."

Andrew held his position against the wall; everything about him remained immobile, except the muscles of his jaw, which moved slowly, steadily. Once again his voice was low, measured. "What have you done? What have you bastards *done?*"

"Stopped you," answered Adrian simply.

"What do you know? What have you been told?"

"The truth. We've no reason to doubt it."

"You need proof for a subpoena!"

"You need probable cause. We have that."

"One deposition! *Nothing!*"

"Others'll follow. What difference does it make? You're finished."

Andrew's voice calmed. He spoke matter-of-factly. "Officers complain. Up and down the zones, officers complain every day——"

"Not this way. There's no fine line between complaints and blackmail. It's very defined, very distinct. You crossed over it."

"*Who have we blackmailed?*" asked Andrew swiftly. "No one!"

"Records were kept, evidence suppressed; the intent was clear. That's in the deposition."

"There *are* no records!"

"Oh, come on, they're *somewhere*," said Adrian wearily. "But I repeat, who gives a goddamn? You're finished."

The soldier moved. He breathed deeply and stood erect against the wall. "Listen to me," he said quietly, his voice strained. "You don't know what you're doing. You say you're a consultant to men who are upset. We both know what that means; we're the Fontines. Who needs resources when they have us?"

"I don't see it that way," broke in Adrian.

"It's *true!*" shouted the soldier. And then he lowered his voice. "You don't have to spell out what you're doing, the Boston newspapers did that. You nail the big fellows, the vested interests, you call them. You're good. Well, what the hell do you think *I'm* doing? We're nailing them, too! You stop Eye Corps, you're destroying the finest young senior officers in the field, men who want to rip out the garbage! Don't *do* that, Adree! *Join* us! I mean that."

"Join——" Adrian repeated the word in disbelief. Then he added quietly. "You're out of your mind. What makes you think that's remotely possible?"

Andrew took a step away from the wall; his eyes were steady on his brother. "Because we want the same thing."

"No, we don't."

"*Think,* for God's sake! 'Vested interests.' You use that a lot, 'vested interests.' I read your summation in the Tesco case; you repeated it continuously."

"It applied. One company owning many, setting a single policy when there should have been competition. What's your point?"

"You use the term negatively because that's the way you find it. Okay, I'll buy that. But I submit there's another way to look at it. There can be *good* vested interests. Like us. Our interests isn't ourselves; we don't *need* anything. Our interests is the country and our resources are considerable. We're in positions to *do* something. I'm doing it. For Christ's sake, don't *stop* me!"

Adrian turned away from his brother and walked aimlessly along the moist planks of the boathouse toward the huge opening that led to the open water. The waves slapped against the pilings. "You're very glib, Andy. You were always very glib and sure and truly confident. But it's not going to work." He turned again and faced the soldier diagonally across the slip. "You say we don't need anything. I think we do; we both need—want—something. And what you want frightens me because I've got an idea what your concept of finest is. Frankly, it scares the hell out of me. The thought of your 'finest senior officers' controlling the country's hardware is enough to send me running to the library to reread the Constitution."

"That's arrogant horseshit! You don't know them!"

"I know the way they operate, the way you operate. If it'll make you feel better, you made some sense in San Francisco. I didn't like it, but I recognized it." Adrian walked back along the slip. "You're not making sense now, which is why I'm warning you. Save what you can of your neck, I owe you that much. Get out as gracefully as you can."

"You can't force me," said Andrew scathingly. "My record's one of the best. Who the hell are *you?* One lousy statement from a disgruntled officer in a combat zone. Bullshit!"

"I'll spell it out!" Adrian stopped by the boathouse doorway, raising his voice. "In five days—next Friday, to be precise—a blanket subpoena will be served on the adjutant general of the Courts of Military Justice. He'll have the weekend to negotiate his arrangements. Arrangements *can* be negotiated, but there's one irrevocable condition. You're *out*. All of you."

The soldier started forward, then stopped, his foot on the edge of the slip, as if he were about to spring across, lunging at his enemy. He held himself in check; waves of nausea and fury seemed to pass over him and through him. "I could . . . kill you," he whispered. "You're everything I despise."

"I guess I am," said Adrian, closing his eyes briefly, rubbing them in weariness. "You'd better get to the airport," he continued, now looking at his brother. "You've got a lot to do. I suggest you start with this so-called evidence you've been sitting on. We understand you've been collecting it for damn near three years. Get it to the proper authorities."

In angry silence the soldier lurched in rapid strides around the slip, past Adrian, and out to the boathouse steps. He began climbing, taking the flagstone stairs two at a time.

Adrian moved swiftly to the door and called out, halting his brother on the border of the lawn.

"Andy!"

The soldier stood motionless. But he did not turn around, or speak. So the lawyer continued.

"I admire your strength, I always have. Just as I admire father's. You're part of him, but you're not all of him. You missed something, so let's understand each other. You're everything I consider dangerous. I guess that means you're everything *I* despise."

"We understand each other," said Andrew, repeating the words in a monotone. He started up across the lawn toward the house.

19

The orchestra and the caterers left. Andrew was driven to LaGuardia Airport. There was a nine o'clock plane to Washington.

Adrian remained on the beach by himself for nearly thirty minutes after his brother left. Finally he wandered up to the house to talk to his parents. He told them he had intended to stay the night but now thought he should leave. He had to get back to Washington.

"You should have gone with your brother," said Jane at the front door.

"Yes, I should have," said Adrian softly. "I didn't think." He said his good-byes.

When he left, Jane walked out to the terrace, carrying the letter brought by the priest. She held it out for her husband, unable to conceal her fear. "A man brought this. About three hours ago. He was a priest. He said he was from Rome."

Victor looked up at his wife. There was no comment in his eyes, and by the lack of it, there was. "Why did you wait?"

"Because it was your sons' birthday."

"They're strangers to each other," said Fontine, taking the envelope. "They're both our children, but they're very far apart."

"It won't last. It's the war."

"I hope you're right," said Victor, opening the envelope and taking out the letter. It ran several pages, the handwriting small but precise. "Do we know a man named Aldobrini?"

"Who?"

"Guido Aldobrini. That's the signature." Fontine held up the last page.

"I don't think so," answered Jane, sitting down in the nearest chair, her eyes on the threatening sky. "Can you see in this light? It's getting darker."

"It is sufficient." Victor put the pages in sequence and began to read.

Signor Fontini-Cristi:

You do not know me although we met many years ago. That meeting cost me the better part of my life. I have spent over a quar-

ter of a century in the Transvaal in holy penance for an act of shame. I did not touch you myself, but I observed and did not raise my voice for mercy, which was an indecent and unholy thing.

Yes, Signore, I was one of the priests with the Cardinal Donatti that dawn at Campo di Fiori. For what we believed was the preservation of Christ's Mother Church on earth, the Cardinal convinced us that there were no laws of God or man or mercy standing between our actions and the preservation of God's Church. All our scholastic training and vows of obedience—not only to our superiors, but to the highest authority of conscience—were twisted by the power of Donatti's influence. I have spent twenty-five years trying to understand, but that is another story not pertinent here. One would have had to know the Cardinal to understand.

I am retired from my cloth. The illnesses of the African forests have taken their toll, and thanks be to Christ I do not fear death. For I have given of myself as fully as I knew how. I am cleansed and await the judgment of God.

Before I face our merciful Lord, however, there is information I must impart to you, for to withhold it now would be no less a sin than that for which I have paid holy penance.

The work of Donatti continues. A man, one of the three defrocked priests who were imprisoned by the civil court for their assault on you, has been released. As you perhaps know, one took his own life, the other died of natural causes while in prison. This third man survives and for motives beyond my comprehension, has rededicated himself to the pursuit of the Salonika documents. I say beyond my comprehension, for Cardinal Donatti was discredited in the highest circles of the Vatican. The Grecian documents cannot affect the Holy Mother Church. Divine revelation cannot be contravened by the hand of mortal man.

This defrocked priest goes by the name of Enrici Gaetamo, and he is taken to wearing the collar denied him by apostolic decree. It is my understanding that his years spent in the criminal institution have done nothing to enlighten his soul or show him the ways of a merciful Christ. On the contrary, I am told he is Donatti incarnate. A man to be feared.

He currently, painstakingly, researches every detail he can unearth relative to the train from Salonika thirty-three years ago. His travels have carried him from the yards of Edhessa, through the Balkans, over the rail routes beyond Monfalcone into the northern Alpine regions. He seeks out all he can find who knew the son of

Fontini-Cristi. He is a man possessed. He subscribes to the code of Donatti. There is no law of God or man that will interfere with his "journey for Christ," as he phrases it. Nor will he reveal to anyone the objective of his journey. But I know, and now you do. And soon I shall depart this life.

Gaetamo resides in a small hunting lodge in the hills of Varese. I'm sure the proximity to Campo di Fiori does not escape you.

This is all I can tell you; it is all I know. That he will attempt to reach you, I am certain. That you be warned and remain safe in God's hands, is my prayer.

In sorrow and personal anguish for my past, I remain,

Guido Aldobrini

There was the sound of thunder over the water; Fontine wished the symbolism were not so crudely simple. The clouds were above them now; the sun was gone and the rains began. He was grateful for the diversion. He looked at Jane. She was staring at him; somehow he had communicated to her his profound uneasiness.

"Go in," he said softly. "I'll follow in a minute or two."

"The letter——?"

"Of course," he answered her unspoken question as he replaced the pages in the envelope and handed it to her. "Read it."

"You'll be drenched. The rain will get stronger."

"It's refreshing; you know I like the rain." He smiled up at her. "Then perhaps you'll help me change the brace while we talk."

She stood above him for a moment, and he could feel her eyes on him. But as always, she would leave him alone when he wished it.

He was chilled by his thoughts, not the rain. The letter from Aldobrini was not the first time Salonika had reappeared. He had said nothing to Jane for there was nothing concrete, only a series of obscurely disturbing—seemingly minor—occurrences.

Three months ago he had gone to Harkness for yet another week of corrective surgery. Several days after the operation he'd had a visitor whose appearance startled him; a monsignor from the Archdiocese of New York. His name was Land, he said. He had returned to the United States after many years in Rome, and wanted to meet Victor because of information he had come across in the Vatican archives.

The priest was solicitous; what struck Fontine was that the cleric knew a great deal about his physical condition, far more than a casual visitor would know.

It was a very odd half hour. The priest was a student of history, he said. He had come across archive documents that raised profoundly disturbing questions between the house of Fontini-Cristi and the Vatican. Historical questions that led to the break between the *padroni* of the north and the Holy See. When Victor was well again, perhaps they could discuss the past. The *historical* past. He had ended his good-byes with a direct reference to the assault at Campo di Fiori. The pain and anguish inflicted by one maniacal prelate could not be laid at the soul of the church, he said.

About five weeks later there'd been a second incident. Victor had been in his Washington office, preparing to testify before a congressional committee looking into the tax concessions enjoyed by American shippers sailing under the Paraguayan flag, when his intercom buzzed.

"Mr. Fontine, Mr. Theodore Dakakos is here. He says he wants to pay his respects."

Dakakos was one of the young Greek shipping giants, an impertinent rival of Onassis and Niarchos, and far better liked. Fontine told his secretary to send him in.

Dakakos was a large man with a blunt, open expression on his face that might become an American football player more than a shipping tycoon. He was around forty years of age; his English was precise, the language of a student.

He had flown to Washington to observe the hearings, perhaps to learn something, he said smiling. Victor laughed; the Greek's reputation for integrity was matched only by the legend of his acute business sense. Fontine told him so.

"I was most fortunate. At a very young age I was given the advantages of an education by a sympathetic but remote religious brotherhood."

"You were, indeed, fortunate."

"My family was not wealthy, but they served their church, I'm told. In ways that today I do not understand."

The young Greek magnate was saying something beyond his words, but Victor could not determine what it was. "Gratitude as well as God, then, moves in strange ways," said Victor smiling. "Your reputation is a fine one. You do credit to those who aided you."

"Theodore is my first name, Mr. Fontine. My full name is Theodore Annaxas Dakakos. Throughout my schooling I was known as Annaxas the Younger. Does that mean anything to you?"

"In what way?"

"The name Annaxas."

"I've dealt with literally hundreds of your countrymen over the years. I don't think I've ever run across the name Annaxas."

The Greek had remained silent for several moments. Then he spoke quietly. "I believe you."

Dakakos left soon after.

The third occurrence was the strangest of all; it triggered a memory of violence so sharply into focus that Fontine lost his breath. It had happened only ten days ago in Los Angeles. He was at the Beverly Hills Hotel for conferences between two widely divergent companies trying to merge their interests. He had been called in to salvage what he could; the task was impossible.

Which was why he was taking the sun in the early afternoon, instead of sitting inside the hotel listening to lawyers trying to justify their retainers. He was drinking a Campari at a table in the outside pool area, astonished at the number of good-looking people who apparently did not have to work for a living.

"*Guten Tag, mein Herr.*"

The speaker was a woman in her late forties or early fifties, that age so well cosmeticized by the well-to-do. She was of medium height, quite well proportioned, with streaked blond hair. She wore white slacks and a blue blouse. Covering her eyes was a pair of large silver-rimmed sunglasses. Her German was natural, not studied. He replied in his own, academic, less natural, as he rose awkwardly.

"Good afternoon. Have we met? I'm sorry, but I don't seem to remember."

"Please, sit down. It's difficult for you. I know that."

"You do? Then we *have* met."

The woman sat down opposite him. She continued in English. "Yes. But you had no such difficulties then. You were a soldier then."

"During the war?"

"There was a flight from Munich to Müllheim. And a whore from the camps escorted on that flight by three Wehrmacht pigs. More pigs than she, I try to tell myself."

"My God!" Fontine caught his breath. "You were a *child*. What happened to you?"

She told him briefly. She had been taken by the French Resistance fighters to a transit camp southwest of Montbéliard. There for several months she endured agonies best left undescribed, as she experienced the process of narcotics withdrawal. She had tried to commit suicide numerous times, but the Resistance people had other ideas. They banked on the fact that once the drugs were expunged, her memories would be motive enough to turn her into an effective underground agent. She was already tough; that much they could see.

"They were right, of course," the woman said, ten days ago at the table on the patio of the Beverly Hills Hotel. "They kept watch over me night and day, men and women. The men had more fun; the French never waste anything, do they?"

"You survived the war," Fontine replied, not caring to probe.

"With a bucket full of medals. *Croix de guerre, Légion d'honneur, Légion de résistance.*"

"And so you became a great motion picture star and I was too stupid to recognize you." Victor smiled gently.

"Hardly. Although I've had occasions to be associated, as it were, with many prominent people of the motion picture industry."

"I'm afraid I don't understand."

"I became—and at the risk of sounding immodest, still am—the most successful madame in the south of France. The Cannes Film Festival alone provides sufficient income for a perfectly adequate subsistence." It was the woman's turn to smile. It was a good smile, thought Fontine. Genuine, alive.

"Then I'm very happy for you. I'm Italian enough to find a certain honorableness in your profession."

"I knew you were. And would. I'm here on a talent hunt. It would be my pleasure to grant any request you might have. There are a number of my girls out there in the pool."

"No, thank you. You're most kind, but, as you said, I am not the man I was."

"I think you're magnificent," she said simply. "I always have." She smiled at him. "I must go. I recognized you and wanted to speak to you, that's all." She rose from the table and extended her hand. "Don't get up."

The handshake was firm. "It's been a pleasure—and a relief—to see you again," he said.

She held his eyes and spoke quietly. "I was in Zürich a few months ago. They traced me through a man named Lübok. To you. He was a Czech. A queen, I'm told. He was the man on the plane with us, wasn't he?"

"Yes. A very brave man, I must add. A king, in my judgment." Victor was so startled he replied instinctively, without comprehending. He had not thought of Lübok in years.

"Yes, I remember. He saved all of us. They broke him." The woman released his hand.

"Broke him? About *what?* My God, the man, if he's alive, is my age or more. Seventy or better. Who would be interested in such old men? What are you talking about?"

"About a man named Vittorio Fontini-Cristi, son of Savarone."

"You're talking nonsense. Nonsense I understand, but I don't see how it might concern you. *Or* Lübok."

"I don't know any more. Nor do I care to. A man in Zürich came to my hotel room and asked questions about you. Naturally, I couldn't answer them. You were merely an Allied Intelligence officer who saved a whore's life. But he knew about Anton Lübok."

"Who was this man?"

"A priest. That is all I know. Good-bye, *Kapitän.*" She turned and walked away, waving and smiling at various girls who were splashing about in the pool and laughing too obviously.

A priest. In Zürich.

. . . *He seeks out all he can find who knew the son of Fontini-Cristi.* . . .

Now he understood the enigmatic meeting at the poolside in Los Angeles. A defrocked priest had been released after nearly thirty years in prison and revived the hunt for the documents of Constantine.

The work of Donatti continues, the letter said. *He currently, painstakingly, researches every detail he can unearth . . . His travels have carried him from the yards of Edhessa, through the Balkans . . . beyond Monfalcone into the northern Alpine regions.*

He seeks out all he can find who knew the son of Fontini-Cristi.

And thousands of miles away in New York City, another priest—very much *of* the cloth—comes into a hospital room and speaks of an act of barbarism that could not be separated from those documents. Lost three decades ago and hunted still.

And in Washington, a young industrial giant walks into an office and for no apparent reasons says his family served the church in ways he did not understand.

". . . I was given . . . advantages . . . by a sympathetic but remote religious brotherhood. . . ."

The *Order of Xenope.* It was suddenly so very clear.

Nothing was coincidence.

It had come back. The train from Salonika had plunged through thirty years of sleep and reawakened. It had to be controlled before the hatreds collided, before the fanatics turned the search into a holy war, as they had done three decades ago. Victor knew he owed that much to his father, his mother, to the loved ones slain in the white lights of

Campo di Fiori; to those who had died at Oxfordshire. To a misguided young monk named Petride who took his own life on a rocky slope in Loch Torridon, to a man named Teague, to an undergrounder named Lübok, to an old man named Guido Barzini who had saved him from himself.

The violence could not be allowed to return.

The rain came faster now, harder, in diagonal sheets blown by the wind. Fontine reached for the wrought iron chair beside him and struggled to his feet, his arm clamped within the steel band of his cane.

He stood on the terrace looking out over the water. The wind and the rain cleared his mind. He knew what he had to do, where he had to go.

To the hills of Varese.

To Campo di Fiori.

20

The heavy car approached the gates of Campo di Fiori. Victor stared out the window, aware of the spasm in his back; the eye was recording, the mind remembering.

His life had been altered, in pain, on the stretch of ground beyond the gates. He tried to control the memory; he could not suppress it. The images he observed were forced out of his mind's eye, replaced by black suits and white collars.

The car went through the gates; Victor held his breath. He had flown into Milan from Paris as unobtrusively as possible. In Milan he had taken a single room at the Albergo Milano, registering simply as: V. Fontine, New York City.

The years had done their work. There were no raised eyebrows, no curious glances; the name triggered no surprises. Thirty years ago a Fontine or a Fontini in Milan would be reason enough for comment. Not now.

Before he left New York he had made one inquiry—any more might have raised an alarm. He had learned the identity of the owners of Campo di Fiori. The purchase had been made twenty-seven years ago; there had been no change of ownership since that time. Yet the name had no impact in Milan. None had heard of it.

Baricours, Père et Fils. A Franco-Swiss company out of Grenoble, that's what the transfer papers said. Yet there was no Baricours, Père et Fils, in Grenoble. No details could be learned from the lawyer who had negotiated the sale. He had died in 1951.

The automobile rolled past the embankment into the circular drive in front of the main house. The spasm in Victor's back was compounded by a sharp stinging sensation behind his eyes; his head throbbed as he reentered the execution grounds.

He gripped his wrist and dug his fingers into his own flesh. The pain helped; he was able to look out the window and see what was there now, not thirty-three years ago.

What he saw was a mausoleum. Dead but cared for. Everything was as it had been, but not for the living. Even the orange rays of the setting sun had a dead quality to them: majestically ornamental, but not alive.

"Aren't there groundkeepers or men at the gates?" he asked.

The driver turned in the seat. "Not this afternoon, *padrone*," he replied. "There are no guards. And no priests of the Curia."

Fontine lurched forward in the seat; his metal cane slipped. He stared at the driver.

"I've been tricked."

"Watched. Expected. Not tricked, really. Inside, a man is waiting for you."

"One man?"

"Yes."

"Would his name be Enrici Gaetamo?"

"I told you. There are no priests of the Curia here. Please, go inside. Do you need help?"

"No, I can manage." Victor got out of the car slowly, each movement a struggle, the pain in his eyes receding, the spasm in his back subsiding. He understood. His mind was refocusing itself. He had come to Campo di Fiori for answers. For a confrontation. But he had not expected it to be this way.

He walked up the wide marble steps to the oak door of his childhood. He paused and waited for what he thought was inevitable: a sense of overwhelming sorrow. But it did not come, because there was no life here.

He heard the gunning of the engine behind him and turned. The driver had swung the car out into the curve, and driven past the embankment into the road toward the main gate. Whoever he was, he wanted to be away as rapidly as possible.

As he watched, Victor heard the metallic sound of a latch. He turned again to the huge oak door; it had opened.

The shock was impossible to conceal. Nor did he bother to hide it. The rage inside him welled; his whole body trembled in anger.

The man at the door was a *priest!* Dressed in the black cassock of the church. He was an old man and frail. Had he been otherwise, Fontine might have struck out at him.

Instead he stared at the old man and spoke quietly. "That a priest would be in this house is most painful to me."

"I'm sorry you feel that way," replied the priest in a foreigner's Italian, his voice thin but firm. "We revered the *padrone* of the Fontini-Cristis. We placed our most precious treasures in his hands."

Their eyes were locked; neither wavered, but the anger within Victor was slowly replaced with incredulity. "You're Greek," he said, barely audible.

"I am, but that's not relevant. I'm a monk from Constantine. Please. Come in." The old priest stepped back to allow Victor to pass. He added softly, "Take your time. Let your eyes roam. Little has changed; photographs and inventories were taken of each room. We have maintained everything as it was."

A mausoleum.

"So did the Germans." Fontine walked into the enormous hall. "It's strange that those who went to such lengths to own Campo di Fiori don't want to change it."

"One doesn't cut a great jewel or deface a worthy painting. There's nothing strange in that."

Victor did not reply. Instead, he gripped his cane and walked with difficulty toward the staircase. He stopped in front of the arch that led to the huge drawing room on the left. Everything *was* as it had been. The paintings, the half-tables against the massive walls, the glazed antique mirrors above the tables, the oriental rugs covering the polished floor, the wide staircase, its balustrade glistening.

He looked over through the north arch into the dining room. Twilight shadows fell across the enormous table, now bare, polished, empty, where once the family had sat. He pictured them now; he could hear the chatter and the laughter. Arguments and anecdotes, never-ending talk; dinners were important events at Campo di Fiori.

The figures froze, the voices disappeared. It was time to look away.

Victor turned. The monk gestured at the south arch. "Shall we go into your father's study?"

He preceded the old man into the drawing room. Involuntarily—for he did not care to activate memories—his eyes fell on the furnishings, suddenly so familiar. Every chair, every lamp, every tapestry and sconce and table was precisely as he remembered it.

Fontine breathed deeply and closed his eyes for a moment. It was macabre. He was passing through a museum that had once been a living part of his existence. In some ways it was the cruelest form of anguish.

He continued on through the door into Savarone's study; it had never been his, although his life nearly ended in that room. He passed by the doorframe through which a severed, bloody hand had been thrown in the shadows.

If there was anything that startled him it was the desk lamp; and the light that spilled downward over the floor from the green shade. It was *precisely* as it was nearly three decades ago. His memory of it was vivid, for it was the light from the lamp that had washed over the shattered skull of Geoffrey Stone.

"Would you care to sit down?" asked the priest.

"In a minute."

"May I?"

"I beg your pardon?"

"May I sit at your father's desk?" said the monk. "I've watched your eyes."

"It's your house, your desk. I'm a visitor."

"But not a stranger."

"Obviously. Am I speaking with a representative of Baricours, Père et Fils?"

The old priest nodded silently. He walked slowly around the desk, pulled out the chair, and lowered his frail body into it. "Don't blame the lawyer in Milan; he couldn't have known. Baricours met your conditions, we made sure of it. Baricours is the Order of Xenope."

"And my enemy," said Victor quietly. "In 1942 there was an M.I.-Six compound in Oxfordshire. You tried to kill my wife. Many innocent people lost their lives."

"Decisions were made beyond the control of the Elders. The extremists had their way; we couldn't stop them. I don't expect you to accept that."

"I don't. How did you know I was in Italy?"

"We are not what we once were, but we still have resources. One in particular keeps his eye on you. Don't ask me who it is; I won't tell you. Why did you come back? After thirty years, why did you return to Campo di Fiori?"

"To find a man named Gaetamo," answered Fontine. "Enrici Gaetamo."

"Gaetamo lives in the hills of Varese," said the monk.

"He's still looking for the train from Salonika. He's traveled from Edhessa, through the Balkans, across Italy, into the northern mountains. Why have you stayed here all these years?"

"Because the *key* is here," replied the monk. "A pact was made. In October of 1939, I traveled to Campo di Fiori. It was I who negotiated Savarone Fontini-Cristi's participation, I who sent a dedicated priest on that train with his brother, an engineer. And demanded their deaths in the name of God."

Victor stared at the monk. The spill of the lamp illuminated the pale, taut flesh and the sad, dead eyes. Fontine recalled the visitor in his Washington office. "A Greek came to me saying his family served their church once in ways he didn't understand. Was this priest's brother the engineer, named Annaxas?"

The old cleric's head snapped up; the eyes became briefly alive. "Where did you hear that name?"

Fontine looked away, his eyes falling on a painting beneath a Madonna on the wall. A hunting scene, birds being flushed from a thicket by men with guns. Other birds flew above. "We'll trade information," he said quietly. "Why did my father agree to work with Xenope?"

"You know the answer. He had only one concern: not to divide the Christian world. The defeat of the fascists was all he cared about."

"Why was the vault taken from Greece in the first place?"

"The Germans were scavengers and Constantine was marked. That was the information we received from Poland and Czechoslovakia. The Nazi commanders stole from museums, tore apart retreats and monasteries. We couldn't take the chance of leaving it there. Your father engineered the removal. Brilliantly. Donatti was tricked."

"By the use of a second train," added Victor. "Mounted and routed identically. Sent three days later."

"Yes. Word of this second train was leaked to Donatti through the Germans, who had no concept of the significance of the vault from Constantine. They looked for treasures—paintings, sculpture, art objects —not obscure writings they were told were valuable only to scholars. But Donatti, the fanatic, could not resist; the Filioque denials had been rumored for decades. He had to possess them." The priest of Xenope paused, the memory painful. "The cardinal's and the German interests coincided. Berlin wanted Savarone Fontini-Cristi's influence destroyed; Donatti wanted to keep him from that train. At all costs."

"Why was Donatti involved at all?"

"Again, your father. He knew the Nazis had a powerful friend in the Vatican. He wanted Donatti exposed for what he was. The cardinal could not know about that second train unless the Germans told him. Your father intended to make use of this fact. It was the only price Fontini-Cristi asked of us. As it turned out, that price brought about the executions of Campo di Fiori."

Victor could hear his father's voice piercing through the decades. . . . *He issues edicts to the uninformed and enforces them by fear.* . . . *A disgrace to the Vatican.* Savarone knew the enemy, but not the extremes of his monstrousness.

The brace across Fontine's back was cutting into his flesh. He had been standing too long. He gripped his cane and walked toward the chair in front of the desk. He sat down.

"Do you know what was on that train?" asked the old monk gently.

"Yes. Brevourt told me."

"Brevourt never knew. He was told part of the truth. Not all of it. What did he tell you?"

Victor was suddenly alarmed. He locked eyes once again with the priest.

"He spoke of the Filioque denials, studies that refuted the divinity of Christ. The most damaging of which was an Aramaic scroll that raised questions as to whether Jesus ever existed at all. The conclusion would appear that he did not."

"It was never the denials. Never the scroll. It was—*is*—a confession written in its entirety that predates all the other documents." The priest of Xenope looked away. He raised his hands; his bony fingers touched the pale skin of his cheek. "The Filioque denials are artifacts for scholars to ponder. As one of them, the Aramaic scroll, was ambiguous, as the scrolls of the Dead Sea were ambiguous when studied fifteen hundred years later. However, thirty years ago at the height of a moral war —if that's not a contradiction in terms—that scroll's exposure might have been catastrophic. It was enough for Brevourt."

Fontine was mesmerized. "What is this confession? I've never heard it mentioned."

The monk returned his eyes to Victor. During the brief silence before he spoke, the old priest conveyed the pain of his immediate decision. "It is everything. It was written on a parchment brought out of a Roman prison in the year sixty-seven. We know the date because the document speaks of the death of Jesus in terms of the Hebrew calendar that places the figure at thirty-four years. It coincides with anthropological scholarship. The parchment was written by a man who wandered blindly; he speaks of Gethsemane and Capernaum, Gennesaret and Corinth, Pontus, Galatia and Cappadocia. The writer can be no one else but Simon of Bethsaida, given the name of Peter by the man he called Christ. What is contained in that parchment is beyond anything in your imagination. It must be found."

The priest stopped and stared across at Victor.

"And destroyed?" asked Fontine softly.

"Destroyed," replied the monk. "But not for any reason you might think of. For *nothing* is changed, yet *all* is changed. My vows forbid me to tell you more. We're old men; we haven't much time. If you can help, you must. That parchment can alter history. It should have been destroyed centuries ago, but arrogance prevailed. It could plunge a great part of the world into a terrible agony. No one can justify the pain."

"But you say nothing is changed," replied Victor, repeating the monk's words, "yet *all* is changed. One cancels the other; it doesn't make sense."

"The confession on that parchment makes sense. In all its anguish. I can tell you no more."

Fontine held the priest's eyes. "Did my father know about the parchment? Or was he told only what Brevourt was told?"

"He knew," said the monk of Xenope. "The Filioque denials were like your American articles of impeachment, charges for canonical debate. Even the most damaging—as you called it—the Aramaic scroll, was subject to the linquistic interpretations of antiquity. Fontini-Cristi would have perceived these issues; Brevourt did not. But the confession on that parchment is not debatable. It was the single, awesome thing that demanded Fontini-Cristi's commitment. He understood and accepted it."

"A confession on a parchment taken out of a Roman prison." Fontine spoke quietly; the issue was clear. "That's what the vault of Constantine is all about."

"Yes."

Victor let the moment pass. He leaned forward in the chair, his hand on his metal cane. "You said the key is here. But why? Donatti searched—every wall, every floor, every inch of ground. You've remained here for twenty-seven years, and still there's nothing. What's left for you?"

"Your father's words, said in this room."

"What were they?"

"That the markings would be here in Campo di Fiori. Etched for a millennium. That was the phrase he used: 'etched for a millennium.' And his son would understand. It was part of his childhood. But his son was told nothing. We came to know that."

Fontine refused a bed in the great house. He would rest in the stables, in the bed on which he had placed the dead Barzini a lifetime ago.

He wanted to be alone, isolated, and above all, out of the house, away from the dead relics. He had to think, to go back over the horror again and again until he found the missing connection. For it was there now; the pattern existed. What remained missing was the line that completed the design.

Part of his childhood. No, not there, not yet. Don't start there; it would come later. Begin with what one knew, one saw, one heard for himself.

He reached the stables and walked through the empty rooms and past the empty stalls. There was no electricity now; the old monk had given him a flashlight. Barzini's room was as he remembered it. Bare, without ornament; the narrow bed, the worn-out armchair, the simple trunk for his few possessions.

The tack room, too, was as he had seen it last. Bridles and leather straps on the walls. He sat down on a small wooden stirrup bench, exhaling in pain as he did so. He put out the flashlight. The moon shone through the windows. He inhaled deeply and forced his mind back to the horrible night.

The shattering of machine gun fire filled his ears, evoking the memory he abhorred. The swirling clouds of smoke were there, the arched bodies of loved ones in succeeding instants of death, seen in the blinding light of the floodlamps.

Champoluc is the river! Zürich is the river!

The words were screamed, then repeated, twice, three times! Roared up at him but aimed higher than where he was, above him, as the bullets pierced his father's chest and stomach.

Champoluc is the river!

The head raised? Was that it? The head, the *eyes*. It's always in *the eyes!* A split fraction of time before the words poured out, his father's eyes had *not* been on the embankment, *not* on *him*.

They had been leveled to his right, on a diagonal. Savarone had been staring at the automobiles, into the *third automobile*.

Savarone had seen Guillamo Donatti! He had recognized him in the shadows of the back seat of the car. At the instant of death, he knew the identity of his executioner.

And the roars of fury had poured forth, up at his son, but beyond his son. Up and beyond and . . . what *was* it? What *was* it his father had done at that last instant of life? It was the missing connection, the line that completed the pattern!

Oh, Christ! Some part of his body. His head, his shoulders, his hands. What *was* it?

The *whole* body! My God, it was the gesture in *death* of the *whole body!* Head, arms, hands. Savarone's body had been stretched in one final gesture! *To his left!* But not the house, not the lighted rooms so viciously invaded, but beyond the house. *Beyond the house!*

Champoluc is the river. . . .

Beyond the house!

The *woods* of Campo di Fiori!

The *river!* The wide mountain stream in the forest! Their own personal *"river"!*

It was part of his childhood. The river of his childhood was a quarter of a mile beyond the gardens of Campo di Fiori!

Sweat fell from Victor's face; his breath was erratic, his hands trembled. He gripped the edge of the stirrup bench in the darkness. He was spent, but certain; it was all suddenly, totally clear.

The *river* was not in the Champoluc, nor in Zürich. It was minutes away from *here*. A brief walk down a forest path made by generations of children.

Etched for a millennium.

Part of his *childhood*.

He pictured the woods, the flowing stream, the rocks . . . the rocks . . . the *rocks*. The *boulders* that bordered the stream in the deepest section of the water! There was one *large* boulder used for diving and jumping and lying in the sun, and *scratching initials,* and childish *messages,* and secret *codes* between very young brothers!

Etched for a millennium. His *childhood!*

Had Savarone chosen *this rock* on which to etch his message?

It was suddenly so clear. So *consistent.*

Of course he had.

21

The night sky turned gradually to gray, but no rays of the Italian sun broke through the overcast. Instead, there would be rain soon, and a cold summer wind whipping down from the northern mountains.

Victor walked down the stable road into the gardens. It was too dark to make out the colors. Then, too, there were not the rows of flowers bordering the paths as there had been; he could see that much.

He found the path with difficulty, only after examining the uncut grass, angling the beam of his flashlight into the ground, looking for signs of the past. As he penetrated the woods beyond the garden familiar things came back to him: a gnarled olive tree with thick limbs; a cluster of white birches, now concealed by beechwood vine and dying spruce.

The stream was no more than a hundred yards away, diagonally to his right, if memory served. There were birches and tall pines; giant weeds formed a wall of tentacles, soft but uncomfortable to the touch.

He stopped. There was a rustle of bird wings, the snap of a twig. He turned and peered into the black shapes of the overgrowth.

Silence.

Then the sound of a small animal intruded on the quiet. He had probably disturbed a hare. Strange, he should assume so naturally that it was a hare. The surroundings jogged memories long forgotten; as a boy he had trapped hares in these woods.

He could smell the water now. He had always been able to smell the moistness when he approached the stream, smell it before he heard the sound of the flow. The foliage nearest the water was thick, almost impenetrable. Seepage from the stream had fed a hundred thousand roots, allowing rampant, uncontrolled growth. He had to force back limbs and spread thickets to approach the stream.

His left foot was ensnared in a tangle of ground vine. He stepped back on his right and, with his cane, worked it free, losing his balance as he did so. The cane whipped out of his hand, spiraling into the darkness. He grabbed for a branch to break his fall; the small limb cracked, stripping itself from its source. On one knee, he used the thick stick to push himself off the ground; his cane was gone; he could not see it. He held onto the stick and threaded his way through the mass of foliage to the water's edge.

The stream seemed narrower than he remembered. Then he realized it was the gray darkness and the overgrown forest that made it appear so. Three decades of inattention had allowed the woods to impinge upon the water.

The massive boulder was on his right, upstream, no more than twenty feet away, but the wall of overgrowth was such that it might have been half a mile. He began edging his way toward it, crouching, rising, separating, each movement a struggle. Twice he butted against hard obstacles in the earth, too high, too thin and narrow, for rocks. He swung the beam of the flashlight down; the obstacles were iron stakes, rusted and pitted as though relics from a sunken galleon.

He reached the base of the huge rock; its body extended over the water. He looked below, the flashlight illuminating the separation of earth and flowing stream, and realized the years had made him cautious. The distance to the water was only a few feet, but it appeared a gulf to him now. He sidestepped his way down into the stream, the thick stick in his left hand prodding the depth.

The water was cold—as he remembered, it was always cold—and came up to his thighs, lapped over his waist below the brace, sending chills throughout his body. He shivered and swore at the years.

But he was *here*. It was all that mattered.

He focused the flashlight on the rock. He was several feet from the edge of the bank; he would have to organize his search. Too many minutes could be wasted going over areas twice or three times because he could not remember examining them. He was honest with himself: He was not sure how long he could take the cold.

He reached up, pressing the end of the stick into the surface of the rock. The moss that covered it peeled easily. The details of the boulder's surface, made vivid by the harsh, white beam of the flashlight, looked like thousands of tiny craters and ravines.

His pulse accelerated at the first signs of human intrusion. They were faint, barely visible, but they were there. And they were his marks, from more than half a century ago. Descending lines scratched deeply into the rock as part of a long forgotten boyhood game.

The V was the clearest letter; he had made sure his mark was vivid, properly recorded. Then there was b, followed by what might have been numbers. And a t, again followed by what were probably numbers. He had no idea what they meant.

He peeled the moss above and below the scratchings. There were other faint markings; some seemed meaningful. Initials, mainly; here and there, rough drawings of trees and arrows and quarter circles drawn by children.

His eyes strained under the glare of the flashlight; his fingers peeled and rubbed and caressed a larger and larger area. He made two vertical lines with the stick to show where he had searched and moved farther into the cold water; but soon the cold grew too much and he climbed onto the bank, seeking warmth. His hands and arms and legs were trembling with cold and age. He knelt in the damp overgrowth and watched the vapor of his breath diffuse itself in the air.

He went back into the water, to the point where he had left off. The moss was thicker; underneath he found several more markings similar to the first set nearer the embankment. V's and b's and t's and very faint numbers.

Then it came back to him through the years—faintly, as faintly as the letters and the numbers. And he *knew* he was right to be in that stream, at that boulder.

Burrone! Traccia! He had forgotten but now recalled. "Ravine," "trail." He had always scratched—recorded—their journeys into the mountains!

Part of his childhood.

My God, what a part! Every summer Savarone gathered his sons together and took them north for several days of climbing. Not dangerous climbing, more hiking and camping. For them all, a high point of the summers. And he gave them maps so they knew where they had been; and Vittorio, the eldest, would indelibly, soberly record the journeys on the boulder down at the stream, their "river."

They had christened the rock The Argonaut. And the scratchings of The Argonaut served as a permanent record of their mountain odysseys. Into the mountains of their boyhood.

Into the mountains.

The train from Salonika had gone into the mountains! The vault of Constantine was somewhere in the mountains!

He balanced himself with the stick and continued. He was near the face of the rock; the water came up to his chest, chilling the steel brace beneath his clothes. The farther out he went the more convinced he became; he was *right* to be there! The faint scratching—the faded scars of half lines and zigzags—were more and more numerous. *The Argonaut's* hull was covered with graffiti related to journeys long forgotten.

The cold water sent a spasm through the base of his spine; the stick fell from his hands. He slapped at the water, grabbing the stick, shifting his feet in the effort. He fell—glided, actually—into the rock and righted himself by pressing the stick into the mud below for balance.

He stared at the sight inches from his eyes in the water. There was a short, straight, horizontal line deeply defined in the rock. It was *chiseled*.

He braced himself as best he could, transferred the stick to his right hand, manipulating it between his thumb and the flashlight, and pressed his fingers into the surface of the boulder.

He traced the line. It angled sharply downward into the water; across and down and then it abruptly stopped.

7. It was a 7.

Unlike any other faded hieroglyphics on the rock; not scratches made by awkward, youthful hands, but a work of precision. The figure was no more than two inches high—but the impression itself was a good half inch deep.

He'd *found* it! *Etched for a millennium!* A message carved in rock, *chiseled in stone!*

He brought the flashlight closer and carefully moved his trembling fingers about the area. My God, was this *it?* Was this the *moment?* In spite of the cold and the wet, the blood raced to his head, his heart accelerated. He felt like shouting; but he had to be *sure!*

At midpoint of the vertical line of the 7, about an inch to its right, was a dash. Then another single vertical line . . . a 1, followed by yet another vertical that was shorter, angling to the right . . . and intersected by a line straight up and down. . . . A 4. It was a 4.

Seven—dash—one—four. More below the surface of the water than above it.

Beyond the 4 was another short, horizontal line. A dash. It was followed by a . . . Z, but not a Z. The angles were not abrupt, they were rounded.

2.

Seven—dash—one—four—dash—two. . . .

There was a final impression but it was not a figure. It was a series of four short, straight lines joined together. A box . . . a square. A perfect geometric square.

Of course, it *was* a figure! A *zero!*

0.

Seven—dash—one—four—dash—two—zero.

What did it *mean?* Had Savarone's age caused him to leave a message that meant nothing to anyone but *him?* Had everything been so brilliantly logical but the message itself? It meant *nothing*.

7—14—20. . . . A date? Was it a *date?*

My God! thought Victor. 7–14. July 14! His birthday!

Bastille Day. Throughout his life that had been a minor source of amusement. A Fontini-Cristi born on the celebrated day of the French Revolution.

July 14 . . . two-zero . . . 20. 1920.

That was Savarone's key. Something had happened on July 14, 1920. What was it? What incident had occurred that his father considered so meaningful to his first son? Something that had a significance beyond other times, other birthdays.

A shaft of pain—the second of what he knew would be many—shot through his body, originating, once again, at the base of his spine. The brace was like ice; the cold of the water had chilled his skin and penetrated the tendons and muscle tissue.

With the sensitivity of a surgeon, he pressed his fingers around the area of the chiseled numbers. There was only the date; all else was flat and unspoiled. He took the stick in his left hand and thrust it below the water into the mud. Painfully, he sidestepped his way back toward the embankment, until the level of the water had receded to his thighs. Then he paused for breath. The flashes of pain accelerated; he had done more damage to himself than he had realized. A full convulsion was developing; he tensed the muscles of his jaw and throat. He had to get out of the water and lie down. Lurching for the overhanging vines on the embankment, he fell to his knees in the water. The flashlight spun out of his hand and rolled over some matted fern, its beam shooting out into the dense woods. He grabbed a cluster of thick, exposed roots and pulled himself up toward the ground, pushing the stick behind him into the mud for propulsion.

All movement was arrested in a paralyzing instant of shock.

Above him, in the darkness on the embankment, stood the figure of a man. A huge man dressed in black, and motionless, staring down at him. Around his throat—in jarring counterpoint to the pitch-black clothing—was a rim of white. A priest's collar. The face—what he could see of it in the dim forest light—was impassive. But the eyes that bore down at him had fire in them, and hatred.

The man spoke. His speech was deliberate, slow, born of loathing.

"The enemy of Christ returns."

"You are Gaetamo," said Fontine.

"A man came in an automobile to watch my cabin in the hills. I knew that automobile, that man. He serves the heretic of Xenope. The monk who lives his life in Campo di Fiori. He was there to keep me away."

"But he couldn't."

"No." The defrocked priest elaborated no further. "So this is where it was. All those years and the answer was here." His deep voice seemed to float, beginning anywhere, ending abruptly in midstatement. "What did he leave? A name? Of what? A bank? A building in the Milan factories? We thought of those; we took them apart."

"Whatever it was, it has no meaning for you. Nor for me."

"Liar," replied Gaetamo quietly, in his chilling monotone. He turned his head right, then left; he was remembering. "We staked out every inch of these woods. We ran yellow strings from stake to stake and marked each area as we studied it. We considered burning, cutting . . . but were afraid of what we might destroy. We damned the stream and probed the mud. The Germans gave us instruments . . . but always nothing. The large rocks were filled with meaningless markings, including the birthdate of an arrogant seventeen-year-old who had to leave his conceit in stone. And always nothing."

Victor tensed. *Gaetamo had said it.* In one brief phrase the defrocked priest had unlocked the door! *An arrogant seventeen-year-old,* leaving his mark in stone. But *he* had not left it! Donatti had found the key but had not recognized it! The reasoning was so simple, so uncomplicated: a seventeen-year-old carving a memorable day on a familiar rock. It was so logical, so essentially unremarkable. And so *clear.*

As the memory was now clear. Most of it.

7–14–20. His seventeenth birthday. It came back to him because there had been none like it in his life. My God, thought Victor, Savarone was incredible! *Part of his childhood.* It was on his seventeenth birthday that his father had given him the present he had wanted so badly he had dreamed of it, pleaded for it: The chance to go up into the mountains without his younger brothers. To really do some climbing . . . *above* the usual and—for him—dreary campsites in the foothills.

On his seventeenth birthday, Savarone had presented him with an authentic Alpine pack, the sort used by experienced climbers. Not that his father was about to take him up the Jungfrau; they never really scaled anything extraordinary. But that first trip—*alone with his father*—was a landmark in his early manhood. That pack and that journey were symbols of something very important to him: proof that he was growing up in his father's eyes.

He had forgotten; he was not sure of it even now, for there had been other trips, other years. Had it—that first trip—been in the Champoluc? It must have been, but *where?* That *was* beyond memory.

". . . end your life in this water."

Gaetamo had spoken, but Fontine had not heard him: only the threat had penetrated. Of all men—all priests—this madman could be told nothing. "I found only meaningless scribblings. Childish markings, as you said."

"You found what rightfully belongs to *Christ!*" Gaetamo's words sliced through the forest. He lowered himself to one knee, his immense chest and head inches from Victor, his eyes wide and burning. "You found the *sword of the archangel of hell!* No more lies. Tell me what you've found!"

"Nothing."

"Liar! Why are you *here?* An old man in water and mud! What was in this stream? On this *rock!*"

Victor stared at the grotesque eyes. "Why am I here?" he repeated, stretching his neck, arching his tortured back, his features pinched. "I'm old. With memories. I convinced myself that the answer *might* be here. When we were children we left messages for one another here. You saw for yourself. Childish markings, scribblings, stone scratched against stone. I thought perhaps—— But I found nothing. If there was anything, it's gone now."

"You examined the rock, and then you stopped! You were prepared to leave."

"*Look* at me! How long do you think I can stay in this water?"

Gaetamo shook his head slowly. "I watched you. You were a man who found what he had come to find."

"You saw what you wanted to see. Not what was there."

Victor's foot slipped; the stick that braced him in the water slid in the mud, sinking deeper. The priest thrust out a hand and grabbed Fontine's hair. He yanked viciously, pulling Victor into the embankment, forcing his head and neck to one side. The sudden contortion was unbearable; wrenching pain spread throughout Fontine's body. The wide maniacal eyes above him in the dim light were not those of an aging man in the clothes of a priest but, instead, the eyes of a young fanatic thirty years ago.

Gaetamo saw. And understood. "We thought you were dead then. There was no way you could have survived. The fact that you did convinced our holy man that you were from *hell!* . . . You remember. For now I'll continue what was begun thirty years ago! And with each crack of your bones you'll have the chance—as you did then—to tell me what you've found. But don't lie. The pain will only stop when you tell me the truth."

Gaetamo bent forward. He began to twist Victor's head, pressing the face downward into the rocky embankment, cutting the flesh, forcing the air out of Fontine's throat.

Victor tried to pull back; the priest slammed his forehead into a gnarled root. Blood spurted from the gash, flowing into Victor's eyes, blinding him, infuriating him. He raised his right hand, grappling for Gaetamo's wrist; the defrocked priest clasped the hand and wrenched it inward, snapping the fingers. He pulled Fontine higher on the ground, twisting, always twisting his head and neck, causing the brace to cut into his back.

"It won't end until you tell me the truth!"

"*Pig! Pig from Donatti!*" Victor lurched to the side. Gaetamo countered by crashing his fist into Fontine's rib cage. The impact was paralyzing, the pain excruciating.

The stick. The *stick!* Fontine rolled to his left, his left hand below, still gripped around the broken limb, gripped as one holds an object in a moment of agony. Gaetamo had felt the brace; he pulled on it, wrenching it back and forth until the steel lacerated the surrounding flesh.

Victor inched the long stick up by pressing it into the embankment. It touched his chest; he felt it. The end was jagged. If he could only find the smallest opening between himself and the monster above, space enough to thrust it upward, toward the face, the neck.

It came. Gaetamo raised one knee. It was *enough.*

Fontine shoved the stick up, driving it with every ounce of strength he could summon, impaling it into the stunned body above. He heard a cry of shock, a scream that filled the forest.

And then an explosion filled the gray darkness. A powerful gun had been fired. The screeches of birds and animals swelled in the woods—and the body of Gaetamo fell forward on top of him. It rolled to the side.

The stick was lodged in his throat. Below his neck a huge gaping mass of torn flesh saturated with blood was in his upper chest; he had been blown apart by the gun that had been fired out of the darkness.

"May God forgive me," said the monk of Xenope from the shadows.

A black void came over Victor; he felt himself slipping into the water as trembling hands grabbed him. His last thoughts—strangely peaceful—were of his sons. The Geminis. The hands might have been the hands of his sons, trying to save him. But his sons' hands did not tremble.

PART
TWO

22

Major Andrew Fontine sat rigidly at his desk, listening to the sounds of morning. It was five minutes to eight; the offices were beginning to fill up. Voices rose and fell in the corridors as the Pentagon started the day.

He had five days to think. No, not to think, to *move*. There wasn't that much to think about; it was only necessary to move out and cut *down*. Stop whatever Adrian and his "concerned citizens" had started.

Eye Corps was the most legitimate clandestine unit in the army. It was doing exactly what the dissenters *thought* they were doing, but without tearing down the system, without revealing weakness. Maintain strength and the illusion of strength. It was all important. They'd tried it the other way. Eye Corps wasn't born in Georgetown, over brandy and cigars and pictures of the Pentagon on the walls. *Bullshit!* It was born in a hut in the Mekong Delta. After he had come back from Saigon and told his three subordinate officers what had happened at command headquarters.

He had gone to Saigon with legitimate field complaints, proof of corruption in the supply lines. Hundreds of thousands of dollars' worth of equipment was being drained off all over the Mekong every week, abandoned by ARVN troops at the first sign of hostilities, routed back into the black market. Payrolls were banked by ARVN commanders, drugs bought and distributed by Vietnamese networks out of Hue and Danang. Millions were piped out of the Southeast Asia operation, and no one seemed to know what to do about it.

So he brought his proof to Saigon, right up to the command brass. And what did the brass do? They thanked him and said they would investigate. What was there to investigate? He'd brought enough proof to institute a dozen charges.

A brigadier had taken him out for a drink.

"Listen, Fontine. Better a little corruption than blow the whole ammo dump. These people are thieves by nature, we're not going to change that."

"We could make a few examples, sir. Openly."

"For Christ's sake! We've got enough Stateside problems! That kind of publicity would play right into the antimilitary hands. Now, you've got a fine record; don't louse it up."

That's when it started, when Eye Corps was born. The name itself said it: a unit of men who watched and recorded. And as the months went on, the four of them expanded to five, then seven. Recently, they'd added the eighth man: Captain Martin Greene, in the Pentagon. They were born of disgust. The army was led by weak-kneed whores—*women —afraid* to *offend*. What kind of stature was that for the military leaders of the strongest nation on earth?

Something else happened, too, along the way. As the records grew and the enemies within tagged for what they were, the obvious stared the men of Eye Corps in the face: *they* were the inheritors! They were the incorruptible; they were the elite.

Since regular channels didn't work, they would do it their way. Build up the records, get files on every misfit, every deviate, every corrupter, large and small. Strength lay with those who could confront the misfits and make them crawl. Make them do exactly what strong, incorruptible men wanted them to do.

Eye Corps was nearly there. Almost three years' worth of recorded garbage. Christ! Southeast Asia was the place to find it. They'd take over soon; go right into the Pentagon and take over! It was men like themselves who had the skill and training and the commitment to oversee the vast complexities that were the armed might of the country. It was not a delusion; they *were* the elite.

It was so logical for him, too. His father would understand that, if he could ever talk to him about it. And one day he might. Since his earliest memories, he felt the presence of influence, of pride, of consequence. And power . . . yes, power. It wasn't a dirty word! It belonged to those who knew how to handle it; it was his birthright.

And Adrian wanted to tear it down! Well, the spoiler was not going to tear it down. He was not going to rip Eye Corps apart.

. . . *arrangements can be made.* That's what Adrian had said in the boathouse.

How right he was! Arrangements could be made; but not any arrangements considered by Adrian and his concerned citizens. A lot would happen before then.

Five days. Adrian wasn't trained to consider the options. Practical, physical alternatives, not words and abstractions and "positions." The army would have a hell of a time trying to reach him five days from now if he was 10,000 miles away in a combat zone, involved in operations covered by an umbrella of security. He had enough clout to do that; to get over there and build that umbrella.

There was a weakling in Saigon who had betrayed them. Betrayed the rest of Eye Corps. To learn who he was—and he was one of six—was the first reason to get over there. Find him . . . then make a decision.

Once he was found—and the decision made—the rest was easy. He'd brief the remaining men of Eye Corps. The stories would be integrated, synchronized.

Even the army needed proof. And there was no way it could get that proof.

Here in Washington, Eye Corps' eighth member could take care of himself. Captain Martin Greene was steel and leather. And smart. He could hold his own against any flak leveled at him. His people had come from the Irgun, the toughest fighters in Jew history. If the D.C. brass gave him any static, he'd cut out for Israel in a second, and the Jew army would be better for it.

Andrew looked at his watch. It was a little past eight, time to reach Greene. He couldn't take the chance last night. Adrian and his civilians were trying to find an unknown officer who worked at the Pentagon. Outside telephones could not be trusted. He and Marty would have to talk; they couldn't wait for their next scheduled meeting. He would be on a plane for Saigon before the day was over.

They had agreed never to be seen together. If they met by chance at a conference or a cocktail party, both pretended they were meeting for the first time. It was vital that no connection between them be apparent. When they did meet, it was in out-of-the-way places and always by pre-arranged schedule. During the meetings they would combine whatever damaging information they'd culled from Pentagon files during the week, seal the pages in an envelope, and mail it to a post office box in Baltimore. The enemies of Eye Corps were being catalogued everywhere.

In times of emergencies, or when one needed the other's immediate advice, they sent word to each other by placing a "mistaken" call through the Pentagon switchboard. It was the signal to invent some excuse, get out of the office, and head for a bar in downtown Washington. Andrew had made the "mistaken" call two hours ago.

The bar was dark and cheap and gaudy, with booths in the back that afforded a clear view of the entrance. Andrew sat in a booth by the back wall, toying with his bourbon, not interested in it. He kept looking up at the entrance fifty feet away. Whenever the door opened, the morning sun burst through briefly, a harsh intruder on the interior darkness. Greene was late; it wasn't like him to be late.

The door opened again and the silhouette of a stocky, muscular man with broad, thick shoulders was arrested in the glare. It was Marty; he was out of uniform, dressed in an open white shirt and what appeared to be plaid trousers. He nodded to the bartender and started toward the rear of the bar. Everything about Greene was powerful, thought Andrew. From his thick legs to the shock of bright-red hair, shaped in a bristling crew cut.

"Sorry it took me so long," said Greene, sliding into the booth opposite Andrew. "I stopped off at the apartment to change. Then I went out the back way."

"Any particular reason?"

"Maybe, maybe not. Last night I took the car out of the garage and thought I picked up surveillance—a dark-green Electra. I reversed directions; it was still there. I went home."

"What time was it?"

"Around eight thirty, quarter to nine."

"It figures. It's why I called you. They expect me to contact someone in your section; set up a meeting right away. They probably had half a dozen others followed."

"Who?"

"One of them's my brother."

"Your *brother?*"

"He's a lawyer. He's working with——"

"I know *exactly* who he is," interrupted Greene, *"and* who he's working with. They're about as subtle as jackals."

"You never mentioned him to me. How come?"

"There was no reason to. They're a bunch of hotheads over at Justice. They were organized by a Black named Nevins. We keep close tabs on them; they mess around with hardware contracts more than we'd like. But they haven't got anything to do with *us.*"

"They do now. It's why I called you. One of the six in Nam broke. They've got a deposition. A list. Eight officers, seven identified."

Greene's cold eyes narrowed. He spoke slowly, quietly. "What the hell are you saying?"

Andrew told him. When he finished, Greene spoke without moving an inch of his powerful body.

"That Black son of a bitch, Nevins, flew to Saigon two weeks ago. The matter wasn't related."

"It is now," said the major.

"Who has the deposition? Are there copies?"

"I don't know."

"Why is the subpoena being delayed?"

"Again, I don't know," said Andrew.

"There must be a reason! For Christ's sake, why didn't you ask?"

"Hold it, Marty. Everything came as a shock——"

"We're trained for shock," interrupted Greene icily. "Can you find out?"

Andrew swallowed part of his bourbon. He had not seen the captain like this before. "I can't call my brother. He wouldn't tell me if I did."

"Nice family. May the brothers live and be well. Maybe I can do better. We've got people at Justice; procurement covers itself. I'll do what I can. Where are our files in Saigon? They're the bottom line."

"They're not in Saigon. They're in Phan-thiet on the coast. In a fenced-off area of a warehouse, I'm the only one who knows the location. A couple of cabinets among a thousand G-Two crates."

"Very smart." Greene nodded his head in approval.

"I'll check them the first thing. I'm flying out this afternoon. A sudden inspection trip."

"Very nice." Greene nodded again. "You'll find the man?"

"Yes."

"Check Barstow. He's a smartass. Too many decorations."

"You don't know him."

"I know the way he operates," said Greene.

Andrew was stung by the similarity of words. His brother had applied them to Eye Corps. "He's a good man in the field——"

"Bravery," interrupted the captain, "hasn't got a goddamn thing to do with it. Check Barstow first."

"I will." Andrew smarted under Greene's pronouncements. He had to get some of his own back. "What about Baltimore? I'm worried about that."

The envelopes in Baltimore were picked up by Greene's twenty-year-old nephew.

"He's perfect. He'd kill himself first. I was up there last weekend. I would have known."

"Are you sure?"

"It's not worth discussing. I want to know more about that goddamned deposition. When you crack Barstow make sure you get every word he put down. They probably gave him a copy; see if he's got a military lawyer."

The major drank again, averting Greene's narrow eyes. Andrew did not like the captain's tone of voice. He was actually giving orders; he was out of line. But on the bottom line Greene was a good man to have around in a crisis. "What can you find out over at Justice?"

"More than that Black bastard would ever guess. We've got funds set up for the mavericks who interfere with armaments contracts. We don't care who makes a few extra dollars, we want the hardware. You'd be surprised how the lowly paid government lawyers take to Caribbean vacations." Greene smiled and sat back in the booth. "I think we can handle this. The subpoena won't mean a damn thing without our records. Line officers bitch all the time, what else is new?"

"That's what I told my brother," said Andrew.

"Him I can't figure," said Greene. And then the captain leaned forward. "Whatever you do in Nam, think it out. If you use prejudice, get your facts and do it by remote."

"I think I've had more experience in those areas than you." Andrew lighted a cigarette; his hand was steady in spite of his increased irritation. He was pleased with that.

"You probably do," said Greene casually. "Now, I've got something for you. I figured it could wait till our next meeting, but there's no point in holding it."

"What is it?"

"A congressional tracer came in last Friday. From a pol named Sandor; he's on the Armed Services Committee. It concerned you, so I pulled it."

"What did they want?"

"Limited. Your rotation schedule. How permanent you were in Washington. I inserted a routine response. You were high-echelon material, War College candidate. Very permanent."

"I wonder what—"

"I haven't finished," interrupted Greene. "I called this Sandor's aide and asked why the congressman was interested in you. He checked his papers and said the request came from a friend of Sandor's, a man named Dakakos. Theodore Dakakos."

"Who is he?"

"A Greek shipper. In your family's class. He's got millions."

"Dakakos? Never heard of him."

"These Greeks are pistols. Maybe he wants to give you a present. Like a small yacht or your own battalion."

Fontine shrugged. "Dakakos? I can buy a yacht. I'll take the battalion."

"You can buy that, too," said Greene, sliding across the seat out of the booth. "Have a prosperous trip. Call me when you get back."

"What are you going to do?"

"Find out everything there is to know about a Black son of a bitch named Nevins."

Greene walked rapidly past the booths toward the entrance. Andrew would wait five minutes before leaving. He had to get to his apartment and back. His plane left at one thirty.

Dakakos? Theodore Dakakos.

Who was he?

Adrian got out of the bed slowly, one foot after the other, as quietly as possible so he would not wake her. Barbara was asleep, but her sleep was fitful.

It was barely nine thirty in the evening. He had picked her up at the airport shortly after five. She'd canceled her Thursday and Friday seminars, too excited to lecture detached summer students.

She had been awarded a grant to assist the anthropologist Sorkis Khertepian at the University of Chicago. Khertepian was in the process of analyzing artifacts taken from the site of the Aswan Dam. Barbara was exhilarated; she had to fly down and tell Adrian all about it. She was intensely alive when things went right in her world, a scholar who would never lose her sense of wonder.

It was strange. Both he and Barbara had entered their professions in a sense of outrage. His was traced to the acid streets of San Francisco, hers to a brilliant mother denied her rightful place in a midwest college because she *was* a mother. A woman who had no place in the higher offices of a university. Yet each had found values that far outweighed the anger.

It was part of the bond between them.

He walked quietly across the room and sat down in an armchair. His eyes fell on his briefcase on the bedroom desk. He never left it in the sitting room at night; Jim Nevins had cautioned him about being careless. Nevins was at times a little paranoid about such matters.

Nevins, too, had come to his profession in outrage. It was the outrage that often sustained him. Not merely the frustrations of a Black man climbing over the barriers erected by a skeptical white establishment, but the anger of a lawyer who saw so much illegality in the city where laws were made.

But nothing outraged Nevins more than the discovery of Eye Corps. The idea of military elitists suppressing evidence of massive corruption for their own ends was more dangerous than anything the Black lawyer could think of.

When Major Andrew Fontine's name appeared on the list, Nevins had asked Adrian to remove himself. Adrian had become one of his closest friends, but nothing could stand in the way of prosecuting Eye Corps.

Brothers were brothers. Even white brothers.

"You look so serious. And so naked." Barbara swept her light-brown hair away from her face, and rolled on her side, hugging the pillow.

"I'm sorry. Did I wake you?"

"Heavens, no. I was only dozing."

"Correction. Your snoring could be heard on Capitol Hill."

"You lie through your legal teeth. . . . What time is it?"

"Twenty of ten," he answered, looking at his watch.

She sat up and stretched. The sheet fell away to her waist; her lovely, full breasts separated, their slow expansion, the movement of the nipples holding his eyes, arousing him. She saw him watching her and smiled, pulling the sheet over her as she leaned against the headrest.

"We talk," she said firmly. "We have three days to wear ourselves to a frazzle. While you're out during the day slaying bears, I'll preen myself like a concubine. Satisfaction guaranteed."

"You should do all those things nonacademic ladies do. Spend hours at Elizabeth Arden's, wallow in milk baths, eat bonbons with your gin. You're a tired girl."

"Let's put me aside," said Barbara smiling. "I've been talking about me all night—almost. How's everything down here? Or shouldn't you say? I'm sure Jim Nevins thinks the suite is bugged."

Adrian laughed, crossing his legs. He reached for a pack of cigarettes next to a lighter on the armchair table. "Jim's conspiracy complex remains undaunted. He refuses to leave case files at the office anymore. He keeps all his important papers in his briefcase, which is the biggest damn thing you ever saw." Adrian chuckled.

"Why does he do that?"

"He doesn't want copies made. He knows the crowd upstairs would take him off half the cases if they knew how much progress he was making."

"That's astonishing."

"It's chilling," he said.

The telephone rang. Adrian got out of the chair quickly and crossed to the bedside table.

It was his mother. She could not hide the anxiety in her voice. "I've heard from your father."

"What do you mean, you've *heard* from him?"

"He flew to Paris last Monday. Then he went on to Milan——"

"*Milan?* What for?"

"He'll tell you himself. He wants you and Andrew here on Sunday."

"Wait a minute." Adrian's mind raced. "I don't think I can do that."

"You *must.*"

"You don't understand, and I can't explain right now. But Andy's not going to want to see me. I'm not sure I want to see him. I'm not even sure it's advisable under the circumstances."

"What are you talking about?" His mother's voice was suddenly cold. "What have you done?"

Adrian paused before answering. "We're on the opposite sides of a . . . dispute."

"Whatever it is, it doesn't matter! Your father *needs* you." She was losing control. "Something happened to him. Something *happened* to him! He could barely talk!"

There were several clicks on the line, followed by the urgent voice of a hotel operator. "Mr. Fontine, I'm sorry to break in, but there's an emergency call for you."

"Oh, God." His mother whispered over the line from New York. "Victor——"

"I'll call you back if it's got anything to do with him. I promise you that," said Adrian swiftly. "All right, operator. I'll take——"

It was as far as he got. The voice now on the line was hysterical. It was a woman, crying and screaming and barely coherent.

"*Adrian!* My *God, Adrian!* He's *dead!* He was *killed!* They *killed him!* Adriannnnnnn!*"

The screams filled the room. And the terror of the screams filled Adrian with a shock he had never felt before. . . . Death. Death that touched *him.*

The woman on the telephone was Carol Nevins. Jim's wife.

"I'll be right there!"

"Call my mother," he told Barbara, as he dressed as fast as he could. "The North Shore number. Tell her it's not dad."

"Who is it?"

"Nevins."

"Oh, my God!"

He raced into the corridor and down to the elevators. He kept his finger on the button; the elevators were slow—*too* slow! He ran to the exit doors, crashed them open and leaped down the angling staircase to the lobby. He sped to the glass doors of the entrance.

"Excuse me! Pardon me! Let me through, *please!*"

Out on the curb he ran to his right, to the lighted sign of an empty taxi. He gave the address of Nevins's apartment.

What had happened? What in God's name *had happened?!* What did Carol mean? *They killed him! Who* killed him. Jesus! Was he *dead?!*

Jim Nevins dead? Corruption, yes. Greed, of course. Mendacity, normal. But not *murder!*

There was a traffic light at New Hampshire, and he thought he would go mad. Two more blocks!

The cab plunged forward the instant the light flickered. The driver accelerated, then halfway down the block came to a sudden stop. The street was jammed with traffic. There were circling lights up ahead; nothing was moving.

Adrian jumped out on the street and began threading his way as fast as possible between the cars. Across Florida Avenue police cars blocked the entrance. Patrolmen were blowing whistles, signaling with iridescent orange gloves, funneling the traffic west.

He ran into the blockade; two police officers several yards away at either side yelled at him.

"No one goes past here, mister!"

"Get back, buddy! You don't want to go in there!"

But he did want to go; he had to go! He ducked between two patrol cars and raced toward the swirling lights near a mass of twisted metal and shattered glass that Adrian instantly recognized. It was Jim Nevins's car. What was left of it.

An ambulance's rear doors were open; a stretcher on which a body lay strapped, covered completely with a white hospital blanket, was being carried from the wreckage by two attendants. A third man, holding a black medical bag, walked alongside.

Adrian approached, pushing away a policeman who held out a prohibiting arm. "Get out of the way," he said firmly, but with his voice trembling.

"Sorry, mister. I can't let——"

"I'm an attorney! And that man, I *think,* is my friend."

The doctor heard the desperation in his words and waved the officer away. Adrian reached down for the blanket; the doctor's hand shot out and held his wrist.

"Is your friend Black?"

"Yes."

"With identification that says his name is Nevins?"

"Yes."

"He's dead, take my word for it. You don't want to look."

"You don't understand. I *have* to look."

Adrian pulled back the blanket. Nausea swept over him; he was at once hypnotized and terrified at what he saw. Nevins's face was half ripped off, blood and bone more apparent than flesh. The area of the throat was worse; half his neck was gone.

"Oh, Jesus. My *God!*"

The doctor replaced the blanket and ordered the attendants to continue on. He was a young man with long blond hair and the face of a boy. "You better sit down," he said to Adrian. "I tried to tell you. Come on, let me take you to a car."

"No. No, thanks." Adrian suppressed the sickness and tried to breathe. There wasn't enough air! "What happened?"

"We don't know all the details yet. Are you really a lawyer?"

"Yes. And he was my friend. What happened?"

"Seems he made a left turn to go into the apartment driveway and halfway across, some outsized rig rammed him at full speed."

"Rig?"

"A trailer truck, the kind with steel gridwork. It barrel-assed down like it was on a freeway."

"Where is it?"

"We don't know. It stopped for a couple of moments, its horn blasting like hell, then pulled out. A witness said it was a rental; it had one of those rent-a-truck signs on the side. You can bet the cops have APB's out all over the place."

Suddenly, Adrian remembered, amazed that he was able to do so. He grabbed the doctor's sleeve. "Can you get me through the police to his car? It's important."

"I'm a doctor, not a cop."

"Please. Will you try?"

The young doctor sucked air through his teeth, then nodded his head. "Okay. I'll take you over. Don't pull any shit, though."

"I just want to see something. You said a witness saw the truck stop."

"I *know* it stopped," replied the blond-haired doctor enigmatically. "Come on!"

They walked over to the wreck. Nevins's car was caved in on the left side, metal stripped everywhere, windows shattered. Foam had been sprayed around the gas tank; white globules had drifted through the smashed windows.

"Hey, Doc! What are *you* doing?" The policeman's voice was tired and angry.

"Come on, kid, get back. You, too!" A second patrolman yelled.

The young doctor raised his black bag. "Forensic washout, fellas. Don't argue with me, call the station!"

"What?"

"What forensic?"

"Pathology, for Christ's sake!" He propelled Adrian forward. "Come on, lab man, take the samples and let's get out of here. I'm beat." Adrian looked into the car. "See anything?" asked the doctor pointedly.

Adrian did. Nevins's briefcase was missing.

They walked back through the cordon of police to the ambulance.

"Did you really find anything?" asked the young doctor.

"Yes," answered Adrian, numbed, not sure he was thinking clearly. "Something that should have been there, but wasn't."

"Okay. Good. Now I'll tell you why I took you over."

"What?"

"You saw your friend; I wouldn't let his wife see him. His face and neck were blown apart with broken glass and metal fragments."

"Yes . . . I know. I saw." Adrian felt the wave of nausea spreading over him again.

"But it's a pretty warm night. I think the window on the driver's side was rolled down. I couldn't swear to it—that car's totaled—but your friend could have taken a short blast from a shotgun."

Adrian raised his eyes. Something inside his head snapped; the words his brother said seven years ago in San Francisco seared into his brain.

". . . *There's a war out there . . . the firepower's real!*"

Among the papers in Nevins's briefcase was the deposition taken from an officer in Saigon. The indictment of Eye Corps.

And he had given his brother five days' warning.

Oh, God! What had he done?

He took a cab to the precinct police station. His credentials as an attorney gained him a brief conversation with a sergeant.

"If there's foul play involved, we'll find it," said the man, looking at Adrian with the distaste the police reserved for lawyers who followed up accidents.

"He was a friend of mine and I have reason to believe there was. Did you find the truck?"

"Nope. We know it's not on any of the highways. The state troopers are watching for it."

"It was a rental."

"We know that, too. The rental agencies are being checked. Why don't you go home, mister?"

Adrian bent over the sergeant's desk, his hands on the edge. "I don't think you're taking me very seriously."

"Fatality sheets come into this station a dozen an hour. Now, what the hell do you want me to do? Suspend everything else and put a whole goddamned platoon on one hit-and-run?"

"I'll tell you what I want, sergeant. I want a pathology report on all cranial injuries sustained by the deceased. Is that clear?"

"What are you talking about?" replied the police officer disdainfully. "Cranial——"

"I want to know what blew that man apart."

23

The train from Salonika had claimed its last sacrifice, thought Victor, as he lay in his bed, the morning sun streaming through the oceanside windows of the North Shore house. There was no reason on earth why any further life should be lost in its name. Enrici Gaetamo was the last victim, and there was no sorrow in that death.

He himself had very little time remaining. He could see it in Jane's eyes, in the eyes of the doctors. It was to be expected; he had been granted too many reprieves.

He had dictated everything he could remember about that day in July a lifetime ago. He had probed forgotten recesses in his mind, refused the narcotics that would numb the pain because they would equally numb the memories.

The vault from Constantine had to be found, its contents evaluated by responsible men. What had to be prevented—however remote it might be—was a chance discovery, exposure without thought. He would charge his sons. Salonika was now theirs. The Geminis. They would do what he could not do: find the vault of Constantine.

But there was a piece of the puzzle that was missing. He had to find it before he spoke with his sons. What did Rome know? How much had the Vatican learned about Salonika? Which was why he had asked a man to visit him this morning. A priest named Land, the monsignor from New York's archdiocese who had come to his hospital room months ago.

Fontine heard the footsteps outside the bedroom, and the quiet voices of Jane and the visitor. The priest had arrived.

The heavy door opened silently. Jane ushered in the monsignor, then went back into the hallway, closing the door behind her. The priest stood across the room, a leather book in his hand.

"Thank you for coming," Victor said.

The priest smiled. He touched the leather cover of the book. *"Conquest with Mercy. In the Name of God.* The history of the Fontini-Cristis. I thought you might like this, Mr. Fontine. I found it in a bookshop in Rome years ago."

The monsignor placed the book on the bedside table. They shook hands; each, Victor realized, was appraising the other.

Land was no more than fifty. He was of medium height, broad in the chest and shoulders. His features were sharp, Anglican; his eyes hazel beneath generous eyebrows that were darker than his short, graying hair. It was a pleasant face with intelligent eyes.

"A vanity publication, I'm afraid. A custom of dubious value at the turn of the century. It's long been out of print. The language is Italian——"

"An obsolete northern idiom," completed Land. "Court Victorian would be the English equivalent, I think. Somewhere between 'you' and 'thee.' "

"You have the advantage over me. My knowledge of languages is not nearly so erudite."

"It was sufficient for Loch Torridon," said the priest.

"Yes, it was. Please sit down, Monsignor Land." Victor gestured to the chair by the bed. The priest sat. The two men looked at each other. Fontine spoke.

"Several months ago you came to my hospital room. Why?"

"I wanted to meet the man whose life I had studied so thoroughly. Shall I speak frankly?"

"You wouldn't have come here this morning if you meant to do otherwise."

"I was told you might die. I was presumptuous enough to hope you'd allow me to administer last rites."

"That *is* frank. And *was* presumptuous."

"I realized that. It's why I never returned. You're a courteous man, Mr. Fontine, but you couldn't conceal your feelings."

Victor examined the priest's face. There was the same sorrow he had remembered in the hospital. "Why did you study my life? Does the Vatican still investigate? Wasn't Donatti's cause rejected?"

"The Vatican is always engaged in study. In examination. It doesn't stop. And Donatti was more than rejected. He was excommunicated, his remains refused the sanctity of Catholic burial."

"You answer my last two questions. Not the first. Why you?"

The monsignor crossed his legs, clasping his hands in front of him on his knees, his fingers entwined. "I'm a political and social historian. Which is another way of saying that I look for incompatible relationships between the church and its environs at given periods of time." Land smiled, his eyes reflective. "The original reason for such work was to prove the virtue of the church and the error of any who opposed her.

But virtue wasn't always found. And it certainly wasn't found in the countless lapses of judgment, or morality, as they were exposed." Land's smile had gone; his admission was clear.

"The execution of the Fontini-Cristis was a lapse? Of *judgment? Morality?*"

"Please." The priest spoke swiftly, his voice soft but emphatic. "You and I both know what it was. An act of murder. Impossible to sanction and unforgivable."

Victor saw once again the sorrow in the man's eyes. "I accept what you say. I don't understand it, but I accept it. So I became an object of your social and political examinations?"

"Among many other questions of the time. I'm sure you're aware of them. Although there was a great deal of good during those years, there was *much* that was unforgivable. You and your family were obviously in this category."

"You became interested in me?"

"You became my obsession." Land smiled again, awkwardly. "Remember, I'm American. I was studying in Rome, and the name Victor Fontine was well known to me. I had read of your work in postwar Europe; the newspapers were filled with it. I was aware of your influence in both the public and the private sectors. You can imagine my astonishment when, in studying the period, I found that Vittorio Fontini-Cristi and Victor Fontine were the same person."

"Was there a great deal of information in your Vatican files?"

"About the Fontini-Cristis, yes." Land gestured his head toward the leather-bound volume he had placed on the bedside table. "As that book, somewhat biased, I'm afraid. Hardly as flattering, naturally. But of you, there was substantively nothing. Your existence was acknowledged: the first male child of Savarone, now an American citizen known as Victor Fontine. Nothing more. The files ended abruptly with the information that the remaining Fontini-Cristis had been executed by the Germans. It was an incomplete ending. Even the date was missing."

"The less written down, the better."

"Yes. So I studied the records of the Court of Reparations. They were far more complete. What began as curiosity turned into shock. You made accusations to the tribunal of judges. Accusations I found unbelievable, intolerable, for you included the church. And you named a man of the Curia, Guillamo Donatti. That was the link that was missing. It was all I needed."

"Are you telling me Donatti's name was nowhere in the files of the Fontini-Cristis?"

"It is now. It wasn't then. It was as if the archivists couldn't bring themselves to acknowledge the connection. Donatti's papers had been sealed, as usual with excommunicants. After his death, they had been found in possession of an aide——"

"Father Enrici Gaetamo. Defrocked," interrupted Fontine softly.

Land paused. "Yes. Gaetamo. I received permission to break the seals. I read the paranoid ramblings of a madman, a self-canonized fanatic." Again the monsignor stopped briefly, his eyes wandering. "What I found there took me to England. To a man named Teague. I met with him only once, at his country house. It was raining and he repeatedly got up to stoke the fire. I never saw a man finger a watch so. Yet he was retired and had no place to go."

Victor smiled. "It was an annoying habit, that watch. I told him so many times."

"Yes, you were good friends, I learned that quickly. He was in awe of you, you know."

"In awe of me? Alec? I can't believe that. He was far too direct."

"He said he never admitted it to you, but he was. He said he felt inadequate around you."

"He didn't convey it."

"He said a great deal more, too. Everything. The execution at Campo di Fiori, the escape through Celle Ligure, Loch Torridon, Oxfordshire, your wife, your sons. And Donatti; how he kept the name from you."

"He had no choice. The knowledge would have interfered with Loch Torridon."

Land unclasped his hands and uncrossed his legs. He seemed to have difficulty finding the words. "It was the first time I had heard of the train from Salonika."

Victor raised his eyes abruptly; they had been focused on the priest's hands. "That's not logical. You read Donatti's papers."

"And suddenly they were clear. The insane ramblings, the disjointed phrases, the seemingly deranged references to out-of-the-way places and times . . . suddenly made sense. Even in his most private papers, Donatti wouldn't spell it out; his fear was too great. . . . Everything was reduced to that train. And whatever was on it."

"You don't know?"

"I came to. I would have learned more quickly, but Brevourt refused to see me. He died several months after I tried to reach him.

"I went to the prison where Gaetamo was held. He spat at me through the wire mesh, clawing his hands over it until they were bleeding. Still, I had the source. Constantine. The Patriarchate. I gained an audience with a priest of the Elders. He was a very old man and he told me. The train from Salonika carried the Filioque denials."

"That was all?"

Monsignor Land smiled. "Theologically speaking, it was enough. To that old man and his counterparts in Rome, the Filioque documents represented triumph and cataclysm."

"They don't represent the same to you?" Victor watched the priest closely, concentrating on the steady hazel eyes.

"No. The church isn't the church of past centuries, even past generations. Simply put, it couldn't survive if it were. There are the old men who cling to what they believe is incontrovertible . . . in most cases it's all they have left; there's no need to strip them of their convictions. Time mandates change gracefully; nothing is as it was. With each year—as the old guard leaves us—the church moves more swiftly into the realm of social responsibility. It has the power to effect extraordinary good, the wherewithal—spiritually and pragmatically—to alleviate enormous suffering. I speak with a certain expertise, for I am part of this movement. We're in every diocese over the globe. It's our future. We are *with* the world now."

Fontine looked away. The priest had finished; he had described a force for good in a sadly lacking world. Victor turned back to Land.

"You don't know precisely, then, what is in those documents from Salonika."

"What does it matter? At the worst, theological debate. Doctrinal equivocation. A man *existed* and his name was Jesus of Nazareth . . . or the Essenian Archangel of Light . . . and he spoke from the heart. His words have come down to us, historically authenticated by the Aramaics and Biblical scholars, Christian and non-Christian alike. What difference does it really make whether he is called carpenter, or prophet, or son of God? What matters is that he spoke the truth as he saw it, as it was *revealed* to him. His sincerity, if you will, is the only issue, and on that there is no debate."

Fontine caught his breath. His mind raced back to Campo di Fiori, to an old monk of Xenope who spoke of a parchment taken out of a Roman prison.

. . . what is contained in that parchment is beyond anything in your imagination . . . it must be found . . . destroyed . . . for nothing has changed yet all is changed. . . .

Destroyed.

. . . what matters is that he spoke the truth as he saw it, as it was

*revealed to him. . . . His sincerity is the only issue, and on that there is
no debate. . . .*

Or was there?

Was this scholar-priest, this good man beside him, prepared to face
what had to be faced? Was it remotely fair to ask him to do so?

For nothing has changed, yet all is changed.

Whatever those contradictory words meant, it would take exceptional
men to know what to do. He would prepare a list for his sons.

The priest named Land was a candidate.

The four massive overhead blades slowed to a stop, sending metallic
thuds throughout the aircraft. An airman opened the hatch and sprang
the lever that swung the short flight of steps out from the undercarriage.
Maj. Andrew Fontine emerged into the morning sunlight and climbed
down the metal stairs onto the helicopter pad at Air Force Base Cobra
in Phan-thiet.

His paper authorized priority transportation and access to the restricted warehouses down at the waterfront. He would commandeer a
jeep from the officers' pool and head directly to the piers. And to a file
cabinet in Warehouse Four. The Eye Corps records were there; and
they would stay there, the safest place in Southeast Asia, once he saw
for himself that nothing was disturbed. He had two more stops to make
after the warehouse: north to Da-nang, then south again, past Saigon
into the Delta. To Can-tho.

Captain Jerome Barstow was in Can-tho. Marty Greene was right; it
was Barstow who had betrayed Eye Corps. The others agreed; his behavior was that of a man who had broken. He had been seen in Saigon
with a legal officer named Tarkington. It wasn't difficult to understand
what had happened: Barstow was preparing a defense, and if that was
so, a defense meant he would testify. Barstow did not know where the
Eye Corps records were, but he had seen them. Seen them, *hell!* He'd
prepared twenty or thirty himself. Barstow's testimony could finish Eye
Corps. They could not allow that.

The legal officer named Tarkington was in Da-nang. He didn't know
it but he was going to meet another man from Eye Corps. It would be
the last person he met. In an alley, with a knife in his stomach, and
whiskey on his shirt and in his mouth.

And then Andrew would fly to the Delta. To the betrayer named
Barstow. Barstow would be shot by a whore; they were easy to buy.

He walked across the hot concrete toward the transit building. A
lieutenant colonel was waiting for him. At first Andrew was alarmed;

had something gone wrong? The five days weren't up! Then he saw that the colonel was smiling, somewhat patronizingly, but nevertheless in friendship.

"Major Fontine?" The greeting was accompanied by an extension of the hand; no salute was expected.

"Yes, sir?" The handshake was brief.

"Washington cable, straight from the secretary of the army. You have to get home, major. As soon as possible. I'm sorry to be the one to tell you, but it concerns your father."

"My *father?* Is he dead?"

"It's only a matter of time. You have priority clearance for any aircraft leaving Tan Son Nhut." The colonel handed him a red-bordered envelope with the imprimatur of General Headquarters, Saigon, across the top. It was the sort of envelope reserved for White House liaisons and couriers from the Joint Chiefs.

"My father's been a sick man for many years," said Fontine slowly. "This isn't unexpected. I have another day's work here. I'll be at Tan Son Nhut tomorrow night."

"Whatever you say. The main thing is we found you. You've got the message."

"I've got the message," said Andrew.

In the phone booth, Adrian listened to the weary voice of the police sergeant. The sergeant was lying; more credible still, someone had lied to him. The pathology report on Nevins, James, Black male, victim of hit-and-run, showed no apparent evidence of cranial, neck, or upper thorax injuries unrelated to the impact of collision.

"Send the report and the X-rays to me," said Adrian curtly. "You've got my address."

"There were no X-rays accompanying the pathology report," replied the police officer mechanically.

"Get them," said Adrian, hanging up the phone.

Lies. Everywhere lies and evasions.

His was the biggest lie of all; he lied to himself, and accepted that lie and used it to convince others. He had stood up in front of a group of very frightened young lawyers from the Justice Department and told them that under the circumstances, the subpoena on Eye Corps should be delayed. They needed to regroup their evidence, obtain a second deposition; to go to the adjutant general with only a list of names was meaningless.

It *wasn't* meaningless! The moment was right to confront the military and demand an immediate investigation. A man was murdered; the evidence he carried with him removed from the scene of his death. That evidence was the indictment of Eye Corps! Here are the names! This is the gist of the deposition!

Now, *move* on it!

But he could not do that. His brother's name was at the top of that list. To serve the subpoena was to charge his brother with murder. There was no other conclusion. Andrew was his brother, his twin, and he was not prepared to call him killer.

Adrian walked out of the phone booth and down the block toward his hotel. Andrew was on his way back from Saigon. He had left the country last Monday; it didn't take a great deal of imagination to know why. His brother wasn't stupid; Andrew was building his defense at the source of his crimes; crimes that included conspiracy, suppression of evidence, and obstruction of justice. Motives: complex and not without fundamental substance, but still crimes.

But no murder at night in a Washington street.

Oh, Christ! Even now he lied to himself! Or to be charitable, he refused to face the possible. Come on! *Say it, think it!*

The probable.

There was an eighth member of Eye Corps in Washington. Whoever that man was, he was Nevins's killer. And Nevins's killer could not have acted without the knowledge given by brother to brother in a boathouse on Long Island's North Shore.

When Andrew's plane landed, he would learn that the subpoena had not been served. Eye Corps was intact for a while longer, free to maneuver and manipulate.

There was one thing that would stop it, though. Stop it instantly and recharge a group of frightened lawyers who wondered if what happened to Nevins could happen to them; they were attorneys, not commandos.

Adrian would look into his brother's eyes, and if he saw Jim Nevins's death in them, he would avenge it. If the soldier had given the order of execution, then the soldier would be destroyed.

Or was he lying to himself again? Could he call his brother killer? Could he *really?*

What the hell did his father want? What difference did it make?

24

The two chairs were placed on opposite sides of the bed. It was proper this way. It could divide his attention between his sons; they were different people, their reactions would be different. Jane preferred to stand. He had asked a terrible thing of her: to tell his sons the story of Salonika. Everything, leaving out nothing. They had to be made to understand that powerful men, institutions, even governments could be moved by the vault from Constantine. As they had been moved three decades before.

He could not tell the story himself. He was dying; his mind was clear enough to know that. He had to have the simple energy to answer their questions; he had to have the strength to give his charge to his sons. For theirs was now the responsibility of the Fontini-Cristis.

They walked into the room with their mother. So tall, so alike, yet so different. One in uniform, the other in a nondescript tweed jacket and flannel trousers. Blond-haired Andrew was angry. It was in his face, the continuous tensing of his jaw muscles, the firm set of his mouth, the neutral, clouded gaze of his eyes.

Adrian, on the other hand, seemed unsure of himself. His blue eyes were questioning, his mouth slack, the lips parted. He drew his hand through his dark hair as he stared down, his expression equal parts of compassion and astonishment.

Victor indicated the chairs. The brothers looked at each other briefly; it was impossible to define the communication. Whatever had happened to alienate them had to be erased. Their responsibility demanded it. They sat down, the Xeroxed pages of his recollections of July 14, 1920, in their hands. He had instructed Jane to give them each a copy; they were to read them through before seeing him. No moments were to be lost on explanations that could be covered beforehand. He hadn't the strength.

"We won't waste words on sentiment. You've heard your mother; you've read what I've written. You'll have questions."

Andrew spoke. "Assuming this vault can be found—and we'll get to that—what then?"

"I'll prepare a list of names. Five or six men, no more; they are not easily arrived at. You'll bring the vault to them."

"What'll they do?" pressed Andrew.

"That will depend on what the vault contains, *specifically*. Release it, destroy it, rebury it."

Adrian interrupted quietly. The lawyer was suddenly disturbed. "Is there a choice? I don't think so. It doesn't belong to us; it should be public knowledge."

"With public chaos? The consequences have to be weighed."

"Does anyone else have the key?" asked the soldier. "The location of this trip on July 14, 1920?"

"No. It would be meaningless. There are only a few left who knew of the train, knew what was *really* on it. Old men from the Patriarchate; one remains in Campo di Fiori and cannot have much time."

"And we're to say nothing to anyone," continued the major. "No one but ourselves is to know."

"No one. There are those who would trade off half the arsenals in this world for the information."

"I wouldn't go that far."

"Then you wouldn't be thinking. I'm sure your mother explained. Besides the Filioque denials, including the Aramaic scroll, in that vault there is a parchment on which is written a confession that could alter religious history. If you think governments, whole nations, are disinterested bystanders, you are grossly mistaken."

Andrew fell silent. Adrian looked at him and then at Victor.

"How long do you figure it'll take? To find this . . . this vault?" he asked.

"I'd estimate a month. You'll need equipment, Alpine guides, a week of instruction—no more, I should think."

Adrian raised the Xeroxed pages several inches. "Can you estimate how large an area there is to cover?"

"It's difficult to say; much will depend on what you find, what has changed. But if my memory serves, no more than five to eight square miles."

"Five to eight! That's out of the question," said Andrew emphatically, but without raising his voice. "I'm sorry, but it's crazy. It could take years. You're talking about the Alps. One hole in the ground, a box no larger than a coffin, anywhere in a dozen mountains."

"The most logical recesses are limited; they are reduced to one of perhaps three or four passes, high above, I suspect, where we were never allowed to climb."

"I've mapped terrain in half a hundred field situations," said the soldier slowly, so courteously his words bordered on condescension. "You're minimizing an unbelievably difficult problem."

"I don't think so. I meant what I just said to Adrian. Much will depend on what you find. Your grandfather was nothing if not meticulous. He considered all aspects of a situation, and most eventualities." Victor stopped and shifted his position on the pillows. "Savarone was an old man; there was a war going on and no one knew it better than he did. He would leave nothing that was recognizable to anyone in Campo di Fiori, but I can't believe he would not leave *something* within the area itself. A sign, a message—something. He was like that."

"Where would we look?" asked Adrian, his eyes straying for an instant to his brother in the leather chair opposite him. The major was staring at the pages in his hand.

"I've written down the possibilities," said Victor. "There was a family of guides in the village of Champoluc. The Goldonis. They were used by my father, his father before him. And there was an inn north of the village. Run for generations by a family named Capomonti. We never traveled to the Champoluc without staying there. These were the people closest to Savarone. If he spoke with anyone, it would be to them."

"That's over fifty years ago," protested Adrian softly.

"Families in the mountains are closely knit. Two generations isn't a particularly wide gap. If Savarone left word it would be passed on from father to eldest child. Remember that: *child*. Son *or* daughter." He smiled weakly at them. "What else occurs to you? Questions may trigger further memories."

The questions began but they triggered nothing. Victor had traced and retraced all he could. Whatever else remained was beyond memory.

Until Jane caught something. And as he listened to her words, Victor smiled. His blue-eyed, English Jane was remarkable for details.

"You wrote that the tracks of the railroad wound through the mountains south of Zermatt and descended into Champoluc, past flagging stops. Clearings between stations for the convenience of climbers and skiers."

"Yes. Before the war. Nowadays, vehicles are more flexible in the snow."

"It seems logical that a train carrying a vault, described to you as heavy and awkward, would find it necessary to stop at one of those clearings. For it to be transferred to another vehicle."

"Agreed. What's your point?"

"Well, there are, or *were,* only so many stops between Zermatt and Champoluc. How many would you say?"

"Quite a few. At least nine or ten."

"That's not much help. I'm sorry."

"North of Champoluc, the first clearing was called Eagle's Peak, I believe. Then Crow's Lookout, and Condor's——" Victor stopped. *Birds.* The *names* of *birds.* A memory had been triggered, but it was not a memory that reached back three decades. It was barely days ago. In Campo di Fiori. "The painting," he said softly.

"What painting?" asked Adrian.

"Beneath the Madonna. In my father's study. A hunting scene, with *birds.*"

"And each clearing on the tracks," said Andrew swiftly, sitting forward in the chair, "is—or was—described in part with the name of a bird. What were the birds in the painting?"

"I don't remember. The light was dim and I was trying to find a few moments to think. I didn't concentrate on that painting."

"Was it your father's?" asked Adrian.

"I'm not sure."

"Can you call?" said the major, his question less a request than an order.

"No. Campo di Fiori is a tomb without lines of communication. Only a postal box in Milan, and that under the name of Baricours, Père et Fils."

"Mother told us an old priest lives there. How does he exist?" The soldier was not satisfied.

"I never thought to ask," replied the father. "There was a man, a driver who picked me up in Milan. I assumed he was the monk's contact with the outside. The old priest and I talked most of the night, but my concerns were limited. He was still my enemy. He understood that."

Andrew looked over at his brother. "We stop at Campo di Fiori," said the soldier curtly.

Adrian nodded and turned back to Victor. "There's no way I can convince you to turn this over to the others? To responsible scholars?"

"No," answered Victor simply. "The scholars will come later. Before then, nothing. Bear in mind what you're dealing with. The contents of that vault are as staggering to the civilized world as anything in history. The confession on that parchment is a devastating weapon, make no mistake about it. No *committee* can be asked to assume the responsibility at this stage. The dangers are too great."

"I see," said Adrian, sitting back in his chair, looking at the pages.

"You mention the name Annaxas, but you're not clear about it. You say the 'father of Annaxas was the engineer on the train,' killed by the priest of Xenope? Who is Annaxas?"

"In the event those papers fell into hands other than yours, I wanted no connections made. Annaxas is Theodore Dakakos."

There was a snap. The soldier was holding a wooden pencil in his hand. He had broken it in half. Father and brother looked at him. Andrew said one word.

"Sorry."

"I've heard the name," continued Adrian. "I'm not sure where."

"He's Greek. A very successful shipper. The priest on that train was his father's brother, his uncle. Brother killed brother. It was ordered by Xenope, the location of the vault buried with them."

"Dakakos knows this?" asked the soldier quietly.

"Yes. Where he precisely fits in, I don't know. I know only that he's looking for answers. And for the vault."

"Can you trust him?" asked the lawyer.

"No. I trust no one where Salonika is concerned." Victor inhaled deeply. It was difficult to talk now; his breath was shorter, his strength going.

"Are you all right?" Jane crossed quickly in front of Adrian to her husband. She leaned over and placed her hand on his cheek.

"Yes," he answered, smiling up at her. And then he looked at Andrew and Adrian, holding each with his eyes.

"I don't ask what I ask of you lightly. You have your own lives, your interests are your own. You have money." Victor raised a hand quickly. "I hasten to add that this, too, was your right. I was given no less, nor should you be. In this respect we are a privileged family. But this privilege extracts responsibilities from those who enjoy it. There must inevitably come periods when you're asked to suspend your own pursuits for an unexpected urgency. I submit to you that such an urgency now exists.

"You've separated. Opponents, I suspect, philosophically and politically. There's nothing wrong with that, but these differences are insignificant compared to what faces you now. You're brothers, the grandsons of Savarone Fontini-Cristi, and you must now do what *his* son can't do. There's no appeal from privilege. Don't look for it."

He was finished. It was all he could say; each breath was painful.

"All these years, you never said——" Adrian's eyes were questioning once again; there was awe and sadness in them. "My God, how you must have felt."

"I had two choices," replied Victor, barely audible. "To be productive or die a neuter. It was not a difficult choice."

"You should have killed them," said the soldier quietly.

They stood outside in the drive in front of the North Shore house. Andrew leaned against the hood of his rented Lincoln Continental, his arms folded across his pressed uniform, the afternoon sun bouncing off the brass buttons and the insignia.

"He's going," he said.

"I know," answered Adrian. "He knows it, too."

"And here we are."

"Here we are," agreed the lawyer.

"What he wants is easier for me than it is for you." Andrew looked up at the windows of the front bedroom on the second floor.

"What does that mean?"

"I'm practical. You're not. We'll do better working together than apart."

"I'm surprised you concede I might help. It must hurt your vanity."

"There's no ego in field decisions. It's the objective that counts." Andrew spoke casually. "We can cut the time in half if we divide the possibilities. His recollections are disjointed, he wanders all over the place. His terrain-recall is confused; I've had some experience in that." Andrew straightened up, away from the car. "I think we'll have to go back, Adrian. Seven years ago. Before San Francisco. Can you do that?"

Adrian stared at his brother. "You're the only one who can answer that. And please don't lie; you were never any good at lying. Not with me."

"Nor you with me."

Their eyes locked; neither wavered.

"A man was killed Wednesday night. In Washington."

"I was in Saigon. You know that. Who was he?"

"A Black lawyer from Justice. A man named——"

"Nevins," completed Andrew, interrupting his brother.

"My God! You *knew!*"

"*About* him, yes. About his being *killed*, no. Why would I?"

"Eye Corps! He took a deposition on Eye Corps! It was with him! It was taken from his car!"

"Are you out of your goddamned mind?" The soldier spoke slowly, without urgency. "You may not like us, but we're not stupid. A target like that man, even remotely linked to us, would bring on the I.G. investigators by the hundreds. There are better ways. Killing's an instrument; you don't use it against yourself."

Adrian continued to look at his brother, searching his eyes. Finally, he spoke. Softly, barely above a whisper. "I think that's the most cold-blooded thing I've ever heard."

"What is?"

" 'Killing's an instrument.' You mean it, don't you?"

"Of course I do. It's the truth. Have I answered your question?"

"Yes," said Adrian quietly. "We'll go back . . . before San Francisco. For a while; you have to know that. Only until this is over."

"Good. . . . You've got things to straighten up before we leave, and so do I. Let's say a week from tomorrow."

"All right. A week from tomorrow."

"I'm catching the six o'clock plane to Washington. Want to come along?"

"No, I'm meeting someone in town. I'll use one of the cars here."

"It's funny," said Andrew, shaking his head slowly, as if what he was about to say wasn't funny at all. "I've never asked for your telephone number, or where you lived."

"It's the District Towers. On Nebraska."

"The District Towers. All right. A week from tomorrow. I'll make the plane reservations. Straight through to Milan. Is your passport current?"

"I think so. It's at the hotel. I'll check."

"Good. I'll call you. A week from tomorrow." Andrew reached for the door handle. "Incidentally, what happened to that subpoena?"

"You know what happened. It wasn't served."

The soldier smiled as he climbed into the car. "It wouldn't have worked anyway."

They sat at a corner table in the St. Moritz sidewalk café on Central Park South. They were partial to such places; they would select pedestrians and invent instant biographies.

They invented none now. Instead, Adrian decided that his father's instructions to tell no one about the train from Salonika would not include Barbara. His decision was based on his belief that were their roles reversed, she would tell him. He wasn't going to leave the country for five to ten weeks without saying why. She deserved better than that.

"So there it is. Religious documents that go back fifteen hundred years, an Aramaic scroll that made the British government go half out of its collective mind in the middle of the war, and a confession written on a parchment two *thousand* years ago that contains God only knows what. That vault's caused more violence than I want to think about. If what my father says is true, those documents, that scroll—the parchment, most of all—could alter a large part of history."

Barbara leaned back in the chair, her brown eyes leveled at him. She watched him without replying for several moments. "That seems highly unlikely. Documents are unearthed every day. History doesn't change," she said simply.

"Have you ever heard of something called the Filioque Clause?"

"Certainly. It was incorporated in the Nicene Creed. It was the first issue that separated the Western and Eastern church. The debate went on for hundreds of years, and led to the Photian schism in . . . the ninth century. I think. Which in turn brought about the schism of 1054. The issue ultimately became papal infallibility."

"How the hell do you know that?"

Barbara laughed. "It's my field. Remember? At least the behavioral aspects."

"You said the ninth century. My father said fifteen hundred years——"

"Early Christian history is confusing, date-happy. From the first to the seventh centuries there were so many councils, so much seesawing back and forth, so much debate over *this* doctrine and *that* law, it's nearly impossible to sort out. Do these documents concern the Filioque? Are they supposed to be the denials?"

Adrian's glass was suspended on the way to his lips. "Yes. That's what my father said; he used the term. The Filioque denials."

"They don't exist."

"What?"

"They were destroyed—ceremonially, I believe—in Istanbul, in the Mosque of Saint Sophia early in the Second World War. There's documentation . . . witnesses, if I remember correctly. Even charred fragments confirmed by spectrochemical analyses."

Adrian stared at her. Something was terribly wrong. It was all too simple. Too negatively simple. "Where did you get that information?"

"Where? You mean *specifically* where?"

"Yes."

Barbara leaned forward, moving her glass absently in thought. Her forehead was creased. "It's not my area, but I can find out, of course. It goes back several years. I *do* remember that it was quite a shock to a lot of people."

"Do me a favor," he said rapidly. "When you get back, find out ev-

erything you can about that fire. It doesn't make sense! My father
would know about it."

"I don't know why. It's awfully academic stuff."

"It still doesn't make sense——"

"Speaking of Boston," she interrupted. "My answering service had
two calls from someone trying to locate you. A man named Dakakos."

"Dakakos?"

"Yes. A Theodore Dakakos. He said it was urgent."

"What did you say?"

"That I'd give you the message. I wrote down the number. I didn't
want to give it to you. You don't need hysterical phone calls from
Washington. You've had a horrid few days."

"He's not from Washington."

"The phone calls were."

Adrian looked up from the table, past the miniature hedges in the
boxes bordering the café. He saw what he was looking for: a telephone
booth.

"I'll be right back."

He walked to the phone and called the District Towers in Washington.

"Front desk, please."

"Yes, Mr. Fontine. We've had several calls from a Mr. Dakakos.
There's an aide to Mr. Dakakos in the lobby now waiting for you."

Adrian thought quickly. His father's words came back to him; he had
asked his father if he could trust Dakakos. *Where Salonika is concerned, I trust no one. . . .*

"Listen to me. Tell the man in the lobby you just heard from me. I
won't be back for several days. I don't want to see this Dakakos."

"Of course, Mr. Fontine."

Adrian hung up. His passport was in Washington. In the room. He'd
go by way of the garage. But not tonight; that was too soon. He'd wait
until tomorrow. He'd stay in New York tonight. . . . His father. His
father should be told about Dakakos. He called the North Shore house.

Jane's voice was strained. "The doctor's with him now. Thank God
he allowed them to give him something. I don't think he could have
stood it much longer. He's had spasms——"

"I'll phone you tonight."

Adrian walked out of the booth and threaded his way between the
strollers back into the café, to the table.

"What *is* it?" Barbara was alarmed.

"Get in touch with your service in Boston. Tell them to call Dakakos and say we missed each other. I had to fly to—hell, Chicago. On business. That was the message for you at the hotel here."

"You really don't want to see him, do you?"

"I've got to avoid him. I want to throw him off the track. He's probably tried to reach my brother."

The path in Rock Creek Park. It was Martin Greene's idea, his selection. Greene had sounded strange on the telephone, somehow defiant. As though he didn't care about anything anymore.

Whatever was gnawing at Greene would vanish in the time it took to tell him the story. My God, would it! In one afternoon, Eye Corps had taken a giant step! Beyond anything they could have imagined. If the things his father said about that vault—the lengths powerful men, entire *governments* went to possess it—if it was all only half true, Eye Corps was in the catbird seat! Unreachable!

His father said he was going to prepare a list. Well, his father didn't have to; there *was* a list. The seven men of Eye Corps would control that vault. And he would control the seven men of Eye Corps.

Christ, it was incredible! But events did not lie; his father did not lie. Whoever possessed those documents, that parchment from a forgotten Roman prison, had the leverage to make extraordinary demands. Everywhere! An omission of recorded history, kept from the world out of unbelievable fear. Its revelation could not be tolerated. Well, fear, too, was an instrument. As great a one as death. Often greater.

Bear in mind that the contents of that vault are as staggering to the civilized world as anything in history. . . .

The decisions of extraordinary men—in peace and in war—supported his father's judgment. And now other extraordinary men, led by one extraordinary man, would find that vault and help shape the last quarter of the twentieth century. One had to begin to think like that, think in large blocks, concepts beyond ordinary men. His training, his heritage: All was coming into focus, and he was ready for the weight of enormous responsibility. He was primed for it; it was his with a vault buried in the Italian Alps.

Adrian would have to be immobilized. Not seriously; his brother was weak, indecisive, no contender at all. It would be enough to slow him down. He would visit his brother's rooms and do just that.

Andrew started down the Rock Creek path. There were very few strollers; the park was not a place for walking at night. Where *was* Greene? He should have been there; his apartment was a lot closer than the airport. And Greene had told him to hurry.

Andrew walked out on the grass and lighted a cigarette. There was no point standing under the spill of the park lamps. He'd see Greene when he came down the path.

"Fontine!"

The soldier turned around, startled. Twenty yards away at the side of a tree trunk stood Martin Greene. He was in civilian clothes; there was a large briefcase in his left hand.

"Marty? What the hell——"

"Get over here," ordered the captain tersely.

Andrew walked rapidly into the cluster of trees. "What's going on?"

"It's gone, Fontine. The whole goddamned thing. I've been calling you since yesterday morning."

"I was in New York. What are you talking about?"

"Five men are in a maximum security jail in Saigon. Want to take a guess who?"

"*What?* The subpoena wasn't served! You confirmed it, *I* confirmed it!"

"Nobody needed a subpoena. The I.G. crawled out of the rocks. They hit us on all points. My guess is that I've got about twelve hours before they figure I'm the one in procurement. You, you're marked."

"Wait a minute. Just wait a minute! This is crazy! The subpoena was canceled!"

"I'm the only one who benefits from that. You never mentioned my name in Saigon, did you?"

"Of course not. Just that we've got a man here."

"That's all they'll need; they'll put it together."

"How?"

"A dozen different ways. Locking in and comparing my checkout times with yours is the first that comes to mind. Something happened over there; something blew everything apart." Greene's eyes strayed.

Andrew breathed steadily, staring down at the captain. "No, it didn't," he said softly. "It happened over here. Last Wednesday night."

Greene's head snapped up. "What *about* Wednesday night?"

"That Black lawyer. Nevins. You had him killed, you stupid son of a bitch. My brother accused me! Accused *us!* He believed me because I believed it myself! It was too stupid!" The soldier's voice was a strained whisper. It was all he could do to keep from lashing out at the man staring up at him.

Greene replied calmly, with assurance. "You're getting the right total but the wrong numbers. I had it done, that's true, and I've got that bastard's briefcase, including the deposition against us. But the contract was so remote the people who did it don't know I exist. To bring you up to date, they were caught this morning. In West Virginia. They've got laundered money that can be traced to a company up for fraud. And we're not it. . . . No, Fontine, it wasn't me. Whatever it was, happened over there. I think you blew it."

Andrew shook his head. "Impossible. I handled——"

"Please. No burdens. I don't want to know, because I don't give a damn anymore. I've got a suitcase at Dulles and a one-way ticket to Tel Aviv. But I'm going to do you one last favor. When everything hit, I called a few friends at I.G., they owed me. That deposition from Barstow we worried so much about wasn't even in the prize money."

"What do you mean?"

"Remember the routine congressional inquiry? The Greek you never heard of——?"

"*Dakakos?*"

"That's right. Theodore Dakakos. Over at I.G. they call it the Dakakos probe. It was him. Nobody knows how, but that Greek was the one who got everything there was to get on Eye Corps. He funneled it piece by piece into the I.G. files."

Theodore Dakakos, thought Andrew. Theodore Annaxas Dakakos, son of a Greek trainman slain thirty years ago in the Milan freight yards by a priest who was his brother. Extraordinary men went to extraordinary lengths to control the vault of Constantine. A calm swept over the soldier.

"Thanks for telling me," he said. Greene held up the briefcase. "By the way, I made a trip to Baltimore."

"The Baltimore records are among the best," said Fontine.

"Where I'm going, we may need some quick firepower in the Negev. These could get it."

"Very possibly."

Greene hesitated, and then asked quietly, "You want to come along? We can hide you. You could do worse."

"I can do better."

"Stop kidding yourself, Fontine! Use some of your well-advertised money and get out of here as fast as you can. Buy sanctuary. You're *finished.*"

"You're wrong. I've just begun."

25

Washington's noonday traffic was slowed further by the June thunderstorm. It was one of the deluges without spells of relief that allowed pedestrians to dash from doorway to awning to doorway. Windshield wipers did little but intrude on the sheets of water that blanketed the glass, distorting all vision.

Adrian sat in the back seat of a taxi, his thoughts divided equally in three parts, on three people. Barbara, Dakakos, and his brother.

Barbara was in Boston, probably in the library archives by now, researching the information—the extraordinary information—about the destructions of the Filioque denials. If those ancient documents had been in the vault from Constantine, and proof of their destruction established beyond doubt . . . had the vault been found? A equals B equals C. Therefore A equals C. Or did it?

Theodore Dakakos, the indefatigable Annaxas, would be scouring the Chicago hotels and law firms looking for him. There was no reason for the Greek not to; a business trip to Chicago was perfectly normal. The distraction was all Adrian needed. He would go up to his rooms, grab his passport, and call Andrew. They could both get out of Washington, avoiding Dakakos. The assumption had to be that Dakakos was trying to stop them. Which meant that somehow Dakakos-Annaxas knew what their father had planned. It was easy enough. An old man returns from Italy, his life expectancy short. And he summons his two sons.

One of those sons was Adrian's third concern. Where was his brother? He had telephoned Andrew's apartment in Virginia repeatedly throughout the night. What bothered Adrian, and the admission wasn't easy for him, was that his brother was more equipped to deal with someone like Dakakos than he. Move and countermove was part of his life, not thesis and antithesis.

"Garage entrance," said the cab driver. "Here it is."

Adrian dashed through the rain into the District Towers's garage. He had to orient himself before walking toward the elevator. As he did so, he reached into his pocket for the key with the plastic tag; he never left it at the front desk.

"Hi, Mr. Fontine. How are ya?"

It was the garage attendant; Adrian vaguely remembered the face. A sallow, twenty-year-old hustler with the eyes of a ferret.

"Hello," replied Adrian, pushing the elevator button.

"Hey, thanks again. I appreciated it, ya know what I mean? I mean it was real nice of you."

"Sure," Adrian said blankly, wishing the elevator would arrive.

"Hey." The attendant winked at him. "You look a lot better'n you did last night. A real broiler, huh?"

"What?"

The attendant smiled. No, it wasn't a smile, it was a leer. "I tied one on, too. Real good. Just like you said."

"What did you say? You saw me last night?"

"Hey, come on. Ya don't remember even? I gotta admit, you was fried, man."

Andrew! Andrew could do it when he wanted to! Slouch, wear a hat, draw out his words. He'd pulled that caricature dozens of times.

"Tell me, I'm a little hazy. What time did I get in?"

"Jee-*sus!* You was flat out. Around eight o'clock, don't you remember? You gimme——" The attendant stopped; the hustler in him prevented full disclosure.

The elevator doors opened. Adrian walked inside. So Andrew had come to see him while he was trying to call *him* in Virginia. Had Andy found out about Dakakos? Had he already left town? Maybe Andy was upstairs now. Again the realization was disquieting, but Adrian felt a certain relief at the prospect. His brother would know what to do.

Adrian walked down the corridor to the door of his suite and let himself in. As he did so, he heard the footsteps behind him. He whipped around and saw an army officer standing in the bedroom door; not Andrew, a colonel.

"Who the hell are you?"

The officer did not immediately reply. Instead, he stood immobile, his eyes angry. When he did speak there was a slight drawl in his cold voice.

"Yeah, you do look like him. Put on a uniform and straighten you up and you could *be* him. Now, all you have to do is tell me where he is."

"How did you get in here? Who the hell let you in?"

"No question for a question. Mine comes first."

"What comes first is that you're trespassing." Adrian walked rapidly to the telephone, crossing in front of the officer. "Unless you've got a warrant from a civilian court, you're going to march into a civilian police station."

The colonel undid one button on his tunic, reached inside, and took out a pistol. He snapped the safety catch and leveled the weapon.

Adrian held the telephone in his left hand, his right poised above the dial. Stunned, he stopped all movement; the expression on the officer's face had not changed.

"You listen to me," said the colonel softly. "I could shoot both your kneecaps off just for looking like him. Can you understand that? I'm a civilized man, a lawyer like you; but where Eye Corps' Major Fontine is concerned, all the rules go out the window. I'll do anything to get that son of a bitch. Do you read me?"

Adrian slowly put down the telephone. "You're a maniac."

"Minor compared to him. Now, you tell me where he is."

"I don't know."

"I don't believe you."

"Wait a minute!" In his shock, Adrian had not been sure of what he'd heard. Now he was. "What do you know about *Eye Corps?*"

"A lot more than you paranoid bastards want me to know. Did you two really think you could pull it off?"

"You're way off base! You'd know that if you knew anything about me! About Eye Corps we're on the same side! Now, for God's sake, what have you got on him?"

The officer replied slowly. "He killed two men. A captain named Barstow, and a legal officer named Tarkington. Both killings were made to look *kai-sai*—whore-and-booze oriented. They weren't. In Tarkington's case it was inconsistent. He didn't drink."

"Oh, Christ!"

"And a file was taken from Tarkington's Saigon office. Which *was* consistent. What they didn't know was that we had a complete copy."

"Who's 'we'?"

"The Inspector General's Office." The colonel did not lower his pistol; his answers were delivered in a flat Southwestern drawl. "Now, I just gave you the benefit of a doubt. You know why I want him, so tell me where he is. My name's Tarkington, too. I drink and I'm not mild-mannered and I want the son of a bitch who killed my brother."

Adrian felt the breath leave his lungs. "I'm sorry——"

"Now you know why this gun is out and why I'll use it. Where did he go? How did he go?"

It took Adrian a moment to focus. "Where? How? I didn't know he *was* gone. Why are you sure he is?"

"Because he knows we're after him. We know he got the word; we made the connection this morning. A captain named Greene in the Pentagon. In procurement. Needless to say, he's gone, too. Probably halfway across the world by now."

. . . *halfway across the world* . . . the words penetrated, the realization began to surface. *Halfway across the world. To Italy. Campo di Fiori. A painting on the wall and the memories of a half a century ago. The vault from Constantine!*

"Did you check the airports?"

"He has a standard military passport. All military. . . ."

"Oh, Jesus!" Adrian started for the bedroom.

"Hold it!" The colonel grabbed his arm.

"Let me go!" Fontine shook off the officer's hand and raced into the bedroom. To the bureau.

He pulled open the right-hand top drawer. From behind the colonel's hand shot out and slammed it, trapping his wrist.

"You pull out anything I don't like, you're dead." The colonel released the drawer.

Fontine could feel the pain and see the swelling on his wrist. He could not think about either. He opened a large leather case. His passport was gone. So, too, his international driver's license and his Banque Genève checkbook with the coded numbers and photograph on the flap.

Adrian turned and walked across the room in silence. He dropped the leather pouch on the bed and continued to the window. The rain outside came down in torrents against the glass.

His brother had stalled him. Andrew had gone after the vault, leaving him behind, wanting no assistance at all, never having wanted it. The vault from Constantine was Andrew's final weapon. In his hands a deadly thing.

The irony was, reflected Adrian, that the army officer behind him in that room could *help*. He could break down bureaucratic barriers, provide instant transportation;—but the army officer could be told nothing about the train from Salonika.

There are those who would trade off half the arsenals in this world for the information. His father's words.

He spoke quietly. "There's your proof, colonel."

"I guess so."

Adrian turned and faced the officer. "Tell me, as one brother to another—how did you lock in on Eye Corps?"

The colonel put away the gun. "A man named Dakakos."

"Dakakos?"

"Yes, he's Greek. You know him?"

"No, I don't."

"The data came in slowly at first. Right into my department, marked for me by name. When Barstow broke and gave his deposition in Saigon, there was Dakakos again. He sent word to my brother to get to Barstow. Eye Corps was covered both over here and over there——"

"By two brothers who could pick up a phone and keep it all together," said Adrian, interrupting. "Without bureaucratic interference."

"We figured that. We don't know why, but this Dakakos was after Eye Corps."

"He certainly was," agreed Adrian, marveling at Dakakos's clarity of method.

"Yesterday, *everything* came in. Dakakos had Fontine followed to Phan-thiet. To a warehouse. We've got Eye Corps' records now, we've got the proof——"

The telephone rang, interrupting the army man. Adrian barely heard it, so total was his concentration on the colonel's words.

It rang again.

"May I?" asked Adrian.

"You'd better." Tarkington's eyes became cold again. "I'll be right next to you."

It was Barbara, calling from Boston. "I'm in the archives. I've got the information on that church fire in forty-one that destroyed the Filioque——"

"Just a minute." Adrian turned his head toward the officer, the phone between them. He wondered if he could sound natural. "You can get on a line in the other room, if you like. It's just some research I asked for."

The ruse worked. Tarkington shrugged and walked to the window.

"Go ahead," he said into the phone.

Barbara spoke as an expert does, scanning a report whose form is familiar; her voice rose and fell as salient points were enumerated. "There was a gathering of elders on January 9, 1941, at eleven o'clock in the evening at the Mosque of Saint Sophia, Istanbul, a ceremony of deliverance. According to the witnesses a consigning of holy property to the heavens . . . sloppy work here; it's all narrative. There should be direct quotes and literal translations. Anyway, it goes on to verify the act and list the laboratories in Istanbul and Athens where fragments of the ash were confirmed for age and materials. There you are, my doubting Thomas."

"What about those witnesses? The narrative?"

"I'm being overly critical. I could be more so; the report should include authorizing credentials and graphic plate numbers, but that's all academic lacework. The main thing is, it's got the archival seal; you don't buy that. You can't play games with it. It means someone beyond reproach was at the scene and confirmed the burning. The Annaxas grant got what it paid for. The seal says it."

"What grant?" he asked quietly.

"Annaxas. It's the company that put up the money for the research."

"Thanks. I'll talk to you later." He hung up. Tarkington was standing by the window, looking out at the rain. This was the man he had to get away from; he had to get to the vault!

Barbara was right in one respect. Dakakos-Annaxas got *exactly* what he paid for: a false report in the archives.

He knew where he had to go.

Campo di Fiori.

Dakakos.

Dakakos, Dakakos, *Dakakos!*

The name burned into Andrew's brain as he watched the coast of Italy go by 30,000 feet below. Theodore Annaxas Dakakos had destroyed Eye Corps for the sole purpose of destroying *him,* eliminating *him* from the search for a vault buried in the mountains. What triggered his decision? How did he do it? It was vital to learn all he could about the man himself. The better one knew his enemy, the better he could fight. As things stood, Dakakos was the only barrier, the only contender.

There was a man in Rome who could help. He was a banker who showed up with increasing frequency in Saigon, a large-scale buyer who bought whole piers, shipped the contents back to Naples and sold the stolen goods throughout Italy. Eye Corps had nailed him and used him; he had provided names that went right back to Washington.

Such a man would know about Dakakos.

The announcement came over the Air Canada loudspeaker. They would begin their descent into Rome's Leonardo da Vinci Airport in fifteen minutes.

Fontine took out his passport. He had bought it in Quebec. Adrian's passport had gotten him through Canadian customs, but he knew it would be worthless after that. Washington would flash the name Fontine to every airport in the hemisphere.

Ironically, he made a connection with several army deserters at two in the morning in Montreal. The exiled moralists needed money; morality could not be proselytized without hard cash. A stringy-haired intellectual in a GI field jacket took him to an apartment that reeked of hash, and for $10,000 he got a passport within an hour.

Adrian was so far behind he'd never catch up.

. . . He could dismiss Adrian. If Dakakos wanted to stop one of them, he obviously wanted to stop both. The Greek was no match for the soldier; he was more than a match for the lawyer. And if Dakakos didn't stop Adrian, the lack of a passport would slow him down more than enough. His brother was out of the picture, no contender at all.

The plane touched ground. Andrew unbuckled his seat belt; he would be among the first out of the aircraft. He was in a hurry to get to a telephone.

The evening crowds on the Via Veneto were heavy, the sidewalk tables under the awnings of the Café de Paris nearly filled. The banker had secured one near the service door, where the traffic was concentrated. He was a gaunt, middle-aged, impeccably dressed man, and he was cautious. No listener could overhear anything said at that table.

Their greeting was perfunctory, the banker obviously anxious to have the meeting over with as quickly as possible.

"I won't ask why you're in Rome. No address, out of your celebrated uniform." The Italian spoke rapidly in a monotone that gave no emphasis to any word and thus emphasis to all. "I honored your demand to make no inquiries. It wasn't necessary. You're a hunted man."

"How do you know that?"

The slender Italian paused, his thin lips stretched into a slight smile. "You just told me."

"I warn you——"

"Oh, stop it. A man flies in unannounced, says he'll meet only in crowds. It's enough to send me to Malta so I won't run into you. Besides, it's all over your face. You're uncomfortable."

The banker was essentially right. He *was* uncomfortable. He would have to adjust better, be more relaxed. "You're clever, but then we knew that in Saigon."

"I never saw you before in my life," replied the Italian, signaling a waiter. *"Due* Campari, *per favore."*

"I don't drink Campari. . . ."

"Then don't. Two Italians who order Campari on the Via Veneto are not conspicuous. Which is precisely what I intend to be. What did you wish to discuss?"

"A man named Dakakos. A Greek."

The banker raised his eyebrows. "If by Dakakos you mean Theo Dakakos, he is indeed Greek."

"You know him?"

"Who in the world of finance doesn't? You have business with Dakakos?"

"Maybe. He's a shipper, isn't he?"

"Among many other interests. He's also quite young and very powerful. Even the colonels in Athens think twice before issuing edicts unfavorable to him. His older competitors are wary of him. What he lacks in experience he makes up for in energy. He's a bull."

"What are his politics?"

The Italian's eyebrows once more rose. "Himself."

"What are his interests in Southeast Asia? Whom does he work for out of Saigon?"

"He doesn't work *for* anyone." The waiter returned with the drinks. "He ships middle-manned supplies to the A.I.D. in Vientiane. Into northern Laos and Cambodia. As you know, it's all intelligence-operated. He pulled out, I understand."

That was it, thought Fontine, pushing away the glass of Campari. Eye Corps had tagged the corruption in AID, and Dakakos had tagged *them.* "He went to a lot of trouble to interfere."

"Did he succeed in interfering? . . . I see he did. Annaxas the Younger usually does succeed; he's perverse and predictable in that department." The Italian raised his glass delicately.

"What was that name?"

"Annaxas. Annaxas the Younger, son of Annaxas the Strong. Sounds Theban, does it not? The Greek bloodlines, however insignificant, are always on the tips of their tongues. Pretentious, I think."

"Does he use it a lot?"

"Not often for himself. His yacht is named *Annaxas,* several planes are *Annaxas—One, Two, Three.* He works the name into a few corporate titles. It's an obsession with him. Theodore Annaxas Dakakos. The first son of a poor family raised by some religious order in the north. The circumstances are cloudy; he doesn't encourage curiosity." The Italian drained his glass.

"That's interesting."

"Have I told you something you didn't know?"

"Maybe," said Fontine casually. "It's not important."

"By which you mean it is." The Italian smiled his thin, bloodless smile. "Dakakos is in Italy, you know."

Fontine concealed his surprise. "Is he really?"

"So you *do* have business with him. Is there anything else?"

"No."

The banker rose and walked rapidly into the crowds of the Via Veneto.

Andrew remained at the table. So Dakakos was in Italy. Andrew wondered where they would meet. He wanted that meeting very much; almost as much as he wanted to find the vault from Salonika.

He wanted to kill Theodore Annaxas Dakakos. The man who had destroyed Eye Corps did not deserve to live.

Andrew got up from the table. He could feel the bulge of papers in his jacket pocket. His father's recollections of half a century ago.

26

Adrian shifted the soft leather suitcase into his left hand and fell behind the surge of passengers in the wide corridor of London's Heathrow Airport. He did not wish to be among the first in the passport line. He wanted to be in the middle group, even the last section; he would have more time to look around, be less conspicuous doing so. He wondered who among the scores of people in the terminal had him in their sights.

Colonel Tarkington was no fool; he'd know within minutes of the application that one Adrian Fontine was at the emigration offices in Rockefeller Center waiting for the issuance of a substitute passport. It was entirely possible that an IG agent had picked him up before he'd left the building. If no one had, he knew it was only a question of time. And because of that certainty, Adrian had flown to London, not Rome.

Tomorrow he would begin the chase, an amateur against professionals. His first step was to disappear, but he wasn't sure how. On the one hand it seemed simple: a single human being among millions; how difficult could it be? Then came second thoughts: one had to travel across national borders—that meant clearly one had to have identification; one had to sleep and eat—that meant shelter and purchases, places that could be watched, alerted.

It wasn't simple at all; not if the single human being in question had no experience. He had no contacts in the underworld; he wouldn't know how to behave if he met them. He doubted that he could approach someone and say the words *"I'll pay for a false passport,"* . . . or *"Get me to Italy illegally,"* . . . or even *"I won't tell you my name but I'll give money for certain services."* Such boldness belonged in fiction. Normal men and women did not do such things; their awkwardness would be laughed at. But professionals—the sort he was up against—were not normal. They did such things quite easily.

He saw the passport lines. There were six in all; he chose the longest. Yet as he walked over to it, he realized that the decision was amateurish. True, he had more time to look around, but conversely, so did others.

"Occupation, sir?" asked the immigration officer.

"I'm a lawyer."

"Here on business?"

"In a manner of speaking. Also pleasure."

"Anticipated length of stay?"

"I'm not sure. No more than a week."

"Do you have hotel accommodations?"

"I didn't make reservations. Probably the Savoy."

The official glanced up; it was difficult to tell whether he was impressed or whether he resented Adrian's tone. Or whether the name Fontine, A. was on a concealed list somewhere in the drawer of his lectern, and he wanted to look at the face.

Regardless, he smiled mechanically, stamped the pages of the newly issued passport, and handed it to Adrian. "Have a pleasant stay in Great Britain, Mr. Fontine."

"Thank you."

The Savoy found him a room above the court, offering to switch him to a suite on the Thames side as soon as one became available. He accepted the offer, saying he expected to remain in England for the better part of the month. He would be traveling around—away from London for much of the time—but would like a suite available during the period of his stay.

What astonished him was the ease with which he lied. It all flowed casually, with a certain businesslike assurance. It wasn't an important maneuver, but the fact that he was able to do it so well gave him a sense of confidence. He had seized an advantage when it was presented; that was the important thing. He had spotted an opportunity and acted on it.

He sat on the bed, airline schedules scattered over the spread. He found what he wanted. An SAS flight from Paris to Stockholm at 10:30 A.M. And an Air Afrique from Paris to Rome. Time: 10:15 A.M. The SAS left from the de Gaulle field, the Air Afrique from Orly.

Fifteen minutes between flights, departure before arrival, from adjacent airfields. He wondered—almost academically now—if he was capable of conceiving a deception, organizing the facts and executing the manipulation from beginning to end.

Odd things would have to be considered. Items that were part of the . . . "dressing," that was the word. Part of the ruse that would draw the proper attention in a crowded, bustling airport. He picked up a Savoy note pad and wrote:

Three suitcases—unusual.
Overcoat—conspicuous.

Glasses.
Hat—wide-brimmed.
Small paste-on beard.

The last item—the beard—caused him to smile uncomfortably, embarrassed at his own imagination. Was he crazy? Who did he think he was? What did he think he was doing? He moved the pencil instinctively to the left of the line, prepared to cross it out. Then he stopped. He wasn't crazy. It was part of the boldness he had to absorb, the unnatural with which he had to be comfortable. He took the pencil away and without thinking wrote the name: "Andrew."

Where was he now? Had his brother reached Italy? Had he traveled halfway around the world without being found? Would he be waiting for him at Campo di Fiori?

And if he *was* waiting, what would they say to each other? He hadn't thought about that; he hadn't wanted to think about it. Like a difficult summation in front of a hostile jury, he could not rehearse the words. He could only marshal the facts in his head and trust his thought processes when the moment came. But what did one say to a twin who was the killer of Eye Corps? What was there *to* say?

. . . *Bear in mind, the contents of that vault are as staggering to the civilized world as anything in history.* . . .

His brother had to be stopped. It was as simple as that.

He looked at his watch. It was one in the morning. He was thankful that he had gotten little sleep during the past several days. It would make sleeping possible now. He had to rest; he had a great deal to do tomorrow. Paris.

He walked up to the desk clerk in the Hôtel Pont Royale and handed him the room key. He hadn't been to the Louvre in five years; it would be a cultural sin to avoid it since it was so close by. The clerk agreed politely, but Adrian saw the shaded curiosity in the man's eyes. It was further confirmation of what Adrian suspected: he was being followed; questions were being asked.

He walked into the bright sunlight on the rue de Bac. He nodded, smiling, at the doorman and shook his head in response to the offer of a taxi.

"I'm going to the Louvre. I'll walk, thanks."

At the curb he lit a cigarette, turning slightly as if to avoid a breeze, and let his eyes wander over to the large windows of the hotel. Inside, through the glass, obscured by the sun's reflection, he could see the clerk talking to a man in a light-brown topcoat. Adrian was not certain, but he was fairly sure he had seen that gabardine coat at the airport two hours ago.

He started east down the rue de Bac, toward the Seine and the Pont Royale bridge.

The Louvre was crowded. Tourists mingled with busloads of students. Adrian climbed the steps past Winged Victory and continued up the staircase to the right, to the second landing, and into the hall of nineteenth-century masters. He fell in with a group of German tourists.

The Germans moved in unison down to the next painting, a Delacroix. Adrian was now in the center of the group. Keeping his head below the level of the tallest German, he turned and looked between the sagging bodies, beyond the impassive faces. He saw what he was both afraid and wanted to see.

The light-brown topcoat.

The man was fifty feet away, pretending to read from a museum pamphlet, relating it to an Ingres in front of him. But he was neither reading nor relating; his eyes kept straying up from the paper to the crowd of Germans.

The group turned the corner into the intersecting corridor. Adrian was against the wall. He parted the bodies in front of him, excusing himself, until he was past the guide and free of the group. He walked swiftly down the right side of the enormous hall and turned left into a dimly lit room. Tiny spotlights shone down from the dark ceiling on a dozen marble statues.

It suddenly occurred to him that if the man in the light-brown gabardine topcoat came into that room, there was no way out.

On the other hand, if the man entered there was no way out for him, either. Adrian wondered which of them had more to lose. He had no answer and so he stood in the shadows at the farthest end of the room, beyond the shafts of light, and waited.

He could see the group of Germans go past the doorway. Seconds later there was the blur of the light-brown topcoat; the man was running, actually running.

Adrian went to the door, paused long enough to see the Germans swing left into yet another intersecting corridor, turned right and walked rapidly toward the hall to the stairs.

The crowds on the staircase were denser than before. There was a contingent of uniformed schoolgirls entering the steps. Behind the girls was the man in the light-brown gabardine topcoat, frustrated in his attempt to pass and reach the steps.

It was suddenly clear to Adrian. The man had lost him and would wait at the exit.

There remained the obvious: reach the main doors first.

Adrian hurried down the steps, doing his best to look unhurried; a man late for a lunch date.

Out on the steps in front of the entrance a taxi was disgorging four Japanese. An elderly couple, obviously British, was walking across the pavement toward the cab. He ran, overtaking the couple, and reached the taxi first.

"*Dépêchez-vous s'il vous plaît. Très important.*"

The driver grinned and started up the car. Adrian turned in the seat and looked out the rear window. On the steps the man in the light-brown topcoat stood looking up and down, confused and angry.

"Orly Airport," ordered Adrian. "Air Afrique."

There were more crowds and more lines but the line he was in was short. And nowhere in sight was the light-brown topcoat. No one seemed interested in him at all.

The Black girl in the Air Afrique uniform smiled at him.

"I'd like a ticket to Rome on your ten fifteen flight tomorrow morning. The name's Llewellyn. That's two *l*'s in front, two in back, with a *y*. First class, please, and if it's possible, I'd like seat location now. I'll be very rushed in the morning, but hold the reservation. I'll pay in cash."

He walked out the automatic doors of the Orly terminal and hailed another taxi.

"De Gaulle field, please. SAS."

The line was longer, the service slower, there was a man staring at him beyond a row of plastic chairs. There'd been no one looking at him like that in Orly terminal. He wondered; he hoped.

"Round trip to Stockholm," he said arrogantly to the SAS attendant behind the counter. "You have a flight tomorrow at ten thirty. That's the one I want."

The attendant looked up from his papers. "I'll see what we have, sir," he replied in muted irritation, his accent heavily Scandinavian. "What would be the return date?"

"I'm not sure, so leave it open. I'm not interested in bargains. The name's Fontine."

Five minutes later the tickets were processed, the payment made.

"Please be here an hour prior to departure, sir," said the clerk, smarting under Adrian's impatience.

"Of course. Now, there's a small problem. I have some valuable, very fragile objects in my luggage. I'd like——"

"We cannot take responsibility for such things," interrupted the attendant.

"Don't be a damn fool. I know you can't. I just want to make sure you have 'Fragile' stickers in Swedish or Norwegian or whatever the hell it is. My bags are easily recognized——"

He left the de Gaulle terminal convinced he'd alienated a very nice fellow who would complain to his colleagues about him, and got into a taxi.

"The Hôtel Pont Royale, please. Rue de Bac."

Adrian saw him at a table in a small sidewalk café on the rue Dumont. He was an American, drinking white wine, and looked like a student who would nurse a drink because of the price. His age was no problem; he seemed tall enough. Adrian walked up to him.

"Hello!"

"Hi," replied the young man.

"May I sit down? Buy you a drink?"

"Hell, why not?"

Adrian sat. "You go to the Sorbonne?"

"Nope. L'École des Beaux Arts. I'm a bona-fide, real-life painter. I'll sketch you for thirty *francs*. How about it?"

"No, thanks. But I'll give you a lot more than that if you'll do something else for me."

The student eyed him suspiciously, distastefully. "I don't smuggle anything for anybody. You'd better beat it. I'm a very legal type."

"I'm more than that. I'm a lawyer. A prosecuting attorney, as a matter of fact. With a card to prove it."

"You don't sound it."

"Just hear me out. What can it cost? Five minutes and some decent wine?"

At nine fifteen in the morning, Adrian emerged from the limousine in front of the glass doors of SAS at de Gaulle terminal. He was dressed in a long, flared Edwardian overcoat of white fabric; he looked like an ass, but he couldn't be missed. On his head he wore a matching white, wide-brimmed fedora, the cloth pulled down over his face in Barrymore style, his features in shadow. Beneath the hat were huge dark glasses that covered far more than his eyes, and below his chin was a blue silk scarf, billowing above and out of the white coat.

The uniformed chauffeur scrambled around to the trunk of the limousine, opened it, and called for skycaps to serve his very important passenger. Three large, white leather suitcases were stacked on a hand rack, to Adrian's complaints that they were being scuffed.

He strode through the electronically parted doors and up to the SAS counter.

"I feel like hell!" he said scathingly, conveying the effects of a hangover, "and I would appreciate as little difficulty as possible. I want my luggage to be loaded last; please keep it behind the counter until the final baggage call. It's done for me all the time. The gentleman yesterday assured me there'd be no trouble."

The clerk behind the counter looked bewildered. Adrian slapped his ticket envelope down.

"Gate forty-two, sir," the clerk said, handing back the envelope. "Boarding time is at ten o'clock."

"I'll wait over there," replied Adrian, indicating the line of plastic chairs inside the SAS area. "I meant what I said about the luggage. Where's the men's room?"

At twenty minutes to ten, a tall, slender man in khaki trousers, cowboy boots, and an American army field jacket came through the doors of the terminal. On his face there was a pronounced chin beard; on his head a wide Australian bush hat. He entered the men's room.

At eighteen minutes to ten, Adrian got out of the plastic chair and walked across the crowded terminal. He pushed the door marked "Hommes" and entered.

Inside a toilet stall they awkwardly manipulated the exchange of clothes.

"This is weird, man. You swear there's nothing in that crazy coat?"

"It's not even old enough to have lint. . . . Here are the tickets, go to gate forty-two. You can throw away the baggage stubs, I don't care. Unless you want the suitcases; they're damned expensive. And clean."

"In Stockholm no one busts me. You guarantee."

"As long as you use your *own* passport and don't say you're me. I gave you my tickets, that's all. You've got my note to prove it. Take my word for it, nobody'll press you. You don't know where I am and there's no warrant. There's nothing."

"You're a nut. But you've paid my tuition for a couple of years, plus some nice living expenses. You're a good nut."

"Let's hope I'm good enough. Hold the mirror for me." Adrian pressed the beard on his chin; it adhered quickly. He studied the results and, satisfied, put on the bush hat, pulling it down on the side of his head. "Okay, let's go. You look fine."

At eleven minutes to ten, a man in a long white coat, matching white hat, blue scarf, and dark glasses strode past the SAS desk toward gate forty-two.

Thirty seconds later a bearded young man—obviously American—in a soiled field jacket, khaki trousers, cowboy boots, and bush hat slipped out the door of the men's room, turned sharply left into the crowds, and headed for the exit door. Out on the pavement he rushed to a waiting taxi, got in and removed the beard.

"The name's Llewellyn!" he shouted to the Air Afrique attendant at the lectern by the departure gate. "I'm sorry I'm late; did I make it?"

The pleasant-faced Black smiled and replied in a French accent. "Just barely, *monsieur*. We've given the last call. Do you have any hand luggage?"

"Not a thing."

At twenty-three minutes past ten, the ten fifteen Air Afrique flight to Rome taxied out toward runway seven. By ten twenty-eight it was airborne. It was only thirteen minutes late.

The man who called himself Llewellyn sat by the window, the bush hat on his left in the adjacent, empty first-class seat. He felt the hardening globules of facial cement on his chin, and he rubbed them in a kind of wonder.

He had done it. Disappeared.

The man in the light-brown topcoat boarded the SAS flight to Stockholm at ten twenty-nine. Departure was delayed. As he walked toward the economy section, he passed the fashionably dressed passenger in the long white overcoat and matching white hat. He thought to himself that the man he followed was a fucking idiot. Who did he think he was, wearing that outfit?

By ten fifty the flight to Stockholm was airborne. It was twenty minutes late, not unusual. The man in the economy section had removed his topcoat and was seated in the forward area of the cabin, diagonally behind the target of his surveillance. When the curtains were parted—as they were now—he could see the subject clearly.

Twelve minutes into the flight the pilot turned off the seat-belt sign. The fashionably dressed subject in the first-class section rose from his aisle seat and removed the long white overcoat and matching white hat.

The man diagonally behind in the economy section bolted forward in his seat, stunned.

"Oh, shit," he muttered.

27

Andrew peered through the windshield at the sign caught in the dull wash of the headlights. It was dawn but pockets of fog were everywhere.

MILANO 5 KM.

He had driven through the night, renting the fastest car he could find in Rome. The journey at night minimized the risk of being followed. Headlights were giveaways on long stretches of dark roads.

But he had not expected to be followed. In Rock Creek Park, Greene said he was marked. What the Jew did not know was that if IG wanted him that quickly, they could have picked him up at the airport. The Pentagon knew exactly where he was; a cable from the secretary of the army had brought him back from Saigon.

So the word to take him had not been given. That it would within days, perhaps hours, was not the issue; of course it would. But he was the son of Victor Fontine. The Pentagon would not be hasty issuing any formal orders for arrest. The army did not bring charges against a Rockefeller or a Kennedy or a Fontine lightly. The Pentagon would insist on flying back the Eye Corps officers for corroborating testimony. The Pentagon would leave nothing to chance or error.

Which meant he had the time to get out. For by the time the army was prepared to move, he would be in the mountains tracing a vault that would change the ground rules as they had never been changed before.

Andrew stepped on the accelerator. He needed sleep. A professional knew when the body hungered for rest in spite of the high-pitched moment, and the eyes became aware of their sockets. He would find a small boardinghouse or country inn and sleep for most of the day. Late in the afternoon he would drive north to Campo di Fiori and find a picture on the wall. The first clue in the search for a vault buried in the mountains.

* * *

He drove by the crumbling stone gates of the entrance without slowing down, and continued for several miles. He allowed two cars to pass him, observing the drivers; they were not interested in him. He turned around and went past the gates a second time. There was no way to tell what was inside; whether there were any security measures—trip alarms or dogs. All he could see was a winding paved road that disappeared into the woods.

The sound of an automobile on that road would be its own alarm. He could not chance that; he had no intention of announcing his arrival at Campo di Fiori. He slowed the car down, and turned into the bordering woods, driving as far off the road as possible.

Five minutes later he approached the gates. By habit he checked for wires and photoelectric cells; there were none, and he passed through the gates and walked down the road cut out of the woods.

He stayed at the edge, concealed by the trees and the overgrowth until he was in sight of the main house. It was as his father had described: more dead than alive.

The windows were dark, no lamps were on inside. There should have been. The house was in shadows. An old man living alone needed light; old men did not trust their eyes. Had the priest died?

Suddenly, out of nowhere, there came the sound of a voice, high-pitched and plaintive. Then footsteps. They came from the road beyond the north bend of the drive; the road he remembered his father describing as leading to the stables. Fontine dropped to the ground, below the level of the grass, and remained motionless. He raised his head by inches; he waited and watched.

The old priest came into view. He was wearing a long black cassock and carried a wicker basket. He spoke out loud, but Andrew could not see who he was talking to. Nor could he understand the words. Then the monk stopped and turned and spoke again.

There was a reply. It was rapid, authoritative, in a language Fontine did not immediately recognize. Then he saw the monk's companion and instantly appraised him as one might an adversary. The man was large, the shoulders wide and heavy, encased in a camel's hair jacket above well-tailored slacks. The last rays of the sun illuminated both men; not well—the light was at their backs—but enough to distinguish the faces.

Andrew concentrated on the younger, powerfully built man walking behind the priest. His face was large, the eyes wide apart, beneath light brows and a tanned forehead that set off short, sun-bleached hair. He was in his middle forties, certainly no more. And the walk: It was that of a deliberate man, capable of moving swiftly, but not anxious for observers to know it. Fontine had commanded such men.

The old monk proceeded toward the marble steps, shifting the small basket to his left arm, his right hand lifting the folds of his habit. He stopped on the top step and turned again to the younger man. His voice was calmer, resigned to the layman's presence or instructions or both. He spoke slowly and Fontine had no trouble now recognizing the language. It was Greek.

As he listened to the priest he reached another, equally obvious conclusion. The powerfully built man was Theodore Annaxas Dakakos. *He is a bull.*

The priest continued across the wide marble porch to the doors; Dakakos climbed the steps and followed. Both men went inside.

Fontine lay in the grass on the border of the drive for several minutes. He had to think. What brought Dakakos to Campo di Fiori? What was here for him?

And as the questions formed, the single answer was apparent. Dakakos, the loner, was the unseen power here. The conversation that had just taken place in the circular drive was not a conversation between strangers.

What had to be established was whether Dakakos had come alone to Campo di Fiori. Or had he brought his own protection, his own firepower? There was no one in the house, no lights in the windows, no sounds from inside. That left the stables.

Andrew scrambled backward in the wet grass until all sightlines from the windows were blocked by the overgrowth. He rose behind a clump of bushes and removed a small Beretta revolver from his pocket. He climbed the embankment above the drive and estimated the angle of the stable road across the knoll. If Dakakos's men were in the stables, it would be a simple matter to eliminate them. Without gunfire; that was essential. The weapon was merely a device; men collapsed under its threat.

Fontine crouched and weaved his way across the knoll toward the stable road. The early evening breezes bent the upper grass and the branches of trees; the professional soldier fell instinctively into the rhythm of their movement. The roofs of the stables came into view and he stepped silently down the incline toward the road.

In front of the stable door was a long steel-gray Maserati, its tires caked with mud. There were no voices, no signs of life; there was only the quiet hum of the surrounding woods. Andrew lowered himself to his knees, picked up a handful of dirt, and threw it twenty yards in the air across the road, hitting the stable windows.

No one emerged. Fontine repeated the action, using more dirt mixed with small pieces of rock. The splattering was louder; there was no way it could go unobserved.

Nothing. No one.

Cautiously, Andrew walked out on the road toward the car. He stopped before he reached it. The surface of the road was hard, but still partially wet from the earlier rain.

The Maserati was headed north; there were no footsteps on the passenger side of the car in front of him. He walked around the automobile; there were distinct imprints on the driver's side: the shoe marks of a man. Dakakos had come alone.

There was no time to waste now. There was a picture on a wall to be taken, and a journey to Champoluc that had to begin. Too, there was a fine irony in finding Dakakos at Campo di Fiori. The informer's life would end where his obsession had begun. Eye Corps was owed that much.

He could see lights inside the house now, but only in the windows to the left of the main entrance. Andrew kept to the wall, ducking under the ledges, until he was at the side of the window where the light was brightest. He inched his face to the frame and looked inside.

The room was huge. There were couches and chairs and a fireplace. Two lamps were lit; one by the far couch, the second nearer, to the right of an armchair. Dakakos was standing by the mantel, gesturing in slow, deliberate movements with his hands. The priest was in the chair, his back to Fontine, and barely visible. Their conversation was muted, indistinguishable. It was impossible to determine whether the Greek had a weapon; the assumption had to be that he did.

Andrew pried a brick loose from the border of the drive and returned to the window. He rose, the Beretta in his right hand, the brick gripped in his left. Dakakos approached the priest in the chair; the Greek was pleading, or explaining, his concentration absolute.

The moment was now.

Shielding his eyes with the gun, Fontine extended his left arm behind him, then arced it forward, hurling the brick into the center of the window, shattering glass and wood strips everywhere. On impact he smashed the remaining, obstructing glass with the Beretta, thrusting the weapon through the space, and screamed at the top of his voice.

"You move one inch, you're dead!"

Dakakos froze. *"You?"* he whispered. "You were *taken!*"

* * *

The Greek's head slumped forward, the gashes from the pistol barrel on his face deep, ugly, and bleeding profusely. There was nothing that so became this man as a painful death, thought Fontine.

"In the name of God have *mercy!*" screamed the priest from the opposite chair, where he sat bound and helpless.

"Shut up!" roared the soldier, his eyes on Dakakos. "Why did you do it? Why are you here?"

The Greek stared, his breathing erratic, his eyes swollen. "They said you were taken. They had everything they needed." He could barely be heard, speaking as much to himself as to the man above him.

"They made a mistake," said Andrew. "Their signals got crossed. You didn't expect them to wire you their apologies, did you? What did they tell you? That they were picking me up?"

Dakakos remained silent, blinking from the rivulets of blood that rolled down his forehead into his eyes. Fontine could hear the Pentagon commanders. *Never admit. Never explain. Take the objective, the rest is no strain.*

"Forget it," he said quietly, icily to Dakakos. "Just tell me why you're here."

The Greek's eyes swam in his head; his lips moved. "You are *filth*. And we'll *stop you!*"

"Who's we?"

Dakakos arched his neck, thrusting it forward, and spat into the soldier's face. Fontine swung the barrel of the pistol up into the Greek's jaw. The head slumped forward.

"*Stop!*" cried the monk. "I'll tell you. There's a priest named Land. Dakakos and Land work together."

"Who?" Fontine turned abruptly to the monk.

"It's all I know. The name! They've been in contact for years."

"Who is he? *What* is he?"

"I don't know. Dakakos doesn't say."

"Is he waiting for him? Is this priest coming here?"

The monk's expression suddenly changed. His eyelids quivered, his lips trembled.

Andrew understood. Dakakos was waiting for someone, but not a priest named Land. Fontine raised the barrel of the pistol and shoved it into the mouth of the semiconscious Greek. "All right, Father, you've two seconds to tell me who it is. Who's this son of a bitch waiting for?"

"The other one. . . ."

"The other *what?*"

The old monk stared at him. Fontine felt a hard emptiness in his stomach. He removed the pistol.

Adrian.

Adrian was on his way to Campo di Fiori! His brother had broken away and sold out to Dakakos!

The *picture!* He had to make sure the picture was there! He turned, looking for the door of the. . . .

When the blow came it was paralyzing. Dakakos had snapped the lamp cord binding his wrists and lunged forward, his fist pummeling into Andrew's kidney, his other hand wrapped around the Beretta's barrel, twisting Fontine's forearm until he thought his elbow would crack.

Andrew countered by falling sideways, rolling with the force of Dakakos's lunge. The Greek sprang on top of him, crushing him like some elephantine hammer. He smashed Fontine's knuckles against the floor until the gun exploded, the bullet embedding itself in the wooden arch of the doorway. Andrew brought his knee up, pounding the base of Dakakos's groin, crushing the Greek's testicles until he arched his back, grimacing in torment.

Fontine rolled again, freeing his left hand, clawing the bleeding face above, tearing at the hanging flesh. Still, Dakakos would not retreat, would not let up; he slammed his forearms into Andrew's throat.

It was the instant! Andrew arched forward, sinking his teeth into the flesh of Dakakos's arm, biting deeply, as a mad dog would bite, feeling the warm blood flowing into his throat. The Greek pulled his arm up—his hand away—and it was the space Fontine needed. He crashed his knee up once again in Dakakos's groin, and slid his whole body under the giant; as he did so he shot his left hand into the well of Dakakos's armpit, and pressed the nerve with all the force he could summon.

The Greek raised his right side in agony. Andrew rolled to his left, kicking the heavy body away, pulling his arm free.

With the speed born of a hundred fire fights, Fontine was on his haunches, the Beretta leveled, spitting bullets into the exposed chest of the informer who had come too close to killing him.

Dakakos was dead. Annaxas was no more.

Andrew rose unsteadily; he was covered with blood, his whole body wracked. He looked at the priest of Xenope in the chair. The old man's eyes were closed, his lips moving in silent prayer.

There was one shell left in the Beretta. Andrew raised the gun and fired.

28

Stunned, Adrian took the cablegram held out for him by the desk clerk. He walked toward the front entrance of the hotel, stopped, and opened it.

> Mr. Adrian Fontine
> Excelsior Hotel
> Rome, Italy
> My dear Fontine:
>   It is urgent we confer, for you must not act alone. You must trust me. You have nothing to fear from me. I understand your anxieties, consequently there will be no intermediaries, none of my people will intercept you. I will wait for you alone and alone we can make our decisions. Check your source.
>
> > Theo Dakakos

Dakakos had traced him! The Greek expected to *meet*. But where? How?

Adrian knew that once he passed through customs in Rome, there was no way he could stop those looking for him from knowing he'd come to Italy; it was the reason for the next step in his strategy. But that Dakakos would openly contact him seemed extraordinary. It was as though Dakakos assumed they were working *together*. Yet it was Dakakos who had gone after Andrew; gone after his brother relentlessly, ingeniously, wrapping up Eye Corps in a seditious ribbon that had eluded the combined efforts of the inspector general and the Justice Department.

The sons of Victor Fontine—the grandsons of Savarone Fontini-Cristi —were after the vault. Why would Dakakos stop one and not the other?

The answer had to be that he was trying to do just that. Carrots held out in front of the donkey's nose; offers of safety and trust that were translated to mean *control, confinement.*

   . . . I will wait for you alone and alone we can make our decisions. Check your source. . . .

Was Dakakos on his way to Campo di Fiori? How was that possible?

And what was the *source?* An IG colonel named Tarkington with whom Dakakos had set up lines of communication to trap Eye Corps? What other source did he and Dakakos have in common?

"Signor Fontine?" It was the Excelsior manager; the door to his office was open behind him. He had come out quickly.

"Yes?"

"I tried your room, of course. You were not there." The man smiled nervously.

"Right," said Adrian. "I'm here. What is it?"

"Our guests are always our first consideration." The Italian smiled again. It was maddening.

"Please. I'm in a hurry."

"A few moments ago we had a call from the American embassy. They say they are calling all the hotels in Rome. They are looking for you."

"What did you say?"

"Our guests are always——"

"What did you *say?*"

"That you had checked out. You *have* checked out, *signore.* However, if you wish to use my telephone. . . ."

"No, thank you," said Adrian, starting toward the entrance. Then stopped and turned to the manager. "Call the embassy back. Tell them where I've gone. The front desk knows."

It was the second part of his strategy in Rome, and when he conceived it, he realized it was merely an extension of what he had done in Paris. Before the day was over the professionals who followed him would know exactly where he was. Computers and passport entries and international cooperation made for swift relays of information. He had to make them all think he was going somewhere that he wasn't.

Rome was the best place to start. Had he flown to Milan, the IG men would dig into their files; Campo di Fiori would appear. He could not allow that.

He had asked the front desk of the Excelsior to draw up a route for a drive south. To Naples, Salerno, and Policastro, along roads that would take him east through Calabria to the Adriatic. He had rented a car at the airport.

Now Theodore Dakakos had joined the hunt. Dakakos, whose relays of information were faster than those of United States Army Intelligence, and far more dangerous. Adrian knew what the United States Army wanted: the killer for Eye Corps. But Dakakos wanted the vault from Constantine. It was a greater prize.

Adrian drove through Rome's melodramatic traffic back to Leonardo da Vinci Airport. He returned the rented car and bought a ticket on Itavia Airlines for Milan. He stood in line at the departure gate, his head down, his body slouched, seeking the protective cover of the crowd. As he was jostled forward—and for reasons he didn't know—the words of an extraordinary lawyer came back to him.

You can run with the pack, in the middle of the pack, but if you want to do something, get to the edges and peel away. Darrow.

In Milan he would call his father. He'd lie about Andrew; he'd invent *something,* he couldn't think about that now. But he had to know more about Theodore Dakakos.

Dakakos was closing in.

He sat on his bed in Milan's Hotel di Piemonte as he'd sat on the bed at the Savoy in London, staring at papers in front of him. But these were not airline schedules, they were the Xeroxed pages of his father's recollection of fifty years ago. He was rereading them—not for any new information; he knew the contents—but because the reading postponed the moment when he would pick up the phone. He wondered how thoroughly his brother had studied these pages, with their rambling descriptions and hesitant, often obscure reflections. Andrew would probably pore over them with the scrutiny of a soldier in combat. There were names. Goldoni, Capomonti, Lefrac. Men who had to be reached.

Adrian knew he could not procrastinate any longer. He folded the pages, put them in his jacket pocket, and reached for the telephone.

Ten minutes later the switchboard called him back; the phone 5,000 miles away in the North Shore house was ringing. His mother answered and when she said the words, she did so simply, without the trappings of grief, for they were extraneous, the grief private.

"Your father died last night."

Neither spoke for several moments. The silence conveyed a sense of love. As though they were touching.

"I'll come home right away," he said.

"No, don't do that. He wouldn't want you to. You know what you have to do."

Again there was silence. "Yes," he said finally.

"Adrian?"

"Yes?"

"I have two things to tell you, but I don't want to discuss them. Can you understand that?"

Adrian paused. "I think so."

"An army officer came to see us. A Colonel Tarkington. He was kind enough to speak only with me. I know about Andrew."

"I'm sorry."

"Bring him back. He needs help. All the help we can give him."

"I'll try."

"It's so easy to look back and say 'Yes, I see now. I realize.' He always saw the results of strength; he never understood its complications, its essential compassion, I think."

"Let's not discuss it," reminded the son.

"Yes. I don't want to discuss——. Oh, God, I'm so *frightened!*"

"*Please,* mother."

Jane breathed deeply, the sound carried over the wire. "There's something else. Dakakos was here. He spoke to your father. To both of us together. You must trust him. Your father wished it; he was convinced of it. So am I."

. . . *Check your source.* . . .

"He sent me a cable. He said he'd be waiting for me."

"At Campo di Fiori," completed Jane.

"What did he say about Andrew?"

"That he thought your brother might be delayed. He didn't elaborate; he talked only about you. He used your name repeatedly."

"You're sure you don't want me to come home?"

"No. There's nothing you can do here. He wouldn't want it." She paused for a moment. "Adrian, tell your brother his father never knew. He died thinking both his Geminis were the men he believed them to be."

"I'll tell him. I'll call again soon."

They said quiet good-byes.

His father was dead. The source was gone, and the void was terrible. He sat by the telephone, aware that perspiration had formed on his forehead, though the room was cool. He got up from the bed; there were things to do and he had to move quickly. Dakakos was on his way to Campo di Fiori. So was the killer of Eye Corps, and Dakakos did not know that.

So he sat down at the desk and began writing. He might have been back in his Boston apartment, jotting down items in preparation for the next day's cross-examination.

But in this case it was not the next day. It was tonight. And very few items came to mind.

* * *

He stopped the car at the fork in the road, picked up the map, and held it under the dashboard light. The fork was detailed on the map. There were no other roads until the town of Laveno. His father had said there were large stone gateposts on the left; they were the entrance to Campo di Fiori.

He started the car up, straining his eyes in the darkness, waiting to catch a glimpse of erected stone in the wall of forest on his left. Four miles up the road he found them. He stopped the car opposite the huge, crumbling stone pillars and aimed his flashlight out the window. There was the winding road beyond as his father had described it, angling sharply, disappearing into the woods.

He swung the automobile to the left and drove through the gates. His mouth was suddenly dry, his heart accelerated, its beat echoing in his throat. It was the fear of the immediate unknown that gripped him. He wanted to face it quickly, before the fear controlled him. He drove faster.

There were no lights anywhere.

The enormous white house stood in eerie stillness, a deathlike splendor in the darkness. Adrian parked the car on the left side of the circle, opposite the marble steps, shut off the motor and, reluctantly, the headlights. He got out, took the flashlight from his raincoat pocket, and started across the rutted pavement toward the stairs.

Dull moonlight briefly illuminated the macabre setting and then disappeared. The sky was overcast but no rain would come; the clouds were everywhere above, but thin and traveling too fast. The air was dry; everything was still.

Adrian reached the bottom step and switched on his flashlight to look at his watch. It was eleven thirty. Dakakos was not there. Nor his brother. Either or both would have heard the car; neither nor both would be asleep at this hour. That left the old priest. An old man in the country would have gone to bed by now. He called out.

"Hello in there! My name is Adrian Fontine and I'd like to talk to you!"

Nothing.

And not nothing! There was movement. A pattering, a series of scratches accompanied by tiny, indistinguishable screeches. He swung the flashlight to the source. In its beam was caught the blurred, rushing figures of rats—three, four, five—scampering over the ledge of an open window.

He held the flashlight steady. The window was smashed; he could see jagged edges of glass. He approached it slowly, suddenly afraid.

His feet sank into the earth; his shoes crunched broken glass. He stood in front of the window and raised the flashlight.

He lost his breath in an involuntary gasp as two pairs of animals' eyes were suddenly caught in the blinding shaft. They darted up, startled yet furious, and a terrible muted screeching was heard as the creatures fled into the darkness of another part of the house. There was a crash. A crazed, frightened animal had collided with an unstable object of china or glass.

Adrian breathed again, then shuddered. His nostrils were filled with an overpowering stench, a putrid, rotting aroma that caused his eyes to water and his throat to swell and choke. He held his breath and he climbed over the window ledge. He pressed his open left hand against his mouth and his nose, filtering the foul stench; he cast the beam of the flashlight over the enormous room.

The shock of it staggered him. The figures of two dead men, one in torn robes strapped to a chair, the other half-naked on the floor, were hideous. The clothes were torn by animal teeth, flesh ripped out by animal jaws, dried blood made moist by animal urine and saliva.

Adrian reeled. Vomit spewed out of his mouth. He lurched to his left; the light caught a doorway and he lunged into it gasping for breath, for air that could be swallowed.

He was in the study of Savarone Fontini-Cristi, a man he never knew, but now hated with all the hatred of which he was capable. The grandfather who had triggered a chain of killing and suspicion that in itself brought more death and greater hatred.

Over *what? For* what?

"Goddamnnn youuu! . . ."

He screamed uncontrollably; he gripped the high back of an old chair and threw it crashing to the floor.

Suddenly, in silence and in full knowledge of what he had to do, Adrian stood immobile and aimed the flashlight on the wall behind the desk. To the right, he remembered, beneath a painting of the Madonna.

The frame was there, the glass shattered.

And the painting was gone.

He sank to his knees, trembling. Tears welled his eyes and he sobbed uncontrollably.

"Oh, *God,*" he whispered, the pain unbearable. "Oh, my brother!"

PART
THREE

29

Andrew pulled the Land Rover off to the side of the Alpine road and poured steaming hot coffee into the lid of the thermos. He had made good time; according to the Michelin map he was ten miles from the village of Champoluc. It was morning; the rays of the early sun shot up from behind the surrounding mountains. In a little while he would drive into Champoluc and buy the equipment he needed.

Adrian was far behind. Andrew knew he could slow down for a while, think things out. Besides, his brother was walking into a situation that would paralyze him. Adrian would find the bodies at Campo di Fiori and panic; his thoughts would be confused, indecisive. He wouldn't know what to do next. His brother wasn't trained to confront death from violence; it was too far removed from him. It was different for soldiers: It was different for him. The physical confrontation—even the bloodshed—primed his senses, infused him with an intense feeling of exhilaration. His energies were peaked, he was confident, sure of his movements.

The vault was as good as his. Now was the time to concentrate. Study each word, each clue. He took his father's Xeroxed pages and held them up, catching the morning light through the windshield.

. . . In the village of Champoluc was the family Goldoni. According to current Zermatt records, they exist still and are scattered throughout the area. The present head of the family is one Alfredo Goldoni. He resides in the house of his father—and father before him—on several acres of land at the base of the mountains in the west outskirts. For generations, the Goldonis have been the most experienced guides in the Italian Alps. Savarone employed them frequently, and beyond this, they were "northern friends"—a phrase my father used to distinguish men of the land from those in the marketplace. His trust was placed in the former far more quickly than in the latter. It is possible that he left information with Alfredo Goldoni's father. With his death, arrangements would be made to pass this information on to the surviving eldest child—whether man or woman—as is the Italian-Swiss custom. Therefore, should Alfredo not be the eldest, look for an older sister.

North, into the mountains—between the railroad clearings Krahen

Aüsblick and Greier Gipfel, I believe—is a small inn run by the family Capomonti. Again, according to Zermatt (I made no inquiries in the Champoluc district to avoid raising suspicion) the inn, too, still exists. I gather it has been somewhat expanded. It is currently under the management of Naton Lefrac, a descendent by marriage of the Capomontis. I remember this man. He was not a man then, of course, for he was one or two years younger than I, the son of a merchant who dealt with the Capomontis. We became quite good friends. I recall clearly that he was much beloved of the Capomontis and the hope was that he would marry a daughter of the house. Obviously he did so.

As children—and young men—we never went into the Champoluc without staying at Locanda Capomonti. I have recollections of warm welcomes and laughter and roaring fireplaces and much comfort. The family was simple—in the uncomplicated sense—and extremely outgoing and sincere. Savarone was particularly taken with them. If there were secrets to leave in the Champoluc, old Capomonti would have been a rock of silence and trust. . . .

Andrew put down the pages and picked up the Michelin road map. Once again he traced the minute markings of the Zermatt railroad, his concern returning. Of the many clearings his father recalled, only four remained. And none bore the name of *hawk*.

For the hunting picture in the study at Campo di Fiori was not as his father remembered; it did not show birds being flushed from bushes. Instead, there were hunters in overgrown fields, their eyes and weapons leveled forward as hawks flew lazily above in the distant sky; an artist's comment on the futility of the hunt.

His father said that the clearings were called Eagle's Peak, Condor's Lookout, and Crow's Summit. There had to be a clearing with the name hawk in it. But if there had been, it no longer existed. And a half century had gone by; obscure railroad clearings below Alpine passes scores of miles apart were not landmarks. Who recalled the precise location of a trolley stop thirty years after the tracks were covered with asphalt? He put down the map and picked up the Xeroxed pages again. The initial key was somewhere in these words.

We stopped in the center of the village for a late lunch, or afternoon tea, I cannot remember which—and Savarone left the restaurant to check the telegraph office for messages—I do remember that. When he returned he was very upset, and I feared our trip to the mountains would be canceled before it began. However, during the meal another message was delivered and Savarone was both placated and relieved.

There was no more talk of returning to Campo di Fiori. The dreadful moment had passed for an anxious seventeen-year-old.

From the restaurant we dropped by the shop of a merchant whose name was German in sound and spelling, not Italian or French. My father was prone to order supplies and equipment from this man because he felt sorry for him. He was a Jew and for Savarone, who fought bitterly against the czarist pogroms and dealt on a handshake with the Rothschilds, such thinking was indefensible. There is a blurred memory of an unpleasant incident at the store that evening. What the unpleasant incident specifically entailed, I have no recall, but it was most serious and provoked my father to quiet but definite anger. A sad anger if, again, memory serves. I seem to have the vague impression that details were withheld from me, but now, so many years later, it is only an impression and could well be false.

We left the merchant's shop and proceeded by horsecart to the Goldoni farm. I remember showing off my Alpine pack with its straps and hammer and cleats and forged double-clamps for the ropes. I was terribly proud of it, believing it signified manhood. Again there is a dim impression that while at the Goldonis' an undercurrent of distress was prevalent, but not obvious. I cannot tell you why this feeling remains after so many years, but I relate it to the fact that I had difficulty holding the attention of the male Goldonis while exhibiting my new pack. The father, an uncle or two, and certainly the older sons seemed distracted. Arrangements were made with one of the Goldoni sons to meet us the next day and take us into the mountains. We stayed at the Goldonis for several hours before leaving to resume our journey by cart to the Locando Capomonti. I do recall it was dark when we left, and, as it was summer, the hour had to be past 7:30 or 8:00.

What were the facts, thought Andrew. Man and boy arrived at the village, had something to eat, bought supplies from a disliked Jew, went to the house of the guides they were hiring, and a spoiled child was insulted because not enough attention was paid to his mountain-climbing equipment. The relevant information was reduced to the name Goldoni.

Andrew finished the coffee and screwed the lid back on the thermos. The sun was higher now; it was time to move. Exhilaration filled him. All the years of training and experience and decisions in the field had prepared him for the next few days. There was a vault in the mountains and he would find it!

Eye Corps would be paid in full.

The soldier turned the ignition and gunned the motor. He had cloth-

ing and equipment and weapons to buy. And a man named Goldoni to
see. Perhaps a woman named Goldoni; he'd know shortly.

Adrian sat in the darkness behind the wheel of the stationary car and
wiped his mouth with his handkerchief. He could not erase the taste of
sickness in his throat any more than he could erase the sight of the ravaged bodies inside the house from his mind's eye. Or the stench of death
from his nostrils.

Sweat rolled down his face, produced by tension he had never
known, a fear he had never experienced.

He felt the need to vomit returning; he suppressed it by inhaling rapidly. He had to find some semblance of sanity, he had to function. He
could not remain in darkness, in an immobile car for the rest of the
night. He had to pass through the shock and find his mind again. It was
all he had left: the ability to think.

Instinctively, he pulled the pages of his father's memories from his
pocket and switched on the flashlight. Words had come to be his refuge;
he was an analyst of words—their shadings, their subtle interpretations,
their simplicity and complexity. He was an expert with words, as much
an expert as his brother was with death.

Adrian separated the pages, reading slowly, meticulously. Child and
man had come to the village of Champoluc; there were immediate impressions of discord, perhaps more than discord. *When he returned he
was very upset . . . I feared for our trip.* There was the shop of a Jew,
and anger. *What the unpleasant incident specifically entailed, I have no
recall . . . it was most serious and provoked my father.* And sadness. *A
sad anger if, again, memory serves.* Then the anger and the sadness
faded away, replaced by vague feelings of distress and embarrassment;
the child was not heeded by those whose attentions he sought. *The father, an uncle or two, and certainly the older sons were distracted.*
Their attentions were elsewhere—on the anger, the discord? The
sadness? And these obscure recollections were in turn displaced by
memories of warmth, and an inn north of the village, *a warm welcome,
which was like a dozen other similar welcomes.* This peaceful interlude
was followed a short while later once again by vague feelings of distress
and concern.

*At the Capomonti inn there is little I can recall specifically except a
warm welcome, which was like a dozen other similar welcomes. One
thing I do remember was that for the first time in the mountains I had
my own room, no younger brothers sharing it with me. It was a
significant departure and I felt quite grown up. There was another meal,*

and my father and old Capomonti drank a good deal of whiskey after-
ward. I recall this because I went to bed, thinking of the next day's
climbing, and later heard loud, belligerent voices below, and wondered
if the noise might wake the other guests. It was a small inn then and
there were perhaps three or four others registered. This concern was un-
usual for I had never seen my father drunk. I do not know to this day if
he was, but the noise was considerable. To a young man on his seven-
teenth birthday, about to be given the present of his life—a real climb in
the Champoluc—the thoughts of a weakened, angry father in the morn-
ing were disturbing.

It was not the case, however. The Goldoni guide arrived with our
supplies, shared breakfast with us, and we departed.

A Capomonti son—or it might have been young Lefrac—drove the
three of us several miles north in the horsecart. We bade him good-bye
and it was agreed he would meet us at the same place late in the after-
noon on the following day. Two days in the mountains and an overnight
camp with adults! I was overjoyed for I knew we would make camp at a
higher altitude than was ever possible with younger brothers in tow.

Adrian put down the pages on the seat of the car. The remaining
paragraphs described sketchily remembered hills and trails and views
that seemed to overlap. The journey into the mountains had begun.

Specific information might well lie in these rambling descriptions.
Isolated landmarks might be revealed, and a pattern emerge; but which
landmarks, which patterns?

Oh, God! The painting on the wall. Andrew had the painting!

Adrian suppressed his sudden alarm. The painting from Savarone's
study might narrow down the location of a clearing, but what then?
Fifty years had passed. A half century of ice and water and summer
thaws and natural growth and erosion.

The painting on the wall might well be one clue, perhaps the most
important. But Adrian had the feeling that there were others as vital as
that painting. They were contained in the words of his father's testament. Memories that survived fifty years of extraordinary living.

Something had happened fifty years ago that had nothing to do with a
father and son going into the mountains.

He had found part of his mind again. He was exercising his ability to
think. The shock and the horror were still there, but he was passing
through to the beginnings of sanity.

. . . Bear in mind, the contents of that vault are as staggering to the
civilized world as anything in history. . . .

He had to reach it, find it. He had to stop the killer from Eye Corps.

30

Andrew parked the Land Rover by a fence bordering a field. The Goldoni farmhouse was two hundred yards down the road, on the left; the field was part of the Goldoni property. There was a man driving the tractor along rows of upturned earth, his living body turned in the seat, watching the progress behind him. There were no other houses in the area, no other people in sight. Andrew decided to stop and speak to the man.

It was shortly past five in the afternoon. He had spent the day wandering about Champoluc, buying clothes, supplies, and climbing equipment, including the finest Alpine pack available, filled with those items recommended for the mountains, and one that was not. A Magnum .357-caliber pistol. He had made these purchases at the much-expanded shop referred to in his father's recollections. The name was Leinkraus; it had a mezuzah on the doorframe of the front entrance. The clerk behind the counter allowed that Leinkraus had been selling the finest equipment in the Italian Alps since 1913. There were now branches in Gstaad and Lake Lucerne.

Andrew got out of the Land Rover and walked to the fence, waving his hand back and forth to get the attention of the man on the tractor. He was a short, stocky Italian-Swiss, ruffled brown hair above the dark eyebrows, and the rugged, sharp features of a northern Mediterranean. He was at least ten years older than Fontine; his expression was cautious, as if he were not used to unfamiliar faces.

"Do you speak English?" Andrew asked.

"Passably, *signore,*" said the man.

"I'm looking for Alfredo Goldoni. I was directed out here."

"You were directed correctly," replied the Italian-Swiss in more than passable English. "Goldoni is my uncle. I tend his land for him. He can't work for himself." The man stopped, offering no further clarification.

"Where can I find him?"

"Where he always is. In the back room of his house. My aunt will show you to him. He likes visitors."

"Thank you." Andrew turned toward the Land Rover.

"You're American?" asked the man.

"No. Canadian," he replied, extending his cover for any of a dozen immediate possibilities. He climbed into the vehicle and looked at the man through the open window. "We sound the same."

"You look the same, dress the same," countered the farmhand quietly, eyeing the fur-lined Alpine jacket. "The clothes are new," he added.

"Your English isn't," said Fontine. He turned the ignition.

Goldoni's wife was gaunt and ascetic-looking. Her straight gray hair was pulled back, the taut bun a crown of self-denial. She ushered the visitor through the several neat, sparsely furnished rooms to a doorway at the rear of the house. There was no door attached; where once there'd been a sill in the frame, it had been removed, the floor leveled. Fontine walked through; he entered the bedroom. Alfredo Goldoni sat in a wheelchair by a window overlooking the fields at the base of the mountains.

He had no legs. The stubs of his once-massive limbs were encased in the folds of his trousers, the cloth held together by safety pins. The rest of his body, like his face, was large and awkward. Age and mutilation had extracted their price.

Old Goldoni greeted him with false energy. A tired cripple afraid of offending a newcomer, grateful for the all-too-infrequent interruption.

The introductions over, the directions and the journey from town described, and wine brought by a sullen wife, Fontine sat down in a chair opposite the legless man. The stumps were within an arm's reach; the word *grotesque* came repeatedly to his mind. Andrew did not like ugliness; he did not care to put up with it.

"You don't recognize the name Fontine?"

"I do not, sir. It's French, I think. But you're American."

"Do you recognize the name Fontini-Cristi?"

Goldoni's eyes changed. A long-forgotten alarm was triggered. "Yes, of course, I recognize it," replied the amputee, his voice also changing, his words measured. "Fontine; Fontini-Cristi. So the Italian becomes French and the possessor American. It's been many years. You're a Fontini-Cristi?"

"Yes. Savarone was my grandfather."

"A great *padrone* from the northern provinces. I remember him. Not well, of course. He stopped coming to Champoluc in the late twenties, I believe."

"The Goldonis were his guides. Father and sons."

"We were everyone's guides."

"Were you ever a guide for my grandfather?"

"It's possible. I worked the mountains as a very young man."

"Can't you remember?"

"In my time I have taken thousands into the Alps——"

"You just said you remembered him."

"Not well. And more by the name than by the person. What is it you want?"

"Information. About a trip to the mountains taken by my father and grandfather fifty years ago."

"Are you joking?"

"Hardly. My father, Victor—Vittorio Fontini-Cristi—sent me from America to get that information. At great inconvenience to me. I haven't much time, so I need your help."

"It's freely given, but I wouldn't know where to begin. A single climb fifty years ago! Who would remember?"

"The man who led them. The guide. According to my father he was a son of Goldoni. The date is July fourteenth, 1920."

Fontine could not be sure—perhaps the grotesque cripple merely suppressed a sharp pain from his massive stumps, or shifted his legless clump of a body in reflection—but Goldoni *did react*. It was the *date*. He reacted to the date. And immediately covered that reaction by talking.

"July of 1920. It's two generations ago. It's impossible. You must have something more, how do you say, specific than that?"

"The *guide*. He was a Goldoni."

"Not I. I was no more than fifteen years old. I went into the mountains young, but not that young. Not as a *prima guida*."

Andrew held the cripple's eyes with his own. Goldoni was uncomfortable; he did not like the exchange of stares and looked away. Fontine leaned forward. "But you remember something, don't you?" he asked quietly, unable to keep the coldness out of his voice.

"No, Signor Fontini-Cristi. There's nothing."

"Just a few seconds ago, I gave you the date: July fourteenth, 1920. You knew that date."

"I knew only that it was too long ago for me to think about."

"I should tell you, I'm a soldier. I've interrogated hundreds of men; very few ever fooled me."

"It wouldn't be my intention, *signore*. For what purpose? I should like to be helpful to you."

Andrew continued to stare. "Years ago there were clearings on the railroad tracks south of Zermatt."

"A few are left," added Goldoni. "Not many, of course. They're not necessary these days."

"Tell me. Each was given the name of a bird——"

"Some," interrupted the Alpiner. "Not all."

"Was there a *hawk?* A hawk's . . . *something?*"

"A hawk? Why do you ask that?" The outsized amputee looked up, his gaze now steady, unwavering.

"Just tell me. Was there a clearing with 'hawk' as part of its name?"

Goldoni remained silent for several moments. "No," he said finally.

Andrew sat back in the chair. "Are you the eldest son of the Goldoni family?"

"No. It was obviously one of my brothers who was hired for that climb fifty years ago."

Fontine was beginning to understand. Alfredo Goldoni was given the house because he had lost his legs. "Where are your brothers? I'll talk with them."

"Again, I must ask if you joke, *signore.* My brothers are dead, everyone knows that. My brothers, an uncle, two cousins. All dead. There are no Goldoni guides left in Champoluc."

Andrew's breathing stopped. He absorbed the information and inhaled deeply. His shortcut had been eliminated with a single sentence.

"I find that hard to believe," he said coldly. *"All* those men dead? What killed them?"

"Avalanche, *signore.* A whole village was buried in sixty-eight. Near Valtournanche. Rescue teams were sent from as far north as Zermatt, south from Châtillon. The Goldonis led them. Three nations awarded us their highest honors. They were of little good to the rest. For me, they provide a small pension. I lost my legs through exposure." He tapped the stumps of his once muscular legs.

"And you have no information about that trip on July fourteenth, 1920?"

"Without particular details, how can I?"

"I have descriptions. Written down by my father." Fontine withdrew the Xeroxed pages from his jacket.

"Good! You should have said so before! Read them to me."

Andrew did so. The descriptions were disjointed, the pictures evoked contradictory. Time sequences jumped back and forth, and landmarks seemed to be confused with each other.

Goldoni listened; every now and then he closed his puffed, creased eyes and turned his neck to one side, as though conjuring up his own visual recollections. When Fontine finished he shook his head slowly.

"I'm sorry, *signore*. What you have read could be any of twenty, thirty different trails. Much that's there doesn't even exist in our district. Forgive me, but I think that your father has confused trails farther west in Valais. It's easy to do."

"There's nothing that sounds familiar?"

"On the contrary. Everything. *And* nothing. Fragments of many locations for hundreds of square miles. I'm sorry. It's impossible."

Andrew was confused. He still had the gut feeling that the Alpiner was lying. There was another option to pursue before he forced the issue. If it, too, led nowhere, he would come back and face the cripple with different tactics.

. . . *Should Alfredo not be the eldest, look for a sister.* . . .

"Are you the oldest surviving member of the family?"

"No. Two sisters were born before me. One lives."

"Where?"

"In Champoluc. On the Via Sestina. Her son works my land."

"What's the name? Her married name."

"Capomonti."

"Capomonti? That's the name of the people who run the inn."

"Yes, *signore*. She married into the family."

Fontine got out of the chair, putting the Xeroxed pages into his pocket. He reached the door and turned. "It's possible I'll be back."

"It will be a pleasure to welcome you."

Fontine got into the Land Rover and started the engine. Across the fence in the field, the nephew-farmhand sat motionless on the tractor and watched him, his vehicle idling. The gut feeling returned; the look on the farmhand's face seemed to be saying, *Get out of here. I must run to the house and hear what you said.*

Andrew released the brake and pressed the accelerator. The Land Rover shot forward on the road; he made a rapid U-turn and started back toward the village.

Suddenly his eyes riveted on the most obvious, unstartling sight in the world. He swore. It was so obvious he had not taken notice.

The road was lined with telephone poles.

There was no point in looking for an old woman on the Via Sestina; she would not be there. Another strategy came to the soldier's mind. The odds favored it.

"*Woman!*" shouted Goldoni.

"Quickly! Help me! The telephone!"

Goldoni's wife walked swiftly into the room and gripped the handles of the chair. "Should I make the calls?" she asked, wheeling him to the telephone.

"No. I'll do it." He dialed. "Lefrac? Can you hear me? . . . He's come. After all these years. Fontini-Cristi. But he does not bring the words. He seeks a clearing named for *hawks*. He tells me nothing else, and that's nothing. I don't trust him. I must reach my sister. Gather the others. We'll meet in an hour. . . . Not *here!* At the inn."

Andrew lay prone in the field across from the farmhouse. He focused the binoculars alternately on the door and on the windows. The sun was going down behind the western Alps; it would be dark soon. Lights had been put on in the farmhouse; the shadows moved back and forth. There was activity.

A car was being backed out of a dirt drive to the right of the house; it stopped and the farmhand-nephew got out. He raced to the front door; it opened.

Goldoni was in his wheelchair, his wife behind him. The nephew replaced her and started wheeling his legless uncle across the lawn toward the automobile, whose motor was idling.

Goldoni was clutching something in his arms. Andrew focused the binoculars on the object.

It was a large book; but it was more than a book. It was some kind of heavy, wide volume. A ledger.

At the car Goldoni's wife held the door while the nephew grabbed the grotesque amputee under the arms and swung the carcass across into the seat. Goldoni twitched and squirmed; his wife drew a strap across him and buckled it.

Through the frame of the open door's window, Andrew had a clear view of the legless, former Alpine guide. The center of focus once again was the huge ledger in Goldoni's arms, held almost desperately, though it were a thing of extraordinary value he dared not let go. Then Andrew realized there was something else in Goldoni's arms, something infinitely more familiar to the soldier. A shaft of glistening metal was wedged between the large volume and the Alpiner's thick chest. It was the barrel of a small, powerful shotgun; a model particularly identified with warring Italian families in the south. In Sicily. It was called the *lupo,* the "wolf." It was without much accuracy beyond twenty yards, but at short range could blow a man ten feet off the ground.

Goldoni was guarding the volume in his arms with a weapon more powerful than the .357 Magnum in the soldier's Alpine pack. Briefly, Andrew focused on Goldoni's nephew; the man had a new addition to

his garb. Jammed into his belt was a pistol, the large handle indicative
of its heavy caliber.

Both Alpiners were guarding that ledger. No one could get near it.
What was——

Christ! Suddenly, Fontine understood. *Records!* Records of *journeys
into the mountains!* It couldn't be anything else! It never occurred to
him—*or* to Victor—to ask if such records were kept. Especially in light
of the years; it was simply not a consideration. My God, a half century
had passed!

But according to his father, and *his* father, the Goldonis were the
finest guides in the Alps. Such professionals with such a collective reputation to uphold *would* keep records; it was the most natural thing to
do. Records of past trips into the mountains, going back decades!

Goldoni had lied. The information his visitor wanted was in that
house. But Goldoni did not want the visitor to have it.

Andrew watched. The nephew collapsed the wheelchair, opened the
trunk of the car, threw it in, and ran to the driver's side. He climbed
behind the wheel as Goldoni's wife closed her husband's door.

The car lurched out of the drive and headed north toward Champoluc. Goldoni's wife returned to the house.

The soldier lay prone in the grass and slowly replaced the binoculars
in the case as he considered his options. He could race to the hidden
Land Rover and go after Goldoni, but to what purpose, and how great
a risk? The Alpiner was only half a man, but the *lupo* in his hands more
than made up for his missing legs. Too, the surly nephew wouldn't hesitate to use the pistol in his belt.

If the ledger carried by Goldoni was what he suspected, it was being
rushed away to be hidden. Not to be destroyed; one did not destroy a
record of such incalculable value.

If. He had to be sure, certain of his judgment. Then he could move.

It was funny. He had not expected Goldoni to leave; he had expected
others to come to him. That Goldoni did leave meant that panic had set
in. A legless man who never went anywhere did not race away into the
indignity and discomfort of the outside world unless the motive was extraordinary.

The soldier made up his mind. The circumstances were optimum;
Goldoni's wife was alone. First, he would find out if that ledger was
what he thought it was; then he would find out where Goldoni had
gone.

Once he learned these things, the decision would be made: whether
to follow or to wait.

Andrew rose from the grass; there was no point wasting time. He started for the house.

"There is no one here, *signore*," said the stunned, gaunt woman, her eyes frightened. "My husband has gone with his nephew. They play cards in the village."

Andrew pushed the woman aside without replying. He walked directly through the house to Goldoni's room. There was nothing but old magazines and out-of-date Italian newspapers. He looked in a closet; it was at once ugly and pathetic. Trousers hung, the cloth folded, the folds held in place by safety pins. There were no books, no ledgers like the one the Alpiner had clutched in his arms.

He returned to the front room. The sullen, frightened wife was at the telephone, depressing the bar in short, panicked jabs with her bony fingers.

"The wire's cut," he said simply, approaching her.

"No," the woman whispered. "What do you want? I have nothing! *We* have nothing!"

"I think you do," answered Fontine, backing the woman against the wall, his face inches above hers. "Your husband lied to me. He said he couldn't tell me anything, but he left in a hurry carrying a very large book. It was a journal, wasn't it! An old journal that described a climb in the mountains fifty years ago. The journals! Show me the journals!"

"I do not know what you talk about, *signore!* We have nothing! We live on a *pensionare!*"

"Shut up! Give me those records!"

"*Per favore. . . .*"

"Goddamn you!" Fontine grabbed the woman's straight gray hair and yanked it forward, then suddenly, brutally backward, crashing her head into the wall. "I haven't got time. Your husband lied to me. Show me where those books are! *Now!*" He wrenched the hair again, and again slammed her skull into the wall. Blood appeared on her wrinkled neck, tears welled in her unfocused eyes.

The soldier realized he had gone too far. The combat option was now defined; it wouldn't be the first time. There'd been no lack of uncooperative peasants in Nam. He pulled the woman away from the wall.

"Do you understand me?" he said in a monotone. "I'll light a match in front of your eyes. Do you know what happens then? I'm asking you for the last time. Where are those records?"

Goldoni's wife collapsed, sobbing. Fontine held her by the cloth of her dress. With a trembling arm and frenzied, shaking fingers, she pointed to a door in the right wall of the room.

Andrew dragged her across the floor. He withdrew his Beretta and smashed the door with his boot. It crashed open. There was no one inside.

"The light switch. Where is it?"

She raised her head, her mouth open, the breath coming shorter, and moved her eyes to the left. *"Lampada, lampada,"* she whispered.

He pulled her inside the small room, releasing the cloth of her dress, and found the lamp. She lay trembling, curled up on the floor. The light reflected off the glass-enclosed bookcase on the opposite wall. There were five shelves, and on each a row of books. He rushed to the case, grabbed a knob in the middle and tried to raise the pane of glass. It was locked; he tried the others. All locked.

With his Beretta he smashed the glass of two panels. The light from the lamp was dim but sufficient. The faded, handwritten letters and numbers on the brown binding were clear enough.

Each year was divided into two six-month periods, the volumes differing in thickness. The books were handmade. He looked at the upper left panel; he had not broken the glass and the reflection of light obscured the lettering. He smashed it, clearing the fragments of glass away with repeated thrusts of the steel barrel.

The first volume read 1907. There was no month noted underneath; that was a system which had evolved.

He raced the barrel over the volumes to the year 1920.

January to June was there.

July to December was missing. In its place, filling the space, was a hastily inserted volume dated *1967*.

Alfredo Goldoni, the legless cripple, had outrun him. He had removed the key from the locked door that held the secret of a journey into the mountains fifty years ago, and raced away. Fontine turned to Goldoni's wife. She was on her knees, her gaunt arms supporting her shaking, gaunt body.

It would not be difficult to do what he had to do, learn what had to be learned.

"Get up," he said.

He carried the lifeless body across the field and into the woods. There was still no moon; instead the air smelled of impending rain, the sky pitch black with clouds, no stars in evidence. The beam of the flashlight wavered up and down with his footsteps.

Time. Time was the only thing that counted now.

And shock. He would need shock.

Alfredo Goldoni had gone to the inn of the Capomontis, according to the dead woman. They had all gone there, she said. The *consigliatori of Fontini-Cristi* had gathered together. A stranger had come among them bringing the wrong words.

31

Adrian drove back to Milan but he did not go to the hotel, he followed the highway signs to the airport, not entirely sure of *how* he was going to do what he had to do, but certain that he would do it.

He had to get to Champoluc. A killer was loose and that killer was his brother.

Somewhere in the vast complex of the Milan airport was a pilot and a plane. Or someone who knew where both could be found, for whatever price was necessary.

He drove as fast as he could, all the windows open, the wind whipping through the car. It helped him control himself; it helped him not to think, for thought was too painful.

"There's a small, private field on the outskirts of Champoluc, used by the rich in the mountains," said the unshaven pilot who had been awakened and summoned to the airport by a well-tipped clerk on the night shift for Alitalia. "But it's not operational at these hours."

"Can you fly in?"

"It's not so far away, but the terrain's bad."

"Can you *do* it?"

"I'll have enough petrol to return if I cannot. That will be my decision, not yours. But not one *lira* will be given back; is that understood?"

"I don't care."

The pilot turned to the Alitalia clerk, speaking authoritatively, obviously for the benefit of the man who would pay such money for such a flight. "Get me the weather. Zermatt, stations south, heading two-eighty degrees sweep to two-ninety-five out of Milan. I want radar fronts."

The Alitalia clerk shrugged and sighed.

"You'll be paid," said Adrian curtly.

The clerk picked up a red telephone. *"Operazioni,"* he said officiously.

The landing at Champoluc was not as hazardous as the pilot wanted Adrian to believe. The field, it was true, was not operational—there was no radio contact, no tower to guide a plane in—but the single strip was outlined, the east and west perimeters marked by red lights.

Adrian walked across the field toward the only structure with lights on inside. It was a semicircular metal shell, perhaps fifty feet long, twenty-five feet high at its midpoint. It was a hangar for small private aircraft. The door opened, brighter light spilled out on the ground, and a man in overalls was silhouetted in the doorway. He hunched his shoulders, peering out into the darkness; then he stretched, stifling a yawn.

"Can you speak English?" asked Fontine.

The man did—reluctantly and poorly, but clearly enough to be understood. And the information Adrian was given was pretty much what he expected. It was four in the morning and there was no place open at all. What pilot was crazy enough to fly into Champoluc at such an hour? Perhaps the *polizia* should be called.

Fontine withdrew several large bills from his pocket and held them in the light of the doorway. The watchman's eyes riveted on the money. Adrian suspected it was over a month's pay for the angry man.

"I came a long way to find someone. I've done nothing wrong except hire a plane to fly me here from Milan. The police are not interested in me, but *I must* find the person I'm looking for. I need a car and directions."

"You're no criminal? Flying up at such an hour——"

"No criminal," interrupted Adrian, suppressing his impatience, speaking as calmly as he could. "I'm a lawyer. An . . . *avvocato*," he added.

"*Avvocato?*" The man's voice conveyed his respect.

"I must find the house of Alfredo Goldoni. That's the name I've been given."

"The legless one?"

"I didn't know that."

The automobile was an old Fiat with torn upholstery and cracked side windows. The Goldoni farmhouse was eight to ten miles out of town, according to the watchman, on the west road. The man drew a simple diagram; it was easy to follow.

A post-and-rail fence could be seen in the glare of the headlights, the outlines of a house farther in the distance. And there was a dim wash of light coming from the house, shining through windows, dimly illuminating cascading branches of pine trees that fronted the old building near the road. Adrian removed his foot from the Fiat's accelerator, wondering whether he should stop and walk the rest of the way on foot. Lights on in a farmhouse at a quarter to five in the morning was not what he expected.

He saw the telephone poles. Had the night watchman at the airport called Goldoni and told him to expect a visitor? Or did farmers in Champoluc normally rise at such an early hour?

He decided against approaching on foot. If the watchman had telephoned, or the Goldonis were starting their day, an automobile was not the alarming intruder a man alone, walking quietly in the night, would be.

Adrian turned into a wide dirt path between the tall pines; there was no other entrance for a car. He pulled up parallel to the house; the dirt drive extended far back into the property, ending at a barn. Farm equipment could be seen through the open barn doors in the wash of the headlights. He got out of the car, passed the lighted front windows covered by curtains, and walked to the front door. It was a farmhouse door—wide and thick, the upper section a panel by itself, separated from the lower to let in the summer breezes and keep the animals out. There was a heavy, pitted brass knocker in the center. He used it.

He waited. There was no response, no sounds of movement within.

He rapped again, louder, with longer spaces between the sharp metallic reports.

There was a sound from behind the door. Indistinct, brief. A rustle of cloth or paper; a hand scratching on fabric? What?

"Please," he called out courteously. "My name's Fontine. You knew my father, and his father. From Milan. From Campo di Fiori. Please let me speak to you! I mean no harm."

Only silence now. Nothing.

He stepped back onto the grass and walked to the lighted windows. He put his face against the glass and tried to see through the white sheer curtains beyond. They were in opaque folds. The blurred images inside were further distorted by the thick glass of the Alpine window.

Then he saw it, and for a moment—as his eyes adjusted to the blurred distortion—he thought he had lost his mind for the second time that night.

At the far left side of the room was the figure of a legless man writhing in short, spastic twitches across the floor. The deformed body was large from the waist up, dressed in some kind of shirt that ended at the huge stumps, what remained of the legs hidden in the cloth of white undershorts.

The legless one.

Alfredo Goldoni. Adrian watched now as Goldoni maneuvered himself into a dark corner at the far wall. He carried something in his arms, clutching it as though it were a lifeline in a heavy sea. It was a rifle, a large-barreled rifle. Why?

"Goldoni! Please!" Fontine cried out at the window. "I just want to *talk* to you. If the watchman called you, he must have told you that."

The report was thunderous; glass shattered in all directions, fragments penetrating Adrian's raincoat and jacket. At the last instant he had seen the black barrel raised and had lurched to the side, covering his face. Thick, jagged points of glass were like a hundred pieces of ice across his arm. But for the heavy sweater he had bought in Milan, he would have been a mass of blood. As it was, his arms and neck were bleeding slightly.

Above, through the billows of smoke and the shattered glass of the window, he could hear the metallic snap of the rifle; Goldoni had reloaded. He sat up, his back against the stone foundation of the house. He felt along his left arm and removed as much of the glass as he could. He could feel the rivulets of blood on his neck.

He sat there, breathing heavily, ministering to himself, then called out again. Goldoni could not possibly negotiate the space between the dark corner and the window. They were two prisoners, one intent on killing the other, held at bay by an invisible, unclimbable wall.

"Listen to me! I don't know what you've been told, but it's not true! I'm not your enemy!"

"Animale!" roared Goldoni from within. "I'll see you dead!"

"For God's sake, why? I don't want to harm you!"

"You are Fontini-Cristi! You are a killer of women! An abductor of children! *Maligno! Animale!*"

He was too late. Oh, Jesus! He was *too late!* The killer had reached Champoluc before him.

But the killer was still loose. There was a chance.

"One last time, Goldoni," he said, without shouting now. "I'm a Fontini-Cristi, but I'm not the man you want dead. I'm not a killer of women and I've abducted no children. I know the man you're talking about and he's not me. That's as clear and as simple as I can put it. Now, I'm going to stand up in front of this window. I haven't got any gun—I've never owned one. If you don't believe me, I guess you'll have to shoot. I haven't got time to argue any longer. And I don't think you do, either. Any of you."

Adrian pressed his bleeding hand on the ground and rose unsteadily. He walked slowly in front of the shattered glass of the window.

* * *

Alfredo Goldoni called out quietly, "Walk in with your arms in front of you. There's no way you'll live if you hesitate or break your step."

Fontine came out of the shadows of the darkened back room. The legless man had directed him to a window through which he could enter; the cripple would not risk the manipulations required of him to open the front door. As Adrian emerged from the darkness, Goldoni cocked the hammer of the rifle, prepared to fire. He spoke in a whisper.

"You're the man and, yet, you are not the man."

"He's my brother," said Adrian softly. "And I have to stop him."

Goldoni stared at him in silence. Finally, his eyes still concentrated on Fontine's face, he uncocked the rifle and lowered it beside him in the corner.

"Help me into my chair," he said.

Adrian sat in front of the legless man, bare to the waist, his back within the reach of Goldoni's hands. The Italian-Swiss had removed the fragments of glass, applying an alcohol solution that stung but did its work; the bleeding stopped.

"In the mountains blood is precious. Our countrymen in the north call this fluid *leimen*. It's better than the powder. I doubt the medical doctors approve, but it does the trick. Put on your shirt."

"Thank you." Fontine rose and did as he was told. They had spoken only briefly of things that had to be said. With an Alpiner's practicality, Goldoni had ordered Adrian to remove his clothes where the glass had penetrated. A wounded man, uncared for, was of little good to anyone. His role of rural physician, however, did not lessen his anger or his agony.

"He's a man from hell," said the cripple as Fontine buttoned his shirt.

"He's sick, though I realize that's no help for you. He's looking for something. A vault, hidden somewhere in the mountains. It was carried there years ago, before the war, by my grandfather."

"We know. We've known someone would come someday. But that's all we know. We don't know where in the mountains."

Adrian didn't believe the legless man and yet he could not be sure. "You said killer of women. Who?"

"My wife. She's gone."

"Gone? How do you know she's dead?"

"He lied. He said she ran away down the road. That he took chase and caught her and keeps her hidden in the village."

"It's possible."

"It is not. I can't walk, *signore*. My wife can't run. She has the swollen veins in her legs. She wears thick shoes to get around this house. Those shoes are in front of your eyes."

Adrian looked down where Goldoni gestured. A pair of heavy, ugly shoes were placed neatly at the side of a chair.

"People do things they don't think they can do——"

"There's blood on the floor," interrupted Goldoni, his voice trembling, pointing to an open doorway. "There were no wounds on the man who calls himself a soldier. Go! Look for yourself."

Fontine walked to the open door and went inside the small room. A glass bookcase was smashed, sharp fragments everywhere. He reached inside and removed a volume behind one of the shattered panels. He opened it. In clear handscript were pages detailing successive climbs into the mountains. The dates extended back beyond 1920. And there was blood on the floor by the door.

He was too late.

He walked swiftly back into the front room.

"Tell me everything. As quickly as you can. *Everything.*"

The soldier had been thorough. He had immobilized his enemy, rendered them helpless through fear and panic. The major from Eye Corps had mounted his own invasion of the Capomonti inn. He had done so swiftly, without a wasted move, finding Lefrac and the members of the Capomonti and Goldoni families in an upstairs room where they were holding their hastily summoned conference.

The door of the room had crashed open, a terrified desk clerk propelled through it so harshly he fell to the floor. The soldier entered quickly, closing the door before any in the room knew what was happening, and held them all rigid at the point of a gun.

The soldier then issued his demands. First, the old ledger describing a journey into the mountains over fifty years ago. And maps. Minutely detailed maps used by climbers in the Champoluc district. Second, the services of either Lefrac's son or eighteen-year-old grandson to lead him into the hills. Third, the granddaughter as a second hostage. The child's father had lost his head and lunged at the man with the gun; but the soldier was expert and the father subdued without a shot.

Old Lefrac was ordered to open the door and call for a housemaid. Proper clothing was brought to the room and the children dressed under gunpoint. It was then that the man-from-hell told Goldoni his wife was a prisoner. He was to return to his house and remain there alone, sending his driver—his nephew—away. If he stopped to reach the police, he would never see his wife again.

"Why?" asked Adrian quickly. "Why did he do that? Why did he want you back here alone?"

"His separates us. My sister returns with my nephew to her house on the Via Sestina; Lefrac and his son remain at the inn. Together we might make each other bold. Apart we're frightened, helpless. A gun against a child's head is not easily forgotten. He knows that alone we'll do nothing but wait."

Adrian closed his eyes. "God," he said.

"The soldier's an expert, that one." Goldoni's voice was low, the hatred seething.

Fontine glanced at him. *I have run with the pack—in the middle of the pack—but now I have reached the edges and I will peel away.*

"Why did you shoot at me? If you thought it was him, how could you take the chance? Not knowing what he did."

"I saw your face against the glass. I wanted to blind you, not to kill you. A dead man can't tell me where he's taken my wife. Or the body of my wife. Or the children. I'm a good shot; I fired inches above your head."

Fontine crossed to the chair where he had thrown his jacket and took out the Xeroxed pages of his father's recollections of fifty years ago. "You must have read that journal. Can you remember what was written?"

"You can't go after him. He'll kill."

"Can you *remember?*"

"It was a two-day climb with many crossing trails! He could be anywhere. He narrows down the place he seeks. He travels blindly. If he saw you, he'd kill the children."

"He won't see me. Not if I get there first! Not if I *wait* for him!" Adrian unfolded the Xeroxed pages.

"They've been read to me. There's nothing that can help you."

"There has to be! It's *here!*"

"You're wrong," said Goldoni, and Adrian knew he was not lying. "I tried to tell *him* that, but he wouldn't listen. Your grandfather made his arrangements, but the *padrone* did not consider unexpected death, or human failing."

Fontine looked up from the pages. Helplessness was in the old man's eyes. A killer was in the mountains and he was helpless. Death would surely follow death, for surely his wife was gone.

"What were these arrangements?" asked Adrian softly.

"I'll tell you. You're not your brother. We've kept the secret for thirty-five years, Lefrac, the Capomontis, and ourselves. And one other

—not one of us—whose death came suddenly, before he made his own arrangements."

"Who was that?"

"A merchant named Leinkraus. We didn't know him well."

"Tell me."

"We've waited all these years for a Fontini-Cristi to come." So the legless man began:——

The man they—the Goldonis, Lefrac, and the Capomontis—expected would come quietly, in peace, seeking the iron crate buried high in the mountains. This man would speak of the journey taken so many years ago by father and son, and he would know that journey was recorded in the Goldoni ledgers—as all who employed the Goldoni guides would know. And because that climb lasted for two days over considerable terrain, the man would specify an abandoned railroad clearing known as *Sciocchezza di Cacciatori*—Hunter's Folly. The clearing had been left to nature over forty years ago, long before the iron crate had been buried, but it had existed when father and son journeyed to Champoluc in the summer of 1920.

"I thought those clearings were given——"

"The names of birds?"

"Yes."

"Most were, not all. The soldier asked if there was a clearing known by the name of the hawk. There are no hawks in the mountains of Champoluc."

"The painting on the wall," said Adrian, more to himself than for the benefit of the Alpiner.

"What?"

"My father remembered a painting on a wall in Campo di Fiori, a painting of a hunt. He thought it might be significant."

"The soldier did not speak of it. Nor did he speak of why he sought the information; only that he had to have it. He wouldn't mention the *search* to me. *Or* the ledgers. Or the reason why the railroad clearing was important. He was *secretive*. And, clearly, he did not come in peace. A soldier who threatens a legless man is a hollow commander. I didn't trust him."

Everything his brother had done was contrary to the memory of the Fontini-Cristis as these people remembered them. It might have been so simple had he been open with them, had he *come in peace;* but the soldier couldn't do that. He was always at war.

"Then the area around this abandoned clearing—Hunter's Folly—is where the vault is buried?"

"Presumably. There are several old trails to the east that lead away from the tracks, up to the higher ridges. But which trail, which ridge? We do not know."

"The records would describe it."

"If one knew where to look. The soldier doesn't."

Adrian thought. His brother had traveled across the world, eluding the Intelligence network of the most powerful nation on earth. "You may be underestimating him."

"He's not one of us. He's not a man of the mountains."

"No," mused Fontine quietly. "He's something else. What would he *look* for? That's what we have to think about."

"An inaccessible place. Away from the trails. Ground that would not be traveled easily for any of several reasons. There are many such areas. The mountains are filled with them."

"But you said it a few minutes ago. He'd narrow down his . . . options."

"*Signore?*"

"Nothing. I was thinking of—never mind. You see, he knows what *not* to look for. He knows that the vault was heavy; it had to be transported—mechanically. He starts with something *besides* the record book."

"We weren't aware of that."

"He is."

"It will do him little good in the darkness."

"Look at the window," said Adrian. Outside, the first morning light could be seen. "Tell me about this other man. The merchant."

"Leinkraus?"

"Yes. How was he involved?"

"That answer went with his death. Even Francesca doesn't know."

"Francesca?"

"My sister. When my brothers died, she was the eldest. The envelope was given to her. . . ."

"*Envelope? What envelope?*"

"Your grandfather's instructions."

. . . *Therefore, should Alfredo not be the eldest, look for a sister, as is the Italian-Swiss custom.* . . .

Adrian unfolded the pages of his father's testament. If such fragments of truth came through the distance of years with such accuracy, more attention had to be paid to his father's disjointed remembrances.

"My sister has lived in Champoluc since her marriage to Capomonti. She knew the Leinkraus family better than any of us. Old Leinkraus

died in his store. There was a fire; many thought it wasn't acci-
dental."

"I don't understand."

"The family Leinkraus are Jews."

"I see. Go on." Adrian shifted the pages.

. . . *The merchant was not popular. He was a Jew and for one who
fought bitterly . . . Such thinking was indefensible.*

Goldoni continued. The man who came to Champoluc and spoke of
the iron crate and the long-forgotten journey and the old railroad clearing was to be given the envelope left with the eldest Goldoni.

"You must understand, *signore.*" The legless man interrupted himself. "We are *all* family now. The Capomontis and the Goldonis. After
so many years and no one came, we discussed it between ourselves."

"You're ahead of me."

"The envelope directed the man who had come to Champoluc to old
Capomonti. . . ."

Adrian turned back the pages. *If there were secrets to leave in the
Champoluc, old Capomonti would have been a rock of silence and
trust.*

"When Capomonti died, he gave *his* instructions to his son-in-law,
Lefrac."

"Then Lefrac *knows.*"

"Only one word. The name Leinkraus."

Fontine bolted forward in his seat. He remained on the edge, bewildered. Yet something was triggered in his mind. As in long, complex
cross-examination, isolated phrases and solitary words were suddenly
brought into focus, given meaning where no meaning had existed previously.

The *words.* Look to the words, as his brother looked to violence.

He scanned the pages in his hands, turning them rapidly until he
found what he was looking for.

. . . *There is a blurred memory of an unpleasant incident . . . what
the unpleasant incident specifically entailed, I have no recall . . . serious and provoked my father . . . a sad anger . . . impression that details were withheld from me. . . .*

Withheld. Anger. Sadness.

. . . *provoked my father. . . .*

"Goldoni, listen to me. You've got to think back. Way back. Something happened. Something unpleasant, sad, angry. And it concerned
the Leinkraus family."

"No."

Adrian stopped. The legless Goldoni had not let him finish. "What do you mean 'no'?" he asked quietly.

"I told you. I didn't know them well. We barely spoke."

"Because they were Jews? Is that the way it came down from the north in those days?"

"I don't understand you."

"I think you do." Adrian stared at him; the Alpiner avoided his eyes. Fontine continued softly. "You didn't have to know them—at all, perhaps. But for the first time, you're lying to me. Why?"

"I'm not lying. They weren't friends of the Goldonis."

"Or the Capomontis?"

"*Or* the Capomontis!"

"You didn't like them?"

"We didn't *know* them! They kept to themselves. Other Jews came and they lived among their own. It's that simple."

"It's *not*." Adrian knew the answer was within reach. Hidden, perhaps, from Goldoni himself. "Something happened in July of 1920. What was it?"

Goldoni sighed. "I can't remember."

"July fourteenth, 1920! What *happened*?"

Goldoni's breath was shorter, his large jaws taut. The massive stumps that once were legs twitched in his wheelchair. "It doesn't mean anything," he whispered.

"Let me be the judge of that," said Adrian.

"Times have changed. So much has changed in a lifetime," said the Alpiner, his voice faltering. "The same was felt by everyone."

"July *fourteenth, 1920!*" Adrian zeroed in on his witness.

"I tell you! It is meaningless!"

"*Goddamn you!*" Adrian leaped from the chair. Striking the helpless old man was not out of the question. Then the words came.

"A Jew was beaten. A young Jew who entered the church school . . . was beaten. He died three days later."

The Alpiner had said it. But only part of it. Fontine backed away from the wheelchair. "Leinkraus's son?" he asked.

"Yes."

"The church school?"

"He couldn't enter the state school. It was a place to learn. The priests accepted him."

Fontine sat down slowly, keeping his eyes on Goldoni. "There's more, isn't there? Who gave the beating?"

"Four boys from the village. They didn't know what they were doing. Everyone said so."

"I'm sure everyone did. It's easier that way. Ignorant children who had to be protected. And what was the life of one Jew?"

Tears came to the eyes of Alfredo Goldoni. "Yes."

"You were one of those boys, weren't you?"

Goldoni nodded his head in silence.

"I think I can tell you what happened," continued Adrian. "Leinkraus was threatened. His wife, his other children. Nothing was said, nothing reported. A young Jew had died, that was all."

"So many years ago," Goldoni whispered as the tears fell down his face. "No one thinks like that anymore. And we have lived with what we did. At the end of my life, it grows even more difficult. The grave is close at hand now."

Adrian stopped breathing, stunned by Goldoni's words. The *grave* is close. . . . The *grave*. My God! Was that *it?* He wanted to jump out of the chair and roar his questions until the legless Alpiner remembered! *Exactly.* But he could not do that. He kept his voice low, incisive.

"What happened then? What did Leinkraus do?"

"Do?" Goldoni shrugged slowly, sadness in the gesture. "What could he do? He kept silent."

"Was there a funeral? A burial?"

"If there was, we knew nothing of it."

"Leinkraus's son had to be buried. No Christian cemetery would accept a Jew. Was there a burial place for Jews?"

"No, not then. There is now."

"*Then!* What about then? Where was he *buried?* Where was the *murdered son* of Leinkraus *buried?*"

Goldoni reacted as though struck in the face. "It was said the father and the brothers—the men of the family—took the dead son into the mountains. Where the boy's body would not be further abused."

Adrian got out of the chair. There was his answer.

The grave of the Jew. The vault from Salonika.

Savarone Fontini-Cristi had found an eternal truth in a village tragedy. He had used it. In the end, not letting the holy men forget.

Paul Leinkraus was in his late forties, the grandson of the merchant and a merchant himself, but of a different time. There was little he could relate of a grandfather he barely knew, or of an era of obsequiousness and fear he had never known. But he was a man of acumen, bespeaking the expansion for which he was responsible. As such, he had recognized the urgency and the legitimacy of Adrian's sudden call.

Leinkraus had taken Fontine into the library, away from his wife and child, and removed the family Torah from the shelf. The diagram filled the entire back panel of the binding. It was a precisely drawn map that showed the way to the grave of Reuven Leinkraus's first son, buried in the mountains on July 17, 1920.

Adrian had traced every line, then matched his drawing with the original. It was precise; he had his last passport. To where, he was certain. To what, he could not know.

He had made a final request of Leinkraus. An overseas telephone call to London for which, of course, he would pay.

"Your grandfather made all the payments this house can accept. Make your call."

"Please stay. I want you to hear."

He had placed a call to the Savoy in London. His request was uncomplicated. When the American embassy opened, would the Savoy please leave a message for Colonel Tarkington of the inspector general's office. If he was not in London, the embassy would know where to reach him.

Colonel Tarkington was to be directed to a man named Paul Leinkraus in the town of Champoluc in the Italian Alps. The message was to be signed Adrian Fontine.

He was going into the mountains on the hunt, but he had no illusions. He was not ultimately a match for the soldier. His gesture might be only that: a gesture ending in futility. And very possibly his own death; he understood that, too.

The world could survive very well without his presence. He wasn't particularly remarkable, although he liked to think he had certain talents. But he wasn't at all sure how the world would fare if Andrew walked out of the Champoluc with the contents of an iron crate that had been carried on a train from Salonika over thirty years ago.

If only one brother came out of the mountains and that man was the killer of Eye Corps, he had to be taken.

The call finished, Adrian had looked up at Paul Leinkraus. "When Colonel Tarkington makes contact with you, tell him exactly what happened here this morning."

Fontine nodded to Leinkraus in the doorway. He opened the door of the Fiat and climbed in, noticing that he had been so agitated upon his arrival that he'd left the keys in the car. It was the kind of carelessness no soldier would be guilty of.

The realization caused him to reach over and pull down the panel of the glove compartment. He put his hand inside and took out a heavy, black, magazine-clip pistol; the loading mechanism had been explained to him by Alfredo Goldoni.

He started the ignition and rolled down the window, suddenly needing the air. His breath came rapidly; his heartbeat vibrated in his throat. And he remembered.

He had fired a pistol only once in his life. Years ago at a boys' camp in New Hampshire when the counselors had taken them to a local police range. His brother had been beside him, and they had laughed together, excited children.

Where had the laughter gone?

Where had his brother gone?

Adrian drove down the tree-lined street and turned left into the road that would take him north to the mountains. Above, the early morning sun was hidden behind a blanket of gathering clouds.

The sky was angry.

32

The girl shrieked and slipped on the rock; her brother whipped around and grabbed her hand, preventing the fall. The plunge was no more than twenty feet, and the soldier wondered whether it might be better to break the grip between them and let her fall. If the girl snapped an ankle or a leg, she wouldn't go anywhere; she certainly could not make it down through the trails to the flat ground and the road below. It was twelve miles behind them now. They had covered the initial terrain during the night.

He could bypass the initial trails of that journey into the mountains fifty years ago. If others began the search, they wouldn't know that; he did. He could read maps the way most men read simple books. From symbols, colors, and numbers, he could visualize terrain with the accuracy of a camera. There was no one better in the army. He was a master of everything *real*, from men to machines to maps.

The detailed map used by climbers in the Champoluc district showed the railroad from Zermatt angling west around the curve of the mountains. It straightened out for approximately five miles before the station at Champoluc. The areas directly east of the final flat stretches of track were heavily traversed throughout the year. These were the first trails described in Goldoni's journal. No one concealing anything of value would consider them.

Yet farther north, at the start of the railroad's western curve, were the old clearings that led to the numerous trails specifically listed in the pages he had ripped out of the Goldoni ledger for July 14 and 15 of 1920. Any of these might be the one. Once he saw them in daylight, and studied the possibilities, he could determine which of the trails he would trace.

Those selections would be based on fact. Fact one: The size and weight of the vault mandated vehicle or animal transportation. Fact two: The train from Salonika made its journey in the month of December—a time of year when the weather was bitter cold and the mountain passes clogged with snow. Fact three: The spring and summer thaws, with their rushing waters and erosion of earth, would call for a recess in the high ground to hide the vault, enveloped by rock for protection. Fact four: That recess would be away from frequently traveled areas, high above an established route, but with an offshoot trail that could be negotiated by an animal or a vehicle. Fact five: That trail had to emanate from a section of the track where a train could pull to a stop, the ground level on both sides flat and straight. Fact six: The specific clearing, in current use or abandoned, would lead into the crisscrossing trails recorded in the Goldoni ledger. By retracing each one to the tracks and picturing the feasibility of traveling over it—in the cold and snow, by animal or vehicle—the number of trails would be further reduced until there was one that led to the hiding place.

He had time. Days, if he needed them. He had supplies for a week strapped to his back. The stump, Goldoni, the woman, Capomonti, and Lefrac and his family were too frightened to make a move. He had covered himself brilliantly. The unseen was always more effective than the observable in combat. He had told the terrified Swiss that he had associates in Champoluc. They would be watching; they would get word to him in the mountains should a Goldoni or a Campomonti or a Lefrac reach the police. Communications were no problem for soldiers. And the result of their reaching him would be the execution of his hostages.

He had fantasized the presence of Eye Corps. Eye Corps the way it had been—efficient, strong, quick to maneuver.

He would build a new Corps one day, stronger and more efficient, without weakness. He would find the vault from Salonika, carry the documents out of the mountains, summon the holy men and watch their faces as he described the imminent, global collapse of their institutions.

. . . *The contents of that vault are as staggering to the civilized world as any in history.* . . .

That was comforting. It could not be in better hands.

They were on a flat stretch now, the first elevation to the west no more than a mile away. The girl fell to her knees, sobbing. Her brother looked at him, his eyes conveying hatred, fear, supplication. Andrew would kill them both, but not for a while. One disposed of hostages when they no longer served a purpose.

Only fools killed indiscriminately. Death was an instrument, a means to be used in reaching an objective or completing an assignment, and that was all it was.

Adrian drove the Fiat off the road into the fields. The rocks ripped the undercarriage. He could drive no farther; he had reached the first of several steep hills that led to the first plateau described on the Leinkraus diagram. He was eight and a half miles north of Champoluc. The grave was precisely five miles beyond the first of the plateaus that were the landmarks of the journey to the burial ground.

He got out of the car and walked across the field of tall grass. He looked up. The hill in front of him sprang suddenly out of the ground, an impromptu bulge of nature, more rock than greenery, with no discernible path on which to scale it. He knelt down and retied the laces on his rubber-soled shoes as tightly as he could. The weight of the pistol was heavy in his raincoat pocket.

For a moment he closed his eyes. *He could not think. O God! Keep me from thinking!*

He was a mover now. He got to his feet and started to climb.

The first two railroad clearings proved negative. There was no way animal or vehicle could traverse the routes from the Zermatt railway to the eastern slopes. Two more clearings remained. The names on the old Champoluc map were Hunter's Folly and Sparrow's Rook; no mention of hawk. Still, it had be one of them!

Andrew looked at his hostages. Brother and sister sat together on the ground, talking in quiet, frightened whispers, their eyes darting up at him. The hatred was gone now, only fear and supplication remained. There was something ugly about them, thought the soldier. And then he realized what it was. Across the world in the jungles of Southeast Asia, people their age fought battles, weapons strapped to their backs over uniforms that looked like pajamas. They were his enemy over there, but he respected that enemy.

He had no respect for these children. There was no strength in their faces. Only fear, and fear was repulsive to the major from Eye Corps.

"Get up!" He could not help himself; he shouted angrily at the sight of these pampered, weak brats with no dignity in their faces.

Christ, he despised the spineless!

They would not be missed.

Adrian looked back across the ridge to the plateau in the distance, thankful that old Goldoni had given him gloves. Even without the cold, his bare hands and fingers would have been a bleeding mass of flesh. It wasn't that the climb was difficult; a man used to minimum exercise in the mountains would find it simple. But he had never been in the mountains except on skis, where tows and trams did the uphill work. He was using muscles rarely employed and had little confidence in his sense of balance.

The last several hundred yards had been the most difficult. The trail in the Leinkraus diagram was landmarked: a cluster of gray rock at the base of a crystalline schistose embankment that all climbers knew should be avoided, for it cracked easily. The crystalline rock evolved into a cliff that rose about a hundred feet from the schist, its edge sharply defined. To the left of the crystalline sheet were abrupt, dense Alpine woods that grew vertically out of the slope, a sudden, thick forest surrounded by rock. The Leinkraus trail was marked off at ten paces from the embankment. It led to the top of the wooded slope whose ridge was the second plateau: the end of the second leg of the journey.

The trail was nowhere to be found. It had disappeared; years of disuse and overgrowth had concealed it. Yet the ridge could be seen clearly above the trees. That he could see it was an indication of the angle of ascent.

He had walked into the dense Alpine underbrush and made his way, yard by yard, up the steep incline, through nettled bush and the skin-piercing needles of the pines.

He sat on the ridge, breathing heavily, his shoulders aching from the constant tension. He estimated the distance from the first plateau to be at least three miles. It had taken nearly three hours. A mile an hour, over rocks and down miniature valleys, and across cold streams, and up endless hills. Just three miles. If that were so, he had two miles to go, perhaps less. He looked up. The overcast had lasted the entire morning. It would continue on throughout the day. The sky above was like the North Shore sky before a heavy squall.

They used to sail in squalls together. Laughing as they bested the weather, sure of their abilities in the water, pitting themselves against the rain and the wind of the Sound.

No, he would not think of that. He got to his feet and looked at his tracing of the Leinkraus diagram, copied from the inside binding of a family Torah.

The diagram was clear but the rising terrain beyond him wasn't. He saw the objective—due northeast, the third plateau, isolated above a sea of Alpine spruce. But the ridge he was on swept to the right, due *east,* leading into the base of yet another mountain of boulders, away from any direct line to the plateau in the distance. He walked around the ledge past the border of the dark, sloping woods he had climbed through. The drop below was sheer and the rocks beneath rose like a bubbling river of stone. The trail as marked in the diagram went from forest to ledge to forest; there was no mention of intersecting rock.

Geological changes had taken place in the intervening years since any member of the Leinkraus family had journeyed to the burial ground. A sudden shift of nature—a quake or an avalanche—had eliminated the trail.

Still, he could see the plateau. What separated him from it seemed impenetrable, but once through it—and over it—he could make out a winding trail on the higher ground that led to the plateau. It was doubtful that that had been altered. He slid down the embankment onto the river of stone, and awkwardly, trying to keep his feet from slipping into a hundred miniature crevices, climbed toward the forest of spruce.

The third clearing was it! *Sciocchezza di Cacciatori!* Hunter's Folly! Long abandoned but once perfect for removing the vault. The trail from the mountains to the Zermatt railway was passable, and the area around the tracks was flat and accessible. At first Andrew had not been sure; in spite of the level ground on either side of the tracks, the stretch was short, blocked by a curve. Then he remembered: his father had said that the train from Salonika had been a short freight. Four cars and an engine.

Five railway units could easily pull beyond the curve and come to a stop in a straight line. Whatever car the vault had been in could have been unloaded without difficulty.

But what now convinced him he was near his goal was an unexpected discovery. West of the tracks were the unmistakable signs of an abandoned road. The cut through the woods was defined, the trees in the cut shorter than those surrounding them, the brush closer to the ground. It was no longer a road—not even a path—but its former existence was undeniable.

"Lefrac!" he yelled at the eighteen-year-old. "What's down there?" He pointed northwest, where the cut in the forest sloped.

"A village. About five, six miles away."

"It's not on the railroad line?"

"No, *signore*. It's in farm country, below the mountains."

"What roads lead into it?"

"The main road from Zürich and——"

"All right." He stopped the boy for two reasons. He had heard what he wanted to hear, and twenty feet away the girl had gotten to her feet and was edging toward the woods on the eastern side of the tracks.

Fontine took out his pistol and fired two shots. The explosions thundered throughout the woods; the bullets detonated the ground on either side of the child. She screamed, terrified. Her brother lunged at him in a frenzy of tears; he sidestepped and smashed the barrel of his pistol on the side of the boy's head.

Lefrac's son fell to the ground, sobs of frustration and anger filling the silence of the abandoned railroad clearing.

"You're better than I thought you were," said the soldier coldly, raising his eyes, turning to the girl. "Help him. He's not hurt. We're heading back."

Give the captured hope, reflected the soldier. The younger and more inexperienced they were, the more hope they should be given. It reduced the fear which was, in itself, detrimental to rapid travel. Fear was an instrument, too. Like death. It was to be used methodically.

He retraced the trail from the Zermatt tracks for a second time. He was certain now. There was nothing that would prevent an animal or a vehicle from negotiating it. The ground was clear and mostly hard. And more important, the terrain rose directly toward the eastern slopes, into the specific trails recorded in the faded pages of the ledger. Light snow and layers of frost covered the earth. With every yard the soldier in him told him he was nearing the enemy zone. For that was what it was.

They reached the first intersecting trail described by the Goldoni guide on the morning of July 14, 1920. To the right, the trail angled downward into some kind of forest, a thick wall of dark green, laced with a roof of white. It seemed impenetrable.

It was a possible hiding place. That mountain forest would not be tempting to the casual climber, and without interest for the experienced. On the other hand, it *was* forest—wood and earth, not rock—and because it was not rock he could not accept it. The vault would be protected by rock.

To the left, the trail continued up, veering obliquely into the side of a small mountain above them. The trail itself was wide, on solid rock, and bordered by foliage. Boulders rose sharply to the right, forming an abrupt sheer of heavy stone. An animal or a vehicle still had space to walk or roll; the direct line from the Zermatt tracks was unbroken.

"Move it!" he shouted, gesturing to the left. The Lefrac children looked at each other. To the right was the way to Champoluc—the way back. The girl grabbed her brother; Fontine stepped forward, broke the grip, and propelled the girl forward.

"*Signore!*" The boy shouted and stepped between them, his arms raised in front of him, his young palms flat—a very penetrable shield. "Don't do that," he stammered, his voice low, cracking with young fear, his own anger challenging himself.

"Let's go," said the soldier. He had no time to waste on children.

"You hear me, *signore!*"

"I heard you. Now, move."

At the western flank of the small mountain the width of the rising trail abruptly narrowed. It entered an enormous, natural archway cut out of the boulders and led to the face of a hill of sheer rock. The geologically formed archway was not only the logical extension of the trail, but the mountain of rock beyond must have been irresistible to novice climbers. It could be scaled without great effort, but was sufficiently awesome by its breadth and height to be a good start for the higher regions. Perfect for an enthusiastic seventeen year old, under the watchful eye of a guide and a father.

But the width under the arch *was* narrow, the rock floor too smooth, especially when heavier snows fell. An animal—a mule or a horse—might cross under but there was considerable danger that hooves would slip.

No vehicle could possibly get through.

Andrew turned and studied the approach they had just made. There were no other trails, but about thirty yards back on the left the ground was flat and filled with Alpine brush. It extended to a short wall of rock that rose up to the ridge of the mountain. That wall, that short cliff, was no more than twenty feet high, almost hidden by shrubs and small, gnarled trees growing out of the rock. But the ground beneath that cliff, beneath that ridge, was flat. Natural obstructions were everywhere else, but not there, not in that particular spot.

"Walk over there," he ordered the young Lefracs, both to keep them in sight and to provide perspective. "Go into that flat area between the rocks! Spread the bushes and walk in! As far as you can!"

He stepped back off the trail and studied the ridge above. It, too, was flat, or at least appeared so. And it was something else, something that might not be noticed except, perhaps, from where he stood. It was . . . defined. The edge, though jagged, formed a nearly perfect semicircle. If that circle continued, the ridge itself was like a small, out-of-the-way platform on a small, unimportant mountain, but still high above the lower Alpine hills.

He judged the height of Lefrac's son as five-ten or -eleven. "Raise your hands!" he shouted.

Arms extended, the boy's hands were just below the midpoint of the short cliff.

Suppose the method of transport was not an animal but a vehicle. A heavy-wheeled piece of machinery, the carriage a plow, or a tractor. It was consistent; there was no part of the route from the Zermatt tracks or up the Goldoni trail that such a piece of equipment could not traverse. And plows and tractors had winch machinery. . . .

"Signore! Signore!" It was the girl; her shouts conveyed a strange exaltation, a cross between hope and desperation. "If this is what you *look* for, let us *go!"*

Andrew raced back into the trail and toward the Lefracs. He sped into the tangled shrubbery to the face of the rock.

"Down there!" The girl shouted again.

On the ground in the light snow, barely seen through the underbrush, was an old ladder. The wood was rotted, the steps swollen out of their sockets in half a dozen places. But otherwise it was intact. It was not now usable, but neither had it been abused by man. It had lain in that shrubbery for years, perhaps decades, untouched except by nature and time.

Fontine knelt down and touched it, pried it off the ground, watched it crumble as he lifted it. He had found a human tool where none should be; he knew that not fifteen feet above him . . .

Above him! He whipped his head up and saw the blurred object crashing down. The impact came; his head exploded in a flashing of pain, followed by an instant of numbness, a hundred hammers pounding. He fell forward, struggling to shake the effects of the blow and find light again.

He heard the shouts.

"Fuggi! Presto! In la traccia!" The boy.

"Non senza voi! Tu fuggi anche!" The girl.

Lefrac's son had found a large rock on the ground. And in his hatred he had lost his fear; holding the primitive weapon in his hand, he had crashed it down on the soldier's head.

The light was returning. Fontine started to get up and, again, he saw the unfocused hand descending, the rock slashing diagonally down.

"You little fuck! You fuck!"

Lefrac's son released the rock, hurling it into the soldier's body— anywhere, a final assault—and ran out of the snow-covered shrubbery onto the trail after his sister.

Andrew recognized the pitch of his own fury. He had felt it perhaps a dozen times in his life, and it had always been in the molten heat of combat when an enemy held an advantage he could not control.

He crawled out of the brush to the edge of the trail and looked below. Beneath him on the winding path were brother and sister, running as best they could over the slippery trail.

He reached under his jacket to the holster strapped to his chest. The Beretta was in his pocket. But a Beretta would be inadequate; it was not that accurate. He pulled out the .357-caliber Magnum he had bought at the Leinkraus store in Champoluc. His hostages were about forty yards away. The boy took the girl's hand; they were close together, the figures overlapping.

Andrew squeezed the trigger eight times in succession. Both bodies fell, writhing on the rocks. He could hear the screams. In seconds the screaming subsided into moans, the writhing became twists and lurches at nothing. They would die, but not for a while. They would go no farther.

The soldier crawled back through the shrubs into the flat *cul de sac* and removed the pack from his back, slipping the straps off slowly, moving his bleeding head as little as possible. He opened the pack and slipped out the canvas first-aid kit. He had to patch the broken skin and stop the bleeding as best he could. And move. For Christ's sake, *move!*

He had no hostages now. He could tell himself it made no difference, but he knew better. Hostages were a way out. If he came out of the mountains alone, they'd be watching. *Jesus,* they'd be watching for him —he was a dead man. They'd take the vault and kill him.

There was another way. The Lefrac boy had said it!

The abandoned road west of the abandoned clearing called Hunter's Folly! Past the tracks, down to a village whose main road led to Zürich.

But he was not going to that village, to that road that led to Zürich, until the contents of the vault were his. And every instinct he possessed told him he'd found it.

Fifteen feet above.

He unwound the ropes clamped to the outside of the pack and spread the grappling hook from its axis; the prongs locked into position. He stood up. His temple throbbed and the wounds stung where he'd applied the antiseptic, but the bleeding had stopped. He was focusing clearly again.

He stepped back and lobbed the grappling hook up to the ledge. It caught. He yanked on the rope.

The rock splintered; fragments plummeted down, followed by larger sections of limestone. He sprang to the side to avoid the falling hook; it embedded itself through the thin layers of snow into the ground.

He swore and once more heaved the hook skyward, arcing it over the ledge, far into the flat surface above. He tugged in swift, short movements; the hook caught. He pulled harder; it held.

The line was ready; he could climb. He reached down, grabbed the straps of his pack and slipped his arms through, not bothering to secure the front clamps. He yanked on the rope a last time; he was satisfied. He jumped as high as he could, thrusting his legs out against the stone, allowing himself to swing back into the rock as he manipulated his hands—one over the other—in rapid ascent. He swung his left leg over the jagged ledge, and pushed his right hand against the stone beneath, forcing his body into a lateral roll that propelled him onto the surface. He started to get up, his eyes traveling to the source of the grappling hook's anchor.

But he remained kneeling in shock as he stared at the strange sight ten feet away, in the center of the plateau. Embedded in the stone was an old, rusted metal star: a Star of David.

The grappling hook enveloped it, the prongs moored around the iron. He was looking at a grave.

He heard the echoes throughout the mountains like repeated, sharp cracks of thunder, one right after another. As if bolts of lightning had sliced through the roof of the forest, splitting the wood of a hundred trees around him. But they signified neither lightning nor thunder; they were gunshots.

In spite of the cold, perspiration streamed down Adrian's face, and despite the darkness of the forest, his eyes were filled with unwanted images. His brother had killed again. The major from Eye Corps was efficiently going about his business of death. The screams that followed the shots were faint, muted by the forest barrier, but unmistakable.

Why? For God's sake, *why?!*

He could not think. Not about things like that. Not now. He had to think only on one level—the level of motion. He had made a half-dozen attempts to climb out of the dark labyrinth, each time allowing himself ten minutes to see the light of the forest's edge. Twice he had allowed himself extra time because his eyes played tricks, and in each case there was only further darkness, no end in sight.

He was rapidly going out of his mind. He was caught in a maze; thick shafts of bark and unending, prickling branches and cracked limbs creased his face and his legs. How many times had he gone in circles? He could not tell. Everything began to look like everything else. He'd *seen* that tree! That particular cluster of branches had been his wall five minutes ago! His flashlight was no help. Its illuminations imitated themselves; he could not tell one from another. He was lost in the middle of an impenetrable slope of Alpine woods. Nature had altered the trail in the decades since the Leinkraus mourners made their final pilgrimage. The seepage of melting summer snows had spread, inundating the once-negotiable forest, providing a bed of moist earth receptive to unlimited growth.

But knowing this was as useless as his flashlight's distortions. The initial reports of gunfire exploded from over *there*. In *that* direction. He had very little to lose except his breath and what remained of his sanity. He began to run, his head filled with the echoes of the gunfire he had heard seconds ago.

The faster he ran the straighter seemed his course. He slashed a path with his arms, bending, breaking, cracking everything that got in his way.

And he saw the light. He fell to his knees, out of breath, no more than thirty feet from the forest's edge. Gray stone, covered with patches of snow, rose beyond the dense trees and surged out of sight above the highest limbs. He had reached the base of the third plateau.

And so had his brother. The killer from Eye Corps had done what Goldoni believed he could not do: He had taken long-forgotten descriptions written down a half century ago and refined them, made them applicable to the present search. There was a time when brother would have taken pride in brother; that time had passed. There remained only the necessity of stopping him.

Adrian had tried not to think about it, wondering if he'd be capable of accepting it when the moment came. The moment of anguish unlike anything in his imagination. He was accepting it now. Calmly, strangely unmoved, though filled with a cold sadness. For it was the only eminently logical, undeniable response to the horror and the chaos.

He would kill his brother. Or his brother would kill him.

He got to his feet, walked slowly out of the forest and found the path of rock diagramed on the Leinkraus map. It wound up the mountain, a series of wide curves to lessen the angle of ascent, veering always clockwise until it reached the top. Or almost the top, for at the base of the plateau was a sheet of rock that Paul Leinkraus recalled was quite high. He had made the journey only twice—in the first and second years of the war—and was very young. The sheet of rock might not be as high as he remembered it to be, for the memory was in the context of a boy's perspective. But they had used a ladder, he recalled that clearly.

A solemn service for the dead and a young boy's sense of life were incompatible, Leinkraus had admitted. There was another way to the plateau, hardly practical for old men, but explored by a youngster lacking the proper respect for religious observance. It was at the very end of the seemingly vanished path, well past an enormous natural arch that was the continuation of the mountain trail. It consisted of a series of jagged rocks that followed the line of the narrowing summit, and necessitated sure feet and a willingness to take chances. His father and older brother had scolded him severely for using it. The drop was dangerous; probably not fatal, but sufficiently deep to break an arm or a leg.

If an arm or a leg were broken now, thought Adrian, the danger *was* fatal. An immobilized man was an easy target.

He started up the winding path, between the intermittent rocks, crouching to conceal his body below their height. The plateau was three hundred to four hundred feet above the path, the distance of a football field. A light snow began to fall, settling itself delicately on the thin layer of white that already covered much of the rock. His feet slipped continuously; he balanced himself by grabbing shrubs and projections of jagged rock.

He reached the midpoint of the climb and pressed his back into a concave flute of stone to catch his breath unseen. He could hear sounds above him, metal against metal, or rock against rock. He lunged out of the recess and ran as fast as he could, up and around the next four bends of the trail, falling once to let untrapped, unswallowed air fill his lungs, to give his aching legs a chance to rest.

He pulled the Leinkraus diagram from his pocket and checked off the curves on the map; he had covered eight, he thought. Whatever, it wasn't any farther than a hundred feet to the arch, symbolized by an inverted U on the diagram. He raised his head, his face bitter cold from the temporary pillow of frost and snow. There was a straight stretch of trail, bordered on both sides by gray, gnarled shrubbery. According to the map, there were two more hairpin curves above that stretch and then the arch of rock. He jammed the diagram into his pocket, feeling the steel of his gun as he did so. He pulled his legs up under him into a crouch and raced on.

He saw the girl first. She was lying off the trail in the shrubs, her eyes wide, staring at the overcast sky, her legs stretched rigidly in front of her. There were two bullet holes above each knee, the blood matted about the cloth. A third puncture could be seen above her right breast, below her collar bone; blood had formed a solid stream down her white Alpine jacket.

She was alive, but in such a degree of shock that she did not blink her eyes against the particles of falling snow. Her lips were moving, trembling, melted snow forming rivulets of water at the edges. Adrian bent over her.

At the sight of his face, her eyes blinked into focus. She raised her head in convulsion, coughing the start of a scream. Gently, he pressed his gloved hand over the mouth, supporting her neck with his other hand.

"I'm not him," he whispered.

The brush above them moved. Adrian whipped up, releasing the girl as carefully as he could, and sprang back. A hand edged its way over the snow—what was left of a hand. It was bloodstained flesh, the glove blown off, the fingers shattered. Fontine crept over the girl and up into the tangled, gnarled shrubbery, ripping the intertwined branches apart. The boy lay on his stomach in a bed of wild mountain grass. A straight line of four bullet wounds angled diagonally along his back, across his spine.

Adrian rolled the youth carefully over on his side, cradling his head. Once again he gently pressed a hand over a mouth in shock. The boy's eyes locked with his and within seconds Adrian's meaning was clear: He was not the killer. That the boy could speak at all was extraordinary. His whisper was nearly covered by the growing wind, but Fontine heard him.

"Mia sorella."

"I don't understand."

"Sister?"

"She's hurt. So are you. I'll do everything I can."

"Pacco. The pack. He wears a pack. *Medicina."*

"Don't talk. Save your strength. A pack?"

"Si!"

. . . *An Alpine pack is not a mere collection of straps and leather casing. It is a work of master craftsmanship.* . . . His father had said that.

The boy would not stop. He knew he was dying. "A way out. The Zermatt railroad. A village. Not far, *signore.* North, not far. We were going to run."

"Shhh. Don't say any more. I'm going to put you next to your sister. Keep as warm as you can."

He half carried, half dragged the boy over the grass to the girl. They were children; his brother murdered children. He removed his raincoat and jacket, tearing the lining of the jacket in order to tie the strips around the girl's wounds. There wasn't much he could do about the boy's, so he avoided his eyes. He covered them both; they held each other.

He put the heavy pistol in his belt beneath the heavy black sweater and crawled out of the sanctuary of the bushes. He raced up the path to the arch, his eyes stinging but his breath steady, the pain in his legs gone.

It was one against one now. The way it had to b̶

33

The sound of cracking came louder, hammerlike and furious. It was directly above him, above the sheer sheet of rock that sprang up, facing the small, defined plateau on the north side. The ground at his feet was disturbed; snow and earth were intermingled, footprints and broken shrubbery formed a semicircle beneath the overhang. Fragments of rock signified the method of ascent: A rope had been thrown above, with a hook attached, and the first throw or throws had not been successful.

A rotted ladder lay in the snow-laced, gray bushes, a number of its steps torn from the frame. It was the ladder Paul Leinkraus remembered. It was at least twenty feet long, on end, slightly higher than the sheet of rock in front of which Adrian crouched.

The burial ground is really a surface of shale. It cracks easily under the force of a pick to the earth beneath. The child's coffin was placed in the ground and a thin layer of concrete spread over it. The words of Paul Leinkraus.

Above him, his brother had broken through the layer of concrete described by Leinkraus. The hammering stopped; a metal instrument was thrown aside on the hard surface. Large particles of cement plummeted down, kicked by impatient feet, joining the fragments of rock on the ground and the bushes. Adrian got to his feet quickly and pressed himself into the miniature cliff. If he was seen, he was dead.

The spray of cement stopped. Adrian shivered; he knew he had to move. The cold was penetrating the black sweater, his breath formed billows of vapor in front of his face. The brief, light snowfall was letting up; a shaft of sunlight broke through the clouds, but brought no warmth.

He edged his way around the sheet of rock until he could go no farther, blocked by a projecting boulder bulging out of the mountaintop. He stepped forward onto the shrub-covered, snow-layered ground.

Suddenly, the earth gave way. Adrian leaped back and stood motionless, petrified, at the side of the boulder. The sounds of falling rock carried on the wind. He heard the footsteps above—heavy, abrupt—and held his breath so no steam would emerge from his mouth or nostrils. The sound of footsteps stopped—except for the wind, only silence remained. Then the footsteps started again—less heavy, slower. The soldier's alarm had subsided.

Adrian looked down in front of him. He had come to the end of Paul Leinkraus's path; there was only mountain now. Below, beyond the edge of broken earth and wild grass, was a drop, a wide, sweeping crevasse whose empty space separated the ground of the summit from the shallow ledge of earth across from it that led to higher regions. The crevasse was far deeper than Leinkraus remembered; it was well over thirty feet to a floor of jagged rock. The boy had been reprimanded by his elders, but not so truthfully as to frighten him, or instill a fear of the mountains.

Adrian swung his body around and, clinging to the uneven surface, inch by inch, testing each, he moved out, pressing his chest and legs into the boulder, holding whatever sharp point he could grasp. On the other side was a narrow mass of indiscriminately formed rock that angled sharply up to the flat surface of the peak.

He was not sure he could reach it. A small boy could walk on the ledge away from the immediate base of the projecting boulder; it would not give way under his weight. A grown man was something else. It had not taken Adrian's weight; it would not take it.

The distance from the central point of the boulder—where he was—to the first promontory of rock was about five feet. He was over six. If he could angle his fall, with his arms outstretched, there was a good chance his hands would reach. More of a chance if he could narrow the distance.

The muscles of his feet were in agony. He could feel cramps forming in both insteps: the strain on his calves swelled his skin, the tendons beneath arching nearly beyond endurance. He forced all thoughts of pain and risk out of his mind and concentrated only on the inches he could cover around the massive boulder.

He had gone no more than a foot when he felt the ground sinking beneath him—slowly, in minute, hypnotizing stages. Then he could hear—actually *hear*—the cracking of stone and frozen earth. He thrust out his arms at the last half second. The ledge fell away and for a moment he was in the void, suspended. His hands clutched out crazily; the wind whipped against his face in midair.

His right arm crashed over the jagged rock somewhere above him. His shoulder and head slammed into the rough, shagged surface. He clamped his hand around the sharp stone, arching his back instinctively to absorb the shock of the impact.

He swung like a puppet on the string of his own appendage, his feet dangling. He had to drag himself up. *Now!* There were no seconds to waste! No time to adjust to his own disbelief!

Move!

He clawed the uneven cliff with his free left hand; his feet pumped insanely until his right shoe caught a tiny ridge that supported his weight. It was enough. Like a panicked spider he scaled the wall of jagged rock, throwing his legs one after another over the diagonal incline, slamming his body into the base of the inner surface.

He was out of sight from above, not out of hearing. The sounds of the falling ledge brought Andrew to the edge of the plateau. The sun was behind him on his right, casting his shadow across the crevasse, over the rock and snow. Again, Adrian held his breath. He had a window on his own lantern show, played out in the now-blinding Alpine sun. The soldier's movements were not only clear, they were magnified. Andrew held an object in his left hand: a climber's folding shovel.

The soldier's right arm was angled at the elbow; the shadow of his forearm joined the shadow of his upper body. It took little imagination to visualize what the right hand held: a gun. Adrian moved his own right hand to his belt. The pistol was still there; he was grateful for its touch.

The shadow moved about the ledge above, three steps to the left, four to the right. It bent down and then stood up again, another object now in its right hand. The object was thrown off; a large fragment of cement plummeted down no more than two feet from Adrian's face and crashed on the floor of jagged rock below. The soldier stood motionless during the object's fall, as if counting off seconds, timing the descent. The last rolling spatters finished, the soldier walked away. His shadow disappeared, replaced by the harsh reflections of the sun.

Adrian lay in his recess, unaware of his discomfort, his face drenched with sweat. The curve of uneven rocks above his head swept sharply up, like a primitive spiral staircase in an ancient lighthouse. The sweep was about twenty-five feet in length; it was difficult to estimate for there was nothing beyond but sky and blazing sun. He could not move until he heard sounds from above. Sounds that meant the soldier was occupied, digging again.

They came. A loud crushing of stone, the scraping of metal against metal.

Andrew had found the vault!

Adrian crawled out of his shelter and, hand over hand, silent foot after silent foot, made his way up the jagged rock staircase. The ledge of the plateau was directly above; below was no longer the crevasse but a sheer drop of several hundred feet to the winding mountain pass. There were, perhaps, eight inches between him and the open space. The wind was steady. Its sound was a low whistle.

He reached for the pistol in his belt, removed it and—as Goldoni had instructed—checked the safety. It was in upright position, locked.

He snapped it level with the trigger and raised his head over the ledge.

The flat surface of the plateau was an oval, extending thirty-five feet or more in length, twenty or so in width. The soldier crouched in the center, next to a mound of earth covered with fragments of cracked cement. Beyond the dirt, partially concealed by the soldier's broad back, was a plain wooden casket with metal borders; it was remarkably preserved.

There was no vault. There was nothing but earth, the fragments of cement, and the coffin. But no vault!

Oh, my God, thought Adrian. We were *wrong! Both wrong!*

It wasn't possible. It was not possible. For if there were no vault, the killer from Eye Corps would be in a rage. He knew Andrew well enough to know that. But his brother was not angry. He was crouched in thought, his head angled down; he was staring at the grave. And Adrian understood: The vault was below, still in the earth. It had been buried beneath the coffin, that casket its final protection.

The soldier got to his feet and crossed to the Alpine pack which lay upright against the coffin. He bent over, unsnapped a strap, and pulled out a short, pointed iron bar. He returned to the grave, abruptly knelt by the edge, and reached down with the bar. Seconds later he yanked the bar up, letting it fall on the ground, and removed a gun from his jacket. Swiftly, but carefully, he angled the weapon down into the grave.

Three explosions followed. Adrian ducked his head below the edge of the plateau. He could smell the acrid odor of the gunfire, see the billows of smoke carried above him on the wind.

And then the words came and his whole body was locked in a fear he never believed he could experience. It was the shock of the knowledge of his own immediate execution.

"Put your head up, Lefrac," was the soft-spoken command, delivered in a monotone of ice. "It'll be quicker that way. You won't feel a thing. You won't even hear any noise."

Adrian rose from his narrow perch, his mind blank, beyond fear now. He was going to die; it was as simple as that.

But he was not what the soldier above him expected. Not *whom* the soldier expected. The killer from Eye Corps was suddenly, completely

gripped in shock of his own. It was so total that his eyes widened in disbelief, his hand trembled and the weapon in its grasp wavered. He took
an involuntary step backward, his mouth gaping, the skin on his face
bloodless.

"You!"

Wildly, blindly, without thought or feeling, Adrian whipped up the
heavy Italian pistol from the ledge of rock and fired at the stunned
figure. He squeezed the trigger twice, three times. The gun jammed. The
spits and smoke from the barrel-housing singed his flesh, stung his eyes.
But he had hit the soldier! The killer from Eye Corps reeled backward,
holding his stomach, his left leg buckling beneath him.

But Andrew still had the pistol in his hand. The explosion came; a
crack of air detonated above Adrian's head. He lunged at the fallen
man, crashing the jammed pistol down in the area of the face. His right
hand shot out, grabbing the hot steel of Andrew's gun, slamming it
against the hard surface of the plateau. His own pistol found its mark;
the bridge between the soldier's eyes erupted; blood flowed into the
corners of his sockets, blurring his vision. Andrew's pistol flew out of his
hand. Adrian sprang back.

He aimed his gun and squeezed the trigger with all his strength. It
would not operate, it would not *fire*. The soldier got to his knees, rubbing his eyes, his mouth emitting grunts of fury. Adrian lashed out his
foot, catching the killer from Eye Corps at the temple; the soldier's
neck arched back, but his legs shot forward, twisting, kicking, slamming
into Adrian's kneecaps, causing him to lurch to the side, his knees suddenly in agony.

Adrian could not stay on his feet. He rolled to his right as the major
leaped up, still wiping his eyes. Andrew sprang off the ground, hands
now outstretched like rigid hooks, directly at his intruder's neck. Adrian
recoiled farther, crashing into the casket at the side of the grave. The
soldier's lunge was uncontrolled; the screaming pitch of his anger
caused him to lose his balance, and he fell, one arm plunged into the
mound of earth and fragments of concrete. The earth flew; an eruption
of dirt and snow and rock.

Adrian dove over the open space of the grave; on the opposite side
was the iron bar. The soldier followed; he lunged up, screaming at
Adrian, his hands locked above his head into a hammer—a monstrous
bird screeching in for the kill. Adrian's fingers were on the bar, and he
lashed it up at the plummeting figure.

The point plunged into the soldier's cheek, stunning him. Blood burst
again from Andrew's flesh.

Adrian lurched away as fast as his exhausted, aching legs could propel him, dropping the bar. He saw the soldier's pistol lying across the flat stone surface; he lunged for it. His fingers wound around the handle; he raised it.

The iron bar came slicing through the air, creasing the skin of his left shoulder, tearing the sleeve half off his sweater. The shock sent him reeling back to the edge of the sheet of rock. He had brought the hand with the gun across his chest in panic; he knew the instant he did so it was the fraction of a second the soldier desperately needed. A wall of earth and stone came at him, the space between himself and the killer from Eye Corps was filled with debris. It smashed into him; sharp pieces of rock pummeled his face, his eyes. He could not see.

He fired. His hand recoiled violently from the explosion of the weapon; his fingers arched from the vibration.

He tried to get to his feet; a boot hammered into his neck. He caught the leg as he fell back, his shoulders over the edge of the sheet of rock. He rolled to his left, holding the leg until he felt the barrel of the gun against the flesh.

He pulled the trigger.

Flesh and bone and blood filled his universe. The soldier was blown off the ground, his right leg a mass of red-soaked cloth. Adrian started to crawl but he could not; there was no strength left, no air in his lungs. He raised himself on one hand and looked over at Andrew.

The major writhed back and forth, moans coming from his throat, his mouth filled with blood and saliva. He pushed himself off the ground, halfway to his knees, his eyes staring insanely at what was left of his leg. He looked over to his executioner. And then he screamed.

"*Help me!* You can't let me *die!* You *don't have the right!* Get me the *pack!*" He coughed, holding his shattered leg with one hand, his other trembling, gesturing at the Alpine pack against the coffin. The blood flowed everywhere, saturating his clothes. The poisons were spreading rapidly; he was dying.

"I don't have the right to let you live," said Adrian weakly, gasping for air. "Do you know what you've done? The people you killed?"

"Killing's an *instrument!*" screamed the soldier. "That's all it is!"

"Who decides when the instrument's used? *You?*"

"*Yes!* And men *like* me! We know who we are, what we can do. People like you, you're *not*——. For Christ's sake, *help me!*"

"You make the rules. Everybody else follows."

"Yes! Because we're willing to! People everywhere, they're not willing. They want the rules made for them! You can't deny that!"

"I do deny it," said Adrian quietly.

"Then you're lying. Or stupid! Oh, *Christ* . . ." The soldier's voice broke, interrupted by a spasm of coughing. He clutched his stomach and stared at his leg again, and then at the mound of dirt. He pulled his eyes away and looked at Adrian. "Here. Over *here*."

The major crawled toward the grave. Adrian rose slowly to his feet and watched, mesmerized by the horrible sight. What was left of his compassion told him to fire the weapon in his hand, end the life that was nearly finished. He could see the vault from Salonika in the ground; slats of rotted wood had been pulled away, revealing the iron beneath. Strips of metal had been shattered by gunfire, a coil of rope lay on top. There were torn pieces of heavy cardboard with faint markings that looked like circles of thorns around crucifixes.

They had found it.

"Don't you understand?" The soldier could barely be heard. "It's there. The answer. The *answer!*"

"What answer?"

"*Everything.* . . ." For several seconds his brother's eyes lost muscular control; they rolled in their sockets, and for an instant the pupils disappeared. Andrew's speech had the inflections of an angry child; his right hand extended into the grave. "I have it now. You can't interfere! Anymore! You can help me now. I'll let you help me. I used to let you help me, remember? You remember how I *always used to let you help me?*" The soldier screamed the question.

"It was always your decision, Andy. To let me help you, I mean," said Adrian softly, trying to understand the childlike rambling, hypnotized by the words.

"Of course my decision. It had to be *my decision*. Victor's and mine."

Adrian suddenly recalled their mother's words . . . *he saw the results of strength; he never understood its complications, its compassion.* . . . The lawyer in Adrian had to know. "What should we do with the vault? Now that we've got it, what should we do with——"

"*Use it!*" The soldier screamed again, pounding the loose rock at the edge of the grave. "*Use* it, use it! Make things *right!* We'll tell them we can ruin *everything!*"

"Suppose we can't? Suppose it doesn't matter? Maybe there's nothing there."

"We tell them *there is!* You don't know how to do it. We tell them anything we *want* to tell them! They'll *crawl*, they'll *whine*. . . ."

"You want them to do that? To crawl and whine?"

"Yes! They're weak!"

"But you're not."

"No! I've *proved* it! Over and over and *over again!*" The soldier's neck arched and then snapped forward convulsively. "You think you see things *I* don't see. You're *wrong!* I see them but they don't make *any difference,* they don't *count!* What you think's so goddamned important . . . *doesn't . . . matter!*" Andrew spaced out the words; it was a child's cry of defiance.

"What's that, Andy? What is it I think is so important?"

"*People!* What they *think!* It doesn't *count,* doesn't *matter.* Victor knows that."

"You're wrong; you're *so* wrong," interrupted Adrian quietly. "He's dead, Andy. He died a couple of days ago."

The soldier's eyes regained part of their focus. There was elation in them. "Now everything's *mine!* I'll do it!" The coughing returned; the eyes wandered again. "Make them understand. They're not important. Never were. . . ."

"Only you."

"Yes! I don't hesitate. *You do!* You can't make up your mind!"

"You're decisive, Andy."

"Yes, *decisive.* That's important."

"And people don't count, so naturally they can't be trusted."

"What the hell are you trying to say?" The soldier's chest expanded in pain; his neck arched back, then shot forward, mucus and blood coughed through his lips.

"That you're *afraid!*" shouted Adrian. "You've always been afraid! You live scared to death that someone'll find that out! There's a big crack in your armor . . . you *freak!*"

A terrible, muted cry came from the soldier's throat; it was at once guttural and clear, a cross between a roar of final anger and a wail. "That's a *lie!* You and your goddamned words. . . ."

Suddenly there were no more words. The unbelievable was happening in the blinding Alpine sunlight, and Adrian knew only that he would move or die. The soldier's hand was in the grave. He whipped it out. In his grip was a rope; he lurched off the ground, swinging the rope violently. Tied to the end was a grappling hook, its three prongs slashing though the air.

Adrian sprang to his left, firing the enormous weapon at the crazed killer from Eye Corps.

The soldier's chest exploded. The rope, held in a grip of steel, swung in a circle—the grappling hook spinning like an insanely off-course gyroscope—around the soldier's head. The body shot forward, over the sheet of rock, and plummeted down, its scream echoing, filling the mountains with its pitch of horror.

With a sudden, sickening vibration the rope sprang taut, quivering in the thin layer of disturbed snow.

There was the sound of cracking metal from the grave. Adrian whipped his eyes over to its source. The rope had been lashed to a steel band around the vault. The band snapped. The vault could be opened.

But Adrian did not go to it. He limped to the edge of the plateau and looked over the sheet of rock.

Suspended below was the soldier's body, the grappling hook imbedded in his neck. A prong had plunged up through Andrew's throat, its point protruding from the gaping mouth.

He filled the large Alpine pack with the three steel, airtight containers from the vault. He could not read the ancient writing etched in the metal. He did not have to; he knew what each container held. None were large. One was flat, thicker than the other two: within it were the documents compiled by the scholars of Constantine 1,500 years ago, studies that traced what they believed was a theological inconsistency—raising a holy man to one substance with God. Questions for new scholars to ponder. The second container was short, tubular; it held the Aramaic scroll that had so frightened powerful men thirty years ago that strategies of global war were secondary to its possession. But it was the third container, thin, no more than eight inches wide, ten high, that held the most extraordinary document of all: a confession written on a parchment, taken out of a Roman prison nearly 2,000 years ago. It was this receptacle—black, pitted, a relic of antiquity—that was the essence of the vault from Salonika.

All were the denials; only the confession on the Roman parchment could produce an agony beyond men's minds. But that was not for him to judge. Or was it?

He put the plastic bottles of medicine into his pockets, threw the pack down on the ground, lowered himself over the edge of the sheet of rock—next to the soldier's body—and dropped to the earth beneath. He strapped the heavy pack on his back and started down the trail.

The boy was dead. The girl would live. Together they would somehow walk out of the mountains, of that Adrian was convinced.

They traveled slowly—a few steps at a time—down the trail toward the Zermatt tracks. He held the girl so that as little weight as possible was forced on her wounded legs.

He looked back up the mountain trail. In the distance the soldier's body hung suspended against the white sheet of rock. It could not be seen clearly—only if you knew where to look—but it was there.

Was Andrew the final death demanded by the train from Salonika? Were the documents in that vault worth so much life? So much violence for so many years? He had no answers.

He only knew insanity was given unearned stature in the name of holy things. Holy wars were primeval; they always would be. And he had killed a brother for their part of an unholy war.

He felt the terrible weight on his back. He was tempted to remove the steel containers and heave them into the deepest gorge in the mountains. Broken, left to wither into nothing with the first touch of air. Swept away by the Alpine winds into oblivion.

But he would not do that. The price had been too steep.

"Let's go," he said to the girl, gently placing her left arm around his neck. He smiled at the child's frightened face. "We're going to make it."

PART FOUR

34

Adrian stood by the window overlooking the dark expanse of Central Park. He was in the small staff lounge at the Metropolitan Museum. He held the telephone to his ear and listened to Colonel Tarkington in Washington. Across the room sat a priest from the Archdiocese of New York, the monsignor named Land. It was shortly past midnight; the army officer in Washington had been given the private number of the museum. He was told that Mr. Fontine expected his call, regardless of the hour.

Official documentation of events surrounding Eye Corps would be issued by the Pentagon in due time, the officer told Adrian. The administration wanted to avoid the scandal that would result from charges of corruption and insurrection within the armed forces. Especially as a prominent name was involved. It did not serve the interests of national security.

"Stage one," said Adrian. "Cover-up."

"Perhaps."

"You're going to settle for that?" asked Fontine quietly.

"It's your family," replied the colonel. "Your brother."

"And yours. I can live with it. Can't you? Can't Washington?"

There was silence on the other end of the line. Finally the officer spoke. "I got what I wanted. And maybe Washington can't. Not now."

"It's never 'now.' "

"Don't preach to me. Nobody's stopping you from holding a press conference."

It was now Adrian who was momentarily silent. "If I do, can I demand official documentation? Or would a dossier suddenly appear, describing——"

"Describing in psychiatric detail," interrupted the colonel, "a very disturbed young man who ran around the country living in hippie communes; who aided and abetted three convicted army deserters in San Francisco. Don't kid yourself, Fontine. It's on my desk."

"I thought it might be. I'm learning. You're thorough, aren't you? Which brother's the lunatic?"

"It goes much further. Family influence used to avoid military ser-

vice; past membership in radical organizations—they're using dynamite
these days. Your odd behavior recently in Washington, including a relationship with a Black attorney who was killed under strange circumstances, said Black lawyer suspected of criminal activities. Lots more.
And that's only you."

"What?"

"Old truths—documented truths—are dragged up. A father who made
a fortune operating all over the world with governments many believe
are inimicable to our interests. A man who worked closely with the
Communists, whose first wife was killed years ago under very odd circumstances in Monte Carlo. That's a disturbing pattern. Questions are
raised. Can the Fontines live with *that?*"

"You make me sick."

"I make myself sick."

"Then why?"

"Because a decision had to be made that goes beyond you and me
and our personal revulsions!" The colonel raised his voice in anger,
then controlled himself. "I don't like a lot of bullshit players upstairs. I
only know—or think I know—that maybe it isn't the time to talk about
Eye Corps."

"So it goes on and on. You don't sound like the man I talked to in a
hotel room."

"Maybe I'm not. I only hope for the sake of your righteous indigna-
tion you're never put in a position like this."

Adrian looked at the priest across the room. Land was staring at the
dimly lit white wall, at nothing. Yet it was in his eyes, *it's always in the
eyes.* A desperation that consumed him. The monsignor was a very
strong man, but he was frightened now. "I hope I never am," he said to
the colonel.

"Fontine?"

"Yes?"

"Let's have a drink sometime."

"Sure. We'll do that." Adrian hung up.

Was it up to him now? wondered Adrian. Everything? Was the time
ever right to tell the truth?

There'd be one answer soon. He'd gotten the documents from the
vault out of Italy with the colonel's help; the colonel owed him that
much, and the colonel did not ask questions. The colonel's payment was
a body suspended in front of a sheet of rock in the mountains of
Champoluc. Brother for brother. Debt paid.

Barbara Pierson had known what to do with the documents. She contacted a friend who was a curator of relics and artifacts at the Metropolitan. A scholar who had devoted his life to study of the past. He had seen too much of antiquity to make judgments.

Barbara had flown down from Boston; she was in the laboratory with the scholar now. They'd been there since five-thirty. Seven hours. With the documents from Constantine.

But there was only one document that mattered now. It was the parchment taken out of a Roman prison 2,000 years ago. The parchment was everything. *Everything*. The scholar understood that.

Adrian left the window and walked across the room to the priest. Two weeks ago, when his father was close to death, Victor drew up his list of men to whom the vault of Constantine was to be delivered. Land's name was on that list. When Adrian contacted him, Land began saying things to him he had never said to Victor Fontine.

"Tell me about Annaxas," said Adrian, sitting down opposite the priest.

The monsignor looked away from the wall, startled. Not by the name, thought Fontine, but by the intrusion. His large, penetrating gray eyes under the dark brows were momentarily unfocused. He blinked, as if remembering where he was.

"Theodore Dakakos? What can I tell you? We first met in Istanbul. I was tracing what I knew was false evidence. The so-called destruction by fire of the Filioque documents. He found out I was there and flew up from Athens to meet the interfering priest from the Vatican archives. We talked; we were both curious. I, why such a prominent man of commerce was so interested in obscure theological artifacts. He, why a Roman scholar was pursuing—*allowed* to pursue, perhaps—a thesis hardly in the Vatican's interests. He was very knowledgeable. Each of us manuevered throughout the night, both of us finally exhausted. I think it was the exhaustion that caused it. And the fact that we thought we knew one another, perhaps even liked one another."

"Caused what?"

"The train from Salonika to be mentioned. Strange, I don't remember which of us said it first."

"He *knew* about it?"

"As much, or more, than I. The trainman was his father, the single passenger; the priest of Xenope, his father's brother. Neither man ever returned. In his search he found part of the answer. The police records in Milan contained an old entry from December 1939. Two dead men on a Greek train in the freight yards. Murder and suicide. No identification. Annaxas had to know why."

"What led him to Milan?"

"Over twenty years of asking questions. He had reason enough. He watched his mother go insane. She went mad because the church would give her no answers."

"Her church?"

"An arm of the church, if you will. The Order of Xenope."

"Then she knew about the train."

"She was never supposed to have known. It was believed she didn't. But men tell things to their wives they tell no one else. Before the elder Annaxas left early that morning in December of 1939, he said to his wife that he was not going to Corinth, as everyone believed. Instead, God would look favorably on them for he was joining his brother Petride. They were going on a journey very far away. They were doing God's work."

The priest fingered the gold cross hanging from a cord on the cloth beneath his collar. His touch was not gentle; there was anger in it.

"From which he never came back," said Adrian quietly. "And there was no brother in the church to reach because he was dead."

"Yes. I think we can both imagine how the woman—a good woman, simple, loving, left with six children—would react."

"She'd go out of her mind."

Land let the cross drop, his eyes straying back to the wall. "As an act of charity, the priests of Xenope took the mad woman in. Another decision was made. She died within a month."

Fontine slowly sat forward. "They killed her." It was not a question.

Land's gaze returned. There was a degree of supplication in his eyes now. "They weighed the consequences of her life. Not against the Filioque, but in relation to a parchment none of us in Rome ever knew existed. I'd never heard of it until this evening. It makes so many things so much clearer."

Adrian got out of the chair and walked back to the window. He was not ready to discuss the parchment. The holy men no longer had the right to direct inquiries. The attorney in Adrian disapproved of the priests. Laws were for all.

Down in Central Park, along a dimly lit path, a man was walking two huge Labrador retrievers, the animals straining at their leashes. He was straining on a leash of his own, but he could not let Land know it. He turned from the window. "Dakakos put it all together, didn't he?"

"Yes," replied Land, accepting Adrian's refusal to be led. "It was his legacy. He vowed to learn everything. We agreed to exchange information, but I was more forthright than he. The name Fontini-Cristi surfaced, but the parchment was never mentioned. The rest, I assume, you know."

Adrian was startled by the priest's words. "Don't assume anything. Tell me."

Land flinched. The rebuke was unexpected. "I'm sorry. I thought you knew. Dakakos took over the responsibility of Campo di Fiori. For years he paid the taxes—which were considerable—fended off buyers, real-estate developers, provided security, and upkeep——"

"What about Xenope?"

"The Order of Xenope is all but extinct. A small monastery north of Salonika. A few old priests on diminished farmland, with no money. For Dakakos, only one link remained: a dying monk at Campo di Fiori. He couldn't let it go. He extracted everything the old man knew. Ultimately, he was right. Gaetamo was released from prison; the banished priest, Aldobrini, came back from Africa dying of assorted fevers and, finally, your father returned to Campo di Fiori. The scene of his family's execution. The terrible search began all over again."

Adrian thought. "Dakakos stopped my brother. He went to extraordinary lengths to trap him, expose Eye Corps."

"To keep him from the vault at all costs. The old monk must have told Dakakos that Victor Fontine knew about the parchment. He understood that your father would act outside the authorities, use his sons to find the vault. He had to. Weighing the consequences, there was no other course. Dakakos studied both of you. Actually he had you watched for several years. What he found in one son shocked him. Your brother could not be permitted to go further. He had to be destroyed. You, on the other hand, were someone he felt he could work with, if it came to that."

The priest had stopped. He inhaled deeply, his fingers once again around the gold cross on his chest. Thought had returned to him and it was obviously painful. Adrian understood; he had experienced the same feeling in the mountains of Champoluc.

"What would Dakakos have done if he'd found the vault?"

Land's penetrating gaze settled on Adrian. "I don't know. He was a compassionate man. He knew the anguish of seeking painful answers to very painful questions; his sympathy might have guided his judgment. Still, he was a man of truth. I think he would have weighed the consequences. Beyond this I can't help you."

"You use that phrase a lot, don't you? 'Weighing the consequences.'"

"I apologize if it offends you."

"It does."

"Then forgive me, but I must offend you further. I asked your permission to come here, but I've changed my mind. I'm going to leave." The priest got out of the chair. "I can't stay. I'll try to put it simply——"

"Simply *put*," interrupted Adrian harshly, "I'm not interested."

"You have the advantage," replied Land quickly. "You see, I'm interested in *you*, in what you perceive." The priest would not be stopped; he took a step forward. "Do you think doubts are erased because vows are taken? You think seven thousand years of human communication is somehow voided for us? Any of us, whatever the vestments we wear? How many gods and prophets and holy men have been conjured over the centuries? Does the number lessen the devotion? I think not. For each accepts what he can accept, raising his own beliefs above all others. My doubts tell me that thousands of years from now scholars may study the remnants of what we were and conclude that our beliefs—our devotions—were singularly odd, consigning to myth what we think most holy. As we have consigned to myth the remnants of others. My intellect, you see, can conceive of this. But now, here, in my time—for me—the commitment is made. It's better to have it than not to have it. I do believe. I am convinced."

Adrian remembered the words. "'Divine revelation cannot be contravened by mortal man'?"

"That's good enough. I'll accept that," said Land simply. "Ultimately, the lessons of Aquinas prevail. They're not the exclusive property of anyone, I might add. When reason is exhausted, at its last barrier, faith becomes the reason. I have that faith. But being mortal, I'm weak. I haven't the endurance to test myself further. I must retreat to the comfort of my commitment, knowing I'm better with it than without it." The priest held out his hand. "Good-bye, Adrian."

Fontine looked at the outstretched hand and accepted it. "You understand that it's the arrogance of your 'commitment,' your beliefs, that disturbs me. I don't know any other way to put it."

"I understand; your objection is noted. That arrogance is the first of the sins that lead to spiritual death. And the one most often overlooked: pride. It may kill us all one day. Then, my young friend, there'll be nothing."

Land turned and walked to the door of the small lounge. He opened it with his right hand, his left still holding the gold cross, enveloping it. The gesture was unmistakable. It was an act of protection. He looked once more at Adrian, then walked out of the room, closing the door behind him.

Fontine lighted a cigarette, then crushed it out. His mouth was sour from too many cigarettes and too little sleep. Instead, he went to a coffee maker and poured himself a cup.

An hour ago Land, testing the metal rim of the hot plate, had burned his fingers. It occurred to Adrian that the monsignor was the sort of man who tested most things in life. And yet he could not accept the final test. He merely walked away; there was a kind of honesty in that.

Far more than he had shown his mother, reflected Adrian. He had not lied to Jane; it would have been useless, the lie known for what it was. But neither had he told her the truth. He had done a far crueler thing: he had avoided her. He was not yet ready for confrontation.

He heard footsteps in the corridor outside the lounge. He put his coffee down and walked to the center of the room. The door opened and Barbara entered, the door held for her by the scholar, still in his laboratory smock, his horn-rimmed glasses somehow magnifying his face. Barbara's brown eyes, usually so filled with warmth and laughter, were sharp with professional involvement.

"Doctor Shire's finished," she said. "May we have coffee?"

"Sure." Adrian went back to the table and poured two cups. The scholar sat down in the chair from which Land had risen just minutes ago.

"Black, if you please," said Shire, placing a single page of paper in his lap. "Your friend has left?"

"Yes, he left."

"Did he know?" asked the old man, accepting the coffee.

"He knew because I told him. He made his decision. He left."

"I can understand," said Shire, blinking his old eyes beyond the glasses in the steam of his coffee. "Sit down, both of you."

Barbara took the coffee but did not sit. She and the scholar exchanged looks; she walked to the window as Adrian sat across from Shire.

"Is it authentic?" asked Fontine. "I imagine that's the first question."

"Authentic? As to time and materials and script and language . . . yes, I would say it will survive those examinations. I'm going under the assumption that it will. Chemical and prismatic analyses take a long time, but I've seen hundreds of documents from the period; it's authentic on these points. As to the authenticity of the contents. It was written by a half-crazed man facing death. A very cruel and painful form of death. That judgment will have to be made by others, if it's to be made at all." Shire glanced at Adrian as he placed the coffee cup on the table beside the chair and picked up the paper on his lap. Fontine remained silent. The scholar continued.

"According to the words on that parchment, the prisoner who was to lose his life in the arena on the following afternoon renounced the name of Peter, given him by the revolutionary named Jesus. He said he was not worthy of it. He wanted his death to be recorded as one Simon of Bethsaida, his name at birth. He was consumed with guilt, claiming he had betrayed his savior. . . . For the man who was crucified on Calvary was *not* Jesus of Nazareth."

The old scholar stopped, his words floating, suspended, as if broken off in midsentence.

"Oh, my God!" Adrian got out of the chair. He looked at Barbara by the window. She returned his gaze without comment. He turned back to Shire. "It's that specific?"

"Yes. The man was in torment. He writes that three of Christ's disciples acted on their own, *against* the carpenter's wishes. With the help of Pilate's guards, whom they bribed, they took an unconscious Jesus out of the dungeons and substituted a condemned criminal of the same size and general appearance, dressing him in the carpenter's clothes. In the hysterical crowds the next day, the shroud and the blood from the thorns were sufficient to obscure the features of the man under and on the cross. It was *not* the will of the man they called a messiah——"

" 'Nothing is changed,' " interrupted Adrian softly, remembering the words. " 'Yet all is changed.' "

"He was involuntarily removed. It was his intention to die, not to live. The parchment is clear on that."

"But he didn't die. He *did* live."

"Yes."

"He was *not* crucified."

"No. If one accepts the word of the man who wrote the document—under the conditions he wrote it. Barely on the brink of sanity, I should think. I wouldn't accept it merely because of its antiquity."

"Now you're making a judgment."

"An observation of probability," corrected Shire. "The writer of the parchment lapsed into wild prayer and lamentations. His thoughts were lucid one moment, unclear the next. Madman or self-flagellating ascetic? Pretender or penitent? Which one? Unfortunately, the physical fact that it's a document from two thousand years ago lends a credibility that would certainly be withheld under less striking circumstances. Remember, it was the time of Nero's persecutions, a period of social, political, and theological madness. People survived more often than not on sheer ingenuity. Who was it, *really?*"

"The document spells it out. Simon of Bethsaida."

"We have only the writer's word for it. There is no record of Simon Peter's having gone to his death with the early Christian martyrs. Certainly it would be part of the legend, yet there's no mention of it in biblical studies. If it were so, and overlooked, it's an awesome omission, isn't it?"

The scholar removed his glasses and wiped the thick lens with a corner of his smock. "What are you trying to say?" Adrian asked.

The old man put the glasses back on his face, magnifying his thoughtful, sad eyes. "Suppose a citizen of Rome, scheduled for a most horrible form of execution, invents a story that impugns the hated mark of an upstart, dangerous religion, and does so in a believable manner. Such a man might find favor with the praetors, the consuls, with a caesar himself. A great many tried it, you know. In one form or another. There are remnants of scores of such 'confessions.' And now one of them in its complete form comes down to us. Is there any reason to accept it more than the others? Merely because it *is* complete? Ingenuity and survival are commonplace in history."

Adrian watched the scholar closely as he spoke. There was a strange anxiety in the words. "What do *you* think, doctor?"

"It's not important what I think," said Shire, momentarily avoiding Adrian's eyes.

There was silence; it was profoundly moving. "You believe it, don't you?"

Shire paused. "It's an extraordinary document."

"Does it say what happened to the carpenter?"

"Yes," replied Shire, staring at Adrian. "He took his own life three days later."

"Took his *own life?* That's contrary to everything——"

"Yes, it is," interrupted the scholar softly. "The consistency is found in the time factor: three days. Consistency and inconsistency, where's the balance? The confession goes on to say that the carpenter reviled those who interfered, yet still at the end called upon his God to forgive them."

"That's consistent."

"Would you expect otherwise? Ingenuity and survival, Mr. Fontine."
Nothing is changed, yet all is changed.

"What's the condition of the parchment?"

"It's remarkably well preserved. A solution of animal oil, I think, pressed into a vacuum, covered by heavy rock glass."

"And the other documents?"

"I haven't examined them, other than to distinguish them from the parchment. The papers that I presume trace the Filioque agreements as seen by its opponents are barely intact. The Aramaic scroll is, of course, metallic and will take a great deal of time and care to unravel."

Adrian sat down. "Is that the literal translation of the confession?" he asked, pointing to the page of writing in the scholar's hand.

"Sufficiently so. It's unrefined. I wouldn't present it academically."

"May I have it?"

"You may have everything." Shire leaned forward. Adrian reached out and took the paper. "The parchment, the documents; they're yours."

"They don't belong to me."

"I know that."

"Then why? I'd think you'd be pleading with me to let you keep them. Examine them. Startle the world with them."

The scholar removed his thick glasses, his tired eyes creased with exhaustion, his voice quiet. "You've brought me a very strange discovery. And quite frightening. I'm too old to cope with it."

"I don't understand."

"Then I ask you to consider. A death was denied, not a *life*. But in that death was the symbol. If you raise that symbol into question, you risk casting doubt on everything that symbol has come to mean. I'm not sure that's justified."

Adrian was silent for a moment. "The price of truth is too steep. Is that what you're saying?"

"If it's true. But again, there's the terrible absolute of antiquity. Things are accepted because they exist. Homer creates fiction, and centuries later men trace sea routes in search of caves inhabited by one-eyed giants. Froisart chronicles history that never was and is hailed a true historian. I ask you to weigh the consequences."

Adrian got out of the chair and walked aimlessly to the wall. The same area of the wall that Land kept looking at: flat, dimly lit white paint. Nothing. "Can you keep everything here for a while?"

"It can be stored in a laboratory vault. I can send you a receipt of acknowledgment."

Fontine turned. "A vault?"

"Yes. A vault."

"It could have stayed in another."

"Perhaps it should have. For how long, Mr. Fontine?"

"How long?"

"How long will it remain here?"

"A week, a month, a century. I don't know."

He stood by the hotel window overlooking the Manhattan skyline. New York pretended to sleep, but the myriad lights below on the streets denied the pretense.

They had talked for several hours, how many he didn't really know. *He* had talked; Barbara had listened, gently forcing him to say it all.

There was so much to do, to go through, before he found his head again.

Suddenly—the sound somehow terrifying—the telephone rang. He wheeled around, too aware of the panic he felt, knowing it was in his eyes.

Barbara got out of her chair and walked calmly over to him. She reached up and held his face with her hands. The panic subsided.

"I don't want to talk to anyone. Not now."

"Then don't. Tell whoever it is to call in the morning."

It was so simple. The truth.

The telephone rang again. He crossed to the bedside table and picked it up, sure of his intention, confident of his strength.

"Adrian? For God's *sake!* We've been tracing you all over New York! A colonel at I.G. named Tarkington gave us the hotel."

The caller was one of the Justice lawyers recruited by Nevins.

"What is it?"

"It's happened! Everything we've worked for is falling into place. This town is blown apart. The White House is in panic. We're in touch with the Senate judiciary; we're after a special prosecutor. There's no other way it can be handled."

"You've got concrete evidence?"

"More than that. Witnesses, confessions. The thieves are running for cover. We're back in business, Fontine. Are you with us? We can *move* now!"

Adrian thought only briefly before he answered. "Yes, I'm with you."

It was important to keep moving. Certain struggles continued. Others had to be brought to a close. The wisdom was in deciding which.

Date: 2/25/20

LP MYS CLELAND
Cleland, Jane K.,
Antique blues

ANTIQUE BLUES

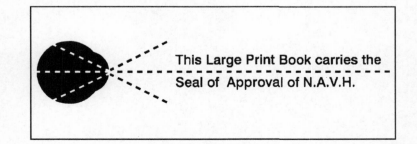

This Large Print Book carries the Seal of Approval of N.A.V.H.

ANTIQUE BLUES

JANE K. CLELAND

THORNDIKE PRESS
A part of Gale, a Cengage Company

Farmington Hills, Mich • San Francisco • New York • Waterville, Maine
Meriden, Conn • Mason, Ohio • Chicago

LIBRARY OF CONGRESS CIP DATA ON FILE.
CATALOGUING IN PUBLICATION FOR THIS BOOK
IS AVAILABLE FROM THE LIBRARY OF CONGRESS

ISBN-13: 978-1-4328-6807-9 (hardcover alk. paper)

Published in 2019 by arrangement with Macmillan Publishing Group, LLC/St. Martin's Press

Printed in Mexico
Print Number: 02   Print Year: 2019

This is for G.D. Peters.
And of course, for Joe.

AUTHOR'S NOTE

This is a work of fiction. While there is a Seacoast Region in New Hampshire, there is no town called Rocky Point, and many other geographic liberties have been taken.

CHAPTER ONE

"The makeup didn't quite cover Lydia's black eye."

I paused just outside the study. I knew the voice. Trish Shannon, my friend Mo's mother, was talking about Mo's kid sister.

I was on my way to the loft to spend some time with Mo's just-purchased Japanese woodblock print, but hearing Trish, I peeked through the one-inch gap between the door and the jamb in time to see Trish brush aside tears. Even though she was in her late sixties, Trish's face was unwrinkled, her complexion creamy. When she retired from her pro golf career, she stopped dyeing her hair, and now, twenty years later, it was mostly silvery white peppered with a few streaks of darker-than-night black.

Frank, Mo's dad, a well-regarded blues guitarist, slapped his chair arm. "Son of a bitch."

"We don't know it was Cal."

"Who else? You think Lydia has someone else in her life who hits her?"

"To be fair, we've never seen her with a black eye before. She says she fell down."

"He treats her like dirt, and now he's hitting her? I'll kill him. That's what I'll do, the son of a bitch. Then our baby girl won't have to worry about falling anymore."

Trish smoothed her skirt, then met Frank's eyes. "I'll help."

"Josie?" Mo called from somewhere in back of me, maybe the kitchen.

I scooted to the teak-and-iron spiral staircase that led to the loft. "In here!"

Mo hurried around the corner. Mo's raven-black hair was newly cut into a stylish wedge.

"I know, I know," I said with more composure than I felt. "The party is outside, but I wanted to see the print again, so I thought I'd sneak up to the loft."

Mo flushed. She was a new collector, a bit awed at having taken the leap from admirer to buyer, and the fact that I, the owner of Prescott's Antiques and Auctions, respected her purchase, tickled her.

"I'm thrilled you like it enough to want to see it again. There's no need to sneak, though!"

"Thanks, Mo. Maybe I'll grab Ty. I'd like

10

him to see it, too."

"Mo?" Trish called. "Is that you?"

Mo poked her head into the study.

"Do you have a minute?" Frank asked.

"Sure." Mo turned to me. "Go on ahead. I'll catch up with you."

Mo disappeared into the study, closing the door, and I made my way to the back-yard. Garden-party fun swirled around me, the kind of hum and buzz that comes from fifty people clinking glasses, laughing, and walking across the flagstone patio.

I spotted Ty over by the shed chatting with an attractive woman in her late twenties. She had wavy reddish brown hair that fell to below her shoulders, and curves galore. The whitewashed shed was designed to look like a miniature house, complete with dormer and blue shutters. Ty stepped inside, reappearing seconds later carrying an old-style wooden croquet set.

At the woman's direction, Ty delivered the croquet set to a couple standing on the grass. He smiled at something the redhead said, then left her and walked to the bar. By the time I reached him, he was talking to Lydia, Mo's sister. Lydia was wearing oversized sunglasses, all the better to hide a black eye. She was taller than Mo by several inches, and thinner by several pounds. Her

11

hair was as black as Mo's and cut in an easy-to-maintain short bob. As if Ty felt my presence, he turned in my direction, and when our eyes met, he smiled. My heart gave an extra thump. Ty and I had been a couple for ten years, and I still felt the new-love thrill every time I saw his face. I waggled a finger, asking him to join me. Ty said something to Lydia and crossed the patio.

He smiled down at me. "What's up, cutie?"

"I want you to see Mo's print." As we set off for the loft, I added, "Am I interrupting? Were you getting ready to play croquet?"

"No, although I will if you want to."

I took his hand. "I like croquet. We used to play it when I was a kid."

"Let's buy a set."

"That's a great idea. Our first game for our new life together."

He squeezed my hand. "Speaking of which . . . any more thoughts about the wedding?"

"I'm in favor of it."

"Good."

"But I want to disappear on a Friday and reappear on Monday, married, and you want a proper wedding and a big reception. I just hate being the center of attention."

12

"You're supposed to be the center of attention on your wedding day."

"I don't want to have to perform."

"You're too modest. You give touching toasts. You deliver inspirational speeches."

"Maybe, but I'm never comfortable. I want to enjoy my own wedding."

"Good point."

I didn't know what to do. I didn't want to disappoint Ty, but I didn't want to disappoint myself either.

"Now what?" I asked.

"Now we think." Ty kissed my forehead. "We'll figure it out."

I twirled my engagement ring. We might be struggling a bit with wedding plans, but I was super-excited to be engaged.

When we reached the top of the loft stairs, I blinked, momentarily blinded by the dazzling sunlight streaming in through the wall of windows.

"Nice poster," Ty said.

"It's a Japanese woodblock print, not a poster."

"I was joking."

"Oh." I took a step closer. "It shouldn't be hanging here. The inks break down in sunlight."

"It's holding up fine so far. What's the artist's name again?"

13

"Utagawa Hiroshige, one of Japan's most revered nineteenth-century artists. This print is called *Meguro Drum Bridge and Sunset Hill.* It comes from the series *One Hundred Famous Views of Edo,* which many experts consider to be his finest work."

The winter scene was rendered in shades of white, blue, and brown, with a touch of coppery orange in the shadows. Faint sparkles glittered across the sky. A dark orange rectangular signature cartouche was positioned on the right side, halfway up. A second rectangular cartouche, also in dark orange, was positioned at the top right, abutting a square poem-card. All three contained black calligraphy. The poem-card featured a subtly gradated orange-and-blue design of what appeared to be a shimmering orange sunset reflected on undulating blue water. The vibrant and bold colors in the print were also gradated, especially the blues in the sky and river. I stepped back to consider the picture itself, not the technique. Snowflakes spun against a steel-blue sky. Five people crossed a lapis river on a snow-covered bridge, none of their faces visible. Some were turned aside. Others were hidden by umbrellas. All were hunched over as they trudged through a storm.

"If it's from a series named *One Hundred*

Famous Views of Edo," Ty asked, "how can this one be number one-eleven?"

"I know . . . it's funny. Actually, there are a hundred and eighteen in the series."

"What's Edo?"

"Tokyo. It was renamed in 1868."

"Do you know everything?"

I laughed. "Would that it were so. I looked it up when Mo told me she acquired it. Hiroshige designed it in 1857. Original prints from this series are extremely scarce. Only seven complete sets are known to be extant. No one knows how many sheets were printed from each image in the first place, probably no more than a few hundred, so it's rare to see one, and it's super-rare to see one in such good condition. More than a hundred and fifty years of framing and reframing, packing and moving, exposure to light, curious hands touching and stroking, coffee spills, and so on take their toll."

"You think it's a fake."

"Let's just say that I want to know more about it."

We stood for a while longer, taking in the snow-tipped trees and pristine white hillside, and the people, solitary figures on a snowy bridge.

"I like that," Ty said, pointing to the square poem-card. "He really captured the feeling of moving water."

"The technique is called *bokashi.*" I squinted, and the illusion of undulating water strengthened. "The detail is amazing."

"Bokashi," a man said. "The mark of a master."

I turned quickly. Cal and Lydia were climbing the stairs to join us. Lydia still wore her sunglasses.

Ty and I had seen Lydia several times during the dozen-odd years Mo and I had been friends. At thirty, Lydia was the youngest-ever director of Hitchens University's Technology Transfer Department. She traveled the world negotiating private industry's use of university-owned patents and intellectual property. She was articulate and poised, and not the least bit shy about sharing her opinions. To call her direct was like calling the ocean wet — it was true, but missed the point. I didn't warm to her, but I appreciated that I always knew where I stood with her and that her opinions were always informed and thoughtful. I'd met her boyfriend, Cal Lewis, before, but Ty hadn't. Since Cal and I shared an interest in art and antiques, and he was smart, educated, classically handsome, and utterly charming, I couldn't account for the fact

16

that every time I spent any time with him, I felt like I needed a shower.

"Hey, Lydia," I said, smiling. I allowed my smile to fade some. "Cal."

"Josie!" he said.

He kissed my cheek, and I fought an urge to rub the cooties away.

"I don't know if you've ever met my fiancé, Ty Alverez. He used to be police chief back when you were in high school."

Cal extended his hand for a shake. "And now?"

"Homeland Security. How about you?"

"Assistant professor at Hitchens, art history. I'm also the assistant director of the Langdon Art Museum on campus."

I turned to Ty. "We've been there. Do you remember? They specialize in Asian art."

"Last winter. You liked one of the fishbowls."

Cal smiled at me, and I had to stop myself from backing up a step, a visceral reaction.

"If you liked it," Cal said, "it must be special."

"Everything in the museum is special."

"Is that your specialization?" Ty asked. "Asian art?"

"My dissertation was on the nature of kami in Japanese artifacts. I study the sacred energy communicated from artist to art."

17

He laughed. "You can blame it on the navy. I was stationed in Japan, at Yokosuka, and I got interested in the concept that objects like vases and pots have souls."

Lydia pushed up her glasses. "I love that idea . . . pots have souls."

Cal turned to me. "Isn't that why you were attracted to the fishbowl? Because it spoke to you on a subliminal, emotional level?"

"Not really. I'm awed by objects of great beauty and inspired by the artists and makers who create them, but there's nothing mystical about it. The craftsmanship of that fishbowl . . . well, it's breathtaking." I turned to the print. "Same with this woodblock print. The way Hiroshige was able to create the sense of quiet and isolation — the stillness of a snowstorm. It's an astonishing accomplishment. Where did you find it?"

"A Boston gallery. I heard through the grapevine that it was included in an estate sale they acquired. I got there before they even catalogued the collection. They only deal in contemporary art, so I was able to get a great price. I tried to get my museum to buy it."

"They didn't want it? I'm surprised."

"The only Hiroshige they'd consider is an original *The Great Wave off Kanagawa.* Are

18

you ready for their logic? It's the only work famous enough to add clout to their fundraising, which is, evidently, their sole concern. Absurd!"

"Well, at least you know the print found a good home with Mo."

"That's bull. All fine art should be in museums, not in the hands of greedy and selfish collectors."

My jaw tightened. "Mo doesn't have a greedy or selfish bone in her body."

"All collectors, by definition, are greedy and selfish." He held up a hand like a traffic cop. "I'm not overlooking the fact that I'm the one who sold it, which makes me an accessory to the crime. I get it . . . but Mo's rapaciousness and my complicity are irrelevant. The fact that Mo is a decent woman and I'm a pragmatist aren't germane to the broader point."

"Josie?" Mo called from downstairs.

I leaned over the railing. "Hey, Mo."

"I can't come up now, but I need to talk to you at some point. My insurance company needs an appraisal."

"What about the gallery it came from?"

"Rheingold . . . they're not certified whatevers. You are."

"I'd love to. Thank you, Mo."

Mo's gaze shifted to a spot over my left

shoulder, and her expression darkened. I glanced back. Her eyes were searing into Cal's face with such ferocity, I could almost smell the singed flesh.

Cal smiled at me, but his eyes remained cold. "I can make it easy for you, Joz. Type up my statement of authenticity on your letterhead, attach the receipt, and boom — you're done."

"Thanks, but the insurance company needs to know the print's value, not just whether the seller says it's genuine and the sales price."

"I negotiated a fair price. That sets the value."

"Come on, Cal," Lydia said. "You know better than that." She turned to me. "I deal with this issue all the time. Just now, for instance, I have to figure out how to price a promising but unproven compound. Do I consider what it might be worth to a pharmaceutical company hot for a new diabetes medication? Do I look to past sales for comparable compounds? Do I try to gauge the likelihood of success and discount the price accordingly? I have to deal with imperfect information, insufficient evidence, conflicting expert opinions, and plenty of uncertainty. In other words, how much is a compound with no known value worth?"

Cal laughed. "More than a Japanese woodblock print."

"I rely on data," Lydia said, her eyes fixed on my face, ignoring Cal's comment. "How about you?"

"The same. I always say I'm in the research and analysis business."

"Josie?" We all looked down at Mo. "I've got to get back to the party. I'll bring the print to your place Monday after school, if that's all right."

I told her that would be fine and thanked her again. After one more scorching look at Cal, she headed out.

I turned to Cal. "By any chance, do you know how many impressions of the print were made?"

"No. Sorry."

"How did you authenticate it?"

"I was able to verify provenance. You'll read the details in the statement I gave Mo. Here's the one-minute version: A few years after trade opened with Japan, Abner Barnes went on a fact-finding mission for a Boston merchant, seeking importing or exporting opportunities. That was in 1861. He bought this print for his private collection. It has remained in the Barnes family until now. And, of course, the *bokashi* in the title cartouche proves it's a first edition."

"Why did the Barnes family sell it?"

"Probably the current Barnes is an assistant professor tired of earning a quarter of what his lawyer girlfriend does, so when his dad died, he decided to liquidate the estate." He snickered. "How about you, Ty? I know Josie's at the top of her game. What do you think about having less power and earning less money than Josie?"

Ty glanced down at me and smiled, then turned back to Cal. "Josie and I work in different fields. Each has to be judged on its own merit. As Homeland Security's director of training for the tri-state area, I have plenty of power, and I earn a good living. From what I hear, it's tough to get an assistant professorship, and even tougher to land an assistant director slot in a museum, so it sounds like you're doing well, too."

Cal's mouth twisted into a sardonic grin. "Good deflection, Ty. Sounds like you've had some practice saying it." He winked at me, and I moved closer to Ty. "Speaking of practice, do you play tennis, Ty? Lydia here can't even give me a game."

"No. I never caught the bug."

"How about rock climbing? That's my new favorite hobby. I can get up that wall faster than anyone."

"Which wall?" Ty asked. "I used to climb

quarries for fun. I'd love to give it a try."

"Middleton Gym, on Islington. We should meet there someday. I like a good race."

"Not me. I like to take it slow, plan each move, and execute according to the plan."

"You're not a risk taker."

"Not hardly."

"Which makes for a good security analyst," Lydia said. She play-punched Cal's arm. "And good husband material."

"If you don't mind spending life bored." Cal placed his arm around Lydia's shoulders and squeezed, a little too hard for my taste. "What do you think, baby? You look like you're ready for some champagne."

"Definitely." She raised her hand, a mini-wave good-bye. "Nice chatting."

We stood at the railing and watched them return to the party. As soon as they were out of earshot, Ty began laughing.

"I can't help it," I said. "I hate him."

"I know. I think it's funny."

"Poor Lydia."

"She seems to like him."

Lowering my voice even further, I repeated what I'd overheard, that Trish and Frank thought Cal hit her, that he had escalated from generalized nastiness to physical abuse. "I don't understand staying with a man who hits you."

23

"Maybe she thinks she deserved it."

"Ick."

"Ick?"

"A technical term for dismay." I leaned my head against Ty's shoulder. "I love you."

Ty raised my chin with his index finger, leaned down, and kissed me.

CHAPTER TWO

Gretchen, Prescott's office manager, had hung wind chimes on the inside of our front door years earlier, and they jangled merrily as Mo stepped inside. She held a large red leather portfolio.

After she said hello to everyone, she unzipped the portfolio and lifted out the woodblock print. I placed it on an easel we keep in a corner next to the bank of file cabinets.

Sasha, my chief antiques appraiser, walked toward it slowly, her concentration absolute. "I never thought I'd see a Hiroshige close up."

Fred, my other antiques appraiser, joined her. "Look at the color saturation."

Mo stood nearby beaming like a new mother listening to people coo over her baby.

Following Prescott's protocol, I video-taped the print, front and back, describing it carefully, including its measurements, then uploaded the file to our cloud storage. Gretchen printed a receipt and logged the print into our computer database.

"Do you have time for coffee?" I asked Mo.

She glanced at the clock mounted near the ceiling, a Chessman original. It read 4:35.

"A quick one. My mom's book club meets at the house tomorrow, and I told her I'd make my irresistible chocolate swirl cupcakes before dinner tonight."

"What makes them irresistible?" Cara, our grandmotherly receptionist, asked.

"Sanding sugar. It adds a sweet crunch."

A gleam of interest lit up Cara's eyes. "I've used pearl sugar, but never sanding."

"Pearl is good, too. Sanding is coarser."

"I'm going to try it." Cara looked at me and smiled. "I'll bring up coffee."

I thanked her and pushed open the heavy door to the warehouse.

Mo paused ten steps in, taking in the rows of shelves. A walk-in safe in the corner held our most valuable objects, but our inventory of vintage goods and collectibles was organized by type and stored on open shelving.

"This is incredible, Josie. As long as we've

26

been friends . . . I had no idea."

"Thanks. We sell a lot, so we need to stock a lot."

Hank, Prescott's Maine Coon cat, dashed over and mewed imperatively. He wanted to know where I'd been. "This handsome fellow is Hank." I scooped him up for a cuddle. "Have you been a good boy, Hank?" Angela, the newest addition to our feline family, scampered in our direction. "And this beauty is Angela." She followed us up the stairs. "She's my little angel."

Upstairs, I took one of the yellow brocade Queen Anne wing chairs, and Hank curled up on my lap. I stroked his tummy, activating his purring machine. Mo sat across from me on the matching love seat. She extracted an envelope from her bag and handed it over. I unfolded the documents, the receipt, and Cal's statement of authenticity, which required that I stop petting Hank. Annoyed, he jumped down.

Cal had paid $25,500 to the Rheingold Gallery in Boston for the print, a bargain but not a steal. Stapled to the receipt was a copy of Mo's check to Cal for $28,050, giving him a 10 percent finder's fee, a fair reward for locating the print and negotiating its price.

"Have you purchased anything else

27

through Cal?"

"No. I had no plans to buy anything, but I just fell in love with this print. Besides, between the way Cal found it, you know, just out of the blue, and my godmother leaving me some money, it felt like it was meant to be."

"I know just what you mean. Serendipity. I'm sorry to hear about your godmother, though."

"Thanks. Edith Winslow. She was a dear, one of my mom's golf instructors, and the person who convinced her to go pro. She died about six months ago and left me twenty-five thousand dollars. Wasn't that incredibly generous of her?"

"I bet every time you look at the print, you think of her."

Mo smiled. "Exactly."

I heard the click-clack of Gretchen's heels crossing the concrete and mounting the stairs. Gretchen was the only one among us who wore stilettos every day. She came into the office and lowered the silver tray onto the mahogany butler's table.

"Cara's on the phone, so I deputized myself."

I thanked her and poured from the silver pot into Minton cups.

Mo added a thimbleful of cream to her

coffee and stirred. She waited until the sound of Gretchen's heels faded away, then said, "Lydia thinks paying for an appraisal is a waste of money."

"Your insurance company won't issue the rider without it."

"She said that I don't need insurance, that the print isn't valuable enough to worry about. That since I live at home — that's a nice way for her to get in a dig about my divorce — and the house is secured six ways to Sunday, I shouldn't bother. What do you think? If you were me, would you get the appraisal?"

"Yes. Forget the insurance implications. It's the only way to know what an object is truly worth."

"Lydia's smart and sensible, but she doesn't always consider the whole picture. That example she gave yesterday, about what a new compound might be worth to a pharmaceutical company . . . When you rely so heavily on data and expert opinions, you risk forgetting about the people who are sick."

I felt uncomfortable. If I didn't tread carefully, I'd find myself enmeshed in someone else's family feud.

"You know what I like best about teaching first grade?" Mo continued. "It means something. I teach kids to read. I teach them to empathize. I make good citizens. All Lydia makes is money."

"She *does* help bring new medications to market. Anyway, it's not a competition." I smiled. "Anyone who teaches with as much passion as you do is a hero in my book. So is anyone who volunteers as much as you do."

"Thank you, Josie. I don't know why I let Lydia get under my skin. I'm a grown woman. It's about time I start acting like it."

"You're doing great, Mo!"

Mo sipped her coffee. "I had brunch with Steve yesterday."

I leaned back. "Really? That's a surprise."

I liked Mo a lot. She hadn't confided in me about why she and Steve had split up, but from the scuttlebutt that had made its way around New Hampshire Children First!, I gathered that Steve had a roving eye, and Mo got tired of being lied to.

"I know," Mo said. "I called him about a month ago. I don't know where I found the courage. We've gone out a few times since then. Do you think I'm weak?"

"No! Why would you ask that?"

She placed her cup on the tray. "I'm thinking of getting back with him."

"You must love him very much."

"Everyone will laugh at me."

"I'm not laughing. I think it's romantic. Besides, who cares what other people think? It's your life."

"Not everyone is as nonjudgmental as you are."

"I don't know about that — but thank you. Good luck, Mo. I'll be rooting for you both."

"Thanks." She reached for her coffee cup. "Do you know Nora Burke?"

"No. Who is she?"

"A book club friend I saw yesterday." She set her cup down without drinking. "After I left Steve, three people told me they'd seen him with another woman, at a candlelit dinner, all lovey-dovey in the park, that sort of thing. They thought they were doing the right thing."

"What did you think?"

"That they enjoyed it a bit too much."

"That's awful. Why do you ask? Is Steve seeing Nora?"

"What? No. Sorry . . . I was thinking of something else. I don't know who he was seeing — or even if the accusations were true. He denied it then, and he still does. We broke up because of money." She waved it aside. "Never mind. I need to go." She took one last sip and stood. "This is some of the best coffee ever. What's your secret?"

"Arabica beans, freshly ground. Cara tells me it's the single most important factor."

I walked Mo out.

The trees that ringed the parking lot were dressed in their autumn best. Some leaves glowed like topaz. Others glistened like opals. I took in a deep breath of warm, clean air. September in New Hampshire is perfect, with temperatures in the seventies most days. Everywhere you look, you're surrounded by a mural painted in iridescent pinks, incandescent reds, radiant oranges, and glittering golds, as showy as a peacock. October is perfect, too, a little cooler, with the autumn foliage fading but still teeming with color. Then winter sets in.

Mo leaned against her car, an old Saab. She stared off into the woods for a moment, past the white steeple of the Congregational church next door, toward the ocean.

"Are you going to this year's volunteer appreciation luncheon?" I asked.

Mo turned toward me, shielding her eyes from the sun with the side of her hand. "Sure. How about you?"

"I wouldn't miss it."

That's where Mo and I first met. About a year after I moved to New Hampshire, a dozen years ago, I'd joined the fund-raising committee of New Hampshire Children First! Mo had been wrangling horses in the charity's therapeutic horse-riding program for a few years, starting when she was eighteen. That first year, we sat next to one another at the charity's annual volunteer appreciation luncheon. I'd been stunned to receive the Fund-raiser of the Year award. Mo had received the charity's highest honor, Volunteer of the Year.

Mo opened the driver's side door. "Those kids . . . those horses . . . they've gotten me through more than one dark day."

"You've gotten those kids through some dark days, too."

She gave me a quick hug. I stood and watched until she turned left out of the lot, toward the interstate.

Rheingold Gallery was located on Newbury Street in the tony Back Bay section of Boston. I only knew of it from one mention in an industry publication, *Antiques Insights.* Each issue of the magazine included a column called "Small Victories." The snippet, which I recalled seeing in one of last spring's issues, had compared traditional Japanese art with the hot new Superflat movement. Rheingold had recently acquired some important contemporary works, and the "Small Victories" author had been impressed with Rheingold's catalogue copy, referencing it as an example of how to shrewdly adapt antiques insights to modern-era art. I parked in the garage under Boston Common and walked the few blocks to the address.

Through the plate-glass window, I saw an attractive woman in her forties leaning against a teak desk chatting with a tall man some years younger. She wore a teal-and-beige Chanel tweed suit. Her sandy blond hair was pinned up in a French twist. He wore jeans and an off-white linen shirt, un-tucked. His hair was long.

The paintings perched on easels in the window were abstracts, some geometric and symmetrical, others comprised of seemingly random slashes of color. I recognized a dramatic Jun Inoue painting, a combination of graffiti and *shodo,* traditional Japanese calligraphy.

I entered the gallery. The woman smiled, then turned her attention back to the man.

A younger woman with waist-long dirty-blond hair and big brown eyes approached me and asked if she could show me anything in particular.

I didn't reply for a few seconds, taking in

34

the gallery's minimalist style, noting the bold colors and the simplicity. "Thanks. I'm interested in learning about a Japanese woodblock print you sold last week."

"Oh, sorry. We only deal in midcentury modern and contemporary art."

"This was part of an estate you bought."

She looked confounded. "That's not possible. I'd know if we bought an entire estate."

"The Barnes estate."

"I'm afraid there's some mistake."

I pulled the receipt from my bag and held it so she could see it.

"This isn't . . . This doesn't make sense."

"Is the owner around? Or a manager?"

She glanced at the older woman. "Sylvia owns the gallery. Sylvia Rheingold. And you are . . . ?"

"Josie Prescott. I'm an antiques appraiser from New Hampshire."

Sylvia patted the man on his upper arm, said something to him, and leaned in for an air kiss. He grinned and left.

"This is Josie Prescott," the young woman said. "She has a receipt . . . You need to look at it."

I held it up.

"Thank you, Heidi, that's all." Sylvia waited until Heidi disappeared behind a

35

partition. "Where did you get this?"

"From a friend who hired me to appraise it."

Her brow creased, and she met my eyes straight on. "This isn't our receipt. It's our logo, but not our format."

"Do you know Cal Lewis?"

"No."

"Cal told me he heard through what he called the grapevine that you bought the Barnes estate, which included a Hiroshige woodblock print."

"I rarely buy estates. I don't have the capacity to catalogue and sell objects that are out of my niche, which, as you can see, is rather narrow."

"Since you didn't sell this print and you don't know Cal Lewis, it seems to me I might have stumbled into a bramble patch."

"Who is Cal Lewis?"

"He's an assistant professor at Hitchens and the assistant director of their on-campus museum. He's a fairly well known expert in Asian artifacts, mostly Japanese vases and pots." I was tempted to add that I had no clue why he would do such a thing — or why he thought he could get away with it — but didn't.

"If he was going to try some kind of con job, why wouldn't he choose a gallery that deals in Japanese art?"

"I don't know."

"Should I expect other appraisers to contact me to ask about sales I didn't make?"

"I don't know that either. I'll ask him and let you know what he says."

From her skeptical look and the derisive twist of her mouth, I could tell she was wondering if I was involved, and I bristled.

"I'm just the messenger," I said, "as upset as you are, maybe more so."

Sylvia's scorn faded. She nodded slowly. "Can I get a copy of this document?"

"I'll ask the owner for permission, and if she says it's all right, I'll email it to you."

I extracted a business card from my tote bag and handed it over.

Sylvia stared at it for a moment, then raised her eyes to mine. "Whatever is going on here . . . it's not good."

I slipped the receipt into my bag. "I'm sorry to drop this Pandora's box on your doorstep. I'll be in touch soon."

CHAPTER THREE

As soon as I reached I-95 on my way back to New Hampshire, I pulled onto the shoulder and called Ellis Hunter, Rocky Point's police chief, and my friend.

I told him what I'd discovered at the Rheingold Gallery. "Given that Cal hits women, or, rather, given that there are allegations that Cal hits women, I'd love for you to keep me company while I talk to him."

"Is this an official request?"

"No. I'm asking as your friend. I don't know what's going on, Ellis. It's possible that Cal was the one who got conned, that he's not the con man. But he's supposed to be an expert in Japanese objects, so that doesn't gel. To make matters more confusing, Cal said he knew the print was a first edition because of the *bokashi* in the signature cartouche. That's not how you determine authenticity."

38

Ellis asked about *bokashi,* and I explained how it was used in the poemcard.

"Did you tell Mo?"

"No."

"How come?"

"Because I didn't want to upset her. For all I know, he simply misspoke."

"Is the print a fake?"

"Probably."

"What makes you think so?"

"Forget that Cal lied about where he bought it and misrepresented the importance of the *bokashi,* the colors are surprisingly vivid, especially the blues. Without further analysis, there's no way to tell what particular pigment was used in this work, but typically, the inks in traditional Japanese woodblock prints are among the most light-sensitive in the world. Dyes and pigments that fade quickly are called fugitive, and blue, whether indigo or Antwerp or one of the organic pigments, is among the most fugitive of all."

"Couldn't the print have been kept out of the light all these years?"

"Yes. That's why I said probably."

"Let's say it's a fake. Would Cal have known?"

"Most likely, although there's a fair chance that he was merely overconfident and did a cursory job on his authentication, then lied about where and how he acquired the print to give it a loftier pedigree than it deserves. Of course, it's also possible someone lied to him and he fell for it. If so, he got snookered good."

"What does your gut tell you?"

"He seemed resentful that he earns less than Lydia. I could see him trying an end-around to pocket a little extra cash."

"You don't like him."

"What are you? A cop?"

"And a good one. The way you tell it, he's got ethics problems, attitude problems, and a temper. No wonder you want me there when you talk to him."

Ellis and I circled the Shannons' house to meet up with Mo and Cal in the garden. The sound of ocean waves lapping against the boulders that lined the shore lulled me, like always. Sun-tipped sequins darted across the dark blue water. Nothing relaxed me like the sight and sound of the ocean.

As we turned the corner, the soft hum of a guitar caught my attention. Frank sat with his back to us playing a blues tune I knew but didn't know. Frank was tall and fit and loose-limbed. His craggy features and weathered skin made him look like an outdoors man, a rancher maybe. He wore dark blue cargo shorts and a sky-blue polo shirt.

We walked across the flagstones, and Frank, hearing our footsteps, looked over his shoulder. He smiled and stood up, placing his guitar on a thick maroon towel he'd laid on top of a black wrought-iron table.

"Josie. Good to see you."

"You, too, Frank. That was beautiful. What is it?"

" 'I Believe I'll Dust My Broom.' "

"I love it. I don't know if you've ever met Ellis Hunter?"

"Never had the pleasure."

Ellis said, "Nice to meet you."

"I called Mo a little bit ago. She was going to ask Cal to meet us here. I have a couple of questions about Mo's Japanese print." I glanced around. "Have you seen them?"

"Mo, not since breakfast. Cal, not since yesterday." He surveyed Ellis's face, pausing at the dark red scar that ran in a jagged line from his right eyebrow to his eye, a relic, I suspected, from his days as a New York City homicide detective. "Hunter . . . you're the police chief." He turned toward me. "You've brought a police chief to ask Mo questions about her print? That doesn't sound good."

41

"Ellis is a friend," I said, telling one truth while avoiding another.

"Fair enough." Frank flashed a smile. "Actually, I'm glad to see you. I was going to call. I'm thinking I want to sell this baby." He pointed toward his guitar. "You handle musical instruments, don't you?"

"Sure." I smiled. "It would be an honor."

"Good. It's a 1930 Martin OM-45 Deluxe. They only made fourteen that year, and I think this one was built for Robert Johnson, a pretty famous blues man back in the day."

"Why do you want to sell it?"

"Estate planning. It's hard to believe, but I'm closing in on seventy. If anything happens to me, I don't want Trish to have to deal with it."

"I'll be glad to handle the sale, but if you'd rather not sell right now, we could appraise it for you, so when either of you is ready, you'll have a good idea of its value."

"That sounds like a smart first step. Let's do it."

I smiled. "Excellent!"

"I'll get it cased up, and check on Mo, too. Sometimes she gets working on those lesson plans of hers and loses all track of time."

I found my iPad in my tote bag. "I'll have

42

my office prepare the paperwork. Tell me what it is again."

Frank dictated the model number and Robert Johnson's name, while I typed.

I keep a miniature flashlight attached to my belt, so I'll always have it handy when I need to examine the undersides of tables and insides of drawers, and I used it now to peer into the sound hole to confirm the serial number, 45317, then videotaped the guitar.

When I was done, Frank lifted it clear, bundled up the towel, and went inside.

"You look excited," Ellis said.

I typed a note to Gretchen asking her to prepare the appraisal documents.

I looked up. "Want to guess why?"

"Because you're excited."

"I never could get anything past you."

"What do you know about guitars?"

"Nothing."

"And that makes you an ideal choice for appraising them."

I hit the SEND button. "Don't be sassy. I know how to appraise valuable objects. I never know anything about anything until I learn it."

"Too bad everyone doesn't share that attitude. Lots of people think they know things when they don't."

43

"And most of those people don't hesitate to share their opinions. Except they don't call them opinions. They call them facts."

One corner of Ellis's mouth twitched. "I know you . . . you're talking about someone in particular. Who?"

"Cal. You'll see."

Frank came out with two black guitar cases in hand. "I can't find her. I called her cell, too." He lowered the cases to the table. He patted the one closest to him. "This is my working case. The guitar's in it. The other case is the original, from Martin." He looked around the yard. "Mo said something the other day about playing some game, croquet or badminton, I forget which. She might be in the shed hunting down birdies or wickets. I'll check."

Ellis's phone vibrated. He glanced at the display. "I need to take this."

Ellis sat on a wrought-iron bench while Frank and I crossed the lawn to the shed. Frank opened the door and switched on the light. The left side was full of lawn care equipment, including a riding lawn mower. Tools hung on pegboard hooks. Sports gear was housed on the right. Two kayaks were suspended from the ceiling; three bags of golf clubs rested on a wooden platform; six tennis racquets, four badminton racquets, and a mesh bag of birdies hung from brackets above the croquet set; and a rolled-up badminton net and silver poles leaned against the wall.

Mo wasn't there.

He turned off the light and shut the door. "What time did she say she'd meet you?"

"Five."

He glanced at his watch. "That's now." He stared into the shrubbery that surrounded the shed as though he might spot Mo hiding under a bush. "It's not like her to miss an appointment."

"It's not urgent. I can come back another time."

"I guess."

"Do you have Cal's number?"

"No, but Lydia will. She's in the living room, working. She left work early today. She didn't want to risk getting stuck in traffic and being late for Trish's book club. Sometimes I think Lydia likes the book club more than Trish does."

We walked across the lawn to the patio. Ellis was reading something on his phone.

"We're going to ask Lydia for Cal's phone number," I told him.

He met my eyes and nodded. "Why don't I wait here."

I knew Ellis well enough to understand

45

his unspoken message. He didn't want to spook Lydia into refusing to give me Cal's number.

I followed Frank into the house, through the mudroom, down a corridor, and into the living room.

Frank stopped about ten feet from where Lydia sat in a red leather club chair. Her feet were curled up under her. She was reading from a legal brief. There was a faint purple smudge under her right eye.

Frank cleared his throat. "Lydia?"

She looked at me, then back at Frank. "Is something wrong?"

"Do you know where Cal is?"

"Why?"

"Mo arranged to meet Josie and him. Neither one of them showed up."

"Maybe they got the location wrong." She met my gaze. "Or you did."

"It's possible, I suppose," I said. "Do you have his phone number?"

"Sure."

She called it out, and I entered it into my phone. Frank and Lydia kept their eyes on my face as I waited for the call to connect. It went directly to voice mail. I listened to Cal's voice invite me to leave him a message.

"Hi, Cal. This is Josie. Josie Prescott. I

46

thought you, Mo, and I were going to meet up today at the Shannons' house. At five. In the garden. Did I misunderstand the location? Give me a call, please! I have a few questions about the woodblock print. Thanks!"

Lydia tapped the brief against her leg. "What questions?"

"Technical stuff. Were you with Cal when he bought it?"

"No. We're not joined at the hip."

"So you don't know where he is now?" Frank asked.

"No. What's going on?"

I smiled. "Just a couple of questions. Could Cal be at Hitchens?"

Her shoulders lifted an inch, then dropped. "Maybe. We're not scheduled to get together until tomorrow."

"If you talk to him, ask him to call me, okay?" She said she would, and I turned toward Frank. "Why don't we check the garden again?"

"Sure."

I glanced over my shoulder as we left the room. Lydia was already back at work, flipping pages, shaking her head over some point in the brief.

Ellis stood facing the ocean, his back to us.

He was on his phone.

Mo and Cal weren't in sight.

"I wonder where they are," Frank said. "I don't like it. Mo doesn't make mistakes about locations any more than she forgets appointments."

"I know."

"I'll go ask Trish if she knows anything."

"Want to sign the appraisal authorization? Then I'll stow the guitar and meet you back here."

Frank read the agreement, signed the electronic form, and headed into the house.

I opened the modern case to confirm that the guitar was inside, latched it closed, and carried the two cases to my car. I wrapped each of them in protective blankets and secured them in the trunk.

When I got back to the garden, I took another look around. Neither Mo nor Cal had shown up. I walked past Ellis, back on the phone, toward the ocean. When he saw me, he raised his index finger. I gave him a thumbs-up.

Riffles of whitecaps ran along the surface, a light chop. Farther out to sea, the water looked black and deadly. I reached the low fieldstone wall that protected the unsuspecting or the preoccupied from the twenty-foot drop. I looked to the right, south. Instead of the tan thick-grained sand that covered most of New Hampshire's coastline, overlapping eight-foot granite boulders ranged along the bottom of the cliff and stretched ten feet into the ocean. Glossy ribbons of bottle-green seaweed were wedged between some of the boulders.

I glanced at Ellis. He was nodding at something someone was saying. I turned north and watched the frothy waves batter the boulders and the cliff. When the water ebbed, I spotted a heap of clothing lying on a boulder, something pink and flowery. I tried to imagine how it got there, then gasped and tripped, scraping my knee on the rough stone wall. It wasn't a pile of clothing. It was a body.

I spun toward Ellis. He must have seen panic on my face, because he ended his call and started jogging toward me.

I turned back to the rocky shoreline.

"What is it?" Ellis called as he ran.

I could see it was a woman. Her face was turned toward the shore, toward me. I squinted to try to discern her features.

"Oh, God," I whispered, pointing at the boulder, fighting tears, my throat closing.

Ellis stood next to me, and together we stared at Mo's broken body.

49

I sat on the lawn with my back to the stone wall and my head between my knees, waiting for the gold flecks dancing in front of my eyes to disappear. Tears streamed down my cheeks. Ellis was on the phone barking orders. After a few seconds, the specks floated away. I found a tissue in my tote bag and wiped the wetness from my face, then used the wall to hoist myself upright.

A police boat cut its engines fifty feet from shore, glided for a few seconds, then dropped anchor. I recognized the medical examiner, Dr. Graham. I'd seen her before, but I didn't know her. She was petite and about my age, midthirties. From all reports, she was totally by-the-book and as thorough as all get-out.

Two men I didn't know, both in their thirties, and both wearing official Rocky Point police windbreakers, lowered a dinghy. It landed in the water with a loud plop. One of the police officers climbed in, followed by a younger man wearing a Rocky Point Crime Scene Technology jacket. The police officer on the larger boat helped the doctor navigate her way into the dinghy. She stepped down, setting it rocking. He passed two black bags, a big one stamped with the department's gold logo, and a smaller one, more the size of a camera case, to the tech. Once the dinghy settled down, the police officer rowed toward the boulders.

"No!" Trish screeched to the heavens, shattering the stillness.

I spun around. Ellis stood on the patio, his face lined with concern, his hand on Trish's shoulder. Frank kept his eyes on Ellis's face and his arm under Trish's elbow, ready to catch her if she fainted, which from her ashen complexion seemed like a realistic possibility.

"No!" Trish screamed again, her head back, her eyes scrunched closed.

Lydia had a death grip on the back of a wrought-iron chair. She looked as scary-pale as her mother.

Ellis said something I couldn't hear.

Trish shrieked again, and Frank embraced her. She howled again and again, her cries growing louder. Her legs buckled. Frank walked her to a bench.

I hadn't had enough time to process the fact that Mo was dead, that my friend was dead, and witnessing Trish's tortured reaction made the horror worse, more palpable. It felt wrong to watch something so private, so harrowing. I looked away. As Trish's screams faded to whimpers, I fought back a fresh wave of tears. After a few seconds, I had myself under a modicum of control.

The medical examiner was squatting on the boulder, leaning over Mo's body. She wore turquoise plastic booties. The tech did, too. He was video-recording Mo's corpse and the craggy rocks. The dinghy was moored ten feet away, roiling in the increasingly choppy water. The police officer who'd rowed the doctor and technician in sat in the boat watching them work.

On the lawn overlooking the crime scene, Ellis was listening to Claire Brownley, a detective I'd known for years.

Lydia, ignoring Detective Brownley, spoke to Ellis, and Ellis nodded.

"Daryl!" Ellis called, and a young police officer hustled over, listened for a moment, then ran ahead and opened the kitchen door.

Lydia whispered something to Frank. He helped Trish stand and placed his arm

52

around her shoulders, said something to her, and led her into the house. Lydia dragged along behind, her shoulders bowed.

Ellis resumed his conversation with the detective. I was curious about what they were discussing. No one was paying any attention to me. Keeping my eyes on the ocean, I sidestepped past beds of late-blooming roses until I was partially hidden by clusters of tall grass. I walked backward past the rosebushes, then turned inland. I skirted the patio by staying on the far side of the hedges and bushes. I paused behind a tall lilac bush, close enough to hear but not so close as to intrude.

Frank burst out of the kitchen and headed straight to Ellis with Lydia on his heels.

"I heard Cal's name on that police officer's radio," Frank told Ellis, his tone so sharp it could have poked a hole in iron, "and I came on the fly. Have you located him?"

"Not yet," Ellis said. "He told the Art Department secretary that he'd be back for a student conference. He didn't show up."

"That son of a bitch."

"Daddy, please."

"Enough. Your sister's dead." He froze her with an icy stare. He turned to Ellis. "I need to get back to Trish. So he's on the run.

Now what?"

"Now we find him."

"Whatever you need, you just let me know. You name it, you got it."

"Thank you."

Frank met Lydia's stony gaze. "Stay and tell him everything you know about Cal."

"Of course." She turned toward Ellis. "Cal had nothing to do with what happened to Mo."

Ellis waited until Frank was back inside. "Are you all right to talk? We can wait a little."

Lydia lifted her chin. "I'm fine. Upset, of course, but I can talk."

A boat engine revved high, then quieted, and we all turned toward the ocean. A second police boat pulled up beside the first one.

"I appreciate your cooperation," Ellis said. "Do you know where Cal is?"

"No."

"When did you last talk to him?"

"This morning. I stayed at his place. We're not scheduled to see each other again today because tonight is my mom's book club. Oh!" She touched her mouth. "I need to call everyone to cancel."

"We'll talk to them as they arrive. To be sure I understand — Cal isn't expecting you back at his apartment later?"

"No. On book club nights, unless Cal attends, I stay here." She shook her head, a small, sad motion. "My mom's pals can toss back wine with the best of 'em. I try to keep up, so I never drive afterward. I called Cal earlier and left a message. I told him what happened and asked him to come over, to help me." She glanced at the side of the house that led to the driveway. "I'm sure he'll be here any minute." She closed her eyes for a moment. "I can't believe this is happening . . . I just can't believe it."

"Why don't you go see how your folks are doing? I'll catch up with you later."

Lydia took in a deep breath. "I'll go in when we're done. Daddy's right — if I can help, I want to. What else can I tell you?"

"When did you last see Mo?"

"Let me think." Lydia rubbed her forehead. "Yesterday, maybe."

"Last night?"

"No. I was with Cal from after work until this morning. I stayed here the night before, so I would have seen Mo at breakfast."

"Do you have your own home?"

"I keep a studio apartment near campus. I don't use it much."

"How was Mo feeling yesterday?"

"About what?"

"In general. Did she seem the same as always?"

"I guess. I didn't notice anything in particular, and I think I would have if something was different."

"Was Mo dating anyone?"

"Not that I know of. She's recovering — she *was* recovering from a bruising divorce. It was final last October, and she's been slow to bounce back."

"Why was it bruising?"

Lydia snorted, half harrumph, half derisive chortle. "Her ex, Steven Jullison. He calls himself Stevie, and that tells you just about everything you need to know about him. He's a first-grade teacher, which feels right since he acts about six most of the time. The precipitating event that made Mo finally toss him out was that she found out he was going on overnight playdates with some hottie."

"Who?"

"I don't know."

"Do you know where Mr. Jullison lives now?"

"No. As far as I know, though, he's still teaching at Rice Dixon Elementary School."

Ellis extracted a notebook from his pocket and flipped to an empty page. He wrote something, then asked, "He didn't want the divorce?"

"I don't know, but I doubt it. If they got divorced, the hottie would expect Stevie to marry her, and he was chronically responsibility averse. Also, Mo supplemented their modest incomes by drawing from her trust fund. Stevie wouldn't like the idea of having to live on his own income. The divorce was her idea, but she took it hard. She was heartbroken."

"Was she depressed?"

"Sure. Isn't that a symptom of heartbreak? That and feeling like a rusty used car in a new-car lot."

"How did the depression manifest itself?"

"She cried a lot."

I felt a stab of sadness. Poor Mo.

"Would you say that she was beginning to find her footing, or was she still running low to the ground?"

"What are you suggesting? That Mo killed herself?"

"I'm not suggesting anything. Was she beginning to be more like her old self?"

"Not noticeably."

"What did Mo do for work?"

"She was a teacher, too. Third grade."

"At the same school?"

"Yes." Lydia pointed at the low stone wall. "Look at that wall. I told Daddy to make it higher, but Mom liked the view."

"You think it was an accident."

"Mo always was a little klutzy. She had two left feet."

"Who were her best friends?"

"I don't think she had best friends, not in the way you mean. She didn't do a lot of girly things, like go shopping or have spa days or anything like that. She spent a lot of time at New Hampshire Children First!, volunteering." She glanced around and walked to one of the tables. "I'm okay to keep talking, but I need to sit."

Ellis pulled out the chair opposite her. I stepped back from the lilac bush and took a few careful steps toward a boxwood hedge. By separating some eye-level branches, I could keep them both in view.

"How did she and Cal get along?" Ellis asked.

Lydia stiffened. "Mo could be a complete bitch, excuse my French."

I was so appalled at Lydia's heartlessness, I stumbled into the hedge. A twig scraped my ear, a small scratch.

"She didn't like him?" Ellis asked.

I righted myself and resumed my observation. Lydia was sitting with her hands clasped in her lap. I wondered if she truly believed what she was saying or if she had a secret motive for bad-mouthing her just-dead sister.

"She couldn't stand him. She acted like she was the grown-up and I was just a little kid."

"That sounds annoying."

"And then some."

"Were the hostilities open?"

"Cal wasn't hostile. Mo tried hard to bring out his bad side, thinking I'd wise up, but he doesn't have a bad side. He's a good guy, funny and witty. Ask anyone — he's charming and smart." She waved her hand dismissively. "Mo didn't want to believe that he was good to me or good for me. She thought his sarcasm was just mean."

"How did you get that shiner?"

Lydia touched her bruised cheek. "I fell. I guess clumsiness runs in the family."

"It sounds like Mo was out to derail your relationship. How come?"

"Jealousy, maybe."

"What can you tell me about the Japanese woodblock print?"

"Nothing. I mean, I don't know much about art. Mo was thrilled with the purchase."

"Thank you." Ellis closed his notebook. "Can you think of anyone else I should talk to?"

"Josie Prescott. Mo thought the world of her."

Tears welled when she spoke my name.

"Her colleagues at her school," Lydia continued. "The people she volunteered with. I don't know who else."

Ellis thanked her again and slipped the notebook into his pocket. A uniformed officer waited on the grass. I knew him. Griff was close to retirement, and laid-back. The other officer, Daryl, who was still in with the family, was younger, in his early thirties, and earnest. Ellis caught Griff's eye, and the older man hurried toward him.

"Walk Ms. Shannon inside, Griff, and stay with the family. If anyone thinks of anything that might help, call me immediately. Send Daryl out."

Lydia walked into the house without saying another word, and Griff followed.

I came out from behind the bush.

Ellis spotted me and took a few steps in my direction. "Let's walk to the wall." When we reached it, he asked, "Were you able to hear?"

"Yes."

"Did everything gel with what you know?"

"Mostly."

"What's off?"

"Mo introduced her ex to me as Steve,

60

not Stevie, and that's what she called him every time I was with them. And Mo wasn't the least bit klutzy." I blinked away tears. "I've seen her ride horses a dozen times. She was graceful and confident, a natural athlete. Why would Lydia lie about those things?"

"What do you think happened to Mo?" Ellis asked, pretending he hadn't heard my question.

"She grew up here. She wouldn't have misjudged the wall."

"Was she a drinker?"

"No. I've never seen her have more than a glass of something, wine or beer, usually."

"What does 'usually' mean?"

I smiled. "I saw her down half a margarita once."

"Did she do drugs?"

"Not that I ever saw."

Ellis's phone vibrated. He pulled it from his pocket and glanced at the display. "It's the medical examiner. Thank you, Josie. You don't need to stay. I'll be in touch later." He called to Daryl, waiting on the patio. "Make sure Josie gets to her car without being overrun by reporters." He turned away and answered his phone with a crisp "Hunter."

I didn't want to leave. I wanted to know

what the medical examiner was telling Ellis, what other questions he'd ask Mo's family, and whether Cal would finally show up as Lydia expected, and if not, how Ellis planned to track him down. I scanned the ocean starting from the south, my eyes moving slowly north, wanting to capture one last mental picture of the crime scene. I felt queasy, imagining Mo's terror as she plummeted onto the boulders. Shivers of fear and upset pricked at me. Mo hadn't tumbled off the wall. She hadn't killed herself. That left murder. The second police boat turned on its side lamps, and streaks of white light shimmied across the midnight-blue water. Twilight was closing in. Where was Cal? Had he witnessed Mo's fall and slunk away like a coward? That sounded like Cal. He was a bully, all bluster and no action. The medical examiner sat in the dinghy, her back to me, her phone to her ear. The police officer rowed her back to the mother boat, his oars cleaving the water as if it took no effort at all.

Daryl cleared his throat. "Josie?"

I stood for a moment longer, fighting tears, staring at the ocean, watching the remaining sliver of orange sun disappear below the horizon.

I turned toward Daryl. "I'm ready."

Yellow-and-black police tape separated the driveway from the street. Daryl raised it for me, then followed me to the road.

Reporters, some new to me, others I'd seen on TV or in person, called out questions, asking what I'd seen and what I knew. I ignored them all. Wes Smith, a reporter for Rocky Point's hometown newspaper, the *Seacoast Star,* stood apart from the group, near his newish red Ford Focus, surveying the scene with unrelenting intensity. Three women and one man stood off to the side, talking quietly among themselves. I recognized two of them, a stately woman Trish's age named Abby Young and the redhead who'd organized croquet at Mo's garden party. Abby was a frequent visitor at the tag sale, cruising the aisles seeking out objects that featured the letter *Y.* A petite blonde in her early thirties nodded in agreement to whatever Abby was saying. One of the men kept his hand on the blonde's shoulder. He was tall and lanky with bushy brown hair, a thick mustache, and a pointy chin. I gathered that members of the book club had arrived and didn't want to leave.

Daryl walked me to my car. He opened my door. "You okay?"

"Not really. Mo was my friend."

"I'm sorry for your loss."

"Thank you."

I tilted my head toward Abby and the others. "Those folks are all in the book club."

Daryl half turned to see whom I was referring to. "Yes."

I slid behind the wheel.

"Would you like an escort home?" he asked.

"Thank you, Daryl. I'll be all right."

He shut my door and stepped back.

I'm good in a crisis — rational, methodical, and careful. It's after the crisis has passed that I fall apart. *Oh, Mo,* I thought, fighting more tears. I didn't want to cry. My phone vibrated. It was a text from Wes: *Meet me in Tiller's lot. Now.* Since Wes's web of contacts was legendary, remarkable in both depth and breadth, there was a chance he had already garnered facts I could use in trying to understand what had happened to Mo. Wes ran a tight ship, though: If I wanted information, I'd have to give information. And I would. I glanced at the rearview mirror. Daryl hadn't moved, and when he caught my eye, he semisaluted. I raised a hand in response. Wes's car was nowhere in sight.

I turned onto Main Street, drove into Tiller's Shopping Plaza's parking lot about three miles down the road, and parked facing the street next to Wes's Focus.

"What's going on?" he demanded. "All I know is what I heard on my police scanner — that someone is dead. Who is it?"

"Oh, God, Wes . . . it's Mo. Did you know her? Mo Shannon?"

"No. Did she fall? Or was she pushed?"

"I have no idea."

"How do you know her?"

"She's a friend. We volunteered together for years."

"Why were you there today?"

"An antiques thing." My eyes filled again, and I gulped.

Wes peppered me with questions I couldn't answer, until finally he gave up. His tone turned stern. "You hear something . . . you call me."

"You, too, Wes. Please. Mo was a good friend."

I watched him zip away, back in the direction of the Shannon house.

Ty had left me a voice mail about an hour earlier. "I just got called down to Washington, God only knows why. Urgent, but no details. I'm at my house right now, packing. I'm hoping to make the eight o'clock shuttle so I can be at the office first thing in the morning. I'll talk to you soon. Love you."

I called him back and got him in the car.

"Traffic is horrendous," he said, "so I shouldn't stay on the line long."

"That's okay. We can talk later." I gave him a thirty-second rundown on Mo. "I'm stunned and so, so sad, and completely confused about what could have happened to her. And now you're leaving town. Do you know when you'll be back?"

"No. I don't even know why I'm going. I'm so sorry, babe. I know how much you liked Mo. Me, too. Let me pull over and check — maybe I can delay going down there for a day or two."

"No . . . you take care of business."

"Are you sure?"

"Yes. I'll be fine."

"You should call Zoë and see if she's around."

"Good idea. Do you think you're in trouble?"

"Why would I be in trouble?"

"What else could it be if it's urgent, without information?"

"I can think of four thousand two hundred and twelve reasons, and that's just offhand. I better go . . . I'll call you at bedtime."

We said our good-byes, and I slid my phone into my tote bag.

I sat for a minute, watching nothing in particular, allowing the anguish I'd been

66

quelling to sweep over me, and then the tears came. I leaned against my steering wheel and sobbed. I cried until I ran out of tears. I patted my eyes dry with another tissue and blew my nose. I sat until I felt less shaky, then tapped the radio button. I wanted to listen to something so I wouldn't have to think. The radio was set to the Hitchens University station, which played classical music and broadcast professors' lectures.

I recognized the student host. His name was Greg Lindsay, and he was a regular.

"According to a tweet just sent by Wes Smith, a reporter with the *Seacoast Star,* a source within Rocky Point's medical examiner's office says that it looks like Mo Shannon's death was a homicide. We've reached out to Wes for more details, and will bring you updates about this shocking development as soon as we get them."

My throat closed. *Someone killed Mo.* I'd known it, yet somehow I simply couldn't comprehend it. I coughed, choking, then sipped some water. Mo had spent her life doing the right thing, and all it got her was killed. Crisis-calm descended on me yet again. My throat opened, and in one savage surge, anger supplanted sorrow. Anger was easier to deal with than grief. Anger inspired action. Grief was debilitating. My hands curled into fists.

I had no doubt that if Mo's print could talk, we'd learn who murdered her.

CHAPTER FIVE

Zoë, my landlady, neighbor, and friend, was the soup queen. She could take any mélange of fresh or leftover ingredients and make a delicious soup. I'd never been in her house when soup wasn't in the fridge or simmering on the stove.

It was almost eight when I called to tell her about Mo and ask if I could come over for dinner. "I know it's late. We can order pizza. My treat."

"I'm so sorry, Josie. What a terrible thing. Of course come over. We've already eaten, but I can offer you leftover roast chicken and just-made chicken soup."

"Even better. I'll bring the fixings for martinis."

"Good. Come whenever."

After a hot bath and a cold martini, I walked across our shared driveway. As soon as I opened the door, I was enveloped by the aroma of bay leaves and thyme. Zoë's chicken noodle soup. My favorite.

Zoë was tall, close to six feet, and willowy. She had short near-black hair and big brown expressive eyes. She wore a white fitted T-shirt and low-cut jeans. She could have just walked off the pages of a trendy fashion magazine.

As Zoë served up a portion of salad, I poured martinis from my silver bullet-shaped shaker — gin, of course, the good stuff, Bombay Sapphire, which I kept in the freezer, shaken with a capful of Limoncello, a concoction of my dad's creation. I used an atomizer to spray vermouth inside chilled glasses, another trick I learned from my dad. I filled them nearly to the top with the frozen liquor. I rimmed the lip of my glass with a curlicue of lemon rind, then tossed it in. I slid two oversized green olives into Zoë's drink. They spiraled to the bottom.

Zoë sipped her martini. "Yum." She stirred the soup. "Ellis called. He hopes to be home by nine."

I glanced at the wall clock. It read 8:50. "Home?"

Zoë's olive skin took on a rosy hue. "It's official. He's moving in this weekend."

"That's wonderful!"

"Thanks."

I wanted to ask why she'd changed her

mind about living with Ellis, but I didn't. Yes, she'd worried for years that her kids would grow attached to him, and then he'd leave, but her announcement had a flavor of celebration, and I didn't want to say anything or ask anything that smacked of criticism.

As if she could read my mind, she said, "The kids adore him. They're older now, and he's been in their lives for as long as they can remember."

"Are you thinking of getting married?"

"Not now. You know I'm seriously gunshy. I married a man everyone but me knew was a loser, which to this day makes me question my judgment. Ellis comes with his own baggage. He gave his heart and soul to his wife. When she died, he lost more than the love of his life. He lost his footing. Our solution is to proceed by baby steps."

"You're so sensible."

"And I make a mean chicken soup." She stirred the pot. "How are you doing?"

"Not good. You met Mo — you know."

"Lots of times. She was lovely."

"I just can't —" I broke off as Ellis walked in through the back door. He looked all in.

"Hey, Josie."

"Hey."

He turned to Zoë and opened his arms.

71

She slipped into his embrace, resting her head on his shoulder for a moment.

She smoothed his hair. "Hungry?"

"Starving. First, though, a beer."

He kissed her and walked to the fridge. Zoë got a bowl from the cupboard.

"Any news?" I asked Ellis.

He found a Redhook pale ale and took a long draw before he answered. "I don't know about news, but I know who I want to talk to. Cal Lewis. He hasn't surfaced. You haven't had a callback, have you?"

"No."

"Neither has Lydia."

"Why not ask Wes to run an article about the situation?"

He drank some more. "Too risky. If Cal saw his name in the paper associated with murder, he might panic."

"I heard the headline that it was murder, but I didn't really think . . . I mean, I knew . . . I just can't fathom . . ." I stopped speaking and closed my eyes for a moment. I couldn't speak for several seconds, and when I did, my voice sounded harsh, unlike my own. "Is it official?"

"Not yet, but it will be by morning. The ME found contusions on Mo's neck that aren't consistent with a fall."

My anger bubbled just below the surface.

"Cal's not stupid. Once he hears that Mo is dead, he'll know I told you he was supposed to meet us."

He finished his beer and tossed the bottle into the recycling bin. "As far as I know, Cal is a family friend who might have insights into what happened to Mo, nothing more."

"In other words, he's a person of interest, but you don't want him to know it."

Ellis smiled. "Wes will hear from someone, not me, that Cal is a family friend who might have insights into what happened to Mo."

"There must be an echo in here."

Ellis walked to the stove. "This soup sure smells good."

I could take a hint, so I let it go.

The soup was as soothing and satisfying as always. The reheated chicken was moist because Zoë had long since adapted my mom's technique — she warmed it in gently simmering poaching liquid, a combination of white wine, lemon juice, Dijon mustard, and minced garlic, with a dash of hot sauce and more than a dash of onion powder.

I texted Wes as soon as I got home: *Where's Cal Lewis? Do you know? As you ask around, make it clear that Cal is a family friend who might have insights into what hap-*

73

pened to Mo. He's not a suspect or even a person of interest.

I was glad to sow the seed Ellis planted, not only to help him but because I wanted to know, too. I trudged up to bed, exhausted, angry, and sad.

The next morning, I stopped at my favorite bakery, Sweet Treats Bakery & Tea Shoppe, en route to work. I wanted a blueberry muffin, and no one made them like Sweet Treats. The owner, a woman named Noeleen McLoughlin, told me that they flash-froze blueberries picked locally in July. Maybe that was the trick. I got in line, and with one whiff of the cinnamon and vanilla wafting throughout the shop, I was transported back to my mother's kitchen, to before she died when I was only thirteen. Sweet Treats smelled like love. I unzipped my jacket. The bakery was deliciously warm, a welcome respite from the morning chill.

I checked my iPhone as I waited my turn. Wes had texted an urgent request to meet. I replied that anytime after ten worked for me. That would give me ample time to get updates from my staff. When my turn came, I ordered a dozen blueberry muffins because everyone loved them as much as I did, then spotted a honey-dipped doughnut, golden brown and dripping with sticky glaze, and ordered a dozen of those, too.

Just before I reached my car, with ideas for authenticating Mo's print whirling in my head, I stopped short. I hadn't thought of it until now, but with Mo dead, I didn't know who owned the Japanese woodblock print. We'd need to put our appraisal on hold unless Ellis asked us to continue as part of his investigation. Frustrated at the thought of anything slowing me down in my effort to help find Mo's killer, I called Ellis and explained my concern.

"Do you know Theo Caswell?" he asked.

"Not well, just to say hello to at Chamber of Commerce meetings and summer concerts on the green, that sort of thing, but he seems like a good guy. Family law, right?"

"He's Mo's lawyer. I'm meeting him at noon. I'll call you afterward and let you know what he says. If the heir doesn't want to go forward with the appraisal for some reason, I'll get a court order."

"Maybe I should come with you, in case either of you has questions about the antique."

"Sure, if you don't mind hanging out in his reception area until and unless."

I assured him that I didn't mind a bit. "On a different topic . . . Zoë told me you're moving in. Congratulations!"

"Thanks. I'm psyched. Zoë's a catch."

I smiled. I loved a man who told the truth.

As soon as I walked into my company's front office, Gretchen said, "Oh, Josie . . . I was so sorry to hear about Mo. It's shocking."

"Thank you, Gretchen." I made eye contact with my staff, one at a time. "I'm not going to pretend I'm feeling fine. I'm not. Mo's death is a terrible loss. She was a good friend and a truly remarkable woman. I'm pretty shaken up."

Gretchen's beautiful emerald eyes moistened. "What happened?"

"I wish I knew, but I don't." I turned toward Sasha. "We need to hold off on appraising Mo's print. I hope to learn who inherited it soon."

"Of course."

"I'm assuming it's in the safe." She nodded. "Where are you with the appraisal?"

"All I've done so far is reach out to museums that have Hiroshige prints in their collections. I want to hear how they approached authentication."

"Good. If you hear back from anyone you've already contacted, go ahead and talk to them, but keep our interest vague."

76

She tucked her baby-fine brown hair behind her ears. "All right."

I turned to Fred. His black square-framed glasses sat on his desk. He was experimenting with contacts.

"Talk to me about Frank's guitar."

"I doubt it's real."

I leaned against the guest table. "I'm sorry to hear that."

"Martin is one of the most highly respected guitar brands in the world, which makes it among the most copied."

"Copied, sure. But counterfeited?"

"Yup." He tapped a paper on his desk. "Martin is aggressive in quashing illegal copies, so if you're going in that direction, you need to counterfeit. So far, I've located three guitars that made their way into reputable antiques auctions and were later revealed to be fakes."

"Like Matisse — he said he painted fifteen hundred canvases, and twenty-five hundred of them were sold in America."

"I think that's a perfect analogy. I've verified that only fourteen OM-45 Deluxe guitars were produced by Martin in 1930 because the economy tanked in '29. Before then, in the mid-1920s, the guitar market was booming, and Martin employed the most innovative designers and the finest craftsmen in the world. The minute the stock market crashed, demand for high-quality guitars plummeted. Martin laid off all but its most skilled workers, which explains both why there were only fourteen built that year, and why the quality is so high. For this appraisal, I think we need to locate every one of those fourteen."

"Can you?"

"Probably not. Martin keeps good records. All the inventory was sold to various shops around the country, but every one of those stores is out of business. None of the owners or their heirs is popping up in any search, including those done by the security company that does our background checks. I'll keep plugging away, but I'm ninety percent sure tracking sales from Martin is a nonstarter."

"That's terrific work, Fred. And impressively fast. What's your plan B?"

"I'll start by posting a request for information on guitar forums and blogs. The online community is large and enthusiastic."

"Excellent."

"Also, we need to ask Mr. Shannon where he bought it and whether he has a receipt or a prior appraisal. For obvious reasons, I didn't want to bother him."

"Agreed. Do you have any context yet for

determining value?"

"Oh, yeah." He grinned. "Get ready to have your mouth water. One of the fourteen sold at auction a few years ago for three hundred and sixty-six thousand dollars. If we can confirm that Robert Johnson, one of the first inductees in the Rock and Roll Hall of Fame, had owned and used Frank's guitar, its price will skyrocket."

"Let's get Davy up here to examine the instrument itself, but since this is a private appraisal, not preparation for a sale, keep it on the qt."

Davy Morse was our go-to expert on plucked or strummed string instruments. Based in New York, he was an expert's expert: experienced, knowledgeable, insightful, and ethical. He was a Juilliard-trained guitar player, and he'd gone on to earn a certificate in sound engineering. After spending eight years touring nationally with two Broadway shows, he'd hung out his shingle as a consultant. His projects varied from serving as a guest curator to designing a guitar for wheelchair players and from appraising vintage instruments to helping video game designers get the music right.

I smiled at Sasha to include her in my comment. "Good job, both of you."

I left them to their work and pushed

through the heavy door into the warehouse. Angela came romping up the center aisle to say hello, and I gathered her up. As I kissed the top of her furry little head, I thought, not for the first time, that there was no greater solace than cuddling a cat.

Wes stood on top of the dune with his back to the street. I drove onto the sandy shoulder and rolled to a stop. At the sound of my door closing, Wes turned around. He watched me crab-walk up the shifting sand.

"How come you asked about Cal Lewis?" Wes asked, skipping hello, as always.

"Hi, Wes. Nice to see you."

"You, too. So what gives?"

"You're welcome."

Wes grinned. "Thanks for the tip."

"Did you find him?"

"Not yet. I've only been working on it a few hours, but I reached enough people who should have seen him to be able to report that he disappeared around four thirty yesterday."

"Disappeared?"

"So it seems. He left Hitchens just after his three o'clock class. That's around four fifteen. He told the department secretary that he was going to grab some sushi but would be back in time to meet with a

80

student. No one on campus has seen him since. Do you think he killed Mo?"

"I don't know. He overheard Mo hire me to appraise the woodblock print he sold her. If he was aware it was a fake, he'd know that meant the jig was up."

"Did he really think Mo wouldn't get it appraised?"

"Never underrate the power of arrogance. Cal thought his stamp of approval would be sufficient. Mo's sister, Lydia, told her the print wasn't worth appraising. I haven't asked her, but I bet he primed her naysaying pump."

"What a doofus."

"Did the police figure out where he went for sushi?"

"Not yet, but I learned that he was a regular at Little Tokyo, in Durham, about ten minutes from campus."

"I'll bet he didn't go there yesterday."

"No bet."

"Even assuming the print is a fake, why would he disappear? If he got called out on it, all he'd have to say is sorry, I screwed up, and return the money."

"How much money are we talking?"

"Twenty-eight thousand, more or less."

"Then I know why he took off — he's broke. He has thirty-one dollars in his checking account."

"How can you possibly know that? Banking information is confidential."

"Thanks," Wes said as if I'd given him a compliment.

I didn't push it. "Maybe he has another account."

"I'll keep digging, but he uses direct deposit for his paychecks, and this account is where they go."

"Then he must have planned his escape."

Wes pulled a spiral-bound notebook from his pocket and flipped it open. He tapped a minipen out of the wire casing and scrawled something. "I'll check on withdrawals and whether he has other accounts. Why would he kill Mo? Just because he couldn't refund her money?"

"Not exactly. Because it would have been humiliating to admit he didn't have the money."

"Money's the root of all evil."

"Not according to the Bible. The *love* of money is the root of all evil, not money itself, and that's exactly what I'm saying about Cal."

"You used the word 'escape' earlier. Did Cal escape or flee? Is there any chance he's a victim here?"

"What kind of victim?"

82

"I don't know. I'm just asking."

"I don't know either, but it's a good question, Wes. What about the Shannons' neighbors? Did anyone see anything?"

"Nope. We've got us a big fat doughnut hole. Everyone was at work or otherwise occupied. One guy is out of the country on a business trip to Brazil — he left the night Mo died. I'll follow up when he gets back. A few of them have security cameras, but they're all aimed at their own houses, not the street. Then there's Mo's phone. According to my police source, three calls came from the faculty lounge the day Mo died, one at three ten, one at three eighteen, and one at three twenty-four. The first one came from Edna Fields, Mo's principal. She says that she wanted to give Mo a heads-up about a new student transferring in the next day. When she learned Mo had already skedaddled, she decided to call her. She left Mo a message. Steve Jullison, Mo's ex-husband, made the second call. He volunteered that he called to ask about a lesson plan — Mo had mentioned a nifty new exercise she'd come up with, and she'd offered to share it with him. They spoke for about three minutes. The third call lasted only one minute, but no one is admitting making it. I figure Steve called her twice.

He didn't call about any lesson plan — paleeze! He was trying for a little nookie with the missus. She agreed, but he had to check his calendar. He did so, then called her right back to confirm the date. What do you think?"

"Where is that coming from, Wes?"

"Logic. Why else wouldn't someone admit calling her?"

"I have no idea. Neither do you."

Wes chuckled.

"God, Wes, you're something like something I've never seen. Why did the principal call Mo from the faculty lounge, not her office?"

"When she didn't find Mo in the lounge, she decided to cross that item off her to-do list then and there. There's a faculty phone listing tacked to the wall, so it was easy to do."

"I can't believe your police source gave you all this detail. Or that they got it so quickly."

"They can move fast when they need to. And why wouldn't they give it to me? They're trying to nail a killer, and they know media exposure can help." Wes wiggled the pen back into place. "What else you got?"

"Nothing. You?"

He pocketed his notebook. "Nada. Catch ya later!"

Wes jiffled down the dune, hopped in his car, and drove off, traveling north, toward the town center.

I stood a while longer, thinking about family dynamics. There was some weirdness between Mo and Lydia.

The sun disappeared behind a tendril of fast-moving gray clouds, and I shivered as a blast of unexpectedly cold air blew in off the ocean. Time to go.

CHAPTER SIX

Theo Caswell was in his late thirties. He was movie-star handsome, with longish brown hair and penetrating brown eyes. His office was in a new, all-glass building on Ocean Avenue, not far from Rocky Point's police station.

Theo stood behind his mahogany desk, which was angled to provide a sweeping view of the ocean.

He smiled at me. "Josie! This is a surprise. A good one, but a surprise."

Ellis offered his hand for a shake. "Thanks for meeting with me so promptly. I asked Josie to join me in case a question came up about any antiques. She'll wait outside."

"Josie's welcome to stay. Mo's beneficiary has already informed me that she plans on making the contents of the will public. Have a seat."

Ellis and I got ourselves settled in matching blue guest chairs; then Theo sat down behind his desk.

"Mo's will isn't complicated. She bequeathed all her clothing to Goodwill, and all her jewelry, financial assets, and household goods to New Hampshire Children First! She estimated that her jewelry was worth about ten thousand dollars. She had around fifty thousand in cash and mutual funds. She thought her household goods would sell for a few thousand dollars. A trust that had been set up by her mother when she was a child provided a monthly income of roughly three thousand dollars. That income was also willed to New Hampshire Children First! Should the organization cease operations or fail to meet certain ethical metrics, the income would revert to her sister, Lydia Shannon, or Ms. Shannon's heirs."

Ellis rubbed the side of his nose. "Who assesses the ethical metrics?"

"I do."

"So there's some arrangement for ongoing compensation for you."

"Yes. A token amount for what is expected to be minimal work — a yearly look at their tax filings and annual report, and a review of whether any complaints had been filed against the organization. I don't anticipate any problems. New Hampshire Children

87

First! has been in existence since 1922. It's well funded by multiple sources. There haven't been any complaints filed, ever. There's no reason to expect this record of excellence to change." Theo crossed his legs. "Mo called me last Friday to tell me she'd acquired an antique print, planned to ask Josie to appraise it, and would send me a copy of the appraisal when it was done. I explained that there was no urgency, from my perspective, since the print would be included in the category of household goods." He swiveled to face me. "How much is it worth?"

"I don't know. Mo asked us to appraise it, but I put it on hold when she died. It's in our safe. If it's real, it's worth around twenty-five to thirty thousand dollars, maybe more because it's in remarkable condition. Christie's sold the same print a few years ago for a little more than ten thousand dollars, but it was quite faded."

"*If* it's real?"

"It hasn't been properly authenticated, so there's no way to tell."

"I'll alert New Hampshire Children First! that it's in your possession."

"I know the director well. Helene Roberts. I'd be glad to talk to her about the appraisal."

"I'll let her know to expect your call."

"When did Mo prepare the will?" Ellis asked.

"She revised her will the same day her divorce was final, last October."

"Was the divorce contested?"

"Nominally. They filed jointly based on irreconcilable differences, but there were some skirmishes."

"What about?"

"I got the impression that her ex would have been glad to reconcile."

"Mo wasn't interested?"

"No way, no how."

"Was adultery involved?"

"So Mo claimed. Steve denied it."

"Did you believe him?"

Theo flipped his palms up, a "who knows" gesture. "I gave up long ago trying to get a handle on other people's relationships. My impression, for what it's worth, was that Mo adored him."

"Then why wouldn't she reconcile?"

"Pride, probably. That's usually the reason. She quoted her sister a lot. 'Lydia says I'm a fool,' that sort of thing."

Ellis asked a few more questions: who Steve's lawyer had been, did Theo know any of Mo's friends, and did Mo have any enemies. All he got for his effort, though, was the name of the lawyer. When Ellis was done, he stood, so I did, too. He thanked Theo for his time and asked for a copy of the will, which Theo had already prepared for him.

When Ellis and I reached the street, he asked if I'd heard anything or thought of anything that might help in the investigation.

"The German word for a mixing spoon is *Kochlöffel*. When someone was a busybody, you know, always sticking their noses in other people's business, my dad called them a *Kochlöffel*. Mo told me Lydia tried to convince her not to waste money having the print appraised, that it wasn't valuable enough to bother with. Mo told Theo Lydia thought Steve was a loser, that Mo shouldn't get back with him. If my dad were here, he'd say that Lydia was a *Kochlöffel,* always wanting to stir the pot. Are you surprised that you can't find Cal?"

"Are you?"

"Yes. It's not so easy to disappear nowadays, what with computers tracking our every purchase and security cameras everywhere." I waited a moment for him to comment, but he didn't. "Do you think he's on the run?"

"I think it's too early to say."

"Is Mo's death going to be ruled a homicide?"

"It looks that way."

"It's possible that whoever killed Mo killed him, too."

"What makes you think so?"

"Nothing. I mean, nothing specific. It's logical, though, isn't it?" My phone vibrated. I rustled around in my tote bag until I found it, then glanced at the display. I didn't recognize the number. "I should take this."

"Sure."

With my eyes steady on the pink rambling roses that grew in the sandy soil near the dunes, I answered the call. It was Theo Caswell, and he wanted me to know that Helene Roberts looked forward to talking to me. I thanked him, and that was that. I repeated his message to Ellis, promised I would keep him posted, and we headed for our cars.

Helene Roberts had taken the reins of New Hampshire Children First! nearly two decades earlier, when she was in her late thirties, and she had transformed it from a one-program charity into a leading medical research and treatment institution. The nonprofit's mission to help children with emotional, physical, and learning disabilities hadn't changed; the vision of how to achieve it had, and both the overarching strategy and the detailed tactics had been designed and implemented by Helene. I admired her as much as anyone I'd ever known. She was a leader and a mentor, and good through and through.

I arrived at Helene's office around two. The administration building was housed in an old farmhouse. Jasper Jackson, the last survivor of his family, had donated the thirty-five-acre property to New Hampshire Children First! in the 1970s.

Helene met me in her private study, which had originally been the back parlor. She looked the same as always — polished and professional. Her light brown hair was cut short. Her blue eyes radiated intelligence and kindness. She wore a blue-and-white checked blouse, with the sleeves rolled up to her elbows and navy-blue slacks. Her only jewelry was a simple pearl pendant with matching earrings and a gold wedding band. Blue plastic-framed reading glasses hung from a thin black nylon lanyard around her neck.

Helene placed her hands on her old-fashioned green leather desk blotter. "I'm devastated about Mo. Just devastated."

"Me, too. It's beyond awful."

"I couldn't believe it when Mr. Caswell told me we were her beneficiary. I've already asked the board to begin brainstorming ideas — I want to come up with a special way to acknowledge her generosity, maybe renaming the horse-training grounds for her."

"That's a lovely idea."

"And I understand we're now the owners of an important Japanese woodblock print. Would you recommend we sell it?"

"It hasn't been appraised, so I don't know its value. If you'd like, I'll complete the appraisal, pro bono, of course. Then I can make a recommendation."

"That's wonderful of you, Josie. Please do."

I explained I'd need her to sign the authorization, then called Gretchen to explain how to word it. Twenty minutes later, the form had been signed, and I was on my way back to my office.

As soon as I stepped inside, Gretchen told me that she'd read on the *Seacoast Star* blog that Mo's funeral was scheduled for Tuesday at two, and I asked Cara to put it into my calendar.

"Why the delay?" I asked.

"The teachers at Mo's school get out early

93

on Tuesdays. This way, they can attend the service."

"That's sensible and thoughtful." I shook my head. "You all know how much I cared about Mo, so you can understand how I'm feeling right now. I understand that life goes on and work needs to continue. I appreciate your patience if I'm scattered for the next little while."

"Of course," Gretchen said.

There were other sympathetic reactions, too, and I acknowledged them all, grateful for their support.

After a moment, I caught Sasha's eye. "So . . . we're back on with the Hiroshige print. Have you heard anything from those curators you contacted?"

"Yes," she said, "and it's about what I expected. There's no master list, so tracing a print's history is nearly impossible. Since we have no information except Cal's statement, which seems to have no backup, we're in a tricky spot. I'll start researching the Barnes family now. It's possible someone will know something. Fred and I are talking about various digital analyses options. Other than that, I suspect we'll need to test the materials."

The phone rang, and we all turned toward Cara.

She put the call on hold. "It's Frank Shannon, Josie."

"I'll take it upstairs." I jogged through the warehouse and dashed up the steps.

"I hope this isn't a bad time," he said.

"Not at all. How are you?"

"Worse than you can imagine. You always hear that the death of a child is a parent's worst nightmare, but that's not the half of it. It's a nightmare you can't wake up from. I need to think about something other than my darling daughter for a bit, so I was hoping that maybe I could tell you some about the guitar's history. I know it would help me to get out of my own head."

"Oh, Frank, I'm so sorry. I wish I could do more. It was on our list to ask you about the guitar, but we planned to wait until after the funeral to schedule a time. Are you sure you're ready? We can put it on hold for a week or so."

"Like I said, I'm a hot mess, and doing nothing makes it worse. If you have the time, I'd like to do it today."

"I can come to the house now, if you'd like."

"Nah. Let's go out. If Trish sees me doing business, she'll get upset. She has her way of grieving, and I have mine, and that's that. To tell you the truth, I could use a drink.

95

Do you have a favorite watering hole?"

"The Blue Dolphin lounge is a good place to talk. Do you know it?"

"Sure. Trish is a fan of the restaurant. Four thirty work for you?"

I told him it did, and I felt a familiar rush of adrenaline, the one I always felt at the start of a complex appraisal. I hoped Frank had juicy secrets to share.

CHAPTER SEVEN

The Blue Dolphin was my favorite restaurant. The three-story brick building had been designed in the mid-eighteenth century to fit into the slender, rounded corner lot. I pushed open the heavy wooden door and greeted Frieda, the hostess.

I paused at the arched entry to the lounge. Frank wasn't there. The lounge was a wood-paneled room with an oversized fireplace and bay windows overlooking the Piscataqua River. I nabbed my favorite table, a small one in the corner. From where I sat, I could see clear across to Maine. A light breeze was blowing, and in the glare of the late-afternoon sun, the burnt-sienna and gold leaves blazed like fire.

Jimmy, the bartender, greeted me by name and called that he'd be right over.

Jimmy had red hair and freckles, and he smiled a lot. He was just that kind of guy. He'd been one of the first people I'd met when I'd moved to Rocky Point, and one of the most welcoming.* Frank's reflection appeared in the window, and I looked over my shoulder, smiled, and waved. He wore black Dockers and a white linen shirt, very urbane, but he walked with the rolling gait of a country man.

Jimmy came out from behind the bar, said hello to Frank like he knew him well, flicked cocktail napkins toward us as if he were skipping rocks on the surf, and took our order: a dry martini, Bombay Sapphire, up with a twist, for me; a double Johnnie Walker Green on the rocks with a splash for Frank.

Frank's eyes followed Jimmy as he walked back to the bar. "Thanks for meeting me on such short notice."

"I'm glad it worked out."

Frank reached a hand up and massaged the back of his neck. "I'm stiff from not sleeping."

"It's horrible losing someone you love, but it's worse when it's unexpected, I think."

"Sounds like you have experience. Who'd you lose without notice?"

"My dad." I looked out the window. The sun was sinking fast. I could make out the

* Please see *Deadly Appraisal.*

98

trees across the river, but barely. I didn't want to talk about my dad. He'd died the year before I moved to New Hampshire, and despite the passage of time, or maybe because of it, since no one I knew now had known him, the wound still festered. "It was a long time ago."

Jimmy arrived with our drinks.

Frank raised his glass. "May the road rise up to meet you."

I touched my glass to his. "May the sun shine warm upon your face."

"God help me. God help us all." He took a healthy swallow. "I never thought I'd have to bury one of my daughters." He drank some more. "I adored Mo. She never said a bad word about anything or anyone, including Lydia. Not one. And Lydia gave her plenty of cause." He jiggled his glass, propelling the ice into a ferocious whirlpool. "They never got along, not really, not like sisters." He drank some more. "Sorry to be maudlin. Hell, look at me, using a word like 'maudlin.' The first time I heard that word was when Tommy Gale died. Tommy was my bass player, best in the business, and he died in his sleep at age thirty-one. Whoever heard of that? He had some kind of heart condition no one knew about. After a week or so, I was still moping about, and Trish told me to stop being maudlin. I waited until she went in the other room and looked it up. Foolishly sentimental. That's what it means. Foolishly sentimental." He shook his ice again. "The next day I drank a toast to Tommy and hired a new bass player." He tilted his glass toward me. "To Tommy."

I clinked. "To silver light in the dark of night."

He clinked. "Hear, hear."

"Tell me about the guitar. How did you come to own it?"

"It came from Abbot's Musical Instruments in Jackson, Mississippi. Man, I wanted that guitar. Looking at it through the window, I could tell it was the best I'd ever play, and I was right. I tried it out and knew I had to have it. It was Ricky Joe who bought it, though, 'cause he had the cash beans. My career took off the day I got hold of it. When you play the blues with a guitar like that, work finds you."

"When was that?"

"Nineteen seventy-three."

"Do you have a receipt?"

Frank finished his drink. "Well, now we're getting down to it."

I waited. Waiting was an important part of listening.

He finished his drink and set it down.

100

"You ready for another?"

"No, thanks. I'm good."

He raised his glass to catch Jimmy's attention, pointed to his chest, indicating he was the only one ordering a refill, then focused on me. "No, I don't have a receipt."

"How much did you pay?"

"It was priced at twenty-eight thousand dollars, a fortune at the time."

"You didn't buy it, did you?"

"You got good ears."

"I noticed how you worded it, if that's what you mean. Was it a gift? From a woman you don't want Trish to know about?"

"Let's just leave it that I got it from Abbot's in the seventies. Can't you appraise it without a receipt?"

"Sure, but it's completely possible that Abbot's records go back that far." I sipped some of my martini. "We can call them."

"Maybe it's best you don't."

"Why?"

"Let's let it lay and talk about what you can do, not what you can't."

"Come on, Frank."

"I never got in trouble keeping my mouth shut."

"If I can't confirm provenance you'll never be able to sell your guitar for top dollar —

101

or insure it for fair market value."

"Explain to me about provenance. What do you need, and why does it matter?"

"In the antiques world, provenance means that we can document a clear trail of owner-ship from the moment of creation to now. There's two options. Go from the producer forward or from the current owner back-ward. From what we've learned so far, it looks like the first option is closed to us. That leaves only the second approach: to work from the current owner — you — backward."

"I don't like it."

"Without clear title, you're leaving money on the table. You'll lose half the value, maybe more. Plus, the Robert Johnson as-sociation probably goes down the tubes."

Jimmy swung by with Frank's drink. Frank thanked him and swallowed a third of it in one long gulp.

"Did you steal it, Frank?"

His eyes shot daggers at me. "Hell, no!"

"You can tell me — the statute of limita-tions has long passed."

"I've never stolen nothing in my life."

"Then what's the big secret?"

"Trish can't know. Not ever."

"I can create a side document for the ap-praisal, but if you ever want to sell it, the world will have to know."

"Give me a minute to think on this."

Frank stood, took another long slug of whiskey, and walked out of the lounge with an unconscious swagger. Two middle-aged women sitting at a table near the front pointed and whispered. It wasn't every day you saw a local celebrity strut by.

While I waited for Frank to return, I checked messages. Wes had emailed asking if I had any new information. Ty had texted that he missed me and would call just before bed. Given that a lot of Ty's work was top secret, I hoped he'd be able to tell me why he'd been called down to Washington, but I wouldn't be surprised if he couldn't say a word. I opened my photo management app and scrolled through the images until I found some from last summer's New Hampshire Children First! volunteer picnic. My eyes filled, and I closed them for a few seconds. I understood the term "heartache." Frank came back into the lounge. I slid my phone into my bag.

One of the women at the table near the front, a full-figured brunette, reached out an arm to touch Frank's hand and said something. Frank paused to chat, smiling and laughing. He'd been a professional charmer for a lot of years, and he still was, despite the fact that his daughter had just died. It took a certain kind of man to steel himself like that. I'd learned the hard way that most people who use charm as currency do so because they have nothing else of substance to offer. Charm disarms and can minimize a multitude of sins. Watching his performance made me wonder if I could trust him.

Frank sat down and drank some whiskey, a sip this time. "There are only three people in the world who know how I came to own this guitar: Ricky Joe McElroy, C. K. Flint, and me. I'm telling you because I want to know the truth about the guitar's value. I'm trusting you to keep the information private until and unless I pull the trigger."

"We'll need to contact the store and those two people, and maybe others, but I can absolutely promise we won't release the information to the public without your okay."

"You trust your staff that much?"

"It's what we do, Frank. We keep secrets for a living."

"I'm probably being silly, anyway. For all I know those boys spread the story all over Mississippi." He finished his drink in two long swallows and slapped the glass on the table. "It's more than forty years ago, but a lie started has to be maintained. I promised Trish the year before I'd never gamble again. That was after I got into some trouble, it doesn't matter what kind, and got roughed up some. She told me she wanted no part of a gambler, period, end of story, and I promised her that my gambling days were over. I kept that promise for a while, a few months, I guess. I told Trish I bought the guitar at Abbot's for a hundred and twenty bucks, all I had and then some, that the owner was dumb as a doornail and didn't know what he had, that it was probably worth double what I paid. If Trish knew I'd been lying to her for all our lives, there'd be hell to pay. Maybe worse than hell. Here we go, then — I won the guitar fair and square in a poker game on June fifth, 1973. That's a date I'll never forget. My life got changed that day. Ricky Joe's family owned McElroy Rubber Corporation. Mostly, they made tires. About two months later, Ricky Joe took himself off to Idaho to go hunting and never came back. Last I heard, he married a girl from Boise and they're living the good life on the trust fund his granddaddy set up. C. K. was a good guy, not too bright, but a hard worker. He got himself a job at the local lumberyard right out of high school, and as far as I know, he's still there.

I came from the other side of the ditch. I got myself licensed as an electrician, but I hated the work. All I ever wanted was to play the blues and get out of Mississippi. That night, I was down thirteen thousand, can you believe it? I didn't have a pot to piss in, but I was drunk, and I had the gambling fever on me. Ricky Joe offered me double or nothing. C. K. wasn't playing. He was sitting in a corner shaking, just hearing the numbers we were tossing about. I said I wouldn't do double or nothing, but I'd do double or give me that Martin guitar you just bought at Abbot's for twenty-eight thousand dollars. Ricky Joe said done. When I won, Ricky Joe cried like a baby, pissin' and moanin' about how he didn't mean it, how he couldn't do it, how his daddy would skin him alive, how he'd give me thirty thousand, thirty-five thousand, but I wasn't having any of it. I wanted that guitar so bad I could feel the strings under my fingers. I'll tell you this, though — the thought that I might have lost sobered me up and straightened me out. I made Ricky Joe take me to his house there and then, and he made C. K. come as a witness. I grabbed that guitar and the case it came in, and told both those boys sayonara. I went home, convinced Trish that our future was waiting for us out west, and we caught the next bus to L.A. That was an easy sell because Trish was starting to think she had a future in golf, and L.A. was a happening place back then for that dream. And that's the end of that tall tale."

"That's quite a story."

"It's the truth, so help me God."

"So Ricky Joe has the receipt."

"I guess. He probably had it back then. God knows whether he kept it."

"Abbot's must have a record of the sale."

"Or they don't."

"C. K. can verify you won it like you said."

"If he remembers."

"I'll need to verify the events somehow, Frank."

"Sure. Just don't tell Trish." He gave the ice one last spin and downed the rest of his drink. "The owner of the store is the one who told Ricky Joe about the Robert Johnson connection, unless he made it up."

"What's his name? Abbot's owner?"

"I don't recall, if I ever knew it, which I doubt I did."

"What did Ricky Joe tell you about the history of the guitar?"

"That Abbot's bought the guitar off some gal who was somehow connected to one of Johnson's girlfriends. Johnson was quite the ladies' man."

"You don't make things easy, Frank."

"Nothing worth a damn is easy."

I clinked his empty glass with mine. "Words to live by."

My phone vibrated. It was a text from Wes: *Urgent. Call now.*

CHAPTER EIGHT

When Wes said something was urgent, usually it signaled nothing more than his eagerness to be first in line. Usually wasn't always, though, so I pushed my half-full drink aside and assured Frank his secret was safe. He stood when I did and insisted on paying, a gentleman. I offered condolences again, and he got misty-eyed and hugged me.

I sat in my car and called Wes. He answered before I even heard a ring.

"I need some info pronto."

"I'm fine, Wes. How are you?"

"Good, good. You were right. Cal didn't go to Little Tokyo. My police source tells me they have him driving down Market Street at four thirty-five."

"What do you mean they 'have him'?"

"On security camera footage. From Harrison Foodmart's parking lot cameras. He whizzed by."

"To get to the Shannons' from Market, you need to take either the interstate or Route 1. If he took I-95, he'd have to pay a toll. What about tollbooth cameras or E-ZPass?"

"Nothing."

"So if he went to Mo's, he took Route 1, which is lined with stores and restaurants and doctors' offices. Surely there are a bunch of security cameras."

"You'd think. They're still checking, but they've got nothing at this point. He might have taken back roads in order to avoid the cameras."

"I suppose it's possible. It's also possible he didn't go to Mo's. For all we know, he's en route to Vegas."

"Good one, Joz! Where do you think he is for real?"

"Have you checked for out-of-state family?"

"He has a sister in Wyoming, and his mom is in an assisted living facility down in Myrtle Beach, but he's not close to either of them. The reason I called . . . Cal hasn't used a credit card or his cell phone . . . how would you find him?"

"You said in your message that it was urgent. What's urgent about that?"

"Don't you want to know what he's up

110

to?" Wes sounded staggered. "I thought you'd be flattered. Every once in a while you come up with a smart idea."

Talk about damning with faint praise. I decided to ignore it. "If I were looking for Cal, I'd ask Lydia who his friends are. I'd talk to people at Hitchens and at the campus museum. I'd look through his desk and his computer. I'd see who contacted him, say in the last three months, and vice versa."

"These are stock approaches. The police and I are tripping over one another. I need a new approach. Give me an idea that's smokin'."

"What about Lydia? If Cal is in touch with anyone, it would be her. Can you tell if he's called her cell or sent her email? Or maybe she's taken out a bigger-than-usual withdrawal to sneak him cash."

"The police are all over it. I don't call that a smokin' hot idea."

"We could —" I stopped myself as an idea rattled me.

"We could what?" Wes prodded.

"I need to go. Sorry." I hit the END CALL button.

Much to my surprise, I had come up with a smokin' hot idea, and I was keeping it for myself.

Sitting in my home office, I reread the document I'd just created and smiled, satisfied. It was good. I emailed it to myself for safekeeping, then printed two copies, slid them into a clear plastic sleeve, and left them by the front door. I crossed the driveway, climbed the steps to Zoë's porch, and rang the bell.

The porch light came on, and I stood in a seashell-pink circle of light. All Zoë's outside bulbs were pink. Ellis opened the door.

"Just the man I want to see." I stepped inside. "Got a sec?"

"Sure."

I spoke to his back as he walked down the hall toward the kitchen. "I need to run something by you."

Ellis stopped. "Privately?"

"Kind of."

"Is that you, Josie?" Zoë called.

"Hey, Zoë! I need to talk to Ellis for a minute. I'll come say hello after."

"Anything wrong?"

"Nope. Just a little business."

Ellis led the way into a parlor off the living room. Zoë called it her thinking room. He slid the pocket door closed. We sat across from one another on matching ladder-back chairs fitted with traditional blue-and-white toile cushions.

I handed him a copy of my flyer and watched him read it. It didn't take him long since most of the space was taken up by photographs. One was a shot of Mo's Japanese woodblock print. The other was a photo of Cal Lewis I'd nabbed from Hitchens University's faculty page. In the photograph, Cal sat in front of a haphazardly filled bookshelf, his chin resting on his hands, his elbows on his paper-strewn desk, a scholar hard at work, or a man wanting to create that impression.

When he looked up, I said, "I think I'd like to post this online. What do you think?"

"This flyer implies Cal has knowledge about the print."

"But not necessarily that he did something wrong. I worded it carefully." I read the headline aloud: "Did you sell this man this Japanese woodblock print?"

"It'll make him rabbit. Just do a regular call for sightings, for the print, not the man."

"The print is a dime a dozen. Everyone and her mother has sold one of these."

"Then we'll have a lot of sifting to do." He leaned back, refusing to be hurried, recognizing my impatience because he'd

113

seen it before. "When we know more about what we're dealing with, then we can talk about publishing someone's photo. It's premature and is likely to do more harm than good. For now, I'm going to ask you to hold off."

Meeting his unrelenting scrutiny, I could hear the last faint sizzle of my smokin' hot idea fizzling out.

Ellis and I walked into the kitchen. He poured himself a cup of tea from the art deco Clarice Cliff ceramic teapot I'd given Zoë last Christmas. He raised a cup in my direction, silently asking if I wanted some.

"No, thanks."

Zoë sat at her kitchen table with her feet up on a chair, flipping through an L.L.Bean catalogue.

I slid into another chair and pointed at the catalogue. "What are you looking for?"

She grinned. "Nothing, but I'll know it when I see it. Any news on why Ty was called to D.C.?"

"Not yet. I hope he'll be able to tell me something when I talk to him later."

"Give him my love."

"I will."

She tossed the catalogue aside. "The kids want to go on a hayride. Want to come? I'm thinking Sunday, around three."

"Great! Let's plan on dinner at my place afterward."

"Sold!"

I revised the flyer, eliminating all references to Cal, and emailed the new version to Wes. My cover note read:

Hey, Wes!
I'm giving you a head start. I'll be mailing this flyer to my entire list in an hour.
You're welcome.

Josie

Two seconds after I hit SEND, Ty called.

"Hey, cutie. How's my best girl?"

"Saying I'm the best implies that you have other girls and they aren't quite up to snuff."

He laughed, a deep rumble. I smiled. I loved Ty's laugh.

"What makes you think I'm joking?" I asked.

He laughed harder. Ty's laugh was infectious, and I caught it. I walked into the living room and plunked down on the couch. After a moment we both quieted down.

"What's so funny?" I asked.

"Stop. Don't start me off again."

"Okay. Are you all right? You sound beat."

115

"I am. It's been a day. All good, but a lot coming at me from a lot of different directions, leaving me with too many balls to juggle and too much to think about. I'm a single-minded man — give me a task, no one does it better. Give me politics, and I'll go fishing. The executive committee brought me down to Washington because they wanted my opinion on a reorg idea. It looks like all training will be under the purview of a national director, a new position. They want to assess best practices on a local level, sift all the findings through one assessment model, come up with a unified program, and roll it out nationally. Instead of eighteen local directors reporting to five regional managers, the eighteen will report to three regional managers, organized geographically East, West, and Central. Those three regional managers will report to the new national director."

"But different areas have different needs."

"That's a concern I raised. And they agree. They think this approach will translate into quicker decision-making."

"What do you think?"

"I think it's a gamble."

"They want you for East."

"Yes. I'd be based in Rocky Point. They nosed around some about whether I might be interested in the national director position."

My heart stopped, then started again, a slow drumbeat, the kind of low, steady thumping that signals danger. I hate change. Any change. I forced myself to think about Ty, not myself. He was brilliant. Responsible. Experienced. Wise.

"Congratulations."

"Thanks."

"What did you say?"

"I kept it vague . . . you know . . . 'That's something to think about,' that sort of thing. They were just putting out feelers. Nothing was offered."

My pulse quieted, just a bit. "Why wouldn't you leap at the opportunity?"

"Because the director will have to be based in D.C. My home is wherever you are, and you need to be based in Rocky Point."

"Wow. That's like the most romantic thing I've ever heard. Say it again."

"My home is wherever you are. Not to sound cheesy or anything, but you are my heart. I love you."

Outside, a car drove by, and in the glare of its headlights, I spotted a deer in the forest across the street. It froze for a second, then turned tail and fled, disappearing into the night.

"No, I don't."

"You don't love me?"

I laughed. "I see you're not a mind reader. I adore you, Ty, and you know it. I don't need to be based in Rocky Point. I'm Prescott's owner. I can be based wherever I want."

"You're a little bit of a control freak. How could you possibly move to Washington?"

"I'd open a second venue and leave my staff in charge of the flagship location."

"That's crazy."

"Why?"

"Because you don't know anything about the D.C. market."

"I'm a quick learner. And where you go, I go."

"I don't have to go."

"Don't you want a promotion?"

"Sure."

"Then apply. We'll figure it out."

"Why can't we do this with our wedding plans?"

"We will."

CHAPTER NINE

Thursday morning, I woke to pelting rain just before six. I rolled over and pulled the blanket over my head, trying to recapture the slow, dreamy haven of sleep, but it was gone.

I took my coffee to my study and booted up my computer. I wanted to see which media outlets had picked up my call for sightings. The Portsmouth newspaper had a short article on page 8. Two local blogs, one with a newsy bent; the other one, antiques focused, ran it as a major story. All the major antiques sites and publications highlighted it. It was the lead story on the *Seacoast Star*'s home page. Wes featured the photograph of Mo's Japanese woodblock print alongside the headline.

HELP SOLVE A MURDER
HAVE YOU SEEN THIS ANTIQUE
JAPANESE WOODBLOCK PRINT?

Next to it, a secondary article discussed the mysterious disappearance of Cal Lewis, stating he hadn't used any of his credit cards or withdrawn any money from his bank account. There was no direct inference that Cal's absence was related to the call for sightings, but the implication was clear: Cal bought the print somewhere and sold it to Mo. Mo was killed. Cal went missing. Learning where Cal bought the print might help track down Mo's murderer. I was glad Wes did it, but I was also glad that it would be Wes, not me, who had to explain the placement to Ellis.

The article about Mo's print ended with an instruction to contact me with information. I texted Wes: *Great story. I'll let you know if I hear from anyone.*

Fred was at his desk when I arrived around seven thirty, a rare occurrence. Fred was a night owl, often coming in close to noon and staying late into the evening. Since his wife, Suzanne, the general manager at the Blue Dolphin,* almost always worked the dinner shift, his proclivity suited their schedules. Protected by the overhang, I straddled the threshold and shook out my

* Please see *Lethal Treasure*.

umbrella before stuffing it into the chinoiserie umbrella stand.

I staggered and pressed my palm against my chest. "Call a doctor! I'm seeing a mirage."

"Ha, ha. I can't believe I'm here either, but duty calls. I have an eight A.M. call to Monsieur Pierre Gagnon in Paris. Evidently, he's the owner of one of those fourteen Martin guitars."

"Great work. Speaking of the guitar, I have an update." I sat down. "I spoke to Frank Shannon, and there are aspects of the situation he doesn't want known." I filled him in. "You reach out to Abbot's and go backward from there. I'll work to connect the dots between Frank and Ricky Joe and C. K. Keep written records as usual, but report only to me."

"Got it. And I'll continue tracing the guitars."

"Good. Any news from Davy?"

"He's due up tomorrow at ten."

"Perfect."

Gretchen's wind chimes jingled, and Fred and I looked up.

Trish straddled the threshold. She shook out her umbrella, then placed it in the holder. She looked amazingly put-together considering the ordeal she'd endured the last few days. Her eyes were clear. Her hair was neatly styled. She wore a hint of blue-gray eye shadow, and her lips shone with a rosy gloss.

"I hope I'm not too early," she said. "I saw cars in the parking lot and thought I'd take a chance that you were here."

"I'm glad you did. Trish, I don't know if you've ever met Fred, one of Prescott's antiques appraisers. Fred, Trish Shannon, Mo's mom."

Fred stood and stepped around his desk. He looked as stylish as ever in his slim-fit, perfectly tailored Italian-made suit.

"I'm so sorry for your loss, Ms. Shannon. Josie's told me wonderful things about Mo."

Trish's eyes moistened as she shook Fred's hand. "Thank you."

I walked to the coffee machine. "I see Fred made a pot of coffee. Would you like a cup? We can take it to my office."

She accepted the offer, and I balanced everything on a tray. Fred opened the warehouse door. Upstairs, I used my elbow to flip on the overhead light in my office, then slid the tray onto the butler's table. Trish sat on the love seat. I poured her a cup, and she grasped it as if she needed the warmth.

"I saw this morning's *Seacoast Star.*

Reading that article about Cal, positioned as it was, directly next to the call for sightings . . . well, it was upsetting." She lowered her cup to the tray. She hadn't taken a sip. "I thought you might know something. The police aren't telling us anything."

"No . . . I'm sorry."

"Never mind. The real reason I stopped by . . . I wanted to let you know that Mo's funeral is next Tuesday."

"I heard."

"Will you be there?"

"Yes, of course."

She paused for a moment. "Mo left instructions that she wanted to be cremated and have her ashes scattered on the beach. We'll do that privately. The service, though, is public, and I was hoping . . . *we* were hoping that you'd deliver one of the eulogies. Her principal is going to talk about her work with the children. Helene will talk about her volunteer efforts. And our minister, of course." She must have seen my surprised expression, because she added, "Whenever Mo spent time with you, she mentioned it, recounting things you said that stuck with her, reporting on your accomplishments . . . Mo didn't have close friends, not in the conventional sense. She was too busy helping other people.

Please . . . will you give the eulogy, as her friend?"

There was only one possible reply. "I'd be honored."

"Thank you." She closed her eyes, just for a second. "May I ask one more thing? As Mo's friend, you might know more than me . . . Did she ever mention Steve? Her ex? I mean lately. Did she?"

"Why do you ask?"

"Lydia told me that Mo was thinking of getting back together with him. I couldn't believe it. I still can't. But Lydia would know more about that than I would. Daughters don't always confide in their mothers, not when they think their mothers would disapprove. Lydia says Mo wouldn't have told me her plans because she was ashamed of her weakness. Loving a man who treated her so poorly."

"That seems a bit strong. I don't know any specifics, but it seems to me that loving someone, flaws and all, doesn't make Mo weak. It makes her loving."

"I agree, theoretically, at least." Trish smoothed her skirt and drank some coffee. "My only concern for my children has always been their ultimate happiness. I know that's trite, to say, 'I only want you to be happy,' but it's true. That's all I've ever wanted for my girls."

"You've had your doubts about Steve."

"Of course. If a man cheats once, he's likely to do so again."

"I hear that Steve denied he cheated."

"Wouldn't you?"

"I don't know. Regardless, people change." Trish placed her cup on the tray and stood. "Do you believe that?"

I stood, too, and led the way to the door. "Yes. We get better. Stronger. More capable. At least, we do if we want to. Wisdom, you know? Think about yourself. Aren't you different now than you were when you were twenty?"

"Dramatically, but I've never thought of myself as wise. Just road weary."

"Mo did. Besides loving you, she admired you." That was true, and I would repeat it in my eulogy.

"Thank you, Josie. That's nice of you to say."

She paused halfway across the warehouse and touched my elbow. "Your speaking on Tuesday means a great deal to me. And to Frank."

"Thank you for asking me."

I walked her out and watched her drive away.

I took Mo's print from our mammoth walk-in safe and brought it up to my office, hoping it would inspire me to write the perfect eulogy. I set it on a burled walnut easel next to the display case that housed my rooster collection.

The colors in the print, while vibrant in tone, were muted in hue, like my mood. The people on the bridge were anonymous, interchangeable. It depicted existential isolation. Or, I supposed, if I wanted to put a positive spin on it, it portrayed self-sufficiency. Mo was self-sufficient, but she didn't see herself that way. I was aware that there is often a gap between how people view us and how we view ourselves. Hiroshige portrayed Edo as cold and lonely. Mo was warm and personable. Perception. What we see. What we believe. It didn't matter to Mo whether people saw themselves as weak or bad; she saw their strength and goodness, no matter how deeply those qualities were hidden. She truly believed that people were essentially decent, and she had a knack for getting people to believe in their own capabilities. That's what I would talk about in Mo's eulogy. I sat at my desk jotting notes about Mo, recalling examples of her generosity and grace, picturing her gentling the horses and laughing with the children.

I turned toward the window beside my desk. My old maple was in full autumn regalia. Even the steady rain couldn't diminish the brightness of the burnished-gold and dusty-pink leaves. I thought again about Steve. If they'd really been close to reuniting, he might have insights he could share, anecdotes that would bring my eulogy to life. If nothing else, the eulogy provided a good excuse for asking how he was doing.

There was no phone listing for Ricky, Rick, Rich, Dick, Richard, or R. J. McElroy in Boise, Idaho, which meant nothing. He could be one of the nearly 50 percent of the population who no longer used a landline. He might have moved. The phone could be listed in his girlfriend's or wife's name. I Googled additional variations of Ricky Joe's name and came up dry.

I bit the corner of my lip as I ran through the options. It only took a minute to settle on a plan. I decided to call all the McElroys in Boise whose phone numbers were listed in the white pages, then, if that didn't pan out, call the McElroy Rubber Company, which was still in business, and try to sweet-talk Ricky Joe's contact information out of someone.

The first two calls were duds. The third number was listed to an S. McElroy. My call went to voice mail.

"This is Sandy! Ricky Joe and I aren't home, but we'd love to call you back. Leave us a message!"

"My name is Josie Prescott, calling for Ricky Joe." I gave my phone number. "It's important that we talk. This relates to something that happened in Mississippi in the early seventies. There's no problem. I'm not selling anything. I'm an antiques appraiser, and I simply need to verify a date." I repeated my phone number and hung up.

I toyed with calling C. K. Flint, the man who'd sat in a corner shaking while Frank won himself a guitar, but I didn't. It would be better to talk to Ricky Joe first. But there was no harm in seeing if C. K. had a listed phone. He did. He still lived in Jackson, and the phone was listed under his name.

I swung back to my computer and brought up a browser. Rice Dixon Elementary School, where Mo had taught and Steve still did, started its day at 7:50. Classes ended at 3:00. I glanced at the clock on the monitor. It read 9:27.

I had plenty of time to think how to phrase my question to Steve.

I had plenty of time to think how to phrase my question to Steve.

CHAPTER TEN

Janson's Antiques Mall was an antiques lover's dream. Two dozen independent antiques and collectibles dealers rented space in a big old red barn set in a five-acre field on the far western edge of Rocky Point. Matt Janson, the owner, was an entrepreneur, not an antiques dealer, and I admired the heck out of his business acumen. Matt told me that the barn was about a hundred years old and had been a bear to renovate. While he was bringing the building up to code, he'd expanded its footprint, nearly tripling the usable space. He'd laid blacktop over a chunk of land for a parking lot and started advertising in local papers and offering discounts to tourists if tour operators made his mall an official stop on their bus tours.

I made a point of stopping by every few weeks. Because we carry some of this and some of that, I know a little bit about a lot of things and am eager to buy anything I can resell at a profit, including things we need to clean, repair, or otherwise refurbish. I often found bargains at Janson's because dealers who specialize usually don't bother to research objects outside their sphere of interest, and I have a nose for value.

I parked near one of three chartered buses. This time of year, we call the tourists who travel through our neck of the woods leaf peepers. Whenever I overhear their oohs and ahs as they realize the colors really are as spectacular as they look in the movies, I always feel a little jolt of pride, as if I had done something to earn their delight.

I pushed open one of a pair of heavy plank doors and entered another world. Matt used reclaimed wood, recessed lighting, and cinnamon-scented incense to create the aura of an idealized country home. Each of the twenty-four vendors had his or her own separate shop, closed in on three sides and open to the central corridors, except at night, of course, when individual pocket doors provided security. The dividing walls were eight feet high, tall enough to create a real feeling of separation, but with the ceiling soaring to thirty feet at the apex, nothing felt closed in. Six units ran along the two long outside walls. Eight more units filled the center, back-to-back, four facing east and four facing west. Two more units ran along the back wall, sharing the space with a corridor that led to public restrooms and a private dealers' room, outfitted with a kitchen and individual lockers. The final two spots took up the space on either side of the entry doors.

I checked my coat and dripping umbrella in the coat room, then faced the information booth, deciding where to start. The place was jam-packed, typical for a rainy Thursday in September.

Matt spotted me and came out from behind the information desk. He was a big man, about six-three, and fit. He was around fifty. His hair was dirty blond, showing a little gray around his temples. He wore it long, gathered at the back of his neck in a ponytail. He moved to New Hampshire because he fell in love with a woman from Rocky Point named Fay. That was twenty-five years ago. He and Fay just had their first grandchild, a girl named Joy.

"Good to see you, Josie. Weren't you here last week?"

"You have a good memory."

"And a knack for deductive reasoning. When something breaks a pattern, it catches my attention."

"I didn't know I was so predictable."

"Sure you did. You cruise through hoping for bargains every few weeks, not every week. So what's up?"

I handed him a copy of the flyer asking for information about Mo's print. "I need to know who sold this Japanese woodblock print."

He stared at the image, taking in the tranquility, the snow, the colors. "It's beautiful. Quiet." He raised his eyes. "It was owned by that girl who was killed. What makes you think the print was sold here?"

"Nothing. I'm checking everywhere. You have a couple of folks who specialize in art prints, and others who sell whatever comes their way, so I thought it couldn't do any harm to ask."

"And you get antsy sitting behind a desk."

"Don't you know it. How's Joy?"

"Perfect. Gorgeous. She just turned three months old."

"Do you have a picture?"

"Is snow white?" Matt slid his phone from a case attached to his belt, tapped, swiped, and handed it over.

The photo showed Joy cooing in Matt's arms. In the photo, Matt was looking at Joy with awe, as if he were holding a twinkling star in his hands.

133

"Oh, Matt! What a wonderful photo." I handed back the phone. "Congratulations."

"Thanks. I've got a bad case of PGS — Proud Grandfather Syndrome." He grinned. "Luckily, there's no cure."

"You're completely adorable, you know that, don't you?"

"In an embarrassing sort of way."

I scanned the room. "I'm glad to see you're so busy, Matt. You're going to have to build an annex."

"Nope. A second location."

"Where?"

"That depends on you."

"Me?"

"Any chance you're free for lunch on Monday?"

I met his eyes and felt a trill of excitement rush through my veins. "Sure." I dug my phone out of my bag and brought up my calendar. "Where and when?"

"What's your favorite restaurant?"

"The Blue Dolphin."

"Sold. When do you like to eat lunch?"

"Twelve thirty."

"Sold again."

Matt extended a hand, his expression hard to read, somewhere between solemn and exhilarated. We shook.

A middle-aged clerk behind the information booth spoke the words "Christmas ornaments" as she typed them into a computer while a young woman wearing a red beret looked on.

"Do you really have all the dealers' inventories?"

Matt grinned. "Yup."

To get twenty-four independent dealers to trust him with their inventory records was akin to completing a jigsaw puzzle in the dark — until you'd tried it, you couldn't fully appreciate the patience and imagination required.

"How on God's earth did you get them to agree?"

He laughed. "It's in the contract. I won't lease to anyone who doesn't want to participate. It's all upside from their perspective. They enter a one-sentence description of an object, the date it's offered for sale, and its asking price, and we send them customers."

"What happens when the piece is sold?"

"The listing automatically transfers to the archives at the moment of sale."

"So you know how long it took for an object to sell."

"Right."

"Can the archive be searched?"

"Sure. Dealers do it all the time. We also maintain a second archive comprised of all that information, plus the actual sales price. As you know, most dealers offer discounts, but they don't want their competition to know about it. By creating a second archive, we were able to build a Chinese wall separating the information we collect and make available to all leaseholders from the information most of them want to keep confidential. The dealers can search their own records, but no one else's."

"Except you."

He grinned again. "I'm a big believer in squirreling away data. Just because I don't know the information's value today doesn't mean I won't figure it out tomorrow."

"You're a smart man."

"The harder I work, the smarter I get."

"Amen to that." I pointed to the flyer. "Could you search for sales of this print in the archives?"

"Sure. Follow me." He leaned over the information booth counter and pulled an iPad from a lower shelf. He entered the query. Seconds later he had the answer. "A Hiroshige woodblock print was sold on September second at ten after one. No others this year. The name of the print isn't listed. The asking price was fifty dollars." Matt looked up. "Do you need me to go back further than a year?"

"No. Not at this point anyway." I did a quick calculation. "September second . . . that was the Sunday of Labor Day weekend. Who sold it?"

"Rose's Treasures. Number seventeen." He slid his iPad back onto the shelf. "So what do you think? Do you like my software?"

"I love it. Is it proprietary, or did you tweak an off-the-shelf package?"

"A hundred percent proprietary."

My dad always said that contrary to popular belief, it wasn't the devil who lurked in details — it was God. In other words, he explained, talk is cheap. I'd just learned that Matt was more than a dreamer; he was a doer, a rare breed.

"I'm seriously impressed, Matt."

He smiled like he meant it and presented his knuckles for a fist bump.

I'd known Rose Mayhew, the owner of Rose's Treasures, for years, having chatted with her frequently during my periodic buying trips. She was tall and thin, with shoulder-length wavy gray hair and gray-blue eyes. She dealt exclusively in sterling silver, from refined Edwardian coffeepots and hanging decanter labels to utilitarian sets of flatware and miscellaneous objects like antique candle snuffers and vintage key rings. The only items I'd bought from her were outside her area of specialization, including a hand-colored nineteenth-century map of Florida she'd priced at twenty dollars and a pair of brass hurricane lamps I'd found for ten dollars.

Rose was ringing up sales. Three people waited in line. I stepped to the side. When she was done, she glanced around, deciding where to go next. She spotted me and came over to where I was standing just outside her booth.

"Can I help you with something, Josie?"

"Sorry to bother you while you're so busy." I held up the flyer. "I'm trying to find out where this print came from. According to the inventory database, you sold a Hiroshige on September second."

"I did?" she asked, her eyes on the flyer. "Let me think . . . I remember finding a few prints in a box of silver pieces last summer, but I don't recall selling any of them." She raised her eyes to my face. "You know me. If it's not made of silver, I don't pay attention."

"I'm trying to confirm its provenance. Can you tell me where you bought that box?"

Her lips compressed into one thin line.

It's much harder to buy good quality items than it is to sell them, so if you have a reliable source, you never reveal it. If your purchase came from a one-off situation, a garage or moving sale, for example, you might be willing to share that information to someone you trust, like me.

"Sorry."

If it turned out that her Hiroshige print was actually the one Mo purchased, I could revisit my request for information, couching it in terms of ethics and promising to mention her shop by name in any articles we wrote on the subject, a rare promotional opportunity for a small business. Now, though, since I had no reason to think Mo's print came from her shop, I could let it slide.

"I understand. September second was the Sunday of Labor Day. Did you have help that day? Someone who might have made the sale?"

"Yes, Artie helps out every Sunday. He's here today, too — leaf peepers." A customer standing by a locked display case was glancing around, looking for help. "I need to get back to work. I'll ask Artie to step out to talk to you."

I thanked her. I was tempted to ask her to check whether the sale was made with a credit card, but if I could avoid bothering her again, I would. While I waited for Artie, I examined the ceiling. Matt had installed security cameras at strategic points around the perimeter. If Artie couldn't help, maybe the cameras could.

Artie couldn't. Artie was long retired, with a soldier's stance, straight and proud. His hair was white and cut short. He studied the flyer for a moment, then shook his head.

"I used to be a whiz at connecting the objects I sold with their buyers. Not anymore. I don't even remember selling it. Sorry."

I thanked him and returned to the information booth. I explained what I needed to Matt. A few taps later, he swung his iPad around so I could see it.

"This is the camera closest to booth seventeen. The camera takes photos every three seconds. Here's the record starting at eight minutes after one."

I clicked through the photos. At ten past one, I saw Rose hand a plastic-sheathed art print to a dealer I recognized, Jonathan Newson. Jonathan was the owner of Newson's Rare and Vintage Art, booth two. I thanked Matt and darted through the crowd to Jonathan's booth.

Jonathan was about forty. He was short and stout, with a few strands of brown hair artfully arranged over his bald pate.

I eased into his booth and sidestepped to the bin of prints labeled BY ARTIST, G–K. I flipped through and found a faded copy of Hiroshige's *Meguro Drum Bridge and Sunset Hill.* The print was encased in a clear plastic envelope. A diamond-shaped white sticker near the top read *$130/918.*

Jonathan stood near a framed copy of Van Gogh's *Starry Night* mounted on the back wall. He was talking to an older man, pointing to a starlit swirl, then the church steeple. The older man said something. Jonathan waved over a middle-aged woman leaning against the front counter. He left her to finish the sale, and I swooped in.

After we exchanged a quick hello, I showed him the flyer. "Have you sold a *Meguro Drum Bridge and Sunset Hill* lately?"

"No. It's weird that you ask, though, since I just bought one."

"The one in the bin. I saw it."

"I thought it might be genuine. It had the look, you know? Fugitive blues."

"How did you determine it wasn't real?"

"I removed the backing and found 'Morty's Art Prints' stamped on the back."

"Ouch. Does the number 918 mean you bought this print this month?"

"That's right. September 2018. It's my

141

old-fashioned inventory system."

"What do you think of Matt's computer-ized system?"

"It's terrific. We get a lot of referrals from the information booth. I don't care about the reports, though. I'm a Luddite. I like being able to rifle through the bins myself and see how long prints take to sell, re-familiarize myself with the inventory . . . you know. I'm an art lover, which means I'm visual. I'm in the business because of the objects, not the reports. But those refer-rals — that's worth the price of admission." Jonathan tapped the flyer. "Is this about that dead girl?"

"Mo Shannon," I said, wanting to speak her name aloud, wanting Jonathan to hear it. "I don't know. At this point, I'm just try-ing to track the print. Have you heard of any sales?"

"Just hers."

Jonathan's assistant came up. "Excuse me for interrupting. Mr. Donovan has a ques-tion."

I thanked him again and slipped away.

Appraising an antique is like any other detective work — you follow leads and rely on luck and experience to help you navigate unknown terrain, and you expect most of your efforts to fail. While I was used to running into brick walls, I never liked it, and today was no exception. As I walked to my car through the driving rain, I tried to put a positive spin on the situation. I'd moved forward — I now knew where Mo's Hiroshige *hadn't* been purchased. You go through enough false starts, all that's left is the truth.

CHAPTER ELEVEN

I reached the Rice Dixon Elementary School at a quarter to three and parked in an empty spot near the rear of the ungated employee parking lot. The rain had slowed to a drizzle, but the sky remained dark. A line of idling cars ran along Bracebridge Road, parents waiting to pick up their kids. I used the time to call work and check my email. Everything was under control. I texted Ty that I loved him, then checked the *Seacoast Star*'s website for breaking news. Wes had posted an update about the medical examiner's findings.

Mo had been strangled, then tossed or pushed off the cliff. From the angle of the contusions on Mo's neck, Dr. Graham stated that whoever had strangled her had stood in front of her and that he or she was taller than Mo. Or, the doctor added, the killer was standing above her, on an incline, for example. *Or a low wall,* I thought.

At three, kids started pouring out of the front doors. Two minutes later, the teachers started exiting from a side door. Steve came out about three ten, a large army-green backpack slung over one shoulder. He held the door for the pretty redhead I'd seen at Mo's garden party and standing behind the police line the evening Mo died. She was laughing at something Steve said. She replied, he nodded, and she walked to a blue Toyota.

I got out of my car and stepped into the traffic lane so Steve would be sure to see me. The drizzle had softened into mist. Steve spotted me and stopped short. His brows raised in surprise, and he smiled.

Steve was just as handsome as the last time I'd seen him, with the same jaunty stride and open demeanor. He looked like the kind of guy it would be easy to talk to, who you wanted to talk to. He was just shy of six feet with nicely trimmed brown hair and brown eyes. He'd played Double-A baseball for the Frisco RoughRiders for two years right out of college and was on his way to the big leagues when he blew out his knee sliding into home.

"Hey, Steve. Long time, no see."

"I'll say."

"You've heard about Mo."

145

"Sure." He glanced around, maybe checking for stragglers who might be tempted to listen in. "I'm pretty broken up about it, to tell you the truth. You get divorced, everyone thinks you don't have feelings for your ex anymore. Not true."

"Mo said you were back in touch. She was excited about it."

He met my gaze, but he didn't reply.

I took a step closer. "It must be awful, not being able to talk about her."

He ran his fingers through his hair. "You got that right."

"Do you have a few minutes now?"

"I can't." He saw my disappointment and glanced at his watch. "I'd love to talk with you, Josie. I just meant I can't now. I'm on my way to a meeting. It's the Cub Scouts. Can you believe I'm a Cub Scout leader?"

"Yes. I bet you're great at it. How'd you get involved?"

"I got drafted. A friend of mine has a seven-year-old son, and their troop leader got a new job in Arkansas." He looked around again. "I've got to go."

"Trish asked me to give one of the eulogies."

"Good. Mo deserves the best."

"Can you talk later?"

He held my gaze for two seconds. "How's

146

coffee in the morning?"

"Perfect."

"I need to be to school by seven thirty. Can you meet at Sweet Treats at quarter to seven?"

I told him quarter to seven was great, and he walked to his car. I stood on sodden leaves until he drove to the exit and paused at the top of the driveway before turning. I saw his eyes in his rearview mirror. I waved good-bye, and he waved back. He turned right. A minute later, the redhead in the Toyota drove by. She stared at me as she passed, and I felt the fervor of her curiosity. She turned left out of the exit.

I was glad to get back inside my car. At first the mist had felt refreshing. Now it just felt cold.

The rain had started up again by the time I got back to my office around quarter to four.

Fred reported that Abbot's no longer existed. The store was sold after the owner died in the mid-1980s, and the buyer changed the name. He didn't keep any of Abbot's business records.

"Who inherited?" I asked.

"Abbot's sister, Gertrude Joan Mays."

I offered to call Ms. Mays so Fred could continue tracking guitars, and he agreed.

Gertrude Joan Mays lived in Florence, Mississippi, a nice suburb south of Jackson. I got her number from information and dialed. The man who picked up the phone was laughing so hard, he barely got "Hello" out.

"Ms. Mays, please."

"Hold on." I heard a televised laugh track followed by a clatter as the receiver hit a table, then scraping sounds, as if a chair were being dragged across a tile floor, then a shout. "Gertie Joan! Telephone!"

"What's so funny?" a woman asked him.

"Those sports bloopers. I can't see straight, I'm laughing so hard."

"Hello?" she said into the phone.

"Ms. Mays?"

"This is Gertie Joan Mays."

I explained my reason for calling.

"Abbot's Musical Instruments. That was my brother's business."

"The new owner said he didn't have the sales records. Do you?"

"I haven't touched those boxes in nearly thirty-five years."

I sat up. "Are they organized by date?"

"I don't know. I had the manager empty the file cabinets and deliver the boxes here."

"How many boxes are there?"

"Two dozen. Maybe more. How about if I

take a gander and see what I've got there?"

"That would be fantastic."

"Tell me exactly what I'm looking for."

"Two things. First, information about how and when Abbot's acquired a 1930 Martin OM-45 Deluxe guitar. Probably there's a record that Abbot's bought it from an individual. Second, the sale of that guitar in late May or early June 1973. I don't know when Abbot's acquired it except that it had to be before then. The buyer was a man named Ricky Joe McElroy."

"McElroy Rubber?"

"That's the family."

"I didn't know Ricky Joe played guitar. It was Frank Shannon, Ricky Joe's best friend, who was the guitar player in that crew."

I felt the ice crack beneath my feet. Every town was a small town, and the Jackson metro area was no exception — and I'd just given Gertie Joan a nifty tidbit to share. I needed to cram the genie back in the bottle.

"Gertie Joan! May I call you Gertie Joan?"

"Of course, hon."

"Gertie Joan, surely you remember what it was like in the early seventies. Everyone was a guitar player back then."

"Ain't that the truth! My boy, Charlie Craig, among them. Now he's a banker. I heard Ricky Joe moved out west somewhere,

I don't know where. Tell me again why you need those receipts?"

"The current owner wants to know what the guitar is worth in case he ever wants to sell it. Without clear title, it's hard to sell a valuable object for top dollar."

"I'm on it. It'll give me something to do besides listen to my husband laugh at ridiculous volleyball bloopers."

CHAPTER TWELVE

Sasha asked me to come downstairs, saying she wanted to show me something.

I met her at the worktable housing Mo's print. She handed me a loupe.

"Look at the woodgrain in the sky behind the snowflakes, on the left."

I eased the loupe into place and examined the print. "Got it . . . it whorls to the right, then to the left." I removed the loupe. "Since woodgrain is like a fingerprint, if you can verify a documented original has woodgrain that matches this pattern, we're well on our way to authenticating Mo's print."

Sasha smiled. "I've contacted three museums that have documented originals."

"Great job, Sasha!" We walked back to the office. "Have there been any responses to our call for sightings?"

"Only fakes or restrikings so far."

"I'll keep cruising around asking dealers.

151

Let's all keep our fingers crossed that —" I broke off when Cara's voice came over the intercom.

"Josie, it's a Mr. McElroy from Idaho."

I grabbed the phone. "Thanks, Cara. I'll take it upstairs. Tell him I'll be with him in a minute."

I thanked Sasha for the update and ran for the staircase.

Upstairs, I pushed the flashing button. "Thanks for holding, and thanks for calling back."

"Your message was pretty mysterious. What gives?"

"Did you buy a guitar from Abbot's in May or June 1973?"

"Tell me again who you are."

I did so, adding in a bit about the importance of provenance.

"You're working for Frank Shannon. I can't believe it. I didn't think Frank would ever sell that thing."

"My client, whom I can't name, isn't selling the guitar. Lots of people want objects appraised for reasons that have nothing to do with selling them, for instance, estate planning purposes or insurance. What can you tell me about the purchase?"

"It cost me two arms and a leg, broke my heart, and got me out of Mississippi. I lost it in a poker game to Frank Shannon and woke up in the real world. You should have heard my daddy on the subject. I haven't gambled since, not even on lotto."

"Did you buy it at Abbot's Musical Instruments?"

"Yup. That's the place."

"Do you have the receipt?"

"Hell, no. I burned that sucker. Last I heard about Frank, he made it to L.A., married Trish, and scored a big-time record deal. I follow his tour schedule some, thinking that if he ever got to Boise, I'd stop by and give him hell. How are they doing?"

"I'm sorry. As I said, I can't reveal a client's name. Do you recall anything about the guitar — for instance, the brand?"

"Yup. It was a Martin OM-45 Deluxe. I dream about it sometimes."

"Do you know where Abbot's got it from?"

"You're asking about the Robert Johnson connection. I don't know anything other than what I heard from the owner, that Robert Johnson gave it to some girlfriend, and that woman's heir sold it to him. I always thought it was just sales hype myself, but Frank sure took it to heart."

"Thank you, Ricky Joe. You've been very helpful."

"Tell Frank I said hey, no hard feelings."

"Thanks again. Bye." I pressed the END CALL button and dialed C. K. Flint's number. If he was still at the lumberyard, there was a good chance he worked the seven-to-three shift. If so, given the different time zone, he might be at home.

He was. I explained who I was and why I was calling.

"I never was at that store. I don't know nothing about it."

"It's okay, C. K. Everything was on the up-and-up. I just need to confirm what I've heard."

"I don't remember nothing." He slammed the phone down.

I stared at the receiver for a moment before I lowered it into the cradle.

C. K. was scared. It didn't matter why. What mattered was that he hadn't verified Frank and Ricky Joe's story. I sure hoped Gertie Joan came through.

I walked downstairs to get a cup of coffee.

"Sasha, are you done with Mo's print for now?"

"Yes. Should I put it back in the safe?"

"Actually, it reminds me of Mo . . . I'm working on her eulogy. I'll take it back upstairs."

Her eyes softened. "I understand."

A woman stepped into the office. I recognized her as the petite blonde I'd seen standing with the book club members the day Mo died. Her complexion was creamy. Her eyes were hazel, changing from amber to moss green to cocoa as she moved from shadow to light.

"Josie?" she said. "I've seen your photo in the paper. I'm Nora Burke."

"Nice to meet you." Mo had asked if I knew Nora, and once again, I wondered why. "I've heard your name. You're in Trish's book club."

"For longer than I care to remember. I hope it's okay that I'm here . . . I need a birthday gift for my dad. A friend said you're fabulous at honing in on just the right thing."

"We try, that's for sure. Have a seat. Would you like some coffee? Or a cold drink?"

She sat at the guest table. "No, thanks."

I took the chair across from her. "So tell me about your father. What does he do for a living?"

"He's an architect. Very cerebral."

"Any hobbies?"

She flushed. "He writes poetry. I know . . . weird, huh?"

"I think it's wonderful. The world would be a better place if more people wrote poetry."

155

The phone rang, and Cara picked up. The second line chimed in almost immediately. Gretchen answered that one. Eric walked into the office from the warehouse, reading something from a clipboard. He looked up, saw Nora, and his brow wrinkled. He glanced at the clock. Eric lived with the fear that he'd done something wrong or forgotten to do something or had otherwise let someone down.

Eric took a step toward us. "Am I late? Are you Melissa Sayers?"

"No. I'm Nora Burke, here to see Josie."

"Sorry." From his sheepish demeanor, I knew he was afraid I was mad at him for interrupting my conversation with Nora. "Gretchen and I have some interviews scheduled for part-timers."

I stood up and smiled. "That's good to hear. We always need reliable workers." I turned to Nora. "Let's go to my office."

Nora followed me into the warehouse, pausing to take in the rows of shelves, the worktables spaced along the perimeter, the walk-in safe, and the loading dock at the back. She smiled when she noticed the kitty domain delineated by the comfy rugs abutting the wall not far from the spiral stairs that led to my office.

"This place needs its own zip code."

I smiled. "We get a lot of work done here, that's for sure. I was going to bring something upstairs. Let me just grab it."

"Sure."

I slipped on gloves and picked up Mo's print. Upstairs, I placed it on the easel, then tucked the gloves behind it.

Nora stood by the love seat, considering it. "This is Mo's Japanese woodblock print. I saw the picture in the *Seacoast Star.*"

"Yes."

"I'm surprised Mo liked it. It looks so, I don't know . . . lonely."

"That's how some people react to it. Mo saw it as quiet, peaceful. To me, and I think to Mo, it communicates serenity, not isolation."

"To each his own. I guess. I'm more a Renoir sort of girl myself."

"Moments of joy. Lots of music. Lighthearted pleasure on beautiful days."

"Exactly."

"That's why they make both chocolate and vanilla ice cream — people have different tastes." I stood in front of the wing chair. "Have a seat."

When Nora sat down, I did, too.

"Back to your dad . . . Does he write on a computer or longhand?"

"Longhand. He has a leather-bound journal. When he fills one up, he buys another."

"A traditional man who values traditional things. Let me show you some options." I reached for the phone and dialed Gretchen's extension. "Gretchen, would you bring me the Parker and Conklin fountain pens and the rosewood lap desk?"

"Sure! I'll be up in a flash."

I cradled the receiver and turned back to Nora. "These pens are more than gorgeous. They're truly rare. And the lap desk . . . Well, you'll see. Just touching it makes you want to write something!"

"Thanks." She looked at her feet for a moment, then raised her eyes. "That friend I mentioned who recommended Prescott's . . . it was Mo. She talked about you all the time. She thought you were so smart."

I winked away an unexpected tear. "I admired her, too."

"Have you learned anything about the print?"

"Not yet."

"How about her murder? Have you heard whether the police are close to catching the killer?"

"No, but I think they're following up on some leads."

"Like what?"

"I wish I knew. Have you heard anything?"

"Me? No."

"Do you know Cal Lewis?"

"I've met him a couple of times at book club meetings."

"Somehow I just can't picture Cal participating in a book club."

Nora laughed. "I see you know him. He comes for the cocktails and nibblies. He likes to correct our wrong opinions."

"I can hear him now. If you saw the *Seacoast Star,* you must have read that Cal is missing."

"I did. The whole situation is so upsetting and confusing. What do you think is going on?"

I leaned back, resting my head on a side wing. "I think Cal is in trouble."

Nora leaned forward. "What kind of trouble?"

"I have no idea, not specifically. It's possible that Cal went missing on purpose, which suggests that he has some involvement with the print he doesn't want to acknowledge, or maybe even that he knows what happened to Mo. The only other possibility is that something happened to him and he's unable to communicate with his employer or his girlfriend or the police. Either way — the way I see it, he's in trouble."

"Maybe he just got fed up with the day-to-day and decided to start over somewhere else. I feel like that sometimes."

"What do you do?"

"I'm an accountant. I love numbers. It's people I struggle with. If they don't like the results, they blame the messenger. Some days I wish I'd gone into construction like my husband. Nails and hammers don't talk back."

"But the people who hire the contractors do. I'm not sure you can ever get away from people, with all their foibles, unless you go off the grid completely." I laughed. "Somehow I can't picture Cal living off the land, and if all he wanted was to start over somewhere new, why hasn't he used his credit cards or withdrawn money from his bank account?"

"Because he doesn't want to be found."

"That's possible, I suppose. Unusual, but not unheard-of. A guy goes out for a pack of cigarettes and just keeps on truckin'. It's harder nowadays to disappear, though."

"Whatever is going on, Lydia must be beside herself."

I heard the familiar click-clack of Gretchen's heels as she walked across the concrete floor and came up the stairs. She lowered a black-velvet-covered tray to the butler's table. Each fountain pen rested on its own black velvet pillow beside the lap desk.

"Can I get you anything else?" Gretchen asked. "Coffee?"

Nora still didn't want anything to drink.

I thanked Gretchen, and as her steps receded, I picked up the Parker pen. "This pen works perfectly, from accepting a full supply of ink to writing evenly, without sputtering."

Nora leaned forward. I moved the pen a bit to catch the light, and the ornate gold filigree barrel and mother-of-pearl insets glimmered.

"Because of its scarcity and superb condition, this one is pricey — two thousand dollars." I laid it down and picked up the Conklin. "This one has an uncommonly large black hard-rubber crescent-filler and a gold trefoil filigree overlay. It works, too, and it's also rare. It's priced at a thousand dollars."

"I had no idea. Thousands of dollars for a pen?"

"I know. It's amazing. They'll probably sell to collectors, not users. Which is why I think this lap desk might be exactly right for your dad. It's only ninety dollars, because it has no pedigree. It's handmade of oak." I lifted the lid. "There's room inside for papers, or your dad's current journal. It's simple, and I think it's gorgeous, but that's an issue of taste and opinion. Go ahead and pick it up. Place it on your lap and see what you think."

She used two hands to lift it. "Oh! It's light. It looks so substantial, I thought it would be much heavier." She lifted the lid and lowered it. "I think my dad would love it. You said the price is ninety dollars? Is there any way you can do better?"

"I'm sorry, no. We work hard to price our objects properly, and we never discount them."

"Ninety dollars seems fair . . . It's just that it's more than we typically spend on birthday gifts." She returned the lap desk to the tray. "The pens are fabulous, too." She stood. "I can't thank you enough for taking the time to show me these. I'm going to talk to my sister about the lap desk and see what she thinks."

I stood, too. "Good idea."

I walked Nora downstairs and opened the front door. Puddles dotted the asphalt. Water dripped from the eaves and trees. The sky remained leaden. I watched her walk to her car, sidestepping to avoid pools of water.

A puff of exhaust caught my eye. A black sedan, mostly hidden by chest-high brush, was idling on the shoulder of Ellerton, just beyond our parking lot. Nora got behind the wheel of her white Chevrolet Cruze, and three seconds later, prisms appeared in the puddles as light glinted off the metal parts of her phone. She rested it against the steering wheel. The black car was hard to spot. Evidently, Nora hadn't noticed it.

It looked like someone was following Nora. Why? She had asked a lot of questions about Cal, but still . . .

She backed out of the space and drove up to the exit, her left-turn light flashing, waiting for a break in the traffic. The black car edged forward.

I was too far away and the foliage was too thick to see who was in the black car, but one thing was clear — someone actually was following Nora, and it looked like she didn't know it.

I ran for the warehouse door, sprinted across the open area, charged up the steps to my office, grabbed my tote bag, and raced downstairs.

"I'll see you all later!" I called as I dashed out the door.

CHAPTER THIRTEEN

By the time I got to my car, both Nora's Chevy and the black sedan were gone. I turned left, toward the interstate, and on a long stretch of straightaway, I spotted the black car. I sped up. At a curve in the road half a mile farther down the road, I recognized Nora's Chevy, four cars in front of the black vehicle, a Lexus, which was now three cars ahead of mine.

We sailed past the entry ramp for the interstate. Nora turned right onto Main Street, the most direct route to Rocky Point's central business district. She parked in front of Sweet Treats bakery. The black sedan and I continued on.

As we circled the village green, I tried to read the Lexus's license plate, but it was streaked with mud, no surprise on this rainy day. I could see two men, one behind the wheel and one in the rear, but I couldn't discern enough of their faces to identify individual features.

When the Lexus rolled to the curb, I did, too, keeping my distance.

Five minutes later, Nora, carrying a white box tied with red string, got back into her car.

Nora headed toward the ocean, making what seemed like random turns. The Lexus closed up. I hung back.

A few minutes later, Nora turned onto Old Mill Pond Road, then spun into the entry road of the Pond View condominium complex, a gated community overlooking the pond.

The Lexus continued down Old Mill Pond Road. So did I. As I passed the entry, I slowed to a crawl so I could see what Nora was doing. She'd reached the ornate black iron gate, and the two sections were moving sideways. I was in time to see her raise her visor — she'd used a remote clipped to it to open the gate.

The Lexus was far ahead now. It turned onto Market Street, which led back to Rocky Point's town center. I turned, too. A half mile farther along, it turned left onto a short road called Langley Lane. I'd passed it a hundred times, but I'd never been on it. I thought it probably connected to Main Street, which ran parallel to Market. Only after I followed the Lexus onto Langley did I discover my mistake. Langley was a curvy road that ended at a dense thicket. The Lexus had already turned around and was driving back the way we'd come. I U-turned at the dead end. Around the first curve on my way back, I gasped and slammed on the brakes — the Lexus sat sideways across the road, trapping me. I plunged forward, then, thanks to my seat belt, jerked back. My head whacked into the headrest.

The driver got out of the car and stood for a moment, facing me. I pushed the door-lock button and felt around in my tote bag for my phone, keeping my eyes on his long, bony face. I took two photos in quick succession, one of the man, the other of the vehicle, then tapped 9-1-1, keeping my hand on the SEND CALL button, but not pushing it.

The driver wore a gray suit that needed pressing. His hair was brown and cut short. He had deep-set eyes that even from this distance seemed hard enough to crack the windshield. The back passenger window lowered, and the occupant turned to watch. At this distance, I could only discern that it was a man.

The driver said something to the passenger, then walked toward me. My pulse speeded up, and my mouth went dry.

I lowered my window two inches as he approached.

The air was thick, damp, and cold. I shivered.

He leaned down to meet my eyes. "You're following us."

"No, I'm not."

"If you're not following us, you're following Nora Burke. Why?"

"I'm not doing anything wrong."

He spun toward the thicket as if he'd heard something. I kept my eyes on his face. He exuded power. After a minute, he turned back to me.

"My boss wants to talk to you. Come sit in his car."

"Who's your boss?"

"Chester Randall."

"I don't know him."

"He knows you. You're Josie Prescott, a local businesswoman. He's a local businessman. He thinks you might have a lot in common."

"What kind of business?"

"Entertainment."

"Who are you?"

"Mr. Randall's driver."

"What's your name?"

"Come on. Mr. Randall's waiting."

"Why were you following Nora?"

"Ask Mr. Randall."

"I'm not comfortable getting into his car, but if he wants to meet at Rocky Point Diner, I'll be glad to talk to him there. I have time now."

"You have nothing to worry about."

He tried to open my door. When he couldn't, his brows drew together and he stared at me. I was glad the glass separated us. I couldn't tell if his eyes were super-dark brown or black. They were cold and emotionless. I didn't reply.

"I'll ask."

He walked back to the car, opened the driver's side door, and leaned in. Entertainment covered a vast spectrum of activities. Somehow I didn't think Chester Randall owned Pirate's Cove Miniature Golf. A minute later the driver returned.

"Okay. We'll follow you."

I exhaled, and only then did I realize I'd been holding my breath.

I drove directly to Rocky Point Diner. The parking lot was half full, and since I was a regular, I knew that most of the people inside would be older folks out for the early bird special and families taking advantage of the weekday kids-eat-free offer. I parked as close to the front door as I could.

I grabbed my iPad, brought up a browser, and Googled "Chester Randall Rocky Point NH."

Chester Randall owned the Colonial Twist, some kind of restaurant, on Ocean Terrace, a short street that ran between Ocean Avenue and Warren, forming a T at both ends, serving as a nifty shortcut from the beach to the village. His signage must be minuscule and his building undistinguished. His photo showed a portly man in his sixties, with a welcoming smile and a full head of brown hair. I checked for restaurant reviews and didn't find any, but at least I knew that Chester Randall was for real. I got out of my car, wishing I'd grabbed my coat when I'd left the office. It was get-in-your-bones cold, more like November than September.

I stood near the hostess stand, watching Chester Randall walk toward the door. He was tall and broad, and big all over.

He stepped inside and extended his hand for a shake. "You run a good business, Josie Prescott. I'm glad to know you."

I shook his hand. He had a firm grip. "Thanks."

He took charge, asking the hostess for a quiet booth in the back, then stepping aside, so I could follow her. The hostess dropped two menus on the table and told us our server would be with us soon. I slid onto the banquette.

Chester took off his raincoat, hung it neatly on a hook by our booth, and sat across from me. He wore a brown suit, a yellow shirt, and a tan tie with fine brown stripes.

He picked up a menu. "I tend to eat late, so maybe I should have a little snack, just to hold me over. How about you?"

"I'll just have coffee. Thanks. You want to tell me why you blocked the road, trapping me?"

"In a minute . . . Let me order first."

The waitress came over. Her name tag read PHYL. She wore a pink uniform with a white frilly apron and sensible white tie-up shoes.

Chester looked up from the menu. "Is the chicken soup any good, Phyl?"

"People seem to like it."

"Not for nothing, Chester, but I love it."

"Good. The lady will have a coffee. I'll have a Coke and a bowl of chicken noodle soup, with extra crackers."

Phyl took the menus away.

Chester shook his head. "You're not wearing a coat." I could almost hear him tut-tut.

170

"This weather . . . You're going to catch cold."

"My mother always said you catch a cold from germs, not bad weather."

"Yes, but in bad weather, germs have an easier time getting in, so you wear a coat to help keep them out."

"Chester, you're very persuasive." For some reason, his concern touched me. As the only child of only children, I'd grown up without an extended family. I had a fleeting thought: If I'd been lucky enough to know one of my grandfathers, I bet he would have been a lot like Chester. "And very sweet."

"Shhh. That's the kind of thing you don't want getting around."

Phyl came back with our drinks. She dropped a paper-covered straw next to Chester's Coke and set down a shallow bowl filled with tubs of half-and-half. I took one, gave it a little shake, and poured it in. Chester picked up his straw and examined it as if he'd never seen one before. He began to pick at the end with a fingernail. I was a ripper, tearing into Christmas gifts — and paper-covered straws — with abandon. When he'd separated the end bits, he scooched the wrapper down enough to extract the straw. Chester was a patient and

171

meticulous man.

We each took a sip of our drinks. Chester smoothed out his straw wrapper. When he raised his eyes to mine, his manner had changed from grandpa to all business.

"So, why I blocked the road." He folded his fingers on the table. "Do you know Cal Lewis?"

"Why?"

"That's no answer."

"That's the only answer you'll get until you tell me why you want to know."

"I need to talk to him about a business thing. How well do you know him?"

"What is this, Chester? The third degree?"

"You're a little cagey, huh?"

"Circumspect."

"Careful. I like that."

Phyl brought Chester's soup and a saucer piled high with cellophane-wrapped packages of saltines.

Chester thanked her. He shook some pepper onto his soup. "So where's Cal?"

"I don't know. Does Nora?"

"I think so. I think they're an item."

"Get out of town."

He blew on a spoonful of soup. "For real."

Ideas and contradictions ricocheted through my brain. Cal was with Lydia. Nora was married. Chester was following Nora,

172

who had nothing to do with Cal. Except maybe she did. Maybe that was why Mo had asked if I knew her — Mo had resented her so-called friends for passing along sightings of Steve with another woman, and here she was facing the same dilemma, debating whether to tell Lydia that she'd seen Cal with Nora. Chester probably read the *Seacoast Star,* like everyone else in Rocky Point, so he knew I was interested in Cal. Nothing made any sense. Unless Nora really was involved with Cal, or Chester genuinely thought she was. There was only one reason I could think of why Chester would care if Nora and Cal were an item.

I drank some coffee. "You're involved with Nora. You're following her because you think she's two-timing you with Cal. Three-timing, really, since she's married."

"You were right. This is delicious." He tore open a packet of crackers. "I've been happily married to the love of my life for forty-two years. I'm not involved with Nora. I'm pretty sure she's involved with Cal, though."

"Why do you care?"

"Business."

"What business?"

"Mine. What's Cal to you?"

"Nothing. Cal is Lydia's boyfriend. Lydia is Mo's sister. Mo Shannon. I'm sure you've

173

read about her . . . She was murdered. Mo was my friend."

Chester blew on another spoonful of soup. "My condolences."

"Thank you."

"Is Cal involved in Mo's death?"

"I don't know. He's MIA, that's for sure."

"I assumed he went missing to avoid me."

"Why would he want to avoid you?"

"He owes me money."

I lowered my cup so quickly it clattered on the saucer. "He does?"

"Do you know my restaurant, the Colonial Twist?"

"I didn't even know there was such a place until I Googled you just now. You don't have any Yelp reviews."

"My customers prefer it that way."

"You let Cal run a tab?"

Chester placed his spoon on a napkin beside the bowl, lining it up. "Do you have a few more minutes? I want to show you the Colonial Twist. I think you'll be interested."

I agreed.

Chester caught Phyl's eye and drew a few lines of text in the air. Phyl delivered the check on the run.

I reached for my wallet.

He held up a hand to stop me. "Allow me. Please."

"I invited you."

He smiled and placed three dollar bills under the salt shaker. "Next time."

"Thank you, Chester."

Two minutes later, we were in our cars, traveling toward a restaurant I'd never heard of and knew nothing about. Before heading out, I texted Cara to tell her where I was going, just in case.

CHAPTER FOURTEEN

Chester led the way to Ocean Terrace. Halfway down the block, he turned into a long driveway, passing eight-foot-high fieldstone columns. He wound his way around a Tudor-style mansion and parked in a roomy lot at the rear. There were about twenty cars scattered throughout the space. If the name Colonial Twist appeared anywhere, I couldn't see it.

I got out, locked my car, and leaned against the still-damp hood.

"I don't care if you're having the party of the year, I'm not going home with you, Chester."

He smiled. "This isn't my home. This is my restaurant. Come on in."

"You don't believe in signage?"

"Adds to the allure. If you don't know it's here, you're not in the know."

"How does anyone know it's here?"

"Word of mouth. I opened with the sup-

176

port of some important customers, and they spread the news."

"I go out for an occasional cocktail and dinner, and I didn't know about it."

"You're not my target customer."

"Why not?"

"You're too wholesome."

I laughed. "You're not bringing me to a strip club, are you?"

"Where the girls wear go-go boots like back in the sixties and do the Twist?"

I laughed louder. "While wearing skimpy Revolutionary War–era clothing. The Colonial Twist, get it?"

He guffawed. "You have quite an imagination, Josie. No, we're just a fancy white-tablecloth joint."

"Just because I'm a regular at a diner doesn't mean I don't like to get dressed up now and again."

"I'm glad to hear it. You're welcome anytime."

The door was impressive. It was made of walnut and was ten feet high, with a hammered pewter handle. Chester pushed a square silver metal panel affixed to the wall, and the heavy door swung out. Inside, a middle-aged man wearing a twentieth-century British uniform welcomed us. His helmet was white with red feathers. His

177

jacket was red with epaulets and black insets at the wrist. His slacks were black. An attractive woman in her twenties smiled as we stepped over the threshold. She wore a knee-length black long-sleeved sheath, conservative pumps, and pearls. She took Chester's coat and handed him a chit.

The entryway was paneled in dark wood with dentil crown molding and box molding below a marquetry chair rail. The ceiling was painted sky blue. Three ceiling fans kept the air moving. The blades were shaped like palm fronds, constructed of a tan grassy material. I felt as if I'd stepped through the looking glass.

The doorman opened a second door located at the end of the entryway, and Chester gestured that I should precede him. We crossed into a beautifully appointed lounge. The room featured the same wood paneling as the entryway. Oversized black leather couches and beige corner chairs with tufted upholstery were grouped into conversation areas. Red-and-blue Oriental rugs covered the hardwood floor. A gas fire blazed in a fieldstone-enclosed fireplace. Nineteenth-century paintings hung on the walls, including a still life depicting a bountiful harvest, a landscape of rolling hills and a meandering stream, and a hunting scene, the hounds frisking around the horses. On the right, a bar ran half the length of the room. Two men sat on leather stools at the far end. Beyond the bar was the restaurant. Heavy wine-colored velvet drapes covered the windows. Vivaldi's *Four Seasons* played softly in the background.

I turned slowly, taking it all in. "I'm gobsmacked, Chester. I can't wait to come back for drinks with my fiancé."

"Wonderful! I want to show you something else, but first, let's toast to our new friendship. What's your pleasure?"

The bartender, a man in his fifties with wavy brown hair, strolled toward us. He wore a long-sleeved white shirt under a tartan plaid vest and black slacks.

"I'm not speechless often, but seeing this place . . . well . . . I think a Bombay Sapphire on the rocks with a twist is in order."

"Maker's Mark for me, Jeremy."

Chester pulled out a stool for me. I climbed up, and he followed.

The bar railing was cylindrical, made of brass, with foot-high elephant heads mounted on the braces that attached the railing to the bar.

I pointed to an elephant head. "That's fabulous."

179

"I had it made by a retired ironworker. I described what I wanted, and he did the rest."

Chester swiveled to face me. "The Colonial Twist is a profit-making enterprise. We offer a full bar but a limited menu, only four items: a ribeye steak, a grilled chicken Caesar salad, my mother's lasagna, and lobster alfredo primavera. I also run the Colonial Club, a nonprofit social club. The proceeds from the club are used to teach ex-cons to cook. We then help them get internships and jobs."

"You have convicts working here?"

"No. That program is run out of a different facility over in Durham. We have a stellar track record, and I'm proud of it. More than ninety percent of our students never go back to prison."

Jeremy placed a linen cocktail napkin in front of me. Real linen, winter white and crisply ironed. He centered my heavy cut-crystal glass on the napkin.

"That's terrific, Chester."

He touched the rim of his glass to mine. "To new friends."

I raised my glass. "To new friends."

"We also partner with other local non-profit organizations to help them do their good works — the Rocky Point Computer

180

Literacy Foundation, New Hampshire Children First!, and the Harmonics Glee Club, among a dozen others."

"I'm involved with New Hampshire Children First! myself. It's a fabulous organization."

"You see . . . I knew we'd get along." He slid off his stool and picked up his drink. "Follow me. You can bring your drink."

He set off for the end of the bar. I carried my drink, wrapped in the napkin, and trailed along.

At the end of the bar, another uniformed doorman stood by a door on the right. He pushed it open, and we passed through into a square, windowless room. An older woman, wearing the same style of black sheath as the younger woman at the front, stood behind an ornately carved hostess stand. She smiled at us but didn't speak. To her right was a double set of doors. A security camera was mounted overhead.

"You have ID on you?" Chester asked me.

"Sure. Why?"

"Because everybody has to sign in."

I met his eyes across the top of my glass. I swallowed some gin, then went up on tiptoe and leaned in close so he could catch my whisper. "This sounds like a setup."

"What kind of setup?" he whispered back.

"You're making a porn movie. You've got Cal tied up in there. You plan on holding me for ransom." I drank some more gin. "And that's just off the top of my head."

He guffawed again. "I love your imagination, Josie Prescott! It's not a setup. No porn. No Cal. No kidnapping."

"I don't want to sign in."

"Rules are rules."

"Let's go back to the bar."

"You need to see this."

"Then show me." I drank some more. "I'm kind of a privacy fiend, Chester. I show my ID to my banker and at the airport when I want to board a plane. Nowhere else." I lifted my head to the security camera and waved. "Plus, you've already got me on film."

Chester considered my request for ten seconds. "Why not? I can make an exception."

Chester made a whirling motion with his hand, and the doorman sprang forward and pulled open the doors, revealing a casino, all glitz and glam, mirrors, and gilt.

My mouth opened, then shut. "You're kidding me."

"Nope. The nonprofit Colonial Club runs the casino. The earnings pay for the good works."

I began a slow inspection. The place was about a quarter full, more men than women, most of them in their fifties or older, all of them well dressed, well kempt, and totally absorbed with the action. Ice clinked in glasses, chimes and bells rang out from the slots, conversation purred softly, riddled with occasional exclamations of pleasure or dismay, and the dealers calling out the odds and the bets and the winning combinations spoke in well-modulated tones. All the dealers, both men and women, were dressed like Jeremy. Women in black sheaths and pearls and men in tuxedos walked the floor serving drinks, clearing empties, pushing in chairs, and picking up any stray bits of litter. The ceiling was mirrored. Security cameras were mounted everywhere, in the light fixtures, above the paintings hanging on the walls, and over every doorway. I counted three blackjack tables, two roulette wheels, a craps table, and half a dozen rows of slot machines. Four oval felt-covered poker tables were positioned behind a brass railing. To my left was a booth labeled TICK-ETS. Next to it was another booth, the sign reading CHIPS.

I turned to face Chester. "Is this legal?"

"Hell, yes. We use tickets and chips, not cash."

"People buy tickets at one booth and redeem them for chips at a second."

"Exactly. It's on the up-and-up."

"If I have winnings, I reverse the process."

"And pay out we do. We have a payout rate of nearly ninety-seven percent."

"I don't know the industry, but that sounds impressive."

"It is."

Six people sat at a roulette table. No one was talking. Everyone's eyes were fixed on the spinning red-and-black wheel.

"That's why Cal owes you money. He lost."

"Big-time. Sixty-two thousand dollars."

"My God! That's probably more than he earns in a year!"

"It's a problem."

"You let people play on tick?"

"Only when I know them. He's never stiffed me before."

"Has he lost that much before?"

"Not that much, no. But he's lost over twenty grand before. More than once."

"He lives on his salary. How did he raise the money?"

"He took to dealing art."

"Japanese woodblock prints."

"I don't know the specifics. What I do know is that he has a reliable source, or so

184

he told me. He was cautious about it. He didn't want to flood the market and make a stir."

"Counterfeits." The roulette wheel slowed to a stop, and the dealer slid piles of chips to the winners. "Why are you showing this to me?"

"Maybe you're a gambler. I need new blood."

I laughed. "You're a piece of work, Chester Randall. I'm sorry to disappoint you, but I don't gamble. Not the way you mean."

"No harm in trying."

"I can tell when someone's pulling my leg." I shook my glass a bit, spinning the ice, then drank some gin. "What do you do with people who don't pay their debts?"

"I don't break kneecaps, if that's what you're asking. I work out a payment plan."

"How did you get onto Nora?"

"He brought her here a couple of times. They seemed pretty simpatico, if you catch my drift. When it became clear he wasn't going to pay up, I got her name from the door. Unlike some people I could name, Nora had no problem signing in. Nora is a lively girl."

"Lively? That's a word with multiple meanings. Which one do you intend?"

"The tight-skirt-cling-to-your-man-bat-your-lashes-drink-oodles-of-champagne kind of lively."

"That's a very colorful description, and paints a profoundly different picture than the straight-arrow young woman I know. Did you research her at all?"

"She's been married to a man named Kevin Burke for seven years, and she works at Hitchens University, in financial aid."

"Why haven't you approached her directly?"

Chester laughed again. "I can tell you've never had an affair. I've seen how she looks at Cal. She'd never give him up."

"That condo complex she turned into — is that where she lives?"

"Yes. I was hoping she'd go to Cal's hidey-hole for a little canoodle before going home."

"What makes you think he hasn't taken off for California or Bali or somewhere?"

"Same reason I think he's alive. If he'd left town or died, she'd be upset. Instead, she glows like a girl in love. He's safe and sound, and she knows where."

"You should be a detective. Have you shared these insights with the police?"

"Nah. If I had any evidence . . ."

"Why are you telling me, Chester?"

"Two reasons. First, I admire you. I have

186

for years. I read the papers. I know who you are and what you've accomplished. Your TV show is one of my wife's favorites. She says she wishes she had a daughter like you. We have three sons, wonderful boys, all of them, and she loves them like nobody's business, but a woman wants a daughter, too, and if she had her pick, that daughter would be you."

I looked away, embarrassed at the tears that sprang to my eyes. After a moment, I turned back. "Please thank your wife for me. That's one of the nicest compliments I've ever received."

"I will. She'll be pleased. Second, I think you're going to find Cal, and when you do, now that we know each other and you see I'm a good guy, I think you'll tell me where he is."

"What makes you think I can find him?"

"Because you'll know how to trace him through the art he's selling. I wouldn't even know where to start."

"You've given me an idea, Chester. I may actually be able to help." I looked around some more. "Why all the cloak-and-dagger if the casino is on the up-and-up?"

"This is a private club, and I think you'll agree that I've created a nice atmosphere, different from what you find in public casinos. Tourists in droopy shorts and sandy flip-flops don't fit."

" 'Nice' isn't the word I'd use to describe this place. 'Sophisticated,' maybe. Not 'nice.' "

"I'm modest."

I smiled. "Is there an initiation fee?"

"Sure. Ten thousand."

My eyes widened. "Ten thousand dollars? Are you telling me Cal paid you ten thousand dollars?"

"No, his other girlfriend did. Lydia Shannon. She bought him a membership."

"Lydia's a gambler?"

"She likes a game or two. Blackjack, mostly. She came the first time as her father's guest."

Frank still gambled, and that meant he'd lied to Trish. I knew it wasn't any of my business, but I felt disappointed nonetheless. "Does Lydia lose?"

"All gamblers lose."

"Does she lose so much she needs to run on tick?"

"No."

"How about Frank?"

"He's a disciplined player. If he loses a thousand, he shrugs it off. If he wins a thousand, he tips the dealers big and walks away. Usually."

"Usually?"

"He's had his moments."

"How bad?"

"Why?"

"I'm trying to get a feel for the situation."

"He lost upwards of a hundred thousand about a year ago, but we've worked it out."

"That's a big number." I watched the poker players for a few seconds. Three men, all wearing sport coats and ties, and a woman wearing a red turtleneck dress were examining their cards. They all had piles of chips in front of them. Four cards sat faceup in the middle of the table. I could almost feel the intensity of their deliberation as they weighed their options. "That looks like Texas Hold'em."

"It is."

I finished my drink. "If I find Cal before you do, I'll let you know."

"Thank you. And vice versa."

We shook on the deal, and Chester walked me out.

"It was a pleasure meeting you, Josie Prescott."

"You, too, Chester Randall."

I turned left out of Chester's Tudor enclave toward Ocean Avenue. When I reached Ocean, I pulled onto the sandy shoulder and called Wes.

He answered on the first ring, sounding out of breath, which he probably was. Wes always moved at warp speed.

"Whatcha got?"

"Do you know the Colonial Twist?"

"No. What is it, a dance?"

"A restaurant and bar. High end. The owner is Chester Randall. He also runs a nonprofit social club called the Colonial Club."

"Here in Rocky Point?"

"Yes. Can you find out about them — and him?"

"Is this connected with Mo?"

"I don't know. Maybe."

"Tell me the names again."

I did so. "Thank you, Wes."

"You owe me, big-time."

"You know I give you what I can as soon as I can."

"See that you do." Wes's tone morphed from pugnacious pit bull to kid brother in the snap of a finger. "Listen, I need a favor."

"Sure. What?"

"I'm applying to be a justice of the peace. I need references who'll attest to my good moral character. I know, it's stupid, but what can I say . . . it was Maggie's idea. She transferred into her bank's compliance division, and she works with lawyers all the time. It turns out justices of the peace can take depositions, and she thinks that since I ask questions for a living as a reporter, I might be pretty good at it. I don't know. I think it sounds pretty lame."

"I think it's a great idea, Wes. I bet you'll be applying to law school within a year."

"No way."

"Never say never. And of course I'll write you a reference."

"Thanks. I'll send you the paperwork. The thing is . . . I'm doing it because we can use the extra money. I mean . . . well . . . Maggie is pregnant."

My eyes filled. I was as excited for Wes as if he'd been my brother for real. "Oh, Wes!"

"Can you believe it? I'm going to be a father."

"You'll be a wonderful father. How is Maggie feeling?"

"Better than ever. She says she loves being pregnant. Don't tell anyone, okay? She's only three months along. She wants to hit four months before we spread the word."

"All right. Give her my love."

"Will do, and I'll get you the skinny on the Colonial duo. Also, do you remember how you asked about Lydia, whether she'd been in touch with Cal? I don't have any information — yet. As to Cal or Lydia withdrawing an out-of-whack amount of money, nope. And he doesn't have any other accounts, not even a savings account. He's always short, and she always has plenty of cash, with no unusual transactions between them. You got anything for me?"

"No."

"Catch ya later."

After he hung up, I texted Ellis: *Chester Randall at the Colonial Club knows Cal.*

I sat for a minute longer, then drove home.

CHAPTER FIFTEEN

Ty called while I was sitting in the living room, doing nothing. It was about ten.

"I had a good day," he said. "How about you?"

His voice had pep in it, and a secret.

"You sound very cheery. What's going on?"

"The powers that be asked me to head an ad hoc committee to begin to think about the new training strategies."

"Congratulations! Who's on the committee?"

"That's the best part. I get to choose my own team, and our meetings will all be conducted via videoconference from my office in Rocky Point."

I pulled a creamy white wool afghan up over my thighs. My mother had crocheted it about a year before she died.

"They're letting you work on a national project from New Hampshire? No wonder you're excited."

"Sean, you know, my boss's boss, took me aside and said he was eager to see how it worked, that if there were no glitches or delays, it could help make the case for more remote assignments."

"Oh, Ty. This is such fabulous news! How will you decide who should be on your committee?"

"A little of this and a little of that. I want representation from each geographic region and area of expertise. I'll tell you more about it tomorrow. I should be home by noon."

The next morning, I was up and out by six. I checked the thermostat I'd mounted outside my kitchen window. It was sunny, but only forty-two degrees. I put on my Thinsulate vest. I could see my breath as soon as I stepped onto the porch.

I walked along the street for a quarter mile until I reached the spinney and turned in. A hundred yards down the path, I came to a fork. The right tine wended its way through the trees to the meadow beyond. The left tine swung hard for fifty feet to an old stone wall, then turned north and ran along it for two miles. I turned left.

The path was thick with fallen leaves, and

where the sun broke through the leafy canopy, deep shadows and bright swaths of light dappled the ground. I loved crunching through the woods in fall.

I knew a few divorced couples who stayed in touch, but I knew more who didn't. I had no idea where Steve and Mo fell on the spectrum of affinity. Mo seemed to think that the fire between them still smoldered, but I had no way of knowing if she'd been in dreamland on that front. From my brief conversation with Steve yesterday, I'd sensed genuine grief, but I might have misread his reaction. If their divorce had been as acrimonious as Lydia implied, there was no reason to think that Steve would be receptive to helping me with her eulogy. So my task was simple, though unpleasant: Before I did anything else, I needed to feel him out about Mo.

I walked for more than a mile before turning back. I spent most of it thinking about Steve, wondering how Mo's death was affecting him. He said that he still cared about her, and that made sense to me. Even after a breakup, if you've loved someone, her death had to hit you like the flu. If they were thinking about a do-over, it had to be worse, like something inside of you died, too.

When I arrived at Sweet Treats, at twenty minutes to seven, the takeout line stretched to the door, but three of the eight tables were empty. I grabbed one by the side wall. A moment later, Steve stepped inside, and I raised a hand to catch his attention.

Noeleen, the owner, was working the front and stopped to greet us.

She was short, about my height, and full-figured, and she was always cheerful and kind. Her hair was ash blond. Her eyes were dark blue.

"So good to see you, Josie! Steve! What can I bring you to drink?"

"Tea, please. Irish Breakfast. With milk."

"Steve? Coffee?"

"You better believe it. Thanks, Noeleen."

Steve swung his backpack to the side, tossed his coat on the back of the chair, and sat down.

"You're a regular here," I said.

"As is everyone who's ever eaten Noeleen's cinnamon buns."

"True. The doughnuts wipe me out, too. And her muffins."

Noeleen returned with our drinks, a mug of coffee for Steve, and a gilt-edged white

196

porcelain teapot for me. The cup and saucer matched the teapot. We ordered food. Steve chose an egg-and-sausage scramble on a cinnamon bun. I went with an order of three honey-glazed doughnut holes and a fruit salad.

I watched Noeleen chat her way to the back, then turned to Steve. "May I ask you something that's totally none of my business?"

He leaned back. "That's a heck of a question to spring on a man before he's finished his first cup of coffee."

I stirred some sugar into my tea.

He drank some coffee, his eyes on my face. "What the heck. Shoot."

"Were you and Mo getting back together?"

"Maybe. We were in touch. Why?"

"As I told you, I'm giving one of the eulogies. I was hoping you might help me, but I need to know what I'm stepping into before I ask. I like you, Steve, and I don't want to put you in an uncomfortable position. Who initiated getting back in touch?"

"She did. I might have if she hadn't." He shook his head. "The breakup is all on me, and so is our not getting back together right away. You know that I've been living with a woman named Kimberly Larson?"

"No, I didn't. I heard you denied playing

around."

"Any lies told in the course of divorce proceedings don't count."

"Situational ethics."

"A branch of philosophy I know well."

"Was Kimberly the woman you got involved with while you were still married to Mo?"

"Yes."

"I bet Kimberly has a seven-year-old son, a Cub Scout."

"Ryan. He's a good kid, which makes the whole situation pretty much a nightmare."

Noeleen brought our food, and the sweet aroma of vanilla enveloped me. She refilled Steve's coffee and asked if we needed anything else. We didn't. I poured more tea and stirred a few drops of milk into the mahogany brew.

"Mo wanted me to leave Kimberly before we got back together. I wanted to see if our reconciliation was for real first. Hedging my bets, I guess you could say. She didn't want any part of that plan. She said she didn't trust me, and if I wanted her to, I had to earn it. We were dickering over the terms when she died. We had plans to meet for dinner that night."

"Really? Do the police know?"

"No, and I hope they never find out. I

didn't kill her. I didn't see her. I don't know anything."

"Where were you supposed to meet?"

"Abitino's. Do you know it?"

"Yes. I love it. When did you make plans?"

"That afternoon. I called her from the faculty lounge."

"So Kimberly wouldn't see Mo's number on your cell phone."

"Makes me sound like a jerk, doesn't it?"

I smiled to take the sting out of my words. "Pretty much."

"It gets worse. I nearly got caught. Kimberly walked into the lounge just as I was hanging up. I had to lie about the call. I said I called the car dealership to schedule a tune-up."

"What did you say when she asked why you didn't use your own phone?"

"My cell was in my briefcase in my classroom, and I'm lazy. The phone was right there, so I used it."

"You're quick on your feet."

"Liars have to be."

"You really do sound like a jerk, Steve. I wonder why I like you so much."

"I'm a lot of fun to be around, quick-witted, and I don't lie to you."

I laughed. "I knew there was a reason. Now I see there are three. Did you get a tune-up?"

"No, as I explained to Kimberly the next day, I got the date wrong. The car's not due for service until December. Slick, wouldn't you say?"

"Super slick. What time were you supposed to meet Mo for dinner?"

"Eight. She was doing some baking for her mother first. I waited until eight thirty, then called her from the restaurant phone. I told the hostess I forgot my cell. I didn't leave a message. I figured I'd see her at school the next day and find out what went wrong."

"I'm surprised the police haven't asked you about it."

"Why? The restaurant was packed, the hostess was a high-school kid who was just trying to keep up, and I made the reservation using the name Baker."

"Why Baker?"

"It's easy to spell, easy to remember, and common."

"What did Mo think about your using a made-up name?"

"She didn't know. I made a point to always get there first."

"What did you tell Kimberly about where you were going?"

"To a Cub Scout training session."

"Was there one scheduled?"

"Yup. And my buddy Don promised to cover for me."

"Oh, what tangled webs we weave . . ."

"No joke, Josie. It was a mess and getting messier by the day. The only good news is that almost no one knows Kimberly and I are involved. I insisted on that. Talk about awkward. My ex-wife teaches in the classroom next to my current girlfriend, the 'other woman' who broke up my marriage, and she doesn't know we're living together."

"And Kimberly is putting pressure on you to marry her."

"Like a vise."

Hearing so many sordid details, I was almost sorry I'd asked Steve for help. I was glad he was only a casual friend. "What are you going to do?"

"Punt."

The attractive redhead I'd seen organizing croquet with Ty, standing with the book club members, and walking with Steve in the school parking lot entered the shop, glanced around, and beelined for our table, brushing past people waiting for takeout. She was even prettier close up under Sweet Treats's golden recessed lighting than she'd been in harsh sunlight or fading twilight, or under a cheerless gray sky. She looked less chunky and more like an athlete, big-boned and curvy, but sinewy and powerful, too. Her hair was a rich coppery red warmed with glints of gold. Her eyes were green, more olive than Gretchen's startlingly bright emerald.

"I thought I'd find you here!"

Steve lumbered to his feet. "Kimberly!" He kissed her cheek. "Josie, this is Kimberly Larson. Kimberly, this is Josie Prescott, an old friend."

I smiled. "Hi."

She smiled, too, but hers seemed pasted on. "It's so nice to meet you. Steve loves this place for breakfast."

I smiled some more, aware of her unspoken message: She was alerting me that she knew Steve's preferences, and that I'd better not encroach.

I felt like waving my engagement ring under her nose but settled for a verbal cue instead. "I saw you at Mo's party. My fiancé helped you carry the croquet set. Ty."

"I thought you looked familiar!" Her stiffness relaxed a notch. "Ty was a doll to do the heavy lifting for me." She turned to Steve. "Can I join you for a quick cup of coffee? I know we don't have much time."

Steve squeezed her shoulder. "Josie and I were in the middle of something. I'll catch up with you at school, okay?"

Kimberly's cheeks flushed. "Oh, sure. Sorry."

She left without a final glance at me. I wasn't her issue; Steve was. I watched to see which way she turned once she hit the sidewalk. She walked diagonally across the street and entered the central parking garage.

I looked back at Steve as he sat down again. "She didn't just happen to be walking by. She parked in the garage."

"She tried to get me to tell her why I was leaving so early this morning. She must have followed me. Jeez . . . I don't have a girlfriend, I have a stalker."

"Given your track record, who can blame her?"

"Touché. One way or the other, I expect I'll get an earful later. I need to go in a minute. School bells stop for no man. You said you were going to ask for my help with the eulogy. Specifically, what can I do for you?"

"I'd love an anecdote . . . something that explains Mo's specialness. I feel as if all I have at hand is a collection of banal generalities."

I'd always heard that eyes are windows to the soul, but Steve's weren't. His revealed

203

nothing. He could have been deciding whether he wanted a refill on his coffee.

"You're doing this for me, to give me a chance to grieve, to share how much I loved her."

"For both of us. And for Mo."

He nodded. "Thank you for asking. I'd like to help. Very much."

I dug around in my tote bag for my card case and handed over a business card.

He stood and slipped the card into his shirt pocket. "I'll email you today, or tomorrow at the latest." He glanced around, caught Noeleen's eye, and scribbled in the air.

"This is on me," I said.

He grinned, and the boyish charm I remembered was writ large upon his face. He was cute as a bug.

"Thanks."

"One last question: What do you think about Lydia?"

He reached for his backpack. "From the top of Lydia's world-class brain to the bottom of her empty heart, she is certain she knows what's best for everyone, in every case, all the time." He slung the backpack over his shoulder. "That kind of arrogance really doesn't work for me. We butted heads a lot."

"I appreciate your candor, Steve."

Noeleen brought the check and thanked us for coming.

I left the tip on the table and walked Steve to the door before joining the line at the cash register. He repeated his promise to be in touch soon, then left, heading away from the garage. Evidently he'd found on-street parking. His gait as he walked away didn't match his nonchalance. He'd seemed weighed down, maybe from guilt, or possibly because his lies had finally caught up with him.

I could see why Mo wanted to get back with him, though. He was smart and quick, up to her intellectual weight. He had an unusual magnetism, too. When he talked to you, his focus was white-hot, and Mo would have melted under the heat of his attention.

"Fancy meeting you here."

I switched gears. Lydia was in line waiting to order. I hadn't seen her arrive. Her shoulders drooped. She had new wrinkles around her mouth and eyes. She'd ditched the sunglasses, and her makeup did a good job of covering whatever remnants of the bruise remained.

"Lydia. How are you doing?"

"It's tough. My mother does nothing but cry. My father paces around like a big cat in a small cage. And Cal is still missing." She moved forward one step. "I've been locked up at home . . . Have you heard anything?"

"No."

The line crept forward again.

"I saw you with Stevie just now. Giving comfort to the enemy?"

"Why is he the enemy?"

"That's good. If you don't want to answer a question, ask one instead."

Lydia was exhausting. "I wasn't avoiding the question. Even though Mo and Steve were divorced, I thought he might be upset, and I wanted to offer my condolences. I like him. I always have, so naturally I don't consider him an enemy, but I was curious why you did. If you don't want to tell me, that's fine."

The line edged ahead. In another minute, it would be her turn.

Lydia kept her eyes on the man in front of her. "Is he all broken up about Mo's death?"

"Yes."

"Yeah, right. I hear from Mo's lawyer that she donated that Japanese woodblock print to New Hampshire Children First! What do you think they'll do with it? Sell it? Or make it the centerpiece of a shrine for Mo?"

I told myself that Lydia must be awash in a sea of misery, that no one could possibly be so mean-spirited unless they themselves were suffering unendurable pain. These rational musings didn't affect my emotional reaction, though. I fought an instinct to flee without speaking another word, to escape the bitterness that seemed to envelop her like a shroud.

"I don't think they've decided yet. I'll see you on Tuesday, Lydia. Again, my condolences."

I walked to the cash register and paid the bill, relieved to get away.

CHAPTER SIXTEEN

Davy Morse's vintage Mustang swung into our lot about ten fifteen. Davy was around sixty. He was shorter than most men, about five-four, and thin, with a full head of close-cut gray hair. He wore a blue baseball cap backward with some writing stitched on it. I couldn't make out the words. He spotted me looking out the window and waved. I waved back and opened the front door.

"Hey, Davy! Long time, no see."

He spread his arms wide. "You sure called me up here at the right time of year. These colors are bitchin'. You hear about the foliage, but man, this is something."

"When I first moved here, I thought it looked like a tapestry." I took a step toward him. "It's good to see you, Davy. How's Ruby?"

"Good, good. She sends regards. What's it been since I looked at that mandolin for you? Three years? Four? It was winter, I remember that. Ruby was with me, and she still talks about freezing her bippy off."

As he stepped inside, I read the words on his cap: METAL FOREVER. He wore a leather bomber jacket over a light blue denim work shirt, jeans, and Frye boots.

"Everyone! You remember Davy Morse."

Fred stood and walked around his desk to greet him.

Sasha, on the phone, smiled, and her eyes lit up.

Gretchen, a celebrity-gossip junkie, smiled at Davy as if he were a rock star.

Cara stood and fussed at him. "You must be tired after your long drive."

"Heck, Cara, I'm not tired. I'm hungry. Do you have any of those gingersnaps of yours?"

"I brought in a fresh batch today!"

"Bless you." He kissed her cheek.

Cara laughed. She brought the tin of cookies to the guest table. Davy rubbed his hands together and pried open the lid. He took a cookie and popped it in his mouth. He made yum sounds, his eyes half-closed.

"Even better than I remembered. You're a wizard, Cara!"

Davy ate gingersnaps and chatted with every member of the staff. I stood by the wall and watched their interactions, appreciating Davy's deft control of the content. He had a gift for making people feel comfortable. When the conversations began to wane, I stepped forward.

"Davy? Sorry to interrupt. What do you say we go to my office and I fill you in?"

"Sounds like a plan."

"Fred, did you set up a studio?"

"This afternoon at four. We should leave here around three forty."

"Good."

I pushed open the door and entered the warehouse. Davy followed. Upstairs, we got settled in the seating area, with Davy on the love seat.

"We're appraising a 1930 Martin OM-45 Deluxe guitar. Right now, I'm working on the provenance, while Fred is tracking down the fourteen made that year. We need you to authenticate this particular instrument. Fred told me we need to worry that this one might be a counterfeit."

"He's right, and no one knows how many forgeries are out there. To complicate the issue, Martin makes its own authentic replicas, which sell for seventy thousand, by the way, so there's serious motivation to create fakes."

"If ours is real and we can verify provenance, what are we looking at?"

"Four hundred thousand. Maybe more depending on who owns it, condition, and so on. Whose is it?"

"I can't tell you."

"Is it for sale?"

"No."

"I'll play it, and I'll know."

"Fred said you'll only need two days to know if it's authentic."

"With any luck, I'll only need an hour, but to make it official, I'll use my fifty-one-point checklist."

"Let's get you started."

I used my desk phone to call Fred and ask him to bring the guitar and both cases to station three, the worktable closest to Hank and Angela, then led the way downstairs.

Halfway down, I paused and turned to look at him. "Ty and I are getting married in June. Will you and Ruby come up?"

"Yes."

"Really?"

"Don't sound so surprised!" He took my hand and squeezed it. "You're the real deal, Josie. I'm your friend."

I squeezed back. "What a nice thing to say. Do you think there's any chance you can bring Shelley with you?"

"Never say never."

Shelley was a friend from my days working at Frisco's in New York City. After I got caught up in the big price-fixing scandal that rocked the high-end antiques auction world, my so-called friends fled as if I had a contagious disease, all except Shelley.

We reached the table before Fred.

Davy squatted beside Angela, sleeping in Hank's basket.

"Who's this beauty?" he whispered. "I haven't met her before."

"She's our newest baby. Her name is Angela. Isn't she a doll? She's a complete love bunny."

He eased a finger under her chin and stroked gently. I could hear her sleepy-time purr from where I stood.

Fred came up, giving Angela a wide berth so as not to disturb her. He hoisted the case containing the guitar onto the worktable and placed the original case next to it. Fred unlatched the working case.

"See ya later!" Davy whispered to Angela.

Davy stood five feet from the guitar and examined it with laserlike intensity. He walked to the table and lifted the guitar from the case, setting it in the center of the worktable. He adjusted the light and leaned in close, studying it. Fred was observing Davy's technique like a disciple.

212

When he was done, Davy carried the guitar to a nearby stool. He began strumming a bluesy number I didn't recognize.

I moved to stand beside Fred. "Do you know what he's playing? It's beautiful."

Davy looked up. " 'Devil Got My Woman,' a Skip James tune."

After a few more seconds, I touched Fred's arm. "I'm going to leave you to your work."

Fred nodded, but I wasn't certain he heard me.

As soon as Ty and I were seated at the Blue Dolphin's best table, a big one by the window, I reached across the snowy-white linen tablecloth and took Ty's hand in mine. "So I have an idea. Let's get married on the beach, just the two of us. Plus witnesses, of course. By a judge. Max can hook us up with a judge. Or Ellis can."

"Okay."

I laughed. "Just like that? You agree?"

"Sure. Then we'll have a blowout party."

"Yes. This way, we each get what we want most."

"Sold."

"This was so easy."

He kissed my hand. "I knew we'd figure it out. When?"

"June twenty-first. It's a Thursday. We get married on the beach in the morning, then disappear, just the two of us. We'll check into Wentworth by the Sea. On Saturday, the twenty-third, we have a party, maybe here at the Blue Dolphin. I won't get stressed. Everything will be perfect."

"Done. Except we may have more people than the restaurant can hold."

"We'll put up a big tent in the back, and the Blue Dolphin can cater it."

"Good. I'll think about the invite list. I have a feeling some folks may come up from D.C."

"Davy said he and Ruby would come from New York and that he might be able to convince Shelley to come, too."

"I want a conga line."

I laughed. "You've got it."

"We're getting married in June."

"I always wanted a June wedding. We need to book the honeymoon suite at the hotel."

"I hope it's available. June weddings are so popular, we may be too late."

"Call me Ms. Flexible. I don't care if we get a suite. Any room will do."

"Let's check out the options now. Today."

"Really? Today?"

He took my hand and kissed it again. "Yes, today. Eat fast."

Ty turned onto Bow Street while I called Wentworth by the Sea. I clicked through their interactive phone system until I reached Sarah Collins, an event planner. She could see us at five. I made the appointment.

The dash clock read 2:47. "I'd like to stop by my office for a few minutes. How should we coordinate?"

"I'll go home and unpack and check in with my team. How about if you drive yourself home? You can leave your car there, and we'll go to Wentworth together."

"That'll work! I'll be home by four thirty at the latest."

Ty rolled to a stop at Prescott's front door.

I paused, my hand on the door handle. "I'm excited, Ty. We're making plans for our wedding."

"Me, too."

"It's really happening. June will be here before we know it."

He stroked my cheek with his index finger, and I closed my eyes, relishing the moment.

I sat at the guest table and stretched out my legs. When Gretchen was off the phone, I

215

asked, "How did the interviews for a new part-timer go?"

"Great. We've identified two solid candidates." She smiled, her eyes twinkling like sparklers on the Fourth of July. "Eric has a flair for asking just the right questions worded in just the right way."

"That's good to hear. Will you bring them both in for training?"

"Assuming their references check out."

"Let me know if and when they come in. I want to welcome them and —" I broke off as the wind chimes tinkled. Steve Jullison opened the door. I stood up. "Steve!"

He closed the door behind him. "Do you have a minute to talk?" His eyes communicated urgency.

"Sure. Come to my office."

Upstairs, Steve stopped at the end of the love seat to assess Mo's woodblock print. He didn't approach the easel. He didn't speak. After a few seconds, he angled his head to the side. After a minute more, he turned to face me.

"I don't have long — I came straight from school, and I'm meeting Kimberly and Ryan at four. I thought of something you might be able to use in your eulogy, but I don't want Kimberly, Frank, Trish, or anyone to know I talked to you."

"I'm good at keeping secrets, but why? What's wrong with the world knowing Mo married a man classy enough to be able to talk about her good points even if their marriage didn't work out?"

"None of them would see it as classy. They'd see it as smarmy." He flipped a palm, dismissing his thorny breakup and possible reconciliation from our conversation. "When Mo and I were first married, I asked her what it was about Japanese woodblock prints that spoke to her. She said it was the duality. Muted colors that communicate vibrancy. Isolated settings packed with life. Two dimensions communicating a three-dimensional narrative. Here's the thing, Josie . . . this duality can be seen in Mo herself. You know — she was kind of reserved, a loner, yet she loved being around people, that sort of thing."

"Oh, Steve, that's so beautiful. And so true. That describes Mo to a T."

"Use it. Just pretend you asked her the question, not me."

"But you're the one who —"

He held up a hand to stop my objection. "Do it, Josie. Do it for her folks."

I smiled. "All right. I will."

I walked him out, then ran back upstairs to write it down. When I delivered Mo's eulogy, I wouldn't speak Steve's name aloud, but I'd be thinking it.

I had almost an hour before I needed to go home, so I decided to make another stop to ask about Mo's print.

Murphy's Interiors was Rocky Point's oldest furniture store. It was known for the quality of its offerings and the knowledge of its salespeople. About five years ago, Murphy's integrated boutiques within the store, similar to how department stores invited fashion designers to open branded mini retail shops inside their walls. One of the boutiques was an interior design firm named Branson Wills.

Anita Wills was a licensed interior designer, a favorite of architects. Anita was Chinese American, in her forties. She wore a purple sweater dress and black ankle-high boots. She and Sasha had been classmates at Hitchens, earning their Ph.D.'s in art history the same year. Eli Branson, her business partner, spent most of his time overseas, hunting for unique pieces. They often carried antiques, one-of-a-kind objects. I rarely found bargains in their shop, but I often found inspiration.

Branson Wills occupied a spot about halfway back on the left, just after Quentin's

Spy Shop. I threaded my way through an array of opulent and utilitarian offerings from Biddington Silk Flowers, Seacoast Living Home & Hearth, French Heart Linens, and Rocky Point Gardens and Patio Furniture.

Anita stood under a teak pergola talking to a couple I didn't know. My phone vibrated, startling me. It was Wes. I stepped aside to answer the call.

"Where are you?" he demanded, as brusque as ever.

"I'm fine, Wes. Thanks. How are you?"

"Good, good. So you asked about Chester Randall, the Colonial Twist, and the Colonial Club. I couldn't find any dirt." Wes sounded disappointed. "He's active in Rotary International and at St. Teresa's Catholic Church. His business is solvent. His charity's paperwork is up-to-date. People like him. You're supposed to be giving me leads, not busywork."

"Some leads don't pan out, you know that. I'm glad to hear Chester's on the up-and-up."

"You owe me, Josie. Pay up."

I was tempted to wriggle out of answering, but I didn't. Our relationship chugged along nicely because we honored our unspoken quid-pro-quo arrangement. If I didn't give Wes some quid pretty darn soon, it wouldn't be long before he stopped providing the pro quo.

I told him what I'd learned from Chester about Nora and Cal. "The thing is . . . she's married."

"That adds a lump of coal in the stocking, doesn't it? Maybe her husband killed Cal."

"I don't know anything about Nora's husband, except that he works in construction and his name is Kevin Burke."

"I'll find out. What do you know about her?"

I filled him in about what little I'd gleaned, and he said, "Talk soon," and hung up.

I still owed Wes, but I was catching up.

I turned back toward Anita. She was sitting at her desk. The couple sat across from her in matching Louis XVI eighteenth-century-style chairs. She placed a book of design options — an idea book — on the desk, facing them, and they began flipping pages, pausing occasionally to comment on various design styles. Anita sat, listening, gathering data for her custom design. I walked toward her, staying far enough away so my approach wouldn't feel intrusive, but not so distant that she wouldn't notice me.

Anita spotted me, smiled, said something

to her clients, and stood to greet me.

"Josie, it's so good to see you."

"And you, Anita. I'm sorry to bother you. I see you're with clients, so I'll only take a minute. I'm hoping you can help me with an appraisal I'm working on — a print from Hiroshige's 'One Hundred Famous Views of Edo.' Have you sold any in the last few months?"

"Josie, you know how much I respect and admire you, but we don't share sales data."

"Let me ask you this — did you ever meet Mo Shannon?"

"The name doesn't ring a bell."

"You must have read about her murder. Or heard about it."

"I don't follow the news. I get too upset."

"I understand, and I'm sorry to have to mention it, but Mo Shannon was a friend of mine. Shortly before she was killed, she bought what is purported to be an original *Meguro Drum Bridge and Sunset Hill*. She asked me to appraise it. She acquired it through a private sale facilitated by a man named Cal Lewis."

Anita's brows drew together. "I don't know anyone by that name."

"How about Nora Burke?"

"I'm sorry. No."

"But you sold one, didn't you?"

221

She met my eyes for a moment. "It's true that we acquired a portfolio of 'One Hundred Famous Views of Edo.' Several images have sold. I'd have to research whether that was one of them."

"Is there any way you can look it up now?"

She glanced at the couple. They were chatting softly.

"I'm sorry, Josie, but I can't. I need to get back to them."

I lowered my eyes to the time display on my phone. Ty was waiting for me. My impatience would have to be contained. I asked if I could come back at ten tomorrow morning for the answer, and she agreed. I thanked her, and we shook on it.

CHAPTER SEVENTEEN

As soon as Ty turned onto Route 1B, he asked, "Do you really like the idea of holding our wedding reception in a tent?"

"It'll be a really nice tent."

"I was thinking of something more elegant."

"We can make the tent elegant, lots of candles and fancy china."

"Okay, then."

"Then on Sunday, we can change out the decorations and have a hoedown, you know, country music and a barbecue, a brunch kind of thing for out-of-towners and our closest friends. We could schedule it for eleven, so people who needed to leave by two or three would still have time to party."

"I like it. We'll have a grand affair to mark the propitious occasion of our marriage, then go back to our jeans and country-dancing roots."

"Yee-haw."

"We have one more major decision — where do you want to go for our honeymoon? I was thinking Paris."

"I want somewhere quiet, where I can just gel. How about St. John?"

Ty began laughing.

I joined in, cackling until my sides hurt. We laughed all the way across the bridge and didn't stop until the sprawling resort appeared in the distance.

"Now what?" I asked when I could talk again.

Ty touched my hand. "We'll figure it out."

As our hilarity faded away, I felt a twinge of guilt. How could I be laughing with Mo so recently dead? *Because life goes on,* I told myself. *Because one event has nothing to do with the other. Because I could feel Mo laughing with me.*

The Wentworth event planner, Sarah Collins, met us in the lobby. She was effervescent.

Her smile was bright and constant. She chatted about everything with ease in one long run-on sentence.

"Follow me . . . I checked availability, and we have one suite available the days you're looking for . . . I'll take you through the lobby so you can have the full experience.

I'm so glad it worked out that I could meet you today . . . Did you notice the grounds? Don't you love autumn in New England? The colors . . . although I love lobster and steamers . . . I was just thinking that I'm in the mood for some . . . the chef here does a wonderful thing with steamers . . . his secret is garlic and vermouth. So here we are!"

The hotel had been restored to its former glory, and it truly was spectacular. High ceilings with plenty of gilt, huge crystal chandeliers, and cushy rugs. The Eastern Turret Flag Officer's Suite had a double shower, a whirlpool tub, and a fireplace in case the nights got chilly.

We booked it for three nights, starting on our wedding day, Thursday the twenty-first.

"It's only six thirty," I said. "How about dropping me at home so I can pick up my car? If you don't mind doing a grocery run, I can do a last-minute check at the office. I should be home by seven fifteen or so."

"Why don't I just drop you at work and pick you up after I'm done shopping?" Ty asked.

"Even better!"

"Any chance you'll make grilled chicken, with your mom's special barbecue sauce?"

The sauce was dark and rich, tangy, and

sweet, and spicy hot.

"That'll work if you don't mind a late dinner. I have some of the sauce stashed in the freezer. The chicken only needs half an hour to marinate, then boom, it's on the grill."

He said he'd get us a nibble as a starter and dropped me at Prescott's front door.

Everyone had left for the day, and the building was dark, except for the night-lights, low-wattage ceiling lamps inside and harsh white lighting aimed at the front door and loading dock.

I stepped into the office, entered the code to turn off the alarm, and pushed open the heavy door to the warehouse. Motion sensors activated a few overhead lights, throwing eerie shadows along the cement floor and shelving. It wasn't bright enough to see much detail, but it was more than adequate to find your way to wall switches for additional lighting if you wanted.

Upstairs, I checked my email. Wes had sent instructions for completing his justice-of-the-peace reference. I agreed with Maggie that Wes would be terrific at taking depositions. The directions said it would take eight to ten weeks for a decision. I did the math. Wes would hear right around Thanksgiving. I was certain he'd be approved, which meant there'd be something else to be thankful for this year. I completed the form and wrote two paragraphs in the comments section stating that I'd known Wes for a dozen years and that he was detail-oriented, hardworking, and ethical. I sent him a copy and submitted the form.

I'd hoped to find a good-news email from Fred telling me he'd tracked another one of the 1930 Martin guitars, but he hadn't written anything. There was nothing from Sasha about Mo's print, either. No one knew better than I did that appraisals took however long they took, and that there was no way to rush the process, but that didn't mean I had to like it. I checked my voice mail. Gertie Joan hadn't called back from Mississippi. Sometimes no news represented good news. Nothing bad had happened, or a bad situation hadn't gotten worse. This was not one of those times. I swiveled to face my window, suppressing my impatience. The sky shone with a soft pink blush as the sun sank below the trees and the autumn-ripe foliage trembled and glimmered in the breeze. As I sat there, twilight faded to dusk.

I brought up the notes I'd scribbled for Mo's eulogy and typed my remarks like a script. I read it to myself, then read it aloud, making eye contact with Mo's print as if it represented the congregation, tweaking it both times. I read it aloud again. It was good. I printed it and turned off my computer. Positioning Mo's woodblock print in clear sight of my desk had served its purpose, helping me connect with her. I was ready to deliver my eulogy, which meant the print could go back to the safe. I switched off my desk lamp, but there was enough light filtering in from the outside lamps and the warehouse nightlights for me to unearth a protective cover, essentially an acid-free, oversized padded envelope, from the supply closet behind my desk and make my way to the easel. I found the gloves I'd placed behind the print, put them on, slipped the print into the envelope, and removed the gloves.

I was three steps from the exit when a close-by clunk, metal on metal, made me jump and spin around. It was loud, too loud to be from the street, the sound floating in the air. I tiptoed to the outside wall, staying clear of the window, and listened carefully. With the window closed and the ventilation system humming, I barely heard the evening sounds, and no traffic, yet I was certain I hadn't imagined the grating thump.

I sidestepped to the left of the window and peered into the night. Bright white light emanating from the rear, where the loading dock was located, illuminated a slice of parking lot on my side of the building. Between that and the rising moon, I was able to see an acorn skitter across the asphalt and a few leaves sweep by, but nothing else. I edged forward to peek the other way, but it was so dark I couldn't even make out shapes. A truck rolling by on Ellerton had hit a rock or a branch, and the cargo, pipes, maybe, crashed into one another. That was as logical a conclusion as any.

I was halfway across the room when the lights flickered, then went out.

"Whoa!"

I was standing in total darkness. I waited for the generator to kick in. One Mississippi, two Mississippi. Five seconds. Ten. Twenty. Thirty. It never took longer than half a minute for the generator to spring into action.

Another metallic clank, this one louder, followed by a sharp, metallic grinding, a sustained metal-on-metal rasping. *A metal ladder.* Someone had perched a ladder against the wall leading to my office. They'd cut the electricity and sabotaged the generator.

It wasn't even seven o'clock. *Why would someone break in so early?*

Scuffing, the sound heavy boots make on metal.

Think.

I could probably make it downstairs before they got in, but then what? When the electricity went off, the doors to the high-end auction venue, tag sale room, loading dock, front office, and safe latched automatically, a fail-safe redundancy. The good news was that the alarm company would be automatically notified. A real person would contact me via office phone and cell within a minute, hoping to hear our safe word. We'd have a good chuckle at the random power outage. If I didn't pick up or they didn't hear the word, they'd alert the police that someone was burglarizing Prescott's, or that we were otherwise under attack.

Another sound, this one more a clomp than a scuff. The intruder was closing in.

The phone rang. It went immediately to voice mail, our night message. My cell would vibrate momentarily. It did so, and a soft light emanated from my tote bag, resting on my desk.

I needed to do something. Go downstairs or stay. Hide or fight. With the doors locked, if I went downstairs, I'd be trapped, a sitting duck. I owned a gun, a Browning 9 mm pistol, and I was a good shot, but it was at home, in my bedside table, so it did me no good here.

Still holding the print, I scooted across the room, grasped my tote bag, dropped to my knees, and crawled under my desk. I positioned the covered print against the modesty panel, centering it so it blocked the view under part of the middle section. If the intruder looked down, he'd see what appeared to be a to-the-floor modesty panel with tapered openings on the sides, not a woman's foot. I felt around in my bag for my phone, saw I had voice mail from the alarm company, and texted 9-1-1: *Break in @ Prescott's. My office. Help.*

Glass shattered, and the thunderous roar was so loud I ducked as if the fusillade were directly overhead. It took all my self-control not to shriek.

My phone! If it vibrated again, the intruder might hear it. I could turn it off, but I might need it. I tapped twice to stop the vibrating. Knowing that the screen would still illuminate, I poked it down to the bottom of my tote bag. I pulled my knees to my chin. My heart battered my ribs. My mouth was arid, and I kept swallowing to fight the urge to cough.

More glass broke, tinkling this time. I pictured little pieces falling to the floor, landing on top of one another.

I opened my eyes and took a breath.

It was happening, and it was happening *now*.

White light shone below the parts of the modesty panel that remained open. A flashlight. More crackling of glass, followed by a heavy thud. The intruder had stepped or fallen over the sill and landed hard. Footsteps crackled until they were at the bathroom door. I scrunched in closer to the modesty panel, trying to make myself invisible, terrified that as the person moved around the light would fall on me.

I peeked.

Someone tall, a man, I guessed, dressed all in black, wearing a ski mask and gloves, stood at the threshold to the bathroom, observing. He stepped back and aimed his light at the open door that led to the spiral staircase, pausing for a moment, perhaps to listen. He walked past the seating area to the far end of the office.

"What the — ?" he muttered.

I didn't recognize the voice, but who could from a two-word whisper? I was still pretty sure it was a man, but it could have been a woman with a deep voice.

Wood from my rooster-collection display case cracked. Something tumbled to the ground, porcelain or glass, and shattered. Tears spilled onto my cheeks, and I bit my bottom lip to keep myself from crying out. My rooster collection had started as my mother's rooster collection. If he'd broken one of my mother's roosters, I'd kill him. I'd hunt him down and kill him. I sat hunched over, weak and feckless, weeping silently into my thighs. I told myself to stop crying, to toughen up, to think. I used the sides of my hands to wipe away my tears.

A siren's squeal broke into my futile thoughts. Finally, the cavalry was on its way.

The air grew still, then loud again as the intruder bolted across the shards of glass to the window, an oscillating stream of light marking his path. A moment later, the light went out. I heard his feet hit the ladder, followed by his pounding retreat. Ten seconds later, there was one last cacophony of metal crashing into metal and dragging along asphalt, then utter silence.

I held my breath and listened.

Within seconds, my brain registered the chirr of katydids and crickets, and I exhaled. I didn't move. I didn't trust that it was over. A brisk wind chilled me, but still I didn't move.

Cal, whose hobby was rock climbing, had come for the print. It had to be Cal. Nora, his lover, told him the print was in my office, and he came for it. Or Trish mentioned to Lydia. Maybe it was Trish herself. She knew it was on display, too. Trish was tall for a woman, a world-class athlete. Even in her sixties, she'd easily be able to climb a ladder and hop a windowsill. But she had no reason to steal the print. Steve did. Steve, who was, according to Lydia, always short of money. He was an athlete, too. He'd seen it just the other day.

I scrambled out from under the desk and stood with my back to the wall, clutching the print to my chest. The darkness was deep and frightening, and there was nothing I could do but wait.

CHAPTER EIGHTEEN

"It looks like a branch fell on a wire," Ellis said, "knocking out the electricity."

"My generator didn't work."

"Someone cut the connection."

We sat on stools on the landing outside my office. The techs had been inside for about twenty minutes. I was hungry and tired and irritable.

"You're saying this was deliberate sabotage?" I asked.

"Yes."

"So the loss of power was a coincidence? Doesn't that seem hard to believe?"

"Not necessarily. Think it through. How long was the intruder inside?"

"It's hard to say. It seemed to last forever, but it was probably only two or three minutes."

"Which means he didn't need the electricity to go off. Our normal reaction time to a call from your security company would be seven to eight minutes. Still, it's a question worth asking, because while the electricity zapping out probably was just a lucky break for him, it did delay our reaction time by about an additional five minutes. The tree branch was lying in the middle of the road, tangled in the downed wires."

"How did you get past it?"

"The guys from your security company were ahead of us, and I followed their lead. We left our vehicles on the side of the road and jogged in. What are the chances that it was an inside job?"

"Zero."

"Your loyalty to your staff is admirable, Josie, but you know better than that. More than ninety percent of art heists are perpetrated by someone who has the key or code or knows his way around the security system."

"No one used a key or security code."

"Still . . . with stats like this, I have to ask."

"My staff is not involved."

"Who, then?"

"Someone after Mo's print."

"Cal."

"That's my guess."

"So you think he's around."

"Don't you?"

Ellis didn't answer right away.

I skewed around to see inside my office. Ty and Eric stood in front of the broken window. Ty held a sheet of plywood in place while Eric pounded nails. Gretchen leaned against my desk watching them work.

Ellis's phone rang, and he took the call. His end was mostly grunts.

Gretchen was number two on the alarm company call list. When I hadn't responded to their calls and texts, they'd called her, and she whipped into action, activating our emergency plan with calm confidence. She called Ty and Ellis to let them know I wasn't responding. She called Sasha, Fred, Eric, and Cara to tell them to stand by for further instructions. She drove to the office to ensure the security company and police were on scene, and she sent me a text saying: *I'm here.*

During the time that Ellis had been consulting with the forensic team, Eric had called Floyd, our glazier. He left a message, and Floyd had called back, promising to be here by nine in the morning to replace the glass in the window and in my display cabinet. Eric assured me he could do the carpentry repairs himself, that the display cabinet hadn't splintered, that only one side panel had broken.

I'd arranged with Russ, our security company's account manager, to station security officers in the parking lot all night, some sitting in cars, others walking the perimeter. I doubted such vigilance was needed, but I'd sleep better knowing the place was secure. He'd already sent over the security camera footage. No one was visible from any of the camera angles. We'd placed cameras to take in all outside access doors and the loading dock, but nothing else. Rocky Point was not a high-crime zone.

My phone vibrated. It was a text from Zoë. She wrote: *Are you ok? Hurry home. Soup is simmering.* I texted back: *I accept!*

I closed my eyes and let a picture of the outside of my building and the surrounding area come into my consciousness.

The generator was housed in a metal shed positioned on a concrete slab on the side of the building farthest from the Congregational church. We'd laid asphalt from the back parking lot to a six-foot-high fieldstone wall that separated the entry to the tag sale from the back. On the rear side of the wall, the unadorned blacktop allowed us access to the shed. On the front side, a flagstone path led from the front parking lot to the tag sale venue door. I'd had the wall built for aesthetic reasons, not for security. An unintended consequence was that anyone working on the generator wouldn't be seen from the front. It simply hadn't occurred to me that someone might sabotage the generator or break into my mezzanine-level office.

A muscle on the side of my neck twitched, and when I realized I was clenching my teeth, I opened my mouth wide. My jaw would be sore in the morning. The intruder had planned the attack carefully. I'd been scared. Now I was angry, but there was no one to be angry at. The best antidote to impotent rage was action. I emailed Gretchen:

This may be a case of closing the barn door after the horse escapes, but let's get bids on adding additional security cameras so we see everything, a 360 view of the building, parking lot, and grounds.

"Maybe," Ellis said, tapping the end call button.

I spun back to face him. "Maybe what?"

"You asked if I thought Cal was around. Maybe. How could he have known that the print was in plain sight?"

"Trish might have mentioned it to Lydia. Lydia might have told him."

"You think Lydia is in touch with Cal?"

"I think it's possible. She loves him."

"She insists she hasn't heard from him since the morning of the day Mo was killed."

"Either she's telling the truth or she's lying to protect him. If she's in touch with him, I doubt she would have fessed up. She probably thinks he's being railroaded."

"How else could he have found out?"

"Nora Burke."

"How is she involved?"

"I hate to gossip."

"Telling the truth to a police officer during an investigation isn't gossip."

"I told you about the Colonial Twist. Did you talk to Chester about Cal?"

"Yes."

"Did Nora's name come up?"

"Come on, Josie. Tell me what you know."

"You're right. Nora went to the Colonial Club with Cal. Chester got the vibe that they were more than mere friends. Nora is married." I gave him her address.

"Who else besides your full-time staff, Nora, and Trish knew the print was on display in your office?"

"Steve." I explained the circumstances of his visit.

"How about regular people? You know, the folks you do business with on a daily basis who might have been in your office while the print was in plain sight."

240

"Like who?"

"Your accountant."

"No."

"Your lawyer?"

"No. Just Davy, our guitar expert. No one else."

"Ty?"

My hackles rose. "No."

"A salesman."

"No."

"A customer."

"No."

"Maybe you want new hardwood and Eric brought up the guy to measure the space."

"No."

"Okay." He stood up and shook out his pant leg. "I have enough for now. Let's plan on talking in the morning."

"I'll be here around eight thirty, or earlier."

Ellis walked into the office to talk to the last remaining crime scene tech. I followed along. Russ leaned against the back wall, ready to escort Ellis and the tech out. No one, not even a police chief conducting an official investigation, was allowed in the warehouse unescorted. I stood just inside the door watching as Ty and Eric finished boarding up the window.

Ty stepped back to assess Eric's handiwork. "Good job, Eric."

Eric flushed, embarrassed at the praise. "It's okay, I guess."

"Thank you — all of you," I said, walking closer.

Gretchen turned at my voice. Her eyes radiated concern. "Are you all right?"

I patted her arm. "I'm fine. Thanks for taking care of everything."

I picked my way to the display case at the end of the room. The damage wasn't as severe as I'd feared. The wood was as Eric described, and only two panes of glass in the display case had shattered. The only rooster that had been broken was a no-name vintage cartoony-looking one I'd bought a year earlier because I'd thought it was cute, but I had no emotional attachment to it. A wooden one had also fallen to the ground, but it wasn't even chipped or cracked.

I squatted and reached into the back of the bottom shelf where I secreted the most valuable of the roosters — my mother's favorites. Her first acquisition, a yellow-and-red ceramic beauty, was among my most cherished possessions. I stroked the rooster's breast and felt my mother's love.

I eased it back into place, then stood and turned around. Ellis and the tech were talking in a low voice. Eric was gathering up his tools. Ty nodded at something Gretchen said. Fatigue weighed down on me. The crisis had passed, and I'd coped well, as always. Gretchen said something to me about covering for me in the morning, and I nodded. People left. After placing Mo's print in the walk-in safe, which Gretchen had offered to do, but which I insisted on doing myself, Ty and I left, too.

Russ semisaluted as we drove toward the exit. I nodded, acknowledging the gesture. I looked to the left, the fast way home. The road was blocked. The utility people didn't seem to have made much progress. Fluorescent orange wooden horses blocked the road. SOUTHERN NEW HAMPSHIRE ELECTRIC was stenciled on the crossbeams in navy blue. Two utility vans sat across the road. Spotlights mounted on the vans' roofs illuminated the road like day. A police cruiser, its rooftop red light spinning, blocked the other side. Ellis's SUV sat nearby. A long, thin, knobby branch lay in the center of the road amid downed wires. The limb was silky gray and spotted with moss. Two men wearing company-branded windbreakers and hard hats stood on the leaf-covered shoulder talking with Ellis.

I dug around in my tote bag for my phone. "Stop for a sec."

He did so, and I jumped out. I walked in front of the SUV and shot a video, panning slowly left to right. I touched the stop button, then took a few still photos of the men, the vehicles, and the log. I tapped through the options to upload the video and photos to the cloud.

"How come?" Ty asked when I was back in the car.

"Posterity. Trust no one. My dad was a skeptical man, and he taught me well."

"What caught your eye?"

"Ellis said he had to jog through the woods because the branch was in the road, tangled in downed wires. That was two hours ago."

"And you wonder why it's still there."

Ty pulled out, turning right, the long way around.

I closed my eyes and leaned back. I was exhausted, to-my-bones weary.

As soon as we got home, I put on my bathing suit, ready for food, drink, and a long soak in my newly installed hot tub. As I shrugged into my heavy red cotton to-the-ankle bathrobe, a cover-up selected more for warmth than glamour, Wes called. I let it go to voice mail. He didn't leave a message. Instead he texted: *Your break-in is tomorrow's lead. Call me. Or text answers: Is it connected to Mo's murder? Was your security sloppy? Any comments?*

I went downstairs and poured myself a martini from the shaker in the fridge, took a sip, and texted back: *I'm fine, thanks. No, my security wasn't sloppy. You may quote me as follows: "No one was hurt. Nothing was stolen. The police and my alarm company responded within minutes, and I'm very grateful."*

He called again, almost immediately, and this time he did leave a message.

"Josie," he said, his tone both aggrieved and impatient, "you didn't respond to my question about a possible connection to Mo's murder. I have a source saying the intruder never left your office, that he had expected Mo's woodblock print to be there. Is that true? And what about your generator? Why didn't it start up when the electricity went off? Also, my source says that the thief didn't tape the window when he broke it, so it shattered, and there was glass everywhere. Confirm it for me, okay? Broken glass everywhere — I love it! That's a great image! Send me a photo!"

Gretchen, I thought. Eric would never talk to a reporter. He was too shy and too scared of making a mistake. Gretchen was effusive and chatty by nature. It wouldn't occur to

245

her to withhold facts.

I texted back: *I have no reason to think Mo's print was involved, and if you write that there is a connection, you're likely to have to print a retraction. Re: generator — no comment. I can confirm that there was glass everywhere. No photos available.*

An hour later, after I'd finished my martini and decimated a bowl of Zoë's minestrone soup and a gooey grilled cheese sandwich, I was snuggling up to Ty in the hot tub. I rested my head against his chest, and as the steamy water bubbled against my back and neck, I felt myself relax for the first time since I'd heard that metallic scraping hours and hours ago.

CHAPTER NINETEEN

I woke before the alarm went off, momentarily confused about where I was. I sat up, clenching the sheet to my chin. The green luminous dial on the old-style alarm clock next to my bed, a relic from my childhood, read 5:52. I heard water running downstairs. Ty was making coffee.

"Hey," I said as I stepped into the kitchen.

"Good morning, sunshine! I'm going to make you banana pancakes."

"You're a man for the ages. Want to marry me?"

"Too late. The girl of my dreams has already got me latched down."

I poured us glasses of orange juice and slid onto the bench on the window side of my farm-style kitchen table. I fluffed up two of the orange-and-blue-plaid pillows and leaned back into the corner, stretching out my legs.

Ty began pulling ingredients from the

cupboard. "How are you feeling?"

Billowy clouds floated in a cerulean sky. I touched the window. The glass was cold. September mornings often started with a shuddering chill.

"Angry. Frustrated. Confused."

"Because of the break-in?"

"Did Cal really think we wouldn't figure out that he was behind the theft? He must think I'm a fool."

"He doesn't think you're a fool. He thinks you're naïve and gullible."

"Thanks."

Ty smiled as he delivered a cup of coffee.

"What a man."

"Just because I poured you a cup of coffee? Talk about a cheap date."

"Does Cal think Chester is naïve and gullible, too? That he could skip out on a six-figure debt and Chester would simply let it go?"

"Maybe he still plans to pay. Didn't you tell me that Chester let him settle his losses over time before?"

"Only because Cal had a viable plan to sell Japanese woodblock prints."

"From what I can tell, Cal's a narcissist, and narcissists have seriously inflated ideas of their own capabilities and importance."

A bantering comment died on my lips as

248

a stunning realization startled me into silence. Chester said Cal sold Japanese prints. Plural. I needed to ask Anita about all sales of prints from *One Hundred Famous Views of Edo,* not only *Meguro Drum Bridge and Sunset Hill.* If I was right, I might be able to find a shop or gallery offering one in the same stellar condition as Mo's and learn the source. If it was Cal, they might have contact information that would lead us to him, especially if they were repeat customers. It was also possible I could find his ad. He might even have one running now. If so, I could respond to it, pretending to be a collector. The clock mounted above the refrigerator read 6:10. I had nearly four hours to wait before my appointment with Anita.

"How long until pancakes?" I asked.

"About an hour, probably. The batter has to rest."

"I'm going to do some research."

I hurried into my study and brought up the *Seacoast Star*'s website. Wes's article read:

Break-in at Prescott's
Police Investigate a Possible
Connection to Mo Shannon's Murder

An unknown intruder shattered Prescott's

249

Antiques & Auctions' mezzanine-level office window at 7:02 p.m. yesterday, according to Russ Barstow, account manager at King Security Corporation (KSC). Josie Prescott, Prescott's owner, was in her private office at the time, but managed to avoid detection. "No one was hurt," Ms. Prescott stated. "Nothing was stolen. The police and my security company responded within minutes." A Prescott's staff member who saw the office after the break-in described it as horrific. "There was glass everywhere."

Southern New Hampshire Electric reports that a downed wire on Ellerton Street, which runs directly in front of Prescott's, caused a widespread loss of electricity, starting at 6:53 p.m. Prescott's was among the nearly 1,000 users who lost service. All service was restored by midnight. When asked why Prescott's generator didn't work, both Prescott and Barstow refused to comment.

A Japanese woodblock print by the celebrated artist Utagawa Hiroshige, titled *Meguro Drum Bridge and Sunset Hill,* which had been owned by murder victim Mo Shannon, was on display in Josie Prescott's private office prior to the break-in. A police source has confirmed that the print, which is valued at more than $25,000, is safe and undamaged.

The police don't know whether the intruder was after that print in particular, but they are working on the assumption that there might be a connection between Mo Shannon's murder and the break-in. "We're pursuing multiple lines of investigation," Rocky Point Police Chief Ellis Hunter said. "It's premature to announce a connection that might not exist."

Anyone with information about Mo Shannon's murder, the downed wire, the non-working generator, or the break-in at Prescott's Antiques & Auctions is asked to call the police at 603–555–3900.

I emailed my entire staff:

Hi All,
If you've seen today's *Seacoast Star,* you know that Wes is quoting someone on our staff. If you're Wes's source, please let this be the last time you speak to him on or off the record. Please don't speak about Prescott's business to him, or to any reporter — or anyone — without talking to me first. No harm has been done here, but I want us all to remain tight-lipped. Remember the old navy ad-

age: Loose lips sink ships.

Thanks,
Josie

I shut my eyes for a moment. Running a business was so complicated. I shook off the momentary apprehension that threatened to distract me, opened my eyes, and got back to work.

I Googled "Buy original 100 Famous Views of Edo print" and got more than 300,000 hits. I went through the first three pages of listings. Despite my search criterion specifying an "original," every one was a repro.

I visited the three largest art auction sites but found no ads for original Hiroshige prints.

I navigated my way to all ten of *Antiques Insights'* most recent "Best of Asian Art" dealers, auction houses, and galleries. I thought I was onto something when I read the promotional copy from a gallery in Zurich offering a near-perfect print, but it was a false alarm. Their "near-perfect" wasn't even close to the vibrant colors found in Mo's print.

I slapped my chair arm, frustrated.

Dealer-to-dealer sales were, universally, the largest component of the antiques market, yet evidently, Cal hadn't gone in that direction. Why not? Probably because he figured he had a better chance of pulling the wool over an amateur collector's eyes than he would a professional dealer, and he wouldn't have to offer any discounts. That made sense.

If I wanted to sell an original Hiroshige for top dollar, I'd advertise on *Antiques Insights'* website. It was expensive, but it was worth it. I opened their search box and asked for an original Hiroshige print. Nothing was available.

I frowned at my monitor, racking my brain for additional alternatives.

It was possible, although unlikely, since I doubted Cal wanted the world to know about his side business, that he had created a website to sell prints directly to consumers. I typed his name into Google. All the listings were connected to his faculty page at Hitchens and his staff listing at the museum. He did, in fact, have a website, but it was simply a shell, a profile of him and a list of his published writing, with links to Hitchens and the museum.

I was missing something. I leaned back and shut my eyes, thinking.

Could Cal have promoted the offering to collectors of Japanese prints, maybe by sending an email to the Langdon Art Museum's house list? Since he was the assistant director, it was reasonable to assume he had access to that list.

I could call the museum director on Monday or even email him now. Lots of people checked their work emails over the weekend. I decided to hold off. I couldn't think of a way to pose the question without risking damaging Cal's reputation, and no way would I do that on spec. Maybe I wouldn't have to wait, though. Ellis might know the answer now. I emailed him and asked if in the police search of Cal's various email accounts they found any record of a sale of a Japanese woodblock print, or a negotiation, or even an inquiry. I also asked if they'd checked with the museum about whether Cal had sent a mailing to its list offering a print for sale.

I stared at my monitor, thinking. Had Chester used the plural "prints" as a figure of speech or a slip of the tongue? Maybe the sale to Mo had been Cal's one and only deal. No. Chester was clear — Cal had spoken about avoiding flooding the market, which meant Cal had more than one print to sell. If I were Cal, how would I go about selling one or more additional prints without making waves, while still maximizing my take?

I remembered Mo's exhilaration at acquiring her print. If a year later Cal approached her saying he'd found another print from the *One Hundred Famous Views of Edo* series, she would have snapped it up. Cal didn't need to advertise if he could go back to satisfied customers.

Assuming he had some, how could I locate them?

I searched *Antiques Insights'* archives and found that fourteen prints from the *One Hundred Famous Views of Edo* series had sold during the last year. I scrolled through the list. Only two were described as originals in perfect condition. *New Fuji Meguro,* number 24, sold in January. The seller was a California gallery. The buyer, who paid $22,750, lived in New Mexico. The second one, *Benten Shrine, Inokashira Pond,* number 87, sold in late June. Both the seller's and buyer's names had been redacted. Typically, galleries and antiques dealers wanted their names to show — it was good for business. Individual sellers and collectors usually did not. Sometimes they were trying to avoid the tax man. Other times they didn't want to alert thieves to where they could find valuable art. The sales price was listed at $24,000.

I had a contact at *Antiques Insights,* Cormac McKenna, known as Mac, who could look up the redacted information, and if I came up with a good enough story, he might pass along the name, but he wouldn't be at work on a Saturday. Still, it couldn't do any harm to email him. Mac might be one of those people who stayed connected to his work email 24/7.

I drafted a subject line that I hoped would get my email read right away:

Urgent. "Benten Shrine, Inokashira Pond," #87

For the text, I wrote:

Hi Mac,
I'm sorry to bother you on the weekend, but I'm investigating a potential fraud case. It's urgent that I know who sold the print "Benten Shrine, Inokashira Pond," #87 listed in your archives.

> Thank you,
> Josie

I reread it, my finger hovering over the SEND button, fretting that Mac would hesitate to respond to what might be a police matter. Then I realized I had no reason to think he would shy away from doing the right thing any more than I would, and sent the email on its way.

I opened a new document and began writing my own ad. After several false starts, I ended up with *Wanted: Any original print from Utagawa Hiroshige's "100 Famous Views of Edo." Must be original in perfect condition. Will pay top dollar.* I created a new Gmail account, using "HiroshigeFan" and some numbers as my name. I also opened a new *Antiques Insights* account. Before posting my ad, though, I needed a phone.

I called Shelley, in New York City.

" 'lo."

"Shelley? It's Josie."

"God, Joz. What time is it?"

I glanced at my monitor. It read 6:50. "Oh, Shelley, it's ten to seven. I'm *so* sorry."

"What day is it?"

"Saturday."

"Have you gone insane?"

"I need a favor. I didn't even look at the clock."

"You've got to get out of New Hampshire, Josie. It's not healthy to be up this early."

I laughed. "Early birds catch worms, Shelley. That's me, an early bird."

She groaned. "Go away, Josie. You just

257

called me a worm. I was out dancing until four. Call again at noon. Or better yet, one."

"That's definitely something I miss about New York. Dancing till four. Where'd you go?"

"Same old, same old. We started at the Flamingo, then went to the Roadhouse."

"Big band, then country. You've got to come up here sometime, Shelley. We have a fabulous country-dancing joint, twice as big as the Roadhouse. The Diamond Cowboy."

"You're such a card. Can I go now?"

"It's urgent. I need a phone. A throwaway with a New York City area code. I'm hoping you'll buy it for me and send it overnight. Use the post office — they deliver on Sundays."

"Okay. Good night."

"The post office closes at one. I'll send you a text to remind you."

"Come for brunch. You can buy it yourself."

"I wish I could. You come for brunch. You can bring the phone with you."

She laughed and hung up.

Shelley was a peach, and I missed her. I sent the text summarizing my request, adding that our next brunch was on me, then, with my ad on hold until I had the phone number, I thought about what I should do next. I might not be able to post my ad, but I could prepare for my talk with Anita.

I used the photo of Cal I'd found on the Hitchens University faculty page and got one of Nora from her church newsletter. I cropped the photo so only Nora showed. Just for good measure, I decided to include a photo of Lydia, too. Her professional headshot from the Technology Transfer Department's Web page was flattering. She looked self-assured and determined, not harsh or ruthless. I downloaded all three images to my phone.

Mac emailed back. He wrote:

Hi Josie,

Good to hear from you.

As you know, we take all cases of fraud extremely seriously and we work hard to ensure that people buying from our site can do so without concern. We vet every ad. In this case, the description of the print, the seller's guarantee, and the price were all in line. What information do you have and what do you hope to learn? Maybe it would be easier if we spoke. 917.555.8762. Now is good for me if it's good for you.

Regards,
Mac

I dialed his number.

"Thanks so much, Mac, for making yourself available on a Saturday — and so early."

"When you have a two-year-old, this is late."

"I didn't know you had a child. That's wonderful! Boy or girl?"

"A boy. Sam. Sam the Man. So . . . Josie . . . what are you saying about this print?"

"I need to learn who sold it. I think it might be a gambler who sells repros as originals to pay down his debt."

"Are the police involved?"

"Yes, but they don't know I've contacted you."

"Will they have to?"

"No. They may need to contact *Antiques Insights,* but no one will know you and I spoke."

"Thanks. If the situation warrants contacting the seller or the buyer about the potential fraud, will you let us do that?"

"Yes . . . with the same caveat. I can't speak for the police."

"That's fair. The seller was Pat Durand." He read off a Gmail address. The phone number started with a 207 area code, Maine. "The buyer is Michelle Michaels." Mac gave me her contact information, an

AOL email account and a Kansas City address.

I thanked him again and promised to keep him posted.

I reviewed my options: tell Ellis about Michelle Michaels and Pat Durand, ask Mac to get Michelle to contact me, or ask Wes to check them both out. There was no choice, not really. Ellis had to know.

I emailed Ellis with an update, keeping Mac out of it, and asked him to let me know what he learned.

There was nothing else I could do until Branson Wills opened at ten. I was halfway out of my chair when I realized I hadn't watched the video I'd shot last night. I opened the file and hit play.

"Oh, wow," I whispered.

I raised my eyes from the screen and stared unseeingly into the woods. I watched the video a second time, horrified at what I was seeing.

After a moment, I brought up the Home Depot's website.

A minute later, my questions answered, I texted Ellis: *Call me. Urgent.*

CHAPTER TWENTY

Ellis called me two minutes later.

"Thanks for calling so quickly, Ellis. Can you meet for a minute?"

"I'm on the porch now."

"I'll be right there."

I stuck my head into the kitchen. "I'm going to talk to Ellis. I won't be long."

Ty held up the coffeepot. "Want a refill?"

"Good idea."

Steaming mug in hand, I slipped on a sweater coat and walked across the driveway to Zoë's porch. Hazy mist rose from the fields, and dew glimmered on the white aster and late-blooming purple flowering raspberries.

Ellis was half-sitting on the railing drinking coffee from a thermos.

"Thanks for meeting me so quickly," I said. "What did the utility people tell you happened last night?"

"A branch took the wires down. They had

to wait for a supervisor to assess the conditions before they could begin repairs. Power was fully restored by midnight."

"Did you look at that branch? I mean really look at it?"

"It's about ten feet long, slender, with smaller branches and twigs running along the whole length of it."

"But no leaves. That branch was covered with moss. It didn't break off a tree — it's been lying on the forest floor for months, probably years. Have they thrown it away yet? It might help prove that someone tampered with the power lines."

"We've got it."

"You knew?"

"I wouldn't say I knew. I'd say we're thorough. Keep in mind, it might be nothing more than some kids who thought it would be fun to create a blackout."

"I think the same person who broke into my place took down the wires."

"Pretty risky."

"Not so much if you wear rubber gloves and stand ten feet away."

"Downed wires can ricochet."

"I don't know whether he got lucky or what; I just know he did it."

"Who's he?"

"Probably Cal."

"Wouldn't he worry about someone driving by and catching him in the act?"

"There's not much traffic at night. This was a deliberate act, Ellis. Someone found the branch and whacked at the wires until they fell. He had a clear plan. First, he disconnected my generator. Second, he knocked down the wires. Third, he broke into my office."

"Fourth, he got away. How?"

"The scraping sounds I heard were from a telescopic ladder being extended. He had to have a ladder, and this model is easy to carry. You can buy one that weighs less than forty pounds at the Home Depot for less than two hundred dollars. He parked at the Congregational church and used the trees as cover. It's only about a hundred yards from my building to the tree line, then a quarter mile on an easy-to-follow path. Figure a minute to collapse the ladder. If it were me, I'd bring a sturdy backpack to carry it — much less unwieldy and much quieter. Add a minute to pack it up and swing it into place. Thirty seconds to pass the tree line, less if he sprints, and another five minutes to reach the church, less if he jogs. Soup to nuts, it wouldn't have taken him longer than seven or eight minutes once he hit the parking lot. As long as he was in the woods, he was safe. It was an audacious and clever plan."

"What happened after he got to the church?"

"He tossed the ladder in his trunk or in the backseat and off he went. Oh! I don't know if the church has security cameras. Do you?"

"Do you think he had a partner?" Ellis asked, ignoring my question.

"No. He didn't need one, not with the generator out of commission. Remember, he thought he had the whole building to himself."

"Could it be a woman?" Ellis asked.

"Sure. I carry things that weigh more than that all the time. I bet you're examining the branch for touch DNA."

"Which I doubt we'll find."

"How about bits of rubber from the gloves?"

"Unlikely, but possible."

"Examine my parking lot and the path — you'll find shards of glass. He walked on them. With all the rain we've had, there may be footprints."

"Good idea."

"You'll check the church for security cameras, too."

Ellis smiled and sat in one of a pair of Adirondack chairs. "Have a seat and tell me what else I'm going to do."

I laughed and sat down. I drank some coffee. "I suggested that you check Cal's emails for references to the Japanese prints."

"Already done. Our computer forensic team tells me no emails about Hiroshige or any Japanese woodblock print have been found on any of Cal's accounts or computers."

"Of course, if Cal used a different device and a new email address, we'd have no way of knowing what he's up to. Will you contact the director of the Langdon Museum and ask if Cal had access to their house list? Mailing the museum members might be a good way to drum up business."

"That's a smart idea. Why did you ask me to look into that buyer, Michelle Michaels?"

"The easiest way to sell another print would be to approach a satisfied customer. Presumably, she is one."

"How did you get her name?"

"I'm reviewing ads offering Japanese woodblock prints going back a year. I think Cal is using that name I wrote you about, Pat Durand."

"Thanks, Josie. I'll follow up."

"I'm going to place a 'Hiroshige print wanted' ad. I'll let you know if I get any nibbles from Pat Durand or anyone else."

"You'll let me know *before* you follow up."

I smiled. "Of course."

We sat in companionable silence for a few minutes. When my mug was empty, I told him good-bye and went home to eat pancakes.

Rocky Point Congregational Church's pastor, Ted Bauer, and I were pals. I frequently walked through the woods that separated our properties to stretch my legs and get some air. Ted was an avid gardener, and in nice weather, I often found him working in his rock garden. Ted's wife, Peg, a tag sale regular, was a nurse. Their routine had her dropping him off at the church en route to her job at Rocky Point Hospital. Her shift started at seven, so I wasn't surprised to see him kneeling on a gray foam pad beside a clutch of lavender phlox. He leaned back on his heels when he heard a vehicle turn into the parking lot, and when he saw it was me, he smiled and stood. Ted was about five-nine and stout, probably thirty to forty pounds overweight. His blond hair had long since turned gray.

"Don't tell me you're getting rid of that beautiful phlox."

"Perish the thought! I'm dividing and

moving some of the clusters. Spreading the wealth, as it were."

I scanned the gutters, then turned to the light poles. "Ted, do you have any security cameras I'm not seeing?"

"No, why?"

"My place was broken into last night. I think there's a chance the thief used your parking lot."

Ted's brows drew close together, and he reached out a garden-gloved hand as if to touch me. "Is everyone all right?"

"Yes, thank you. And nothing was stolen."

"Is this related to the power outage?"

"I think so."

"So this was no casual break-in." His eyes emanated caring. "Is there anything I can do?"

I smiled. "No, thanks, Ted."

"We talk sometimes about installing cameras."

"It's hard to decide what's best."

"Please let me know if we can do something."

I thanked him again and walked to my car. By the time I was buckled in and ready to leave, Ted was already back in his garden, hard at work.

I sat at a worktable in the warehouse and

talked to each of my key staff, one at a time, reassuring them that I was fine, that the break-in was an aberration, and that repairs would be completed shortly. I asked Eric and Gretchen to pass the news along to the part-timers.

Everyone reacted as expected: Sasha listened without comment, twirling her hair nervously; Fred got angry, wishing he could have a few minutes alone with the intruder as soon as he was caught; Eric was anxious, shuffling in place, while nibbling on his bottom lip; Cara was worried about everyone and everything, eager to help in whatever way she could; Gretchen was more concerned about my emotional well-being than the break-in per se.

Gretchen took two steps toward the front office, then stopped. After a moment, she marched back.

"It was me. Wes called me and asked so many questions, some of them so awful . . . you know . . . lurid. I had to stop him."

That sounded just like Wes. "Like what?"

Tears glistened on her long lashes. "He asked if any of us used your office for a little nooky when you aren't there. Isn't that horrible?"

Rage, which had fired up as soon as I heard the panes of glass break, and which had been simmering all night, began bubbling to a boil.

I forced myself to speak calmly. "That's unbelievable, actually. A new low, even for Wes."

"I was shocked, completely shocked. I told Wes no, of course not. Then he asked how I could be so certain." Gretchen raised her chin. "I know I should have ignored him, but I couldn't. I simply couldn't. I said maybe his wife expected to find him there with a sweet young thing and broke in to check."

I laughed, my anger dissipating in an instant. "Well done, Gretchen! What did he say to that?"

"He chuckled as if he'd just been razzing me and I'd landed a winner. After that he started asking questions about what was taken and who had keys and so on. I was so relieved he stopped trying to create a scandal, I said too much."

I stood up and patted her shoulder. "Thank you for telling me. It looks like there was no lasting harm done, and you've learned an important lesson: Don't take the bait. Not that I blame you — Wes is a champion baiter."

"Thank you for understanding. I promise nothing like this will ever happen again."

As soon as she was gone, I set off to the tag sale venue. I'd bought the nineteenth-century building, which had started life as a manufacturer of canvas products like sails and duffle bags, for its bones and location, but every inch had to be upgraded, from the electric and the plumbing to the foundation and the roof. I walked through the warehouse to the inside access door and stepped into a different world. I'd brought the tag sale venue up to code and expanded it, but I'd kept the nostalgic rustic feel. Our warehouse was modern and efficient, the auction venue was luxurious, and the tag sale venue exuded country charm.

After a quick walk-through to confirm that Eric had done his usual capable job setting up the displays, which, of course, he had, I met our newest part-timer, Melissa Sayers. Melissa was new to Rocky Point, the wife of a doctor who'd just accepted a job at Rocky Point Medical Center. She was tall and thin, somewhere around forty, with medium brown hair, cut short. She wore a maroon Prescott's polo shirt and khakis, as we all did on tag sale days. She had the residue of a deep tan and dark brown eyes.

Before leading me up to her, Eric whispered that she'd gotten tired of selling men's suits, which had been her last job, and loved antiques. She'd passed her background check with flying colors and seemed eager to learn. Today, she was scheduled to shadow Eric.

I loved that Eric and Gretchen had taken the initiative to hire her, and I hoped she worked out, as much for their sake as for mine.

Sasha was booting up a laptop in the Prescott's Instant Appraisal booth. I told her she could plan on me staffing it from noon to two, and left.

At nine fifty-seven, I turned into the Murphy's Interiors parking lot. When I reached the Branson Wills boutique, Anita was sitting at her desk, typing into her computer.

She greeted me warmly and invited me to sit.

I brought up Cal's photo and slid my phone across the desk to Anita. She swallowed, twice. Her recognition was apparent.

"You know him."

"Yes. He's a customer."

"This is Cal Lewis, the man I mentioned who sold the print to my friend, Mo. You said you didn't recognize that name. What name did he give you?"

"I'm sorry, Josie, but I'm just not comfortable talking about my customers."

"And I hope you know I feel the same. I'm not asking you to gossip. I never gossip. I hate gossip. This is part of an appraisal that I'm afraid might lead to an investigation into fraud."

"You suspect him of misrepresenting a print?"

"I'm afraid so. Did he buy a Hiroshige print?"

She didn't reply for several seconds. "I hate this."

"So do I. It's important, Anita. You know I wouldn't be asking if it wasn't."

She kept her eyes on my face, thinking it through. "He said his name was Pat Durand."

"Thank you." I took a notebook from my bag. "What did he buy, and when?"

She tapped into her computer. "He's purchased two twentieth-century Japanese woodblock print reproductions, both from *One Hundred Famous Views of Edo.* The first was sold on June nineteenth: *Benten Shrine, Inokashira Pond,* number eighty-seven. He bought the one you asked about, *Meguro Drum Bridge and Sunset Hill,* number one hundred eleven, on August twenty-third. He paid eighteen hundred fifty each time, cash."

"What's his address?"

273

Anita turned to her computer for a moment, then read off a Rocky Point post office box number, 156.

"His phone?"

"None given. I have an email address, though."

She called it out, the same Gmail address I got from Mac.

"I think Cal is ready to sell some more prints. He's gone into hiding, and I'm afraid he's deputized someone into helping him. Can you tell me when you last sold one of these prints?"

"Actually, a woman bought one yesterday, Hiroshige's *Flower Pavilion, Dango Slope, Sendagi,* number sixteen, also for cash, the same price, eighteen hundred and fifty dollars."

"Did she seem agitated?"

"Not so much agitated as . . . I don't know . . . unengaged. I asked her a bunch of normal questions, you know, was she trying to match a color scheme? Was she a fan of all Asian art? She didn't want to talk at all. She wasn't even aware that this portfolio encompassed four seasons, and when I told her, she didn't seem to care. She merely flipped through and picked one in what seemed a random fashion."

"What's her name?"

"I don't know. She didn't want to be on our mailing list."

I brought up Nora's photo on my phone and handed the unit to Anita. "Is this her?"

Anita shook her head. "No. I've never seen this woman before."

"Are you sure?" I asked, surprised. I'd been certain that Nora was Cal's co-conspirator. I swiped the screen to reach Lydia's photo and gave the phone back to Anita.

She stared at the image, then shook her head. "No. I don't recognize her, either."

"Thank you, Anita." I glanced at the ceiling. "Are there any security cameras?"

"Only in the back office. Murphy's isn't concerned about shoplifting. It's up to each of us to decide if we want to install a security system. Cameras are on my list."

"So there's no photograph of her."

"No."

"Can you describe her?"

"Not really. She wore a bulky coat, so I have no sense of her body shape. She wore a hat, black felt with a big brim."

"What color was her hair?"

"I'm sorry. I didn't notice."

"Eyes?"

She opened her palms. "I wish I could be more helpful. I was busy, and she was in a hurry. She was in and out of here in about two minutes. I just don't remember."

I thanked her again and started for the front, then paused. "Did I hear you right before — you bought an entire portfolio."

"Yes. A lovely set, probably from the 1930s. I've been selling them one at a time, mostly to decorators."

"Did you have the portfolio appraised?"

"No, it didn't seem worth it. You know it's more profitable to break the book."

I hated that some dealers embraced a policy of cutting art prints from bound editions, but I understood it. A nondescript nineteenth-century book in decent condition that included ten illustrations of anything from flowers to medical devices might sell for fifty dollars. If the dealer sold each of the prints individually, he might garner a hundred dollars each, netting a thousand.

"You're right, I do understand. The economics are hard to ignore. May I see the prints you have left?"

Anita swiveled toward an oak architectural cabinet, the kind used to store oversized drawings and blueprints. She opened the third drawer and flipped through some plastic-encased images, selecting half a dozen Hiroshige prints. She fanned them out on her desk facing me.

"I have more, but this is a representative sample."

The prints were the same size as Mo's, with the same distinct and spectacularly vibrant colors.

The third one grabbed me, number 76, *Bamboo yards, Kyōbashi Bridge.* A man standing on a wooden boat punted down a nearly deserted river. He was passing under a bridge. A dozen people walked overhead, none of them aware of him any more than he was aware of them. The blues were spectacular, ranging from a deep navy blue in the shadowy water under the bridge to cobalt glistening in the moonlit sky. Hiroshige's prints took my breath away. I looked up. Anita was watching me.

I smiled. "Hiroshige knocks me out."

Anita smiled back. "I could look at them forever. It's the storytelling."

"And the quiet."

"And the colors."

"And the detail."

"All that."

"What makes you think they're from the 1930s?" I asked.

"There were many reproductions featuring this level of craftsmanship created during that period."

She was right. But it was also possible she

was wrong.

"Did you ever consider that they might be authentic?"

Anita looked down at the prints. "Do you think it's possible? The colors are so vivid."

"I know. You almost never see it, but 'almost' is the operative word in that sentence. When I finish appraising Mo's print — her heir asked my company to appraise it — I'll let you know what I learn."

"Thank you. That's very generous of you. Do you think I should hold the others back?"

"I would." I laid the print back down. "You know the importance of provenance, Anita. You also know I would never poach one of your sources. That said, I'm hoping you'll tell me where you got the portfolio."

"You're asking a lot."

"I know."

"Only because you're you, Josie." She swiveled toward her monitor, scrolled down to read something, then turned back to me. "Eli bought the collection from a dealer in Winslow, England, Richardson Antiques."

She gave me Richardson's contact information, and I thanked her.

As I walked out, I considered my next steps. Five paces from my car, a glimmer of an idea came to me with a thud, and I stopped short.

A horn blared. I was blocking traffic.

I mouthed "Sorry" and continued to my car. I leaned against the hood and stared into the middle distance, considering ways and means. The sun warmed my face, and I shut my eyes, enjoying the sensation.

"Okay, then," I said aloud.

I sent two identical emails, one to Ellis and one to Wes:

I have confirmed that Cal is using the name Pat Durand and P.O. Box #156.

I emailed Sasha, too:

It looks like Cal bought Mo's print from Anita Wills. Eli bought a complete portfolio from Richardson Antiques in Winslow, England. Anita thinks the set is a repro from the 1930s. Please contact Richardson's for more information.

I added the antique shop's contact information, reread the message, and hit SEND.

I tossed my phone in my bag and drove back to work.

279

CHAPTER TWENTY-ONE

I was standing in the front office sipping coffee, getting ready for my stint staffing the Prescott's Instant Appraisal booth, when Cara told me a woman named Gertie Joan Mays was on the line. I nearly pounced on the guest-table phone.

"Gertie Joan! I'm so glad to hear from you."

"I hope it's okay that I'm calling on a Saturday. I hate to disturb you on the weekend."

"I'm thrilled you called. Tell me you have good news."

"I have good news."

I sat down, dragged over a pad of paper, and extracted a pen from the Prescott's mug in the center of the table.

"I'm ready when you are."

"Ricky Joe McElroy purchased that guitar on June second, 1973. He paid twenty-eight thousand three hundred and ten dollars.

That's a lot of money."

"It sure is. Did you find the receipt or an entry in a general ledger, or what?"

"Both. I found the receipt, then matched it up to the general ledger."

"Gertie Joan, you're a treasure and a half."

"That's nice of you to say. Gil Paul, that's my brother, bought the guitar on March fifteenth, 1971. So he had it just sitting on the shelf for more than two years. I trailed that one from the receipt to the general ledger, too."

"How much did he pay?"

"Ten thousand five hundred. That makes him look kind of sleazy, doesn't it? Charging Ricky Joe nearly three times what he paid."

"Paying a third is standard in the antiques business," I said. The direct and indirect costs of acquiring, appraising, cleaning, marketing, and merchandizing objects add up quickly. "Who did he buy it from?"

"A woman named Marianne Dowler. There's a note on the receipt in Gil Paul's handwriting that reads 'granddaughter of Estelle Mae Bridges, friend of Rbt. Johnson.' There's an address listed, but no phone number."

Gertie Joan called out the address. In 1971, Marianne Dowler lived in Clarksdale,

Mississippi.

"Fabulous. Did you find any other documentation? Notes, maybe, about provenance . . . you know, the trail of ownership?"

"Nothing like that. Only purchase and sales records."

"Thank you again for looking. I'm so appreciative. I hate to ask you to do more, but I'm going to need the original documents, or at least good clear copies of everything."

"I can't let the originals go, but I'm glad to send you copies. As it happens, I'm one step ahead of you! I took photos with my smartphone and emailed them to you. Is that good enough?"

"Let me check that they came through. May I ask you to hold on for a minute?"

"Sure."

Gretchen wasn't at her desk, so I commandeered her computer, logged into my email account, and downloaded the photos.

"Gertie Joan?"

"I'm here."

"The two sales receipts are perfect. The general ledger shots are a little wiggly, though. Can you get someone to press down on the pages so the writing near the binding is visible?"

"Let me do that now. I'll call you when I send them."

Gertie Joan was a woman of action. Ten minutes after we hung up, two completely legible photos arrived. While I was waiting, I composed an email for her to send me, confirming that she had the original documents in her possession, and that these photographs represented an accurate and complete record of Abbot's involvement with the 1930 Martin OM-45 Deluxe guitar, serial number 45317. I sent it to her, then called to thank her for retaking the photos and ask her to cut and paste my content into an email to me. She opened it then and there, read it aloud, and said it was fine. I had the email less than a minute later.

"Gertie Joan, what's your favorite flower?"

"You're going to send me flowers?"

"A lot of them. A huge bouquet."

She laughed, a tinkling happy sound. "Instead of a big bouquet, I'd like an orchid. I've always wanted one, and now I have the time to take care of it. I understand they're tricky to grow."

"I can make this happen, Gertie Joan. Do you have a certain species in mind? Or a color?"

"Nope. You pick. Make it flashy." She laughed louder. "Just like me."

I was still chuckling as I returned to the

283

tag sale venue. Gretchen was working at one of the cash registers.

I waited until there was a momentary lull. "I need you to investigate orchid options for a novice who lives in Florence, Mississippi. Get her one she can't kill. Better yet, get her lessons on how to keep an orchid alive. She wants a flashy one."

Gretchen's eyes glinted with excitement. This kind of project was right up her alley. "I'm on it."

It was eleven thirty-five, which meant I had enough time to begin the hunt for Marianne Dowler. No Dowlers lived in Clarksdale, but hundreds of Dowlers lived in the South. At eleven fifty-five I threw in the towel. I emailed Fred Gertie Joan's photos and asked him to find Marianne Dowler but not to contact her until we'd spoken. I turned off Gretchen's computer and went to start my turn in the Prescott's Instant Appraisal booth.

I spoke to Fred, taking an early lunch, en route. "I just sent you an email. We're making progress. How's Davy doing?"

"Good. He's at his hotel doing some research."

"Did he give you any hints about what he thinks?"

284

Fred smiled. "What do you say when a client asks you that question?"

I grinned. "I tell them an appraisal is a process."

"That's what he told me when I asked, almost word for word. I know he wants to confirm some of the materials, specifically whether all 1930 Martin OM-45 Deluxe guitars' backs and sides were made with Brazilian rosewood and topped with torrefied Adirondack spruce. He's also checking out the gluing techniques."

"I hate waiting."

"Me, too."

I ran across the warehouse and reached Prescott's Instant Appraisal right at noon.

A man named Finn sat across from me in the Prescott's Instant Appraisal booth. He was in his seventies, short and thin, with scraggly gray hair and leathery brown skin, the kind you get from years of outside work. He told me he was a retired roofer, and his wife was pestering him to divvy up some of their collectibles among their grandkids.

"Once you get on Harriet's radar, the only thing you want is to get off."

"That's why you've brought this Coca-Cola Barefoot Boy tray in for appraisal."

"Exactly. I'm hoping it comes in at something around fifty dollars. My granddaughter Allie likes it a lot, but her sister Naomi got the miniature watercolor Harriet and I picked up on the Isle of Wight in the 1980s. It's a cute little thing, about two by two, a picture of a church. I saw one just like it for sale in the church gift shop the last time we were there for thirty-four dollars. That was three or four years ago now, so I figure with inflation and all I'd be on solid ground valuing it around fifty dollars."

"Are you from the Isle of Wight?"

"Can't you tell by looking at my Irish mug? My mum used to say I had a map of County Clare written on my face. It's Harriet's people that hail from the Isle of Wight."

"So where did you get this tray?"

"Darned if I know. Harriet thinks we bought it at a yard sale when we were first married, around 1975, but I just plumb don't remember."

"Let me take a look."

Branded paraphernalia was a popular collectible. This one featured a Tom Sawyer–looking boy lounging against a tree in a bucolic setting. The boy wore chinos and a long-sleeved blue shirt with the pant cuffs and shirt sleeves rolled up. He also wore suspenders, a broad-brimmed straw hat, and an ear-to-ear grin. He was surrounded by grassy fields. He had a white-bread sandwich in one hand and a bottle of Coke in the other. A cute mutt sat facing him, his eyes fixed on the sandwich. The illustration was rimmed by a double border, two inches of red and a quarter inch of gold. The words DRINK COCA-COLA appeared in white script at both the top and bottom of the image. I inserted a loupe in my right eye and examined the tail of the *C* in "Coca" at the top. A tiny all-cap message divided onto two lines read TRADE MARK REGISTERED.

My heart pattered a bit faster than normal. Each letter was distinct. This was no quick-and-dirty knockoff.

I turned the tray over. The back was black. I removed the loupe and handed back the tray.

"Thanks for bringing this in, Finn. To properly authenticate and value this object, we'd need to take some time with it, but based on my instant appraisal — this tray is evidently the 'real thing.' Are you sitting down?"

"With my feet planted."

"Your tray has the right markings in the right places, properly executed. It's in wonderful condition. If it's real, I would expect it to sell for at least a thousand dol-

287

lars. Maybe twelve hundred."

Finn's eyes popped open, forming perfect little saucers. "That's more than fifty."

"Looks like you'll have some rejiggering to do."

Finn shook my hand enthusiastically and left, carrying the tray as if it were made of pure gold. As he pushed through the outside door, I noticed Frank Shannon standing just inside, his eyes on my face, his expression somber, and I stood up. He jerked his head to the left, silently asking if I could step outside with him. I nodded. The clock over the door told me it was twenty to one.

I turned to the next person in line, a young woman, and smiled. "Someone will be right with you."

I did a 360. Fred was standing near the back, greeting people as they ambled by, offering to answer questions. I raised my arm, caught his eye, and waved him over.

"Cover for me, all right?"

"Sure."

Fred took my place, and I went outside. I found Frank leaning against the trunk of a willow tree, partially hidden by the drooping branches.

"Sorry to bust in on you," he said as I approached. "Trish and Lydia are over talking to Pastor Ted about Mo's funeral. Trish is

288

having a container-load of flowers dropped off Tuesday morning. It's all bull, if you ask me. Mo doesn't need a special send-off to get to heaven. She's already there, standing next to God."

"Oh, Frank." I touched his arm.

"Trish tells me to be quiet, that the send-off is for us, not her. I guess that's right." He turned back to face me. "I stopped by to see that you're all right. I read the *Seacoast Star* article about the break-in."

"Thanks for asking. It was scary, but no harm done."

"Except to a window and a display case."

"Except for that."

"Were any of your roosters hurt when the glass shattered?"

"None I care about."

"Do you think the guy broke in to get Mo's print? Trish told us it was on an easel, in plain sight."

"I don't know."

"Quite a coincidence about the power going out. I hear a branch snapped off a tree. You'd think the power company would do a better job trimming them."

"Where'd you hear that?"

"I don't know. The *Seacoast Star,* I reckon."

"I'm not sure it was a coincidence. Maybe

289

someone wanted Prescott's to be in the dark."

Worry lines appeared on Frank's forehead. "That's quite a thought."

"Josie!"

I looked up. Abby Young, the older woman who'd been part of Mo's book club, was smiling and waving at me.

"Abby! Nice to see you."

"Any *Y*'s for me?"

Ever since the day she found an old wooden figurehead with the letter *Y* carved onto the woman's apron, Abby's been a fan of the tag sale.

"I'm not telling! Finding *Y*'s on your own is part of the fun!"

Her smile faded as she recognized Frank. She patted his arm and walked inside.

"I buy pizza for my staff on Saturdays," I told Frank. "Want to come in for a slice?"

"I'd better not. Thanks, though. Trish wants to play some tennis, to get the kinks out, it she calls it. Athletes, even retired ones, can't stay still for long."

"Not golf?"

"Not since the day she retired. She won't touch a club. She can't stand playing with amateurs. I wonder if it'll be the same for me with guitars."

"I doubt it. So she plays tennis. Is she any good?"

"Better than me, which isn't saying a whole lot. Speaking of guitars . . . any news about mine?"

"Not yet. We're making progress confirming provenance, but it's a process. One step at a time."

"Progress is good." He aimed his index finger at the woods on the other side of the parking lot. "I walked along Ellerton to get here . . . but what about that path? Does it lead to the church?"

"Yes. It's about a quarter mile, a nice walk."

He turned to face me. "You ready for your eulogy on Tuesday?"

"Yes."

"Trish will be glad to hear it."

He squeezed my shoulder and set off. I stood under the willow tree watching him trek across the parking lot and disappear behind a screen of bushes and trees.

A moment later, a soft voice called, "Josie?"

I turned. Steve's girlfriend stood nearby. I remembered her name was Kimberly. She wore a Kelly-green crewneck sweater that set off her titian hair, and brown jeans.

"Do you have a minute?"

I smiled. "Sure. Kimberly, right?"

"Yes." She turned around slowly, taking in the path to the tag sale entrance, the building, the half-full parking lot. "What made you decide to open your own business?"

"Why do you ask?"

Kimberly met my eyes. "Envious, I guess. You're so accomplished. Was it a long-term dream?"

"Not really. I moved to New Hampshire for a fresh start. I worked in antiques before, so I knew something about the business. Are you thinking of starting a company?"

She stared at her feet for a moment. Worry lines wrinkled her brow. "No . . . but I'm thinking I might need a fresh start. Did you get divorced? Is that why you moved?"

I twirled my engagement ring. "I've never been married."

"What, then?"

I didn't want to talk about that horrible year, my last living in New York City, especially to a stranger. You always hear how whistle-blowers endure contempt and mistrust, and that's what happened to me after I reported my boss's collusion with the competition in a price-fixing scheme. Then my dad died. Two weeks later, my boyfriend at the time, Rick the Cretin, announced I was getting to be a downer, his word, and left me cold. My dad always said when you're at the end of your rope, tie a knot and hang on, and if you can't hang on, move on. I lasted a year before moving to New Hampshire to start a new life. I could no longer recall the details of what those miserable people had said about me in my hearing or even the specifics of what they'd done to make me feel so isolated, but the feelings their shunning had engendered were seared into my soul and would stay with me forever. Living well was the best revenge, and I was living well indeed. I had a thriving business and employees I cared about and trusted; I was engaged to a man I adored who adored me; I was involved with New Hampshire Children First!, work that added meaning to my life; and I had good friends, real friends, friends who wouldn't toss me in a Dumpster like yesterday's trash, no matter what. I couldn't imagine why Kimberly was asking about such old news.

I smiled again, hoping she'd let it go and change the subject. "A bunch of things. It worked. I love my life here in New Hampshire. Where are you thinking of going?"

"I don't know. I have a son, and that makes moving tougher." She dismissed the topic with a wave of her hand. "Never mind. What I really wanted was to ask you about

Steve Jullison. Mo's ex. What do you know about him?"

I let my astonishment show. "Me? Why on earth would you ask me that?"

"You two seemed close."

"We're not."

"I don't want to make another mistake." She looked around again. "I'm not doing a good job of asking, but I was hoping you would advise me."

Gretchen advanced toward us from the tag sale entrance, stopping twenty feet away, waiting for my signal.

I raised a finger, indicating I'd be with her in a minute. "I'm sorry I can't help you, Kimberly." I glanced at Gretchen, then smiled at Kimberly. "Duty calls."

I left Kimberly standing there, her pretty face framed by the yellow-gold willow leaves.

"Problem?" I asked Gretchen in a whisper.

"Not exactly. It's Wes Smith. He's on line one. He says it can't wait."

"Thanks."

I trotted to the front office. I felt bad for Kimberly, and sad, too. Maybe it was because her relationship with Steve was secret that she had no one she could talk to, no one she could trust to tell her the truth: *Be careful. If a man cheats on one woman, it's not a stretch to think he might cheat on you, too. Steve is a world-class liar.* I could hear the platitudes most people would dump on her: *You've invested so much time in the relationship, what's a little more? Love is always worth fighting for. Don't give up — Ryan needs a dad.* As I entered the building, I glanced back. Kimberly hadn't moved. Her eyes remained fixed on the ground in front of her.

"Kimberly!" I called.

She looked up.

"Come on in — let's talk some more."

She took a step in my direction. "Are you sure? I don't want to be any trouble."

I smiled. "I've got pizza!"

She came on the run.

CHAPTER TWENTY-TWO

I asked Gretchen to make Kimberly comfortable, told them I'd be back in a flash, and dashed to my office to take Wes's call.

"Hey, Wes. It's me. What's going on?"

"You should have called me." Wes sounded huffy. "What do you know about this Pat Durand person?"

"Nothing other than what I told you — Cal is using that name. I'm not holding back on you, Wes. What about the P.O. box?"

"It's real, and they have security cameras — except they only store the images for ninety days, and guess what? No one's checked the box for the last three months."

"When was the box opened?"

"June eleventh, this year."

Pat Durand opened the post office box three days before he bought the first print from Anita. "No doubt the clerk doesn't remember a thing about him."

"The clerk has trouble remembering his

own name. It gets worse. You need two IDs to open a box. One of them was a lease for an apartment at 965 Ocean View Lane. Duh! There is no Ocean View Lane in Rocky Point. The other ID was for a non-existent Hitchens employee. That one included a picture, but it's still a bust, because all you can see is that the person is white. The photocopy is in black-and-white and pixelated. Between the short hair, long bangs, and bad lighting, you can't even tell if it's a man or a woman. The police are stymied. There are nine full- and part-time workers at Hitchens who have rights to create IDs. They issue thousands of them — all the students, faculty, staff, authorized researchers, visiting professors, select vendors, etcetera, etcetera, but that's not relevant anyway because this one isn't real. Someone jury-rigged the design in Photoshop, adding a photo they probably got off the Internet, printed it out, and laminated it. It's a dead end. Plus which, using a fake name isn't against the law unless you intend to commit a crime like fraud, and the police are a mile away from proving that, even if they can confirm who Pat Durand is or was, which they can't."

"Cal may not be the only person using the name."

"Who else?"

"Someone helping him."

Wes's voice lowered conspiratorially. "Like Nora."

"It's possible. I'm convinced that she knows where Cal is. Do you think she's aware the police are onto her?"

"No. If she has any suspicions, she probably just thinks she's paranoid. When you're having an affair, you're always looking over your shoulder."

"And you know this how?"

"I read a lot. Same as you."

"What about Nora's husband?"

"Kevin. I hear rumors he's the jealous type. Lots of innuendo, nothing specific."

"Who said what?"

"You're asking for my sources?" Wes asked, outraged.

"As if." I laughed. "I'm asking whether people are actually saying things or whether you're reading between the lines."

"Two people told me he keeps her on a short leash, but they both have an ax to grind. One is an ex-girlfriend with a grudge. Kevin dumped her years ago, and she's as bitter now as she was then. The other is one of Nora's coworkers who was hot on her a few years ago and resents her brush-off."

"Are Nora and Kevin happy?"

"I guess. Why?"

"Because if she's happy, it's hard to see why she'd be sleeping with Cal."

"I figure that's just sex, you know? I mean after a few years, sex is just same old, same old, so if you're that kind of person, you go sniffing around. Kevin isn't. Nora is."

"Do you think that's right, Wes? Romance only lasts a few years?"

"Like I said, it depends on the person. For most people, it only lasts a few months."

"That's pretty cynical."

"Nah, I'm not cynical. I'm realistic. I'm a reporter, so I see more of the dark side than you do. You're all about the froufrou."

I started to argue the point, then decided to let it go. "Never mind. Kevin is in construction. Is that right?"

"He's a project manager for Calidale Vista. Do you know them? They're huge."

"Really? I got the impression from Nora that he was one of the guys pounding the nails, not that he was running the show. She told me being an accountant was really tough, that sometimes she wished she was in construction like her husband because nails don't talk back."

"Good one, Joz!"

"Good one, Nora. I'm just repeating what she said. What else have you learned?"

Wes hadn't dug up any dirt. Neither Nora nor Kevin had financial troubles, pending lawsuits, or criminal records. Which didn't mean Nora wasn't having an affair with Cal and helping him commit art fraud any more than it proved Kevin wasn't controlling.

"Have the police talked to that neighbor?" I asked. "The one who was on a business trip to Brazil?"

"Yup. His name is Walter Greene, and he saw two cars parked in front of the Shannons' the day Mo died. One was there when he got home from work about four thirty. He didn't recognize the car, and he didn't see the driver. He can't even say what model or color it was. The second car drove up as he was getting his mail, about quarter to five. That was Cal. Walter knows him by sight. Cal walked onto the Shannons' property. Walter went inside to drop off the mail. He figures the first car drove away while he was inside, because when he went outside again to look around his garden, it was gone. Then a minute or two later, here comes Cal, hustling to his car and leaving. He saw you and Chief Hunter drive up about five to five."

"This is incredible, Wes! We have Cal at the murder scene at the right time."

"I know — it's a definite hot patootie! Cal

300

kills Mo and runs for it. Now we just have to find him."

"I'm stunned. We knew it was possible — and it is."

"It's more than possible. It's likely."

Sadness washed over me. "Cal killed Mo."

"It looks that way. What else ya got?"

"Nothing."

"Okay, then. I'll catch ya later."

I replaced the receiver, then stood, staring at it.

Cal and Nora and Lydia — three such different personalities. Cal was arrogant and narcissistic, with morals so elastic anyone following his play risked whiplash. Nora was smart and methodical, with an unexpected party-girl edge. Lydia was guarded and suspicious, wrapped in a melancholic fog.

I called downstairs and asked Gretchen to load up a tray with pizza and bring Kimberly up.

Gretchen placed the tray on the butler's table. I asked her to tell Fred I was sorry for not coming back to finish my shift, and to let him know I'd try to fill in later in the afternoon.

After Gretchen left, Kimberly reached for a slice of pepperoni. "Thank you for this. And for inviting me in to talk. I've been reading about you and your company for years. I'm a real fan."

"Thank you. I know a little about how hard you work from Mo."

"I'm crushed about her death. That's part of what has me reeling."

"Crushed is a good word for how I'm feeling, too. She was a good friend."

"And a wonderful teacher."

"I know she loved her work. How about you . . . Do you like teaching?"

She patted her lips with a napkin. "Yes."

"I hear some hesitation in your voice."

"You know how it is . . . you can love the work and the schedule . . . but it sure would be nice to make more money. Sometimes I think I should just drive away, to do what you did, to start over."

"Drive away where?"

"That's part of the problem. I love Rocky Point, and I don't want to live anywhere else. I love Steve, too. But if our relationship isn't going to work, I want to know now, not a year or five years from now."

"What does he say?"

"Give it time. Which isn't helpful. It's also hard because I have no one to talk to. Almost no one knows we live together."

"It's hard to make decisions in a vacuum."

"Exactly. What do you think I should do?"

"I don't know." I took a slice of mushroom

pizza. "Did you grow up in Rocky Point? Is this home?"

"Sort of. My mom and I spent summers here starting when I was in grade school. We had a cottage on the beach. My dad came up weekends. We lived just outside Boston, so it wasn't that far for him. Then he got transferred to Dayton. That was about five years ago, and everything changed. They sold the cottage last spring. I tried to buy it, but I couldn't afford the fair market value, and they couldn't afford to let me have it for less."

"That's tough."

"Nothing's easy, right? Rocky Point is a great place to be a kid, and I wanted Ryan to have that same experience."

"Isn't he?"

"Not really. It's different when you live in a single-family house on the water." Kimberly smiled, a memory coming to her. "The girl who lived in the cottage next door to us . . . her name was Chelsea . . . she and I did everything together, all summer, every summer. We played beach volleyball. We went spelunking in the salt caves at the end of the beach. We even went clamming right in front of our houses. Ryan doesn't have any of that. We live in a condo a mile from the shore, without a private lawn or anything."

"Those summers sound heavenly. No wonder you want that for Ryan."

"God, I remember it all like it was yesterday. The lock on one of my bedroom windows was broken, so I never had to worry about getting locked out." She laughed. "That was when we were older. We'd go to the beach late at night to smoke and drink beer. All I had to do was shimmy down a tree."

"Does Chelsea still live in Rocky Point?"

"No. You know how it goes. People move away. They change. Chelsea lives in Colorado Springs now, with her husband and three kids. I emailed her about buying the cottage — I thought it would be fun to go in together — but she wasn't interested. She hasn't been back east since she left for college. If she didn't send Christmas cards, I'd never hear from her."

"It's hard when orbits no longer overlap."

"Is it inevitable?"

"That you lose touch with friends? I think each situation is different. I'm not friends with anyone from Welton, where I grew up. I have one good friend from my years in New York. Regardless, it sounds like you're ready for some stability."

"Desperate is closer to the mark. And I'm not sure Steve can handle that." She stood up. "Thanks for the pizza and for letting me vent. I'm sure it will all work out."

I carried the tray downstairs and led the way to the front office.

Cara was on the phone and raised her hand, catching my attention. I placed the tray on the guest table.

She punched the HOLD button. "I'm sorry to bother you, Josie, but this woman bought a pair of bronze bookends at last week's tag sale. Lincoln. She wants more. I checked the computer. We don't have any more in stock. She's asking where we got them so she can see if more are available. What should I tell her?"

"Find out exactly what she's looking for. Bronze bookends? Only bronze bookends featuring Lincoln? Anything Lincoln? Presidential bronze bookends? Tell her we'll let her know when something she wants comes available, but that we never reveal sources. If she pushes, I'll take the call."

Cara smiled broadly. "I can do it."

"Good — but if you need help, that's okay, too!"

I walked Kimberly out. She paused with one hand on her car door handle to thank me again for the pizza and conversation.

"I don't know that I was any help, but you're always welcome to run things by me. I know how hard it is to be on your own."

She thanked me for the offer and drove away.

Kimberly seemed to have a good heart, but it was clear that she was struggling to juggle her own needs with Ryan's and Steve's. I hoped she'd figure it out.

As soon as I walked back inside, I stopped thinking about Kimberly and started thinking about Marianne Dowler, who'd sold a guitar in 1971.

If Marianne paid taxes, the Mississippi Department of Revenue would know it, and if it was public information, Fred's contact would tell us, but that call would have to wait until Monday. I sent Fred a quick email with the suggestion.

I returned to the tag sale venue, thanked Fred for covering for me, and took over for him at the instant appraisal booth. Afterward, I texted Ty that I wanted to go to the Colonial Twist for dinner. I asked him to make a reservation. I added that he'd need to wear a tie and jacket. Then I got back to work.

Davy Morse, our guitar expert, called around four, saying he was leaving for New York, had some details to confirm, and hoped to get us his report by midweek. I told him that was fine and resisted asking for an interim update.

hoped to get us his report by midweek. I
told him that was fine and resisted asking
(by asking) him about

CHAPTER TWENTY-THREE

Ty and I got to the Colonial Twist about
seven thirty. We were all buffed up. I wore a
short-sleeved cherry-red dress. It had a fitted top and a swirly skirt, and when I wore
it, I felt pretty. Ty wore a brown suit with an
off-white shirt and a green-and-brown-
striped tie. He didn't react to the white-
helmeted doorman or the heavy wooden
door, but two steps into the lounge, he
stopped short.

Every chair in the lounge was taken. A
couple stood by the mantel, laughing.

Ty turned to look at me. "Can you believe
we didn't know this place existed?"

"Can you believe it's this successful
without Chester promoting it?"

"How did he do it?"

"He found himself some well-heeled
gamblers, and word of mouth did the rest."

"Too bad. I thought maybe he'd found an
elixir and we could help him bottle it. We'd

make a million dollars before morning."

We made our way to the bar.

Chester came toward us, hands extended. "Josie! The Colonial Twist is honored."

"You're very kind. Chester, this is my fiancé, Ty Alverez. Ty, Chester Randall." As the two men shook hands, I added, "I see we were lucky to get a reservation."

"I can always make room for friends. Why don't you order a drink? It won't be too long."

The bar was almost as crowded as the lounge, the happy rumble of conversation sprinkled with laughter. I waited by the side wall while Ty elbowed his way to the elephant railing.

As I'd anticipated, all the men wore jackets or blazers and ties. I felt a bit underdressed because most of the women wore evening attire, the little black dresses and sparkly tops you see at cocktail parties. I didn't recognize a soul.

Chester joined me. "A table should be ready in about ten minutes."

"Perfect."

Chester leaned in close to my ear so he wouldn't be overheard. "I was going to stop by on Monday. I heard about the break-in on the news. Are you all right?"

I kept my voice low, too. "Yes, thank you.

I'm fine. It was pretty frightening, though."

"You don't know who did it?"

"No."

He cast his eyes around the room, keeping a professional watch on the servers and his guests. "So . . . do you have any news regarding the whereabouts of our mutual acquaintance?"

"No. How about you?"

"I thought so, but no. I followed his lady friend after she left work yesterday. She drove to a cobbler on Islington. Why does anybody go to a cobbler five miles from her condo, and farther than that from her job, when there's a shoe repair shop a half mile from where she lives? Do you know that stretch of Islington? Down by Hatchett Street? The neighborhood is solidly working class, a little long in the tooth, maybe, but decent. Nora stayed about an hour."

"I can't see Cal living in a working-class neighborhood. He's too proud."

" 'Pride goes before destruction, a haughty spirit before a fall.' When vermin is under attack, it does what's necessary to survive."

"Where did Nora go next?"

"Straight to her condo."

"And you went back to check out the shop."

"That's right. As far as I could tell, it's

just a shoe repair shop. I figure she waited while they replaced a heel and gave her shoes a good shine."

"An hour is a long time for that."

"I know."

Ty walked up carrying my martini and a glass filled with amber liquid. Chester said he needed to check on something and walked toward the restaurant.

I took a sip. The drink was cold and thick, creamy. "Yum. You don't drink beer out of a glass very often."

"This isn't a drink-from-the-bottle kind of place. Plus, they have Allagash White on tap."

"Really! Allagash White. I'm stunned. You're not serious!"

"Sarcasm doesn't become you."

"I wasn't being sarcastic. I was celebrating with you."

"Oh." He raised his glass.

I clinked and said, "Here's to us."

"And to silver light in the dark of night." He touched my glass, then drank. "Ahh! Allagash White. Life is good."

The hostess, another attractive woman in a black dress and pearls, led us to a table in a corner. The cloud-white tablecloth was soft and supple. I could see myself reflected in the silver flatware. Delicate yellow blossoms drifted alongside a tea candle in a shallow bowl of water. To my left, I could see the entry to the casino.

I turned my attention back to Ty. "If I ask nicely, I bet Chester would show you the casino."

"Not tonight. Tonight I just want to be with you."

"You're so romantic."

"I'm in love."

I raised his hand to my cheek and closed my eyes. "Me, too."

The waiter appeared. I chose Mama's lasagna. Ty went for the lobster alfredo primavera. We decided to share a Caesar salad.

The food was wonderful, and the service was even better, there when you wanted it, but unobtrusive. We sat and talked about nothing in particular. It was, all in all, a perfect evening.

"What do you think?" I asked Ty as soon as the waiter cleared our plates.

"Delicious. Next time, I'll try the steak."

"Me, too."

Chester beamed when we told him how much we'd enjoyed ourselves.

I had a new favorite restaurant.

Shelley came through. The disposable phone with a 917 area code arrived just before eleven on Sunday morning. I texted her a thank-you, not wanting to risk waking her again, then dashed to my computer, entered the phone number into my *Antiques Insights* request for a Hiroshige print in perfect condition, paid the fee, and posted my ad.

At two, I sat on the couch, reading "Poor Sherm," a short story by Ruth Chessman that had been featured in *Alfred Hitchcock Mystery Magazine* as a "classic."

Ty came into the room. "You look deep in thought."

"Relationships are complicated."

"What did I do wrong?"

I laughed. "Not you. You're perfect. I was thinking how fragile life is. Blink twice and you miss it."

"You miss your mom."

"And my dad."

Ty sat beside me and kissed the top of my head. I leaned into his shoulder and let the memories come. From the time I was about six until my mom died, our little family of three spent a weekend a season in Dennis, on Cape Cod. We stayed in a beachfront cabin. My folks got the bedroom. I slept on the couch.

During my mother's final pain-ridden

days, we'd gone for one last weekend. It was September, and my mother had insisted that she was eager to go on our annual hayride. My dad, afraid that sitting on hard slats of wood and bouncing along the rough track would be too much for her, arranged with a local farmer for a custom ride. While she napped inside our cabin, Dad and I covered the cart's floor with thick blankets and set up three tranquility chairs, low and cushy. We reclined in style as the farmer drove us slowly along a packed-dirt path that ran alongside his property. My mother kept her eyes on the fire-colored leaves and breathed in the pine-infused scent of fall.

I leaned over and kissed Ty. "Ready for a hayride?"

At three, Ellis, Zoë, her son, Jake, her daughter, Emma, Ty, and I bundled ourselves into hoodies and sweaters and drove to the Allen Farm. We walked along the faux-torchlit path to where an old wagon was waiting, and I took my place next to Ty. For the half hour we rocked along the path, I was young again, and I had my mother near me.

After we got back to my place, I grilled burgers and dogs, and then, as twilight's purple blush enshrouded the meadow like a veil, we sat around the fire pit, watching Jake and Emma play badminton until they could no longer see the birdie.

Later, the kids roasted marshmallows and passed them out to the adults, and as I licked the gooey sweetness from my fingers, I thought I was maybe the luckiest woman in the world.

CHAPTER TWENTY-FOUR

I was first into work on Monday morning.
As soon as I booted up my computer, I
emailed Mac at *Antiques Insights.*

> Hi Mac,
> How did Pat Durand pay for his ac-
> count? What credit card did he use? How
> did his buyers pay him? Did the transac-
> tions go through PayPal? Thanks!
>
> > Josie

Mac's reply came quickly.

> Hi Josie,
> Yes, everything went through PayPal.
>
> > Mac

I looked up from my monitor. PayPal
linked to a credit card. The police — or Wes
— could probably find the record, but that
wouldn't help. I was certain that Cal, using
the name Pat Durand, had acquired the

kind of credit card you prepay in cash and refill as needed. Lots of places sold cards like that, and many of them didn't have security cameras, since tracking buyers would be bad for business. In all likelihood, the post office box had been opened simply because Pat Durand needed an address to get the credit card, but he was paying the bills online. I'd taken one step forward and one step back. I'd learned the details of Cal's operation, but I'd made no progress in tracking him down.

As I began considering next steps, Shelley's phone rang. I grabbed it, then froze with my finger hovering over the ACCEPT CALL button. If it was Cal, he'd recognize my voice. Same with Nora. Same with Lydia. I hoped whoever was calling would leave a voice mail.

The display said it was an unknown number. A few seconds later, an email popped into my newly created Hiroshigefan Gmail account.

Hello!
I see you're looking for an original print from 100 Famous Views of Edo — I have one. Where are you located?

Pat

I knew how I wanted to reply, but I hadn't considered what name I should use. I swiveled toward my window. One of my best friends in grammar school was named Andrea Brewster. We'd called her Andi.

Hi Pat,
Which one do you have? I'm from New York.

Andi

Hi Andi,
"Flower Pavilion, Dango Slope, Sendagi No. 16" in stock. Do you know it?

Pat

I Googled Hiroshige "Flower Pavilion Dango Slope Sendagi No. 16." The print depicted an exquisite cherry blossom scene. Indistinct figures strolled through the orchard, taking in the astonishing, fleeting beauty.

Hi Pat,
I love it! I want it! Can you send photos?

Andi

Hi Andi,
Will do. I'm on the road right now, so it will be a few hours before I can get them

318

to you, though. Okay?

Pat

Hi Pat,
No problem. I'll be running around all day anyway. Are you a dealer?

Andi

Hi Andi,
Yes. And you're obviously a collector of great discernment!

Pat

I didn't roll my eyes, but I could have. Pat was treating our exchange like a mating dance. I represented fresh meat. Flattery, he assumed, would boost the price. I decided to let him think his ploy had worked.

Hi Pat,
Thanks! I try.
Where are you located?

Andi

Hi Andi,
Maine. But I get to NYC often. Are you in Manhattan?

Pat

Hi Pat,
I live in Manhattan, but I happen to be in Boston for a few days. Where in Maine?

Andi

Hi Andi,
Bar Harbor. Too far. I can get to Boston.

Pat

Time to slow it down, to think, to regroup, to consult Ellis.

Hi Pat,
Let me check my schedule and get back to you.

Andi

Hi Andi,
Okay. Talk soon!

Pat

I checked the voice mail on the phone I was now thinking of as Andi's.

"Sorry I missed you. I'm calling about a fabulous Hiroshige print that meets your specifications. I'll email you now."

"What?" I said aloud, confused.

Pat's voice sounded female. *How could that be?* Anita had identified Cal as her cus-

320

tomer, Pat Durand. My brows drew together. It seemed Cal had a partner after all. *Who is she?* It wasn't anyone I knew. She had a faint British accent, as if she'd been reared in England but had lived here for decades.

I called Ellis.

Ellis didn't speak, but he didn't need to. His attitude was apparent from his icy stare.

We sat in a booth at the Rocky Point Diner. We each had a coffee. Outside, the clouds were thickening.

Ellis stretched out his arm, palm up. "Give me the phone."

"Why?"

"I need to have that voice mail analyzed."

"I thought I would text Pat Durand."

"Why text?"

"Whoever is behind this scam might recognize my voice."

His lips tightened. "Yet another reason for you to let us take it from here." He stretched out his arm, palm up. "Give me the phone."

I slid the phone across the table. "I thought I was helping."

"You agreed to consult me *before* you took action." His eyes remained unrelenting. "You don't know what you're getting yourself into, Josie. If Cal or whoever is

321

behind this is a killer, your life may be in danger. Even if he's merely a crook, he may feel cornered and become deadly. These conditions require finesse. To make matters worse, your well-intentioned efforts may chase him deeper into the woods."

I swallowed hard, abashed. "What can I do?"

His hand closed over the phone. "I'll get back to you on that." He relented. "I know you thought you were helping."

He slid out of the booth and left.

I sat in my car and called Max. I explained the situation and asked his opinion. "I know I messed up. How can I make it right?"

"How about if I call Ellis on your behalf and offer your assistance in fielding any calls or texts. I'll make it clear your only interest in this is your appraisal, but that since your interest might run alongside his interest, you're eager to cooperate."

"You make it sound so easy, Max. I'm glad you're on my side."

I was almost back to my office when I remembered Quentin's Spy Shop. I'd passed it each time I visited Anita's boutique inside Murphy's Interiors. I backtracked to Route 1, parked near the front, and went inside. I approached the shop and found my attention riveted to the video playing on a TV just inside Quentin's. A woman was demonstrating how to use a hidden voice recorder built into a lipstick.

Twenty minutes later I was back in my car, the proud owner of a voice-changing machine. One of the settings was a female with a slight British accent. It looked like Cal didn't have a partner after all.

CHAPTER TWENTY-FIVE

Fred was hot on the trail of another guitar, so I called his contact at the Mississippi Department of Revenue, Heather Jan Lassiter. She was surprised at my request.

"As I told your associate, we never release personal information. Individual tax records are personal."

"I don't need to know anything about Ms. Dowler's taxes. I just need her address."

"Her address is personal."

"Darn! I really need to talk to her. There's no possible bad outcome. I'm trying to trace an antique."

"I'm sorry, but I can't help."

I thanked her for her time and hung up.

I called the city clerk's office and spoke to another nice woman who, like Heather Jan, refused to release personal information.

"Is there anyone there close to retirement? Someone who would have been on the job in the early 1970s?"

"Why?"

"I have an off-the-wall question about Clarksdale in 1971. I know, I know . . . that's not something you hear every day, is it?" I laughed. "Who do you think I should talk to?"

"You're right, that's not an everyday request. You should talk to Jay Malc. He's an engineer with the county. He's retiring at the end of the year, and he knows everything about Clarksdale from long before I was born."

She gave me Jay Malc's full name, Jay Malcom Curtis, and his extension number, then transferred me.

Jay Malc Curtis answered on the first ring. He had a deep baritone, a radio voice.

"I'm an antiques appraiser calling from New Hampshire. I have a question that will, I suspect, surprise you . . . To complete an appraisal, I need to speak to Marianne Dowler, and I'm having trouble finding her. I know she lived in Clarksdale in 1971, and I know Clarksdale isn't all that large. Since you've been in the workforce since about then, I was hoping you might know her."

"Know Marianne Dowler! Sure I do. She went by Mari Mae. I haven't thought about Mari Mae in years. We went to the same high school. Mari Mae and I worked together on a science fair project our senior year. She was truly special — smart, hard-working, dedicated."

I did a private fist pump. There was nothing as exhilarating as moving an investigation forward. "Did she leave Clarksdale after school?"

"That's right. She went north to college. She got herself a scholarship at Temple."

"In Philadelphia. Where is she now, do you know?"

"I'm not rightly sure. Mari Mae used to come home now and again — I don't know why, to tell you the truth, since she didn't have any family left. I haven't seen her in . . . I'm guessing it's fifteen years, maybe more. She married a Yankee, I know that for certain. He was from Boston, I think."

I crossed my fingers. "Do you recall his name?"

"Rayburn Sanford. She called him Ray. Said he was her ray of sunshine."

"That's sweet, isn't it? What did she study at Temple?"

"Psychology. She went on and got a Ph.D. From New York University, I think it was, but I'm not sure about that."

"You've been very helpful, Mr. Curtis. May I have your home or cell phone number in case I need to reach you again?"

"Sure."

He called out both numbers.

"When did you graduate high school?"

"Nineteen seventy. Can you believe it? I started here with the county in 1975, and I've been here ever since. More than forty years."

I congratulated him on his retirement, then listened as he told me how he and his wife were going on a cruise to Tahiti to celebrate. While he spoke, I Googled "Marianne Sanford" and "Boston."

Marianne and Rayburn Sanford lived in Amesbury, an affluent suburb of Boston. Ray was a psychiatrist in private practice. Marianne was a professor at Rockport University, with three books and more than fifty peer-reviewed articles under her belt.

I thanked Jay Malc and called Marianne's office number. It went directly to voice mail.

"Dr. Sanford, my name is Josie Prescott." I explained who I was and where my company was located. "I have a question about a guitar you sold to Abbot's Musical Instruments in 1971." I gave her my contact information, then added, "I know this must come as a surprise to you. I look forward to filling you in. I think you'll be pleased!"

I walked into the front office. Gretchen was

smiling at her computer monitor like a cheerleader facing adoring fans.

"You look like you just won the lottery," I said, grinning.

"I think I've exceeded your expectations." She spun the monitor 180 degrees so I could see it. "This is a vanda orchid. Can you believe that color?"

The blossom was dazzling, a rich blue, closer to purple than turquoise, specked with white. The blossoms were large, four inches or more.

"It's gorgeous!"

"Do you think Gertie Joan will like it?"

"How could she not? Where would you buy it?"

"There's a place in Jackson. They've agreed to give Gertie Joan lessons."

"Perfect!"

Matt Janson, the owner of Janson's Antiques Mall who'd asked me to lunch to discuss his plans to expand his business, was waiting by the Blue Dolphin's hostess stand when I arrived for our twelve thirty date. He greeted me warmly, taking my right hand in both of his and giving it a gentle squeeze.

After we ordered and our drinks had arrived, iced tea for him, hot tea for me, Matt said, "I've been impatient waiting for this lunch."

"Tell me what's going on."

"I want us to be partners."

"You do?"

"You said it yourself — I should open a second location. I want us to do it together."

"You need the money?"

"No. I need you."

I leaned back and smiled. "I'm intrigued. Where are you thinking?"

"Where do tourists go?"

"Rocky Point Beach."

"Too close to my current location."

"You're going to Maine."

"Why not Vermont?"

"Too saturated. York Beach?"

"Too close."

"Wow. Portland. A more populated location lends itself to a year-round business."

"Want to go in with me? Now that you have a TV show, you're a big draw. I've had this idea for a while. I've been working up the courage to approach you."

"Ha, ha."

"I'm serious. I didn't want to come to you with a half-baked proposal. At this point, I'm closer to three-quarters baked, so I feel comfortable pitching it."

"How would it work?"

"We'd call it Prescott's Antiques Mall. It would look like my barn. We share start-up costs. I'll be the COO, chief operating officer. You'll be the CEO, chief executive officer. We split the profits. What do you say?"

"I say maybe. I'm interested. I need to think about it."

"Sure. Take as long as you need. But know this, Josie . . . it would be an honor being your partner."

"Thank you, Matt. I feel the same. All I have to do is look at your place to see what you're capable of. You've made a wonderful business there."

"Out of nothing."

"Don't exaggerate. There was a barn."

"And a field. What do you think — should I add a petting zoo?"

"To bring in families? Don't they already shop there?"

"Yeah. But I've got the land."

"I wouldn't do it. Too labor intensive."

"A tea shop?"

"To bring in more women? Aren't they already your primary demographic?"

"They'll stay longer. Make a day of it. Bring their girlfriends."

"Maybe. But only as a concession."

Matt patted my shoulder. "See. I knew we'd be a great team."

I smiled and raised my tea cup for a toast. "To us."

Marianne Sanford called back at four Monday afternoon.

"I can't remember ever being as astonished as I was listening to your message," she said. "I haven't thought of that guitar in a thousand years. Maybe two thousand."

I could hear a hint of Mississippi in her voice.

"I can only imagine. I think the guitar I'm appraising is the one you sold back in 1971. I'm hoping you can tell me its history."

"Why? What possible reason could there be for you asking that question?"

"Provenance. I need to show an unbroken chain of ownership from the time of manufacture to now. Martin sold fourteen of this model guitar that year, but all the stores Martin sold them to are out of business, and their records are long gone. I can't go forward, so I need to go backward. So far I have traced the guitar to Abbot's Musical Instruments, where their records show you as the seller. To continue the chain, I need to know how you acquired the guitar. What can you tell me about it?"

Seconds ticked by. If Dr. Sanford shut me down, our hunt was probably over.

"I'm sorry."

"I understand this may be asking you to think about something you don't want to think about. If it wasn't crucial, I wouldn't ask."

More time passed, a minute or longer.

"I'm sorry," she repeated. "I'm not comfortable discussing it. I'd better go."

She hung up.

I slapped the desk, frustrated with myself. I knew better. You could have all the antiques knowledge in the world, but if you couldn't read people, you were certain to fail, and I'd just messed up. There was some kind of secret associated with Frank's guitar, and I might have squandered my only opportunity to learn it. I should have read her mood better. I should have been more sensitive. I should have eased into my questions. *Shoulda. Woulda. Coulda.*

Pat Durand emailed a photo of *Flower Pavilion, Dango Slope, Sendagi,* number 16, a stock shot, probably an image she — or he — found on the Internet. I realized that since the voice on the message had been female, I was now thinking of Pat as a woman.

I called Max but got his voice mail. In case you were in the throes of a legal emergency,

332

he invited you to call his cell phone. I didn't want to bother him, and I could easily wait until morning. It was probably a good thing to keep Pat Durand on pins and needles.

I stared at the image. Cherry blossom season in Japan is a time of celebration and joy, and it showed in this print. The trees were lush, the blossoms white, tinged with pink. Unlike the loneliness and isolation shown in most of the prints in the series, several people, though their faces were generically drawn, interacted with one another. Others reclined on benches under the trees, their eyes on the blossoms. The print exuded a soothing and reflective mood, evocative of innocence and a more peaceful time.

I confirmed that Pat only sent the one photo. She hadn't included a shot of the print's back, which any reputable dealer would have done. Not only can potential buyers discover flaws such as foxing or water stains, which might be hard to spot in a busy design, but marks indicating authenticity, such as labels, gallery notations, or signatures, can be examined, and if expected marks are missing, that needs to be noted, too.

Cal was not Pat Durand. Cal would know

better. Pat Durand — presumably Cal's partner — was an amateur.

CHAPTER TWENTY-SIX

Tuesday morning, I woke up just before the alarm went off at seven. Ty was organizing a training session at the Portland, Maine, office, and he liked to be at his desk before everyone else, so he left home around six thirty. I stumbled downstairs, poured myself a cup of coffee from the pot he'd left on the burner, and found an I-love-you note on the counter. I pressed it to my chest, to my heart.

At eight, I called Max and got him.

"Your timing is good. I'm just sitting down at my desk with a coffee. How can I help?"

"Two things. I want to run a business expansion opportunity by you and get your read on it, and I got an email from that Pat Durand person. I'd like to arrange a phone call with her — I'm calling Pat 'her' since the voice on the phone is female — anytime tomorrow morning."

"How about you come in at nine and schedule your call to Pat Durand at ten thirty? We can talk about the business thing first. I'll have the police come at ten to get everything set up. Does that work?"

I said I'd bring some of Noeleen's muffins, and I could hear him smack his lips.

At ten, I was in my office. I emailed Pat Durand a thank-you, and asked if she could call me at 10:30 tomorrow morning. Two minutes later, she replied saying 10:30 was perfect.

I'd caught up on emails, and I was deep into reviewing my accountant's latest good-news report when Sasha called to update me on Mo's print. While she hadn't yet located any verified originals we could use to validate the woodgrain pattern she'd spotted in the print, Richardson Antiques in England had been helpful. They'd given her the name of the portfolio's former owner, a widow. It seemed that the widow had found the portfolio in a trunk after her husband's death, that she hadn't seen it or heard about it in twenty-two years of marriage, and that she had no documentation, so Sasha wasn't hopeful she'd get any useful information, but she planned to talk to her anyway.

"As you suspected from the start, we'll need to send it out for a materials analysis," I said. "I want every *i* dotted and every *t* crossed."

Sasha said she'd get quotes, and I thanked her. The fact that the portfolio had been found in a trunk was encouraging. If the prints hadn't been exposed to light, that might explain why the colors were so vivid.

Dr. Marianne Sanford's class schedule was posted on the Rockport University's website. She was teaching Principles of Social Psychology today from 10:00 to 11:15 A.M. The classroom wasn't listed, but her office was, W-396 in Westover Hall. I checked the campus map and saw that Westover Hall was one of four buildings surrounding a spacious stone courtyard. Parking lot 4 was closest. I glanced at the clock on my monitor. It read 10:20. Rockport was only about a twenty-five-minute drive. Call it a half hour each way and a half hour to talk, I should be back by noon or twelve thirty at the latest. Mo's funeral was scheduled for two. I had plenty of time.

Rockport University was located on a thirty-five-acre campus. The entire place, from the ivy-covered fieldstone buildings and meticu-

337

lously groomed grounds to the fresh-faced students and courteous staff, seemed unreal, as if it had been staged for a movie.

The parking security guard cheerfully directed me to a visitor's spot. A gilt-edged sign pointed me toward Westover Hall. A wide marble staircase took me to the second floor. A glass-fronted cabinet listed all this semester's psychology courses. At thirteen minutes after eleven, I stood just outside room W-208, an auditorium-style classroom, where Dr. Sanford was finishing up her lecture.

At eleven fifteen exactly, the double doors burst open and scores of students rushed out. I pressed myself against the wall, avoiding the deluge. The river quieted to a stream, then a trickle, then stopped. Dr. Sanford stepped out. She looked just like the photo posted on Rockport University's website. Her chin-length black hair was curly. Her skin was cocoa brown. She had a model's face: prominent cheekbones, a high forehead, a long, slender nose, and a determined chin. She wore a bone-colored cable-knit turtleneck sweater, black slacks, and black leather ankle boots. She carried a red leather briefcase.

I peeled myself off the wall. "Dr. Sanford?"

"Yes?"

"I'm Josie Prescott. I was hoping you had a moment to talk."

"The antiques appraiser."

"Yes. I'm sorry to barge in on you like this, but it's important."

She leveled assessing eyes at me. I didn't waver.

"Follow me."

I walked alongside her down the wide corridor and around a corner to a door with her name on it. She used a key she took from an outside pocket of her briefcase to unlock it.

Books jammed the shelving that lined both side walls. White sheer curtains allowed the light in, and the office was bright. Her desk was messy. Stacks of folders were squeezed between piles of books and an all-in-one computer. Three framed vintage travel posters were mounted on the back wall. One advertised an Eastern Airlines flight to sunny Florida, bragging that it was only a ten-hour flight from New York to Miami. The second one recommended traveling across Australia on the Trans-Australia Railway. The illustration showed a man wearing a duster and a wide-brimmed hat riding a camel. The third featured a cheetah tracking the viewer, its eyes black and piercing. The copy advertised an African safari organized by Imperial Airways.

Dr. Sanford placed her briefcase on the floor and sat behind her desk. "Have a seat."

"You like to travel."

She smiled, and her face was transformed from severe to playful. "More than anything. If I could, I'd never stop."

"What's your favorite place?"

"Jordan for exotic — leaving the airport, I felt like I was walking into the Bible. Bonaire for diving. Paris for romance." She flipped a hand. "It depends. What's yours?"

"I don't have as much experience. I'm on the hunt, though, for the perfect honeymoon location."

"Congratulations. When are you tying the knot?"

"June."

"Beautiful. What do you like to do?"

"Everything. Nothing. I want to gel and swim and snorkel and hike and have nice dinners."

"Go to Maui."

"Maybe. Hawaii's pretty far, though. I hope you don't mind . . . I'm here to ask for information about the guitar."

"Will it be published?"

"If it's ever sold, information about it will appear in a catalogue. But right now the owner simply wants to know how much it's worth — estate planning."

"You're putting me in a difficult position."

"Why is that?"

"I got the guitar from my mother, who got it from her mother. My grandmother went to a lot of trouble to keep the story of how she came to own it private."

"Is she alive?"

"No."

"If the truth became known, who would it hurt?"

"That's a good question." She thought about it for a moment, her eyes on the travel posters. "No one." She refocused on me. "What do you need to know?"

I found my little notebook at the bottom of my tote bag and flipped it open to a blank page. "What is your mom's name?"

"My mom was Lucille Mae Dowler. My grandmother was Estelle Mae Bridges. Want to guess what my middle name is?"

I laughed as I scribbled their names. "Mae."

"How'd you guess?"

"I'm known for my deductive reasoning skills. Plus a man named Jay Malc Curtis called you Mari Mae. That's how I found you."

"Jay Malc! We went to school together. What a great guy he was! Good through and through."

"He said the same about you." This was the moment of truth. "How did your grandmother come to own it?"

"She got it from a boyfriend, Robert Johnson."

"The blues guitarist?"

"Yes. He and my grandmother were . . . well . . . friends."

"When did he give it to her?"

"My grandmother was a proud woman. She never admitted she had an affair with Robert Johnson, though certainly I assumed she had. My brother and I romanticized their relationship."

"She married your grandfather after Johnson's death."

"That's right. He never knew about their involvement. My grandfather was a hard man."

"Hard in what way?"

"He was sarcastic, sniping, but words weren't his only weapon. He was the kind of man who sees you have a sore spot on your foot and accidentally-on-purpose treads on it. I could tell that my mother despised him, that she could barely stand to be in the same room with him, but she never spoke a bad word about him. My family wasn't known for its openness or its communications skills. I knew there was bad blood, but I honored her reticence by not asking any questions about it." She swiveled to face the windows. "Or maybe I just didn't want to know." She spun back and raised her chin, keeping her eyes on my face. "My father died in 1962. My brother died in 1963. My mother died in 1968. I moved in with my grandmother for my last two years of high school. She died in 1970, a month before my graduation. I went through everything my family owned and sold everything I could, including the guitar, to get money to move to Philadelphia. I won a good scholarship to Temple University, but the stipend only covered about half my expenses, to say nothing of transportation."

"That's a lot of loss in a short amount of time."

"Yes."

"What happened to things like photos and papers, you know, birth certificates and so on?"

"I packed them in boxes and left them in a storage unit back in Clarksdale. For decades, I went home every few years, to visit my family's graves, to attend a high school reunion, that sort of thing. The last time, I went for an old high school friend's fiftieth birthday party. After that, I realized

I'd changed. Clarksdale no longer felt like home, so I transferred everything into plastic tubs and shipped them to my house."

"May I go through the contents? I assure you I won't damage anything or take anything without your permission. I'll only be seeking evidence related to the guitar's ownership."

"No one but me has ever looked through them."

I met her resolute stare. "Please."

"It's a privacy thing. I don't like the thought of anyone pawing through my possessions."

"I understand. How about if you do the pawing? I'll be a witness."

She paused again, her eyes once again on the back wall. After a minute, she came back to me. "I don't know. I want to talk it over with my husband. Ray sees the world unvarnished."

"Of course."

She stood up. "You probably think I'm being silly. Sentimental."

"I respect your instinct for privacy. I believe that finding the truth is always worth the effort, though, and that hiding the truth is always a mistake. But that's me."

"If you asked me about a theoretical situation, I'd say the same thing."

"I understand. Life isn't a theory — it's your life."

She took a step, then stopped. "I believe in living my values. You can come and help me go through things."

I nearly bounced out of my seat, but I spoke with calm composure. "Thank you. When is good for you?"

"Friday. I don't come to campus on Fridays."

I walked beside her to the door. "What time?"

She suggested ten, and I agreed. I wrote down her street address, email address, and home phone number, thanked her again, and left.

I was in my car, backing out of the space at 12:02 P.M.

I was thrilled that Dr. Sanford agreed to let me search for documents about the guitar, but I didn't much feel like celebrating. Instead, I rehearsed my eulogy the whole way back to Rocky Point.

CHAPTER TWENTY-SEVEN

I stopped at home to change from my chinos into something more appropriate for a funeral, settling on a black-and-dark-green tweed pleated skirt with a dark green blouse, a black blazer, and low-heeled black pumps. I drove myself to the church, arriving about ten minutes early, and parked in a spot near the front.

A representative from the funeral home handed me a program. I stepped aside to read it. After Pastor Ted spoke and we sang some hymns, those of us scheduled to deliver eulogies would be brought up to the stage one at a time. I was delivering the third eulogy, after Helena, the director of New Hampshire Children First!, and Edna, Mo's principal.

The usher led me to an aisle seat near the front. Helena sat on the aisle across from me. We nodded, acknowledging one another. Frank, Trish, and Lydia sat alone in the front pew on the right.

The service started shortly after two when Willa Como, a classically trained pianist, stepped onto the stage and sat at the organ. She played the prelude, Bach's Cantata BWV 147, "Jesu, Joy of Man's Desiring." Ted came up next, then Willa played three hymns. I joined in the singing. Helene spoke about Mo's core goodness. Edna spoke about her work ethic and the lives she'd touched through her teaching. Then it was my turn.

The church was about three-quarters full. Trish held a lace-edged white handkerchief to her eyes. Her shoulders shook. Frank sat next to her, holding her hand. Lydia's eyes were fixed on her thighs. She'd lost weight, and she looked frail. Nora and her husband, Kevin, were seated about halfway back on the right, next to the other book club members. Ellis sat in the last row on the left. Detective Brownley sat two rows in front of him on the right. Wes was seated at about the midpoint, on an outside aisle.

My heart rate doubled and my mouth went dry as I climbed the stairs. I thanked my escort and took my notes from my jacket pocket. I swept my eyes across the church. Steve, Mo's ex-husband, stood at the back, half hidden by a stone column.

"Mo Shannon was my friend."

Kimberly, Steve's girlfriend, stepped into the church. The funeral director approached her. She shook her head and waved him away.

"Which makes me one of the luckiest people in the world, because when Mo was your friend, you were set for life."

Kimberly crept forward, her eyes on the crowd, angling her head to see around people.

"Mo only saw the good in people, the potential. She believed that people were essentially decent. She didn't merely mouth the words, she lived the life."

Kimberly sidestepped toward the right. Steve kept his eyes on my face.

"She worked with children, both in her job as a teacher and as a volunteer. You've heard of those successes. I witnessed some awe-inspiring moments, like the time she knelt beside a little boy so scared and hurt after enduring years of abuse, he could barely communicate. She whispered to him, always smiling, a portrait of tenderness and devotion. She comforted him enough to trust her, and he let her place him on a horse, his first time. I watched his frozen expression, the face of silent suffering, soften into a smile of wonder and delight.

They set off, Mo leading the pony around the indoor ring, an image of an angel. Mo loved children, and children loved her."

My eyes filled, and I paused. Kimberly turned her head and spotted Steve, pinning him with her eyes. She walked slowly, deliberately, toward him. Steve leaned against the column. As far as I could see, Steve had no idea Kimberly was in the nave.

"Mo loved Japanese woodblock prints. I asked her what it was about them that spoke to her. She said it was the duality. Muted colors that communicate vibrancy. Isolated settings packed with life. Two dimensions communicating a three-dimensional narrative. This duality could be seen in Mo herself. Mo was reserved and introspective, yet when she walked into a room, people gravitated toward her, wanting to know her. Mo was quiet yet lively. She delved into the dark corners of children's lives, yet all she saw was potential." I paused and looked out into the congregation for a moment. "Mo will stay in my heart forever, a reminder that when we're patient and kind, we bring out the best in one another."

As I descended the steps, I took one last glance at the back. Neither Steve nor Kimberly was in sight.

■ ■ ■

I waited in line to pay my respects to Mo's family. The temperature had dropped during the service into the fifties, and the cold got inside me.

Frank embraced me, a bear hug. "Thank you, Josie."

"Frank . . . my condolences."

He gave me a final squeeze, and I moved on to Trish. Her face was gaunt. Her eyes were swollen and moist.

"I'm so sorry, Trish."

"Thank you for those beautiful remarks, Josie. It helps a bit."

I touched her forearm. Lydia stood two paces away, alone despite the crowd, as rigid as a fence post. She stared at me.

"Lydia, I'm sorry for your loss."

Pastor Ted walked up in time to hear my comment and Lydia's reply.

"I know."

Before I could formulate a response, Pastor Ted nodded at me and touched Lydia's shoulder. "I'll stand here beside you, Lydia."

I acknowledged Ted's kindness with a brief smile and walked slowly to my car, trying to account for Lydia's apparent malice, but I couldn't. She was as sharp as a porcupine needle and just as cuddly, and that was simply who she was, at a garden party, viewing art, or at her sister's funeral. It felt personal, but it wasn't.

"So what did you think?"

I spun toward the voice. It was Wes.

"Hi, Wes. I thought it was a lovely service."

"You got anything for me?"

"No. You?"

He glanced over both his shoulders, then lowered his voice. "I think Lydia's involved."

Incredulity froze my words.

"I know. It's a super-shockeroonie."

"My God, Wes — what do you know?"

He grinned. "Nothing. I'm just thinking aloud." He turned around to face the receiving line. "I mean, jeesh! Look at her. She looks like she's made of stone."

"She's grieving, Wes."

"If your sister was murdered, wouldn't you show a little emotion at the funeral?"

"We shouldn't judge."

"That's what you always say because you're so nice."

I smiled at his backhanded compliment.

Kevin Burke walked Nora to her car. Her eyes were red, and her blond hair was in disarray. She clutched a wadded-up tissue in her hand. Kevin turned her to face him and said something. She wrapped her arms around his shoulders, pressing her cheek into his chest. After a moment, he pulled back and kissed her. She touched his cheek. They looked like a couple in love. Kevin stood beside her car until she belted herself in. As she pulled out of her spot, they waved to one another, and he walked to a pickup truck two rows away. Presumably, they'd driven separately because they came from work. I was about to ask Wes if he had any other news when I noticed Chester's black sedan on the street. With all the traffic, it was easy to miss.

"I have to go," I said.

"Why? What's going on?"

"Nothing. I'll call you."

I jumped into my car and got it started. To distract Wes, I waited for a minute, fiddling with the radio setting, then checking my phone for messages. I gave a quick finger flutter and pulled out, turning left, toward my company. I was six cars behind Nora, and three behind Chester. Vehicles peeled off, and others joined the flow. Soon only one car separated Chester from Nora, and two separated me from him.

A half mile farther on, just after we turned onto Main, Nora sailed through a yellow light. The car ahead of Chester stopped for the red, trapping him. I spun right, turning quickly onto Milo Street, then zipped left onto Lister Road, a residential street that ran parallel to Main. I sped up. At Tapson, I turned left, rejoining Main, only two cars back of Nora. Chester wasn't in sight.

Nora made a right onto Islington. Three miles down, she parked in front of Anthony's Shoe Repair. I drove past her, pulled a quick U-turn, and parked diagonally across the street. I had an unobstructed view of the entrance. Nora leaned her head against her steering wheel, clutching it as if it were a life ring, and wept. After a minute, she sat up and wiped away the wetness with a tissue. Her chest heaved as she inhaled deeply, trying to pull herself together. Another minute passed before she opened her car door.

I slunk down, holding my arm up to block my face while allowing myself a clear view, but it wasn't necessary. Nora was so wrapped up in whatever was going on within herself, she didn't even glance around. She dragged herself into the shoe repair shop as if she were facing the gallows. I agreed with Chester. That Nora used this cobbler made no sense.

The sun slanted off the plate glass window, so I couldn't see inside, but from the steady foot traffic, I could see that the shop was busy.

I waited.

After about ten minutes, I called my office. Cara told me everything was fine and asked about the funeral. Fred, she said, was out meeting with a curator about an unsigned Impressionist-style painting we'd acquired in an estate sale. Eric was outside, overseeing a crew he'd hired to clean the gutters. Cara passed me on to Sasha. Sasha read me catalogue copy for some marbles we'd bought about two years earlier* that were going to be featured in an antique toy auction next spring. I approved it. I spoke to Gretchen next, who gave Melissa Sayers, our new part-time employee, a glowing review. When I was done, I checked the time. Nora had been inside the store for nearly thirty minutes.

I called the Rocky Point Police Department, and Cathy, a civilian admin, told me Ellis wasn't available. She transferred me to his voice mail. "Ellis, I'm at Anthony's Shoe Repair." I gave him the address. "I know how odd this might sound, but Nora Burke went in more than half an hour ago, and she hasn't come out. It's possible she's

* Please see *Glow of Death*.

meeting Cal. Anyway, I thought I should let you know."

I texted Wes: *Can you find out about Anthony's Shoe Repair on Islington?*

Ten minutes later, phone in hand so I wouldn't miss a response from either of them, I got out and looked around. The neighborhood was just as Chester had described it, solidly middle class, decent but uninteresting. Harvey's Market, a discount grocery store, was two blocks down on Islington. Anthony's Shoe Repair was one of a series of small shops that ran for a block. An Italian deli was on one side, and a small convenience store was on the other. Across the street, two-family houses shared driveways and minuscule front yards. Every house was freshly painted, though. There were curtains on the windows and flowers in the gardens. I locked my car, waited for the traffic to slow, and crossed the street.

CHAPTER TWENTY-EIGHT

Anthony's Shoe Repair looked like every other cobbler's storefront I'd ever been in. Cubbyholes lined the left wall, displaying everything from shoe dye, shoe polish, and shoelaces to umbrellas, rain boots, and plastic ponchos. A cash register sat on the counter toward the rear alongside an old-fashioned cast-iron receipt spike, half filled with pink slips. A short old man with rounded shoulders, wrinkles on wrinkles, and a thick white mustache stood behind the counter. I wondered if he was Anthony.

I eased a red umbrella from the stack and pretended to read the label, half turning toward the rear so I could continue my assessment.

Two raised shoeshine chairs abutted the wall to my right, both empty. Next to them was a door bearing a gold-and-black paper sign, the corners curled with age, that read PRIVATE. In back of the old man, a chest-high counter allowed him to pass items back and forth to a man in the rear. That man was taller and broader than the man in front, and about half his age. He stood in profile, hammering something on a worktable I couldn't see.

Nora was nowhere in sight.

A woman hurried in and placed a pink receipt on the counter. The old man held it close to his eyes, then turned to a shelf behind him and found her bag. She paid in cash, and he added the paper to the stack on the spike. The transaction took about a minute.

Where was Nora?

A man in a gray suit that could have used pressing entered the shop and plodded to the door marked PRIVATE. Without saying a word, he opened it and passed through. I had enough time before the door swung closed to see a flight of steps leading down.

I slipped the umbrella back into place and smiled as I approached the counter. "Hi. I'm looking for Nora Burke."

"Who?"

"Nora Burke."

He shook his head. "I don't know a Nora Burke."

"I saw her come in here about forty minutes ago."

"A customer, maybe. She left."

"No. She didn't come out. Her car is here."

He shrugged and turned his back on me.

"I need to talk to her. It's important."

He didn't turn around.

I looked past him. The man in the back was working a wheel, spinning it forward, then backward. It made a grinding noise, louder when he rolled forward than when he rolled back.

I sidled to the door marked PRIVATE, and with my eyes on the back of the old man's head, I patted the air in back of me until I found the doorknob. I turned it slowly and tugged gently. It opened soundlessly. I crossed the threshold and eased the door closed. To my ears, the latch clicking home sounded as loud as a jackhammer. I was standing in a windowless whitewashed stairwell under a single lightbulb covered by a white glass globe. Muted sounds drifted up from the basement, a chair being dragged across a concrete floor, perhaps, followed by a man's rumbling laughter and rustling papers.

I took a step down, and the wood creaked. I froze for three seconds, then continued, leaning heavily on the railing to mitigate the squeals of old wood. Eight steps down, I

358

reached a half-landing. The staircase turned to the left. I counted six additional steps. At the bottom, I stood on a square landing facing a closed door. I placed my ear against the door, and sounds resolved into words.

Two men were talking, one a baritone, the other a tenor.

"You know anyone who's been to Lake Worth, Florida?" the baritone asked.

"Sure. It's a nice residential area, you know, a little suburban, quiet. My aunt is down there and likes it."

"Then my wife won't." He laughed, the same rumble I'd heard at the top of the stairwell. "My Bea likes a little pizzazz."

"Take her to Miami. South Beach."

"That's what I'm thinking."

I took a to-my-toes calming breath and exhaled slowly through my mouth, opened the door, and stepped into a big room with narrow frosted-glass windows running along the front of the building. A stack of metal pipes lined the floor underneath the windows. The room was as large as a basketball court. The two men I'd heard talking were sitting at a battered round table. One held a copy of today's *Seacoast Star;* the other was busy with a crossword puzzle. The table was the kind used at banquets, set for eight or ten. Without a tablecloth, all its nicks and chips showed.

I counted five doors. The one opposite the windows, to my right, was labeled with the same kind of sign as the door I walked through: PRIVATE. Two doors opposite from where I stood read MEN and LADIES, a nonamusing misalignment — men are men, but women better be ladies. To my immediate left were two more doors, both unlabeled.

The man holding the newspaper lowered it to the table and stood. He was big and burly, and nearly bald. "Can I help you?"

"Where am I?"

His forehead creased. "Downstairs."

"I know that, but what is this place?"

"A social club. Who are you?"

"Josie Prescott. Who are you?"

"What do you want?"

"I'm looking for Nora Burke." I sent my eyes around. "Where is she?"

He took two steps toward me. "You're in the wrong place, lady. This is a members-only club. You need to leave."

I turned to the door marked PRIVATE. "What's in there?"

"Nothing for you."

I walked toward it.

"Stop!" he bellowed.

I stopped and met his eyes, and shivers

ran up my spine like a spider. "Sorry." I back-stepped to the staircase door.

"Who are you again?"

"Josie Prescott, an antiques appraiser. I don't want any trouble. I just need to talk to Nora. I thought she was here."

The tenor stood and watched our interaction as if it were a tennis match. My phone vibrated, and the baritone's gaze shifted to my hand. It was Wes, calling from his office at the *Seacoast Star.*

The man stomped toward me and grasped my arm, rotating my hand palm up so he could see the phone display. "Are you kidding me? You're a reporter?"

"No. I told you. I'm an antiques appraiser. This call is about advertising my company's weekly tag sale."

The baritone snatched the phone. I reached to grab it back, but he kept me at bay with one outstretched arm. I stopped trying to recover it, and he pushed me backward, not too hard or far.

"What's your password?"

"Come on. You want me to go . . . I'll go. No harm. No foul."

"That ship sailed by. What's your password?"

"Six eight two eight."

He tapped the numbers in, brought up

361

my text log, and raised his eyes to mine. "This ain't no ad. You asked a reporter to check out Anthony's." He opened the telephone window. "Are you kidding me? Your last call was to the police?" He turned to the other man. "Tell 'em." As the tenor ran for the door marked PRIVATE, the man holding my phone wrenched my tote bag from my hand. He dumped the contents onto the table. He flipped open my wallet and thumbed my license out. "Well, at least you gave your right name." He tossed my phone onto the pile.

Grasping my arm with a viselike grip, he walked me across to one of the unmarked doors, yanked it open, shoved me in, and slammed it shut. His shove catapulted me into some plastic shelving that lined the back wall. I toppled to the ground as empty plastic storage containers and packages of paper goods rained down on me. The snick of the lock turning resonated like church bells. Struggling to my feet, I grabbed the doorknob and pulled. Nothing. I turned it and pushed. Nothing. I pounded on the panels. Nothing.

"Let me out!" I hollered. "Help! Help! Help!"

Silence.

I was trapped.

I heard people calling out instructions, but the words were indistinct.

"Let me out!" I shouted again. "Help! Help! Help!"

Scraping sounds told me things were being moved around. What if they edged a table under the doorknob?

Help didn't come.

Slender threads of light showed me where the door met the frame. I reached for my flashlight, pulled gently to activate the retractable cord, and examined my prison.

The shelving I'd crashed into was made of hard gray plastic. White plastic tubs on the bottom shelves hadn't fallen. Each one contained a pile of food prep, serving, or eating objects, including shish kebob skewers, spatulas, slotted spoons, flatware, steak knives, and two-pronged corn holders. It took me five steps to walk from the door to the back wall and seven side to side. A fluorescent light fixture was mounted overhead, but there was no switch.

I closed my eyes, then opened them. I had no time for self-flagellation. Later, I could beat myself up, but not now.

The rumblings and rasps from outside continued unabated.

Three cabinet hinges were attached on the inside. I could remove them, and the door would fall forward, held in place only by the lock.

I needed a screwdriver. I opened every drawer and cabinet and found lots of pots and pans and dishes, but no tools.

I tried the skewer first, but the point was too thick. I used one of the prongs on a corn holder, and it fit, but snapped off. I tried another, and it snapped off, too. Tears of frustration welled in my eyes. I tried a regular knife. Too wide. A butter knife. Too rounded. I reached for a fork, certain the tine would be too large and too blunted, but it fit as if it had been designed for the job. It took less than a minute to remove the two screws. I placed them and the two parts of the hinge in a bowl and started work on the middle hinge.

The noise stopped as suddenly as it had started.

The quiet was even more alarming than the noise had been. They'd left me locked in a dark closet. I told myself to keep focused on the task at hand, to work the problem, to not make things worse by succumbing to paralyzing fear.

Five minutes later, I slipped the last hinge and set of screws into the bowl. I tapped the door, once, twice, then pushed harder. It collapsed at a crazy angle, the lock holding the left side mostly in place. On the right, a two-foot gap allowed me to view part of the room. I eased my head and shoulders through and looked around.

The place was deserted. The door to the room marked PRIVATE stood open, revealing another large room, an outside loading dock with the doors ajar, and the alley that ran behind the building.

Using the flats of both hands, I thrust the door forward, and it opened an additional inch. I rammed it with my shoulder, and the wood around the lock cracked. I rubbed my shoulder. I'd have a heck of a bruise in the morning. I kicked the door, hard, and finally it gave and broke away from the lock, taking some of the frame with it. It landed on the ground with a loud smack.

The contents of my tote bag were heaped on the table, just as I'd last seen them. The bag was on the floor. I grabbed my phone to check the time — unbelievably, only fifteen minutes had passed. I swiped my arm across the table, and everything tumbled into my bag. I was about to dial 9-1-1 when I heard footsteps and froze.

I listened hard but didn't hear anything else. I unlocked my phone. Wes had texted *I'm on it,* a simple reply to my request for information about Anthony's Shoe Repair. I started to call 9-1-1 but couldn't think of what to say. There was no emergency. I decided to call Ellis from my car instead. I started for the stairs, then paused to look into the other room.

Six- and eight-foot rectangular meeting tables were positioned in staggered rows. Dozens of standard-issue metal meeting-room chairs were shoved against the walls. Half a dozen had fallen over. Playing cards were strewn across a felt-topped round table. A roulette wheel sat on another round table. The social club was really an illegal gambling joint, and at the thought that the police were en route, the staff and players had abandoned it willy-nilly. Evidently, Nora was more of a gambler than I realized. Or Cal was here and she'd come to visit him.

I took a step toward the open room and stopped short, groaning in pain. Sharp daggers stabbed at my upper back and left shoulder. I took stock. I did a deep knee bend. I rotated my shoulders forward and backward. I lifted my arms, then swung them back. Nothing was broken. Everything hurt. I ignored the pain and continued walking, pausing in the doorway to send my eyes around.

With people adding cheer and energy, the

room might have been more appealing, although I doubted it. The walls were empty. The windows were painted black. The overhead lighting was harsh. Big, bulky security cameras dotted the ceiling. Rainbows prismed from a mirrored disco ball, circa 1973, coloring the barren tables and scuffed off-white linoleum floor.

I crossed the room, stepped outside onto the concrete platform, and choked on the stench of garbage emanating from a row of old metal trash cans that lined the wall on the left.

A cold east wind whipped through the alley, and I rubbed my upper arms.

The alley was narrow, barely wide enough to accommodate a delivery van. Two cars were parked a few buildings away, their tires up on the weed-filled shoulder. The asphalt was pitted. Tufts of weeds had sprouted in the cracks.

No one was in sight.

Steps at either end of the platform allowed easy access from the alley to the loading dock. I spotted a door on the right two paces from the stairs. I edged my way along the building, hoping to find a window in the door so I could peek in, but it was solid. I tried the knob, turning it gently. It was locked.

I wanted to see if Nora's car was gone. I considered circling the block but decided it would be quicker to go through the building. I was three steps into the casino when I heard footsteps on the concrete loading dock. I dashed to the side wall, detonating spikes of pain in my thighs. Peering through the open doors, I could see a triangle of platform and alley, but not the door. Lydia, still wearing the navy-blue suit she'd worn to church, her small blue purse dangling from her shoulder, climbed down the stairs and hurried to one of the cars. A few seconds later, a car engine turned over; then a vehicle drove by, hitting potholes and kicking up pebbles.

I backed up to the wall and slid to the ground as I tried to make sense of the images and ideas rattling around in my head.

Lydia was here.

That singular fact had to be explained. Lydia had parked in the alley, which meant she knew about the back door or entered the casino through the loading dock. I glanced around. Streaks of violet and yellow light reflecting off the disco ball mottled the floor. What did Lydia have to do with this dilapidated ersatz grandeur? This place was a dump by any standards, depressing and demoralizing. Why would Lydia come here to gamble when she was a member of the upscale Colonial Club? She wouldn't. Lydia wasn't here to gamble — she was here to see Cal. Maybe Lydia came for solace and found Cal with Nora. I used the wall to heave myself upright.

My squabble with the baritone hadn't felt like an emergency; this did. I rooted through my bag for my phone and dialed 9-1-1. I reported that something was wrong in the basement of Anthony's Shoe Repair, then sank onto a gray metal folding chair to wait. A moment later, I realized that Nora and Cal might be injured. I needed to check, to see if I could help.

I zigzagged my way across the casino, avoiding tables and chairs. A dull ache radiated from my back to my legs, adding a layer of misery to the pricks of pain punctuating every step.

I approached the inside door near the closet, the only one I hadn't identified. I held my breath and listened for ten seconds, hearing nothing but the random clicks and creaks of an old building settling, the whirring of a refrigerator in back of me, and a dog barking somewhere outside. I turned the knob. The door opened silently, and I stepped over the threshold into a dimly lit short hall. A closet door on the left stood open. A man's trench coat hung on the rod. A pair of black wingtips sat on the floor.

Three paces down the hall, I came to a bathroom on the right. The fixtures were old and dingy. Two more steps brought me to the end of the hall and the entryway to a room. I stood on the threshold to survey the space. A bureau rested against the front wall, to my right. Drawers were half open, clothes flung aside. A round oak table stood directly in front of me, with two old ladder-back chairs ranged around it. Papers were strewn across the top, and some had fallen to the floor, including a half-hidden issue of *Antiques Insights.* I recognized the cover and felt a judder of comprehension. That was the issue where Rheingold Gallery had been highlighted in the "Small Victories" column. A mattress lay on the floor in back of the table, the bedding all tangled. Leaning out to see to the left, my mouth went desert-dry.

A river of blood had pooled on the vinyl tile.

Cal lay on the floor, faceup, dead. I swallowed a scream. I clamped my teeth onto my bottom lip. His eyes were open. His mouth was closed. The top of his head was dented and matted with blood. Horrified, I covered my mouth with my hand.

I stepped into the room, one tentative step. There was nowhere to hide, no kitchenette, no extra closet, no oversized cupboards. Nora wasn't here. No one was here. I approached Cal's body and squatted, and a blaze of pain jagged up my back. I took his wrist in my hand and felt for a pulse, just in case. There was none.

I stood, stunned. *Cal is dead.* The words echoed in my brain. *Cal is dead.* I couldn't bear to look at his bloody corpse, but I couldn't look away. *Cal is dead.* It took a minute or more before I was able to think. Seemingly unrelated facts and observations clattered against one another as I stared, unseeing, at his body.

I turned to the clutter on and near the table. The issue of *Antiques Insights* answered the niggling question about why Cal chose Rheingold Gallery. He didn't study his options — he simply scanned the article, saw that Rheingold sold Japanese art, and figured it would serve his purpose just fine. Maybe he visited the gallery's website and discovered its logo was easy to download. He never expected to be challenged because he never expected Mo to appraise the print. I walked around the room, examining every flat surface. I crouched over to see into the open drawers. There wasn't a computer in sight. Lydia hadn't been carrying anything except a small shoulder bag. Someone else had been here and had ransacked the place. Nora?

Someone hammered on the outside door, breaking into my inchoate thoughts.

Before I could decide what to do, footsteps pounded down the stairs, and a moment later, the inside door was flung open. Two uniformed officers I didn't know burst into the hall with their guns drawn, aiming them at my chest.

CHAPTER TWENTY-NINE

Four hours later, just after nine, I sat chin deep in my hot tub griping to Ty about being kept at the police station for two hours. One jet shot hot bubbles at my left shoulder blade. Others were aimed at my lower back and legs. I'd hung scores of miniature Japanese lanterns along the path from the back door and around the patio and hot tub, and streaks of muted orange stippled the churning water. Ty sat on the wooden deck, his legs dangling toward the lawn, cooling down in the chill night air.

He drank water from a plastic bottle. "Two hours isn't unreasonable."

"Spoken like an ex-cop. I finished my statement in thirty minutes. I looked at mug shots and worked with a sketch artist for another hour. Then they had me sit around and do nothing until I begged to be sprung."

"You refused medical treatment, so they assumed you were okay."

"I was. I am. What does that have to do with wasting my time?"

"They needed you to be available in case more questions came up, and don't forget, you found the body."

I huffed, leaned my head against the rubberized edge, and closed my eyes.

"I can tell the difference between a recalcitrant witness and a weary one." Ty's voice softened. "You're in the weary category. Are you sure you're okay, babe?"

I opened my eyes. "You're so wonderful, Ty. I'm fine." I closed my eyes again. "Weary is the right word, though. Along with a little beat up. Mental note to self: Next time you're locked in a closet, don't use your shoulder to batter down the door."

"Good tip."

"Ellis was surprised that I couldn't ID the thug who tossed me in there."

"Because you couldn't ID him or because he's not in the system?"

"Because he's not in the system. The whole operation operated without any official notice. They're trying to figure out who owns the building and who ran the casino."

"What about the old man upstairs?"

"Anthony. He doesn't know anything about anything, so he says. When I called

Ellis saying that Nora had gone into the shoe repair shop and hadn't come out, he sent Detective Brownley to check. Anthony was as uncommunicative with her as he'd been with me. Ellis was asking for a search warrant when I called nine-one-one."

"What's Anthony's problem?"

"Follow the money. I'm sure someone is paying him off to play dumb, and he doesn't want to ruffle any feathers. He has a sweet deal, and he knows it."

"Anthony's Shoe Repair. That's a helluva front for an illegal gambling club."

"You'd think Rocky Point is a hotbed of gambling. First, Chester's nonprofit casino, now this no-name place located under a genuine business. What's the world coming to if sweet little Rocky Point has turned into a gambling mecca?"

"Don't be naïve. Rocky Point has always been a gambling mecca. Lots of places are. People like to gamble. Let's start with state-sanctioned lottery games. In Rocky Point, there's Gibbon's Tavern, where you'll find a poker game any night of the week in the back room and bingo run through churches and service clubs four or five days a week. And let's not forget the high-stakes mah-jongg game Liz runs out of her suburban colonial."

"How do you know all this?"

Ty kissed the top of my head. "I know everything."

I pretend-slapped my forehead. "Silly me to have forgotten that."

"I've seen you enjoy a good game of gin."

"So true. It was my dad's game. I never play for money, though."

"Who won?"

"Him. All the time. I am a woman of many talents. Cards isn't one of them."

"You're good at all the important things."

I smiled and opened my eyes. "I bet Lydia's still at the station. I was waiting in the lobby when they brought her in. I didn't notice any blood on her clothes, but I'm not sure I would have spotted anything on that dark material."

"Any sign of Nora?"

"None, and Ellis wouldn't tell me a thing. When I reached street level outside Anthony's, her car was gone. I called Wes on my way to the police station to ask if he knew where Nora was. I'd already asked him to check out Anthony's Shoe Repair. I added the building and the casino to his list."

"What did he say?"

I deepened my voice, mimicking an indignant Wes. " 'What do you mean you didn't take any photos?' "

Ty laughed.

I splashed around a little. "Wes had no idea where Nora was and would see what he could ferret out about the other things. Once we know who owns or runs the place, we'll probably know why Cal was staying there. The answer might be nothing more than opportunistic convenience. Cal was a gambler. He knew the social club had an extra room in the back. He asked for a favor, and the powers that be said sure."

"How do you figure Lydia knew where he was?"

"No doubt they've been in touch all along."

"If she helped him avoid the police, they're going to charge her with obstructing justice."

"They've already got her for murder."

"They'll add it on."

"It's horrible. Worse than that, actually, when you think about it, because if she was helping him stay clear of the police after he killed Mo, the justice she obstructed involved her sister. I know she's cold, but surely she cares about finding Mo's killer — unless she killed her, too."

"It's rare that siblings kill one another."

"But not unprecedented. Lydia saw Mo as an obstructionist to her relationship with

Cal. Or maybe Mo found out that Cal had conned her. She warned Lydia she was going to tell the police what he'd done. She would have, too. Mo was that kind of honorable."

Ty lowered himself back into the tub, settling next to me. "And everyone knows that love is blind. If Mo represented a threat to Cal, Lydia would have struck before Mo could follow through."

"I understand. I'd do anything to protect you."

"Would you lie to the police? Hide a killer?"

"Yes."

Ty placed his arm around my sore shoulder and gently stroked my upper arm. "Me, too."

"Good." I snuggled in closer. "One thing Ellis did tell me was about Michelle Michaels, the buyer of the other woodblock print that Pat Durand sold on *Antiques Insights.* I was right — Pat Durand contacted her about buying another print, but she wasn't interested. She said no before Pat told her which one she was selling, so it's just another dead end. It does support the conjecture that both Cal and his female partner were using the name Pat Durand, though. Which is interesting but doesn't bring us any closer to finding her. Ellis also told me that Cal didn't have access to the Langdon Museum's house list. Only the director and the marketing team do. At Ellis's request, the director checked — no mailing has gone out in a month."

"Sometimes knowing what the bad guy *isn't* doing helps you find out what he *is* up to."

"Ellis told me about other dead ends, too. The forensic team didn't find anything significant on the log used to down the wires, and there were so many footprints on the pathway through the woods that they couldn't sort them out. They did find glass shards along the path, though."

"That's something."

"I guess."

We sat quietly for a while. Wisps of misty fog descended on the meadow.

I sank farther underwater, letting the steamy water lap up over my chin. "Maybe Cal's murder has nothing to do with the print. Let's say Lydia hotfooted it to Cal's place immediately after the funeral expecting sympathy; instead, she found him in bed with Nora. Lydia lost it, grabbed something, a baseball bat, for example, and started whaling on him."

"Except there wasn't a bat at the crime

scene, and you said Lydia wasn't carrying anything but a little purse."

"It's possible Nora took it away."

"Lydia kills Nora's lover and she helps cover up the crime? Unlikely."

"True," I said. "Maybe Lydia showed up wanting love, and Cal broke up with her."

"Why?"

"He decided he liked Nora better. No, that doesn't fit. Nora was pretty into her husband when I saw them in the parking lot after the funeral."

"She was putting on an act — she has a guilty conscience."

I slapped the water. "Or . . . or . . . or . . . this is all conjecture, Ty. We don't have any evidence of anything. Not a shred. Lydia didn't use a baseball bat. If Cal played softball, he'd have had a glove. There wasn't one."

"You looked?"

"I noticed. I noticed something else, too. There was no computer. Call me crazy, but I can't see Cal going to the public library to check his email. Ellis told me his phone is missing, too."

"Interesting. Was Cal Pat Durand?"

"I guess we'll find out if Andi Brewster's call goes through as scheduled — after all, dead men can't take phone calls." I repositioned myself to allow the steam and pulsing bubbles to hit my neck. After a moment, I continued. "Ellis asked us to move the call from Max's office to the police station so their tech people can try to trace it. He agrees that Cal might have been working with a partner."

"Lydia."

I rested my head against Ty's shoulder. "Or Nora."

"Are you going to be able to handle it — my achy shaky baby?"

"Ha! There's nothing wrong with me that two ibuprofen and a good night's sleep won't cure." I yawned. "Speaking of sleep . . . I think I'm done. I'm getting pruny."

Ty stood up, and water cascaded from his bathing suit. He reached out a hand and helped me onto the deck. He wrapped a towel around me, and I rubbed myself dry. The night noises soothed me, the birds saying their final good nights and soft rustlings from the woods. I slid my feet into my flip-flops. Ty turned off the jets, drew the cover over the tub, and led the way inside.

As I stepped into the kitchen, a thought struck me with the clarity and force of a meteor, and I fell back against the wall. I clenched the towel closer as the implications and ramifications jostled for position in my brain.

Ty walked toward me, his eyes on my face. "You look like you've just seen a ghost."

"Oh, Ty . . . I need to call Ellis right away . . . I just remembered . . . There was a stack of metal pipes in the social club. The murder weapon was right at hand. Talk about an easy way to dispose of a weapon — all you'd have to do is toss it back in the pile."

CHAPTER THIRTY

Wes called at seven twenty Wednesday morning.

"I've got an info-bomb. Can you meet now? At our dune?"

"Yes."

I got to the beach before Wes. Bundled in my sweater coat, I climbed the dune. I was stiff but not gimpy, and my bruises were colorful and tender to the touch but not debilitating. Nonetheless, I was glad I'd taken some more ibuprofen before I set out.

The day was bright and windless. Golden stars flicked across the dark blue ocean surface. The temperature was just shy of fifty. It would be another perfect autumn day. To the north, a man wearing an anorak walked along the shoreline, his golden retriever darting around a jumble of seaweed. To the south, two older women walked in tandem. One was gesturing wildly. The other was laughing. I wondered what was so funny.

A car screeched to a stop. I turned toward the street and watched Wes step out of his car and shrug into a brown leather jacket as he clambered up the dune.

"Hey, Wes. Nice threads. You look very cosmopolitan."

"Thanks. Maggie got it for me."

"How is she feeling?"

Wes flushed with pleasure. "We had a doctor's appointment yesterday. Mom and baby are perfect!"

I touched his arm. "That's wonderful, Wes."

"Yeah. We're stoked. So you sure landed yourself in the middle of this one, huh?"

"What are you talking about?"

"It looks like Lydia's in the hot seat, and you're the key witness. She's been at the police station all night."

"What evidence do they have?"

"MMO, baby. MMO. Motive: Cal was two-timing Lydia with Nora. Means: It's too early for a definitive analysis, but my police source tells me that the ME found residue from something that might be metal and wood splinters in the wound. The wood could have come from the hardwood flooring, but the metal is foreign to the room, so that means the murder weapon was made

of metal or something like metal, and —
hold on to your hat — there's a pile of metal
pipes at the social club."

Evidently, my late-night call to Ellis had
already reaped a benefit.

Wes continued. "Opportunity: You place
her at the scene. What more do they need?"

"What is Lydia saying?"

"Nothing. She's lawyered up."

I turned toward the ocean. "I can't believe
it. Lydia killed him."

"There's more. Your RFI — I've got it."

"What's an RFI?"

"Request for information. Get with the
program, Joz. You asked about Anthony's
Shoe Repair, the building, and the social
club. The building is owned by a holding
company called PDS, Inc. Wait for it . . .
PDS owns *all* the buildings on that block.
The company is based in Bermuda, a tax
haven extraordinaire. The corporate officers
are all employees of a Hamilton law firm.
They're not talking, natch. There's no way
to tell who really owns it. Anthony's Shoe
Repair rents that space from PDS through
a local property manager. They know nothing except the name of their contact, one of
the Bermuda lawyers. They say they had no
clue that anyone was using the basement.
Ditto PDS. Ditto Anthony, and ditto Antho-

ny's employee, the guy in the back, whose name is Boris. You met Anthony, the old man behind the counter. He identified you from your photo and said you were nosy." Wes chuckled. "In any event, the social club doesn't exist in any formal way. It's not a registered business or charity. The utility charges come through on Anthony's bill. He says he never thought to question it, even though his charges quadrupled after the social club opened about ten months ago. Anthony denies it, but the police think whoever ran the social club was slipping him cash to look the other way to people trooping in and out, and to cover the utilities. Anthony is old school. He doesn't take credit cards, and with an all-cash business, no one, not even a forensic accountant, can verify revenue sources or expenses."

"How can Boris not know something?"

"People only see what they want to see. You know that. You ran into exactly the same issue that time Gretchen went missing.* Employees don't turn in their bosses because you don't bite the hand that feeds you."

I didn't want to believe it, but I knew that Wes was right. "I guess . . . but if nothing

* Please see *Killer Keepsakes*.

else, wouldn't you be curious?"

"Sure, but I'm a journalist. Lots of people think asking questions is just looking for trouble, so they steer clear." Wes extracted his notebook and tugged the pen from the wire casing. He opened to a page marked with a slim black ribbon. "Your turn — fill me in. I want the blow-by-blow. Start with leaving the church after Mo's funeral."

I told Wes everything, including why I was following Nora.

"Describe Cal's apartment."

"It was messy. And sad. There was a chest of drawers, a table and two chairs, and a mattress on the floor, that's it. The drawers were open. Clothes and books and papers were scattered everywhere."

"Like he was a slob?"

"More like someone did a quick search."

"I can't believe you didn't take pictures!"

I gave him an "oh-puhleeze" look, and he sighed, Wesian for disappointment.

"I know you didn't see Lydia whack Cal, but did you hear anything?" he asked.

"Only her footsteps as she left."

He flipped his notebook closed and stuffed the pen back in place.

"Catch ya later!" he said, and started down the dune.

I stood at the top a while longer, watching

the frothy waves roll to shore.

I got into work around eight fifteen. I needed to leave for my meeting with Max around quarter to nine, which meant I had plenty of time to check my email and read updates from my staff. The first thing I did was say hello to Hank and Angela and refresh their food and water. While I waited for the coffee to brew I booted up Gretchen's computer, so I wouldn't have to go upstairs.

Cal was killed in a building owned by PDS, Inc. No one knew who was behind PDS. I brought up a search engine and typed "Trish Shannon" and "first golf win." The first hit linked to a photo from a 1974 Los Angeles newspaper. A younger Trish stood on a golf course, her arms high over her head in a V, smiling with unadulterated joy. The caption read NEWCOMER PATRICIA D. WERNER CELEBRATING HER FIRST PROFESSIONAL WIN. Trish was a nickname for Patricia, and Trish changed her name from Werner to Shannon when she and Frank married. Trish's legal name was Patricia D. Shannon, which meant her initials were PDS. Trish owned the building where Cal was killed.

I had just poured myself a mug of coffee

when the front door swung open and Lydia stepped in.

She looked the worse for wear. She was still wearing the same blue suit she'd worn at the funeral, but now it was crumpled and stained along the hem. Her hair was stringy. Her eyes were red and moist, not as if she'd been crying but as if she were struggling to keep them open.

She closed the door. "I didn't know if you'd be in this early."

"I'm not always."

She drew her hand across her brow. I watched her, my mind racing to guess why she was here.

"Can I get you something?" I asked. "Coffee? Tea?"

"Coffee would be good. Black. Do you have a minute to talk?"

I'd never heard her sound so measured and noncombative. "Sure. Have a seat."

She took the closest guest chair. I poured coffee into a Prescott's mug and brought it to the table.

Lydia cupped the mug, staring through the aromatic steam into the coffee as if she hoped to find answers. After a moment, she lifted her bleary eyes. "The police told me you were at Cal's, that you saw me."

"Yes."

"They're probably going to arrest me for murder. The only reason they haven't is that they don't have the murder weapon and your testimony proves I wasn't carrying it when I left. Unless they think I went back to Cal's place after dropping the weapon and his computer in my car trunk. Can you believe they're that stupid? Who'd go back to a murder scene?"

"Someone who forgot something."

She blinked at me. "Like what?"

"I don't know. Cal's phone. Cash. The coveralls she wore while she killed him."

"You saw me — I wasn't the least bit bloody."

"Thus the coveralls."

"Did you see me carrying coveralls?"

"No."

She lifted a hand. "That's my point." She drank some coffee. "What exactly did you see?"

I was sorting through whether there were any parts I should withhold when she spoke again.

"Trying to figure out a good lie?"

I met her steely glare and looked for signs of grief, but I found none.

"I wish I could help you, Lydia, but I can't. I saw two men in the big room at the bottom of the stairs and you, and that's it."

"Who were the men?"

"I don't know. I couldn't identify them. How did you know where Cal was staying?"

"Why wouldn't I know? Cal was my boyfriend. Of course we were in touch."

"The police must have searched your bag, which means they must have found the phone you used to communicate with him."

"They didn't search anything. I wouldn't let them, and they don't have enough for a warrant."

"You wouldn't be talking so openly about being in touch with Cal if the police didn't know about it. How did they find out?"

She raised her chin, in defiance or a dare, I couldn't tell which, and glowered at me. "I told them. My mother owns the building. I stopped by now and then to check on the place. Sometimes Cal went with me, so when he needed a safe place to stay, he thought of that room. He asked if he could use it, and I said yes."

"Then you knew about the casino."

"No. I haven't been there in a while. I was speechless when Cal told me."

"Who owns it?"

"I have no idea."

"Why didn't you close it down?"

"I planned on it, as soon as Cal left."

"I bet the police were livid with you for lying."

"I don't care. I knew Cal didn't kill my sister, and just because the police ask questions doesn't mean you have to answer them."

"How could you possibly know he didn't kill Mo? He was there. He had a motive. He fled."

"He ran because you were hounding him about that print. For God's sake, he was an expert, but oh no! You knew better. You poisoned Mo's mind with your talk of formal appraisals and insurance riders."

I kept my eyes on her face. She seemed to actually believe what she was saying. Denial, thy name is Lydia.

"You must have seen or heard something," she insisted. "Cal was killed minutes before I arrived."

"I didn't."

She placed her mug on the table and stood. "I shouldn't have come. I don't know what I expected. Mercy, perhaps."

"Mercy?"

"Compassion for my grief, understanding for my need to know." She walked to the door. "Forget it."

As I watched Lydia tramp across the parking lot, I wondered whether she'd fibbed.

Despite saying she'd come to hear what I'd witnessed, I thought it was likely that she had a different agenda completely, that she hadn't expected to learn anything new; rather, she'd hoped to confirm that I hadn't seen her kill the man who'd betrayed her.

The lack of blood on her clothing could be easily explained. She could have worn lightweight plastic coveralls, then turned them inside out, rolled them up, and stuffed them into her waistband where they'd be hidden from view by her jacket. I could understand why the police wouldn't formally charge her with Cal's murder until they found where she'd bought them or dumped them, or both, and the weapon she used to kill him, but I bet they were keeping close tabs on her. I peeked out the window. I wasn't surprised to see Detective Brownley drive by in an unmarked car seconds after Lydia left the lot.

I pulled into the little parking lot behind Max's office and backed into a spot by the rear entry.

Every time I stepped into Max's office, I was reminded that people are complex. He always wore traditional tweedy suits and bow ties, yet in furnishings his taste ran to contemporary. Today's suit was gray. His tie was red with black polka dots. His desk was a slab of black granite perched on stainless steel legs. Black-metal-and-stainless-steel bookcases lined one wall. The guest chairs were black leather and slouchy. The carpet was a red-and-gray block print. The art was abstract, mostly oils, all black-and-white geometric shapes or slashes of red or purple or gold.

Max sat at his desk. I sat in one of the comfy leather chairs. I opened the box of muffins I'd picked up en route, and he dove in.

He tapped a yellow legal pad with his fountain pen. "I've reviewed Matt Janson's business plan. Rather than a partnership, I'm going to recommend that you buy Janson's Antiques Mall outright. Offer Matt a good employment contract with a profit-sharing component. He'll work for you, with his first assignment getting the Maine location up and running while continuing to manage the venue he started and overseeing Prescott's. If it doesn't work out or if he quits and cashes out, that's that. You can shake hands and move on."

"I love it . . . but do you think he'll go for it? I'm sure he expects a cut of everything in perpetuity, which he'd have in a partnership."

394

"Sell it as plenty of profit-earning upside with no risk. He's the one who suggested using Prescott's as the brand."

"You're right. What's my next step?"

"Decide if you want to proceed. If so, we'll get going on due diligence."

"I want to proceed."

"Terrific. I have a good feeling about this, Josie." He finished his muffin. "If it works, you'll go from one location to two plus one in development in a few months."

"Thank you, Max. You're a treasure."

"You, too. You're an ideal client." He switched off his desk lamp and stood. "What do you say . . . should we hitch up our wagon and mosey on over to the police station?"

I stood. "Hitch up our wagon? Mosey?"

"I can't help it. I just tried out for *Oklahoma!*"

"I didn't know you could act."

"Who says I can?"

I laughed. "Or sing."

"Ditto."

"You're too funny."

"That I am."

He held the door, and we agreed to drive separately. I called Matt en route and left a message saying that I wanted to move to

the next step and had some ideas to discuss.
I hoped my news would make his day.

CHAPTER THIRTY-ONE

Katie, the police department's IT tech, was ready to go when Max and I arrived. Police Officer Dawn LeBlanc was there, too. Dawn was short and stocky, with shoulder-length medium brown hair, brown eyes, and a sprinkling of freckles across her nose. She worked for a police force in a nearby town and had helped the Rocky Point police with undercover assignments in the past.* Her job was to play Andi Brewster at the meet.

Ellis led us into Interrogation Room Two, and we took seats around the table. An assistant district attorney named Cheryl Tavery fussed a little about the language Max had written absolving me of responsibility and liability for anything and everything, but finally she signed all four copies. After I signed, too, he distributed them, shook

* Please see *Dolled Up for Murder* and *Glow of Death*.

hands all around, and left.

Ellis sat at the head of the table, to my left, with Cheryl next to him, across from me. Katie was next to her at the foot of the table, surrounded by computer and electronic equipment. Cables snaked across the table from her computer to the phone. Dawn sat next to me, on my right, pen and pad in hand.

Ellis slid the phone unit from the center of the table toward me. "I assume you're all right with our using your phone and voice changer. Probably we could forward the number to a police cell phone and get our own voice changer, but why risk it? I'll see you get them back."

"Of course." I placed my voice changer next to the phone, attached the cable, and tapped the voice changer's screen to bring up the southern-woman option. "My job is to role-play the call with Dawn, is that correct? I play Pat Durand. She plays Andi Brewster."

"Yes, but let's start with you explaining the antiques aspect to Dawn."

I pushed my chair out, angling it so I faced Dawn straight on.

I described Hiroshige's woodblock prints, showed her a photo of *Flower Pavilion,* and detailed how I'd tried to create an impression that Andi was a bit overeager and naïve.

"I'm certain Pat Durand is not an art or antiques expert," I said and explained how Pat hadn't sent any photos of the back of the print. "Pat is involved in art fraud, though, and maybe murder."

"And as such, should be considered armed and dangerous," Ellis said. "Thank you, Josie." To Dawn, he added, "Any questions?"

"Only one — what if Pat Durand doesn't answer our call?"

I jumped in. "Pat is expecting Andi's call, so if she doesn't answer, I think you should hang up, then call back a minute or two later, sounding mystified that Pat isn't there, explaining that the previous hangup was you, that you wanted to confirm the time, blah, blah, blah. What do you think?"

Dawn made a note on her pad. "My goal would be to set another time to talk?"

"I wouldn't. I'd try to set a time to meet without any intermediate steps."

Dawn looked at Ellis. "Sounds good to me. What do you think?"

"I like it. Cheryl? Any objections?"

"I'm always in favor of hurrying things along. Make certain you don't say anything that could be interpreted as entrapment."

"Of course."

399

I looked at Ellis, then Cheryl. "Are you sure I can't do it? We know the voice changer works. Why not?"

Cheryl was brusque. "Because it's police business."

Ellis looked at Dawn. "We'd talked about arranging to meet at the gazebo on the village green. The overhang on the roof will allow Katie to hook up her equipment so it's out of sight. But don't mention it to Pat Durand. Get a commitment to meet in Rocky Point tomorrow afternoon around five. Once she agrees, tell her you'll call her back with a location when you know where you'll be." Ellis caught Katie's eye. "We can delay telling her the location until around four or four thirty — does that give you enough time?"

"We'll be done by then. Plus, my assistant, Curt, and I will be wearing Park Department uniforms. We'll cover the gazebo in tarps and put up 'People Working' and 'Wet Paint' signs. Everyone will think we're whitewashing it."

Ellis rubbed his nose. "Good. Josie? Are you ready?"

"Yes. Someone do a ring, ring, beep for me."

"I'll do it," Cheryl said. *"Brrrrng. Brrrrng. Brrrrng.* Please leave a message at the beep.

Beep."

I closed my eyes. "Pat, I'm sorry I'm missing you. That hangup you just got — that was me. When you didn't pick up I got afraid I had the wrong number or the wrong day or something. Anyway . . . maybe I wrote it wrong in my calendar. It doesn't matter! I hope you're doing fine. I really love that print! Love it! The colors are so incredible. It turns out I'm going to be in Rocky Point, New Hampshire, tomorrow, Thursday, so I'm hoping we can connect around five in the afternoon. Give me a call, okay? I probably won't be able to pick up, but I'll get the message for sure. I'll bring cash, so if the print is as beautiful in person as it is in that photo you sent, we can do the exchange right then and there. Talk to you soon — or rather, see you soon! Bye-bye!" I opened my eyes and looked around the room. "How was that?"

Cheryl smiled. "Masterful. I'm glad you're not a defense attorney I have to face in court."

I felt myself blush at the compliment. "Thanks."

"Talk about a hard act to follow," Dawn said. She dragged the phone unit closer. "I'm ready to go. I don't need to practice."

Ellis turned to me. "What could Pat say

401

that might trip Dawn up?"

"Nothing I can think of. If Pat asks why you like the print, just talk about the beauty of the scene and the colors. If she uses any technical terms, feel free to giggle with embarrassment and ask what they mean."

"Dawn?" Ellis asked.

"I'm good."

"Okay. Let's do it."

Dawn looked at Katie.

"The tracer is up. The recording is on."

Dawn put the phone on speaker and dialed. After six rings, a robotic voice invited Dawn to leave a message. The sound reverberated through the room. She hung up. We sat silently for more than a minute; then Dawn hit REDIAL and waited for the beep. She spoke clearly and confidently, parroting my message, her tone warm and excited. When she was done, she replaced the receiver.

"Well done, Dawn!" Ellis said.

"Now all I have to do is actually talk with a southern accent while maintaining that kind of perkiness. I can handle the southern accent, but the perkiness may kill me."

Everyone laughed.

Ellis stood. "Thank you, Josie. I'll walk you out."

"Good luck, everyone."

When we reached the lobby, Ellis stopped. "It goes without saying that you shouldn't talk about this with anyone, and you shouldn't be on the village green tomorrow afternoon."

"You're more than welcome. I'm glad to help."

Ellis grinned. "Thank you. I appreciate your cooperation very much. No offense intended."

"None taken. I won't talk to anyone about this, and I won't go to the village green tomorrow afternoon."

I had a day to find a place where I could see the gazebo without being seen.

I dug my phone and keys out of my tote bag, then locked it in my trunk. Matt had called back saying he was eager to hear my ideas for the new business venture and asking when I'd like to get together. I didn't want to talk to Matt until my mind was clear, so I texted him that I would call him soon to schedule a time.

I crossed the street and climbed a low dune, relishing the warm September sun. The ocean was green today, darker than emerald, lighter than pine. To the north, far from where I stood, a woman rode a gray stallion along the shoreline, and I thought of Mo.

I sat on the sand, letting the breeze tousle my hair, and stared at the horizon. A thought came to me: What if Lydia was telling the truth, that she hadn't killed Cal? The memory of what I'd overheard at the garden party — Frank and Trish agreeing to kill Cal — remained fresh in my mind. I wondered if anyone had checked them out.

I texted Wes: *Do Frank and Trish have an alibi for Cal's murder?*

My phone vibrated. It was Sasha. I took the call. Sasha had news about Mo's print. The prior owner's great-great-grandfather had been a professor of industrial design at Oxford University, specializing in medical instrumentation design. He'd visited Japan as part of a Dutch delegation before and after the country opened to the West.

"Rangaku," I said, referring to a body of knowledge developed by the Japanese through their relationships with the Dutch. "You've done a great job, Sasha."

She also reported on the quotes to test both the paper and the ink. Greyson Chemicals wasn't the cheapest, but we agreed they were the best, so we decided to go with them.

Moments after our call ended, Wes texted

back: *Airtight. Why?*

My phone vibrated. It was Cara. Dr. Sanford, the woman who sold the Martin guitar to Abbot's back in the early 1970s, was on the line. She was close by and wondered if she could stop in.

"Tell her I'll be there in ten minutes."

I had almost reached my car when Nora pulled into the lot. I stood until she parked and got out of her vehicle, then walked toward her. Everything about her looked tense. A muscle on the side of her neck twitched. Her knees were locked.

I said hello and asked how she was.

"Okay, I guess. I'm pretty freaked out, actually. I can't imagine why they want to talk to me."

"Probably they think you know what Cal was doing at that social club."

Her lips tightened. "Why would they think that?"

"I saw you at Anthony's Shoe Repair yesterday, just before Cal was murdered."

She tried to smile, and failed. "I didn't kill him."

"I believe you."

Her tension eased, just a bit. "Why?"

"Because of how you hugged your husband after Mo's funeral. I know how a woman looks when she's giving a man she

405

used to love a good-bye hug. This wasn't that. You hugged him like he was your safe harbor." I took a step closer and lowered my voice. "Did you break up with Cal?"

"I went there to play bingo."

"The police know you were involved with him."

"That's crazy!"

"I'm sorry."

"I don't know what you think you know, but —"

She broke off when I held up a hand. "Don't. Folks at the Colonial Club reported that you and Cal were an item."

Nora seemed to falter. She closed her eyes for a moment. After a few seconds, she turned toward the ocean. "I'm such a fool."

"Indiscreet, perhaps; not necessarily foolish."

"I acted like a giddy teenager."

"What attracted you to him?"

"You've seen Cal, haven't you? He was gorgeous!"

"I suppose."

She turned back to face me. "You didn't think he was good-looking?"

"I don't think appearance has much to do with attraction."

She half-smiled. "It does for me . . . at least at the start. And he seemed so urbane, so debonair. So different from Kevin."

"What changed?"

"Gambling. At first, going to the Colonial Club was exotic and fun. I'd make twenty dollars last an hour, but Cal lost hundreds, thousands, so much money, not once, but over and over again. He finger-popped the whole way through, like it was nothing. After a while, I thought it was, well, pathetic."

"Did he ever ask you for money?"

"No. He wouldn't."

"How about the Japanese woodblock prints? Did he ask you to help sell them?"

She looked mystified. "What prints? Like Mo's?"

I ignored her question. "Was Cal alive when you got to Anthony's?"

"Yes. I told him it was over."

"How did he take it?"

"He was philosophical. He said we'd had a good run, but that his luck always did run out. It took two minutes. Three, maybe. He didn't care, not really. I was so relieved. I'd been afraid he'd argue with me, try to convince me to give it another go. Then I went and sat in on a bingo game. In case anyone saw me there, I needed a cover story." She smiled again, a weak one. "I won five dollars."

"Have you told the police?"

Her smile faded. "Just about playing bingo. There are security cameras all over the casino, so I knew they'd know."

"You should tell them the truth. It will help them set the timeline."

"No way. Kevin will find out. I can't believe I went to the Colonial Club with Cal. If I hadn't done that one thing, no one would know, and everything would be all right."

"The police are good at keeping secrets. You have an opportunity to be a hero here."

She rubbed her temples for a moment. "I've made such a mess of everything."

"You made a mistake, that's all."

She aimed her big, frightened eyes at me. "I wish —"

Nora turned without finishing her thought and walked quickly toward the front door.

I hoped she'd take my advice and tell the police the truth, but I doubted it.

CHAPTER THIRTY-TWO

I was sitting at the guest table when Dr. Sanford arrived about twelve fifteen. She wore black jeans with a red sweater and a gold chain belt, casual chic. I told myself not to get excited, that her calling didn't mean she had news about the guitar's provenance.

She didn't want anything to drink, and I suggested going up to my office. She walked beside me through the warehouse, observant and silent, intelligence radiating off her like heat. Upstairs, she settled onto the love seat. I sat across from her and waited for her to speak.

"I know how easy it is to create a website and a social media history on the fly, so I wanted to visit your company without giving you time to fake a persona. I'm convinced — you're for real."

In her position, I would have done the same thing.

"I'm pleased I've passed muster."

"My husband and I spent yesterday evening going through everything I inherited that could possibly be related to the guitar. I know I said that you and I would look together, but the more I thought about it, the less comfortable I got." She extracted an envelope from her briefcase. "I brought you copies."

"Thank you so much. That's wonderful of you. If you made copies, that implies you found something you thought I could use."

"I did. My grandmother kept a diary. She was a hairdresser by occupation, but a poet by avocation. She had big ideas and big dreams, but back then, a black woman in the Deep South, well, her options were limited." She reached into the envelope for an old photograph, which she laid on the butler's table, facing me. "I found this photo between two pages of her diary."

I reached for it, then hesitated. "May I?"

"Yes. You can keep it. As I said, it's a copy. You can publish it, if you want."

I picked it up. "This is Robert Johnson."

"Yes, a studio shot."

I read the inscription: *To my best girl, Robert Johnson.* "The guitar he's holding sure looks like a Martin OM-45 Deluxe."

Dr. Sanford eased a sheet of paper from

the envelope and handed it over. "Here's a copy of the back."

I squinted at the blurry red mark. "Cloister Studio. San Antonio." I smiled. "San Antonio . . . Robert Johnson recorded fifteen tunes for Vocalion Records in San Antonio in 1936. If he had a record contract, naturally they'd want some publicity shots."

"It gets better." She removed a sheaf of papers from the envelope and slid them onto the table. "These are copies of Grandma's diary, every page that mentioned Johnson. The Post-it Note flags where I found the photo."

I skim-read the first two pages, then looked up. "They were in love."

"It sounds like he was the love of her life."

"Does she explain how she came to own the guitar?"

"Robert got sick. Speculation was that he'd been poisoned by another girlfriend's husband. My grandmother knew he wasn't faithful to her, and she didn't care. I don't understand that. Do you?"

I thought of Nora. "Love can be so powerful, reason goes out the door. It's irresistible, like a tidal wave, so yes, I do understand that."

"That's lust, not love."

"You may be right, but when you're in the middle of it, you call it love. I suspect it's a walk-a-mile-in-her-moccasins thing. I don't judge."

"Perhaps. My grandmother wrote that she offered to nurse him, but he refused. From all reports, Johnson was a prideful man, and he didn't want a woman he loved to see him weak and delirious. It broke her heart. A friend took him to his house on the plantation where he worked, but Robert left his guitar at her place for safekeeping, saying he'd be back for it as soon as he got better. He died two days later. He was twenty-seven."

"That's tragic."

"My grandmother cherished that guitar because of the man who played it." Dr. Sanford stood. "I give you all this information for my grandmother. She hid her love for Johnson her entire life. There's no reason to hide it anymore. She's smiling down on me right now, I just know she is."

"If I get to share your grandmother's story, I promise you I'll honor her love for Robert Johnson."

Dr. Sanford reached out a hand as if to touch my arm, then pulled back. "Thank you."

As we walked downstairs, she asked,

412

"How much do you think the guitar is worth?"

"It's too early to speculate. We're still in the authentication phase. On the face of it, this guitar has everything going for it. It's in perfect condition, it's rare, it's scarce, it's been owned by legendary players, and guitars are enduringly popular. It ticks all the boxes."

"Players — plural. Someone besides Robert Johnson has played it, or is now."

"I'm sorry. I can't say."

"When will you know if it's genuine?"

"Soon, I hope. We're working with a New York–based expert. I expect to hear from him any day."

We walked across the warehouse.

"Will you be able to learn how Robert Johnson acquired it?" she asked.

"I don't think so, but that missing link shouldn't hurt the value. People don't always keep receipts, and if they do, it's not unusual that they get lost over the generations. Life isn't a business, after all."

I pushed open the heavy door to the front office.

"Will you let me know its value when you determine it?"

"I can't. The current owner has only asked me to appraise it, not sell it, and appraisals

413

are confidential."

"I understand."

Dr. Sanford offered her hand for a final handshake, and her grip was firm.

I placed the copies of Estelle Dowler's documents on the guest table. While I waited for Fred to finish a phone call, I swiveled to face the window. A gust of wind whipped through the fallen leaves, funneling them up as if they were caught in a twister, then, moments later, releasing them, and they twirled to the ground like confetti. I should begin thinking about the wedding. There were so many details, from designing invitations and selecting the music to identifying a theme and choosing the caterer. I had catalogue copy to review, too, and Matt Janson's business plan to study. I didn't want to do any of that. I didn't want to do anything. I was on edge. *Don't think — do.* My dad repeated that admonition a thousand times in the months after my mother's death when I was rudderless, and later when I was in college and overwhelmed. Action might not cure anxiety, he said, but it sure helps manage it.

Fred hung up. "That was Davy."

"From your eyes, I can tell you have news."

He grinned. "We've got ourselves a real-deal 1930 Martin OM-45 Deluxe guitar."

"Hot diggity!"

He leaned back, a happy man. "Super hot diggity!"

I pointed to the papers on the table. "Dr. Sanford gave me copies of documents that validate the claim that the guitar was owned by Robert Johnson just before his death."

His eyes fired up. "This might really be something."

I held up crossed fingers. "Any leads you're still following?"

"No. I've verified eight extant guitars, and that's as far as I think we'll be able to get. I primed every pump I could find."

"Eight of fourteen . . . that's like a sixty percent success rate, Fred. Unbelievable."

He grinned again, more broadly this time. "Why are you surprised?"

I laughed. "I'm not. I'm awed."

I asked Fred to research whether Cloister Studio kept any records about Johnson's visit, specifically whether he'd brought his own guitar to the photo shoot or used one they had on hand, like a theater prop. If he'd brought the guitar with him, it would go a long way to showing that he'd actually owned it. The odds that Cloister retained records that detailed were remote, but we

415

had to check.

The phone rang. Trish was on line one.

Trish sounded agitated. "May I come to talk to you? It's urgent."

I told her yes and gathered the documents related to her husband's private appraisal into a pile and handed them over to Fred for safekeeping. He placed them in a drawer, out of sight.

Trish didn't want to go to my private office. "Can we step outside instead? It's so lovely out."

"Sure." I grabbed my jacket.

I led the way to the bench over by the tag sale venue.

Trish sat with her knees together, her back board-straight, and her eyes fixed on the distant woods. Sunlight touched her silver hair, setting it aglow like a halo. I sat at an angle, my right thigh resting on the seat. Her expression was austere, her jaw set, her neck muscles rope-tight.

"Thank you for seeing me with no notice. I needed to talk to you. I need to explain." She met my eyes. "Frank and I have agreed to a policy of no secrets. Never again will we keep things from one another. Not to protect ourselves. Not to shield Lydia. Never." After a few seconds, Trish asked,

"Do you have some good news for us about Frank's guitar?"

Frank told me he didn't want Trish to know about the appraisal, that he didn't want anyone to know. If he'd changed his mind about keeping secrets, he hadn't told me. For all I knew, Trish had found the receipt and was trying to suss out information behind his back.

"I'm sorry, Trish. I can't comment. All appraisals are confidential. I can't even reveal whether we're conducting one or not."

"Really?" I didn't respond, so she added, "It doesn't matter, I suppose. We're leaving New Hampshire. I can't stay in that house. I haven't slept since Mo died. I doze a little, then jerk awake. Frank doesn't even try. He sits in his studio all night, playing guitar or listening to music."

"I'm so sorry, Trish. Where are you going?"

"Mountain climbing to start with. If we get tired enough, maybe we can sleep. We fly to Lucerne in a few days."

I wondered if Ellis knew they planned to leave the country. "Does Lydia go with you?"

"No. I don't know Lydia's plans. She's reeling. We all are, I suppose, but Lydia is less communicative than either of us. So much loss . . . truly, it's almost too much to bear. You know that the police think Lydia might have killed Cal?"

"I heard that, yes."

"She didn't." Trish studied her hands. "It's absurd. Horrifying and absurd." She raised her eyes and scanned the parking lot. "Well, then . . . you're probably wondering why I'm here. Three reasons. First, I couldn't leave without thanking you for Mo's eulogy, for being such a good friend to her."

"I meant every word. Thank you for including me."

She patted my hand. "We're putting all our furniture we want to keep and most of our clothes into storage. I'm hoping you'll sell everything else, all the outdoor furniture, sports gear, and miscellaneous items, like pots and pans and so on, that sort of thing. Will you take it on?"

"Of course. We can buy the objects outright or you can consign them."

"I don't want to think about them again, so I'll ask you to buy them outright."

"All right."

She paused for a moment. "The third thing I want to say . . . that I *need* to say . . . it's my fault you were attacked at that social club." She raised a hand to stop me from

418

interrupting. "I drove Frank and Lydia to do some terrible things." She paused again, this time for several seconds. "You need context to understand, to forgive me. I was worried about Frank's gambling, so I put him on an allowance. Doesn't that sound awful? This was years ago, before we were married even. His royalties and fees are deposited into a bank account that only I can access. He agreed, but still . . . I dole out money to him as if he were a child. I hate it, but I do it, because it's the smart thing to do. It was a good system, and we've built some impressive holdings over the years, but the system broke down. He needed twenty thousand dollars, far more than his allowance, and he knew I'd demand an explanation before I gave it to him, and he also knew that if he told me the truth, I'd refuse."

She stopped talking, and after a moment, I asked, "Was it a gambling debt?"

"No. Frank told me that he only plays a little nowadays, and that he never loses much. It wasn't that. He couldn't tell me because it was a secret. He'd promised Lydia he wouldn't tell."

"Cal. It was Cal's gambling debt."

"Yes . . . and Frank and Lydia were right — I wouldn't have paid a nickel to help

419

Cal." Trish closed her eyes for a few seconds, then took in a deep breath and opened them. She turned toward me. "I'm asking for your compassion, Josie. Cal owed more than sixty thousand dollars. Sixty thousand! Can you believe it? He lost it in one night at the Colonial Club. Lydia wanted to help him, but her trust is set up to provide periodic payments. She can't touch the principal without my permission. She gave Cal forty thousand dollars, all the cash she had available and all the cash advances she could get on her credit cards."

"Lydia went to Frank for help."

"Never underestimate the devotion of a father to his daughter."

"What does Frank's devotion have to do with my getting hurt?"

"I own that building."

"But you didn't hire those thugs."

"No, of course not. But I've been a hands-off owner. When the cat's away the mice will play."

"Lydia runs the casino."

Trish closed her eyes for a moment. "How did you know?"

"She mentioned she stopped in now and again. No one else would know that the space was available and the owner wouldn't catch on."

"She started it as a fun surprise for Cal, a birthday present. A pop-up casino, she called it. Then it proved so popular, she let it continue."

"Did you know she let Cal stay there when he ran for it?"

"No. I was outraged. I still am." Trish stood. "The point is . . . I wanted to say . . . the attack happened in my building, under my watch, except I wasn't watching, and I sincerely hope you weren't hurt."

"Thank you. It could have been worse." I stood, too. "Do the police know you're leaving the country?"

"Our lawyer plans to tell them today."

We walked to the parking lot.

When we reached her car, she paused. "Can you come today? Now? To take everything away."

"Yes."

As soon as I stepped inside, Fred said, "Cloister Studio is long gone — they closed down in 1958. Their photo archives and business records are at the University of Texas, San Antonio. The librarian was helpful, but of no help. The photo Dr. Sanford gave you is the only one they have of Robert Johnson, and there are no relevant business records. That said, here's my estimate

421

of value."

He handed me a sheet of paper on which he'd written *$500,000+*.

"This is a big number."

"And I'm being conservative."

"That's great news. Get the instrument and the extra case ready for pickup or delivery." I turned toward Gretchen. "Please call Frank Shannon and tell him his appraisal is ready. Ask him to stop by — or I can bring everything to him. I'm going to the Shannon house now. Trish wants to sell some things." I faced Fred. "In fact, Fred, why don't you come with me? Get Eric and a couple of other guys, too. Let's take the truck and plenty of packing materials." I turned back to Gretchen. "Don't leave a message — speak only to Frank." As Fred headed into the warehouse, I congratulated him on his thoroughness, then turned to Sasha. "Where are we with Mo's print?"

"Greyson Chemicals expects to finish their materials analysis by the end of business today."

"Good."

I sat at the guest table. Hank sauntered over, jumped into my lap, and curled up. The sounds of a normal workday combined with Hank's soft purr soothed me.

Gretchen hung up. "Frank isn't home — I

reached him on his cell. He says he'll be here at three."

Fred and I drove in my car. The part-timers rode with Eric in the truck. Fred and I video-recorded everything outside and in the shed, and the marked items inside, as per our protocol. While Eric and his team loaded the truck, I met with Trish in the living room.

"Until I've done an appraisal on some of the more valuable objects, like your golf clubs, I can't determine actual value. All I can do is offer you a third of what I expect everything would sell for at the tag sale, and I know that's going to be far less than what things are actually worth. I encourage you to let me appraise things first."

"Thank you, Josie. I appreciate your frankness. As I said, though, I just want everything gone."

I did the calculations, Trish approved the number, and I asked Gretchen to prepare the paperwork. When it arrived, Trish signed the e-forms.

I left the men to their work and drove back to the office.

At three o'clock sharp, Frank thanked Gretchen for the escort to my office and sat on the love seat. I chose the wing chair.

"You didn't need to come up."

"Trish told me about your conversation."

"She said you're going to Switzerland."

"Yeah. It was Trish's idea, and I think it's a good one. Better to work our bodies for a while, then light somewhere new."

"How's Lydia?"

His lips folded together, and he shook his head. "Not good. It's killing me, watching her suffer. When you love someone, their pain is your pain, except more so because it's doubled. You feel it as if it's happening to you, and you see it happening to them."

"You're okay leaving before Mo's killer is found?"

"It's not Lydia, if that's what you're asking."

"I wasn't."

"If there was anything we could do . . . if Lydia wanted us or needed us, we'd stay."

"It's a mess."

"A big one. Life keeps on coming at ya, that's for sure. So what do you have for me about my guitar?"

"Good news. We have great confidence that the guitar is genuine and that it was owned by Robert Johnson. I've documented ownership from you back in time to a woman who had a long-running affair with him. She kept a diary. One entry specifies that Johnson was sick, deathly ill, and that he gave her his guitar for safekeeping. So we have it in his hands, then hers. The only missing link is how he came to own it. That gap won't hurt the value, though."

"That's incredible work, Josie. Lay it on me — what's it worth?"

I smiled. "Five hundred thousand dollars, or more, largely because of the associations with star blues players — you and Johnson."

"Hot damn." Frank grinned. "You've made my day."

"We aim to please, and sometimes we can."

Frank stood and extended his hand. "Well, I guess this is good-bye, then."

I didn't stand, and I didn't take his hand. I kept my eyes on his face. "Before you go, there's something I need to tell you."

His eyes grew wary. He lowered himself to the love seat, perching on the front half of the cushion.

"I know you broke into my place to steal Mo's print, Frank."

"Whoa, girl. You can stop right there."

"Forget the fact that Trish as good as told me — saying you needed twenty thousand dollars to help Lydia settle Cal's debt and asking for my compassion. I knew anyway.

You trained as an electrician, which means you knew where to hit the power line to cause an outage without frying yourself. You also knew how to sabotage my generator."

"Trish told you no such thing. She was upset you got attacked in her building, that's all. As to the rest, you've got an active imagination, Josie. Anyone could have mucked with the power."

"You're the only person who asked if my roosters were okay. How could you know the glass in the display case had been broken if you hadn't seen it? That wasn't part of any news story or broadcast. Your plan was slick, Frank, but I'd already removed the print from the easel, and my security company and the police got here before you could finish looking around. I know you did it. You probably justified it by telling yourself that Mo would have been glad to help her sister. You're a the-ends-justify-the-means sort of guy."

Frank walked to the window. He stood for several seconds staring out over the trees.

"I rely on Trish to take care of this sort of thing," he said, his back to me, "apologies and whatnot. It's not in my nature. I just don't have it in me." Frank turned to face me. "That said, I hate the thought of your place being burglarized. I'd like to pay for

426

the damage."

"You can't." I stood. "Glass can be replaced easily and for not a lot of money. Trust can't be bought at any price."

"I'm sorry."

"For doing it? Or for getting caught?"

Frank didn't comment, and his expression didn't change. He didn't look sorry or ashamed or worried or anything in particular. He just looked like Frank, a man more used to adoring fans than paying the piper.

"Come on. I'll walk you out."

427

CHAPTER THIRTY-THREE

I sat at the guest table thinking that nothing gelled. Disparate facts whirled in my mind's eye like dust particles in the sun. I couldn't stop thinking about trust and betrayal, and about money: earning it, inheriting it, losing it, spending it, protecting it, and gambling it away. And the people. Everything pointed to Lydia as Cal's killer. Mo's, too, really, when you considered that Lydia was on the scene and faced a myriad of issues with her sister. I considered alternatives, experimenting with combinations of people and motives, seeking out patterns, looking for clues in the mundane. People kill because of lust, more than love; revenge, more than hate; and greed, more than longing. The question was who fit that profile, and in one fell moment, the pieces snapped together like a child's puzzle, and I gasped.

"Josie?" Gretchen asked, concerned. "Are you all right?"

I blinked myself back to the here and now. "I'm fine. Thanks."

I allowed myself to sink back into the haze of reflection. Mo had been both a failed romantic and mawkishly sentimental. She viewed the world as she wished it were, with selective vision, whereas Cal had been a realist, astute, intuitive, manipulative, and a deft liar. Mo had loved heedlessly, with all her heart. Cal had been too self-centered to love. Mo had a gentle, trusting soul. Cal had no soul. Steve betrayed Mo, then proceeded to dicker about the terms of their reconciliation. Cal betrayed Lydia, then asked her to bail him out. And she did. Lydia trusted her father. Nora wanted out. The answer was so obvious, I couldn't understand how I could have missed it for so long. *Lust. Revenge. Greed.* Put those three motives together, and a witch's brew of murder boils over.

I knew who killed Mo, and why.

And I thought I knew how to prove it.

I grabbed my tote bag, called out a general "Bye" to my staff, and drove straight to Branson Wills.

I sat in the Murphy's Interiors parking lot searching for a headshot to show Anita. It took less than five minutes to download and

429

crop an appropriate image.

Anita was standing on a low stool twirling an elegant artificial vine around a decorative column. I waited until she stepped down to speak.

"I have another photo to show you."

She took my phone and stared at the photograph, then raised her eyes to my face. "I hate this."

"I know."

"That's the customer who bought *Flower Pavilion,* number sixteen."

I felt like cartwheeling out of the place.

Ellis was on the phone when I poked my head into his office just before five. He pointed at the blond-wood table by the front wall, and I sat facing the window.

"That's right," he said. "Seven o'clock . . . two people . . . thanks."

"You're going out to dinner."

He joined me at the table. "You're some deductive whiz."

"Tonight's Wednesday. What's the occasion?"

"It's sort of a celebration."

"You're blushing."

"Police chiefs don't blush."

"Should I mind my own business?"

"Yes, but I know you won't. It's Zoë's and

430

my 'I love you' anniversary."

"Tonight's the anniversary of the first time you told her you loved her."

One side of his mouth shot up. "And she told me."

"So you're taking her to dinner. That's maybe the sweetest thing I've ever heard. Is it a surprise?"

"No. I told her I think we ought to celebrate more. Life is so busy, it's easy to get into a rut. Better to celebrate the small things."

"I love that, Ellis. I really do."

"Thanks. Dinner isn't a surprise . . ." He reached behind him for a small maroon box. It was from Blackmore's Jewelers, the finest jeweler on the Seacoast. ". . . but this is. What do you think?"

"I think it's fabulous."

He laughed. "Open it."

I lifted the lid. A gold bangle embedded with diamonds rested on a white satin pillow. "Oh, my God, Ellis! This is magnificent!"

"Do you think Zoë will like it?"

I touched his wrist. "I think she'll love it."

"Thanks." He closed the lid and placed it back on the desk. "So, back to business. What can I do for you?"

"I have information about Mo's and Cal's

431

murders."

His tone sharpened. "Talk to me."

"At first, Mo's murder seemed inexplicable. Shift your perspective, though, and the answer is apparent." I explained what I knew, what I suspected, and what I concluded.

"Thank you, Josie. This is incredibly helpful."

"Are you going to let the meet with Pat Durand go forward as scheduled? At five, in the gazebo?"

"Yes. I'll need to verify your information and talk to the DA about a search warrant, but I don't anticipate any problems. Will you be able to help me out tomorrow after the meet? I may need your expertise when it comes to the woodblock print."

I assured him I would, and left.

Fred was alone when I got back to the office around six thirty.

He was reading from a thick sheaf of papers. He handed me a note Sasha had written before she left for the day.

Mo's woodblock print is a fake. A clever fake, but a fake nonetheless.

I raised my eyes. "Have you read the

report?"

Fred nodded. "Yes. The ink is good. The production methodology is consistent with known originals. The woodgrain appearing on the paper is accurate — but there were no lees."

I leaned against the table. "No lees means no wood."

"Right."

"So instead of using a woodblock made of cherry or whatever, someone transferred the real woodgrain pattern onto plastic or Formica or something, and printed from that. What about the paper?"

"It's wrong."

I slid into a guest chair.

"The nuclear residue found in the paper fibers proves that the paper was produced in Japan — but during the years following World War II." He tossed the papers onto his desk. "Why would a counterfeiter think it was worth so much effort?"

"Greed. Let's do the math. All the effort is in the preparation. Once I have the plastic or whatever, I can print at will. Just for the sake of argument, let's say I printed a hundred and twenty copies to start. I keep my inventory out of the light and only sell a dozen prints a year, one a month or so. At twenty thousand dollars each, we're looking at nearly a quarter of a million dollars a year. Each year. For ten years. When I run out, I print more."

"What are you going to tell New Hampshire Children First! about the print's value?"

"Nothing. We'll send this print to the tag sale, priced to move. What do you think? Fifty dollars?"

"It's so beautiful . . . maybe seventy-five."

"That's fine. Work with Sasha to buy us a genuine print in perfect condition." I laughed. "Make certain it comes with an unimpeachable pedigree. New Hampshire Children First! gets a valuable print, and we'll all put this episode behind us."

"That's really great of you, Josie. We'll get started tomorrow."

I thanked him, elated that my business was doing well enough that I could fund the contribution to New Hampshire Children First! I dashed off a note to Anita, telling her that the copy of Hiroshige's *Meguro Drum Bridge and Sunset Hill* that she sold was a fake, and I explained why. I suspected the prints she had held back would be back on the shelf first thing in the morning. I also suspected that she wouldn't change her pricing strategy. Why should she? She was selling them as decorative accessories, in

434

the same way some antiquarian booksellers sell rare books by the yard, not for the content but for the colorful leather bindings.

I wrote Mac at *Antiques Insights,* too.

Hi Mac,
You asked me to let you know the outcome of our appraisal of the Japanese woodblock print I told you about, Hiroshige's "Meguro Drum Bridge and Sunset Hill." Based on a materials analysis, we have concluded that it's a counterfeit. Specifically, the apparent woodgrain is nothing more than a visual effect — there are no lees. Further, the paper, while Japanese, was produced after World War II.

This print was sold by Cal Lewis (who is, apparently, partnering with someone using the name Pat Durand) to my client. While I have no knowledge that other objects sold by Cal Lewis or Pat Durand are fakes, it would seem prudent to have everything he sold under either name appraised. I should mention that Cal Lewis died recently. He was murdered, a crime currently under investigation by the Rocky Point police. You may be hearing from them.

Thanks again, Mac.

Josie

I was sorry to open up such a hornet's nest, but it had to be done.

Ty texted that he was running late; he was about to leave work and was in the mood for Italian. He wanted to know what I thought about going to Abitino's and suggested we meet at eight thirty. I replied that was fine. I took advantage of the time to stop by Rocky Point Paper Palace. I parked across from the village green and went inside.

Racks of greeting cards ran the length of the shop, samples of specialty papers hung on rods against the walls, and binders of special occasion options rested on a long wooden table at the back. At Prescott's, we used Rocky Point Paper Palace for all our invitations and special announcement cards. They were expensive, but their attention to detail and the quality of their workmanship were unparalleled.

The shop's owner, a voluptuous blonde named Brenda Cragan, was a former rock 'n' roll singer who'd traveled with cover bands throughout Asia in her twenties, then quit and used her savings to set herself up in business in Rocky Point. Now, twenty years later, her shop had been featured in national magazines and on lifestyle design TV shows. I'd asked her why she hadn't capitalized on the publicity to expand, and she said she loved her life just as it was.

The shop was busy, even at seven thirty. Brenda was just finishing up a special order at the back.

"Josie!" She leaned forward for a butterfly kiss. "What can I do for you?"

"I need help, Brenda." I felt suddenly shy. "Ty and I are getting married."

"Oh, Josie! That's wonderful. You need wedding invitations."

"Party invitations. We're going to have a very small private ceremony, followed by a very large party."

"Nice. Tell me what you're thinking."

"Something simultaneously elegant and casual. I know that's an oxymoron."

"How do you want people to feel when they open the invitation?"

"Oh, golly, I don't know. Like it's going to be fun! But, you know, not silly. And not stuffy, either." I laughed. "In other words, I have no idea." I took a moment to gather my thoughts. "I want something they haven't seen before, yet more on the traditional end of the spectrum than cutesy."

Brenda reached for a book on a low shelf and flipped through to the back. She peeled back a plastic protector and eased out a sheet of parchment with a deckled edge.

I stroked it. The pale yellow paper was luscious, butter soft, and thick enough to sleep on. "It's gorgeous, but parchment feels too formal."

She flipped forward, pausing at a pale ochre sheet, embossed with flowers. "This might be perfect for a June wedding."

"Too . . . I don't know . . . fussy."

I didn't like a pink flax paper with laser heart-shaped cutouts, either. Or a blue-and-beige-marbled paper.

"I don't want to keep you, Brenda. Maybe I should just flip through."

"It's my pleasure to float ideas, Josie, but if you'd prefer looking on your own, let's do that."

"You know me well."

I started at the beginning and quickly discovered it was easy to eliminate options. What wasn't simple was finding any I liked. At ten after eight, five minutes before I needed to leave to meet Ty, I found the perfect paper. I looked over my shoulder, and as if Brenda could feel my excitement, she turned and met my eyes.

I held up my choice, translucent vellum

decorated with a border of miniature poinsettias.

"I want tiger lilies and hydrangeas instead of poinsettias," I said as she walked up.

"I love it. It's exactly what you described, traditional yet welcoming."

"Do you have a sample I can take? I want to show Ty."

"Of course. Take this one. I have spares in the back." She slipped the vellum into a white envelope. "I'll have a mockup for you in a few days."

"Sounds good!"

As I drove around the village green heading for Abitino's, I passed Ellie's Crêpes,* one of my favorite restaurants. Ellie's was located directly across from the gazebo and would serve as a perfect vantage point to watch Dawn meet with Pat Durand. If I got there by four, I'd have no problem nabbing a window seat.

* Please see *Glow of Death, Ornaments of Death, Blood Rubies, Lethal Treasure,* and *Deadly Threads.*

CHAPTER THIRTY-FOUR

I woke the next morning, Thursday, at six. Wrapped in my favorite pink chenille robe, I yawned my way downstairs and joined Ty for coffee.

He poured me a cup. "You're up early."

"My brain is busy. I get to start planning the merger with Janson's Antiques Mall today."

"What's your first step?"

"Studying his business plan and coming up with a list of questions."

"Are you comfortable taking on a project this big?"

"Yes. Even if we move to D.C., it'll work out fine. Max pointed out that by acquiring Matt's company, I'll be acquiring a top operations guy."

"What do you think about moving to Washington?"

I drank some coffee. "I think I had enough trouble choosing that vellum paper to make any decision bigger than that right now. Except for buying out Matt. That feels like a no-brainer. How about you?"

"I like our life in New Hampshire, but I never want to turn my back on an opportunity."

"If they offer the job and it has to be based in Washington, we can decide then. What's their timeline?"

"Soon."

I reread Matt's business plan just after lunch. Assuming we could come to terms on a buyout, I didn't see how we could lose. He'd thought of everything, from personnel needs to marketing plans and from construction timelines to financing options. He recommended appointing or hiring a general manager for each location to handle the day-to-day, with him overseeing everything. His plan called for me to step back from operations and work more on high-level strategy and promotion. For instance, he thought I could — and should — write a monthly column for *Antiques Insights* magazine, with each article focusing on demystifying some element of the antiques appraisal process. I stared across the room. I would begin by writing about the difference between rarity and scarcity.

I saw the time on my computer monitor — 3:30 — and leapt out of my chair. I'd been so immersed in Matt's ideas for expansion, I'd completely lost track of time, but there was no way I was going to be late to Ellie's.

I got to Ellie's just before four and found Detective Brownley sitting at the table closest to the front window, reading something on her smartphone.

"Detective . . . may I join you?"

Her eyes showed neither surprise nor annoyance. "Sorry. This is Ellis's table. You'll have to ask him."

"Okay." I glanced around. The place was empty. "Where is he?"

"I don't know."

A favorite waitress, a young French woman named Juliette, stood near the kitchen chatting with a cook. I walked to join her.

"Hi, Juliette. Would it be all right if I moved a table near the window? It's so beautiful out — I want to enjoy the view."

"Of course. Will anyone be joining you?"

"No. Just me today."

Juliette selected a table next to the brick wall and rolled it to the front. Detective Brownley looked up but didn't say anything.

I carried a chair and ordered a cappuccino.

My view was perfect. The gazebo, which was draped with plastic, was directly across the street. WET PAINT signs had been taped to the tarp.

Ellis arrived half an hour later, spotted me, and stopped short.

I smiled at him and tapped my forehead. "Great minds."

He met my eyes for a moment, then turned to the detective. "All set?"

"We're good to go on all fronts. Katie's upstairs."

Ellis walked to the back and said something to Juliette I couldn't hear. She opened a door on the side, revealing a staircase I hadn't known existed. Ellis crooked his index finger at me, and I joined him, carrying my cappuccino.

We climbed a steep flight of steps. I paused at the top to look around. The room was set up as a living room, so I inferred that we were in Ellie's home. I hadn't realized she lived above the restaurant.

Katie, the police IT expert, sat at a card table near the front. She wore oversized headphones. A stack of equipment rested on the table. Yellow and blue lights flickered on the bottom box. A man I didn't recognize stood by the window. A Nikon camera hung from a leather strap around his neck. A video recorder rested on a tripod. A pair of earbuds sat on the table.

Ellis pointed to a chair at the far end of the table. "Have a seat."

"Thanks." I sat.

Ellis took another chair and turned it around. He sat backward, resting his forearms on top of the backrest. He lowered his voice. "I told you to stay away."

"You told me to stay away from the village green. I haven't been near the village green all day."

"You're quibbling."

"I am not. More to the point, no one knows I'm here, or as far as I know, that I have any reason to be here."

"Good."

"Did you talk to Anita?"

"Yes. She confirmed what you told me, and we got the search warrant." Ellis's phone rang, and he glanced at the screen, then back at me. "Don't move."

"Why would I? This is the best seat in the house."

He walked toward the staircase and leaned against the wall. I couldn't hear what he was saying. I dug around in my tote bag for my phone to check the time. It was twenty minutes to five.

444

Katie tapped the microphone clipped to her collar. "Go inside, Curt. Tell me whether the paint is dry."

A lanky man in his forties with sandy hair and a goatee appeared from behind a tree and sauntered to the gazebo. He found a separation in the tarp and climbed up and in.

"The paint is dry."

Katie spun a dial. "Good. Talk to me."

"The paint is dry. The paint is dry. Oh why oh why is the paint so dry?"

"Stand by."

Katie spun around and dipped her head, trying to catch Ellis's attention. He got the message and nodded. A moment later, Ellis finished and returned to the worktable.

"We're ready," she told him.

"Good. Dawn is going to touch base with Pat Durand now, confirming the time and telling her the place. She'll call as soon as they connect."

Katie spoke into the mic. "Curt? You can leave the gazebo."

Ellis leaned against a front window frame. Curt stepped out from behind the plastic and ambled along the path. When he reached an old oak, he stretched. He looked for all the world like a worker on a break.

Sun filtered through the trees. Two men

445

in suits walked across a fresh layer of crunchy leaves and sat at one end of a wooden-slat bench. An older couple sat on the other end, their shoulders touching. A young woman pushed a baby stroller along a distant path.

Ellis's phone rang. He swiped the display to accept the call.

"Hunter . . . Good . . . Thanks, Dawn." He tapped the END CALL button and looked at Katie. "Dawn has confirmed the meet."

Katie pushed a button on her microphone. "Curt?"

"Standing by."

"Open it up."

"Will do."

Curt trotted back to the gazebo. He tugged the tarps and down they came, one section at a time. Curt laid them on top of one another and rolled the pile into a bulky ball. Two minutes after he began, he was finished and out of sight.

"Curt, I'm going quiet."

"Got it."

Katie flipped a switch and turned another dial. "Can you hear me, Curt?"

There was no reply.

"Detective Brownley?"

"Loud and clear."

Katie continued her checks.

446

"Daryl?"

"I'm good."

I couldn't see Daryl. Or Griff when she checked in with him. Or Officer Meade, a tall ice-blonde I'd met before.

The cameraman used a remote to activate the video camera and leaned into the viewfinder to tweak the alignment.

Ellis sat at the table, rightwise now, crossing his long legs, his left ankle resting on his right thigh. His eyes were fixed on the gazebo.

Katie kept her eyes on her equipment.

I leaned in close to Ellis. "How was dinner last night?"

He smiled but didn't move his eyes. "Perfect. Thanks."

Ellis picked up the earbuds, then turned to Katie. "Do you have regular headphones?"

Katie reached under her chair and came up with a set of over-the-ear headphones.

"You just happen to have them ready to go?"

"I have two additional pairs available, too. And two more pairs of earbuds. Triple redundancy, a good cop's best friend." Katie slid a switch embedded in the headset band to the on marker and handed them over.

Ellis slid the earbuds toward me. "You

447

okay with earbuds?"

"Yes. Thank you." I lowered my voice. "You're being awfully nice to me."

"I'd rather have you in sight than in trouble."

I eased the earbuds into place. "I never get in trouble."

"Of course you don't."

At one minute to five, Dawn, wearing jeans and a navy-blue windbreaker, strolled along a cross path. The photographer raised his camera and started taking pictures, the clicks a steady staccato beat. Dawn climbed the gazebo steps and stood in the center. After a few seconds, she walked to the far railing and leaned against a column, her back to us. The photographer continued snapping.

At three minutes after five, a woman wearing oversized sunglasses and a black canvas floppy hat that blocked most of her face walked slowly toward the gazebo, looking every which way. She carried a large padded envelope, just the right size to safely transport the Japanese woodblock print.

Dawn spotted her and smiled, a 1,000-watter. "Pat!"

I could hear the south in that one word.

"Andi?"

"That's me, happy as a lark, and rarin' to go."

The woman calling herself Pat climbed onto the gazebo. "Nice to meet you."

"You, too."

Pat patted the envelope. "Here's the print."

Dawn clapped like a schoolgirl. "Yay!"

I bit my lip to keep from laughing. Dawn was one heck of an actress.

Dawn peeked inside, squealed with delight, and slid the plastic-encased print out of the envelope.

"Oh, it's gorgeous, Pat. Look at the colors. They're even bolder than I'd expected. Where did you get it?"

"I can't tell you that, I'm afraid. The previous owner wants confidentiality."

"Really? I'd sure like to know."

"Sorry. I wish I could, but I can't."

"No harm in asking, right?" Dawn tilted her head, faux-thinking, then smiled. "Sold!" She reached into her purse and extracted a large plain white envelope. "Here's the cash."

Before the woman calling herself Pat had time to do more than open the flap, Detective Brownley and three police officers charged the gazebo. Dawn leapt off the platform, landing in a squat on the grass.

She jogged out of the way. Pat tried to follow, but before she reached the edge, all three officers surrounded her.

"No!" she screamed.

Griff grasped her arms from behind her and held her fast. I wished they'd turn her around so we could see her face.

Detective Brownley, wearing plastic gloves, grabbed the white envelope containing the cash. "We need you to come with us to the station."

The woman thrashed in all directions, struggling to get away. "No! No! No!"

It was chilling to watch. A few passersby paused, taking it in, followed by a trickle of people who came off the street. I saw two people holding up their cell phones, video-recording the scene.

The detective dropped the money into a plastic evidence bag and sealed it. She got close to Pat and raised her voice. "Please listen. I can arrest you as a material witness or you can cooperate. We have a search warrant for you, your bag, and your vehicle."

Pat stopped struggling. "Oh, God!" she whispered, as despair overtook panic.

A patrol car pulled up and double-parked, its blue-and-red dome lights spinning.

Detective Brownley said, "We need to check you for weapons. I'm going to ask

Officer Meade to remove your hat and sunglasses, then we'll check your person."

Pat stiffened but didn't object.

Officer Meade snapped on plastic gloves. She pulled the hat straight up and the glasses straight off. She slid her hand under the hat brim and felt all around the crown. She ran her fingers along the glasses' earpieces.

"Nothing."

Detective Brownley extracted a jumbo clear plastic evidence bag from her pocket and shook it open. Officer Meade dropped the hat inside. The sunglasses went into a smaller bag.

Officer Meade did a thorough pat-down. Pat wasn't armed.

Detective Brownley searched the woman's tote bag. After a moment, she whirled a silver key ring over her head like a cheerleader shaking a pom-pom, then tossed the keys to Officer Meade. "Find the car."

Officer Meade jogged toward the street, pushing the unlock button on the fob.

Detective Brownley slipped the woman's tote bag into another evidence bag.

Officer Meade spoke into her collar mic. "We've got the car. It's parked in front of Parlor Ice Cream."

Detective Brownley told the two other

451

officers, Griff and Daryl, "Take her in."

The woman began crying as the officers led her down the gazebo steps, her feet dragging. Once they reached the grass, we had her full face, her eyes round with terror.

The woman we'd known as Pat was, as I'd expected, Kimberly Larson, Steve's secret live-in girlfriend.

As Kimberly shuffled alongside the officers, tears streaming down her cheeks, a thousand pricks of sadness stabbed at me. Kimberly's face was ashen. Reality was setting in.

The things we do for love.

CHAPTER THIRTY-FIVE

I sat on the wooden bench in the Rocky Point police station lobby waiting my turn to be interviewed. I'd been there about twenty minutes when Steve entered with Officer Meade.

His hair was disheveled. His polo shirt was half untucked.

Officer Meade nodded at me, then turned to Steve. "Have a seat. It won't be long."

Steve sank onto the bench beside me. "Jeez, Josie . . . do you have any idea what's going on?"

"I'm not sure about anything. What did you hear?"

"Nothing. The police just showed up with a search warrant, and now they're crawling all over my condo. Have you seen Kimberly? That detective told me she was here."

"I think she's in the back. Is Ryan okay?"

"Yeah, I left him with a neighbor." He leaned back against the hard bench. "I have a bad feeling about this."

Kimberly hobbled in from the corridor on the right as if she couldn't lift her feet. Daryl hovered near her elbow. Kimberly's eyes were puffy and rimmed in red. Her lips were chapped.

Steve shot up, his mouth falling open.

Kimberly saw Steve and moaned, deflating, sinking to her knees as if someone had pulled the plug on a blow-up doll. She keened, a guttural sound of unendurable pain.

Cathy, the admin, leapt up from her desk, her eyes filled with fear. Griff charged out from behind the counter.

As Daryl hoisted Kimberly to her feet, she broke away, hurtling herself toward Steve.

Steve stepped back, gawking.

I swung my feet up onto the bench. I needn't have worried — she only had eyes for Steve.

Daryl tackled her. Griff held her thrashing legs in place.

Between the two officers, they got her upright and half walked, half dragged her down the corridor on the left, toward the interrogation rooms. She didn't speak, but her mewlings continued unabated and echoed in my mind long after she was out of sight.

Detective Brownley came into the lobby and asked Steve to join her. He touched my shoulder as he left, following her down the right-hand corridor.

Moments later, Lydia stepped into the lobby.

She looked better, as if she'd had a long sleep, a hot shower, and a big meal. She marched to the counter without looking left or right, so she didn't notice me. Cathy asked how she could help her.

"I'm Lydia Shannon. I want to see Chief Ellis."

"He's in a meeting right now. I'm his assistant . . . Is there anything I can do for you?"

"No. It's urgent. I must see him."

"Have a seat. I'll give him the message." Cathy picked up the phone.

Lydia turned, saw me, and approached. She stood in front of me, her displeasure patent in her stance and frigid glare.

"I heard on the news that someone involved with Cal in some kind of art fraud scheme has been detained. Who is it?"

"I haven't heard anything official."

"Tell me unofficially."

"No." I got up and crossed the room to the Community News Bulletin Board.

Lydia spoke to my back. "Your sanctimony falls on deaf ears."

I continued reading the announcements and notices until Lydia's name was called and she followed Detective Brownley down the corridor on the right.

No one came for me until just before seven.

Ellis and I stood side by side in front of the one-way mirror in the police station's observation room. Kimberly sat on one side of the long wooden table, staring at her clenched hands. Officer Meade sat in a corner, watching her.

Ellis arched his back, flexing his muscles. "Kimberly isn't talking."

"She hasn't asked for a lawyer?"

"Nope, and she signed the Miranda waiver. If you can get her talking about the woodblock prints, that might be a start."

"She has a son, Ryan. Steve told me he left him with a neighbor. Is he all right?"

"The neighbors are keeping him overnight. Steve called Kimberly's parents, and they're flying in from Dayton in the morning."

"Poor kid."

456

"He has a lot of people who love him."

"Did you find other woodblock prints when you searched Kimberly's car or house?"

"No, just the one she had in her possession. We searched her classroom, too. Her principal opened it up for us. Nothing."

"There has to be evidence that explains her connection to Cal."

"We have a phone we found in her bag. Katie's team is working on it now, and another one turned in by Nora. Nora told me you spoke to her, so I can share that she turned over the phone voluntarily. All she's asking is that we keep her name out of the papers, and I think we might be able to do it. Wes is on board."

"You got Wes to agree to hold back news?"

"Nora's involvement isn't germane to the investigation. It's gossip."

"That may be true, but agreeing to sit on a story doesn't sound like the Wes I know."

Ellis grinned. "I promised him an exclusive."

"That explains it. What does Kimberly say about why she has that phone in her purse?"

"Other than commenting that possessing a phone isn't a crime, nothing."

"She has a point."

He glanced at his watch. "It's been a

couple of hours. They might have something." Ellis picked up a wall-mounted phone and punched in four digits. "Katie, where are you with those phones?" Ellis listened for almost a minute. "Okay. I'll take what you've got."

"Where did the phones come from?"

"Kirby's, a mom-and-pop electronic store in Elliot, Maine. The buyer purchased four phones, a voice changer, and a laptop in a cash transaction the day Mo was killed and Cal disappeared. The store can't help us ID the buyer because they only keep their security camera footage for seventy-two hours, and the clerk doesn't remember a thing about it."

"I bet Cal bought everything, kept one phone, and gave the others to Kimberly, Nora, and Lydia."

"I'm with you on that. The question is, where are the computer and voice changer now?"

"What does Lydia say?"

"Nothing. Unlike Kimberly, Lydia did call her attorney, and he instructed her not to answer any questions."

"Any news on the pipes in the social club?"

"Just another dead end. It was a good lead, and thank you again, but we heard from the property manager that they're getting ready to update the gas line. We've confirmed the delivery with the vendor. All pipes are accounted for, and none contains forensic material. None has been wiped or cleaned in any way."

Katie stepped into the room and handed Ellis a thick folder.

"Thanks, Katie. Anything I should know that's not in this printout?"

"The top sheets are texts and emails from the phones, followed by a list of numbers called."

Ellis ran his thumb down the lists, thanked her for her quick work, and told her she could go. "There are dozens of calls on both of these phones from one of the missing units. That must be the one Cal used." He continued reading. "The emails support that, but they're all from generic addresses and are unsigned." He placed the documents back in the folder. "Ready?"

"Yes."

"Keep it simple. Stick to the print and how she got involved with Cal."

I followed Ellis ten feet down the hall. We paused at the heavy door that led to Interrogation Room One.

Ellis stood at the head of the table and pointed to a chair across from Kimberly. I nodded at Officer Meade, sitting near the back wall, and sat down. Kimberly didn't react. A human-sized cage stood off to my right, and I shifted my chair so I wouldn't see it. Three video cameras were mounted high overhead.

Ellis took a remote from his shirt pocket and aimed it at each video recorder. One by one, pinpricks of red light appeared.

"Ms. Larson, as I've explained, we record all interviews. I've activated the recorders." Ellis stated the date, glanced at his watch, and added the time. "You'll recall that I'm Police Chief Hunter. I've asked Josie Prescott to join us. She's an antiques expert, and I'm hoping she can help me understand the transaction you just participated in. Do you collect Japanese woodblock prints?"

Kimberly didn't move. I had no sense she heard him.

Ellis nodded at me.

"Kimberly?"

She raised her eyes to my face. She still looked worn and upset, but she didn't seem panicky. She wasn't shaking or sniveling or, as far as I could tell, showing any emotion at all.

"As Chief Hunter just explained, the police asked me for help. I can't believe you did this, Kimberly. I know you wanted to

460

earn more money, but selling fraudulent art is no way to do it."

Kimberly's eyebrows pulled together. "What are you talking about? The woodblock print is real."

"How do you know?"

"I know where it came from."

"Where?"

Kimberly raised her chin. "You know better than to ask me that."

"Come on, Kimberly. Let's talk turkey. If it's real, why the fake name?"

"I guess you've never worked in a top elementary school. You're supposed to devote every waking moment to the job. If my students' parents found out I was moonlighting, my principal would never hear the end of it, and neither would I." She pushed her chair back and stood. We all followed suit. "I don't want to talk to you about it. I know you mean well, Josie, but all I did was sell a beautiful woodblock print." Kimberly turned toward Ellis. "I'm leaving."

"Not quite yet."

"Then I've changed my mind. I want a lawyer."

"Certainly."

Ellis announced to a video camera that he was suspending the interrogation, then turned the machines off. Officer Meade escorted Kimberly out to make the call.

"Sorry," I said.

"You did your best."

"Now what?"

"I'll point out to her lawyer the advantages of cooperating with us. He'll raise a ruckus, and we'll let her go. We know Cal was involved in fraud, and that she helped him sell the print, but until we can prove intent, we don't have enough evidence to hold her."

He walked me to the lobby, thanked me again for helping, and headed back inside.

CHAPTER THIRTY-SIX

At eight o'clock Friday morning, I stood with my mouth agape. I was staring at one of Trish's golf club bags, disbelieving what I was seeing.

All the objects we'd bought from the Shannons were in a cordoned-off area of the warehouse awaiting appraisal. I'd brought over two standing work lights and video gear to begin sorting through the objects. Not every piece was worthy of a full appraisal. Each of the three golf bags contained fourteen clubs. From watching an occasional golf game on TV, I knew there was no minimum number of clubs a pro golfer could carry, but the maximum was fourteen. Frank told me Trish hadn't played golf in twenty years, and from what he said and what I could see, once she'd quit the game, she hadn't cared for them anymore. The bags weren't covered, and she'd left them in a non-climate-controlled shed, so I wasn't surprised to see a layer of dust on the heads. What was stunning, though, was that one of them, a driver, was pristine.

I ran to a worktable and brought up the video I'd taken the day before. I captured a still shot of the bag containing the undusty club and blew it up. Looking at the clubs carefully, the distinction between the clean driver and the other clubs was unmistakable. I emailed the image to Ellis, then called him.

I got his voice mail. "Ellis, I just sent you a photo." I explained why I had Trish's golf bags, then added, "I can't help but wonder if I'm looking at the murder weapon."

I sent my staff an email telling them not to touch anything in the Shannon section.

I felt shaken and confused. Trish couldn't have known. Using one of her golf clubs to kill Cal pointed right at Lydia, so Trish never would have sold them to us.

I wanted some air. Outside, the sky was thick with ash-gray clouds, and darkening by the minute, so a walk through the woods to the church would be in the near-dark. Instead, I drove to the ocean and parked in the Rocky Point police station lot. A walk on the beach sounded good. First, though, I walked into the station.

Ellis wasn't in. I left a message saying I'd

464

be on the beach for a while, in case he came in.

The ocean was black and churning. Diagonal lines of white foam surged toward the beach. I watched for a few seconds, then walked along the shore. After about ten minutes, I turned around. A gusty wind blew in off the water, and I shivered. When I reached my car, I felt better, stronger, more like myself.

I walked back into the police station. Ellis was in.

"I just left you a message," he said. "I wanted to speak to you before I sent Detective Brownley and a tech team to your place to get the golf clubs."

"Let me text Cara that it's okay." I did so, and she texted back immediately, saying she'd prepare the receipt. "All set." I looked at him. "Are you all right? You look like you haven't slept in a week."

"That's about how I feel."

"Is Kimberly still here?"

"No. Her lawyer showed up around nine thirty last night, and we let her go about ten."

"Now what?"

"I bring the clubs in for forensic analysis, and I think of more questions to ask people, starting with the Shannons. On the off

465

chance the golf club is the weapon, I need to know who had access to them."

"I was at a party there not long ago, and the shed was unlocked."

"So someone could walk onto the property, take a club, use it to kill Cal, clean it, bring it back, and no one would notice."

"That sounds about right. I have another suggestion, too . . . two, actually. First, ask Kimberly about blackmail."

Ellis leaned back and rubbed his nose. "Tell me."

"The only reason Kimberly would conspire with Cal was if she had to. Sure, she wanted more money, but it would never occur to her to do something sleazy. She walked the straight and narrow until she couldn't anymore. Everything started to unravel that day in the faculty lounge when she came into the room and saw Steve hang up the phone. That could only mean one thing — he'd made a call he didn't want her to know about. She assumed he'd called Mo. She hit redial, and sure enough, Mo picked up. She taught in the room next to hers, so she'd know her voice. Kimberly went to Mo's house after school to confront her, to stake her claim. Cal was there to meet with Mo and me. He arrived early, and he saw Kimberly arguing with Mo. Cal witnessed Mo fall. He threatened Kimberly, saying he'd tell the police he saw her push Mo."

"Did she?"

"I don't know. Maybe. Regardless, I can see Cal blackmailing Kimberly. It's just his style of slimy. If you can get her talking about how she was the victim, maybe she'll come clean. My other idea . . . about covering your clothes if you're going to beat someone with, say, a golf club, and you don't want to end up covered in blood. Rain gear would work, and guess where they sell it? Anthony's Shoe Repair. Talk about convenient."

"These are good ideas, Josie." He stood. "Thanks for coming in."

As I crossed back to the beach, I toyed with texting Wes to ask if Anthony's sold any rain gear in the hours before Cal was killed, but I didn't. I suspected getting Anthony to cooperate would be a delicate operation, one requiring Ellis's deft handling, not Wes's bludgeoning.

The sky was steel gray now, and the air was thick with moisture. The swells were growing and breaking hard, slapping the water with a deafening roar. I didn't want to think about blackmail or the kind of emotional anguish that drove someone to kill. I wanted to do something optimistic.

I called Matt Janson.

"Do you have any time today to talk?" I asked. "It won't take long."

"I'm meeting a friend in Rocky Point for a late breakfast. Can I stop by afterward? Around eleven thirty?"

"Perfect!"

As I pulled into my parking lot, Wes broke into the regular radio program with a news flash. "Kimberly Larson is apparently missing. The police are asking for help in locating her." She wasn't at her teaching job, and she hadn't called in sick. According to Wes's police source, Kimberly had been released from police custody at ten last night, and she hadn't been seen since. She didn't go home. She didn't stay in a hotel. She simply vanished.

I pulled into a spot and called Ellis. "What about Ryan?"

"Steve took him to school. He's fine. We pulled him from class and have him safe. Her parents should be here soon. Why?"

"Because I doubt she'd leave without him. She's up to something, Ellis. Something local. Kimberly's parents owned a summer cottage, which they sold last spring. Since it's September, maybe whoever bought it isn't using it. She told me there was a

468

broken lock on her old bedroom window that she used to come and go when she was a teenager. If it's empty, and the new owners haven't fixed the lock yet, it would make a perfect hideaway."

He thanked me so brusquely, I suspected he was already accessing the state tax records for the address. I grabbed my iPad and found it in two minutes by looking up recent sales on a real estate website. I drove directly there.

The cottage was picture-book charming, with weathered dove-gray siding, a terra-cotta roof, a white picket fence covered with red climbing roses, and a wraparound porch. A red maple grew on the left. The place looked deserted, but I wasn't fooled. It was a perfect lair, and I was convinced Kimberly was there, or had been overnight. There was a one-car detached garage.

I parked half a block away and texted Wes to give him a heads-up.

Five minutes later, Ellis drove up in his SUV, followed by a van filled with uniformed officers and technicians. Ellis pretended he didn't see me, but I knew better. Ellis saw everything. I got out and leaned against a streetlamp to watch them work.

Ellis pressed the doorbell, waited ten

seconds, rang the bell again, waited some more, then pounded on the door.

Officer Meade and a uniformed officer I didn't know, a young man with red hair, walked up the driveway to the garage. Officer Meade tugged on the door, without luck. She went left and he went right, circling the small structure. They paused at windows and peered in. Ellis said something to two men who were balancing a tall metal ladder on their shoulders, and he pointed toward the beach.

Wes arrived a minute later. He took in the scene at one glance, then hustled toward the ocean. I followed more slowly. By the time I reached the sand, Wes was video-recording the action. I stood in back of the garage, far enough away so I wouldn't interfere with the police, but close enough so I wouldn't miss anything.

The two men wedged the ladder into the sandy ground, then leaned it up against the house. One man held it in place while the other scrambled up. When he reached a second-story window, he pressed his nose against the glass and cupped his eyes so he could see inside. After a few seconds, he tried to lift the window, but it didn't budge. He came down the ladder. They moved it to the next window and repeated the process with the same result. One by one, they made their way across the back of the house. When they reached the side window by the red maple, the man on the ladder easily slid it open. He straddled the sill, then disappeared.

Ellis hurried to the front, and I followed.

A minute later, the front door opened from the inside, and Ellis stepped in. Officer Meade followed him, reappearing a few seconds later with what looked like a gold-colored key on a silver ring. She used it on a lock built into the garage doorjamb, and the male officer hoisted the rolling door. They both put on gloves. She reached in and flipped on the light. I could see that no one was inside. Tools hung from a big sheet of brown pegboard along the left wall. A workbench was positioned at the rear. Two big green plastic trash cans stood on the right.

A rumble of thunder exploded overhead, startling me. I'd been so certain Kimberly was here, and I was wrong. Ellis stepped out, talked to Officer Meade, and drove away.

When I got back to my company, I went to my office and sat facing my window, trying to think about what Kimberly was doing.

She said she dreamed of just driving away. Maybe she had. I would have thought she'd take Ryan with her, but maybe I was wrong about that, too.

Wes texted: *Thx for the tip. Kimberly's car found in Rocky Pt Mall parking lot. No sign of her. Any ideas?*

I didn't have a clue, so I didn't text back. Instead, I checked email.

Mac at *Antiques Insights* had written thanking me for the update and letting me know he was working with the Rocky Point police to unravel Pat Durand's crimes.

I had just finished a private meeting with Gretchen, explaining that Ty and I were going to hire a wedding planner, and asking her to help manage the details on a consultant basis for extra pay, when Cara called up to tell me that Matt had arrived.

"Thanks, Cara. Bring him up." I turned back to face Gretchen. "As you can tell, Ty and I know a lot of what we want, but we're wrestling with some things. If you create a timeline with what needs to be done and when, you'll be able to coordinate with the wedding planner, and we'll be certain we don't miss anything."

Gretchen stood, her emerald eyes gleaming. "Thank you for your confidence in me, Josie. I won't let you down."

I listened to the click-clack of her stilettos reverberating through the cavernous warehouse, followed moments later by the steady, sturdy sound of boots. Cara escorted Matt in.

We shook, and I pointed to a guest chair.

"Thanks for coming in, Matt. As I said in my message, I'm interested in proceeding. I've finished reviewing your business plan. It's a winner on all fronts."

Matt leaned back and grinned. "Thanks."

"If you're still of the same mind, I'd like to make an offer to buy you out, then hire you."

He cocked his head. "No partnership?"

"No. Our roles would be as you describe, though. You can have a contract of any length." I smiled. "The terms will be favorable, including a profit-sharing arrangement."

"I'm amenable to discussing it, but I make no guarantee. I've been pretty focused on a partnership."

"I understand. Can we see what develops as we proceed?"

"That's fair. Let the due diligence begin. Do you have someone in mind to run this location?"

"Yes. Our first confidence — I'm trusting you not to repeat this."

"You can. I won't."

"Gretchen. Our office manager."

"That's quite a leap — office manager to general manager in one step."

"She'll be great. Gretchen is one of the most organized and trustworthy people I know. She's confident and poised, and she never pretends to know something she doesn't."

"I wish we could clone her. I'll have to hire from the outside."

"I want to introduce you to my key staff."

When we reached the front office, I waited for Cara to finish her call. "Everyone . . . excuse me for interrupting."

Cara smiled. Sasha and Fred looked up from their computer monitors. Gretchen, who was standing at a file cabinet, turned toward me, a manila folder in hand.

"Do you all know Matt Janson? He owns Janson's Antiques Mall. I visit it periodically and often find hidden gems. Matt, this is Cara, our receptionist and database manager. Sasha is our chief antiques appraiser. Fred is also an antiques appraiser. Eric, our facilities manager, isn't here."

I looked at Gretchen.

"He's meeting with Montgomery's Landscaping Service," she said. "I thought he should visit their headquarters before we signed the contract. One last check."

"Good thinking, Gretchen!" I looked at Matt. "And this, obviously, is Gretchen."

"Nice to meet you all," Matt said, smiling around. He turned to me. "I'll be in touch."

I walked him out, and we shook hands, our eyes meeting, honoring the moment.

CHAPTER THIRTY-SEVEN

Wes was nothing if not thorough. By one, his news reports included a phone interview with Annie Briscoe, a New York City–based dermatologist, who had bought the beachfront cottage from the Larsons last March. The police had alerted Dr. Briscoe earlier that morning that they'd applied for and received a search warrant. She was devastated that her house could have been used by a fugitive. I could admire Wes's journalistic acumen, but her shock and a dime didn't tell us where Kimberly was now.

Ellis stopped by as I was finishing a salad I'd ordered in for lunch.

"Thanks again for the tip about the cottage."

"It was a bust."

"Most tips are. The golf club, on the other hand, that's the real deal."

"Oh, wow."

"The ME matched the shape of the club

head to the shape of the wound. The materials found in the laceration appear to match the graphite and persimmon wood in the club's shaft and head. We have to wait for forensic testing, but Trish confirmed the clubs were made of those materials, and she hasn't cleaned them since she retired. This one club was doused with bleach."

"They can do DNA testing on the wood."

"If they need to."

"Was the shed locked?"

"According to Trish, it's never locked."

"I can't believe it."

"Did Kimberly know about the shed?"

"I saw her in it earlier this month. She opened the door and walked in. I wonder where she is right now."

"I can tell you where she isn't — anywhere requiring a ticket or a passport. She hasn't used her credit cards, an ATM, or her phone. I liked your idea — she'd go somewhere familiar and comfortable, and the cottage sure qualified. Are you sure she didn't mention anywhere else that might fit the bill?"

I thought for a moment, reviewing our conversation. "She said she dreamed of just driving away."

"We found her car, so that's out."

"Maybe she bought a new car."

"With what? According to Steve, she doesn't carry a lot of cash."

"Cal did. He funded her purchase of the woodblock print. It's possible he was flush and she cleaned him out."

Ellis tapped a speed-dial button on his phone. When his call was answered, he said, "Check if any car dealers sold a car to Kimberly . . . Describe her . . . She might be using another name. The dealer might have picked her up at the Rocky Point Mall." He pushed the end call button and smiled at me. "Another good idea. Thank you."

"Spelunking."

"Excuse me?"

"She and her friend Chelsea liked caves."

"What caves?"

I recounted Kimberly's comments.

"What's Chelsea's last name?"

"I don't know. She lives in Colorado Springs with a husband and three kids. Kimberly exchanges Christmas cards with her."

Ellis called Detective Brownley and told her to pull Steve from his class. "Find that Christmas card list."

According to Chelsea Cox, Kimberly's old friend, their favorite cave was Salt Pearl

Cavern at the end of Rocky Point Beach.

As soon as Ellis had that information, he thanked me and left. I waited for him to pull out of the lot, told Cara I didn't know when I'd be back, and drove to Clinton Lane, across from the beach. I parked behind a silver Ford Escape. I took my phone and keys and left my bag in my trunk.

I knew of Salt Pearl Cavern, but I'd never been inside. I didn't like the dark. I'd never thought of my disinclination as a phobia, or even a fear; rather, I simply didn't like the dark. I always left a light on when I left home so I'd never have to enter a dark house, and I'd made certain Prescott's nightlight setting was more than cursory. I couldn't imagine wanting to hike into a cave.

I followed a rocky trail inland for about a quarter mile, then pushed through a dense stand of holly, laurel, and oak. A jumble of four-foot boulders ran from the path to the mouth of the cave. I climbed one and slid down the other side. I sat on pebbly ground, positioning myself so I could see through a crevice between the rocks. I wasn't tempted to contact Wes, knowing his rough-and-ready methods, but I would take photos for him.

The waves pounded the shore, so I didn't

hear Ellis and the other police officers arrive. They walked in single file, silently. I opened the camera on my phone and began snapping away.

Ellis pointed to Daryl, then to the left of the cave mouth. Daryl walked quickly to the left, flattening himself against the granite wall. He signaled Griff to go to the right. Griff got in position. The same two men who'd carried the ladder at the cottage held two huge LED flashlights. Officer Meade handed Ellis an old-fashioned megaphone.

"Ms. Larson, this is Chief Hunter." His voice sounded echo-y and unlike him. "I've consulted the Rocky Point surveyor. He tells me there's only one way in and out of this cavern. It's over, Kimberly. Come out now, with your hands up, and let's talk about what's going on."

Ellis tried again, making his request seem reasonable. Nothing. After two more attempts, he said, "We're coming in."

"No! Don't."

Kimberly appeared at the cave opening, her hands cheek high. She didn't look anything like as upset as she had the day before. Her eyes were clear, and her chin was up.

"Are you alone?" Ellis asked.

"Yes."

"Where's your bag?"

She lowered her hands. "Why?"

"I need to check for stolen property."

"It's mine."

Ellis scanned the desolate area. "How did you get here?"

"I hitchhiked, then walked."

Ellis turned to the men with the flashlights. "Take a look inside. Daryl, cover them."

"Don't!" Kimberly said. "It's sacred ground. I came out so you wouldn't go in. I haven't done anything wrong."

"This isn't your private property, Ms. Larson." He waved them in. "We need to talk."

"I'm done talking."

"Then we can wait together while they search the cave."

Thirty seconds later, Daryl appeared at the mouth holding a wheeling suitcase in one plastic-gloved hand. The suitcase was black and sized to fit in a plane's overhead bin. He held Kimberly's tote bag in his other hand.

Ellis snapped on gloves and eyeballed the insides. He pulled out a set of keys and read from the red tag attached to the ring. He looked up. "Daryl, call Detective Brownley and tell her to check with Milkin Cars." He

481

tossed the keys to Griff and said, "Find the car."

Kimberly took a step toward him.

"Why did you leave your old one in a shopping mall parking lot?" he asked.

She didn't reply.

"Why did you lie just now about hitchhiking here?"

"It's not a lie when someone asks a none-of-your-business question."

Ellis reached back into Kimberly's bag and extracted a narrow blue plastic binder. I saw a logo on the front and some text.

Ellis said, "Greenfield Travel Agency." He opened the binder and flipped through the papers. "Kosovo. Tonight at eleven from Boston's Logan Airport. You and Ryan. Why are you leaving Rocky Point?"

"You keep asking me about things that aren't crimes. So what if I want to take my son to Europe? The only crime I see is searching a woman's bag without her permission."

Ellis didn't comment. He lifted a manila envelope from the bag and opened it. "What have we here?" He pulled out a bundle of cash. "How much is it?"

Kimberly didn't comment.

Ellis turned to Daryl. "Open the suitcase."

"This is outrageous!"

Daryl reached for the zipper. "It's locked. A small padlock."

Ellis looked into the envelope containing the money, then unzipped a side pocket inside the tote bag and poked around. He zipped it back up and unsnapped a change purse. He shook a small key into his palm and handed it to Daryl.

"Am I under arrest?" Kimberly demanded.

"Only if you insist. We have evidence that Cal committed fraud and that you were involved. Your plan to leave the jurisdiction will convince a judge that you had knowledge of your wrongdoing, and that's enough to prove intent. I don't want to arrest you on that charge, though. I think you're a victim here, Kimberly. I think Cal was blackmailing you."

Kimberly began to cry, and she covered her face with her hands. Ellis nodded at Daryl, and he unlocked and unzipped the suitcase. A shiny laptop sat on top of a neatly folded pile of clothes.

Griff hustled along the rocky path. "The key opens a silver Ford Escape parked on Clinton."

The two men with the flashlights reappeared and talked to Ellis. I couldn't hear what they said. After a minute they left.

Ellis turned to Daryl. "No one goes in this cave until the forensic team gives an all clear."

"Got it."

Ellis touched Kimberly's elbow, and she trudged down the path beside him. Griff followed close behind. I kept taking photos until they rounded a corner and disappeared from view.

I slipped my phone into my back pocket and used footholds on the boulder to heave myself up and over. Daryl's eyes widened and he took a step forward when I landed on his side of the rocks, but he didn't say anything, so I didn't either.

By the time I reached my car, the Ford Escape was already hooked up to a police tow truck. I took some more photos, then started emailing them to Wes. I was still at it when the truck drove off. As soon as I finished, I texted Wes. Before I had the car in gear, he called.

He asked where I was, and I explained about Kimberly's connection to Salt Pearl Cavern.

"I can't believe you didn't tell me about it."

"You're welcome for the photos."

Wes sighed.

I ignored his unspoken disapproval. "The last ones show her new car being towed away."

"What new car?"

"Apparently, Kimberly decided to start over somewhere. She needed to figure out the logistics of getting a new identity, so she bought a car for cash. I'm certain she used a different name. The temporary plates are good for twenty days, plenty of time."

"Car dealers require ID."

"Maybe she paid extra . . . you know . . . cash money. Some dealers would be happy to make up a name and address for you, maybe even jury-rig a fake ID they could photocopy for their files. By the time the DMV catches on, she'd be long gone."

"The dealer's going to get in big trouble."

"Possibly. They'll both deny it — he said, she said." I told Wes about discovering the laptop in the suitcase and the plane tickets to Kosovo. "Maybe she'd planned this for a while, and already had a new identity, a passport — you know, a new name for a fresh start."

"Why Kosovo?" Wes asked.

"No extradition treaty."

"Why would Kimberly buy a car on the down-low if she planned to fly to Europe right away?"

"I suspect she wanted time to think things through and get her plans in order. Evidently, she was ready to face the fact that her relationship with Steve was over. If Lydia was arrested, Kimberly might figure she could come back. If she did, the car would be waiting for her at the airport, and off she and Ryan would go. If she decided to stay in Europe, oh, well . . . she lost a little money on the purchase."

He soft-whistled. "She was cooking on all burners, huh?"

Thunder cracked overhead.

"A storm's coming," I said.

"More than a storm! A nor'easter — we're in for it! Rain starts by six, then the temperature plummets. We may get snow."

"Why do you sound so happy?"

"Because Maggie and I are going to hunker down all weekend."

"What a great idea, Wes! Maybe Ty and I will do the same."

He asked for more details — what Kimberly was wearing and how she looked, did Ryan's name come up, or Steve's, and how did she explain having so much cash — and when he ran out of questions, he gave his usual "Catch ya later" and was gone.

A jagged bolt of lightning illuminated the yellow-gray sky, and I drove back to work.

CHAPTER THIRTY-EIGHT

Ty and I spent the weekend at his house. My place was cozy. His was expansive. He once told me he bought the house because of the view from the living room. We sat on the oversized sofa in front of the wall of windows gazing into the forest. By leaving the outside deck lights on, we had a 180-degree view of the crimson, gold, and orange leaves, their colors as true as fire. By the time darkness descended, the rain had picked up, and all I could see was black. We turned out the deck lights and closed the curtains, insulating ourselves from the outside world.

I stacked kindling and logs for a fire while Ty made martinis. I lit it and watched the flames tickle the bark, then sat on the rug and leaned against the double-wide ottoman. Ty placed a tray on the floor and sat beside me.

He kissed my cheek. "We need to decide

on the timeline for selling this place."

"Never."

"Do you want to live here for real?"

"No." I poured us martinis from the silver shaker and handed his over. "I want us to have a home we choose together, but this fire! That view!"

"Do you want us to live at your place?"

"Short term, yes. It's next door to Zoë, and it has a spiffy new hot tub."

"Long term?"

"Once you know whether we're moving to D.C., we'll figure it out."

"Good." He took a sip. "Guess what I did today?"

"You signed up to train as an astronaut."

He laughed. "Where did that come from?"

"I always wanted to be an astronaut."

"Really?"

"Sort of."

"You're a woman of many aspects."

I snuggled into his shoulder and watched the flames leap and curl, a perfect end to a difficult day.

"What did you do?"

"I confirmed our reservation in a gorgeous suite for three nights starting on our wedding day, Thursday the twenty-first."

"Eastern Turret Flag Officer's Suite."

"You have a great memory."

"For some things. For others, I have Gretchen. I've asked her to help us organize the wedding."

"That's a smart idea. I also put twenty sleeping rooms on hold for out-of-town guests . . . and . . . drum roll, please . . ."

I pitta-patted my thighs.

"You said you wanted a honeymoon that offered cosmopolitan amenities and a quiet beach and from-the-shore snorkeling. I've booked us a house on Seven Mile Beach on Grand Cayman Island. We fly out on Wednesday, June twenty-eighth, for ten days."

I sat up and spun around. "The Cayman Islands? That's fabulous!"

Ty grinned like a ten-year-old with a hot new video game. "It's a single-family house and comes with a cook, a housekeeper, and a gardener. The gardener also takes care of the pool. The property includes a full acre of private gardens, winding paths lit by tiki torches, and a twenty-foot-high waterfall."

I placed my glass on the tray and kissed Ty full on the mouth. "Oh, Ty. It sounds heavenly. Magical."

He placed his arm over my shoulder and drew me close. The orange flames curled around and over the logs. Sap crackled and popped.

I leaned my head against his shoulder. "I can't wait."

"Me, too."

"Why do we leave on Wednesday?"

"I know you. After the wedding weekend, you'll want to check in at work for a couple of days."

I smiled. "It's perfect, Ty. Thank you."

I kept checking the *Seacoast Star*'s website all weekend and all day Monday, but there was no new information about Kimberly. The first news came from Ellis, who stopped by my office Tuesday morning.

"I thought you'd want to see this." He handed me a printout of the Rheingold logo. "We found this on the laptop in Kimberly's bag. From fingerprints and the contents of emails, there's no question it was Cal's."

"Was it password protected?"

"Yes. Katie was able to circumvent it, though. Why?"

"If Kimberly couldn't access the computer, she wouldn't have seen the email making Pat's phone date with Andi. Not that it matters whether she knew or not. She couldn't have kept the appointment anyway, since she was teaching. I bet she planned to take the computer to an IT

490

service company and pretend to be so ditzy she forgot her own password."

He laughed. "We found the phone Cal used in Kimberly's suitcase, too."

"More evidence of intent. Anything of interest on the phone?"

"Cal sent a text to the disposable phone that we think went to Lydia. From the time stamp, he sent it during the funeral." Ellis read it aloud. " 'Is it as awful as you expected? See you soon. I miss you.' That helps set the time of Cal's murder."

I touched the printout. "Cal created the Rheingold receipt."

"And the fake Hitchens ID, and the phony lease that was used to open the P.O. box."

"You're building a case."

"One fact at a time."

After Ellis left, I sent Sylvia Rheingold an email explaining that the Rocky Point police had discovered who created the fake invoice, and that since the perpetrator was dead, there was no reason to think there'd be a repeat performance. I was glad I could provide her with some closure.

Wes and I met at our dune just before two thirty. Last weekend, we had a nor'easter. Today we were in the middle of a mini heat wave. The temperature had soared to nearly eighty. The sun sparkled, and the ocean was bright blue and calm.

Wes pulled out his notebook. "So talk to me. How did you know Kimberly was the killer?"

"I remembered something Ty said years ago — there's always a motive for murder. Always. Even if the motive doesn't seem logical to you, it makes sense to the killer. In this case, the only person who wanted Mo out of the picture was Kimberly. She was petrified that Mo and Steve were going to get back together."

"Were they?"

"Maybe. Kimberly was so desperate to find out, she even approached me to ask — after Mo was dead."

"That was kind of dumb of her, huh? Calling attention to herself for no reason."

"She didn't really call attention to herself, at least not directly. She asked about starting fresh in a new location, which makes me think she'd already half given up. You know how that goes . . . Your rational self knows a relationship is over, but your emotional self doesn't want to let go. Her rational self was asking why I moved to New Hampshire, how I set up a business, and so on. Her emotional self clung to the hope she wouldn't have to leave, that the murder

492

cases would go cold, and Steve would propose, and all would be well with the world."

"Stupid."

"Not stupid. Deluded."

"Whatever . . . So you never bought the idea that Lydia was the killer?"

"Not once I thought about Kimberly's motive. How is Lydia doing?"

"Who knows? She talks, but she doesn't say anything worth listening to. She plays her emotions close to her chin."

"I hope she finds her way."

Wes made a note. "Do you think Kimberly killed Mo on purpose?"

"I don't know that it was premeditated, but it's not like Mo simply tumbled over the wall. Remember what the ME said — Mo's death wasn't an accident. Have you heard whether Kimberly has admitted it?"

"Not yet, but smart money says she'll take a deal. She's already admitted she stole Cal's computer, phone, and voice changer. She insists the cash they found in her purse — fifteen big ones, thank you very much — is hers fair and square. She says that she won it from Cal at poker. That's possible, right? Anyway, what she can't explain away is the rain gear she bought at Anthony's. My police source tells me that checking

493

their sales of rain gear was your idea. You nailed it, Joz! Anthony was in the restroom when Kimberly came in, and Boris made the sale. They found the receipt for one pair of booties and one poncho. Boris picked Kimberly out of a photo lineup. According to Boris, the transaction occurred at the right time — just as the funeral was ending. They've got Kimberly cold."

"What does she say?"

"That Boris is wrong, that it never happened."

"And of course she denies taking the golf club."

"Yup."

"It's not going to be an easy case to win."

"They're retracing her steps after leaving the social club. Maybe they'll find the bloody boots and poncho. Most grocery stores and shopping malls have security cameras aimed at their Dumpsters. That's funny, isn't it?"

"Trash removal is big business. Using another guy's Dumpster saves you money. Cameras discourage the practice."

"Back up for a minute . . . Why did Cal need someone else to buy the Japanese woodblock prints for him, anyway? He was doing fine on his own."

"He was doing fine because he was only

494

selling one fake every few months. After he lost so much money, he needed to sell three or four prints right away to cover the debt. He got Lydia to help, but still needed to raise twenty thousand dollars, and that would simply get him caught up. It wouldn't pay her back or help him finance his lifestyle going forward. He had a choice — risk raising a red flag by flooding the market or find a proxy to do it for him."

"And since what he was doing was illegal, he couldn't simply ask a friend to help him out."

"Nor could he hire it out."

"Why did Kimberly go ahead and sell the print after Cal was murdered?"

"Why not? She had a buyer ready to go."

Wes closed his notebook. "The one thing I can't wrap my head around is that you figured everything out because the ink in Mo's print was too blue. Did I get that right?"

"Not just that . . . but, yeah."

Wes's phone vibrated. He read the message and chuckled. "Guess what? The police found security camera footage showing Kimberly tossing plastic cover-ups in the Dumpster behind Harvey's Market, the one that's closest to Anthony's. The timing is right. Their case is no longer hard to prove."

495

Even though I wasn't surprised, I was horrified, and I let it show. "Oh, Wes."

"Yeah . . . it gets you thinking, doesn't it? What else ya got for me?"

"Nothing."

"Catch ya later!"

Wes walked-slid down the dune. I stayed for a while, watching the waves slide to shore.

Kimberly would be found guilty of murder and sentenced to life in prison.

Ryan would move to Ohio to live with his grandparents.

Lydia would get a slap on the wrist.

Life would go on.

I pulled into my parking lot around three thirty and saw Steve leaning against the hood of his car, tapping into his smartphone.

I parked two spaces away. Steve looked up. He wasn't smiling, but neither did he look angry or upset.

He slipped his phone into his pocket. "Hey, Josie."

"Hey, Steve."

"I waited to stop by to thank you . . . I know it seems silly to talk about it now, but I heard your eulogy for Mo. It was beautiful. It meant something to me."

"Thanks, Steve. How are you doing with all this?"

"Worse than I expected. I knew I was going to have to leave Kimberly, whether Mo and I got back together or not. I wasn't happy, and it had been dragging on too long. Sometimes you've just got to rip that Band-Aid off."

"Do you think she sensed it, or was she in denial?"

"Complete denial."

"And then there's Ryan."

"Thinking about what he's going through kills me. I know he'll be okay, but you know . . . How do you get over something like this? He's heading to Ohio at the end of the week."

"You'll miss him."

"A lot."

Sadness enveloped me, and for a moment, I struggled to speak. Murder was always horrible, but some crimes seemed especially malevolent.

"What do you think . . . Will Kimberly plead guilty?"

"Beats me." Steve paused for a moment. "The other reason I came by . . . I'm looking for jobs in Florida. The Sunshine State. I could handle a little sunshine right about now. So I wanted to say good-bye."

497

"Everything is happening so quickly." I extended a hand. "Good luck, Steve."

We shook. I stood by my car and watched him drive away. His world had rocked a little, but after the initial shock wore off, he would go on his merry way, unscathed.

Late that night, Ty and I were relaxing in the hot tub.

We sat quietly for several minutes.

Ty took my hand. "What are you thinking about?"

"Cause and effect."

"Versus coincidence. How come?"

I tried to think how to express what I was feeling. "Have you ever thought about the way so many incidents link back to one singular event? You know, if I hadn't taken that train, I wouldn't have sat next to that person. If I hadn't sat next to that person, I wouldn't have heard about such-and-such a book. If I hadn't read that book, I wouldn't have known that x-y-z was possible. And so on. Have you ever done that?"

"Sure . . . it's kind of fun."

"Exactly. Except sometimes it's not so much fun. Cal came up with the idea to steal Mo's inheritance the minute he heard about it. Isn't that horrible? That one despicable act led to fraud, blackmail, and murder. If Mo's godmother hadn't left her twenty-five thousand dollars, she'd be alive today."

Ty raised my hand to his lips and kissed my knuckles. "You're right. Sometimes it's not so much fun."

EPILOGUE

May

Zoë picked the Sunday of Memorial Day weekend for my shower, thinking that guests would feel less rushed if she scheduled it in the middle of a three-day weekend. I'd asked her to keep it small, and she did.

The theme was "Island Loving," in honor of Ty's honeymoon choice. Nine of us sat on her deck drinking mai-tais and mojitos: Zoë; Gretchen; Sasha; Fred's wife, Suzanne; Cara; Eric's girlfriend, Grace; Helene, the director of New Hampshire Children First!; my cousin Becca,* who'd flown in from England; and me. Zoë had arranged for lunch to be prepared by a catering company that brought its own grill and smoker. We planned on doing the same for Sunday's hoedown, so I was glad for the opportunity to test them out.

* Please see *Ornaments of Death.*

500

I raised my glass. "I have a toast."

Everyone lifted their glasses.

"To Gretchen, the new general manager of Prescott's flagship location!"

We clinked and drank, and people asked for details. I sat back and listened to Gretchen's clear and concise explanation of her new position and its genesis. Suzanne proposed another toast, to me, for the expansion, and we clinked and sipped again.

Sasha leaned forward. "Has Ty decided whether to take the national director position?"

"Yes — he will, and we don't have to move. He was able to negotiate basing the position here."

Applause rippled around the room, and another toast was proposed.

"To Ty's success," Sasha said.

Zoë added, "And to your staying in Rocky Point."

Later, Gretchen sat on my right, notating who gave what gift. Zoë was on my left, handing them to me one at a time. I'd asked Zoë to request donations to New Hampshire Children First! in lieu of gifts, and she had, sort of. I thought her wording was clever:

Josie's asked that instead of a gift, you

bring a donation to her favorite charity,

New Hampshire Children First!

I suggest you do both!
In addition to your donation, bring her
something small to mark this special day.

The gifts were uniformly thoughtful, from monogrammed glasses to a set of rare teas, and from a string of mini-palm-tree outdoor lights to a small silver picture frame. Gretchen gave me a copper watering can. Zoë gave me a white satin-and-lace heart-shaped pillow. She'd had it custom embroidered. The message read:

Josie & Ty
Fairy Tales Do Come True

Zoë handed me the last box, a big one. "What's this? I thought we were done."

"Shelley couldn't come from New York, but she sent this."

I ripped open the turquoise water-patterned giftwrap. Inside the box was a grass skirt. I laughed, shook it out, and stepped into it, lifting my sundress to my waist. Gretchen began humming a hula tune, and I started dancing, shimmying my hips, holding my dress up with one hand, my other arm undulating to the side, an amateur's attempt at hula. I turned slowly, laughing. Photos were snapped and a thirty-second video recorded.

After a minute, I sat down, still wearing the grass skirt. "Shelley embraced the island theme, I see. Hawaii . . . the Caymans . . . it's all the same, right?"

Zoë handed me the box again. "There's more."

I opened a tissue-paper-wrapped package. Inside was a set of ice-blue lingerie, a French lace strapless bra and matching low-cut panties. "Wow. Look at this." I held the set up for everyone to see, then examined the labels. "They're my size. How could Shelley possibly know my size?"

Zoë grinned. "I raided your underwear drawer."

I laughed again, then picked up a white envelope. Inside was a check made out to New Hampshire Children First! and a handwritten note, which I read aloud:

Dear Josie,
I wish I could be there. (Ha!)
I hope you're having a wonderful day. I got you "something blue" in case you didn't have that yet. Very cool idea, ask-

503

ing for donations to your fav charity.

Love, Shelley

"Shelley is prescient," I said. "I didn't have the blue yet."

"What are you doing for the rest?" Cara asked.

"I'm wearing my mother's wedding ring on a chain around my neck. That's something old. My dress is new. Zoë's going to lend me her gorgeous bangle." Zoë lifted her arm, showing off the gold-and-diamond beauty Ellis had given her last fall. "Now I have something blue."

Becca stood. "In England, we add a bit at the end: 'Something old, something new, something borrowed, something blue, and a sixpence for your shoe.' " She handed me a silver coin. "I brought you a sixpence."

"Oh, Becca! That's wonderful." I hugged her, and as I did, I whispered, "I'm so glad you're here. Thank you for coming."

"I wouldn't miss it — or your wedding."

I gave her shoulders a last squeeze before backing up. I sent my eyes around, including everyone in my comment. "I can't tell you how much it means to me that you're all here, including Shelley, in absentia. Thank you."

We ate, and drank some more, and I did

one final hula before calling it a day.

"We raised more than a thousand dollars!"

Ty and I were in the hot tub. I'd told him about the delicious barbecue, demonstrated the hula in my grass skirt, and showed off the gifts, except the lingerie, which he wouldn't see until our wedding day. He congratulated me on my fund-raising success, admired the gifts, and leaned back, resting his head against the bumper and closing his eyes.

I placed my hand against a jet, relishing the pulsating water. "I've changed my mind about our wedding."

He opened his eyes. "What did I do?"

"No, silly! Not about whether to get married, about who to invite. You know I wanted it to be just the two of us on the beach. I've rethought that decision."

He shut his eyes again. "Good."

The next Tuesday, Ty and I walked out of the Rocky Point Community Theater after seeing *Oklahoma!*

He handed me his program. "Max was pretty good."

"I thought he was great. He's a man of many talents. He looked like he was having a blast."

"Any update from Gretchen about the wedding?" he asked.

"The Blue Dolphin is confirmed for catering the luncheon reception, and she's organized chandeliers for the tent."

"Chandeliers?"

"Fancy crystal chandeliers. Hey, you wanted elegant, big fella, you're getting elegant."

"Sweet."

June

My wedding day began with tears. I slept fitfully and was up by seven, gripped by hollow misery. I was burningly upset that my mother couldn't see me in my wedding dress. I was crushed that my dad couldn't walk me down the aisle. I went for a walk in the woods and talked to the sky, to my parents. I told them about Ty and our love and our life together, and by nine, when I got home, I had myself under control.

Zoë arrived a few minutes later and made us scrambled eggs, but all I could do was pick at them. I was jumpy.

At ten, Zoë helped me attach the net veil to the lilies-of-the-valley wreath that sat on the top of my head.

I met her eyes in the mirror. "I wish my parents were here."

She took my hand in hers and squeezed. "They are."

My eyes moistened. "Thank you."

She spread the veil over my shoulders and had me stand. She took a step back and looked me up and down.

"Turn around."

I did so.

I wore a pale peach to-the-ankle sleeveless silk slip dress with a scoop neckline. My sandals were strappy and high-heeled. Becca's sixpence was taped to the bottom of my right shoe.

"I can barely walk in these sandals," I fretted. "If I do a facer in the sand, I'm going to cry."

"I'll be beside you the whole way, and if you fall, I'll pick you up. But how about taking them off once we reach the beach?"

"I'll be barefoot."

"Yes."

"I got a pedicure."

"You're all set, then." She finished her examination. "Oh, Josie . . . you're going to take Ty's breath away."

I smiled.

The limo pulled into the driveway at ten thirty. The driver loaded Ty's and my suitcases into the trunk; then Zoë and I climbed into the back.

Zoë glanced at her watch. "Ellis is picking up Ty at this very minute. Gretchen will meet us at the beach with their boutonnieres and our bouquets. The wedding planner is already at the Blue Dolphin making sure everything is set for lunch."

"It's pretty eccentric for the bride to skip her own wedding luncheon."

"It would be eccentric if the bride skipped it while the groom attended. But since you and Ty both plan on skipping it, I don't think it rises to the level of eccentricity."

I patted her hand. "Thank you, Zoë. Thank you for reassuring me. Thank you for being you."

The limo rolled to a stop along the sandy shoulder next to the dune where Wes and I regularly met. Gretchen was waiting by the tall grass. Zoë got out to coordinate the flowers. I stayed seated.

Through the tinted window I counted twenty-three people, ranged in a loose half circle. Ellis and Ty were already there, their blue-and-orange boutonnieres in place. I didn't see Shelley. Oh, well. Wes stood next to Ty. This would be Wes's first marriage as a justice of the peace.

Zoë opened the door, and I stepped out. The flowers were perfect, blue hydrangeas and orange tiger lilies, their stems stripped of leaves and wrapped in peach satin. I accepted the bouquet from Gretchen, and tears filled her expressive eyes. She kissed my cheek and hurried to join Jack and her toddler, Johnny.

Zoë touched my arm. "Ready?"

"Yes."

As soon as we reached the sand, I slipped off my sandals. The ocean was jade green today, flecked with gold. The ragged line of guests closed in. Out of the corner of my eye, I saw a woman a hundred yards away, running like a demon toward us. It was Shelley. When she reached the group, she eased herself into the line of guests.

Ellis and Ty approached, and from that moment, I saw nothing except Ty. I was mesmerized by the love in his eyes.

Wes came forward, a black leather portfolio in hand. He opened it and began to read: "Friends, we are gathered here together to join this man and this woman in holy matrimony . . ."

We exchanged our vows. After the kiss that marked our marriage, people applauded.

Gretchen had stashed a cooler behind a dune, and she and Cara poured everyone a plastic champagne glass full of bubbly to toast our happiness. After the first round of toasts, Shelley ran up to greet me and meet Ty.

"I'm so sorry I was late, Josie. I got lost — it turns out all dunes look alike."

I hugged her, and she hugged me back, and we rocked from side to side.

"You came!" I whispered. "I can't believe you came! You're in New Hampshire!"

"I guess the cows came home after all, huh?"

I laughed, and we linked arms, and I turned to face the group. "Everyone . . . this is Shelley!"

When we'd finished our drinks, Ty whispered, "Ready?"

"Yes."

I kissed Zoë's cheek, then waved goodbye to everyone, and we left. The limo driver offered congratulations, and we set off, heading north, toward Wentworth by the Sea.

Ty leaned over and kissed me. "You got married barefoot."

"While your toesies were in foot-prison."

He lifted his right leg a few inches to show off his handsome cordovan slip-ons. "They may be in prison, but you've got to admit, these puppies are good-looking."

"True, but I bet your toes are jealous."

Ty leaned forward to speak to the driver.

"Would you pull over for a minute?"

The limo eased onto the shoulder and stopped. Ty stepped out, and I followed.

"What are we doing?" I asked.

"I thought a brief walk on the beach — barefoot — was in order. Toe-parity."

I laughed and kicked off my sandals, and Ty removed his shoes and socks. He took my hand, and we picked our way through the dunes to the soft, warm sand.

We walked for a hundred yards or so; then Ty leaned over and kissed me. "My toes are happy."

"What a relief."

We walked back to the limo, hand in hand, our shoulders touching.

As I slid into my sandals, I took one last look back, memorizing the panoramic view, the dunes with the tall grasses trembling in the breeze, the pink rambling roses, and the sun-specked water, and I knew that glorious image would stay emblazoned in my head and in my heart forever.

ACKNOWLEDGMENTS

Special thanks go to my literary agent, Cristina Concepcion of Don Congdon Associates, Inc. Thanks also go to Michael Congdon and Cara Bellucci.

Thanks to Dan and Linda Chessman, who suggested the officiate and location for Josie and Ty's wedding; Julie Bishop, who selected the orchids for Gertie Joan; and G. D. Peters, who read an early draft of this novel with care and diligence.

The Minotaur Books team also gets special thanks, especially those I work with most closely, including executive editor Hope Dellon, assistant editor Hannah O'Grady, publicity manager Sarah Melnyk, director of library marketing and national accounts manager (Macmillan) Talia Sherer, copyeditor India Cooper, and art director David Baldeosingh Rotstein.

ABOUT THE AUTHOR

Jane K. Cleland once owned a New Hampshire-based antiques and rare books business. She is the author of the Josie Prescott Antiques mysteries, has been a finalist for the Macavity and Anthony Awards, and won the Agatha Award for her book *Mastering Suspense, Structure and Plot.* She has twice won the David Award for Best Novel. Jane is the former president of the New York chapter of the Mystery Writers of America and chairs the Wolfe Pack's Black Orchid Novella Award. She is part of the English faculty at Lehman College and lives in New York City.

The employees of Thorndike Press hope you have enjoyed this Large Print book. All our Thorndike, Wheeler, and Kennebec Large Print titles are designed for easy reading, and all our books are made to last. Other Thorndike Press Large Print books are available at your library, through selected bookstores, or directly from us.

For information about titles, please call:

(800) 223-1244

or visit our website at:

gale.com/thorndike

To share your comments, please write:

Publisher
Thorndike Press
10 Water St., Suite 310
Waterville, ME 04901